PRESIDENTIAL MISSION

THE "LANNY BUDD" NOVELS

IN ORDER OF PUBLICATION

World's End

Between Two Worlds

Dragon's Teeth

Wide Is the Gate

Presidential Agent

Dragon Harvest

A World to Win

PRESIDENTIAL MISSION

Upton Sinclair

The Viking Press · New York

1947

TO

MY FRIENDS AND READERS IN BRITAIN

who during the eight years of Lanny Budd have been carrying a heavy burden, and who are now engaged in installing democratic Socialism, a task of vital importance to the world.

Author's Note

THANKS of both author and readers are due to Mr. Eric Erickson, Swedish-American oil man, for permission to give a glimpse of his strange wartime adventures in Germany. The same to Mr. Kenneth Pendar, United States vice-consul in North Africa, for permission to present him and his experiences, charmingly told in his book, *Adventure in Diplomacy* (Dodd, Mead & Co.).

The same to Mr. Louis Adamic, for permission to have Lanny Budd present at the occasion of a certain dinner at the White House. He told me this story soon after the dinner occurred, and I asked him to write notes of the affair and permit Lanny Budd to be present. The scene was written in accordance with the notes that dealt with the dinner and nothing else. Subsequently, Mr. Adamic expanded the notes into a book, *Dinner at the White House* (Harper & Brothers).

UPTON SINCLAIR

Contents

Book One:
So Nigh Is Grandeur to Our Dust

Book Two:
Now Is the Winter of Our Discontent

Book Three:
A Mad World, My Masters

Book Four:
Still Point of the Turning World

Book Five: Time by the Forelock

Book Six: Doors That Lead to Death

Book Seven:
More Deadly Than a Mad Dog's Tooth

Book Eight: The Devil Is Diligent

Book Nine:
The End of This Day's Business

BOOK ONE

So Nigh Is Grandeur to Our Dust

1

Humanity with All Its Fears

I

LANNY BUDD'S heart was high as he drove northward along the Palisades. Hardly a day during the past six months had passed that he had not imagined this hour when he would make his report to the Big Boss—what he would say and what the Boss would answer. Six months is a chunk out of any man's life, and Lanny's had been crowded with new experiences. He had been all the way round the earth, and most of the trip near the equator, where the distance is greatest. Meantime that earth had been witnessing events of pain and terror, cataclysms so momentous that men would continue to write and talk about them so long as there was anybody on the planet able to know what had happened in its past.

The sun was shining warm on this early April afternoon. Small white clouds drifted across the blue sky, above apple orchards wreathed in pink satin blossoms, to welcome a world traveler home. The well-paved highway wound irregularly along the wooded cliffs, dipping now and then into hollows, or coming out upon open places where a driver could observe the broad sweep of the river, the railroad on the opposite shore, the villages, and the hills dotted with farmhouses and country mansions. Lanny, who delighted in motoring, had not had a steering wheel in his hands for half a year. He had come from the snows of Archangel and the fogs of Newfoundland; and here was warmth, sunshine, beauty, comfort—all the gifts of nature and of civilization which an American of the leisure classes takes for granted and appreciates only after he has been traveling in wild and poverty-stricken lands, or amid scenes of war and destruction.

The warmth seeped in through the traveler's skin, the orchard scents through his nostrils, and the beauty through his eyes. His subconscious mind absorbed these while his conscious mind was busy with the great man he was going to see, the story he had to tell him, and what questions would be asked and what answers given. Lanny had missed so

2

much, in these days when significant events came piling one on top of the other, hardly giving people time to realize any of them. America had been at war for a matter of four months, and it had been one defeat after another, with not a single success. Bataan had just surrendered, and the Japanese were close to India; the Germans were close to Leningrad and to the Suez Canal. Lanny thought: F.D.R. is the man who will know about everything. How much will he tell me. and what will he want me to do?

II

After a drive of an hour and a half the motorist came to the high Poughkeepsie bridge and crossed over to the east bank of the river. He drove through the spread-out city with the queer Indian name and on up the post road to the north. This road was wide and fairly straight, arched by tall elm trees and lined with the fences and gates of country homes. Soon it was a village called Hyde Park, and then it was an estate called Krum Elbow, for the past nine years the "summer White House." Lanny had been here just before setting out upon his long journey. That time he had been smuggled in by the back door in the night and had seen his Chief lying in bed, wearing pongee pajamas and a blue crew-necked sweater, which he wouldn't part with even after the moths had devoured parts of it. Only once had the visitor entered this estate in the normal way, the first time, before he had become a secret agent for the most powerful man in the world.

At the little sentry-box by the entrance gate there had formerly been a State Trooper; now it was wartime, and the United States Army had taken over. The driver stopped his car and gave his name to the sergeant in command. The sergeant had a list, no doubt, and knew it by heart. He surveyed a conventionally dressed gentleman in his early forties, wearing a tropical worsted suit of brown, a tie and a homburg hat to match; a little brown mustache, a friendly smile, and a sun tan not entirely lost in the snows of Russia. "I have to see your driver's license, Mr. Budd," said the man; and then: "I have to look in the trunk of your car." It was a sport car with a rumble seat, and anybody who had been hidden there would have had to be of jockey size. Lanny said: "It isn't locked." The sergeant took a glance and then said: "O.K., sir."

The car sped up the drive, through a lane of shade trees which their owner loved—he was pleased to describe his occupation as "tree grower" instead of President of the United States, a less dependable job. The mansion was something over a hundred years old, two-and-a-half stories, partly brick and partly stone; it had been added to now and then, each time in a somewhat different style of architecture. At the front entrance was a semicircular portico with four white columns, and here was a sentry who gave Lanny an informal salute but did not stop him. His coming must have been announced by telephone, for the door was opened without his having to ring, and a Negro butler took his hat; a woman secretary greeted him cheerfully.

III

In front as you entered this family home was a grandfather's clock, and at the right a circular stairway with carved banisters. The way to the library was at your left, and as you turned in that direction you were confronted by a statue of the President as a youth, a life-size seated figure rising out of a square block of stone. There was a passageway, and a descent of three or four stairs, and at one side a ramp on which a wheel chair might be moved. Wherever the President sat, the wheel chair was near, and a button which he might press to summon his Negro attendant.

The library formed the left wing of the building and was of generous size. There was a fireplace at each end; in front of one was a large flat-topped desk, and sitting behind it was the man Lanny had come to see—a large man, with large shoulders and head and a frank, cheerful face known to most of the world. He was on the alert for his visitor and did not consider it necessary to pretend to be preoccupied; his face lighted up and he held out a welcoming hand from a distance. "Hi, Marco Polo!" In the dozen visits that Franklin Roosevelt had received from his secret agent he had never failed to think up some fancy greeting, and this time it was for a man who had traveled all the way across China. He added: "By golly, I can't tell you how I have missed you!"

"You have had enough to occupy your mind." The visitor smiled. He looked with curiosity at this great, crippled man who carried an Atlas load upon his broad shoulders. F.D.R. was a little thinner, a little more careworn, but never more cheerful, for he liked people to come to see him, especially when they had interesting reports to deliver.

"Make yourself at home," he said and signed to a tall chair beside his desk, one of two "gubernatorial chairs" which he had earned, one for each term he had served in his native state. Lanny saw that the desk had toy elephants and donkeys, billikins, snake rattles, all sorts of odds and ends that admirers sent him; also a formidable stock of official documents which he would have to dig his way through, but not this afternoon. He had come to Hyde Park for a week end of badly needed rest, and talking to Presidential Agent 103 was one of his ways of diversion.

"You are able to get about all right?" was his first comment. "Tell me just what happened."

"My plane cracked up in a terrific storm, and when it hit the sea both my legs were smashed. But they're all right now, and ready for duty."

"I thought to myself when I heard about it: he'll be one man who can understand *my* plight!"

"Believe me, Governor, there wasn't a day in the hospital and afterward that I didn't have that same thought."

"You were luckier than I, you could hope for a comeback."

"I was more lucky than any man had better count on. I don't know if I ever told you that an astrologer had predicted that I would die in Hongkong. I had several close calls there, and almost got converted to a belief in the stars."

"Alston tells me that you were married instead." Then, with a chuckle: "You know the jingle about needles and pins?"

"Plenty of trouble began there, but it wasn't due to getting married. Quite the contrary."

"I wish you happiness, Lanny. You must bring your wife to see us sometime."

"That will give her pleasure indeed. She is, as you may have heard, a writer of short stories, and has given the Nazis some sharp digs. The Russians were delighted by them."

"Send them to me and I'll be glad to read them. Did you see much of Russia?"

"Only Kuibyshev and Moscow, but I had some worth-while talks. You will want to hear first about Stalin, I imagine." Lanny brought up the subject at the first moment, being aware of his Boss's fondness for chatting. The caller didn't want to get diverted, say to the President's great-great-uncle or great-grandfather or whoever it was that was suspected of having been an opium smuggler in the China Seas; or perhaps to the model of his Yankee Clipper which stood in a glass case against one wall of this ample room

IV

Lanny Budd launched himself upon a subject which he could be sure was of importance to the Commander-in-Chief of the American Armed Forces. He reported on a two-hour conference with the mystery man of the Kremlin—not so mysterious if you would read some of his published writings and those of his master, Lenin. But many people find it easier to contemplate a mystery than to read a book, and Lanny doubted Franklin Roosevelt's ever having seen one of Stalin's tomes. He described the oval room which was the Soviet chief's office, and the interview late at night, and the fur coat and boots which had been presented to the emissary from the White House.

"The Embassy here at Washington made inquiry about you and I gave you my O.K.," said F.D.R. To which the visitor replied: "I guessed that must have happened, because Stalin was so frank and gave me several messages for you."

"The thing we want to know most of all, Lanny, is whether they will stick it out in this war."

"As to that I am sure you need have no fear. They have seen too much of Nazi brutality, which is really quite insane. A Russian would as soon trust a Bengal tiger as take the word of a Hitlerite. Stalin's reply to my question was prompt and decisive. They are in this war to the finish, and only beg that you will get help to them as quickly as possible."

"We will do our best, Lanny, but we have almost nothing at present. Our shortage of shipping is paralyzing, and the U-boats are playing the very devil with us. The Russians expect a heavy attack this spring, I assume."

"They do, and cannot be sure where it will come; that is the disadvantage of defensive warfare. The best guess is that Hitler will concentrate on the south because of the oil, which is his greatest need. It will be an overwhelming attack; he has not been nearly so heavily hit as the Soviet communiqués would have us believe. His retreat was strategic, to prepared winter positions, and not many of his troops were sacrificed. He will no doubt throw in everything he has as soon as the ground is dry. There are millions of Russians, now strong and happy, who will be food for the wolves and the kites when the steppes are dry."

The smile had gone from the President's face, and instead there was a mask of grief, which silenced his secret agent. "You know, Lanny, I never dreamed I'd be a war president. It is a thought I could hardly have faced."

Lanny did his best to meet this mood. "Lincoln didn't want it, Wilson didn't want it, I doubt if any of our war presidents ever did or will. You are in the hands of fate, sir; and history will record that you did your job well." Lanny guessed that this was what Roosevelt lived for, the fountainhead from which he drew his courage and confidence; he was making history that men would study and from which they would renew their faith in democratic principles.

The visitor went on with his story. He told everything the Red dictator had said, including the assertion that he was not a dictator. He repeated the questions Stalin had asked about Roosevelt; questions all to the point, revealing a knowledge of America that extended even to Hearst and Colonel McCormick and their newspapers, whose main purpose appeared to be to misrepresent the Soviet Union. Then Lanny underwent an inquisition similar to the one he had gone through in Moscow. What did Stalin look like, what was his manner, what appeared to be the state of his health? Lanny reported that he spoke quietly and paid close attention to every reply. He was in his sixties, but only gray hair and mustache betrayed his age.

"A curious thing," the President said. "I had the impression that he was a big man, but they tell me this is not so."

"I would guess him to be four inches shorter than I, and I am five-ten; but he is sturdily built. His training has been that of a revolutionary, a hunted man under the tsardom, and it must be hard for him to imagine the free institutions which you and I take for granted. It must be hard for him to realize that men born to wealth and comfort like ourselves can be genuinely interested in the abolition of their own privileges. But when I proposed a toast to the progress of democracy throughout the world, Stalin drank to it without hesitation. Of course he has his own definition of the word, and his own idea of how to attain the goal. If he is to be persuaded that our way is better, it will have to be by actions, not by words."

V

Everything about the Soviet Union and then everything about China. F.D.R. stuck another cigarette into the long thin holder which he affected, lighted it with a patent lighter, and started another inquisition. He wanted to know what life was like in the interior of a land which had been at war for ten years. How did the people appear, and what were they doing and saying? Had the travelers seen any signs of starvation, and what had they used for money, and how much did the common people know about what was going on in the outside world? "They all know about *you*," Lanny said with a grin, "and they are all sure you are going to send them several thousand airplanes by next Tuesday."

"Alas, I would not dare tell them how few planes we have, Lanny. I won't tell even you. It will be impossible to get anything to them for some time."

"The intelligent ones realize that. They say they are worse off since we entered the war. They used to get some goods by smuggling or by bribing Jap officials. Now they get nothing."

"It is of the utmost importance that China should not collapse, Lanny. We can only make promises, but we do this with real sincerity. We are surely going to smash the Jap warlords, and then it will be possible for a peaceful and democratic China to exist."

"That is what I told them everywhere. I took the liberty of saying that I was a special emissary of yours, sent to give them assurances."

"You are that wherever you go, Lanny. I understand that you were in Yenan. Tell me about that. I hear such contradictory reports."

So this "Marco Polo" described "Red China," the land in the north and northwest to which the Communist armies had marched when expelled from the rest of the country, and where they were now building a crude, pathetic utopia, mostly in caves chopped out of cliffs where the Jap bombers couldn't reach them. Lanny told of the odd impression this life had made on him; it wasn't Marxist and certainly not Leninist, it was early American utopian; it was a "colony," a "phalanstery," a "commonwealth." Its people did not talk about class struggle; they talked about co-operation and brotherhood and worked at it with apostolic zeal.

"Then they are not trying to socialize industry?" asked the President. The answer was: "It was carefully explained to me that their theoreticians have decided that at this stage they must promote private industry as a means of overcoming feudalism."

"A sort of N.E.P.," commented the other. "That ought to make it easy to get along with them."

"One might think so. But unfortunately the Chungking government wants to perpetuate feudalism under the label of democracy. They maintain a strict blockade of Yenan, and we were told that it would be impossible to get there. We did manage it, but it was an uncomfortable journey, and not without its dangers."

"Every nation wants to continue its civil wars, it appears, even while it is being crushed by the Japs or the Germans."

"Even after it *has been* crushed, Governor. That is the situation in France, and among every group of refugees I have met anywhere."

"It is sad," was the reply. "But the problem seems very simple. We are going to fight Japs and Germans and break their military systems. That is the only thing that counts with us, and we are not going to fight anybody's civil wars, not in China, nor in France, nor in Italy, nor wherever our troops may go. When it is over, we'll see that all the countries have a fair democratic election, and after that they will be on their own."

"Is that the formula, Governor?"

"That is it. Paste it in your hat and look at it every once in a while. Everybody who is willing to help fight Japs and Germans, and Italians, of course, is our ally, and everybody who wants to fight anybody else will have to be sat on for the time being."

"I'm glad to hear it from your own lips, Governor, for I know from previous experience how it is going to be. All sorts of cliques and causes will try to use our armies for their schemes."

"The watchword is democracy. That means government of the people, by the people, for the people—and it means all the people, not just General Whoosis and Prince Highupsky."

"Don't forget to mention that to your State Department and to your generals," was the visitor's dry suggestion.

VI

The busiest man in the world lighted still another cigarette and proceeded to "talk turkey," as he called it. "Tell me, Lanny, what do you want to do next?"

The visitor had prepared for this and replied promptly: "I want to do whatever will be of the greatest help to you."

"We are building a big, and I hope an efficient, Intelligence service. I can turn you over to 'Wild Bill' Donovan, a shrewd and loyal man, and he will make you one of his right bowers."

"If that is where you think I can do the best work. But I was rather hoping you might have some personal mission for me. You know how I feel—my contact with you has been half the fun of all this."

"It's not a thankful sort of job, Lanny. It has no future."

"You mean that I won't get titles and a salary? I have never wanted those. My reward is to sit in this gubernatorial chair and tell you my story, and hear from you what is coming next and what I can do to help it along."

"You would rather go on as a free lance, then?"

"I have never learned to be anything else, and I'm not sure I could become a cog in a machine. I have been thinking about it, and here is the difficulty: the contacts I have in Europe are personal and I am bound by pledges; before I could tell Colonel Donovan anything of importance, I should have to go back there and persuade my friends to give their consent."

"Surely you don't expect to go into Germany any more!"

"I can't see any way to do it. But I have a contact in Switzerland that has proved valuable in the past, and I hope to find the man still alive and on the job. It is the same with an old friend who is working with the underground in Toulon. There should be code letters waiting at my mother's home on the Riviera."

"The situation has been altered greatly since we have been forced into the war. What will you use as your camouflage now?"

"I have given much thought to that all the way across Asia and Europe. I believe I can still get along in neutral countries in my role of art expert. My clients have money, and they will buy paintings if I can find them and get them here."

"But it surely won't seem plausible for an art expert to be rambling about Europe carrying on business in wartime!"

"It will seem more plausible than you might like to believe, Governor. There is plenty of bootlegging and black marketeering going on, and most high-up people still believe that there are special privileges. In London I was offered opportunities to speculate in French industrial shares—I mean, of industries in Occupied France, strictly illegal. I could tell you scores of stories along such lines. All I have to do is to smile knowingly and remind my friends that my father is president of Budd-Erling Aircraft and an influential man in his own country. To those who are sympathetic to our cause I can drop a hint to the effect that I am able to assist my father in getting information. The slightest hint will suffice, for people will realize that such matters would be strictly hush-hush."

"Shall you continue to pose as a secret sympathizer with Fascism?"

"I have worked out a rather complicated technique in the course of the years, and I vary it according to the person I am with. Most of the time I am the art lover, the ivory-tower dweller, the lotos-eater, careless of mankind. Something that will amuse you—I was wearing that role the evening I met the lady who is now my wife, and she gave me a fine dressing down, called me a 'troglodyte.' But most of the time that role satisfies people in the *haut monde*."

"I've an idea you may find it different now that we're in the war, Lanny. People have taken sides."

"I have learned to shade my statements and put on a little smile which makes me enigmatic and mysterious. With those who are Fascists at heart, or without realizing it, I can take the attitude of my former wife, Lady Wickthorpe, who has become a pacifist and humanitarian; she deplores mass slaughter, and perceives so clearly that it cannot help anybody but the Reds. These lofty sentiments break nobody's bones."

"I am told that conditions are changing fast, in France especially. The Germans are making themselves bitterly hated, and the underground is spreading fast."

"I am prepared for that, and I may feel free to make the real truth known to more persons than in the past. I had to use extreme care so long as I was going into Hitlerland; but I've an idea that my visit to Stalin has put an end to all that. It is hard to believe the Nazis wouldn't get a report of it. Indeed, I decided that my goose was cooked last September, when I was brought into Halifax after the plane crash. The hospital people found two passports on me, one of them under an assumed name. The nurses knew about it, and it must have been whispered all over the town. I am bound to assume that the Germans would have agents there, and that the story would get to Berlin. So far as I know, the Führer never had but one American friend, and if that one was revealed to be a spy, it would make a tremendous scandal among the insiders. I rather think I may get echoes from it when I meet the old-time Social Democrat and labor leader who is my contact in Geneva."

"I get your point, Lanny," said F.D.R. "Let it be understood that I don't ask you to go into any German-held territory, or Italian. We have many others who can do that, and at less risk."

VII

They had come to the crucial part of their talk, about which Lanny had been dreaming for half a year. The Big Boss fell silent, looked at him steadily, and began in a grave voice: "I am going to share some information with you, Lanny—top secret. You will understand without my saying it, you are not to drop any hint of it to any person."

"Of course, Governor."

"I have to specify, not even to your wife."

"My wife has never asked me a question, once I had told her that I was pledged."

"Churchill came here just before Christmas, as you probably heard; he brought a large staff, and we threshed out the problems of world strategy. We both agree that Germany is our principal foe and must be beaten first; but we differ as to the best way to get at him. I would like to cross the Channel and seize the Cherbourg peninsula. I would do it this summer, even poorly prepared as we are. The Russians are pleading for a second front; they are in desperate straits, and we fear they may be knocked out of the war. But Churchill won't hear of it; he is afraid of another Dunkerque. He keeps talking about what he calls 'the soft underbelly of Europe.' He is hypnotized by the idea of breaking in by the back door. As you know, he tried it in the last war."

"I have heard him explain his failure, to his own satisfaction."

"I doubt very much if I'll be able to change him. In any case, I am determined that we shall fight this year; and if it can't be Cherbourg, then it'll be French North Africa. In either case, it will be the largest expedition ever to cross an ocean and will involve a colossal amount of work; something like a thousand ships, with landing craft, artillery, air support. Have you picked up any hint of all this?"

"I haven't been any place where there were hints, Governor. I can see the strategy—to make the Mediterranean safe, shorten the route to Suez, and be in a position to take Rommel in the rear."

"Just so. And if we can take Tunis we shall be able to cross to Sicily, and then to Italy."

"Italy would be dreadful country to fight in, Governor. I have motored through it, and it is a bootful of mountains."

"We shall have command of the sea, and soon, I hope, of the air. If we can take the airfields in southern Italy we shall be in a position to bomb southern Germany and the munitions plants which Hitler has built in Austria, imagining them safely out of reach."

"That all sounds fine to me, Governor."

"The main point is that we shall be doing something, and giving our troops actual battle practice, the only way they can learn. Also, we shall be showing the Russians that we mean business; every division that Hitler has to send to stop us will be one more missing from the eastern front."

"You want me to go and spy out the land?"

"Go first to Vichy and meet the leaders, as you did before. Let them talk, and tell you how they feel about us, and what they expect us to do, and what they will do in reply. Then you might meet your friend in Toulon and get acquainted with some of the underground people. Sound them out on the all-important question of their Fleet, and what we have to expect from both officers and men."

"They won't talk to me, Governor, unless I reveal the truth about myself."

"Use your own judgment. If you can meet the right people and get anything of value, you may tell them that you have been sent by me. Tell them that our armies are coming, and soon, but don't say where or when. Give them money, if they are dependable and can use it to our advantage. We must have a new arrangement about money, Lanny, for we are spending it, really spending now. Nothing counts but saving the lives of our men and furthering our objectives."

"I see what you mean, Governor. I don't want any money for myself—"

"I am paid a salary, Lanny, and so is everybody I am putting to work. You are a married man now, and you have to think about a family."

"My wife is very proud of earning all she needs, so put me down as one of your dollar-a-year men. But when it comes to distributing money to the underground, I'm willing of course. I have the good fortune to know one absolutely reliable man, and have no doubt that he will be able to lead me to others."

"I will arrange to have a hundred thousand dollars put to your account in your New York bank. I shall not expect any accounting, except in a general way, when we meet. When you can use more to good advantage, let me know."

"What the underground needs, Governor, is not so much money as arms and explosives."

"When you come back, bring me the names of such persons as are willing to be known to us. I will turn them over to Donovan, and his agents will get in touch with them. We have many ways of getting supplies into France now, and we shall have more. However, I don't want you to go deeply into that sort of thing, which is bound to be dangerous. What I want from you is information from the top people, with whom you have had so much success. It's all right for you to go to Switzerland and see what your German man is doing, and give him whatever money he can use; but don't stay long. I'd rather you would go to North Africa and meet the top people there, and find out what their attitude is now and what it's likely to be when we come. I don't need to go into details, you will understand what is needed."

VIII

So there were the orders, not very different from what P.A. 103 had received in the past and what he had expected now. His quick mind started thinking up questions, but before he could speak his Boss began: "Do you know Robert Murphy?"

"I met him in Vichy, but only casually. You may remember, you advised me to keep away from Admiral Leahy and the rest of our staff because they might suspect that I was the mysterious 'Zaharoff' who was sending reports through the Embassy."

"I have sent Bob as our counselor to North Africa. He has been provided with a staff of vice-consuls, about a dozen. They are carefully chosen men, mostly young; they know French, and of course their consular duties are nominal; they are there to prepare the way for a possible invasion. You will inevitably meet them and form an impression of what they are doing. I am not sending you to watch them, but if you see anything that I ought to know, you will tell me about it; that goes for good things as well as bad, their successes as well as their inadequacies."

"I understand, Governor."

"You will find Bob Murphy a delightful fellow, warmhearted and genial—perhaps too much so for the sort of people he will be dealing with. He is one of what you have called my 'striped-pants boys.'"

"Your cookie-pushers, Governor." Lanny grinned.

"Also, he is one of those liberal Catholics whom you find it hard to believe in. But you will recognize that he is the sort I have to send to Vichy France and to their colonies. You will like him personally, and will discover that he has a nasty job. I need not tell you that the enemy agents are swarming in that region and are pretty well in command of its affairs."

"I realize that. Do you wish me to approach them secretly and pretend that I am still their friend?"

"I leave that to your judgment. I doubt if you could get much from them, because they will naturally assume that you must be their enemy now. I am more interested in what you can get from the French, of all groups. They are bound to know that we are coming sooner or later, and they will be trimming their sails to the new wind. You will encounter many varieties of intrigue."

"Algiers will be a nest of rattlesnakes, Governor; I'll do my best not to get bitten. Am I to give Murphy any hint of what I am doing?"

"Not at the outset, I think. He'll no doubt have his suspicions. Tell me this, can you manage to work your camouflage in that part of the world? Is there any art there?"

"Wherever there are wealthy French residents, there are always paintings, and maybe good ones. I have come upon old masters in unexpected places, and to be looking for them in those colonies would be as natural as looking for spinning wheels and grandfather's clocks in Vermont or New Hampshire. There must also be Moorish art preserved there. I don't know much about it, but I could bone up in the library and be an 'authority' in a week or two. I'll try to interest one or two of my clients in the idea, and then I'll be able to write letters and send cablegrams from the field. That impresses the censors, and of course they inform the authorities, and presently they begin to think that I may really be what I pretend to be."

"Fine!" said the President. "I am beginning to believe it myself."

"But of course I won't be able to interest the State Department gentry in Moorish art. It's up to you to see that I get a passport to all these places you have suggested."

"I'll have Baker attend to that at once. How soon do you think you can go?"

"I ought to have a week or so to attend to personal matters. I want to get my wife settled in New York, and take her to Newcastle and introduce her to my father and his family. My father may have some request to make of me—and that's important, because it provides an extra camouflage and enables me to meet influential people. I suppose you will want me to talk with Professor Alston about this project?"

"By all means. He will have many suggestions to make. Take your time, but no more than is necessary."

"Am I to send you reports in the usual way?"

"Through our chargé when you are in Vichy, through Harrison in Switzerland, and through Bob Murphy in North Africa. I will instruct Bob that letters for me marked 'Zaharoff' are to be forwarded by diplomatic pouch, unopened."

"By the way, Governor, that reminds me—an odd thing. As you know, I amuse myself by delving into psychic phenomena. Most of my friends take it as a sign that I am slightly cracked, but they can't explain the things that happen."

"I have known of such experiences, Lanny, and am not surprised that you are interested in the subject."

"At my mother's home on the Riviera there is an old Polish woman who is a medium. She has been a family pensioner for the past fifteen years. Whenever I go there, I never fail to try a few sittings, and one of the 'spirits,' or whatever they are who never fail to announce themselves, is old Zaharoff. He fusses and frets because I won't pay a debt he owes a man at Monte Carlo, but he never tells me any way to get the money. The last time I was there, about a year ago, he gave me quite a shock by announcing that he was greatly displeased by the way I was making use of his name. You understand, I have never mentioned that fact to a living soul, and I thought you and I were the only two persons who knew that I was 'Zaharoff.' Of course, it may be that the medium got that out of my subconscious mind; anyhow, it makes me uneasy about having other people experimenting with Madame. My stepfather does it continually, and he might talk about it, simply because he wouldn't have any idea how important the secret is."

"I get you," said F.D.R.

"It set me to thinking about the name. The old munitions king didn't have many intimates before his death, and if one of my reports were to fall into the hands of the Gestapo, they might set out making inquiries among the old man's heirs and business associates and thus come upon my name. So I think we had better have a new deal and bury old Sir Basil."

"All right," said the President, "choose a new name." Then, before Lanny could speak, he added: "A North African landing is known as 'Operation Gymnast.' That is top secret, but if ever you get into a spot and want to convince one of our people that you are an insider—somebody like Bob Murphy—you can use it."

"O.K.," replied Lanny. "It might be a good idea for me to have a name along the same line. Suppose we say 'Traveler.' I seem to be earning that fairly."

"So let it be, and I'll give the necessary instructions. Also, I'll list the name with my private telephone service, and any time you call the White House and give the name, you'll reach me if I am available."

"Fine, Governor! Thanks a million."

"The thanks are all yours. And one thing more. Get me a visiting card out of that desk drawer."

Lanny had done this once before and knew where to look. The President took the card and wrote on it with his fountain pen: "My friend Lanny Budd is worthy of all trust. F.D.R." He handed that to the secret agent, saying: "Better sew it up in the lining of your coat or some safe place, and use it only when you are sure it is needed."

The agent replied: "If I get into a jam with the enemy, I'll chew it up and swallow it!" Little did he guess what a seer he would prove to be.

IX

Business first, then pleasure. "If you can spare the time," said the Boss, "you might stay for tea and meet some of the family. You don't have to be so carefully hidden from now on."

Lanny said he would be glad to stay. A button was pressed, and an amiable Negro man appeared, the same Prettyman whom Lanny had seen many times dozing in a chair just outside the President's bedroom door. The master was wheeled from the library, up the ramp, and along the hall to the drawing-room at the other end of the house. There was a tea service waiting, and Lanny met for the first time the tall, active person whom the newspapers were wont to call the "First Lady of the Land," and whose picture he had seen so many times.

The First Lady was splendidly dressed in a pale blue panne-velvet gown, adorned with "diamond clips" in many places. She had the same delicate blond coloring of eyes and skin which had once caused Lanny to say of Bernard Shaw that he was the cleanest-looking person he had ever seen. In her story of her own life she had stated that since she had not been blessed with a pretty face she had had to cultivate other gifts. But Lanny thought her opinion of her own face was certainly a mistaken one; she was not only pretty, she was an exquisite person. Her blue eyes smiled constantly, even when she was occupied with the tall silver tea service. There was no trace of that gaucherie in gestures and posture which news-camera men somehow managed to put into her photographs. Perhaps their employers always chose the worst!

Eleanor Roosevelt had been her name before her marriage—she was Franklin's cousin. She had married him and brought up five children, whom her mother-in-law considered she was spoiling. Her political enemies had considered that these children wanted too much money, and too many divorces; but now the four tall sons were in the service and doing their painful duties, so that clamor was for the most part stilled.

The young Eleanor had played tennis, and the mature Eleanor played politics, and in that game half the country finds fault with whatever you do and attributes it to the worst motives imaginable. The conservative half considered that Eleanor gadded about too much, especially in wartime; they insisted that woman's place was the White House, and that it was a deplorable thing for a President's wife to be filling the place up with all sorts of riffraff—movie actors and dancers and labor leaders and even Negro singers. They found it intolerable that she should go flying about the country, making speeches to women's clubs and "radical" conventions and what not; they didn't like the sound of her voice, rather high-pitched and tremulous over the radio, nor anything that she had said over a period of ten years. They insisted that she made too much money, and refused to pay attention to the statement that it all went to charity. In short, they just didn't like her; and the worst of it was, she didn't appear to mind it in the least, but went serenely ahead to manifest her able personality and give pleasure and advice to millions of the plain people who wanted it.

Now here she was, seated behind a tea-table, smiling brightly. She knew that this caller had been in her husband's service without pay, and was going off again on a dangerous mission. She set out to be agreeable to him, and he had no trouble in believing that it was because she really liked him and was interested in what he had to say. She had heard of his escape from Hongkong, and who wouldn't want to hear about that? Lanny, who liked to talk, told about it; then he told about Ching-ling, the widow of Sun Yat-sen, founder of the modern Chinese Republic. She was another gracious lady, born just halfway round the globe, yet her social ideals and political program were in complete harmony with those of the First Lady of the Americans. So powerful are the forces which are making the modern world, and are making it one world, whether or not anybody wants it so.

Lanny told about the cruise from Baltimore on the yacht *Oriole*, which had taken him to the Orient, and how on the night of the Japanese attack on Hongkong it had endeavored to steal out of the harbor. Four months had passed, and the yacht had never been heard from, so it must be presumed to be lost. The President remarked that of the many vessels which had made that attempt, seventeen were missing. Of course some might have been captured. "We may not know until the war is over, for our barbarous enemy pays no attention to the Hague Convention."

Mrs. Roosevelt asked about Reverdy Holdenhurst, owner of the yacht. She had never met him, but had heard of him. He was one of those "economic royalists" whom F.D.R. had pilloried, and who had responded with bitter hatred. "A strange, unhappy man," Lanny said. "He was not equal to the battle of life, and he knew it, and clung to his money as his one form of distinction. I never gave him any hint concerning my attitude to the New Deal. It was enough that he put his money into Budd-Erling stock and enabled my father to expand more rapidly."

"Let him be admitted into heaven on that basis," remarked the President.

Lanny knew how to make himself agreeable, and also when to take his departure. When he arose, Mrs. Roosevelt said: "Tell your wife that when she is settled I shall be happy to call upon her." Nothing could have been kinder, and he said so. As he drove back to New York he reflected upon the subject of how much a woman could do to make or mar the life of a public man. In how many of his crucial decisions had this man been guided by his wife's advice, by the facts she put before him, and the people whom she introduced to him? What would he have been without her by his side? Would he even have survived his illness? Lanny, who had called himself "a feminist" from his boyhood, found confirmation of his creed.

2

Between Love and Duty

LAUREL CRESTON'S friend Agnes Drury had shared Laurel's apartment in the East Sixties, just off Park Avenue. Now Laurel had been around the world and come back with a husband; they could make room for him, but it was crowded. Laurel had said: "I'm afraid he'll be leaving very soon." Her unmarried friend replied: "I am curious to see what a man is like."

When the man returned from his errand up the Hudson, Agnes was in the kitchenette, preparing the evening meal. The new wife came and put herself in her husband's arms. "Lanny," she whispered, "I have been to the doctor."

"And what?"

"He says it has happened."

"Sure?"

"Absolutely."

"Oh, *grand!*" He held her tightly, and she hid her pleasure in his coat. She was a little woman, and the top of her head just about came to his shoulder. He kissed her soft brown hair. "I am tickled to death," he said. And when she asked: "Really? Truly?" he declared: "It will be an adventure for both of us, and make sure that we have to appreciate each other."

He had a twelve-year-old daughter in England, but hadn't seen her for almost a year, and he had the sad belief that she would mean less and less to him as she grew up. She was Irma's daughter, and Lanny was bored with Irma and her friends and everything they said and thought and did. But a child of Laurel Creston's could grow up to be interested in what Lanny himself said and thought and did. He led his subdued bride to the sofa and put his arms about her, whispering delightful nothings to cheer her up and give her courage for woman's long ordeal. He put off saying: "I have to leave in a week," and instead remarked: "I ran into Mrs. Roosevelt, and she offered to call on you."

Laurel was surprised, and objected: "That wouldn't be proper. I ought to call on her. She is the older woman."

"Well, drop her a line at Hyde Park and fix it up the way you think best. She is worth knowing, and some day you may want to write about her."

The wife didn't say: "Where did you meet her, and how?" If Lanny wanted to tell that, he would do so; if he didn't, she had to assume that he was bound by his orders, and she was bound not to "fish." She was rigid about all duties, an ethical person. She didn't even ask: "Have you found out when you are leaving?" Perhaps he wasn't free to let her know that meeting the First Lady and getting his marching orders had any connection with each other. She had married him with the understanding that he was not free to tell her anything about his job.

II

Their next adventure was to be a visit to Newcastle, Connecticut. Lanny said: "How about driving up this evening? It only takes an hour or two."

The answer was: "I am à little tired and I'd rather rest and start fresh in the morning. I had to get some clothes, you know."

"Haven't you a closet full?" he countered.

"How manlike! Don't you know how fashions change in half a

year? And don't you realize how much your own happiness depends upon my managing to please your family?"

"Really, darling, you don't have to worry about that. They will be delighted with you."

"Their delight may be increased if I look the way they think I ought to. For a man forty-two years old, you are still naïve, Lanny. You told me for how long they tried to get you married to an heiress."

"They gave up that hope long ago. I am sure they will be willing to settle for a bluestocking." He chuckled.

"Maybe so, but all the same I'm taking no chances. Whatever you think of them, I'm sure they think of themselves as very grand people."

He chuckled again. "They surely don't think themselves any grander than your Uncle Reverdy thought *himself*. They wanted me to get married, and when they hear that I am 'expecting,' they will welcome you as the vessel of the Lord."

"We will go the first thing in the morning, and I'll have a chance to make friends with your stepmother before I meet your father. One at a time!"

Lanny telephoned to Newcastle and announced this program, and incidentally gave his father the medical tidings. He had announced their safe arrival on the previous evening, as soon as they had stepped off the plane from Newfoundland. Early the next morning Robbie had sent them a car for their use. That was Robbie's way.

Lanny inspected the spring costume which his wife had purchased, a blue frock and hat to match; he had told her that he liked her in blue, and so she had adopted it. She would take along the very grand fur coat which had been presented to her in Moscow, for you couldn't count upon New England weather in early April. Lanny duly praised her taste, and then they went in to the supper which Agnes Drury had got ready—mostly out of cans, according to the custom of apartment dwellers in Manhattan. Agnes was a trained nurse whom Laurel had met in a boarding-house when she had first come to New York; they had teamed up and got along perfectly, because one went out to a job while the other sat at home and pecked at a typewriter. It would be still more convenient later on, for when Laurel needed help, she would become Agnes's job, and Lanny could be sure that his wife was in competent hands.

Only after they were alone in their room did he tell her: "Darling, I have to be leaving for Europe in about a week."

He saw her blanch. She had known it was coming, but that did not spare her the pain. He added quickly: "I am not going into Germany or any enemy-held country. I have positive orders on that. So there won't be much danger."

"Yes, dear," she forced herself to say. "Do your best to take care of yourself, for my sake." She had had fair notice what she was marrying, and what her lot would be. She would never torment him with grief.

"Millions of men are going into danger," he reminded her, "and mine will be of the least."

"I know. I know, Lanny. I have my job, and I'll do it and not allow myself to brood."

"My headquarters will be at Juan-les-Pins. Write me there; but of course nothing of a confidential nature. The Vichy censorship will read everything. Remember, I am an art expert."

"I understand. When do you expect to return?"

"Usually I stay two or three months, depending upon what I run into. I will write to you frequently, and I may be able to drop you a hint by references to paintings I discover. Be on the watch for a double meaning in any names of painters or their subjects." He didn't say: "That is my code."

III

Next morning they set out on their drive, by one of the bridges across the Harlem River and along the boulevard which borders the Sound. The weather favored them, and the fur coat stayed locked in the rumble seat of the car. They drove to what had once been the little town and now was the crowded port of Newcastle, and onto the higher ground where the masters of the community had their homes. Esther was out in the rose garden, waiting for them, and Robbie, busy though he was, came home at lunchtime to meet his oldest son and newest daughter.

They were pleased with Laurel—how could they be otherwise? She was thirty-three, a settled woman who knew what she wanted, and presumably Lanny was it. She was what is technically known as a "lady," and shared his peculiar ideas and interests. She was going to give him a child, and that was what all his parents wanted—the pair in Connecticut and the pair on the French Riviera. The former got their claim in first, inviting Laurel to come and live with them; but Laurel, forewarned, made it plain that the way of life she had established was necessary to her work. In New York she met the editors and publishers and got their advice. She was going to write several articles about what she had seen in China and Russia and then resume work upon a partly completed novel. Pregnancy wasn't going to make any difference in her life, at least not for some time. A lady who knew her own mind!

There was a whole flock of Budds and Budds-by-marriage who had to drop in and satisfy their curiosity; and there had to be a hurriedly got-up reception for all the friends at the country club. The visiting bride had to be driven to see that vast new fabricating plant which was turning out fighter planes, a new model every two or three months, the way things were going in this mad war. For a year or more the Budd-Erling had lagged behind the Spitfire, but now it was ahead, Robbie proudly announced, and marched his daughter-in-law through drafting rooms and "mock-up" rooms where it was being made absolutely certain that never again would American flyers have to fear anything in the skies. There was a new phrase, "jet propulsion," which Robbie barely whispered; he couldn't show any of that because he had hidden it away somewhere in the deserts of the far Southwest.

Laurel had heard about the Budd-Erling Aircraft Corporation, not merely from her husband but from her Uncle Reverdy. Now that he was presumed to be lost, she, as one of his heirs, would become a stockholder—another way of being important among the Budds. She was seated in a sort of little handcar and was run through the immense plant, amid a considerable racket and what looked like confusion but wasn't. She saw parts of planes coming down from overhead and being welded together; she saw them roll out of doors, taxi under their own power, and take off on test flights. That would be going on all day and all night, while she ate and while she slept and while she finished an anti-Nazi novel. It was part of the immense and horrifying price required to put three dictators out of business; and much as she hated war, she had to reconcile herself to it, and be glad that her new father-in-law had foreseen it for half a century, and had had his own way at least for the past half-dozen years.

She had heard a lot about him, and she now put her shrewd mind to understanding his. He was nearing seventy but refused to make any concession to age. His hair was gray, but his frame was sturdy and unbowed. He was kind and generous to everyone he liked, but he was limited in his interests and set in his opinions, as hard as the concrete of his runways or the steel in the engines of his planes. The world was a place of battle, and his country was going to get on top, and he, the master of Budd-Erling Aircraft, was on top in his country and going to stay there. The way to get along with him was to take those things for granted.

As to Esther Remsen Budd, Lanny's stepmother, the problem was even simpler. Esther, too, was an ethical person, a daughter of the Puritans. The great lady of her town, she took her duties seriously, supported all worthy causes, and would not permit the Republican Party boss to bring to prominence in public life any man who neglected his family or got drunk in public. She quickly decided that this shrewd woman writer was exactly the proper person for her problem stepson, and had a long confidential talk with her, telling about Lanny as she had known him since his youth, and about men in general, and the necessity of managing them. When after a visit of two days the couple set out for New York, the gray-haired woman kissed the brown-haired one and told her that she was a member of the clan and free to call for their help at any time.

IV

Back in the city, Lanny visited the bookstores and found a couple of works on Arab and Moorish art, which he learned was mostly architecture, because the Prophet, seeking to put an end to idol worship, had banned all "images," and the zealots of his faith had interpreted that to include painting. Lanny visited the Public Library and spent a couple of mornings reading diligently and making notes concerning arabesque doorways with carved interlacements, and mosaic floors with designs representing flowers, vines, and geometrical forms made out of pious sentences from the Koran.

Also, there was his friend Zoltan Kertezsi, his associate in art matters for a couple of decades. Zoltan had never met Laurel, nor indeed heard of her; he was astonished when his friend dropped down out of the blue with a wife, and of course he wanted to meet the lady. A lonely old bachelor would stop in at the little apartment now and then, and when he had come to know this woman writer well, he told her a story that he had never told Lanny, the story of his losing the great love of his life. She had been a lady of high degree in Hungary, his native land, and had decided at long last that she did not care to marry a commoner.

This gracious and cultivated art lover, now in his late fifties but still youthful at heart, had been handling the paintings of Beauty's deceased husband, Marcel Detaze, which were stored in a bank vault in Baltimore; he now had accountings to render and suggestions to make.

Also, he could tell Lanny about art in North Africa, French, Spanish, and Moorish, for he had traveled in those regions and had made many acquaintances there. He had long ago got over his surprise that his colleague was able to travel in wartime; he pretended to consider it quite normal, even though he knew that he, Zoltan, could never have got such permissions. A tactful person, he had never questioned Lanny, and would never question Lanny's wife; he would pretend to take it as proper that some persons should enjoy privileges.

Did Lanny's clients have any suspicion concerning his ability to gad about in a severely restricted world? They were all wealthy persons who were accustomed to having their own way. They knew about Budd-Erling and wouldn't be surprised to hear that the son of Budd-Erling enjoyed the confidence of State Department officials. They wouldn't question their art expert, any more than they had questioned their bootlegger in times past, or would question their black-market operators in times soon to come. If somebody brought you what you wanted at a price within reason, you would pay him and take possession, whether it was an old master, an automobile tire, or just a few pounds of butter or cartons of cigarettes.

Lanny didn't have the time for his usual trip to Chicago and points in between. He used the long distance telephone, and had a chat with his plate-glass friends in Pittsburgh and his hardware friends in Cincinnati; with old Mr. Hackabury, the soap man of Reubens, Indiana, and old Mrs. Fotheringay, who filled her Lake Shore mansion with painted babies. He drove out to Tuxedo Park, and discovered that his friend Harlan Winstead was not interested in Arab or Moorish art objects, but thought that a neighbor might be. This Mr. Vernon was invited to lunch; he was building a villa for his favorite daughter, and was charmed by the descriptions Lanny gave of arabesque doorways and mosaic floors with interlacing designs made of Arabic scripts. He suggested that it might be a unique idea to take up such mosaics, carefully numbering each piece on its under side, and restore them as features of a loggia or a patio in an American suburban home.

Lanny pointed out that Algeria was full of ancient Roman ruins, whole cities, and that the Romans also had gone in for mosaics, and without being afraid of either polytheism or nudity. The best of these ruins had been made national property by the French government, but others were on private property and the mosaics might be purchased. Mr. Vernon authorized this well-recommended art expert to make such purchases for him up to a total cost of twenty thousand dollars. He wrote a letter to that effect, which Lanny said would help him in getting a passport from the State Department, though its real purpose was to lull the suspicions of officials in Vichy France and its African possessions. He knew from long experience that there was no baggage so well worth its weight as letters from American millionaires.

V

The President's confidential man, Baker, telephoned to the apartment, and Lanny went to the man's hotel room and got his passport. He made sure that it covered all the places to which he might have to go.

Baker said: "I hope you have better luck than you had with the last ones, Mr. Budd. I can get you passage on a Clipper to Lisbon by way of Puerto Rico and Brazil on Saturday."

Lanny said: "Fine," and that was that.

The time was short. He had to have a conference with Professor Alston. He was ready to fly to Washington for this, but Alston telephoned that he was coming to New York and that Lanny should wait. Meantime there was Jim Stotzlmann, who was F.D.R.'s friend as well as Lanny's. The President had hinted that Jim was another P.A., but had told Lanny not to ask, and Lanny hadn't. This genial fellow, big and yet gentle as a girl, was only a couple of years older than Lanny, but while Lanny had been playing with the fisherboys on the beach at Juan, Jim had been dining with most of the crowned heads of Europe, on board his father's "palatial" yacht—as the newspapers always called it.

In World War I the scion of the Stotzlmann clan had enlisted as a private, and later had become an Army Reserve officer. Now he was a Major, and stationed in New York, busy with mysterious matters having to do with docks and shipping and the prevention of sabotage. They had dinner at Jim's hotel, and Lanny told the story of six months' misadventures. Jim, for his part, told of goings-on in what had become the busiest port in the world. "You can have no idea of the scale on which we are going into this war, Lanny. It fairly takes one's breath away."

"What I want to know about is the junta," Lanny said. That was their name for the group of powerful persons who for the past year or more had been discussing a plan for putting the New Deal out of business by taking physical possession of its principal exponent and keeping him under their control.

"They are still at it," Jim said. "I still can't sleep at night because I can't get the Governor to take it seriously enough."

"I had hoped that since we got into the war their patriotism might have come to the fore."

"Patriotism, heck!" responded the Major. "That gang knows nobody but themselves."

"Do they expect to make a deal with Hitler?"

"They expect to do anything that will keep them from having to fight for Stalin. I'm not free to go into details, Lanny, but that remark was made by Harrison Dengue to a friend of mine barely a week ago. I personally reported it to the Chief, but he just smiled and said: 'Well, his money is fighting, and that's all we care about.'"

"Dengue said he wanted to see me again after I had talked to Hitler and his crowd; but I doubt if I'm ever going into Germany again. This war has been most inconvenient for me." Lanny said it with a smile, and his friend smiled in return; they had met only two or three times, but their points of view were so nearly the same that they could talk in shorthand, as it were.

"Dengue is in Chicago now, and that is one of the headquarters of sedition. I wish you could go out there and make friends with them, Lanny."

"I wish I could, but I have to fly overseas in a couple of days. I turn our great Chief over to your keeping."

"He has promised me to have Hyde Park taken out of the New York Military District and put directly under the care of Washington. That will help, I hope."

"You know, Jim," said Lanny, "the story you told me has haunted me; I doubt if I'll ever get it out of my mind. We've read about how the Roman Republic was overthrown, and so many others in history, but we just can't bring ourselves to realize how easily the same thing might happen in this country. Just imagine that in the next industrial crisis the labor crowd, or what are called the 'radicals,' carried an election, and our big business masters wanted to keep them out; suppose there was an Army cabal, and these men backed it with their money and their newspapers and their radios; suppose they were to seize the newly elected President, hold him incommunicado, and issue orders in his name—what could the rest of us do?"

"That is just what I keep hammering into my friends, Lanny. They all say: 'The people would rise.' But what can the people with shotguns and pitchforks do against modern weapons of war and modern organization? With bombing planes and poison gas a few men could wipe out a whole city; and I know men who are ready to do it—they have said so in plain words."

"I could compile a list of a hundred such," responded Lanny. "It is a danger we shall not be free from so long as capitalism endures; and it is going to die a hard and nasty death."

VI

There was one other man in New York with whom Lanny wanted to have a talk. That was his friend Forrest Quadratt, who had been head of the Nazi propaganda service in America. Forrest knew what was going on, and when he got going he would spill many hints. Lanny telephoned the ex-poet's home, and, as usual, the soft silky voice revealed warm pleasure. "Where on earth have you been all this time?"

"I've been all the way round the world and had a lot of adventures."

"Will you come up to dinner? I'll be alone."

Lanny had been planning to take Laurel and Agnes out to dinner, but duty came before pleasure. He walked uptown and over to Riverside Drive, to the familiar apartment with the study full of books and photographs and other literary trophies. Forrest Quadratt was in his fifties, and had made it his business to meet many of the writers of his time. In his youth he had been a flaming erotic poet, a self-proclaimed genius, and he had become embittered because his word was not taken by the critics. Now he was a self-registered Nazi agent—because the law required this frankness. He had collected large sums from Germany and expended a part of them to pay for a flood of books, pamphlets, and papers. He had written speeches for congressmen to deliver and put into the *Congressional Record*, and then he had them mailed out to the extent of hundreds of thousands of copies free of postal charges.

Lanny told the story of his plane smash-up, his sojourn in the hospital, his yacht trip to the South Seas, and his escape from Hongkong. "I couldn't imagine what had become of you!" exclaimed Quadratt. "So much has been happening in the meantime—the wrecking of all our hopes of peace. Have you heard what has happened to me?"

"I saw no newspapers between Manila and New York, a period of more than four months."

"I have been indicted and convicted, and am under a jail sentence of from eight months to two years."

"Good Lord! What for?"

"They framed me on a preposterous charge. I registered myself as in the employ of German magazines, and they undertook to prove that I was in the employ of the government."

"*Herrgott, noch einmal!* Don't they know that German magazines are government institutions?"

"Of course they know it; but they pretended not to, and so did the jury."

"Well, but you're not in jail!" Lanny looked about him at the elegant apartment.

"I am out on bail, pending an appeal. I have every hope that some court will set aside the conviction. The conduct of the prosecutor was so outrageous that he should be the one to serve the sentence."

"You know how it is in wartime," remarked Lanny sympathetically. "The country goes crazy."

"But this was before Pearl Harbor, Lanny. At any rate, the indictment was. It has been an intensely disagreeable experience."

"I sympathize with you, Forrest; and certainly I hope you get a reversal of the verdict." It was hard for Lanny to put the proper amount of feeling into his tone, for he knew what would have happened to a German citizen in Berlin who had made a fortune by serving American magazines or American government agencies in circulating pro-Allied propaganda throughout the Fatherland. That was the advantage which the ruthless men had over the mild and honorable in this world; and how the balance was to be righted was a problem indeed!

Lanny sat watching the rather small man with the round, smooth-shaven face, the thick spectacles, and the hesitating manner. He saw that the convicted agent was a worried man indeed. He spoke with great rapidity, as if he were afraid he would not be allowed to finish; but Lanny let him pour out a stream of troubles. All his German friends in this country were interned and incommunicado, and all activities had come to a stop. Forrest didn't say what they weren't able to accomplish, but left the son of Budd-Erling to make queries as to his meaning. The Americans who were in sympathy with his ideas were many of them no longer working, because it was so difficult to get money. The unscrupulous F.B.I. agents were dogging everybody's footsteps, trying to get something on them. "I have reason to believe they are going to try to frame something else against us; possibly a sedition charge, which carries a much heavier penalty. They are after Father Coughlin now and seem determined to put him out of business."

In short, the skies over Forrest Quadratt's head looked black. He had failed in everything he had attempted, and his appetite for an excellent dinner was spoiled. The might of the Western world was going to be thrown against the Fatherland, and the only hope the ex-poet could see was in the forthcoming spring offensive against Russia, which might wipe out that nest of vipers soon enough to save Germany from a two-front war. Lanny tried subtly and carefully to find out if there might not be another hope, that of replacing Franklin D. Roosevelt as Commander-in-Chief of the American Armed Forces. Lanny mentioned that he was getting in touch with that powerful personality, Mr. Harrison Dengue, but Forrest didn't take the bait; he wasn't going to discuss the junta, even if he knew anything about it.

Could it possibly have occurred to him that the son of Budd-Erling might have changed his point of view when he discovered himself under the Japanese bombs and shells? Certainly Forrest must have known that Budd-Erling was now turning out a superior type of fighter plane, and he must have been warned that the Federal Bureau of Investigation was employing many sorts of agents and disguises in its secret war on American Nazism. It might be that Berlin had informed him that Lanny had visited Stalin. Lanny waited for some hint on the subject, but none came. He decided at last that he was wasting his evening. He excused himself, went home, and took his two ladies out to a late supper.

VII

Charles T. Alston came up from Washington, and Lanny went to his hotel and took him for a drive in the park, a safe place for a confidential talk. This quiet little gray-haired man was much sought after by reporters, for he had been one of the members of the original "brain trust," away back in the days when a former Assistant Secretary of the Navy was elected Governor of New York State, and had the unprecedented idea of inviting some college professors to join his cabinet and advise in the management of the most populous and wealthy state of the Union. Later Alston had been taken to Washington, where he became a "fixer," charged with settling the wrangles of jealous bureaucrats, and later on of statesmen, generals, and admirals who got into one another's hair.

Earlier in his career this professor of geography had served on the staff of advisers which Woodrow Wilson had taken to the Paris Peace Conference, and there he had become Lanny Budd's first and only employer. Lanny had been nineteen then, and now he was forty-two, but he still addressed Alston as "Professor" and still looked up to him as an authority on all affairs of government and politics. Alston, for his part, still thought of Lanny as the brilliant and fashionable youth who had chattered in French with generals and duchesses, while Alston had painfully studied the language from textbooks and wondered how to find out whether you pronounced the final "s" in Reims, and what was the difference, if any, between the sounds of *dedans* and *des dents*. The geographer from the "sticks" had felt the same secret awe of Lanny that Lanny had felt for him.

First Lanny had to repeat the story of his adventures on the plane trip and in Hongkong and Yenan and Moscow. He had had to tell it to F.D.R., and to Robbie, and Zoltan, and Jim, and the end was not yet. Alston wanted to hear everything that Ching-ling had said, and Mao Tse-tung, and Stalin, and others in the Soviet Union. He asked questions, and incidentally imparted a few secrets. "We have to be sure that what we are sending the Russians actually reaches the front; for we are sustaining grave losses on the route to Murmansk, so great that we may have to discontinue it."

"Of course I didn't see anything with my own eyes," responded the younger man. "I can only tell you what Stalin and the others said. They beg for everything we can spare, and are certain that they will be pushed to the uttermost this summer."

"Did they give any hint of the possibility of having to quit?"

"All the way through China and Siberia and Russia proper, we never heard any word but of resistance to the last gasp. You can count upon that as a gift from Hitler. He is the most hated man that has appeared upon the stage of history for many centuries."

VIII

After Alston was through asking questions, it was Lanny's turn, and he had accumulated quite a list. "Professor," he began, "there is something that has been troubling my mind for nearly half a year. You telephoned me at the hospital in Halifax that you had received the information you wanted from Germany. Did you mean that, or were you just putting my mind at rest?"

"I meant most of it, Lanny. We got some information and expect to get more."

"Are you free to tell me anything about it?"

"The rule still holds, that we never speak the words atomic fission except when it is absolutely necessary. But I can say this: we are ahead of the Germans and expect to keep ahead."

"But you can't be absolutely sure?"

"Nothing can be absolutely sure in matters of scientific research. We know what the signs are at the moment, but nobody can know what some German physicist may have hit upon last night."

"I keep thinking there may still be something I can do about it."

"The Chief was quite positive that he didn't want to send you into Germany again, Lanny."

"He told me that. But I told him about my German contact in Geneva, and he was willing for me to go there."

"It would be foolhardy for us to risk taking *any* German into our confidence in this matter. The outcome of the war might depend upon it, and the whole future of humanity."

"Let me tell you a little about this man. I have known him since before Hitler. He was vouched for by the woman who later became my second wife. I have never told you about her; not even my mother or my father knows about her. She was a devoted Socialist Party member, and her first husband was murdered by the Nazis; she became a worker in the underground, and died in Dachau concentration camp, in spite of my best efforts to save her. The man I am talking about helped me in trying to rescue her; before that he was in Spain and proved his loyalty in the fires of that civil war; he rose to be a *capitán*. That surely ought to be enough evidence of his trustworthiness."

"I grant you that, Lanny. But what can he do now?"

"He had quite an extraordinary contact in Germany, apparently someone in Göring's own headquarters. He was able to give me the date of the invasion of Holland and Belgium, and later that of Norway, and I sent this information to the President. The last time I saw this man, about a year ago, he told me he had lost that contact but hoped to get another. He might have it now."

"That is just where the trouble comes in, Lanny. He may have a new contact that he trusts, and it may turn out to be a Gestapo agent playing with him. We simply cannot take such chances with the atomic bomb."

"I grant you that, Professor. But let us consider whether there might not be some information my man could get without having to know what it is for."

"That would be difficult, for the reason that the information is so highly technical that any scientist would know at once what the man was after and could infer what stage we had reached in our research."

"Let me make a suggestion or two. If we could find out whether the Germans have increased their production of graphite, wouldn't that tell us something?"

"In the first place, the fact that we are using graphite to moderate the speed of neutrons is one of the most priceless of our secrets; and second, German production wouldn't tell us much, because graphite is used for many war purposes and comparatively little of it is needed as a moderator."

"Well, then, how about heavy water? That, as I understand it, is difficult to produce and not much of it exists."

"That is true. If your man could find out if and where the Germans are making heavy water in large quantities, we should have a number-one bombing target."

"And how about Professor Schilling? Can his name be mentioned?"

"I fear we have to say no to that. Schilling is a nuclear physicist and nothing else, and we know that the Nazis have him at that job. We cannot risk having anybody know that he is on our side."

"If I could find out where a number of such physicists are employed, wouldn't that be important?"

"We already have that information, I believe; but I do not know what use is being made of it. I am only admitted to the fringes of these ultra-secret matters."

"This is true, is it not, that the quantity production of fissionable material would require a large plant; and if my man could find out where such a plant is located, wouldn't that be worth while?"

"I have to admit that that would be a major achievement."

"This is the way it appears to me: the Germans must know that we know the possibility of atom splitting, and they would certainly expect us to try to find out about what they are doing. I don't have to give my man any hint that we are working on the project. Can't I just tell him what has been in the scientific journals prior to the war, and ask if he can find out any more on this subject?"

"I should say there would be no harm in that; but it would be an exceedingly dangerous matter for your man and for his contacts."

"That is up to him. I will tell him the facts, as I have always done, and leave it to him to use his judgment. I suppose the same thing goes for jet propulsion, which Robbie tells me he is working on very secretly; and for rocket projectiles, and so on. The Germans are known to be working on these, and it surely wouldn't be any news to them that we are trying to catch up."

"If your man were able to get us real news about these matters, we'd award him a D.S.M. when the war is over."

"To award him American citizenship might be more to the point," opined Lanny. "We shall see."

IX

They talked about the presidential agent's own job, what information he might get in Vichy territory, and what use was likely to be made of it. Alston said that he agreed with the Chief in thinking that they ought to open a second front across the Channel in the summer of 1942, if only for the sake of its effect upon the Russians. "Even if we could do no more than establish a bridgehead, it would pay us in the long run, however costly. But between you and me, Lanny, I don't think we are going to be able to budge Churchill on this issue. I appreciate him as a propagandist, but he fancies himself also as a military strategist, and I fear he is somewhat vain on the subject. Certainly I have found him hard to argue with; he does all the talking."

"I can imagine it," responded Lanny with a grin. "He was so glad to get his troops off that shore, no doubt the idea of sending them back again gives him nightmares."

"He argues that our American troops are utterly untested, and who can be sure they would stand the punishment they would get from the Panzers and from the overhead strafing?"

"To say nothing of the subs on the way across, Professor. You can be sure that Hitler would throw in everything he has to make good the promises he has fed to his own people. It would be a life and death matter for him."

"I have listened to the arguments of the military men on both sides; there is very little agreement among them. We shift in our discussions from Cherbourg to Dakar, to Casablanca, Algiers, and Tunis. Then Churchill takes us to Salonika and the Vardar valley, and even to his old stamping ground of Gallipoli. Then we come back to Cherbourg. But this much I can tell you quite surely: no information that you bring us and no contacts that you make in Unoccupied France and in North Africa will be wasted. We shall surely be landing there before this war is over, and meantime we have to defend ourselves there, to the extent of keeping Laval out of power and Franco properly worried."

"The Governor seemed to think there was no longer any danger of a German attack upon Gibraltar."

"It would appear that the time for that has passed. Franco's demands were more than Hitler was willing to meet; and now, I think, Franco has been brought to realize that we mean business, and he will continue to hold his precarious seat upon the fence."

"F.D.R. didn't seem very clear in his mind whether I am to be an American patriot or a sympathizer with Fascism in my secret heart. It will hardly be possible to play both roles, at least not for long."

"Nobody can tell you about that, Lanny. You will have to go and find out what changes a year has made, and what your probable sources of information are, and then make your own decision as to which side of the fence to be on. A lot of Frenchmen will be doing the same, I fancy."

"No doubt about that!" agreed the P.A. with a touch of bitterness.

X

Parting time was at hand. On Lanny's last day at home Agnes went off to her work, and thoughtfully arranged to dine with a friend and go to a movie so that Laurel might be alone with her husband. But when they were alone they found that they didn't have much to talk about. Lanny couldn't talk about his work, and neither of them wanted to say how unhappy he or she was. Romeo had told them that "parting is such sweet sorrow," but neither found it true. Their hearts ached, and there was nothing sweet about it.

Lanny felt free to say that he was going to Vichy France, to see what the Pétainists were doing and planning. There was no danger about it—that tottering regime was doing its best to remain friends with America, and besides, they all thought that Lanny was one of them. So there was nothing for a wife to worry about; she would do her work, and Mother Nature would do Mother Nature's work, and by midsummer at the latest Lanny would return and perhaps be able to stay and see her through her confinement. Meantime they mustn't make things hard for each other. Laurel agreed, and when tears stole into her eyes she turned her head away and found an excuse to slip out of the room.

She had used the few days to make a rough draft of an article about what she had seen in "Red China." Lanny read this, and they had a subject to occupy their minds. For the past year or two few Americans had been able to get past the blockade which the Central Government maintained against their Yenan rival, and so this article would be something of a scoop; but its political point of view would work against it, because Laurel had been fascinated by the new life she had seen in that half-barren mountainous land, and editors of big-circulation magazines didn't fancy telling their readers that the outcome of this war might be a socialized world. Nor was it in accord with Allied propaganda to suggest that supplies being flown to Chungking at heavy cost were not being used against the Japs but were being saved for use in a future civil war. Laurel said: "I won't doctor the article. If the big-circulation editors don't want it, I'll give it to one of the small-circulation editors." Not so good for the future of a budding novelist!

As soon as Lanny left she was going to Baltimore to visit her aunt, Millicent Holdenhurst, and tell the story of the *Oriole* so far as she knew it. That would be a sad duty, and they talked about what she would say. Once more they discussed the possibility that the passengers and crew of that yacht might have got off in small boats and be stranded on some one of the thousands of islands large and small which pepper the map of that part of the world. It had happened to many people, and every now and then you read in the papers about some castaway who had found his way back to civilization. The natives took care of them and did not eat them—or, at any rate, those who were eaten did not get reported.

Inevitably that led to the strange experience which had befallen the newly married couple, flying from Yenan to Ulan-Bator over the great Gobi Desert. Laurel had fallen into a spontaneous trance, the only time that had ever happened to her. Or perhaps she had just been talking in her sleep, who could say? Anyhow, Lanny had heard what purported to be the voice of Lizbeth Holdenhurst, saying that the yacht had gone down with all on board. Could you believe that? Certainly you had to think about it, after so many strange psychic experiences had come to you.

XI

Lanny had a desire to try a séance with his wife but had refrained from suggesting it. She had had a warning of danger in advance of his last flight overseas, and he was afraid that might happen again and leave her possessed with fear. Now, on this last evening, she told him that her curiosity was greater than her fear, and she wanted to try one more trance. There was nothing he could say to that; if he were to invent some pretext for objecting, she would know that his fear was greater than his curiosity.

They shut off the telephone and plugged the doorbell, and Laurel stretched herself out on the couch and closed her eyes. Lanny sat by with notebook on his knee and pencil poised in proper psychical-research fashion. Laurel moaned and sighed several times and then lay still; and presently there came stealing into the room, from eternity, or God only could say where, a voice—what the researchers have labeled a "control." The most urbane and agreeable of controls imaginable was the lately deceased Otto Hermann Kahn, former senior partner of the international banking firm of Kuhn, Loeb and Company. Why he had picked Laurel Creston for his manifestations he did not say, and probably did not know; he professed to be skeptical about the whole affair. A weird joke upon himself as well as upon them!

"Well, well, here we are again!" chuckled the voice. "The last time was Hengyang, if I remember correctly. How people do get about nowadays! It is all I can do to keep up with you."

"Tell us how you do it," countered Lanny, for when you are dealing with the "spirits" you have to enter into the spirit of their occasion. "I would tell you if I could," was the reply. "But I am as much at a loss as yourself. Will you pardon me if I refuse to believe any of this?"

"Of course. I don't believe it either. But here we are, Mr. Kahn."

"Do call me Otto," suggested the voice. "Surely we do not have to stand on formalities at this late date."

"With pleasure, Otto. But you will understand that I think of you as being older than myself."

"You will catch up in due course, and you will discover that you are neither so wise nor so important as you appear to your fellow men."

So they bantered, as they would have done if they had met in the drawing-room of that opera *diva* who had been Otto's dear friend in the happy days when it had been the custom for international bankers to take the good the gods provided them. Lanny listened with one half his mind, while with the other half he thought: Could this really be Otto Kahn, or was it just the subconscious mind of Laurel Creston at play, or possibly a mingling of Laurel's with Lanny's and perhaps others? Laurel was a novelist, and her mind was perfectly capable of making up light drawing-room conversation; if you dived into her subconscious mind, her memory mind, her racial mind, who could guess what masses of material might be hidden there, and what connections it might have with other mindstuff, either living or supposed to have "passed on"?

Presently the voice remarked: "There is an old man here whom I used to know well and who says he used to know you. Do you remember Zaharoff?"

"Oh, very well indeed. How are you, Sir Basil? My very best wishes!"

"He says he cannot summon the energy to speak to you directly.

He is worried about his money; he always thought too much of it and didn't get any fun out of it, as I learned to do. He breaks in to say it is somebody else's money, and he wants it paid."

"Yes, I know all about it, Otto. You will have to explain to him that the international banking system has not yet been extended to the spirit world. Perhaps you and he can work up something of the sort. Let me suggest another partner, a friend who has just come into your world, an active capitalist with whom you used to do business. That is Reverdy Johnson Holdenhurst. Have you seen anything of him?"

"I haven't, but I remember him well and will inquire for him. However, I am not interested in money any more. I have musical and artistic friends who have come over, and they are much better company, now that they are not always looking for subsidies or financial aid from me. You know how it was. I used to be an 'angel.' And now I am a ghost! How odd!"

"Tell me about yourself, Otto. You will understand, I am sure, how curious we are about the future world, and how hard we find it to understand."

"What you will find hardest to understand is that I don't understand it either. One moment—here is an old lady who asks to give you a message. Her name is Marjorie."

"Oh, yes. She was my wife's grandmother."

"She still is, she wishes to inform you. She wants you to know that she is better pleased with your conduct of late. It is nice indeed that one gets along with one's grandmother-in-law. I congratulate you."

"I have no fewer than eight grandmothers in the spirit world. You see, I have been married three times. Oddly enough, I never met a single one of those ladies and cannot even recall their names. If you meet any of them, give them my regards and tell them that I am a tireless experimenter with psychic matters and should be happy if they would present themselves and give me an opportunity to exchange information."

This was in the modern drawing-room line of conversation, as anyone should perceive; but apparently it gave offense, for Lanny suddenly heard a severe old lady's voice: "Young man, you are being flippant!" and then silence. Lanny sat wondering: Was that Marjorie's voice, or was it by chance that of Robbie's mother, or Beauty's mother, or one of the grandmothers of Irma, or of Trudi in Germany? As the silence continued, he wondered what had become of Otto Kahn; had Marjorie by chance hit him over the head with a lump of ectoplasm? Not a sound, until Laurel began to moan and sigh, and presently she came out of her trance and opened her eyes and inquired: "Well, what happened?"

Lanny read her his notes and they had some good laughs; they could both take comfort because there had been no prophecies of doom or destruction. So it would be just an ordinary plane trip, and a visit to Lanny's mother on the Riviera, and some chats with French politicians, generals, capitalists, and other "V.I.P.'s"—very important persons, as the Army was calling them. Then Lanny would fly back again, not precisely with the wings of a dove, but he would come to his beloved and be at rest. So he told himself, and her.

In the morning came a girl from Robbie's office who would ride in the rumble seat of the car while Lanny drove with his wife to the airport. She would drive Laurel back to the apartment and then take the car to Newcastle. Laurel exchanged a last embrace with her husband, and stood on the pier at the great airport and watched the gray-painted plane glide out into the Sound and lift itself into the air. She told herself that everything was all right, it was one more trip, like thousands and tens of thousands of others. She held back her tears and conversed politely with the girl. But when she got back to the apartment and was alone, she wept copiously into the pillow which bore the impress of Lanny's head.

BOOK TWO

Now Is the Winter of Our Discontent

3

And Only Man Is Vile

I

P.A. 103 had been placed in the care of "Pan-Am," with his expenses mysteriously paid. He was not being routed by way of Bermuda because he was in the black books of the British government, which had become suspicious of his intimacy with Rudolf Hess and other leading Nazis. Lanny's route was via San Juan in Puerto Rico, and thence to the port of Belém in Brazil; he would cross the ocean to a place called Bolamo in Portuguese West Africa, and from there go on to Lisbon. It wasn't as roundabout as it looked on the maps, and anyhow, distances aren't so important when you rise eight thousand feet into the air and there are no enemy planes to bother you.

He was traveling in a million-dollar contrivance, one of mankind's most surprising achievements. He was one of thirty-three passengers who were provided with every comfort and were looked after by nine young men and one young woman, all carefully trained and clad in natty blue uniforms. Each passenger had an upholstered seat, which at night was made into a bed. There was a buffet where you might help yourself to a variety of tasty foods; there were magazines to read, and a push button which would bring you the services of the good-looking young stewardess. The cabin was soundproof, so you might chat with your fellow passengers, or play cards, checkers, or dominoes. If you were restless you might stroll in the long corridor, and sometimes members of the crew would come down into the cabin and let you ask them foolish questions.

When you travel on land planes you don't see much of the places where you alight; you see only the airport, and each is much like the previous one. But on a seaplane you have a good look at harbors and their shipping, and the vast improvements being made in wartime. If the weather is at all rough, it may take a while to bring the rather fragile machine up to the dock; if the reports from the next station happen to be unfavorable, you may have a wait of a day or two and have time to stroll around. So Lanny learned about parts of the earth which he had never seen before; and while up in the air he diligently acquired information about Moorish art and architecture in their period of greatest flowering. He was genuinely interested, so business and pleasure were one and the same.

The title of the book Lanny was reading attracted the attention of a well-groomed young gentleman who gave his name as Faulkner and said he was an instructor in archeology at the University of Chicago. He was on his way to Volubilis, to investigate new excavations which had recently been made there. Lanny doubted it from the first moment and guessed that he was working on "Operation Gymnast," perhaps under the orders of "Wild Bill" Donovan. But a P.A. asked no questions, and they chatted about the traces of Carthaginian ruins which are to be found in North Africa. Possibly Dr. Faulkner was as good in guessing about Lanny as Lanny about him; but he, too, kept away from dangerous subjects. When they parted in Lisbon, Lanny said: "My business may bring me to Volubilis before long, and if so, we'll meet again." And they did.

II

The traveler had been told to report to the consulate in Lisbon, where arrangements were made for his plane passage, first to Madrid and from there to Vichy. He had to wait a couple of days, and this gave him time to observe what another year of neutrality had done to the spy center of Western Europe. The dictator who ruled Portugal was taking no chances, especially since the vast indefinite power of America had been thrown into the scales. The former college professor saw to it that his newspapers published an equal amount of Axis and Allied news, side by side, and he allowed all parties to spend their money in his capital, provided they did not call names or engage in fisticuffs. British and American and German and Italian planes came in at the same airport, and their flyers drank at the same bars, but without speaking. Refugees of all nations and all creeds ate in the cafés while their money lasted, and when it was gone they tried to find someone to take pity on them. Wages were fifty cents a day.

Not a happy place, not a beautiful place, but one that was useful to a great many people. Lanny avoided the spies and played his own game, visiting the art museum and making inquiries as to private collections and old masters that might be on the market. As an art expert he was no pretender; he knew what to look at, and what prices should be; if he found anything good he might cable, and meantime he could be sure that careful note was being made of his activities and that word concerning them would go to Paris and Madrid and Vichy, London and Berlin and Rome. Dossiers would be compiled, and wherever somebody might wish to make use of him, his hobbies and his weaknesses would be known, and a list of his family connections and friends.

Then to the great city of Madrid, which in Lanny Budd's view was surely the most unhappy place in all Europe. Here had been committed the first wholesale murder of the modern age; the murder of a nation, of a free people and their hopes. Lanny had been here several times. He had seen the beginning and the progress of this crime, and his soul ached with longing to see the end of it. In the best hotel in the city, where he spent the night, the hot-water spigot ran cold and the water was stained with rust. In the elaborately gilded dining-room the meal cost twenty-five dollars and was none too good, but the band played American jazz and the ladies were loaded with diamonds and pearls and the men with gold lace and jeweled decorations. The food choked Lanny, because he knew that in the back alleys of this phony capital the poor were dropping dead from malnutrition, and millions of the enemies of the regime were in prisons and concentration camps. More than three years had passed since the ending of the civil war, but the idea of amnesty was unknown to Franco, and wholesale shootings went on in the prison courtyards night after night. Soldiers were everywhere, and a surplus of swaggering officers and strutting armed Falangists, the Party gangsters.

Lanny knew art collectors here, and high-up personalities whom it was his duty to call upon. General Aguilar would receive him even though his country was now at war with the General's dear friends and patrons, Herr Hitler and Signor Mussolini. Over the usual *copitas de manzanilla* the white-whiskered old *conquistador* told Lanny about a very beautiful Madonna and Child by Murillo, which a friend of his might be willing to part with; incidentally the General did his best to persuade Lanny to part with information about what America was planning to do in aid of the Bolsheviks and against the defenders of the Faith. A son of Budd-Erling Aircraft couldn't pretend to be ignorant on the subject, so Lanny gave figures—slyly exaggerated—as to the output of his father's plant. He added that he was ashamed of these activities and had done everything in his power to persuade his father to reject the filthy lucre which the fanatical Roosevelt was pouring into his lap.

"What does that *Presidente* of yours think he can do?" demanded the General. "Does not a man have to be truly mad to imagine that he can conquer the whole continent of Europe? Even Napoleon couldn't do it from France, and Roosevelt is three thousand miles across the sea!"

III

The plane which took the traveler to the small capital of Unoccupied France was in no way up to American standards of comfort, but it flew, and it set him down safely on the broad plain of the Allier River. Springtime was in full flood and the country was so beautiful that its inhabitants were a shame, or so Lanny thought. Into this small watering place and summer resort a good part of the *haute bourgeoisie* of Paris and other cities of northern and northwestern France had been driven by bombing and terror. Here they pawned their jewels and furs and lived the same wasteful lives that had brought their country to ruin. Food was supposed to be rationed, but the black market ruled, and a corrupt and enfeebled government was powerless against it. The Germans left enough food for those who could buy it, for they wanted the help of that same *haute bourgeoisie*.

Lanny found lodgings, not without difficulty, and surely not without price. He did not ask official favors, but set to work at his private business of exchanging American dollars for French works of art. He had established contacts on two previous visits and knew where to go; he could be certain that his arrival would be noted and that politicians and officials would seek him out. They might guess that he was there for ulterior purposes, but they couldn't prove it and would treat him with French courtesy. Wonderful is that power called "social position"; the elegance, the aloofness, the assurance that come with the possession of wealth—and not crude wealth, but wealth that your family and your friends and your class have possessed for generations, so that it is like the air you breathe and do not have to think about.

From the newspapers of Vichy, Lanny gathered that he had arrived in the midst of great events. Pierre Laval had once more become head of the government; the aged Marshal Pétain had been reconciled with him again, something Pétain had vowed, a little more than a year ago, he would never do. Lanny knew enough about this puppet world to be sure that the political pot must be bubbling furiously; the wretched newspapers and radio of Vichy wouldn't tell him about the real events, but he was sure to find out soon.

Sitting in one of the little iron chairs at a round iron table of one of the sidewalk cafés, sipping a poor imitation of coffee, Lanny heard his name pronounced in eager tones, and turned to see M. Jacques Benoist-Méchin, journalist-snob and little brother to the rich. He had risen by eager subservience to the Nazis, and was named in the papers as a member of Laval's new cabinet. Lanny had seen a good deal of him on previous visits, and now was prepared to have him demonstrate that success had not turned his head and that he still remembered old friends. *"Est-ce bien vous, M. Budd!* What brings you to town?"

They had a chat; brief, for the new minister had pressing duties, but to the point. He was in a position to speak with authority. He declared that Herr Hitler had established a New Order for the tormented old Continent, and it was nothing short of imbecility to fail in recognizing that fact. France's only future lay in loyal collaboration, and men who persisted in resisting this course were to be treated like poisonous serpents. *"Écrasons l'infâme!"* exclaimed the cultivated M. Jacques. He was tall, slightly stooped, wore spectacles, and smoked a pipe; his manners were airy and elegant in the extreme.

Lanny assented promptly. He said he was heartsick over the part which his country was playing in this situation; and that he had come back to France, where he had lived most of his life, because he could no longer stand the atmosphere of violence and fanaticism which he found in his own America. Lanny rather guessed that this wretched careerist might not believe what he said, any more than Lanny believed what the careerist said; yet he put on a tone of ardent friendship—such a pleasure to see you again; won't you come to my soiree and meet some of my friends? So men and women lived in this dog-eat-dog world.

Lanny knew that Benoist-Méchin was one of Darlan's men, and it was Lanny's desire to see the Admiral, but without seeking the meeting. He asked after the great man's health, and Benoist-Méchin said he was sound as a nut. "I notice that he is not in the new cabinet," Lanny ventured. And the other replied: "He did not wish to be. He remains commander of all the land, sea, and air forces, and retains his title as heir apparent to the Maréchal. He has always preferred to be the military man and to leave the world of intrigue to the politicians."

Lanny would have liked to add: "To you!" but he doubted the journalist's sense of humor.

I V

The visitor could feel quite certain that an intriguing politician would not fail to inform his powerful military patron that the son of Budd-

Erling was in town, loaded with information concerning affairs in Yankeeland. There came to Lanny's lodgings a messenger with a note from the Admiral, very cordially inviting him to call, and that, of course, was equivalent to a royal command. Lanny strolled through the pleasant sunshine to the Hotel Belgique, where the Ministry of Marine was quartered—all the summer hotels had been turned into government offices, and officials had their headquarters in bedrooms and filed important documents in stacks on the beds. But of course the Commander-in-Chief of the Armed Forces of France had rooms in accordance with his dignity, and his visitor was ensconced in a comfortable chair beside a large flat-topped desk.

Jean Louis Xavier François Darlan was his name, and he came from Brittany, which is a Catholic and Royalist corner of France. He had hated the Republic which he had sworn to protect, and which among his friends he had referred to as *la salope*, the slut. As a loyal Frenchman he had hated the Germans also; but now that they had won, they represented law and order for Europe, so it had not been too difficult for the Admiral to transfer his loyalty to the new masters and his hatred to the British, who had treacherously attacked and in part destroyed his Fleet in an action which the British called Oran and the French Mers-el-Kébir. Darlan would say that his policy was for the protection of France, and France alone; that was what Pétain tirelessly repeated in his radio talks. But when you spoke with them privately you would discover that they did not love France so much as they hated and feared the Soviet Union and the collectivist ideas which were spreading over Europe. It was a continuation of the political point of view which Lanny had heard expressed in a hundred French drawing-rooms prior to the outbreak of the war: "Better Hitler than Blum."

Now this policy was working itself out; Hitler was saving France from the Bolsheviks, and Frenchmen who didn't like it were being thrown into concentration camps or shot at once. When an act of sabotage was committed, the Nazis would seize twenty or fifty perfectly innocent Frenchmen who had the misfortune to live in the neighborhood. A week after Pierre Laval took power, thirty such "hostages" were executed by a firing squad at Rouen, and the very next day twenty more were shot at St. Nazaire. A government of Frenchmen had to stand this, and even defend it! No wonder the land was a seething caldron of hate! An American art expert who had dropped down out of the skies had to watch every step and guard every word.

He told the Admiral that he, Lanny Budd, was a man of peace, and therefore hated and feared the Red terrorists and their dupes who were making America a land impossible to live in; he was returning to his mother's home in France because he believed in the New Order and wished to live under it. He was going to disregard the request which the American State Department had just issued that American nationals in France return to their native land at once; he was confident that his mother, too, would pay no attention to this request. While he was saying this, Lanny was wondering, with cold chills running over him: Does Darlan know that I have been to Russia and talked with Stalin? If this should be brought up, Lanny had his story ready—that he had promised his friend Rudolf Hess that he would try to use his father's influence to get into the Red Empire and find out what he could about conditions there and the intentions and plans of its masters. Hess was one man with whom Darlan would be unable to check!

But no such question was asked. The fact that Lanny's mother had lived for more than forty years in France, and that Darlan had met her some twenty years ago and remembered her well, made it seem natural that she and her son should love France; also, the idea of a "parlor Pink" was less familiar to a Frenchman than to an American. The pipe-smoking Admiral listened while this American told him of the rage against Roosevelt's policies which was seething in the hearts of a great number of Americans, and of the possibility that some of them might take drastic action to draw their country out of the mess before it was too late. When the Admiral asked if M. Budd had any idea where the Americans were planning to attack, Lanny tried no evasions, but answered quite truthfully that he had heard on good authority that the American military leaders were in a state of confusion, and that their discussions ranged all the way from the English Channel to Dakar and from there to the Vardar valley in Greece. The Frenchman said that was in accordance with his own information, and this, naturally, raised the value of Lanny's stock.

Darlan was a man of medium height, solidly built, smooth-shaven, alert, and with bright blue eyes. When his pipe was not in his mouth it was in his hand or on his desk. People described him as having a "poker face," but perhaps that was only when he was negotiating with opponents; certainly Lanny had never found it so in their social relations. The host brought out a bottle of his favorite Pernod Fils brandy, and when he had had a couple of swigs his eyes lighted up with the fires of *la gloire*, and he said just what Benoist-Méchin had said, that France was going to have its own kind of New Deal, *la Nouvelle Ordre*, and from now on traitors and the dupes of traitors were going to have a hard time of it. This referred especially to the puppet government which the British had set up in London under that arch-traitor, Charles de Gaulle. "Seadogs" are supposed to have their own special brand of profanity, and Darlan produced it both in French and English when he named this abhorred personality.

"You hear fools discussing what is going to be done with the French Fleet, M. Budd," pronounced Admiral Darlan. "Well, you may tell them for me, its master, that the French Fleet is going to defend the honor and the glory of France. It is not going to be surrendered, and it is not going to run away, and it is not going to be scuttled. To the last vessel and the last man, it is going to fight whatever enemies may dare to interfere with it."

And there was something for "Traveler" to put into a report, marked "Personal for the President"!

V

Having been accepted as a friend of the great Darlan, the American visitor was *persona grata* to the busy politicians and pullers of wires such as Pierre Pucheu and Fernand de Brinon and Paul Marion and Joseph Barthélemy—collaborators all, who had cast their lot with the Nazis and had risen to power and importance in their service. Now they were basking in the sunlight of success, but at the same time a chill of doubt was shrinking their hearts. When they had taken the gamble of making friends with Hitler, they had assumed that Britain was done for and must soon quit; but Britain had refused to quit, and now, nearly two years later, had the help of the great new power overseas. What was that going to mean? The collaborators listened gladly to an American who told what they wanted to hear, that it wouldn't be long before the American people awakened to the fact that in trying to oppose Herr Hitler they were merely helping Comrade Stalin.

In return for the pleasure of hearing such words, these gentlemen invited Lanny to their homes and introduced him to their ladies. M. de Brinon, a Secretary of State to the Premier, had a charming *amie* whom he had put on the public payroll with the title of "Chief of the Private Secretariat." In her salon Lanny listened to a buzz of gossip that was like the sound of a large hive of bees at swarming time. France had been deprived of most of her wealth and power, but it appeared that the more her resources were reduced, the more furiously her public men fought over what was left. M. Leroy-Ladurie, member of the new cabinet, told the visiting stranger his grave doubt as to the capacities of M. Pucheu, a fellow member, and M. Pucheu, without being informed of this, murmured to Lanny some of the charges which in past times had been made against the character of M. Leroy-Ladurie. M. Benoist-Méchin abhorred M. de Brinon, a rival journalist risen by treachery to a post equal to his own; and so it went. Lanny came away from this evening affair comparing the company to a flock of buzzards he had observed while on a motor trip through the American Far West, squabbling over the carcass of a donkey which had perished in the desert.

However, this state of affairs was convenient for a secret agent, who had no trouble in getting the information he had come for. He heard from the lips of Fernand de Brinon himself the story of how that worthy had brought about the restoration of Pierre Laval. The Nazi governor of Paris was Otto Abetz, red-headed German intellectual who had a French wife as well as a French mistress, and who made a specialty of posing as a friend of Latin culture. Lanny had known him well in the old days when Abetz had lectured in Paris to the elegant, fashionable ladies on how France and Germany must unite to save Europe from Bolshevism. *"Le Couple France-Allemand"* was the slogan. Now this dear friend of Marianne had fallen into disfavor with the Gestapo and the Schutzstaffel, because France wasn't contributing her fair share to the defense of Germany. Herr Hitler was demanding more food, more manufactured goods, more French workers for the factories of Germany, more fighters for his Anti-Bolshevik Legion. The good and kind Herr Abetz was about to be replaced by some such man as Jacques Doriot, one-time Communist agitator who had turned against his gang and was now the most ruthless of Fascist bullies. And instead of the noble-minded old Maréchal, Vichy would have a *Gauleiter* such as now was ruling Poland.

It had been M. de Brinon's duty to bring this information to the old Maréchal and to persuade him to restore Laval to power. It had taken much running back and forth of collaborators between Paris and Vichy, but at last the victory had been won, and the patriotic gentlemen who had saved *la patrie* for a second time were now reaping their rewards.

They were going to make a thorough job of the "coupling" this time. There would be no more nonsense of trying to serve two masters, no more provocation to those upon whom the future of France depended. The French workers who were so desperately needed in the German factories would be forced there by shutting down great numbers of factories at home; and to keep them in order meantime, there would be a new police force, special troops trained by the Germans, who had learned the job with their own SA and SS.

All this Lanny learned from Benoist-Méchin, another Secretary of State to the Premier, whom he invited to lunch and provided with a bottle of the best wine to be found in the town. This high cabinet member revealed that he was going to be entrusted with the presidency of a committee to organize the "Tricolor Legion" and put down once for all the traitorous movements which the puppet De Gaulle was seeking to spread throughout France. The nucleus of the new body was to be the already-existing "Anti-Bolshevik Legion" organized by Jacques Doriot and Eugène Deloncle. "Believe me," said Benoist-Méchin, "these are fighting men, and they mean business."

"I know, I met Deloncle years ago," replied Lanny, "at the home of my old friend Denis de Bruyne."

"Oh, you know De Bruyne?" inquired the cabinet minister. And when Lanny replied that the family were among his oldest friends, the other said: "Then you know Charlot, too."

"He is practically my godson. I have lost track of him since the armistice."

"He is in Vichy now; a *capitaine*, and one of my helpers in the organizing of the new Legion."

"That is indeed pleasant news for me, M. Benoist-Méchin. The last I had heard of Charlot, he was reported captured by the Germans."

"They released him, as they have done many others for whom we were able to vouch."

"I have known him since he was a little chap," Lanny explained. "His mother was one of my dearest friends. It is hard for me to realize that four or five years have passed since I was trying to save him from the French police, when he and his father and brother were charged with taking part in the activities of the Cagoule."

"Thank God those dreadful days have passed!" exclaimed the new minister. "France has found her soul again!"

VI

Lanny lost no time in getting into touch with Charlot. They embraced and kissed each other in French fashion, and it wasn't altogether hypocrisy on the secret agent's part. A strange duality and duel in the human heart; Lanny loathed everything that Charlot believed; he wanted to see it exterminated from the earth; he wanted to see the advocates of it killed, so long as they were bearing arms in its defense, and here was Charlot, wearing one of its uniforms! Yet, he was Marie de Bruyne's son, and Marie had been the first woman Lanny had loved with all his soul. On her deathbed she had committed her two boys to the joint care of Lanny and her husband—a curious scene, possible only in predominantly Catholic countries.

Lanny still thought of Charlot as the boy he had first met in the lovely garden of the Château de Bruyne; a boy well brought up, so polite that it would have seemed odd to an American, but not to Lanny; a boy studious yet full of fun, gentle, affectionate, and adoring Lanny Budd as a model of what a gentleman ought to be. Charlot had been taught all those things which a member of the "two hundred families" should believe, and if Lanny had tried to teach him otherwise he might have broken up the home, which he had no right to do. He had felt obliged to let those boys work out their own destiny, and the result had been that Charlot, ardent and impetuous, had become one of the young French aristocrats who were determined to overthrow *la salope*. His father had helped to finance the organizing of the reactionary secret society called the Cagoule, and in the fighting which had taken place in the streets of Paris some years ago Charlot had got a slash across the cheek and still bore the honorable scar.

It was hard to realize that he was thirty-five years of age. He still looked young, and his step was springy, his expression intense. He hadn't had to fight the Germans, having been stationed in Alsace, where the armies had been surrounded and immobilized until the armistice. "They treated us officers reasonably well," he said. "And of course it didn't take *le père* very long to make them realize that I had been working for Franco-German understanding from a long way back."

"How is your father?" Lanny asked. The answer was: "Physically as well as you could expect for a man over eighty; but he is in a situation that is painful to talk about—" Charlot stopped and hesitated; he saw a look of concern on his old friend's face and added: "You have a better right to know than anybody else, Lanny. He has fallen into the hands of an unscrupulous woman who is plundering him unmercifully."

"That is truly sad, Charlot. He has had a weakness that way most of his life. It caused your mother great unhappiness."

"I have known about that for a long time. It seems to grow on some men with age. I suppose it is nature's way of punishing them. Anyhow, there is nothing I can do, for he will not let me talk to him about it. Perhaps if you could go to Paris you might have better success."

That led to the subject of Lanny's attitude to the unhappy world situation. "A dreadful thing, Lanny, that your country should have got into the war on the side of Bolshevism. Do tell me that you have not gone over to that greatest of enemies."

"You know my attitude, Charlot, and I cannot change. I am a man of peace and do not take part in any wars. I am here looking for paintings worthy to go into a great American collection."

"I am so glad to hear that, Lanny. I could not bear to think of you as an enemy. But if your country helps the Bolsheviks to take all Europe, what will become of the art of painting?"

"I hope that we shall have enough specimens safe in America, where the Bolsheviks cannot get at them. So the art can be revived."

VII

The *capitaine* talked for a while about his important assignment, the Tricolor Legion. Lanny perceived that Pierre Laval was planning the same thing in Vichy France that Hitler had done in Germany, the organizing of a private army, a military force of his Party, to replace the army of his country and make permanent his personal grip on power. It was to be a complete outfit, including a youth movement, with banners and slogans and songs. The grown men would have machine guns and hand grenades and rubber truncheons with which to beat their prisoners in the barracks and jails. Charlot's eyes lighted up with fanatical fervor as he told about it; at last they were going to put down the labor unions and their revolutionary propaganda, and make sure that the traditional France would survive and dominate Western Europe. Lanny found the German Nazis strange and terrible people, but he found even more fantastic these Fascists of the Spanish and French Catholic pattern, who were building this machinery of repression in the name of Jesus Christ.

Of course he wouldn't give a hint of all that. He would be warmhearted and sympathetic, as he had always been with the De Bruyne family. He asked about Charlot's older brother, Denis, *fils,* and here was another family tragedy difficult for the younger to talk about. Lanny had known for some time that Denis did not put the same trust in the Germans as his brother did; Denis had thought it his duty to defend his country against the invader. He had fought and been wounded, and had escaped to the south, hoping that France would go on fighting in North Africa. Said Charlot with grief in his voice: "Lanny, I am afraid he has fallen under the spell of the Gaullists. The last I heard of him, he was in Algiers. I wrote, pleading with him, but have not had any reply."

"It is something that happens in civil wars, Charlot." Lanny knew that, as a traditionalist, the *capitaine* would be impressed by precedents. "I know how in the American Civil War brothers argued with each other; some went north and some went south, and more than once it happened that they met on the battlefield."

"I know, Lanny, but think of the disgrace of this! After the wanton attack which the British made upon our unprepared and unresisting Fleet! Now they have set up this wretched puppet, a man who was a mere major general, and yet presumes to constitute himself the government of France!"

"I understand how you feel, Charlot. Let me tell you that I am hoping to go to North Africa. I have an assignment from a client who is collecting Moorish art. If I do, I will make an effort to find Denis and see if I can do anything to influence him."

"Oh, please do!" exclaimed the younger brother. "I cannot talk to him, but he has such respect for your judgment! It is not too late. He might come back here and see what we are doing. I can arrange for him to meet the Maréchal and hear from his Commander-in-Chief personally where his duty lies."

"I'll let you hear from me without fail," Lanny promised.

VIII

The visitor didn't make an attempt to see the old marshal himself. He knew that pathetic figure only too well, and everything that he could and would say. Nothing useful, nothing new, for at the age of eighty-five he did nothing but repeat what he had been saying all his life. If you disagreed with him he would become greatly excited and his attendants would interrupt to protect him; if you just listened, he would pause, and his head would begin to nod and he would fall into a doze. Now he had surrendered all real power to the evil Laval, and would serve as a figurehead to make the masses of the French people, who adored him as the hero of Verdun, believe that *la patrie* was in the hands of an all-wise and all-benevolent father, a deputy of God.

What Lanny wanted to do was to make his report and move on from this health resort before it became unhealthy for him; before his visits attracted too much attention from the Gestapo and caused them to look up his recent doings. But just as he was making inquiries about travel accommodations to the south, he ran into Count René de Chambrun, descendant of the Marquis de Lafayette and husband of Pierre Laval's only daughter. He was sitting in one of those iron chairs in front of a café, an agile little man who always made Lanny think of a jockey. He was a lawyer and a tireless errand boy for his great *beau-père*.

Now he said: "By the way, M. Budd, I mentioned your presence in town to the Premier, and he expressed the hope that he might see you before you depart."

That, of course, was an honor, and Lanny responded: "I know how busy he must be, and feared that I might be breaking in on important matters of state."

"He always finds time for his old friends, M. Budd, and especially those who bring news from abroad."

Next morning Lanny received a telegram requesting him to call the Premier's secretary, and when he did so he was invited to be on hand at the end of the working day, to be taken out to Chateldon for the night. He accepted with pleasure. Sitting in the well-cushioned seat of a custom-built Daimler and speeding over the Allier plain toward the mountains, he listened while Pierre Laval poured out his indignation against Franklin D. Roosevelt, Cordell Hull, and Sumner Welles, because of the extreme discourtesy with which these gentlemen had received the news of the change in the Vichy government. Really, it was as if Laval thought his visitor had had something to do with it, or could do something about it. Lanny broke in, laughing: "*Écoutez, cher Maître*, you must understand that these statesmen are at the opposite pole of thinking from myself. If I could have my way, they would be bounced out on their behinds. Since I cannot do that, I have come back to live in my fosterland, my godmotherland, if you like, the place where I used to be happy and hope some day to be again."

"Yes, yes, I understand, M. Budd. I just need somebody to tell my troubles to. It is incomprehensible to me why those Americans should feel such bitterness toward myself, and should persist in a policy which can help nobody but the Red dictator."

"I can only guess at the minds of the commercial gentlemen who control America's policy. My father is one of them, and even him I cannot understand. It appears that they fear the rivalry of Germany, and the system of government control of foreign trade."

"But it was the Russians who devised that system and taught it to the Germans. And surely the trade rivalry of Britain is a greater menace than that of Germany!"

"Big businessmen do not see very far ahead as a rule. Their motto is, one at a time. I suppose that Russia will be next, and then Britain—who can guess?"

So a smooth-talking agent soothed his victim, and presently the new Premier was telling the wonderful plans he had for the restoration of all France—of course in loyal collaboration with the Germans, for that was the cornerstone of policy. "I desire a German victory," declared Pierre Laval. "Indeed, I consider that a German victory has been achieved, and that to reverse it would involve the total destruction of Europe."

Accordingly, he went on to declare, the government of French North Africa was furnishing food to the army of General Rommel in Italian North Africa and intended to go on doing so regardless of anything that America might say or do. Accordingly, the government had worked out elaborate plans for making the French workers want to go to Germany, and for sending them whether they wanted to or not. Pierre Laval clenched his hairy fists and used the language of a butcher's son in expressing his hatred of the men who were secretly trying to thwart this policy and his determination to stamp their faces into their own excrement.

IX

Just as Lanny addressed Roosevelt as "Governor" because he had once been Governor of New York State, so he addressed Laval as "*cher Maître*" because Laval once had been a practicing lawyer in Paris and liked to look back upon those days when success had somehow been more successful than now. The son of the village butcher and tavernkeeper had found out how to make money by showing the rich how to evade their income taxes, and by getting a "cut" in many great enterprises which wanted to break the laws of the Republic safely. He had come back to the place of his birth and had had the satisfaction of buying the ancient Château de Chateldon which dominated the scene. The estate included a comfortable manor house in which Pierre lived with his long-suffering wife, their adored daughter, and the daughter's noble husband, who had been purchased at a price which some placed at seven figures and some at eight.

Here they were, and they were glad to see the agreeable art expert after the lapse of a year. He had an interesting story to tell about his plane wreck and his yachting trip through the South Seas. He said that he had come out by way of China and didn't mention the Soviet Union, nor did he take too long with his tale, for he wanted Laval to do the talking, and he knew that this family didn't really care very much about anything in the world except the intrigues by which they had got power and the menaces and bribes by which they were keeping it. The greedy and vulgar man with the dark complexion and the slanting eyes, which had caused his enemies to call him "the Mongolian rascal," had not one word of reprobation concerning the wholesale murders of French men and women which the Nazis were carrying on all over the occupied portions of the country. He justified their scheme of compelling the French to print and give to them three hundred million paper francs every day, including Sundays and holidays. This was supposed to be for the upkeep of the German army of occupation, but the Nazi economic commissions were using it to buy up the most important industrial properties of the captive land. Laval was following his old practice of getting a rake-off on many of these—for his services in browbeating the owners into giving way.

The tactful Lanny didn't mention any such aspects of the "collaboration" program. What he said was: "They tell me you gave your enemies a drubbing at Riom while I was making my way through China." That was enough to start the ex-butcher boy off and keep him going all through a dinner *en famille*. Laval didn't say so, but he knew perfectly well that the world considered him to have got much the worst of the proceedings. He had put Daladier and Reynaud and Blum, and the rest of his opponents in the prewar government of France, on trial for their lives. He had done it against his own judgment, for he knew how much he had to hide. Hitler and Abetz and others of his new masters had demanded it, hoping to prove these men guilty of causing the war. Instead, the trial had turned into an effort to prove the defendants guilty of losing the war, a different matter and no crime in Nazi eyes. They had put up such a vigorous defense of their public course that the trial had dominated the news of the world. The Nazis had ordered it stopped, and those too eloquent public men were shut up in fortresses—whether guilty or innocent.

Pierre Laval hated them more than ever now, and his language concerning them was more fitted to the village tavern than to the dinner table of the head of *l'État Français*. The spectacle of a furious man stuffing food into his mouth and then pouring out vituperations, pausing now and then to mop his greasy black mustache—this was one which the fastidious Lanny Budd would not have chosen for his own enjoyment, but only in the line of duty. His well-trained memory was taxed to remember all the secrets of Vichy France—vicious France was an almost inescapable pun. When he was shown to his room he did not dare make a single memorandum, but lay on the bed for an hour going over what he had heard in the course of the long evening.

And back in the town next morning, he sat at his little portable and typed off the most important details—no carbon copy—and sealed the sheets carefully in an envelope marked "Traveler: Personal to the President." This he put in a larger envelope, addressed to the Chargé d'Affaires at the American Embassy—Admiral Leahy, the Ambassador, having been summoned home as a gesture of repudiation of the new government. This missive Lanny had delivered by a messenger, watching from the street to see it handed in at the door. Then his job was done. He went back to his room, packed his few belongings, and set out for the south.

X

The trains were running again—it was the classic boast of Fascism that it caused the trains to run on time. They were jammed with people who were trying to get to some place where they hoped that life would be a little less hard than they had found it where they were. They squatted on the floors or in one another's laps, and slept that way if they could. Lanny had learned in China that the conductor of a train keeps some compartment locked on chance that somebody will pay him a *cumshaw* for the use of it; in France it is called a *pourboire*—for a drink—and Lanny paid enough to keep any conductor properly alcoholized for a week. It was his fate in life to be comfortable while other people were miserable, and he made up for it by having his conscience troubled. Manifestly he couldn't go into fashionable society if he slept on dirty floors, and he couldn't be an alert and capable secret agent if he stinted himself on food. If he wanted to meet the rich and powerful he had to look like one of them, and they are watchful and severe in their judgments.

When he stepped off the "Blue Train" at the famous resort city of Cannes, he was the glass of fashion and the mold of form. He had telegraphed of his coming, and there was his mother waiting to welcome him with the mild enthusiasm permissible to a lady on a public platform. More than a year had passed since she had seen him, and there had been parts of that year when she had given up hope of ever seeing him again. But here he was, cheerful and sound as ever, her adored only son, her own handiwork, yet so different from what she had ever imagined. A man of mystery, and never more so than now, when the world seemed to have gone entirely mad—and what part was her Lanny playing in it?

He was forty-two, and his mother almost sixty; she shuddered at the

very word, but had to face it. For half her life she had had to worry
about what the ladies politely called *embonpoint*. Now the Vichy government had helped her by rationing food, and instead she had to
worry about wrinkles. When you have been "plump," and then lose
ten or twenty pounds, you have more skin than you need to cover
you; and when you come out into the sunlight, how dreadfully the
folds do show! You just have to make up your mind that you are an
old woman, and get along with such love as you have been able to win
in a world where the young are selfish and pleasure-seeking.

But Lanny loved her! He took her in his strong arms and kissed the
powder off her cheeks and exclaimed: "Well, well, old girl! Here we
are again!" And how was Parsifal, and how was Baby Marcel, and had
she heard from Marceline, and had she got the letters he had written
from various parts of the earth? And then it was Beauty's turn: How
was Robbie, and how was his family, and where had he left Laurel,
and what was she doing, and was it really certain that she was preg-
nant? "Lanny, I want you to know right away, I think you have made
a good choice. She is just the woman for you."

"Yes, dear, I am glad to hear you say so. She is wise and sensible
and understands me very well." He refrained from extreme praise,
being wise himself in matters where "the sex" was concerned; his
mother was a jealous goddess, and it wasn't easy for her to see her
place taken by another female—and especially one whom she hadn't
picked out. But it is the way of nature, and if Laurel was going to give
Beauty another grandchild she would be forgiven for having once
called Lanny a "troglodyte," and caused Lanny's mother to want to
scratch her eyes out.

Essence being almost unobtainable, even to the rich, Beauty was
driving herself in an ancient buggy with a middle-aged horse. They
looked extremely odd trotting down the splendid Boulevard de la
Croisette; they had almost the only vehicle, for traffic was confined to
official cars. The small city was packed to the roofs with refugees; they
walked in the two lanes of the wide drive, separated by palm trees;
they sunned themselves in near nudity on the beach below. "The Côte
d'Azur will never be the same again," said Beauty Budd sadly. "But we
take what we can get and are thankful to be alive."

"Are you thinking of going back to the States?" the son inquired,
and as he had guessed, she told him no. People of all nations had always
been polite to her and she couldn't bring herself to be afraid of either
Germans or Italians. This was her home, and who could say that she
had ever done any harm here?

XI

Always a pleasant thing to come back to Bienvenu, the lovely old place which had been Lanny's home for as long as he could remember. It was his headquarters and repository; his books were here, his piano and accumulation of music scores, his treasures of one sort and another. It was always his dream that some day he would be able to live here again and do the things he really liked. But that couldn't be so long as gangsters threatened mankind. Lanny had been forced to the conclusion that it couldn't be until the world had been made over according to the principles of justice and co-operation.

Meantime here was a place of retreat, a shelter where the gangsters had not yet intruded. The dogs came running out, barking their welcome; following them came a lovely little dark-haired boy, Beauty's grandson and Lanny's nephew, whom they called Baby Marcel, but they would have to change that before long. He was the son of Marceline Detaze, and when she had divorced his father she had had his name legally changed to Marcel Detaze; an honored name, that of his grandfather, the French painter, long since dead. The little one remembered his Uncle Lanny from a year ago, with Beauty's help, of course; Uncle Lanny had taught him dancing steps and would teach him more, and now he leaped into Uncle Lanny's arms with a cry of delight.

And here came Beauty's husband, her third, as she wished the world to believe, and it obligingly did so. Parsifal Dingle's hair had grown snow-white, and if he had his way it would have grown long, for he was too busy with God to bother with barbers. But Beauty wouldn't let him be any more eccentric than necessary, and now and then she would pin a sheet about his neck and trim him herself. It was so hard to get about nowadays that people revived the home industries, reverting to an earlier stage of culture. Parsifal was no trouble to anybody. He adored his beautiful wife—she was still that to him if not to herself—and he asked nothing but to sit in the court reading his "New Thought" books or to stroll about the grounds of the estate, keeping himself in tune with the Infinite. A more harmless man never lived, and he was always delighted to see Lanny, who shared his interest in psychic matters and would go over Parsifal's notes and join in speculation concerning what had happened.

There was "Madame," the elderly Polish woman who had lived on this estate ever since Parsifal had discovered her in a dingy "medium parlor" on Sixth Avenue in New York. At a time when bankers and brokers had been throwing themselves out of top-story hotel windows because they had lost everything in the world, this man of God had been busy with the next world, or, as he would say, the world in which yesterday, today, and forever are the same, and which is in us and around us, whether or not we choose to become aware of it. Madame Zyszynski didn't have any ideas of her own on these abstruse matters, but she accepted whatever Parsifal said; she loved this kind gentleman as if he had been her father, and Lanny as if he had been her son.

XII

How delightful the son would have found it to stay here and teach Baby Marcel to dance and to swim, and let Beauty cut the hair of both of them, and let Madame summon the spirits from the vasty deep, and let Parsifal sit by as sage and interpreter, and as healer in case of need. Beauty would have pleaded for it, save that she had tried so often and knew that it was no use. There was something that called Lanny away, and it hadn't taken her shrewd mind many years to guess what the thing must be. Always the call came by mail; there were letters postmarked Toulon which took him westward, and others from Geneva which took him northward. Beauty had studied the handwriting and guessed that the former came from Raoul Palma, whom she had known for twenty years or more as one of Lanny's Leftist friends; the other writing she did not know, but it had peculiarities which were German, and she had noted that Lanny generally went into Germany after getting one of these letters.

She knew much more about this strange son than he guessed. She had become certain that he had never changed his political coloration, as he gave the world to understand; if he had, he would never have become a friend of Laurel Creston's—to say nothing of marrying her. The idea that he was a secret Leftist terrified her, for she knew what danger it meant in times like these. The fact that he refused to take her into his confidence hurt her, but she had to accept his cryptic statement: "A promise is a promise, old darling." She had kept these speculations hidden in the deepest corner of her mind, and even her best friends believed that she believed her son to be an art expert, traveling about the world only in search of beautiful paintings.

Beauty's instructions were never to forward his mail, because of the uncertainty of his movements and of communications in wartime. She put the papers and magazines on a closet shelf and locked the letters up in her escritoire. There was a considerable packet after a whole year, and she didn't make him ask for them, but put them into his hands without delay. He would not look at them in her presence, but would take them off to his study to read and perhaps answer. He would never entrust the replies to the postman who delivered mail at the estate every day, but would find some excuse to go into Cannes and there presumably drop them into an inconspicuous box. All this she had observed for years and had tactfully pretended to observe nothing.

Alone in his study, Lanny set aside a number of unimportant letters and tore open those which had to do with a P.A.'s job. There were three which had come from Raoul, all mailed in Toulon and signed with the code name "Bruges." According to their practice, the text had to do solely with the purchase of paintings; when Raoul wrote that he had located an especially fine Meissonier, it meant that he had important news about the war; when he said that the painting could be purchased for eighty thousand francs, it meant that he wanted Lanny to bring him that amount of money. In the last of his letters, mailed over three months ago, "Bruges" said that he had been distressed to hear about M. Budd's plane accident and hoped soon to hear of his recovery. That didn't surprise Lanny, for the Budd family was well known in Juan-les-Pins and near-by Cannes, and Raoul had many friends in the neighborhood who could tell him what members of that family were doing.

There was only one letter from Bernhardt Monck, and that was six months old. He had discovered a fine work by the Swiss painter Hodler, and since this painter had done most of his work and attained most of his fame in Germany, Lanny could guess what that meant. Monck wanted only five thousand Swiss francs, but each of these was worth more than ten of the depreciated francs of Vichy. Lanny had no way to reach Monck by mail; he would have to go to Geneva, on chance that the old-time Social Democrat would still be doing research work in the public library there.

Raoul's last letter said: "I am still employed by the bookstore." So Lanny wrote a note to "M. Bruges" in care of the Armand Mercier bookstore, Toulon, saying: "I am home again, and much interested in what you tell about having come upon a Meissonier painting. The price is reasonable, if you are sure of its genuineness. Let me know at once if it is available, and I will come." He added: "I don't want to take any chance of finding that it has already been sold, as happened in the case of the Daumier drawings." That was asking Raoul whether there was any chance of Lanny's getting into trouble, as had happened to him on his last visit to Toulon.

According to Beauty's expectation, Lanny came to her, saying: "I have to go into town to attend to some matters at the bank. If you don't mind, I'd like to take the buggy, because I'll buy some presents for our friends whom I have been neglecting." The generous-hearted Lanny, so the friends would all think; but he didn't fool his keen-minded mother, who had been Robbie Budd's side-partner in munitions deals for a couple of decades and knew all there was to know about intrigue. She had observed this business of giving presents to people who needed them and to others who didn't, and she had managed to figure out what it meant. Lanny must be needing money in small denominations which could not be traced through the bank, and this was his way of getting large bills changed. She had even noticed that his pockets were bulging when he came home! Now she said: "All right," and didn't offer him the pleasure of her company on the expedition. She knew that when he had got the money, he would be leaving shortly.

4

We Cannot Escape History

I

LIFE at Bienvenu went on comfortably in spite of war. Foods were rationed, and that was supposed to apply to everybody, but of course it didn't. Beauty had American money, large sums of it because of the sales of her late husband's paintings. Also, she had many friends, and not merely among the fashionable folk. In one of the valleys which ran back from this rocky coast lived Leese, who for thirty years or so had been Beauty's cook and major-domo; she had purchased a farm out of her savings, and while she herself was crippled with rheumatism, she had a swarm of grandchildren and grandnephews, and the war had not got them all. They would load up a one-horse cart with produce, and in the middle of the night drive to the village of Juan-les-Pins; not to the markets, but to Bienvenu, and at the back door of the Villa they would be met by the lame butler whom Lanny had brought from Spain. They would have a price written on a scrap of paper, and José would take that to Madame, who would make a wry face, for the amount grew steadily larger; but no matter, it was in francs, and they were worth less than a cent apiece.

So the cellar and pantry and icebox of Bienvenu were kept full. And then would come Lanny's old friend and ex-tutor, Jerry Pendleton, whose travel bureau had very few patrons these days. Jerry liked to go fishing, and his wife had a *pension* with hungry boarders. When Jerry had a good day he would appear at Bienvenu with, say, a ten-pound *mérou*, or perhaps a basket of *langoustes*. There would be an argument as to whether they should be paid for, and Beauty would insist that if he refused payment she wouldn't let him come again. Sometimes they settled it one way and sometimes the other; in any case there would be a seafood dinner, and then a cold supper, and next day a *bouillabaisse*, something resembling a chowder. Beauty, a generous soul, couldn't bear to think of anybody being hungry, at least not anybody she knew; so she would send baskets of food to the various refugees she had stowed away on the estate and whom she was rapidly pauperizing—without too much resistance on their part.

She had announced her determination to stay in her home regardless of hostilities. But the recent imperative from the State Department had caused many of her friends to depart, and she was uneasy in her mind and asked what Lanny thought about it. He couldn't give any hint of what he knew, but he could say that he didn't consider the French Riviera a likely landing place for an army, at least not for some time to come. The Germans had done some fortifying, but in a halfhearted sort of way, and it would seem that they agreed with Lanny. He pointed out that there was danger in sea travel also, and surely in the air, as he had proved. If the worst came, Beauty could hitch up her bony horse and drive into the hills and stay with Leese until the issue was decided.

II

One evening she said to him: "Come for a stroll with me." She took him out behind the garage, where there was a storeroom, and near one corner of it a little oleander was growing. "I planted that myself one night," she said. "It is a yellow oleander, and we have no other on the place, so it will be easy to remember."

She was speaking in a low tone, and they did not stop. "I took the precaution to bury some money there, and in case anything should happen to me, I want you to know about it. I noted the fact that when the Italians came into Menton they blocked all accounts at the bank, and I thought it might happen here at any time."

"You are right about that," he answered. "You would be in enemy territory, whether Italian or German. You couldn't draw money from New York, and neither Robbie nor I could send you any."

"That was my thought. I have been getting cash from the bank at intervals and hiding it in the house; but I thought the house might be burned, so I wrapped all the money in oilcloth and put it in an aluminum box which won't rust. The oleander grows slowly, as you know, so you won't have trouble digging it up. I thought it wise to plant something, because that explained the ground being freshly dug. I buried it on Saturday night, and told the gardener the plant was a gift and I had put it into the ground at once to make sure it would live."

"Very clever," said Lanny. "How much is there?"

"I didn't count it, but it must be over a couple of million francs."

"*Whew!*" he exclaimed. "Pirate's treasure!"

"I put my jewels in, too. There's no use having them nowadays because I don't go anywhere. I haven't told anybody else about it; it'll be yours if I go. You will remember the place. Yellow stands for gold."

Lanny, amused, recited:

> Bright and yellow, hard and cold,
> Molten, graven, hammer'd, and roll'd;
> Heavy to get, and light to hold;
> Hoarded, barter'd, bought, and sold,
> Stolen, borrow'd, squander'd, doled:
> Spurn'd by the young, but hugg'd by the old
> To the very verge of the churchyard mould;
> Price of many a crime untold:
> Gold! Gold! Gold! Gold!

His mother said: "Wait until you get to be as old as I am!"

III

While Baby Marcel chased the butterflies in the court and in turn was chased by the dogs, the two learned elders sat in canvas chairs in the sunshine, discussing the profoundest problems which engage the mind of man. What are we, really, and how do we come to be, and for what purpose are we placed here, and what becomes of us when we depart? Above all, what is the origin of that strange faculty in us which we call conscience? Why do we have a sense of duty, and what is the basis of its validity, and of our assurance concerning it? If we are as the beasts of the field that perish, why do we owe any obligation to the world, or to our fellow men, or to ourselves? Even the Communists, who spurn the idea of God, owe loyalty to their Party! Even the Nazis, who despise the mass of mankind, are slaves to their own racial ideal!

A retired real estate man from Iowa had found his retreat across half a continent and a wide ocean, and had instituted a monastery with one monk, a psychical research society with one member and one medium. Parsifal Dingle asserted that there was a Spirit in the universe, and that it created and maintained those illusions which we know as the material world. He asserted that it was possible to maintain communion with this Spirit, and he did so, day and night. "God is all and God is love," he would say. "God is alive and God is real." He would prove it by healing the sick and by setting to all men an example of a harmless life. He asserted that everything that ever existed exists always, and he proved this by exchanging daily communications with persons who claimed to have lived long ago.

For years Parsifal had been getting messages from the old-time monks of a monastery in Ceylon known as Dodanduwa, and he had accumulated a mass of notes concerning their ideas and way of life. Now he informed Lanny that these monks had given place to a representative of a rival sect, the Jains, who claimed to be even more ancient than the Hindus, and who worshiped their *tirthankaras*, or saints, as gods. Parsifal Dingle declared that he had never known anything about the Jains and couldn't say whether they were Hindu, Persian, or Arab; but here was this "spirit," a grave and dignified personality, avowing that he had been a holy man of the Jain shrine of Chitaral—the "Rock Temple," it was called—in South Travancore; it had been founded in the ninth century, and he had been present at the ceremonies. Stranger yet, this ancient one declared himself to be a previous incarnation of Parsifal and spoke as if in solilquy—"we" have done this and "we" have done that. It was fascinating, but at the same time a bit uncanny.

Lanny read the notes which his stepfather had carefully written out. It appeared that the Jains, heretics themselves, had spawned numerous other varieties of heresy. The holy man, whose name was Chandragupta, belonged to the sect called Digambaras, and warned his later self concerning the rival Swetambaras, explaining in detail what was wrong with their beliefs. The Jains all held the strictest ascetic views and disputed over such questions as to whether women could attain *Nirvana,* and whether it was permissible to wear white costumes or no costumes at all. Chandragupta brought various authorities to converse with his latest reincarnation; one of them was introduced as Siddharaja, King of Guzerat, who had been the first monarch to be converted to the Jain religion, an event something like the conversion of the Emperor Constantine to Christianity. Parsifal Dingle, ex-realtor from Iowa, had never conversed with a monarch before and had striven to keep his democratic balance.

He had learned much about the Rock Temple and the life there. The original structure on top of the rock was in ruins, but the sculptures on the rock itself were intact. There were thirty figures, all formal and rigid, each representing a saint absorbed in contemplation which would continue to the end of time; each saint was bald-headed, smooth-shaven, narrow-waisted, and wore no garments, not even "holy threads," and each had three tiers of umbrellas carved over his head. Parsifal wondered, he said, what "holy threads" might be; he had been afraid to interrupt with questions, and he did not have access to a large library. Chandragupta was distressed because, some three hundred years after his departure from this life, the temple had been converted into a Hindu shrine, and an image of the goddess Sree Bagavathi had been installed. He scorned this interloper and would talk only about the Jain saints and the inscriptions in the language called Vattezuthu which he had spoken in those days. He had no way of reproducing the script, but had spoken some of the words, and Parsifal had written down the way they sounded to him. All very curious, and some day it might be possible to check on the details.

What did these communications mean? To Lanny's stepfather they could mean only one thing, which was what they claimed to mean. Parsifal was positive that he had never read anything about the Jains; but Lanny wondered if he could not have done this long ago and forgotten. Parsifal read everything he could get hold of about religions, old and new; and what could be more likely than that he might have read a few paragraphs about the Rock Temple? The subconscious mind never forgets, and apparently it has the same impulse toward imaginative creation that has filled the libraries of the world with works of fiction. Of course that left unexplained the problem of how these matters had got into the mind of Madame Zyszynski. The phenomena made it certain that at some level her mind and Parsifal's mind were one, or had some way of becoming one for a time; and that seemed a startling discovery, enough to keep the professors of psychology busy for a long time.

Lanny tried experiments with Madame, as he always did. There came "Tecumseh," the Amerindian control, but he seemed an old and tired Tecumseh, not full of "ginger" as in the old days. He produced "spirits" whom Lanny didn't know, also the same old stock figures, who had nothing new to say. Lanny had been hoping that he might get Laurel Creston's grandmother, or possibly some member of the Holdenhurst family; but no such luck. He had to tell Madame that it had been a good session, otherwise she would have been greatly depressed. He went away wondering why Parsifal continued to have success, while for himself the phenomena seemed to be fading? Was it because of his skepticism, his continued dalliance with what Tecumseh called "that old telepathy"? Did that deprive Madame's subconscious mind of its impulse? Lanny could imagine a child who began to invent stories or to make drawings; if the child's parents said they were good, the child would go on working with delight, but if the parents said that it was all foolishness and a waste of time, what talent the child had might die of inanition.

IV

Lanny awaited a letter from Toulon, and in due course it arrived. "Bruges" said that the painting was still available, but that on account of the decrease in the value of the franc it might be well to bring a little more money. He said that he, Bruges, would be at the usual place, but not to let anybody there know about the painting, as this might cause an increase in the price. "Do not talk about it to anybody but me," said the letter, and Lanny understood that this was a warning of danger. He hardly needed it.

He went into Cannes and withdrew more money in small-denomination bills; and he told his friend Jerry that he wanted a train ticket to Toulon, and a seat, if such a miracle were possible. Jerry, who also knew about *pourboires,* said that it would be possible to anyone who had dollars. A wonderful land was America, and more and more French men and women were wishing they could get to it.

The P.A. came back and told his mother that he was going to take a run to Toulon, he had word of a promising painting. There was nothing she could do but believe him, for he might actually show up with a painting, and she could hardly believe that he had done it just to impress her. She had to be content with his promise: "I'll be back soon."

Beauty drove him into town next morning, and on the road they met the postman. There was a letter for Beauty from a village not far from Berlin. That was Marceline, and the mother, driving, handed it to Lanny, who read it aloud. The daughter wrote that she had left Berlin to get away from the bombs; she had been taking care of Oskar, who had been wounded. Soon he would be well enough to return to the front, and then Marceline was going to try to get permission to visit Juan. "I cannot stand to be away from my baby any longer," she wrote. "Kiss him many times for me, and tell him every day that he has a mother."

That was all. Doubtless Marceline knew that a letter to Unoccupied France would be censored, and perhaps she thought that a brief one would stand a better chance. "She doesn't write often," complained Beauty. "You know that she is not a demonstrative person, and she does not tell me much about her affairs."

"Is she happy with Oskar?" the half-brother inquired.

"If she were not, she would be too proud to say so. She has made her own bed. You know what a quietly self-willed person she is, Lanny. She would listen to what I had to say, and give me some vague answer, and then go ahead and do what she pleased."

"I didn't think she would like the attitude of the Nazis to their women, any more than she liked the attitude of the Italians to theirs."

"Oskar von Herzenberg is hardly a typical Nazi, I should think; he is a Prussian aristocrat."

"His father has been hiring his services to the Nazis, and I never saw any signs of disapproval on the part of the son. If she is happy with him, I'll be surprised."

"It makes quite a problem for me," said Beauty. "That my daughter should become the mistress of a Wehrmacht officer and should take to dancing in a Berlin night club won't leave me many friends among the English or the Americans when they return here. But I can't refuse my home to my daughter, and it would break my heart if she were to take the baby away."

"I think your true friends will forgive you, old darling; and you don't have to worry about the rest." He spoke more cheerfully than he felt, for he had warned Marceline that she would have a hard time with the Allies if she committed herself to the Germans. But there was no use worrying Beauty in advance. He added: "She has not troubled to give me her address. If you write, tell her that I wrote to her the last time I was here. Give her my love and tell her that I hope we can meet." He had not seen his half-sister for three years, and he had been out of sympathy with her for longer than that. But he would never get over his old fondness for her; and he was not forgetting the fact that she might have information about Naziland which would be of use to a P.A.

V

The train to Toulon was in need of paint, and possibly also of coal; it took three hours to cover about seventy-five miles along the coast. Lanny got himself a room at a small, obscure hotel, and then presented himself at the police station. He reported his business as art expert and exhibited the permit to "circulate" with which his Vichy friends had favored him. Those formalities attended to, he strolled to the Mercier bookstore where, a year ago, he had tried in vain to find his friend Raoul. This time he hoped for better luck, and surely meant to do his best to avoid the troubles into which he had then stumbled.

After the French fashion, the store had stands out in front, loaded with secondhand books, and Lanny stopped in front of these and began looking over the titles. He didn't even raise his eyes to the interior of the place; he just picked up one book after another. After a few minutes a man came out from the store, a man several years younger than Lanny, a slender figure, with black hair and finely chiseled, sensitive features, rather pale; the face of an idealist, perhaps an ascetic. When he smiled, you saw that he had even white teeth, and that his dark eyes were alert and attentive. He asked politely: "Can I help you, Monsieur?"

Lanny looked up, but gave no sign of recognition; he looked at the books again, and Raoul Palma's quick eyes glanced one way and the other to be sure there was no one near enough to hear. Then, in a low voice: "In front of the Hôtel de Ville, eight o'clock this evening."

"Right," murmured Lanny, and that was all. The clerk went into the store again, and the book browser moved on down the street.

It was getting late in the afternoon, closing time for dockyards and shops of the arsenal. The streets were thronged with workers carrying their dinner pails, women shoppers with baskets and bundles, and bluejackets from the Fleet with their little round flat hats with a red pompon on top. Lanny, his pockets stuffed with money, stayed in the well-frequented streets, keeping his distance from all comers. He was taking every precaution; when it was time for dinner he resisted the impulse to go to some workingmen's café, where he could enter into conversation and find out what they were thinking; he chose the Grand Hotel, where he would have a table to himself and never be spoken to.

So he reckoned, but, as the saying goes, without his host. Entering by the main doorway, he almost ran into a lady, and there resulted one of those incidents in which both step to the same side and then to the other side. Suddenly he stopped and stared at the lady, who was rather tall and slender, a brunette in her twenties, simply but tastefully clad. "Mademoiselle Richard!" he exclaimed. And the lady, almost speechless, managed to whisper: "Monsieur Budd!"

Lanny, man of the world who had been in many embarrassing situations in his life, was the first to recover his savoir-faire. "*Enchanté, Mademoiselle!*" he said. "I have been wondering if I should ever have the pleasure of seeing your collection of paintings."

Amusement spread over his face, and confusion over hers. He had her at a hopeless disadvantage, and it pleased him to make the most of it. It was in the lobby of this same hotel that he had encountered her, something like a year and a half ago, when she had lured him into her car and driven him up into the hills, where the partisans, the enemies of the Vichy government, had stepped out in the guise of bandits and taken possession of a supposed *collaborateur* and the funds he was carrying. Now he had another load of funds, but he was surely not going for any more drives with strange ladies, no matter how refined in appearance and gracious in manner. Here he had caught her in a situation where he was safe and she was far from safe; it was what is known as a "social situation," and more than that, a political situation. It appealed to his sense of humor, and he could see no harm in having a little fun with her, here in the lobby of a luxury hotel where *tout le monde* surrounded them, and everything was proper and expensive.

The "bandits" up in the hills had gone through a little farce comedy with the lady driver, pretending to frighten her; they had turned her car around and ordered her to drive away and keep silent, upon penalty of death for herself and her family. That hadn't fooled Lanny for very long; he was clear in his mind that "Marie Jeanne Richard" was herself a member of the rebel group. This meant that she was a friend of the cause Lanny was serving, and a very brave and determined person. But he wasn't in a position to tell her so—not yet.

"I trust no harm came to you, Mademoiselle," he said. "I have been intending to look you up and ask about the paintings."

Relief dawned upon her features. Incredible as it must seem, he had really believed her story! She had described herself as the secretary of a wealthy, eccentric "Madame Latour," who owned a collection of fine paintings and kept them up in the wild country behind Toulon, and who had sent her secretary to inform him that some of these paintings were for sale. All right, if Americans were that naïve, Mlle. Richard would play the game with one of them. "A dreadful night, M. Budd! I have never ceased to worry about it. I had no way of finding out what happened to you."

"You did not report the matter to the police?"

"I did not dare to. I thought that if you survived, you would do it."

"I decided that it was not an ordinary crime, that it had a political aspect, and I was afraid it might cause unpleasant publicity for yourself and your employer."

"That was certainly considerate of you, Monsieur. How can I thank you?"

"Very easily, *chère Mademoiselle*. I was about to dine alone, and that is a waste of opportunity. Will you favor me with your company, and tell me a little about life in a great French naval base?"

"Really, Monsieur Budd—" she began.

He saw that she was groping for an excuse. "If," argued he, "I was unconventional enough to go for a motor ride with a strange lady, surely you can risk sitting in the dining-room of a respectable hotel with a strange gentleman. I have an engagement immediately after dinner, so you will be free."

Was it a command? She couldn't be sure. He was a strange gentleman in more than one sense of the word; and she must have reflected that he had only to go to the telephone and call the police to land her in jail upon a charge that would involve the penalty of death for her and her friends. She was completely in his hands. If he had smiled politely and invited her to go up to his room with him, she would have had to obey. But he only wanted her to eat a meal with him!

"*Enchantée, Monsieur*," she replied, returning both his compliment and his smile. She allowed him to escort her into an ornate *salle à manger*, for which she was not properly dressed, and to seat her at a table with ceremony, and to press upon her food which would cost several hundred francs. She knew that he was a rich man—fabulously rich, she doubtless thought, knowing that his father was Budd-Erling, and it was known to all the world that America was pouring out billions of dollars for swift and deadly fighter planes. Well, this was how American multimillionaires treated ladies who caught their fancy; and she could only wonder what was coming next.

VI

It was a rather devilish thing to do to a woman. He treated her as if she were a duchess—he had treated a number of duchesses and knew all about it. He smiled charmingly and asked if she liked the taste of this and that which was put on her plate. Meanwhile he plied her with questions about the paintings in Madame Latour's collection. She did her best, but her confusion grew, and at last she had to tell him that she really didn't know much about paintings and had been kept too busy to study them. He asked about the rich lady, and from what her fortune had been derived; he only let up on his victim when he saw that she was blushing furiously and that the food was threatening to choke her. All the time that smile—or was it a grin? Was he telling her that he was deliberately teasing her, and that it didn't matter much what she answered?

"*Chère Mademoiselle*," he said, with what had suddenly become grave kindness, "it is perhaps difficult for you to realize, in times of stress like the present, that a man can have an abiding faith in the permanence of art, and that he should take it as his duty to assemble a collection which will have enduring value, and which the people of his homeland, groping for culture, may have opportunity to study and imitate. To help in setting a standard of technique and expression for a new nation of a hundred and thirty million people—that is an undertaking for which it should surely be possible to have respect."

"*Vraiment, Monsieur*," she replied. She was studying his face and trying desperately to read his mind. She must have been told by her comrades in this revolutionary *coup de crime* that they had cross-questioned him closely in their mountain hideout and revealed to him that he was suspected of being a Nazi-Fascist agent. Was he now trying to tell her that he was innocent of this charge, and that he really was what he pretended to be, an art expert acting as purchasing agent for American collectors? He had been robbed of fifty thousand francs and had not troubled to mention the matter to the police; he had escaped by bribing one of the band, and that must have cost him still more; yet, apparently, he hadn't told a soul about it—certainly, at any rate, not in the Var. That didn't look like the behavior of a Nazi-Fascist spy; and was he now spending money on a dinner for her in order to say: "I am not what you have thought me"?

Yes, that must be the case. It was hardly likely that he was putting up this meal because he was lonely, or just for the pleasure of teasing her. He was asking for protection. You let me alone and I'll let you alone! And he was doing it in a very clever and altogether charming way. He must have thought of it in a flash, running into her in a hotel doorway. Or could he have somehow found out that she was employed in this hotel, and that this was her time for leaving work? She couldn't ask him that, or hint at it, for she had to go on stoutly pretending that she was the secretary of a wholly imaginary Madame Latour who hid up in mountains with imaginary old masters!

VII

Immediately after dinner Lanny excused himself and left the building. After making certain that he was not being followed, he walked to the headquarters of the city's government, the Hôtel de Ville. In front is a large statue entitled "The Genius of Navigation," and in its shadow Lanny saw his old friend and protégé waiting. When the American approached, Raoul strolled away, and Lanny followed at a distance; two experienced conspirators, they did not join each other until they had made certain they were not being followed, and until they were on a quiet street. This wasn't easy, for it was a balmy night, and most of the population of Toulon lived in the streets. The city was completely "blacked out," but a full moon was shining with dangerous brightness, and it appeared that every nook and shaded spot was occupied by a loving couple; children were under foot everywhere; in short, it was a Mediterranean port.

Raoul's first question was: "Are you all right for a walk?" When Lanny said he was, the other added: "I will take you out to Cap Cépet, and we can talk quietly in the gardens of the *Hôpital*."

First of all, Lanny wanted to know if his friend had heard the story of what had gone wrong when they tried to meet last time. Raoul, speaking English so as to be less apt to be understood if overheard, answered that Julie, his wife, was in Toulon, and had told him everything that Lanny had told to her. "A wretched *contretemps!*" he exclaimed. Lanny smiled and said it would be a story to tell to his grandchildren.

"Have you told anybody about me?" he next inquired.

"Not a soul," the younger man replied. "I am not supposed to know anything about the matter myself. They sent me off on an errand to get me out of the way. They knew that you and I were old friends and that you had helped to support the school."

"I had an idea that the leader of that crowd was a former pupil, but

I couldn't bring him to mind. He was masked, and I had only his voice to guess from."

That might have been a hint for the former school director to talk, but he said: "You know, Lanny, I am under oath."

"That is quite all right," responded the P.A. "I prefer not to know, for if something should happen to him, I might be held responsible." After a moment he added: "Here is something I ought to tell you without delay. An hour ago I was having dinner with Mlle. Richard."

"Richard?" said the Spaniard inquiringly.

"Marie Jeanne Richard is the name she gave me."

"I do not know her."

"She is a good-looking brunette, in her mid-twenties, I should guess; rather tall for a French woman, cultivated, and very good company. She is the person who met me in the hotel last time and told me that she was private secretary to a wealthy lady who had a collection of paintings; so I let her drive me up into the hills—perhaps the silliest thing I ever did in my life. But I thought I knew a lady when I saw one."

"I think I know who she is," said Raoul. "How on earth did you come to dine with her?"

"I ran into her in the entrance to the Grand Hotel. I saw that she knew me, and I thought it would be the part of wisdom to make friends with her and persuade her that I believed what she wanted me to believe—that she was an innocent party in that episode. I think I succeded in that, and perhaps in persuading her that I, too, am innocent."

"That is not possible, Lanny," exclaimed Raoul quickly. "You are in danger. You ought not stay in Toulon tonight!"

VIII

The man of the underground lost all interest in taking his friend to the beautiful gardens on Cap Cépet; he wanted to find some place to hide. But Lanny refused to be worried. Said he: "I have been thinking it over and have things to tell you that may change the situation entirely. You must understand that America's coming into the war has made a great difference in my job. I can no longer go into Germany or German-occupied territory. Even if I wanted to take the risk, my orders are otherwise. I have just been to Vichy and collected a lot of information, but I doubt if I shall wish to go there again, for the reason that those intriguers are getting to be of less importance, and it won't be long before they are of no importance at all. The Americans are coming, Raoul."

"*Sapristi!*" exclaimed the former school director. "You really know that?"

"I do."

"When?"

"That I have not been told, nor the place. But I know they are coming, and in real force."

"That is the point everybody will ask about, Lanny. They all remember St. Nazaire. The people rose to help the British, and then it turned out to be nothing but a commando raid; the British took to their boats again and the Nazis came back and slaughtered the French."

"I know all about it, Raoul. I am authorized to give the assurance that when the Americans come, it will be to stay."

"*Naturellement* that is the most important news in the world to me and my friends. But how can I convince them of it?"

"That's what I'm coming to. I am authorized, at my discretion, to meet some of the underground leaders and put them in touch with our Intelligence service."

"But, Lanny, they are convinced that you are a Fascist agent. It won't be easy to persuade them otherwise."

"It won't be enough if you vouch for me?"

"I am afraid not. It might work the other way and lead them to distrust me. I must tell you, the leader you tried to recognize is a Communist, and you know how it is between the Communists and the Socialists. We have a truce for the struggle against the Nazis and try to keep the agreement loyally, but it is very hard for a Communist to recognize any loyalty or faith except to his own Party. This man is suspicious of me and inclined to oppose any proposition I put before our group. Probably in his heart he suspects me of trying to take the leadership away from him."

"Just like the old rows that used to be fought out in our workers' schools. You saw them in Cannes, and Freddi Robin saw them in Berlin, and I saw them everywhere I went."

"Exactly so, Lanny. I will tell you something horrible that is in my mind—that some day there may be another world war, fought between the Communists and the Socialists."

"Let's not talk about that now, Raoul; we have a war against the Nazi-Fascists, and that is plenty. Tell me this: will your leader respect credentials from President Roosevelt?"

"Ah, mon Dieu, Lanny! If you have that, we can knock him cold!"

"O.K., that is what I will show him. I can tell you now that for the past five years I have been what in inside circles is known as a 'presidential agent'—'P.A.' for short. I report directly to the President, and only one other friend—the man who introduced me to the President—knows what I am. Less than a month ago Roosevelt told me what I was to say to you and others who can be trusted: that the Americans are coming, and not too long a time from now, and coming to stay. I have money which I am authorized to pay to leaders of the underground who can use it effectively."

"Lanny, I would like to sing!" exclaimed the younger man; but instead of that, he whispered: "I'd like to have an hour to get two or three people together and tell them this news. I have an idea they'll be meeting to hear what your Mlle. Richard has to tell them. You ought to keep out of sight. But where?"

"One of the safest places would be a cinema. That will be dark, and nobody is apt to notice me in the short time it takes to enter."

"Bien," said Raoul, "I will take you to the nearest."

"One thing more," added the P.A. "You know you asked me to bring you something, and I have it."

"All right, I'll take it. Wait until we see a chance."

They continued their walk and presently came to a dark alley, into which they stepped. Lanny transferred his bundles of banknotes to his friend's hands, and Raoul stuffed them into his pockets. They strolled farther, until they came to a motion-picture theater, dark, of course. "Come out exactly one hour from now," said the younger man.

IX

The American purchased a ticket and went into the darkened cave, to see a crime-of-passion story, manufactured in Paris—the Germans didn't care how degraded the French became, provided only that their films contained no ideas of liberty or democracy, or the glory of France past or present. They had tried offering newsreels showing Nazis troopers marching and Nazi propagandists speaking bad French, but the audiences had booed and rioted, and after a few experiments the Nazis had given up and just let the Vichyites feed themselves on their own native garbage.

The two conspirators had compared watches, and promptly on the minute Lanny strolled out of the theater. He saw his friend a short way down the street and presently caught up with him. Raoul said:

"I have talked with my friends, and they want to meet you; but they won't reveal themselves to you until they are satisfied."

"Of course not," Lanny replied. "I am quite willing to take a chance on convincing them. Did you tell them how long you have known me?"

"They knew all about that. What makes them suspicious is that you deserted the school and turned into a Fascist so long ago."

"But that was the way I managed to get information. Did you tell them how I brought it to you, and how you fed it to the Socialist press?"

"I told them all that, and that it was on your money they have been operating most of the time. But it's the old trouble—the Reds don't want to have to believe anything good about the Pinks. They'd have a hard time not being pleased if it should turn out that I am a Fascist agent, spying upon them all."

Lanny chuckled. "If that were the case, they'd hardly have much time to be pleased about anything!"

Their walk took them into the "Old Town," near the docks. They went into an alley and came to an ancient arched doorway of stone; it led into a sort of court, and they entered at an unlocked door, turned through an irregular passageway—very old buildings are like that, for reasons long since forgotten. Raoul gave three quick taps upon a door, and when it was opened he led his friend into a room that was completely dark. A voice said: "*Asseyez-vous*," and Lanny, reaching about him, found an empty chair and took it. He did not have to hear another word in order to know that voice; it was the leader of the band that had abducted him, the masked man who had questioned him for an hour or two up in the low mountains, or the high hills, that lie back of this French naval base. Lanny had been sure that his life depended upon that matching of wits, and he was never going to forget the tones of the voice.

"Monsieur Budd," said the man, speaking educated French, "our friend Bruges wishes us to believe that you are a friend of the anti-Nazi cause and a confidential agent of President Roosevelt."

"That is true, Monsieur."

"You will understand that this is a serious matter to us, *une affaire très grave*. All the machinery of government is in the hands of our enemies, and we are being hunted like rats. If we are betrayed, it will mean torture of the worst cruelty our foes can devise."

"I understand that perfectly," Lanny said.

"Therefore you will not take it amiss if we question you closely, and refuse to accept your story until every possible doubt has been removed."

"That is quite reasonable. In such matters it has to be everything or nothing, and you could be of no use to me unless you were prepared to trust me."

"*Très bien. Alors*, let us hear your story."

"First, a question from me. How many persons besides Bruges and myself are in this room?"

"Two men and a woman."

"You know who these persons are, Bruges?" Lanny asked. And the voice of Raoul answered that he did.

X

"*Messieurs et Madame*," Lanny began. "At the age of seventeen I became interested in the labor cause, and very soon I was calling myself a Socialist. After the war, when I came to Juan, I met Bruges, who was then a clerk in a shoestore. We got together a small group and discussed the idea of a school for workers. I helped to raise the money, and later, when I began earning large sums as an art expert, I was able to carry a good part of the burden. I did this as long as the school existed, paying the money secretly to Bruges. After Hitler seized power, I realized that we were in for a long fight, and that I was in a special position to get information because I had met Hitler and had come to know the Nazis."

"Tell us how you came to know Hitler, for that is the crux of the whole matter."

"At the age of thirteen I spent a summer at the Dalcroze School of what is called Eurythmics, a kind of dancing; that was at Hellerau, a village near Dresden, and there I met a German boy named Kurt Meissner. I went to spend the following Christmas with him at Schloss Stubendorf, in Upper Silesia. Kurt grew up to become a famous pianist and composer. My mother was a widow—her husband, the painter Marcel Detaze, was killed in the second battle of the Marne. She took Kurt Meissner as her lover, and he lived at our home in Juan for a matter of eight years. That led to my meeting many Germans and to visiting that country. My friends were the rich and powerful, persons who despised the Nazis, but later, when the Nazis seized power, they did what we in America call 'climbing on the band wagon'—*montant sur le wagon de la musique*."

"We have observed the same thing in France, Monsieur Budd."

"At Schloss Stubendorf I had met a son of the head forester, named Heinrich Jung, and he became a follower of Hitler in the very early days, and visited him in prison. In the course of the years he converted Kurt, and he labored hard to convert me. That was how I came to meet Hitler. I listened to him politely and then told him that I was a non-political person, an art expert. But as the years passed I realized that I had a valuable asset in that ability to go into Germany and meet its leader; and as Hitler's power increased, I began telling Bruges what he was doing and planning. I did the same for a Socialist friend whom I have in England, the playwright Eric Vivian Pomeroy-Neilson. These two men used to put the information into articles for the Socialist and labor press, and I hoped that I was being of some help in awakening the workers to the threat which Nazism meant to them. Am I going into too much detail?"

"*Pas du tout, Monsieur. Continuez.*"

"I had another boyhood friend, Freddi Robin, son of the Jewish financier Johannes Robin. He became a Socialist and founded a workers' school in Berlin. I helped him and went frequently to that school, and there I met a couple of artists, Ludi and Trudi Schultz. When Hitler took power the Nazis grabbed Ludi and killed him—at least he was never heard of again. Trudi became an underground worker, under the same conditions that you face here. For several years I gave her money, just as I have done in the case of Bruges. Then the Gestapo got onto her trail and I helped her to escape to Paris. To finish that story, they seized her in Paris, smuggled her back to Germany, and tortured her to death in Dachau. In the meantime she had become my wife—that was after my divorce from Irma Barnes—and so you can see that there is not much about your present position that I do not understand. I mean the underground life and the danger."

"You are telling us something new, Monsieur Budd. We have had reports on many events in your life, but not about that marriage."

"I am glad to hear that, because it was a secret known only to persons whom I trusted in my effort to rescue Trudi. Not even my father and mother knew about it. The reason was that by that time I had come to realize that the greatest service I could render to my friends of the Left was to use my acquaintances among the ruling classes as a means of finding out their plans. I took to telling these people, including my own families, that I had become disgusted with political developments and had retired to an ivory tower. I became the art expert, interested only in furthering great collections for the American wealthy, and incidentally in earning large commissions. The rich all understand that you desire to become richer; that is what the game of life means to them."

"Is that what you tell Hitler, Monsieur Budd?"

"I always shade my story according to the company I am in. I told Hitler that I was a complete convert to his cause; for years I addressed him as '*Mein Führer.*' I told him about the many sympathizers he had in Britain and America, and I brought him messages from them—all this, of course, before America came into the war. In return, he confided to me a great deal about his plans."

"You did not feel that you were giving him encouragement and perhaps information?"

"That was a problem about which I used to worry. But when I put it up to President Roosevelt, he assured me that what I brought him was worth any price it cost. That settled it for me, because I have complete confidence in his judgment. For five years I have been what is called a presidential agent, and have done exactly what he told me."

XI

That was the matter about which the three judges were waiting to hear. The leader said: "We have great confidence in the President of your country, Monsieur Budd, even though it is a capitalist country. Will you tell us how you came to enter his service?"

"I was sent to him by a member of his 'brain trust,' Professor Charles T. Alston, who had been one of President Wilson's advisers at the Paris Peace Conference, and whom I had served as secretary-translator at that time. President Roosevelt invited me to his home, heard the story I have just told to you, and said that I could be of help to him. Of course I could not refuse his request. I have a confidential way of getting reports to him, and I have sent him more than fifty so far. He has several times offered to pay me, but I told him I made plenty of money, and so I am what is called in Washington a 'dollar-a-year-man.' I did not even collect from him the sums I have paid to Bruges and other contacts which I have. The last time I talked with the President, which was less than a month ago at his home in Hyde Park, he told me that our Intelligence service was supporting the underground movements where our armies were likely to come, and indeed wherever we could hinder and hurt the Germans. He put money into my bank account in New York, and I have just paid some of it to Bruges. I am prepared to pay more if you can show me ways you can make use of it."

"Just what does the President wish us to do?"

"You understand, we have to make a distinction between the two parts of France. In the occupied portion the Germans rule; we are at war with them, and we furnish our friends with arms, explosives, and all means of sabotage. But with Vichy France we are not at war, and it is not according to our code to encourage sabotage in a country with which we maintain diplomatic relations. Naturally, any harm you can do to German agents here is all right with us, though we do not ask for it or direct it. What we particularly want is to keep the French Fleet out of Hitler's hands, and no doubt Bruges has told you that it was I who urged his coming to Toulon in order to make contacts with the sailors and the arsenal workers."

"He has told us that."

"There is nothing more important to the Allied cause, and nothing for which we would be more glad to make expenditures. If you could manage to start the publication of a clandestine paper, or the printing and circulating of leaflets—"

"We are already doing both those things, Monsieur Budd."

"That is good news, and I shall mention it to the President, with your permission."

"Is it your plan to stay in this neighborhood?"

"That has never been my way. I go from place to place, under the pretense of inspecting works of art. I talk with the people I know and listen to the gossip in the salons, and now and then I send in a report."

"You have recently been in Vichy?"

"I was flown there by way of Lisbon and Madrid. I was a guest in Laval's home and I had a long talk with Admiral Darlan, whom my parents have known since World War I. I picked up a lot of information among the collaborators, and that information should by now be in the President's hands. It goes by air."

"Will you tell us how you expect to work with us?"

"The President's instructions were that I should get into touch with the underground wherever I had a contact I could trust; that I should ask permission to send the leader's name to the President, so that he may give it to the new Intelligence service headed by Colonel William J. Donovan in New York. A properly accredited agent will come to you and presumably maintain continuous contact with you."

"We should be glad to co-operate with President Roosevelt, Monsieur Budd; but we must point out that any letter mailed to any place, whether inside or outside of Vichy France, is very likely to be opened and read."

"Quite so, and you have my word that I will never take such a risk. If you decide to trust me with a name and address, I will memorize it, and not put it on paper until I am in a position to be certain that it will be flown in a diplomatic pouch, and will be seen by no eye until it reaches the President's. Give me a code word, and in due course someone will appear who will repeat it."

"Bruges tells us that you have credentials from the President himself."

"The last thing he did before I left his study was to take one of his engraved visiting cards and write with his fountain pen the sentence: 'My friend Lanny Budd is worthy of all trust.' He instructed me to sew that in the lining of my coat and use it in case of need. I am wearing that coat, and will show you the card; but it must be with the understanding that it is precious to me, and I must have your word of honor that, regardless of what your decision about me may be, you will return the card to me. If it were lost or destroyed, I should have to travel back to America to get another."

"You have our word on that, Monsieur Budd."

There came into the P.A.'s voice a little of that humor which on many occasions had been the means of making friends and influencing people. "I will put the coat into your hands, Monsieur Incognito, but perhaps you will leave the cutting of the threads to the lady who is present. It is necessary that there should be no damage to the lining, and the opening should be no larger than necessary. It would look very suspicious if a fashionable gentleman were wearing a coat which showed signs of repairs."

"We will do our best," said the leader of the band. "Bruges, will you take Monsieur Budd into the next room?"

XII

Patiently the P.A. waited, sitting coatless and in darkness for five or ten minutes while the secret group debated his story. When the door was opened again, there was a light in the other room; only a kerosene lamp, but even so it made Lanny blink when he entered. He saw that all four of the persons in the room were smiling. "*Soyez le bienvenu, camarade!*" said the leader. "Here is your coat and here is your card. We have agreed to accept your word, and you are one of us." He added quickly: "My name is Zed. If you think you remember any other name from past times, please understand that it is not to be spoken."

For a year and a half Lanny had been worrying his brain, trying to identify the voice of the masked man whom he had seen only by the light of a flickering campfire. Lanny had tried to recall the voices he had heard and the faces he had seen in the workers' school—hundreds of them in course of the years. Now, at the first glance it came to him, like a flash of lightning on a dark night: Jean Catroux! Sallow, sharp-featured, eager, and contentious Jean! His father had owned a cigar-store, and the son had been a clerk in the daytime and an incessant troublemaker at the school in the evenings. A partisan of the extreme Left, he was one of a small group who kept the place in turmoil and almost brought Raoul to despair. The pupil had been older than the teacher by several years and considered that he knew much more.

The Reds in those unhappy days had joined the *front populaire* and had helped to vote Léon Blum into power. But they sabotaged him by propaganda and waged relentless ideological war upon him. In truth, Blum had given them plenty of cause, for in the dreadful crisis of the Spanish civil war he had given way to the class enemies and shown himself a broken reed. All this came to Lanny in a rush of memories, and it was like a puzzle to which you cannot guess the answer, but when you have heard the answer, you cannot imagine how you failed to guess it.

"I remember, Comrade Zed," he replied at last.

How much had happened in the world in five or six years, and what did it mean for the future? This man had come out on top because he had energy and fervor, because he knew exactly what he wanted and had the courage to take it. Was this an augury, a portent? Were the Socialists going to fail everywhere because they hesitated and fumbled? Were the Reds going to win because the holders of privilege throughout the world wouldn't permit any social change without violence? Anyhow, that was the way it had been here in the Var. Lanny has heard that Jean Catroux had gone to Spain to fight the Fascists; now he was back, hunted as an outlaw by the Vichyites, and helping to prepare the French workers for renewed war upon the Nazi enemy. In that war the Reds would come forward as leaders precisely because they knew what they wanted and had the courage and the fervor.

XIII

The other man was a dockworker, solid and weatherbeaten, with a horny hand and a devastating grip. Lanny, who played tennis and the piano, was able to survive it. The man's name was Soulay, and Lanny had never seen him before. As he expected, the woman proved to be Mlle. Richard. He was told now that her name was Mlle. Bléret, but of course he couldn't know whether that was a real name or another *nom de guerre*. She blushed as he shook hands with her, and her voice was unsteady as she said: "Comrade Budd, we are dreadfully ashamed of what happened on your last visit here."

He answered, with his agreeable smile: "Don't worry about it. The mistake was a natural one, and it taught me a useful lesson." He was thinking what he had thought the first time he had spoken to this young woman, that she was intelligent and attractive, and that he would like to know more about her. There was a difference, however, between this time and last: he was now a married man.

"This we have to assure you," put in Catroux, alias "Zed." "Every franc of the money taken from you was used for the cause."

"I took that for granted," Lanny said. "It appealed to my sense of humor that you expended so much effort to get what Comrade Bruges would have brought to you more quickly."

Possibly this line of conversation did not appeal to Zed; it was one of his exploits for which he would never be awarded a medal of honor. In a businesslike tone he remarked: "Comrade Budd, it will be necessary that we assign you a code name. Obviously we should never speak your real name from now on. Will it be all right if you become '*Monsieur Zhone*'?"

"O.K.," Lanny said, and restrained an impulse to smile. He was familiar with the forms that English names take to a Frenchman. This one would be written "Jones."

"You will continue to communicate through Bruges, and you will give his name and only his to the American Intelligence service. There will be no need for you to mention the rest of this group, even to President Roosevelt. We will decide who is to meet the Intelligence man when he comes."

Again Lanny said "O.K.," and again he was amused to see Comrade Catroux taking charge of the former *patron* of his school. The bourgeoisie giving place to the proletariat! "Arise, ye prisoners of starvation! Arise, ye wretched of the earth!"

XIV

With these four anti-Nazis Lanny sat in consultation. He told them as much as he was allowed to, enough to give them courage in a time of seemingly endless defeat. He described the prodigious war works now under way in the New World, especially the Budd-Erling effort, which he had seen with his own eyes. In return they told him what they desired from the American government, pending the arrival of an army on any one of the shores of *la belle France*. They repeated what Bruges had said already: "Don't send us commandos. Don't come until you mean to stay!"

Without direct questions the visitor gathered a few items concerning these new comrades. Soulay was an old-time labor man and a Catholic. Mlle. Bléret had no special label; she came of a doctor's family in the northeast, and was earning her living here because she had to; she was helping in the fight against the Germans because her mother had been killed in the wanton bombing of refugees on the highways. An odd fact that came out in the course of conversation was that Catroux had met Raoul Palma during the fighting in Spain, and had asked about Lanny Budd and been told that he had lost interest in the workers and gone back to his own class. That was what Lanny had told his friend to say, and it had caused the Red leader's mind to become centered upon this renegade. It might easily have cost Lanny his life.

"Don't worry about anything you may hear about me," he cautioned them. "Remember, not even the Intelligence people who come to you will know about '*Camarade Zhone*,' and you are not to mention me to them. It is my job to travel and to take any role that will help me get information. If you hear of me in the enemy's camp, shake your heads sadly and say that it was to be expected and that no help can be expected from the *haute bourgeoisie*."

He impressed upon them that the main thing was to keep the Fleet out of Nazi hands. He came back to this a second and a third time, assuring them that a crisis was bound to come soon, and advising with them as to how to meet it. One of the crimes of the Laval regime, they told him, was forcing French sailors to teach Germans how to handle these ships; the Germans were learning fast. Lanny said: "That is our President's greatest concern. With your Fleet they might get control of the Mediterranean, and we might lose the war, or, at any rate, have it prolonged for several years."

The answer of these people of the underground was: "Tell your great friend that it will not happen. The French sailors—not the officers but the *marins*—will sink the ships even if they have to go down with them. *Les boches ne les auront. Jamais, jamais!*"

5

Testament of Bleeding War

1

LANNY stayed in Toulon long enough to ask questions about paintings. He once more inspected the collection of the wealthy D'Avrienne family, and gave them another chance to put a reasonable price upon a Nattier which they possessed—a portrait more of costumes than of human features, he told them. Since their views still did not meet, he gave them more time and took the crowded train back to Cannes. He could feel certain that he had done good work in that base of the French Fleet, and that the authorities of the town could have no grounds for suspicion.

His mother was prepared to be told that he was planning next to visit Switzerland. She could not restrain the impulse to protest: "You're not going into Germany, Lanny!" He answered her: "Good heavens! That would be trading with the enemy."

It was all right to trade with the Swiss; they were neutral and were getting rich on the war. To be sure, they had to spend a good part of it on their army, standing guard at all their passes, day and night. Even so, many of them were worried about the future, and some might be glad to have money put to their accounts in one of the great New York banks. On those terms they would part with a painting or two. So Lanny explained, and it made a story—good enough to fool the Swiss, perhaps, but it did not fool Mrs. Beauty Budd Detaze Dingle, who had been in the world a long time.

Lanny's reason for coming back, he said, was to have his clothes pressed and his laundry done; but really he was hoping there might be another letter from Bernhardt Monck. Finding none, he decided to take a chance anyhow. He got his railroad ticket and his Swiss visa, and took the train eastward to the broad rich valley of the River Rhône, familiar to him since childhood, and to invading armies as far back as history records. At the silk-weaving city of Lyon the road divides into three forks, one westward to Vichy, one northward to

Paris, and one eastward to Geneva—three cities which had come to be centers of attention and activity for a secret agent.

The Rhône flows down from Geneva, and the railroad follows its valley. Near the Swiss border is the French town of Annemasse, where the Swiss customs and security agents come aboard to inspect papers and baggage. Lanny's papers were in order; his card from President Roosevelt had been neatly sewed back into the lining of his coat, which the polite Swiss did not examine. He sat looking out of the windows at the rushing green waters of the river, which comes out of Lac Leman, or, to be exact, of which the lake constitutes a forty-five-mile stretch. At the foot of the lake, near the dam over which the water flows, is a small island. On it, slightly less than two centuries ago, there had resided a revolutionary writer, much dreaded and maligned by the powers that then were; but the whirligig of time had brought him revenge, and now the island was known as Rousseau's, and tourists came to see his statue.

On both shores of the lake's outlet there had been a town in ancient Roman days, and before that a settlement of lake-dwellers, whose piles could still be seen at various places. Now there was a fine city in which the old and the new were combined, and in which the American art expert had made a few friends. The League of Nations had had its headquarters here, in a grand building paid for by the Rockefeller family; now it had shut up shop, and too late the Genevans were realizing that it had been an important real-estate asset.

II

Lanny had never had the address of Bernhardt Monck, alias Capitán Herzog, alias Branting, alias Braun; the man of the underground could not afford to be known as receiving letters or visits from foreigners. The Swiss were holding rigidly to their neutrality and were trying to restrict the activities of the secret agents who swarmed into the country. This applied particularly to the Reds and the Pinks, for the government of the country was conservative and, like all such governments, found it easier to get along with well-heeled and well-dressed Fascists than with ex-labor leaders and agitators, refugees who generally were destitute and frequently had jail records. This is something which applies to nearly all governments; F.D.R. had complained to Lanny that he was powerless to prevent it, even in his own State Department.

Lanny put up at the Hotel Beau Rivage, as was his custom. His first duty was to type out a report to his Chief, covering the situation at Toulon and giving the name and address of Bruges as a contact with the underground there. This he double-sealed, as usual, and mailed it to the American Ambassador in Bern. Then he permitted himself the luxury of reading a newspaper—one which really deserved the name. The Swiss papers were no longer permitted in Vichy France, for it had been discovered that nobody wanted to read any others. Lanny learned that Corregidor had fallen to the Japs, and that the Germans had taken Kerch, in the Crimea. Always defeats!

The visiting art expert proceeded to make his presence known to the dealers and the possessors of private collections with whom he had done business in the past. Through one of these he had met an editor of the *Journal de Genève*, and he now invited this gentleman to lunch and to chat about art development during the war. The result was an interview in the paper, for not many Americans appeared nowadays in a land which had depended to a great extent upon tourists for its prosperity. The *Journal* sent a photographer and published a picture of the distinguished art authority, so no reader of the news could fail to know that he was in town.

That was the way Lanny had planned it. In the afternoon he strolled into the library of Geneva's much honored university and possessed himself of an American magazine, something difficult to get on the Riviera. But he found it hard to keep his mind on the pages; every minute or two he would lift his eyes and turn them here and there. He couldn't be sure whether his friend Monck was still in town, or even if he was still alive. This afternoon would tell.

His heart gave a leap when he saw the familiar sturdy figure coming down the aisle. Lanny dived into his magazine again; he knew that Monck would see him and, as usual, would pretend to have some business in the reading-room. Presently he would stroll out, and Lanny would follow after an interval. They had to use extreme care, for this ex-sailor, Social Democrat, and *capitán* in the International Brigade in Spain was a man marked by the Gestapo, and by the security police of Switzerland as well. To be seen with him would be damaging to the reputation of a respectable *connaisseur d'art*.

At a safe distance Lanny followed him out of the building and across the park. Monck stopped in front of an art dealer's window—that being a proper place for Lanny. Making sure they were alone, the German whispered: "Reformation Monument, twenty hours this evening." That was their usual place of assignation, and all Lanny had to answer was: "O.K." The German moved on, and the American went inside to inquire whether there was any new talent appearing in this Alpine land, which, as a rule, was interested more in facts than in fancy, more in morality than in genius.

III

This pair's last meeting had been in the month of March; snow had been falling, and they had had to stamp their feet while talking. Now, more than a year later, it was spring, and happened to be a mild night. Lanny's first words were: "We ought to have a good long talk, *Genosse*." It was the Socialist Party's word for "comrade." "Can we not find some place to sit down?" It was a fact that they had never dared have a real meeting since the old days in Paris. "Have you any reason to think you are being watched at present?" Lanny asked.

"It can happen any time," replied the other. "The Gestapo never sleeps. But perhaps we can get out of town and find a quiet corner."

They walked toward the north, following obscure and poorly lighted streets, conversing in low tones, in the German language, as usual. Monck said: "You have been a long time coming. I had given you up."

"I nearly gave myself up, *Genosse*. I set out for England last September, and was in a plane wreck and had both legs broken. I was invited on a yachting trip while recuperating, and I very nearly got caught by the Japs in Hongkong." He did not mention Russia; this pair of secret agents set each other an example in reticence.

"I had important news for you," said the German, "but most of it is out of date now. I learned that the Nazis intended to attack Russia on the southern front and drive for Caucasus oil. Hitler has been saving up all his resources and is expecting to put Russia out of the war in the next two or three months. The attack should be beginning any day now."

"Presumably the move in the Crimea is a preliminary," Lanny agreed. "You have been able to restore your contacts in Germany?"

"To some extent; but it is all so uncertain, I am brought nearly to despair. You cannot imagine the persistence with which our comrades are hunted, of the cold ferocity with which they are exterminated. A messenger comes at intervals, and then I never hear from him or about him again. A new one comes, and I have the problem all over again. Is he the real thing, or an agent of the enemy?"

"I bring you reinforcements, *Genosse*. I have just left America, and it is unbelievable what is happening there. The country is united at last, and it is really going to win this war."

"Which war? The one in the Far East or the one here?"

"Both of them in the end. This one first."

"That means conquering practically the whole of Europe. You really believe that America has the resources and the will for such a bloody task?"

"I know that it sounds unlikely. I had spells of pessimism myself until I got back home. I saw with my own eyes what was going on at my father's plant; and it is the same all over the land. The whole industrial energy of America is being turned to war work. Huge new factories are going up all through the Middle West, where before was nothing but prairie. There has never been such a tornado of activity in all history."

"But the shipping, *Genosse*—"

"We are going to turn out the ships by mass-production methods. A cargo vessel that used to take a year will now take a month, or perhaps two weeks."

"And the U-boats?"

"We are licking that problem. My father knows about it, but he gave me only a few hints. We are perfecting devices to reveal the presence of submarines; they will not be able to move without our knowing it. Then we shall get them with airplanes from small carriers. This spring the situation is bad, I know, but soon it will be better. And we are going to have an army of eight or ten million men."

"You Americans toss figures like that around. But an army takes years to train—surely a German knows about that!"

"I am not permitted to say anything about the time or the place, *Genosse;* but you may be sure that an army is coming, and it will be much sooner than you think. Take courage and start over again."

"I am a German, but you know that I am a true revolutionist and am not seduced by any touch of pride in what the Nazi armies have achieved. But I have firsthand knowledge of their efficiency, and my mind is not equal to the task of imagining an army brought from overseas being powerful enough to drive the Nazis out of the strongholds they have taken, all the way from Kharkov to Bordeaux, and from Narvik to Tobruk."

"You must not forget the air, *Genosse.* The victories so far have been won by air power, and it has been shown that no army can stand up very long without air cover. We are going to build an air force greater than that of all the rest of the world put together. The construction is under way, and the training; the bases are being built, the techniques are being worked out, and the job is going to be done. Believe me, I am fresh from seeing it and hearing about it from people who know."

I V

They had come up the lake shore to the magnificent building of the League of Nations, now silent and dead except for caretakers. It stood upon a rise of ground overlooking the lake, a vast structure, like three sides of an oblong, and with tall square pillars in front. Wide flights of steps led up to it, and at the foot of these steps was an excellent place for a secret conference, because no one could come near without being seen. The stars afforded light enough so that no one could creep up, but not enough for a passer-by to recognize the conferees.

To Lanny it was one of the most melancholy places in the world; the dead shell of what had been his brightest hope, his most cherished dream. In the old days he had had friends here, and had followed the proceedings, giving mankind credit for more collective intelligence than it possessed. He had hoped and prayed, first that Japan would be forced to retire from Manchuria, then that the insolent Mussolini would be driven back from Albania and Abyssinia. The murder of Spain had ended all those hopes and shattered the cherished dream.

"The world has to learn by blundering," declared Monck, as if he had divined his friend's thoughts. "The only question is whether the blunders will be so great as to destroy the pupil."

"One thing we can count on," his friend replied. "This war will put an end to isolationism in America. Whatever happens from now on, we shall have a part in it."

"Yes, but what sort of part, *Genosse?* What will this military effort do to your democracy? And what has any capitalist land to contribute to mankind except a new set of exploiters?"

"Listen," said the P.A. "I am able to talk more frankly than has been previously permitted. I can tell you that I was in Roosevelt's home less than a month ago and spent a couple of hours going over the situation. I have his word for it that the purpose for which our armies are coming to Europe is to see that the people of each country have a chance to decide their own destiny in a democratic election. Surely we Socialists have nothing to fear from that, and we have no right to ask more."

"If he stands by it, and if he is able to have his way."

"Who will be able to stop him? Churchill has pledged his acceptance of the Atlantic Charter, and Stalin has ratified it."

"Those generalizations are wonderful vote-getters in your country," remarked the sad ex-*capitán;* "but we Europeans have learned that when the diplomats sit down to interpret them, they turn out to mean the opposite of what we had thought."

"Let us win the war first," said Lanny, and added with a smile: "That will be task enough for tonight. What I want to convey to you is that I am working under the President's orders and reporting to him by a confidential route. All the news that you have given me since our days in Paris has gone directly to him, and I can assure you that it has been useful."

"That is indeed of interest to me, *Genosse.*"

"It may make a difference in your own affairs. I told Roosevelt about you, but did not give him your name nor even mention Geneva. He wants your consent to put our Intelligence service in touch with you, so that your reports will no longer be subject to delay. You understand, I have an assignment elsewhere, and coming here at long intervals is far from satisfactory."

"That would be a serious decision for me, *Genosse.* When you deal with a government organization you run risks of broken codes and betrayals. The Americans have a number of agents here, and I know who several of them are. Their point of view is different from mine."

"There is only one point of view now, old man: and that is, to beat Hitler. The arrangement I am suggesting would be of a special kind. There would be some picked man who would come to maintain contact with you; he would be trained and would have some occupation or camouflage that would be completely protective. He would provide you with funds; that is something the President mentioned explicitly. We are prepared to spend money without limit—anything that will get results."

"I don't need money for myself, *Genosse.* I have invested the sums which you turned over to me in Paris. My wife and children managed to get out of Vichy France and are here, and are getting along all right. What I have to think about is the group I am serving."

"As you know, I have never asked questions about that; but this is certain, *Genosse:* no group can have any purpose but to aid in winning this war, and there is no way that you or they can do more than by making this contact. There are certain specific things we need to know, and if you can get the information for us, you will have done as much as any Socialist in the world."

The German sat for a while in thought. Then he said: "I ought to put the matter up to my comrades."

"Why take that risk?" argued the other. "You have admitted that you can never be safe against the possibility of betrayal. You did not have to tell them about me, at least I assume that you have not done so."

"Never."

"Well, then, why tell them about some other Roosevelt agent? They know that you are putting the information to use, and you are the one to judge the best use. If I had been killed in that airplane accident, you would have had no contact whatever. As it was, for fourteen months your work has been wasted."

"I am doing other work for the cause, *Genosse*."

"Very well; but I am talking about this particular kind of work. You have admitted that if the war is to be won, we Americans have to win it; and what can you do more important than to get us information? You might be the means of winning a whole campaign and saving thousands of lives."

Monck thought again for a while. Then he said: "All right, I'll take my chances with you."

V

Living close to the border of Naziland, this labor man had many sources of information, and he reported on the situation as it now stood. The food-rationing system there was working—all systems worked with the Germans; the Führer was making good his promise that his people would be the last in Europe to suffer hunger. But Göring was not doing so well with his promise that no bombs would fall on German cities; they were falling faster and faster and doing great damage. But this had not suggested any idea of defeat to the population, so far as a former Social Democratic official had been able to learn; it merely made them rage at their enemies, calling them *Barbaren* and *Mörder;* they discovered that the bombing of cities was a dastardly and wicked practice. Said Monck: "You would think they had never heard of Guernica and Barcelona and Madrid, to say nothing of Warsaw and Rotterdam, Coventry and London."

Lanny said the Germans had seen only the beginning; the American flyers were already in Britain, learning to use British planes; soon their own would be coming over. Not even the British believed the Americans could make a success of their precision bombing by day; the

British, too, would be shown, predicted the son of Budd-Erling. He said it was important to know the details of damage done to targets of the raids, and Monck undertook to get what information he could. Lanny was amused to note his phrase: "I will endeavor to establish a system."

The most important of all targets was German science. Lanny inquired: "Do you have any contacts with the scientific world?"

"You know how it was with Socialists in the old days," his friend replied. "We had contacts everywhere, with all sorts of people. But the greater number are now in concentration camps, or else they are dead—we cannot always find out which. Some have fallen for the lure of Hitler's phrases; some have had their wills broken by torture, and they are—what is it you Americans say?—stooges. We have had to rebuild our organization on the basis of tiny cells, only two or three persons; one is the leader, and he knows one person to whom he reports. I know only two persons who come to me, and if I say to them: 'Can you establish a contact with, say, an authority on explosives, there will be a long wait, and I may never hear any more about the matter, because the Gestapo has got some man or woman somewhere along the chain."

"A slow and painful way of working," commented the American. "Let us hope that more bombings and a few defeats will weaken the hold of the Nazis upon your people. Meantime I will tell you what we especially want. Did you ever hear of heavy water?"

"I have heard the name, but that is about all."

"In it the hydrogen is what the physicists call an isotope of ordinary hydrogen. All you have to do is to remember the name, *schweres Wasser*, for any physicist will know about it. We have reason to believe that the Nazis have set up a plant for its manufacture on a large scale. That may give an important clue to their plans, and we should like very much to know where that plant is situated and how far its work has progressed. You will be helped by the fact that it is apt to be at some place where hydroelectric power is available."

"O.K.," said Monck. "I have a mental note of it."

"Next, we understand the Nazis are working on a jet-propelled bomb which will carry great distances, perhaps one or two hundred miles."

"I have heard rumors of that, *Genosse*."

"Such bombs might do great damage in a city like London which covers an immense area. We want every possible kind of information about them: the structure of the bomb, where it is manufactured, the location of the launching sites. They will be camouflaged, of course, and difficult to get at. We have heard reports that the Nazis are putting some of their more important manufacturing plants under the ground, or in caves."

"We have many caves in our country. I am told that some of them have been turned into comfortable working places."

"We have saboteurs who are training to go into Germany, and no doubt we shall soon be dropping them from parachutes. Get us every scrap of information you can about war industries and their products, about military plans, about transportation, about German connections here in Switzerland—"

"This is quite a task you are setting me," said this Socialist Party member. He said it with no trace of a smile.

"Get what you can," said Lanny. "No one will ask more. Give me the name you are using here and where a note can reach you. That will be in President Roosevelt's hands in three or four days. How soon there will be a man to contact you, I cannot say, but it should not be long. And above all, put anxieties out of your mind; you will have a new and fresh organization behind you, more powerful than anything the Hitlerites have ever dreamed. We Americans may be too confident, and we may get more than one bloody nose in this war; but it has never occurred to us as a people that we can fail, and I promise you that we won't forget those who have helped us."

Backing up these confident words, Lanny transferred to his friend's pockets a lot of Swiss banknotes of various denominations—he had established his bank credit here long ago for his purposes of picture purchasing. "I took the liberty of buying a diamond ring for your wife," he added. "She will probably not wish to wear it under present circumstances, but it is a convenient thing to have hidden away in case of emergency." He told Monck about his own marriage, and received his congratulations.

VI

Next morning the P.A. took the train to Bern, a lovely old city nestled in a U-bend of the young river Aar. He got himself a room in the Bernerhof, with a fine view of all the Bernese Alps, still covered with snow. However, he didn't see them, because he was absorbed in typing out a report, somewhat longer than usual. He double-sealed it in the usual way, addressed it to the Honorable Leland Harrison, and caused it to be handed in at the door of the American Embassy. Then, his mind at peace, he paid visits to the art dealers, to impress them with his agreeable manner and discriminating taste. He spent part of a day in the Art Museum, and another part inspecting a private collection to which he had no trouble in gaining access. Then he returned to Geneva and took the night train back to Cannes, quite certain that he had re-established himself as a respectable member of society, and that he would have no trouble in getting another visa should he wish to return and inspect other works of art in the Helvetian Republic.

He had promised his mother to telegraph her of his coming, and he did so. One could never be sure whether a telegram would arrive, but this one did, and when he stepped from the train, could you believe your eyes? Marceline! "For crying out loud!" he said, in the slang of his youth, and caught her in his arms and gave her a good substantial kiss. She was an *artiste*, a *danseuse*, used to public appearances, and not bound by stiff bourgeois notions of propriety. She was twenty-five, but to him she would always be "Little Sister," whom he had first greeted when she was two years old, and to whom he had taught dancing steps, just as he had recently been teaching them to her son. She hadn't turned out exactly the way he would have preferred, but she could say that she had never done harm to anybody but herself, and certainly none to him.

They had two stories to tell on that drive behind the ambling family nag. Ladies first, and she chose to ask questions: What sort of wife had he got himself, and for God's sake, why had he come away and left her? Couldn't he make enough money selling the Detaze paintings in America? She had a one-third interest in the proceeds of such sales, so it wasn't precisely disinterested advice—he had learned that her advice seldom was. He had put a lot of money to her credit in a New York bank, and she thanked him for this, but then wanted to know what were the chances of her being cut off from it. Did he think that Beauty was wise in defying the State Department's instructions, and what did he think that she, Marceline, ought to do?

"I am not going back into Germany," she declared, and there her questioning of Lanny halted and his questioning of her began. Had she ceased to love Oskar? She made a sort of *moue* and said that she loved him as much as she was willing to love any man, but she couldn't stand the Germans, especially since America had entered the war. Graf von Herzenberg, Oskar's father, had used his influence to make it possible for her to go on dancing and to enjoy complete freedom, but he couldn't keep the German women from making snide remarks whenever she came near them, and asking her how her countrymen dared to bomb the most beautiful cities in the world and to kill the most cultured people in the world.

"You know, Lanny, I never had the least idea of being patriotic. I'm only half an American, and that by accident; nationalities meant nothing to me, and I hardly bothered to know where the countries were. This war has been horrid, I just didn't want to know about it. But now some Germans have cut me dead, and Oskar can't bring himself to blame them, and I'm not supposed to blame him, and I don't—only I do." This wasn't exactly clear, but it was feminine, and Lanny understood. Many years ago he had read a translation of some Latin verses which had come down from old times, and he remembered a part of them:

> The Germans in Greek are sadly to seek . . .
> All save only Hermann, and Hermann's a German.

In short, Marceline had got tired of her young Prussian aristocrat. He was brave and had killed many Russians, and she didn't mind that, but it was a messy business, and none of hers; quite the contrary, she said, for the Russians loved the dance, and up to a year ago she had rather fancied the idea of going to Moscow. Now, of course, all that was *fini;* all Europe was *fini,* it seemed to her. What sort of reception did Lanny think the daughter of Marcel Detaze would get in New York? Was she an American citizen, or what? And would they give her a passport? What a mess this world was!

VII

"Social life" had come pretty nearly to a stop on the Riviera. It was so much trouble to get to any place, and only the very rich could get the food and wine for entertainment. The Americans were nearly all gone, and the English who hadn't gone were interned. In spite of the best efforts of the government, Frenchmen and Germans did not mix very well; those French who tried it were expecting to get something out of it and were looked upon with suspicion by the rest of the population. The fortunate people were those who could be happy with a book, a violin, a garden, a child.

Parsifal Dingle was one of these, and Beauty was learning to be another. Lanny watched to see what his impatient half-sister would do with the problem. Marceline had a raging appetite for pleasure, and to be in what she called the "social whirl." She hated the war, not because it was killing millions of men and reducing other millions to destitution, but because it was destroying that brightly shining world in which she had won a place by much effort of body and brain. To be an artist did not mean to the daughter of Marcel Detaze what it had meant to her father, to express the deep longings of the human soul for beauty and understanding; it meant to be "somebody," to have a place in the world of wealth and fashion, to be talked about, and to have eyes turn to follow her when she entered a public place. Now the public places were mostly dark because fuel was so scarce, and a dancer at the height of her career was expected to be content with sitting at home and making up a bridge four with people who had formerly been elegant but now were dependent upon her mother for a place to lay their heads.

Marceline was enraptured with her lovely little boy and found the role of an adored mother most intriguing; but she soon tired of answering his questions and decided that this duty was more appropriate to a grandmother. She was pleased to talk with Lanny, so long as he would tell her about people of the fashionable world. She would question him for hours about Robbie's family in Newcastle, the Holdenhursts in Baltimore, and the other important Americans for whom he collected paintings; about Lord and Lady Wickthorpe in London, and Rosemary, Countess of Sandhaven, who had been Lanny's old flame; about Baron Schneider and Mme. de Broussailles and other smart friends in Paris; about the Laval family and the ladies of the Vichy government—anybody, so long as they had "succeeded."

Marceline's attitude was not consciously Fascist; she truly didn't want to have anything to do with politics. She was like so many other people Lanny had known, who were Fascists by instinct, or as you might say, *a priori*. They didn't call themselves Fascists, in many cases they didn't have any idea of being that; the basis of their thinking was the axiom that the Reds must be held down. Three great men had shown how to do it—*Der Führer*, *Il Duce*, and *El Caudillo*. Who else?

Lanny's much indulged "Little Sister" had had her way and had married an Italian army officer, a Fascist devotee. Lanny had warned her that she wouldn't be pleased with this husband's attitude to women, and indeed she hadn't been. She had decided at last that he was a rotter, but she hadn't discovered any connection between his conduct and the political system under which he had been trained. Then she had tried an elegant and haughty Junker, with a dueling scar on his left cheek; this time Lanny hadn't been free to warn her, for he was supposed to have changed his own ideology and couldn't trust Marceline with his secret. She had to make her own mistakes and learn from them if she could.

The idea had occurred to him that she might be an excellent person to go into Germany and collect secrets among the military and governmental classes. She would be paid well for it, and she would like that; but after watching her, he decided that he couldn't trust her. Whether she went to Germany or stayed here on the Riviera she would meet some new man, and whatever his political coloration, she would adopt it, as the way to please him. Doubtless it would be some man of wealth; for after her experience with Vittorio di San Girolamo she had vowed that she would "make them pay." If she broke with Oskar von Herzenberg she would surely decide that two "romances" were enough, and that next time it must be business.

VIII

As always, Lanny would have liked to stay at Bienvenu; but the "hound of heaven" bayed in his soul, and he had to be off again. He told the members of his family about the art commission which obliged him to travel in Algeria and Morocco. A land which he had not seen since boyhood, it shone in his memory with a glory of sunlight because Marcel had painted it. Lanny had been fourteen then, and no boy on earth could have been happier. He had visited all the Mediterranean lands on board the yacht *Bluebird*, made entirely of kitchen soap, or so its owner, Ezra Hackabury, had been wont to declare.

Marcel had made it not merely a pleasure cruise, but a culture cruise, a floating university. He had opened the sensitive lad's mind to the mysteries of human existence on this planet, to awe as well as beauty. For Lanny's then stepfather had been not merely a painter, but a student and thinker. When he painted the ancient ruins of Greece and Rome he tried to make you feel the sorrow of great things vanished forever. When he painted a Greek shepherd in his rags or a Biskra water carrier in his gray burnoose, Marcel was not just getting something exotic and unusual; he had a heart full of pity for lonely men who lived hard lives and did not understand the forces which dominated them.

Lanny took the night train to Marseille, and from there a steamer to Algiers. The latter trip took a little more than a day and a night, and was supposed to be safe. The Allies permitted a supervised trade between Vichy France and its African colonies because they didn't want to have to fight the French Fleet; the Germans permitted this trade because they were secretly getting a part of the goods. However, you could never be sure that a submarine might not make a mistake; so

Lanny spent the night in a steamer chair on deck with a life preserver strapped to one wrist to make sure that nobody else carried it off. The weather was warm in mid-May, and when he was not asleep he could look at the stars and realize the infinite unimportance of the human insect; or he could think about the various North African insects to whom he bore letters of introduction, and how he was going to approach them, and what he expected to get out of them. Thus a philosopher lives upon various planes, and his theories and his practices are frequently not in accord.

In midmorning the mountains of the "Dark Continent" loomed up blue-gray on the horizon, and presently the traveler saw the well-remembered white city spread out on rapidly rising hills. Most Mediterranean cities are like that, for the sea was formed by the dropping of the land in some geologic convulsion. That is the reason real estate in Mediterranean harbors is high in both altitude and price. It is one of the reasons that the workers live in closely packed tenements of anywhere from four to six stories, many of them.centuries old, and which have been repaired about once in a century. The harbor seemed smaller than Lanny remembered it, but that was because Lanny had changed, not the harbor. The city had spread along the shore for miles in both directions. There had been a building boom after World War I, and there was now a modern residential district, with villas and hotels for tourists who came to enjoy the winter climate. The population of the city had been doubled by refugees from France.

IX

Lanny put up at the St. George Hotel, high up on the hillside, overlooking the sea; it was old, English, and very respectable, with beautiful gardens where Marcel had once made sketches. Lanny presented letters of introduction and established his credit at one of the city's banks. He knew how to make himself agreeable, and it wasn't many days before he was in the châteaux and elaborate villas which the plutocracy of Algiers maintained in private parks on the hill slopes surrounding the city. He was not surprised to find these people pro-Fascist in sentiment. It had been his observation that all colonial peoples are conservative, even reactionary. In Hongkong he had found the English more Tory than all but a small handful of diehards in London, and now he found the businessmen of French North Africa asking nothing but to be let alone. They were doing a brisk trade with the Germans; everything they could lay hands on was in demand at the

highest prices ever known. It didn't take a P.A. many days to realize
that these merchants were not going to hold out welcoming arms to
an invading army of democracy.

But they were pleased to welcome a visiting art expert whose
pockets were well lined, who had lived in the great capitals of the Old
World and the New, and who seemed to know everybody you could
mention. He presented himself to the director of the Museum of Antiquities, which is in Mustapha Supérieur, a pleasant garden near the
Governor's summer palace; he gave attention to Algerian antiquities and
Arab art, such as it was, and charmed the director by the knowledge
he had acquired in the New York Public Library. He made inquiry as
to private collections, and when he inspected these he tactfully intimated that he might find American purchasers for worth-while items.
He displayed no special interest in political affairs, but when such subjects were brought up he knew what a proper gentleman was expected
to say. As a result he gained the confidence of important persons, and
it took him only a short while to form a clear picture of the situation.

In the days when the propaganda of *Le Couple France-Allemagne*
had been at its height, the son of Budd-Erling had been guest of honor
at a dinner party in the Paris mansion of Baron Schneider-Creusot.
This "armaments king of Europe" had been a greatly worried monarch, fearing not merely for his crown but for his head, and he had
invited a dozen or so of the leading entrepreneurs to meet an American
who knew Adolf Hitler and might be able to explain this new portent
risen to the east. Among the guests had been M. Jacques Lemaigre-
Dubreuil, an ardent collaborationist and one of the most active businessmen of the country. He was a director of the Banque de France,
he published the reactionary newspaper *Le Jour*, and his wife was the
heiress of Huiles Lesieur, the great vegetable-oil trust. More important
yet, he was organizer and head of the most powerful pressure group
in France, the League of Taxpayers, which was something like the National Association of Manufacturers in the United States, at once a
propaganda and a "slush-fund" group for turning the heat on politicians and legislators to make sure that they did what the "two hundred families" wanted.

Now, at a social gathering, Lanny encountered this gentleman and
was remembered and greeted with cordiality. M. Lemaigre-Dubreuil
was a stocky, solidly built man with an odd husky voice and an aggressive, direct manner, like that of an American "go-getter." When
he learned that Lanny had recently been in New York and Washing-

ton he saw another opportunity to get information. He invited the visitor to lunch at the ultra-smart Golf Club and treated him with great distinction—how charming a Frenchman can be when he takes the trouble! The pair sat on a shaded piazza overlooking a splendid view, and chatted about common friends and the parlous state of the world. M. Lemaigre-Dubreuil found nothing peculiar in the fact that an art expert should be here for the purchasing of Roman and Moorish mosaics. Lanny, on the other hand, didn't have to be surprised by his host's presence in Algiers, for he knew that the principal raw material from which Huiles Lesieur derived its products was the peanut crop of French West Africa. The firm had a great refining plant in Dunkerque, and the Germans had permitted the machinery to be moved to the south, so that it might produce edible oils for the people of France, and not entirely forgetting the firm's German friends.

Lanny asked about Schneider and learned that this owner of several hundred munitions plants was still in Paris; he was feeling his years, which were over seventy. He was ill-content with the kind of gratitude the Germans had shown him; he was distressed as to the fate of France, and, in short, Lanny's informant considered that he was worrying himself into his grave. This was still more true of poor Denis de Bruyne, who was over eighty and in no position to cope with events such as were now overwhelming his country. He was in his château in Seine-et-Oise, near Paris, with his two daughters-in-law and their children. Lemaigre-Dubreuil knew him intimately, and Lanny knew from Denis's lips that some five years ago, when the Cagoulards had been planning to overthrow the French Republic, Lemaigre had been one who knew what was going on.

"I met Charlot in Vichy just recently," Lanny told the vegetable-oil man. "He is active in organizing the Légion Tricolore and seems very hopeful about it. He told me that Denis, *fils,* is in Algeria, and I have been meaning to look for him."

"He is here in the city," volunteered the other, "but I have not seen him. It is rumored that he is a Gaullist."

"*Mon Dieu!*" exclaimed the American. "What a sorrow for the old man! How do you account for such a thing?"

"De Gaulle is a fanatic, but he is also an exceedingly shrewd intriguer, and the broadcasts he is sending from Britain are well contrived to affect French youth. I fear they have done so even more than we realize. It is a calamity, because it can have no result other than a dreadful civil war."

"I will make it a point to see young Denis and try to influence him," Lanny said. "I have known him since he was a boy, you know; his mother was my very dear friend."

The word *amie* can mean two kinds of friendship, and therefore offers a way of carrying delicate intimations; it left Lanny in the position of saying something and yet not quite saying it. When M. Lemaigre-Dubreuil replied: "So I have been told," he, too, had said something and yet not quite said it.

X

In this conversation Lanny followed his practice of giving information in the hope of getting more. He knew that this able Frenchman would be watching every word that both of them spoke; he was not the one to give without getting, and he would not spend a couple of hours and the price of a lunch because of an American's *beaux yeux*, nor yet because of his *beaux arts*. He wanted to know about that young giant of a country and what it was doing and planning. Lanny told him that this giant, who had so much more muscle than brain, was waking up and wiping the sleep from his eyes, but as yet hardly knew what he saw. There was much opposition to the war throughout America, but Lanny feared that this opposition would not be able to do much. He explained the unhappy position of his father, who was forced to turn out warplanes regardless of his own convictions. He had many friends in Germany and had done good business with General Göring; but now the government didn't ask what he thought, they just ordered him to make fast fighters to kill German pilots, and if he should refuse to do it they would take his plant away from him.

It had been the same way in France for many years, the host remarked; businessmen were the prey of military men and politicians, and the dream of M. Lemaigre-Dubreuil's life was that there might some day be a government that was run by and for businessmen; indeed, that was why he had organized his Ligue des Contribuables—of which the last word means, literally, those who contribute. M. Huiles Lesieur said that all the contributing that was ever done anywhere in the world was done by the property owners, the taxpayers, and he and they were tired of it, and surely there must be many in the United States of America who were in the same frame of mind.

Lanny was so sympathetic to this point of view and quoted his father so effectively that his host became confidential and said that the businessmen of both parts of France, fearing disturbances, were transferring funds to North African banks. Lanny said he had heard this in Vichy and wondered why the Germans allowed it. The reply was that there were many Germans, and their ideas and interests were not all the same. There, as in France, politicians wanted one thing and businessmen wanted another, and the latter had to pay, but they managed to get back still more. Businessmen knew that wars came and went, but business continued, and its interests were permanent. There were various kinds of business that were half-French, half-German, and the two halves found no pleasure in fighting each other.

Lanny was here confronting that old situation which his father had explained to him as a small boy. The great cartels, in America called "trusts," were international in ownership and operation, and so were the banks which co-operated with them. The Comité des Forges, a union of the steel and munitions makers of France, used ore from Lorraine, which was French, and coal from the Ruhr, which was German. The French and Germans who owned these vast interests wanted nothing but to make goods and sell them at prices which they fixed in secret with the steel makers of Britain and America. They didn't want to fight each other, they wanted to save their own property from the general wreck. So the French chiefs of the Comité des Forges had got their German colleagues and associates to help them with the Nazi officials. They had let these officials into their companies, and thus obtained permission to ship their wealth to their banks in North Africa. Lanny heard about it from one source after another, and some said that ten billion francs had come to Algiers, and others said twenty billion, and all agreed that it was still coming.

XI

Why should a man of money like Jacques Lemaigre-Dubreuil have become confidential on a subject so delicate as this? Lanny could guess; and before the talk came to an end it was made plain to him. The vegetable-oil man was doing the same thing that Lanny did—telling secrets in the hope of getting more secrets. He had somehow got wind of the fact that the American Army might choose French North Africa as a safe *pied-à-terre* for its attack upon the soft underbelly of Europe, and it had occurred to him that the President of Budd-Erling Aircraft would be apt to know about this and might have dropped hints to his mysteriously traveling son. In short, M. Lemaigre-Dubreuil was "fishing," and Lanny let him jiggle the bait for a long time before he approached it.

Suddenly the Frenchman asked: "Do you know Mr. Robert Murphy?"

This was not the first time the question had been asked of Lanny. The American diplomatic representative, whose title was "Counselor to the Embassy at Vichy stationed in Algiers," was a much-sought-after person, and it would have been natural for an art expert to ask his advice. But Lanny had avoided doing so, because he wanted to feel out the situation for himself and without incurring obligation to any American. Now he answered cautiously that he thought he had met Mr. Murphy in Paris, where the latter had been Counselor to the Embassy before the war broke out; but he doubted if Mr. Murphy would remember him.

"I, too, have known him from the Paris days," said the man of great affairs. "Now he has become my very good friend. He is a charming person."

"So I have been told," replied the P.A. "I gather that he has a rather thankless task with you."

"Oh, we get along perfectly. He is most considerate in the carrying out of his duties."

The special duty of the Counselor and his twelve vice-consuls was to see that the precious supplies which America allotted to French North Africa—such as oil and gasoline without which modern industry comes to a dead stop—were apportioned to the needs of the community and that none of these went to Germany. That would bring Mr. Murphy into conflict with just about everything that M. Lemaigre-Dubreuil wanted in North Africa or anywhere else. If they had become "very good friends," that didn't necessarily mean anything sinister, for a tactful Frenchman would say that in any case and try to pretend that it was so even though it was otherwise. In the same way it might be the Counselor's role to pretend that it was so, even though it was otherwise. The State Department career man would be doing what Lanny was doing, trying to get as much as he could out of the vegetable-oil man at as low a price as possible. And he would be using the same means—that is, being "charming"!

XII

The time came when the host asked the direct question: "Do you think there is much chance of this province becoming a battleground?" A natural question, of course, and entirely innocent. If Lemaigre and his friends of the Comité des Forges were bringing their money into

French North Africa, they would be concerned to know if it would be safe.

Lanny's smile had been prepared in advance. "If I had any idea that Algiers was going to be a battleground very soon, I surely wouldn't be here looking for mosaics." Then, lest this might seem like teasing, he added: "My own opinion would have no value, Monsieur; but my father meets people who are in a position to know, and he tells me that the decision has not yet been taken. There are some who want to risk the chance of a landing in Normandy at once; there are others who think it will be at least a year before we are ready for such a venture. As you know, the Allies are under heavy pressure from the Russians to do something to draw the enemy away from the east."

"We hear much about that so-called 'second front.' "

"That clamor may compel the Americans to make some move this year. My father tells me he has heard the suggestion of Marseille and Toulon, of Genoa and Naples, of Salonika and the Dardanelles. There is a wide range of choice."

"Yes, M. Budd. But I have also heard mention of our own ports, all the way from this city to Dakar."

"It is easy to pick out places on a map," commented the art expert, "but not so easy to estimate the military factors. One, I should guess, would be what resistance was to be expected, here and elsewhere."

It was the most delicate of hints, and a capitalist concerned with the manufacture of vegetable oils was free to take it or leave it. If you have ever watched ants, you have seen them rushing along an ant highway, and when one encounters another coming in the opposite direction they stop for a small fraction of a second and touch each other ever so lightly with their sensitive feelers; when they have made certain that it is a friendly ant and not an enemy, they both hurry on about their affairs, so urgently important to ants. This vegetable-oil ant appeared to be satisfied with what his feelers reported, for he chose to answer: "My friends and I discuss that subject frequently, as you can guess. Opinions differ as to what our policy should be; but this much is certain, the decision would depend in great part upon the nature of the force which attempted a landing. I have heard one of our generals say, and not entirely in jest: 'If they come with one division, we should fire on them; if they come with twenty divisions, we should embrace them.' "

Said Lanny: "On that point, Monsieur, my father's informants are most positive. Wherever the Army comes, it will come with the full intention of staying. You should make your plans upon that basis."

6

A Tangled Web We Weave

I

THE vegetable-oil magnate recommended an assistant to the art expert: an educated Arab, middle-aged and substantial, who had served as steward to a wealthy French lady recently deceased. His name was Hajek, and he spoke reasonably good French. Lanny could suppose that M. Lemaigre-Dubreuil had dropped him a hint that he might watch this plausible American and report on what he was up to; but Lanny didn't mind that, for he was really going to find some mosaics and have them shipped, and if this white-robed and black-bearded half-servant, half-scholar was any good at all, Lanny would keep him busy. The visitor was careful never to talk politics, but he acquired a mass of information on such subjects as the practice of the Mohammedan religion, the various tribes which inhabited North Africa, and their ways of life and history.

All subject races have their underground means of communication, and word spread with surprising rapidity that there was an eccentric American desiring to buy mosaics, wall fountains, and possibly a doorway or two, for transportation across the sea. It was Hajek's duty to interview all callers, and if what they had sounded promising, to make an inspection and report. Should the report sound good, the American lord—so they were calling him in Arabic, as not long ago they had been calling him in Chinese—would hire a conveyance and be driven through the streets of Algiers, which climb the hills in zigzag ramps, and sometimes have a step every few feet, so that only a donkey can make it.

Visiting the Casbah, the vile and filthy native quarter, Lanny was led to an old house which had once been the home of a merchant and now served as lodgings for a score of squalid families. There he found an inner courtyard with a fountain, now used to store junk. On all four sides of the fountain were floors, and when they were cleared of trash and scrubbed, Lanny discovered beautiful iridescent tiles. He had

108

studied enough designs to know what was representative, and he had known good coloring most of his life.

Hajek undertook to find out the price at which these items could be bought. The owner, an Arab, of course decided that he had the world's greatest art treasure, and his price was a quarter of a million francs. Lanny knew about Mediterranean bargaining and took it as a safe rule that the asking price was six times the real price, and for an American even higher. He left the matter to Hajek, who took delight in it, and in the coffee drinking which was part of the ceremony. In the final settlement he would get a rake-off, called *dasturi;* it was the custom, and worth while to an American lord whose time was precious and would not let the sordid details of business interfere too greatly with his pleasures.

The one essential to the bargaining process is that there must be no hurrying. Arabs have a great sense of dignity and are extraordinary conversationalists. They take the same interest in a financial deal that Americans take in a baseball game, and if it is a really big deal, it is like the World Series. The wretched tenants in this decayed mansion knew what was going on and asked eagerly for the score; every gain for their side, the Arab side, was received with pleasure, and every loss with sorrow. All sympathized with the landlord, who lay awake at night in an agony of fear lest the American lord should make some other purchase and depart. The lord encouraged this idea by finding other mosaics which were as good or better.

The news about the battle spread through the bazaars, and it became a betting game—the natives are great gamblers. These negotiations and others went on for two or three weeks, and Lanny carried a notebook with memoranda containing names and addresses, details about the works offered, and the prices with the date of offering; the last was important, for you must know how long to wait before a reduced offer is to be expected. All this must have been convincing to anyone having suspicions as to the good faith of a visiting art expert. Lanny wanted it that way and helped to spread the news by telling his French and American acquaintances funny stories about the difficulties he was having. They all assured him that it was quite in order.

II

There came word of treasures to be uncovered in the old city of Constantine, three or four hundred miles to the east; so Lanny engaged accommodations for himself and his assistant on the fearfully overcrowded and always late French railroad. He took the day train because he wanted to observe the scenery and the people in the interior of the country, which he had never visited. The road ascends along the slopes of the snow-covered Djurdjura Mountains, which form a distant background to the landscape of Algiers. The mountains are brown or gray against a deep blue sky; big trees line the roads, and on isolated points here and there are perched tiny villages of the Kabyles. Everything in this country tells of centuries of invasion and plunder, and the peoples sought safety in the most inaccessible places.

It is this which had determined the building of the city, one of the strangest a world traveler had seen. It stands on a rocky plateau, surrounded by a chasm of something like a thousand feet, through which flows a roaring river; the plateau is four-sided, something more than half a mile on each side, and there is only a narrow isthmus connecting it with the surrounding land. The rocks are red. Maupassant had compared the river and its gorge to a dream of Dante. A city with only one gate, it is said to have withstood eighty sieges. Hajek, proud of himself as an historian, assured his employer that during the first thirty years of the preceding century no fewer than twenty Beys, or rulers of the city, had died by poison, the bowstring, or the sword.

In this small space, less than half a square mile, are crowded a European, an Arab, and a Jewish quarter. Marble of the ancient Roman city had been used for modern buildings, and the white city on red rocks appeared most impressive, until you were inside and investigated its narrow stone-lined alleys filled with men, donkeys, camels, and the filth of all three. The Arabs wore their dirty white robes, as everywhere, and when nature called they just squatted in the street. The Jewish women dressed in bright colors and wore tiny red felt hats, and heavy jewelry, broad bracelets of gold and silver and heavy rings in the lobes of their ears. The war had brought prosperity to all lands to which it had not yet come; and around Constantine were the broad plains which had been wheatfields for at least two thousand years. This part of North Africa had been one of the granaries of the ancient Roman Empire.

Ruins were everywhere in this countryside. Through the centuries they had been plundered to build peasant huts and storehouses. Lanny was shown a few stones which marked where a villa had once stood. He took a chance and offered the peasant owner of the land ten thousand francs for the privilege of digging and taking away whatever he might find. Hajek brought workmen from the city, a donkey train of them, one of the most comical spectacles the art expert had ever beheld. The donkeys were the smallest ever, and each had apparently been conditioned to traveling only in response to a tattoo of strokes from the rider's slipper-clad heels. Each rider sat on the rump of his beast, and in front were strapped saddlebags or baskets. Lanny discovered what these were for—when the work was done the worker would use his wages to buy produce and carry it to town.

A couple of days' digging sufficed to uncover a tessellated floor with a fine representation of the huntress Diana. Lanny stayed right there and saw it taken up piece by piece. With a borrowed camera he took pictures at the start, so it wasn't necessary to mark each piece; but each had to be wrapped in cloth, and the packing boxes had to be small, and then half a dozen of them packed in larger boxes. This was a lot of work, and his commission would hardly pay for the time; but it was a novelty, and he learned a lot about Arabs which would be useful to him later on. Always he had in mind that the American Army was coming and would want every scrap of information. Here, as everywhere in wartime, goods were more precious than money, and G.I.'s exchanging trinkets for fresh eggs would owe thanks to the son of Budd-Erling without having any idea of it.

III

The shipment properly labeled and sent off to Algiers, Lanny wanted to see Timgad. He wouldn't be able to buy antiquities there, but he mustn't miss inspecting the site. He succeeded in finding a motorcar that ran on gas from burning charcoal, and was driven through a land which in many ways reminded him of the American Far West—the combination of wild scenery and a fine road. He passed through the town of Tébessa, a name which he was to hear often before that year 1942 had come to an end, but not having the gift of prevision he did not pay any special attention.

On the slopes of the Aurès Mountains, three thousand feet above the Mediterranean, lies what is left of the outpost town of Thamagudi, built by the Emperor Trajan a hundred years after Christ, and now known as Timgad. The Arabs had conquered and destroyed it, and for more than a thousand years the place had been left to the jackals. Recently the French had restored it as far as possible, clearing away the driven sand and setting up the broken columns. So there are long streets, with paving worn by the feet of the Roman legions; and there are a great gate, a forum, and many arches; everything solid and magnificent, for this had been no haphazard growth, but a planned city, covering a whole mountain slope and occupied by some fifty thousand people.

Lanny was used to Roman ruins, from his childhood on the Cap d'Antibes, and later in England and Spain, but he had never seen anything like this. He inspected the remains of a noble public library—the Roman equivalent of what the Americans call a "Carnegie" library. It had been built at a cost of four hundred thousand sesterces, bequeathed to his native town by the senator Marcus Julius Quintianus Flavus Rogatianus—a gentleman known to the modern world solely because of the inscription found in these ruins.

In his youth Lanny's heart had been touched by a tablet found in Antibes, telling about a "little Septentrion child" who had "danced and pleased in the theater." Here in the forum of this ancient city of the Emperor Trajan he read an inscription from those same ancient days and in that same spirit: "To hunt, to bathe, to play, to laugh, that is to live." How he would have enjoyed being able to do those same things!

IV

Among Lanny's purposes in North Africa was to meet the younger Denis de Bruyne. The Army had been in great part demobilized under the terms of the armistice, and both officers and men were required to wear civilian clothing. Lanny might have found his friend by inquiring among military people, but he could not take the chance of knowing a reputed Gaullist. He employed a device which had worked on previous occasions, bringing it about that his presence in the city was mentioned in the newspapers. So, when he returned to Algiers, he found at his hotel a note in the familiar handwriting of his near-godson. Denis was living in one of the suburbs of the capital and said that he would call wherever Lanny asked. The P.A. wrote, appointing an hour and signing the name "Bienvenu."

It was a pleasant afternoon, and when Denis came they strolled into the extensive gardens of the hotel and found themselves a quiet seat in the shade of a great bougainvillaea vine. They weren't exactly hiding, they were avoiding making themselves conspicuous in this spy-ridden town.

Denis was only a year or two older than his brother, but he looked ten years older; there were lines of care in his face and traces of gray in his hair. He was of medium size, slender but strong. His dark eyes were melancholy and his manner grave, with none of Charlot's humor and *élan.* He had been twice wounded in the course of desperate fighting near Maubeuge, and after he had recovered his health at home, he had had the devil's own time escaping from the Germans and getting into Southern France. He had been hidden for a time on the Côte d'Azur and had come near seeking refuge in Bienvenu, but had decided that it wouldn't be fair to Lanny's mother.

Now the young *capitaine's* position was sad. He had made no open breach with his family, but the difference between his ideas and those of his father and brother made it impossible for them to co-operate, or, on account of the censorship, even to discuss the subject. Mail between Occupied and Unoccupied France was restricted by the Germans to a postcard with various printed statements, of which you crossed out those which did not apply. It was a criminal offense to use any sort of code—it might even carry the death penalty if you conveyed political or military information. So Denis, *fils,* could tell his father and his wife and children that he was well, and he could get the same news from them, but he could not tell them what he was thinking or ask what they were thinking.

The brothers had been inseparable; and now, when Denis learned that Lanny had talked with Charlot in Vichy, it was pathetic to see his excitement. He wanted to hear every word that Charlot had spoken, and when he learned that his brother was helping to organize the Légion Tricolore in the service of Pierre Laval, his despair was pitiful to see. Nor was he comforted when Lanny hinted: "All those factional disputes are going to be wiped out, Denis. The American Army will be coming." Denis didn't ask when or where or how. He was thinking only about his brother and exclaimed: "They will shoot him!"

"No," declared Lanny, "the Americans won't be like that. They will shoot only Germans."

"The French will shoot him, Lanny. They will call him a traitor, and he *is* a traitor! What defense can there be for a man who betrays *la patrie* into the hands of a *fripon* like Laval or for his *apaches* who seize French patriots and turn them over to the Nazis to be tortured and shot?"

Lanny looked about him hastily. "Be careful," he said, moving a little closer. "Remember, I am a foreigner, and I'm supposed to be here buying art works."

V

Lanny had had weeks to think this problem over in advance. He knew that this young officer was the soul of honor. There was no one

Lanny knew better or would trust more completely. The only question was, what his ideas were now, and whether they were such that he could fit in with American policies. If so, a presidential agent would have another contact, and one whose value might prove to be great.

"Denis," he began cautiously, "as you know, I have had nothing to do with political questions for many years. I have told myself that my work as an art expert justified me in keeping aloof, so that I could travel in all countries and meet all sorts of people. Now the fact that my country has been attacked makes that attitude more difficult."

"*Vraiment, cher ami!* I have been wondering how you could expect to keep it. I don't see how any man can keep it in these times."

"I have been doing a lot of worrying over the question. Give me your advice about France. What do you think is going to happen, and what could I do to help?"

"You ask me—and I have been looking forward to asking *you!* I am clear in my mind that De Gaulle is the man to whom France must look for salvation. What troubles me is my own course, whether to try to get to Britain and join him, or to stick it out here and do what I can to influence my friends and others. When I heard that you were here I was greatly pleased because I thought you would be able to tell me about America and what we have to expect from her."

"First, tell me about De Gaulle. You are in a position to hear his broadcasts?"

"This is something secret, of course, for it is considered treason for an officer to listen to them. Vichy has reason to fear his words, for he thrills the soul of every true Frenchman who hears him. To me he has become a symbol of *la France libérée*. What do they think of him in America?"

"One hears many different opinions, and people ask me to find out. Some are troubled because, so they say, he has Communists active in his London committee."

"But what can he do, Lanny? In war you have to accept what allies come to your standard. The Russians are fighting on our side, and even Churchill has had to welcome them. So has Roosevelt, unless I am misinformed."

"We know those men, and we can understand their maneuvers. But nobody that I know seems to have met De Gaulle, and so we find it harder to decide what is maneuver and what is his real belief."

"I do not know him, Lanny, but I have read his book, *Au Fil de l'Épée*, and anybody who has studied it will know that he is a French patriot, *pur sang*. He is the last man in France who would be influenced by Red ideas; he stands for the rights of property, for order and discipline, for the defense of *la patrie* against foes inside and out."

"If Roosevelt can have his way in this war," suggested Lanny mildly, "the slogan is to be democracy."

"I know, and we all use the word, but we give it our own meaning. To the Reds it means confiscation and dictatorship in the name of the proletariat; but Roosevelt means nothing like that, I am sure, and the order-loving people of France will not mean it either. If De Gaulle can have his way, there will be no more venal politicians stirring up the mob as a means of lining their own pockets."

Lanny let his friend talk and weighed his words carefully. Lanny had never seen the book of the new French Jeanne d'Arc—so De Gaulle had described himself—but he had seen extracts quoted. The very title, meaning "to the edge of the sword," repelled the American, who couldn't conceive a man using that title unless he meant to convey a threat. The quotations had had a decidedly Fascist color and indicated that the Colonel de Gaulle—so he had been when the book was published—was calling for something resembling what General Franco had done in Spain: the Fascist temper and technique, without the label, adapted to a Catholic culture and the purposes of the Church hierarchy.

Right now Lanny's attention was on his near-godson and what this London-sponsored crusade meant to him. Lanny was interested to discover that the defeat and enslavement of Marianne hadn't changed the young *capitaine's* social ideas a particle. He still believed in the right of the De Bruyne family, in co-operation with the other hundred and ninety-nine great families, to control French industry and finance, and, through the Army, control the government. He still wanted what Pétain wanted, a Catholic France, benevolently kept in order by the general staff. He would have endorsed the old Marshal's slogan of fatherland, labor, and family. Lanny reflected that it shouldn't be hard for the two brothers to get together after the war was over; they both wanted the same thing, the difference lay only in how they expected to get it.

VI

This realization would modify somewhat the extent to which Lanny could confide in his younger friend, but it didn't change the basic fact that he had here a man of honor who could be of great use to the American Army, if and when it was ready to establish its *pied-à-terre* on French North African soil. If it was proper for General de Gaulle to use Reds, it would be equally proper for a P.A. to use a Catholic. So presently he said: "Denis, I am going to entrust you with a secret, and you must understand that it is the most confidential thing I have ever told you. You are not free to mention it to anybody else without first getting my approval and consent."

"Certainly, Lanny. I hope you are going to tell me that you have decided to be on the side of France in this dark hour."

"That is a part of it," Lanny said and dropped his voice to a whisper. "The rest is that not long ago I had the good fortune to meet President Roosevelt and to gain his confidence. The reason I am here now is to sound out the situation and learn what the Americans have to expect if they should come to this shore."

"You mean that they are coming, Lanny?" This in a tone of excitement. "*When?*"

"If I knew that, I could not say it. But the truth is, the decision has not yet been taken. This much is sure, however; before this war is over, our armies will come here. So no effort that is spent in inquiry and preparation will be wasted. If you accept that, and act upon it, you will surely not be disappointed."

A military man, who knew what secrecy was, could not ask more. Denis laid his hand on Lanny's arm, and Lanny could feel it trembling. "That is the most wonderful news I have ever heard, and you may count upon me to the very death. I had about made up my mind to make a run for it and try to get to Brazzaville; but now I will stay, and you may consider me as under your orders."

"That is more than I would ask, *cher ami*," replied Lanny with a smile. "I am not used to giving orders and am far too uncertain as to my own judgments. Let us say that we shall consult together. You give me the benefit of your knowledge of the local situation, and I will pass it on to the government without naming you or giving any indication of how I got it; that is, of course, unless you wish me to act otherwise."

"What I wish," declared Denis fervently, "is to drive the Nazi *doryphores* out of France, and indeed off the earth."

"*Très bien!*" agreed the American. "But tell me, what is a *doryphore?*"

"Oh, you haven't heard that? A *doryphore* is a potato bug, and we apply it to the Germans because they demand and get nearly all of the French potato crop. In our food-saving campaigns we send the schoolchildren out to pick the bugs off the plants, and they have had the bright idea of carrying signs reading '*Mort aux doryphores!*' The Germans can do nothing about that, so it gives delight to our people, who have not yet been entirely deprived of their sense of mischief."

VII

They skipped their dinner, not wishing to appear together in any café, and continued their conference into the night. Lanny told about his talks with Lemaigre and with others of the ruling group in this colonial capital. (Nominally it was a part of "Metropolitan France," and proud of that fact, but in most ways it resembled a colony.) Lanny was interested to observe the reactions of his old-time friend to the various cliques which were pulling and hauling the community's political affairs. Denis, *fils*, despised the vegetable-oil man as a collaborator, but at the same time he respected him as a man of great affairs and as a friend of Denis, *père*. It was a worthy work that he had done, trying to save the taxpayers of France from being plundered by the mobsters; also, it was the most natural thing in the world that his friends of the Comité des Forges should be trying to save their funds by bringing them to North Africa. In fact, Denis, *fils*, took it for granted that his father would be in on such arrangements.

Once more it was that powerful thing called "social position." The scion of the De Bruynes enjoyed it, in spite of being one of the wicked Gaullists. He went about in the salons and was able to reveal to a P.A. many details of what was going on. The same thing had been true even in the Army; Denis had never said it, for that would have been bad taste, but Lanny had understood that he had been no mere *capitaine*, but a prospective heir to fortune and power, a man who might some day be able to offer social advantages to his major, his colonel, even his general.

What was going to be the attitude of demobilized Army officers to an American landing? Denis reported that to a man they hated the Germans, and "collaboration" was not in their vocabulary. Many of them also disliked the British, but few objected to the Americans, and they would find it easier to tolerate an invasion by them. What stood in the way was their loyalty to the old Marshal. Denis himself despised the "old fraud," as he called Pétain, saying that his piety was "political"—he was a freethinker, and married to a divorced woman. But to most of Denis's brother officers the Marshal was still the hero of Verdun. "You know," explained the *capitaine*, "we French have a notion of what we call 'legitimacy'; our monarchy was based upon it, and the idea survived all the storms of the Revolution. The old Marshal is the legitimate head of our state, and especially of our Army; that authority has been properly handed on to him, and it is hard for us not to recognize it."

"Like the apostolic succession in the Church," commented the American. With anyone else he would have smiled as he said it, but he knew that Denis was one of the faithful and would see nothing humorous in the idea that St. Peter had received power by the laying on of hands of the Lord, and that he had passed on that power to the bishops, and so it had come down, even through the blood-smeared hands of the Borgias. "The apostolic succession in grace conferred by ordination," was the formula.

Lanny inquired as to the attitude of the Navy, and Denis replied that the situation would be far more delicate there. The officers of the Fleet were even more "legitimist" than those of the Army, and their hatred of the British was far more intense because of the pounding they had taken at Mers-el-Kébir. Any expeditionary force would have to be convoyed by the British, and the French would be strongly tempted to resist it. Propaganda was difficult to spread on board the ships, but Denis said he had whispered his ideas among such officers as he could trust. "Navies are always ultra-conservative," he explained, and Lanny said that was true in America, even under the New Deal.

VIII

The time came when Denis asked the inevitable question: "Have you met Mr. Robert Murphy?" Lanny explained that he was working independently, observing the situation from all angles, and this diplomat was one of the objects of his attention. Denis had met him several times and reported that he was a good man for the post; he was gracious and genial and tried to understand all points of view. Denis had attempted to explain to him the position of the Gaullists, and Mr. Murphy had thanked him but had avoided committing himself.

"Apparently," said the *capitaine*, "your government has a prejudice against General de Gaulle which we, his admirers, do not understand and which no one will explain to us. Mr. Murphy would not admit it, and apparently he wanted me to believe that it was the policy of his government to maintain strict neutrality among the different factions of the French. But I happened to know from other sources that elaborate negotiations were carried on with ex-Premier Herriot, at his home in Lyon, urging him to come to North Africa and assume leadership of the Free French. When this plan did not succeed, they approached

General Giraud, who just recently made his escape from the German fortress of Königstein. My understanding is that he is to come to Algiers for that purpose."

"I have heard such a rumor," responded the P.A. "Tell me what you think of him."

"He is a soldier and a man of honor. He will fight for *la patrie* to the best of his ability. But I do not see how he can have any success as a leader of the movement. What claim to legitimacy could he have?"

"I am trying to understand your point of view, Denis. What claim of that sort can General de Gaulle have? When I mention him to Frenchmen here, the response is: 'A mere brigadier-general, self-proclaimed as head of our government.'"

"I know that it is difficult to explain, Lanny. De Gaulle was first in the field and he has managed to get the ear of the people. He seems to us an inspired leader, one of the deliverers whom God has always sent to our nation when the need became extreme."

Lanny would have liked to say that legitimacy and inspiration were different things, and frequently opposite; but he didn't want to hurt his friend's feelings, he merely wanted the "lowdown" on the followers of De Gaulle so as to know how to deal with them, and to report them to the Boss—one who seemed to Lanny to possess both legitimacy and inspiration. The secret agent wanted also to understand Mr. Robert Murphy, and what he was telling members of the "two hundred French families" about the intentions of the American government toward *them*. Lanny could understand why a kindly and trusting career man of the State Department seemed such an excellent choice to Denis de Bruyne; he was a gentleman, and knew how to talk to other gentlemen; he was Catholic, and knew how to deal with Frenchmen of that conservative sort.

Lanny learned from Denis that the Counselor had made M. Lemaigre-Dubreuil his confidential adviser and practically his righthand Frenchman. It had been Lemaigre who had suggested Herriot and had sent agents to that statesman, who called himself a "Radical Socialist"—in much the same way that Southern defenders of property rights in the United States call themselves "Democrats." It had been Lemaigre who had suggested General Giraud, and even, so it was whispered, had persuaded the Germans to let him escape. When Lanny expressed incredulity at this idea, the scion of the De Bruynes explained: "You know how it was before the war, Lanny. Many of our leading men of affairs were intimate with the Germans; they did not wait for *Le Couple France-Allemagne* to be realized officially, but went ahead and introduced it on their own. Now, of course, they have influence among Germans, and if they ask a favor, and pay for it, they may get it. Who can tell what secret pledges General Giraud may have given before he slid down that rope from the fortress window?"

"Now, now, Denis! That is a Gaullist voicing his prejudice!" is what Lanny wanted to say, but he bit off his tongue. His purpose wasn't to educate his near-godson, but only to use him, as he would use everybody he met, at home and abroad, for the safety of the American Army. Every time Lanny walked or drove along the esplanade of Algiers he saw with his mind's eye that Army coming in under the fire of machine guns and cannon. How many guns there were, and how straight they were shooting, might depend upon what Lanny was doing now, and what Mr. Robert Murphy was doing, and all his twelve young vice-consuls, whose trail Lanny kept crossing now and then.

IX

What more could a P.A. do? What questions should he ask, what people should he meet? He racked his brains and those of his old friend. Denis said there was a small group living like the early Christians, not literally in catacombs, but meeting in secret places and arranging to print and distribute leaflets and otherwise wage ideological war upon the Vichyites. There were several of these people with whom President Roosevelt's friend ought to consult, so the *capitaine* insisted. When Lanny objected that he couldn't afford to identify himself with the Gaullists, Denis replied: "They are not Gaullists; that is just a bad name used by the enemies of *la France libérée*. These friends are patriots. There is a Communist among them, and a Catholic priest; there are several small business people, there are students and teachers and some workingmen."

Lanny asked: "What are the chances of there being a spy among them?"

"Who can ever be sure about that? All I can say is that I cannot imagine which of our twelve would be the Judas. If you cannot risk meeting a large group, let me choose three or four of whom I can be absolutely certain."

"That sounds better, Denis. I cannot be sure of coming back to Algiers, and what I must do is to put trusted friends in touch with our Intelligence service. If you give your consent, a specially trained man will be sent here to contact you and arrange to furnish you with money and supplies."

"That would be a serious proposal for an officer of the French Army to accept, even a demobilized officer. I would prefer that you put it before the group I will bring together. You know how it is when you have pledged yourself and accepted a leader."

The other replied: "It will be much better for me to be dealing with a group, and with someone of whom I am not personally quite so fond. Let me meet not more than four other persons and tell them my story—but not all of it. Let me be the judge of that. You say nothing, except to vouch for me personally."

"It's a deal," said the young officer, speaking American. "I will send you a note to this hotel. It will be signed, let us say 'Annette,' for code." That was the name of Denis's devoted young wife, whom he had not seen for a year and a half. "It will be better to use a woman's name," he explained; "for then, if a spy should read it, he will assume that it is an assignation."

"O.K.," said Lanny, and went back to his hotel room. He spent half an hour typing a report. He double-sealed it and addressed it to Mr. Robert Murphy, Counselor of the United States Embassy. Next morning he went walking. On the street he picked up an intelligent-looking Arab lad and offered him twenty francs to deliver the letter to the Consulate, just across the street from the Admiralty. Ten francs when he started, and the other ten afterward, Lanny said. He went up in the *ascenseur* of an office building and saw the letter handed in at the door. He smiled to himself, considering it something of a joke on the genial career man mentioned in the report. Lanny could be quite sure that as an honorable official he wouldn't open the inside letter; but suppose he happened to be psychic!

X

A note from "Annette" made an appointment for the following evening. The spot agreed upon was in the Place Bugeau, near the harbor, and there happened to be a military band concert. After one of those dreadful moist and sticky hot days for which the climate of Algiers is notorious, the night was cool, and a great crowd had come out for fresh air and free entertainment. Lanny had to do some searching before he found his friend. They did not give any sign, but Denis started to walk and Lanny followed at a discreet distance.

He was prepared to be taken into some dark alley and to dive into a cellar of underground conspirators. He didn't relish the prospect; the alleys swarmed with Arab refugees who had no other place to sleep, and the filth was such that you hated to set foot in it. But Denis led the way along the main street, the Rue Michelet, past throngs of people on their way to the movies. He entered number 26, a modern apartment house, and waited in the entrance for his friend. Their goal was the home of Professor Henri Aboulker, a Jewish physician.

In a drawing-room furnished in the demoded French bourgeois style, with heavy fumed oak furniture, the thickest carpets, draperies, and tapestries possible, and gilt on everything that could carry it, the P.A. was introduced to four men: first, the professor himself, nearly seventy, and crippled from World War I; he was a professor at the university medical school. Second, to the professor's son, José by name, a medical student of twenty-two, eager, intelligent, and determined. Third, to M. d'Astier de la Vigerie, middle-aged, very French, slender and dapper, good-looking and aware of the fact, Lanny decided. The fourth man was younger and wore the garb of the Jesuit order; he was the Abbé Cordier, and it soon became evident that he regarded D'Astier as his leader.

The *capitaine* had complied with Lanny's request to say nothing except that here was an old friend and the bearer of important news. Lanny revealed to them that he was an agent of the American government, sent to gather data and report on the prospects in the event of an American landing in French North Africa; he desired to be informed concerning every aspect of the situation, and would arrange for Intelligence agents to get in touch with the most dependable persons. He requested that these friends of his old and very dear friend tell him as much as they were willing about themselves, their organizations, their plans, and their hopes.

They did this freely. The doctor was president of the Algerian Jewish Federation. He reported that the large population of his people were chafing under the shameful restrictions which the local government had imposed upon them—compelled, of course, by the Vichyites, compelled, in turn, by the Nazis. José declared that the Jewish youth were ready to rise to the last one; but they could do nothing until they had arms. If they acted prematurely they would bring on only a frightful pogrom. Lanny replied that all American and British broadcasts to France were warning the population to do nothing until they received orders; and this applied to Jews more than to any others of the population.

D'Astier de la Vigerie was one of the organizers of the "Chantiers de la Jeunesse," an Algerian youth organization with all the Fascist trimmings. He now assured Lanny that this was mostly camouflage, that secret propaganda had been carried on, and that his four thousand young people—their ages up to twenty—despised the *collaborateurs* and would put themselves at the service of the Americans to do whatever was desired. Denis de Bruyne put in the remark that the youngsters adored M. d'Astier and called him "Chief." The Abbé Cordier added that these facts were well known to Mr. Robert Murphy, who was counting upon them in his plans.

All this, of course, was good news and a source of satisfaction to an itinerant investigator. He spent several hours questioning these gentlemen and storing their replies in his mind. The intricacies of French politics presented few mysteries to the son of Budd-Erling, for he had watched them for a long time, and on this African shore he found everything reproduced in miniature. He was somewhat startled to learn that the youth leader and the abbé were royalists, that is to say, followers of the Comte de Paris, the pretender to the throne of a monarchy which had been dead for more than a century. This meant that they were the most fanatical of all French reactionaries, devotees of Roman Catholicism in its unreconstructed medieval form. The group in Paris had been headed by Charles Maurras and Léon Daudet, publishers of ferociously abusive newspapers and tireless conspirators against the Third Republic.

Lanny wondered, had Denis come out of the war a "subject" of this Comte, who was at present a refugee in Spanish Morocco, under the protection of a Catholic-Fascist Caudillo? The American reminded himself that all three of the De Bruynes, father and two sons, had been supporters of the Cagoule, a sort of Ku Klux Klan of France, but far more violent and deadly. Lanny listened to these two conspirators and saw the light of fanaticism in their eyes. He realized that he was keeping dangerous company; but that was a part of the game he was playing, and if the readers of *L'Action Française* were willing to help save the lives of American soldiers, they must surely be allowed to do it. Five years ago F.D.R. had explained to his new agent that there were millions of Catholics who were not French royalists but loyal American citizens, and who controlled a mass of votes without which there could be no Democratic Party. So he had sent his friend Admiral Leahy to pray with the old Maréchal in Vichy, and the Catholic Mr. Murphy to Algiers to line up a Jesuit abbé and the leader of an imitation Fascist youth group against the old Maréchal's supporters in the colony which was the richest jewel in his crown.

Lanny went away from that secret meeting whispering to himself: "Good Lord, we are going to take Algiers with the boy scouts!"

XI

While Lanny was engaged with these activities, he read the miserable newspapers which the censors plus the paper shortage permitted to the people of Algiers. Everything was treated from the propaganda point of view, the German successes played up and the Allied played down. General Rommel had begun a fierce attack against the British line, which had seesawed back and forth over a distance of some five hundred miles and had been established west of Tobruk. After a week or two of fierce fighting, the British were beginning to show signs of weakening, and this made a deep impression upon the rest of North Africa, both the Europeans and the natives. Lanny could see doubt and fear in the eyes of his friends, and exultation in the eyes of the near-Fascists whom he had to pretend to hold as friends.

At the same time the Germans on the eastern front launched the tremendous attack in the Ukraine which they had been preparing for many months. They, too, made gains, and the pro-Vichy newspapers hailed these as the beginning of the end. When the British chose this time to make a twenty-year military alliance with the Soviet Union, this seemed to complete the Vichy case. "You see," said their newspapers and radios, "just as we told you, the British Empire is the devil's ally, and this is a war for the salvation of the Christian world." When the elegant ladies of the colonial plutocracy echoed this in Lanny's presence, he expressed regret that his recently shattered legs made it impossible for him to play a soldier's role in this conflict. These ladies, as a rule, distrusted Americans as socially dubious, but they had learned that the son of Budd-Erling had been honored with the friendship of Admiral Darlan and had even been received by *le vieux lui-même*.

There were successes to counterbalance the Allied defeats, but these the Algiers newspapers did not mention, or if they did, it was only to cast doubt upon them. London issued the claim that eleven hundred bombers had attacked Cologne, and in the short time of an hour and a half had destroyed a great part of the city's industries. Vichy said that claim was absurd on the face of it; there weren't enough airfields in Britain to launch such a number of big planes at one time, and they would have bumped into one another in the sky. It was the same when the American Navy claimed to have destroyed a great part of a Japanese Fleet by air attack near Midway. Nobody from Vichy had been there to see it; nobody but Americans had been there, and it was obvious that they were making up stories to keep their public satisfied.

There was an "Armistice Commission" of the Germans and Italians in Algiers, for the purpose of seeing that the French obeyed the orders of their conquerors. That meant hundreds of Nazis, both military and civilian, and Lanny might have met some of them and sought to trade on his old-time friendship. But he didn't think he could get anything out of any Nazi now, and it seemed to him the part of wisdom to meet as few as he could and to be the ivory-tower art lover, wholly aloof from a cruel war into which his country had been dragged by forces beyond any art lover's control. The Germans would have their doubts about such an attitude, but their spies would be unable to disprove it.

XII

Lanny's various art purchases had been properly packed, and arrangements had been made for shipment, no easy matter, requiring influence and many *pourboires*. In these days of food shortages and black markets, everybody's palm was held out, and you couldn't blame him, poor devil. Robbie Budd's son had been taught from childhood that the way to get along in the world was to have plenty of money and to distribute it freely; this attitude had been confirmed, as a war measure, by no less an authority than the Commander-in-Chief of his country's Armed Forces. Lanny spent; and while he dared not keep any written records, he kept in mind a rough estimate of what he had expended as a P.A., and when he got back to New York he would withdraw that amount from the account which F.D.R. had established for him.

He was going to French Morocco, partly because Casablanca was a convenient place from which to jump off, and partly because he had been told that Moroccan mosaics were even finer than those in Algiers. Also, he reflected that if any of the collaborators had become suspicious of his activities, it would be better that he should manifest interest in more than one part of the African coast. From the Mediterranean port to the Atlantic port was some twelve hundred miles as the planes flew, and he would keep the enemy's mind jumping from one to the other.

The evening before his departure Lanny spent in the home of the Jewish doctor, along with Denis and the other three conspirators. They had gone to work with renewed ardor as a result of his assurances and they had much to report. Later they turned on the long-distance radio set and heard the voice of an announcer: "*Ici Londres.*" He introduced the hero of the Free French, General de Gaulle, and the five conspirators listened to that fervid oratory which had so thrilled French refugees all over the world. It wasn't so good this time, because the orator devoted most of his talk to scolding the American government for continuing in its refusal to recognize his government as the one and only representative of France. It was made quite evident that this Jeanne d'Arc in striped military trousers had little love in his heart for Americans; and this was embarrassing to the four Frenchmen who had agreed that America was the only power in the world that might be able to help the French to freedom.

They talked about the problem, and Lanny explained the position of his government, that to recognize De Gaulle as the sole French authority would mean a formal break with Vichy and would have the effect of closing a window into the Axis world. Lisbon and Stockholm were other such windows, but not to be compared with Vichy. "There are millions of Frenchmen who are loyal to the old Marshal, but who hate the Germans, and these people help us and we can help them," Lanny argued. "But if we should break with Vichy, or force Vichy to break with us, all that would come to an end. I personally am here because of that contact, and the same thing applies to Murphy and his vice-consuls. We don't want to fight you, and surely it's important that we have a chance to come here and tell you so!"

Nobody among the rebels in Algiers could deny the soundness of that argument. Lanny said nothing personal about their hero, but he came away from the broadcast with the conviction that however courageous a soldier the General might be, he was a very poor statesman and no sort of diplomat. When the P.A. put into the hands of Denis de Bruyne the large bundle of medium-sized French banknotes which he had been accumulating for this purpose, he felt obliged to say: "This money is not mine, it is the United States government's; and I have to put upon you the restriction that it is to be used to further the policy of that government, which is that we are not favoring any faction or group of the French, but are appealing to the whole French people to help us in ousting the Nazis, and setting you free to choose your own government in a democratic election."

Denis replied: "That is all we have a right to ask."

XIII

The flight to Casablanca took some five hours, part of it through bumpy air. Soon after the plane left the fertile Algerian plateau the landscape changed, and in place of wheatfields and vineyards on the

terraced mountain slopes the country became lonely and in parts desert. Morocco was a country whose wild tribes had been conquered by
the French and the Spanish only with the greatest difficulty. The rains
were uncertain; when they fell the great land companies made money;
and when they failed, the poor peasants starved or took to wandering
as their forefathers did. Forests were few, and from the plane you
could see herds of cattle, goats, and sheep, tended by solitary white-
clad men. Great gullies had been cut in the land by stormy waters.
Here and there were clusters of mud huts, and on the hilltops little
cubical Moslem shrines with white domes.

In Casablanca, Lanny found a fine modern port, made by a breakwater of which the French were proud. In its business district were
office buildings of whitestone with many balconies, a concession to
the climate; its native quarter was a place of vice and danger. The
shops were known as *souks*, and most of them were the size of a booth,
made of American oil cans cut and flattened. Whining beggars followed Lanny everywhere, calling for *baksheesh*, and he had to learn
to say *"Imshi!"* which, he was told, means " 'Tis naught!" It seemed to
do the business.

Lanny had brought letters of introduction and quickly found out
who had mosaics to show him. He was surprised to learn that the native grapevine worked even at a distance of a thousand miles; the people
knew who he was and what he wanted. While waiting for the indispensable Hajek to arrive, he had a pleasant time inspecting various
art treasures. "Infidels" were not permitted inside the mosques, but
they could stand outside and admire the details of fine buildings,
erected in a far-off age of glory. Mosaics were everywhere, and some
could be bought. It was only a question of time to bargain.

Meanwhile, in the evenings, Lanny visited the homes of the *haute
bourgeoisie* of "Casa," as fashionable and as French as in Paris. They
were pleased to be exclusive, but circumstances forced them to be
curious about Americans, and they all wanted to ask questions of a
son of Budd-Erling. Lanny found them somewhat more free-spoken
than those of their class in Algiers. They were a thousand miles nearer
to America, and perhaps the winds from the broad Atlantic had swept
their heads clear. The wife of a wealthy exporter of wines and olive
oil said to him at her dinner table, in the presence of several guests:
"When are you Americans coming, and will you come with enough?"
The guest smiled enigmatically and asked: "Do you want us to come?"
The reply was: "We'll be polite to you. *Mais pas d'Anglais, s'il vous
plaît!*" No English!

He was still more surprised when he presented a letter that Denis had given him to a certain Lieutenant-General Émile-Marie Béthouart, who, Denis said, was a cousin of his mother's family. Denis wrote: "Lanny Budd was a dear friend of my mother's, and you may talk to him as you would to me." The cautious officer arranged the conference in the home of a friend, and took the guest out to a summer house in the garden, where they could be safe from intruders. There the stiffly corseted officer unbent enough to ask the customary questions: "When?" and "Where?" and "How many?" Lanny had to make his usual reply: "The decision has not yet been taken, but it will be as soon as we can assemble the force."

"This is the absolute essential," declared Béthouart. "It must be enough. You must not fail, and you must not change your minds after you have started."

"That I am authorized to promise," replied the P.A. "I am told that one of your high officers has declared that if we come with one division he will fire on us, and if we come with twenty he will embrace us."

"That was General Weygand, and it explains why he is no longer in command in North Africa. You understand that courage must be combined with discretion."

"*Oui, très bien, mon Général.* Let me inform you that I expect to fly to America in a few days, and what you say will be reported to President Roosevelt personally, and to no one else except under his orders."

"Explain to your great President that the French armies here have not been demobilized as in Algiers; the Germans did not wish the task of controlling the Moors. I command a division, and if your forces land near Rabat they will find my forces lined up on the beaches, but withholding their fire. You must come ashore fast, because otherwise I may be court-martialed and shot. Our commander, General Noguès, does not agree with my point of view, and I doubt if he will let himself be persuaded."

Lanny promised, and when the time came he did his best to keep that promise; but the General came within an inch of seeing himself proved a prophet—too late to do him any good!

XIV

Lanny got word of art treasures in Marrakech, and decided to throw a scare into the negotiators in "Casa." (Everybody demanded a fortune from an American millionaire, and they didn't give way normally.) So Lanny hired a venerable car equipped to run on charcoal, and with a little trailer to carry the fuel for a round trip of three or four hundred miles. The route lay toward the south, through wheatfields alternating with barren stretches, with aloes such as stood by the gates of Bienvenu and giant cactus such as he had seen in the California deserts. The little Mohammedan shrines called *marabouts* were everywhere.

All this scenery was dominated by the Atlas Mountains to the southeast—taller than the Alps, and covered with perpetual snow. As it melted, streams cut great chasms through the land, and the life of the ancient civilizations through the centuries had depended upon catching this water at high levels and spreading it over the land or bringing it to the cities. Aqueducts were everywhere, built out of the stones of the earlier ones. Those in Marrakech were low and appeared like swift-moving brooks. Approaching the city you passed over a bridge a thousand feet long, with twenty-seven graceful stone arches built by the Almohades, rulers of this country some eight hundred years previously.

Marrakech is a vast city, an oasis of palm trees, spread out so that it seems bigger than it is. It has immense estates with high walls, and the owners were living in comfort untroubled by war. It has a mosque and minaret, the Koutoubiya, built of rose-colored stone, and when Lanny stood and watched it at the hour of prayer he marveled at the power of the human spirit, for these beautiful things had come out of the soul of a humble and untutored camel driver of the seventh century. There is plenty of fault to be found with the Koran as a guide to conduct in the modern world, but no one could doubt that it had been superior to the forms of idol worship it replaced.

Lanny had a letter to a Moorish dignitary who lived not many miles from this ancient city. He owned an oasis and had groves of oranges, and palm trees loaded with great clusters of dates; there were herds of camels, goats, and sheep, and at the same time many appurtenances of civilization, including a radio set and a motor truck of Detroit manufacture. The master of this household, who spoke a little French and understood still more, showed the guest about his estate. Near one of the sheep pens Lanny noticed an ancient drinking fountain, and behind it a large plaque with one of the most beautiful mosaics he had yet come upon. He expressed his admiration and asked tactfully if it might be purchased and taken to show Americans what Moorish taste at its best could be. He was told to wait until the morrow, and the matter would be discussed.

XV

He was to spend the evening in this household, and it proved to be interesting. He did not meet any of the women, but he guessed that they were listening behind portieres. He met about a dozen men, tall, dark, and handsome, dressed in ceremonial white for a distinguished guest. There were two lads, grandsons of the master, slender youths who reminded Lanny of himself in the days when he had danced all over the lawns of Bienvenu and the beaches of Juan. There was a banquet, the like of which the world traveler had never seen; ten courses, and he had to eat them all from a low table, sitting with his heels tucked under his thighs: chicken broth with rice; lamb roasted whole on a spit—you tore off chunks with the thumb and two fingers, and it was hot; pigeon pie, sweetened; chicken roasted, with a custard gravy; rice fritters in oil; pigeon stuffed with sweetened vermicelli; *koos-koos*, made of grains chopped up with mutton or chicken and highly seasoned; olives baked in a bowl and covered with poached eggs; caramel custard; and last of all oranges. Before and after each course Negro slaves, wearing large silver earrings, brought you a basin, soap, and towel to wash your hands. Each course was washed down with scented mint or jasmine tea.

Later in the evening Negro slaves played the flageolet, the flute, and the drum, the melody in thirds and sixths; then a troop of graceful youths showed the dancing they had learned in a school maintained by the Giaour, the native governor of this district. Lanny told them about the "eurythmics" he had learned as a boy at the Dalcroze School in Germany, and it turned into quite a lecture on the dance arts of the West. It was impossible for these men to imagine themselves dancing with a lady in their arms, but they knew that it was a custom, to them much more barbarous than eating with your fingers.

Far into the night these Moorish gentlemen conversed with their cultivated guest. They told him that the sooner the Americans came to French Morocco the better it would please the Mohammedan population. They were so pleased with his compliments and interest in their culture that in the morning the master of the family insisted upon presenting him with the mosaic. Lanny protested, and ceased only when he saw that he was committing a discourtesy. The host would have his workmen chisel out the tiles and they would be packed with care and delivered by that wonderful Detroit truck. Lanny took photographs of the fountain, and of the one-story red stone mansion with all the men of the family standing in front of it. He promised to come again and to send some Detaze sketches of North Africa in remembrance of his visit.

He drove back to "Casa" in the rattly tin Lizzie. From there he sent a cablegram to his father: "Am ready to return." It had been agreed that Robbie was to notify Baker, who would see to providing transportation from wherever in the world a P.A. might show up. Lanny made arrangements for the packing and shipping of the various art treasures; he paid off his faithful translator and guide; and two days after the filing of his cablegram he received notice that a place had been reserved for him on a plane flying from Tangier to Lisbon. The Army had charge of everything now, and whenever the President's confidential man asked for something he got it quickly. A passenger was just a different kind of package—but one that had to have food and drink on the way, and a bed to sleep in, and magazines, a checkerboard, writing paper, anything he might fancy, including an aluminum can if he got airsick, and a "Mae West" and rubber boat if he had to land in the middle of the Atlantic Ocean!

BOOK THREE

A Mad World, My Masters

7

Love Is Love Forevermore

I

LANNY BUDD, three times a husband, had learned a lot about women. One of these things was that the chosen one is never to be taken for granted. The three simple words, "I love you," which have been spoken so many millions of times since the human race began, have never once been found monotonous—save only in sad instances where the sentiment is not shared. When a woman has given herself to a man, and especially when she is carrying his child, she wants to know that this enterprise is to be co-operative, and that she has made no mistake in a commitment which, once made, is hard to withdraw from.

Lanny wished his chosen one to be in no slightest doubt on this subject. Therefore, when he was in her presence, he spoke the magical words on every occasion, together with the smiles and gestures which accompany and confirm them. When duty took him away from her, he never failed to write her once a week, using the time which other people took to attend church. This letter had to be written with one eye on the censor, a suspicious anonymous person who kept watch for unusual expressions, names, numbers, anything which might be code. Fortunately the censor had no objection to "man and woman stuff"; you were free to say "I love you," but beware of repeating it too often, for that might be code, and if you made some "x" marks you would surely damn your letter to the furnace fires, even though you might add the explanation: "These are kisses."

All this Lanny had explained in advance. He would never express any political opinion or refer to any military event; he would never say where he was or whom he had met, unless it was some common-place name, like Emily or Sophie. He would say "I have bought a fine painting," but never "I have bought a fine Meissonier," for the censor might think that was the name of an airplane or a tank. He would sign his own name and address the letter to "Miss Laurel Creston," because she was keeping her maiden name as a writer, and also because sweethearts might be more intriguing to European censors than wives. He would add something of a complimentary nature for the severe functionary's benefit: "The French are kind to me; they never lose their interest in art"; or, "You would be surprised to know how many of the people here, in spite of all their troubles, labor to preserve the flame of their culture."

Now, when the plane deposited him at the Washington airport, the traveler delayed only long enough to get Baker on the telephone and ask for his appointment; then he put in a call to New York, and when he heard Laurel's voice he said: "Darling, here I am, safe and well."

"Oh, Lanny!" she cried. "Such a relief! I have been holding my breath."

"Be careful," he cautioned, with a smile in his voice; "you are breathing for two."

"Where are you?"

"In Washington. I have to make a report, and then I'll take the first plane. I'm not sure how long it will be, but I'll keep in touch with you. I am well, and have some interesting adventures to tell you. Incidentally, I love you."

"*Truly?*" It was an invitation to repeat, and he no longer had to worry about the censor.

"Truly, truly, with understanding."

"Understanding of what?" came the greedy query.

"Of the treasure you are, and of my need of such treasure."

II

It had been possible for a P.A. to be taken quietly into the "summer White House" because the reporters stayed in Poughkeepsie and were furnished with a list of the day's guests—from which Lanny's name had been omitted. But it would have been another matter for him to come openly into the real White House, where reporters swarmed all day and most of the night, watching for stories as hawks watch for field mice and baby chickens. He followed his well-established procedure of walking to an appointed street corner at night and stepping into Baker's car when it stopped. A few minutes later he was in that familiar bedroom on the second floor of the President's home, with the big mahogany bed, the chintz curtains drawn back for the night breeze, and the prints of old sailing ships on the walls.

In that bed, half lying and half sitting, with pillows propped behind him, was the large bundle of intelligence, kindness, and fun which was a gift of Providence to the people of the United States—a gift much better than they deserved, for they would never have chosen him if they had known in advance what he was going to do. Or so, at any rate, the worshipful Lanny thought. He had come to center all his hopes for social justice and world order on "That Man in the White House."

Here the man was, clad in a blue-and-white-striped pajama coat, and with a sheet over his crippled legs, as it was a hot night in June. He was a big man with a big head, and with powerful shoulders and arms which he had developed by swimming, and by the necessary labor of lifting himself into whatever positions he took. Always he greeted his visitors with a hearty smile, and none more so than his Number 103, for he knew that he was going to hear a good story, and he was prepared to enjoy every word of it. "Welcome to our city!" was his call. "Our hot and muggy city! Take off your coat and turn the fan on you. Would you like some iced tea, or something with a stick in it?"

"No, thanks," Lanny said. "Anybody who has come from Algiers will not mind Washington." He wanted to get down to business and not take the great man's time. Always there was what he took for a warning—a stack of documents and correspondence on the reading table, and some on the bed where this cruelly burdened man worked until far into the night. "You received my reports, Governor?"

"All in numbered order, received and contents noted. Thanks, as always, old man. Your data have been invaluable."

"That's all I need to hear. Here is a statement of the money I spent. I prepared that on the plane coming here, the best I could from memory. I did not dare to make notes of any sort on my trip. I never have a scrap of writing that the enemy is not free to inspect. I think it would be correct to say that my baggage was gone through once a week at every hotel in Europe and North Africa where I stopped."

"Err in your own favor in these accounts, Lanny. As I have told you before, you ought to be paid."

"I bought a couple of paintings in Vichy and a lot of stuff in North Africa, and my commissions will amount to three or four thousand dollars, which will more than cover my expenses. What I have listed here are the sums I paid to members of the underground. I couldn't tell you exactly how much, because I don't dare to draw money at a bank and hand it over to them. I have to change the large bills by making small purchases, and when I have a lot of small bills I tie them into a bundle and slip them into pockets. So when I go to a rendezvous I look like a badly stuffed sausage. I have made several valuable contacts, but didn't dare say much about them in my reports. I'll tell you, or Colonel Donovan, whichever you say."

"Tell *me!*" exclaimed F.D.R. and grinned like a schoolboy. "Sometimes I read a 'whodunit' to put myself to sleep."

Lanny began with Raoul Palma and his underground group. When he came to Mlle. Richard and his two meetings with her, in the Grand Hotel and then in the unlighted den in the Old Town of Toulon, the auditor remarked: "That is really operatic. To complete the libretto you should go back and fall in love with her." Lanny grinned in his turn and said that the libretto would be ruined by the fact that he had a wife in New York. To this F.D.R. remarked: "By the way, my wife met her, and spoke very highly of her. It is better that a secret agent should have a proper wife—he is not so apt to fall for any of the Gestapo ladies."

"I think my record is clear on that score," said Lanny. "I have had several passes made at me, I suspect."

III

Next the story of Monck, then of Denis de Bruyne, and then of General Béthouart; F.D.R. said for Lanny to stop in at Colonel Donovan's office and give him a detailed report on these persons. What the President wanted especially was to ply the traveler with questions about the political situation in all these various places, how well or ill his declared policies were being carried out, and what Lanny thought the effect of them was likely to be. It was a "blue" time, for the Germans were driving hard into the Ukraine and the British were in what appeared to be a rout in Tunisia; but if this responsible man felt any doubts or fears he did not let his agent and friend get the slightest hint of them. He said: "We are getting ready, Lanny, and we are going to do this job. Don't let anybody tell you anything different."

He put the P.A. through a grilling on the subject of the Vichy leaders. What faith, if any, did they have, and what was going to be their conduct in a showdown? Lanny said: "If you could drop an army into Vichy from the sky, they would all be on your side. As it is, they are prisoners of the Nazis, and they have to force themselves to believe that they are right. Laval said to me, in exactly these words: 'I desire a German victory.' I didn't see any signs of his shaking in his boots, but that will be happening some day, no doubt."

And then the problem of Charles André Joseph Marie de Gaulle, author of *Au Fil de l'Épee* and favorite orator of the British Broadcasting Corporation. There was a clamor in circles in America known as "Liberal" that the State Department should recognize this man of both the sword and the pen for what he so loudly claimed to be, the sole head of the government of France. How shocking of us to trade with those hucksters of Vichy, who had sold the honor and the very life of their country to the Nazi tyrants! This agitation was a thorn in the flesh of F.D.R., it appeared; for he, too, had called himself a "Liberal" through his public career and had fought men of the Laval and Darlan type wherever he had met them in American public life—which was frequently. He seemed to be pleading with Lanny to tell him that he was right in the course he had chosen; Lanny, fresh from the scene, was able to do this.

"I was unable to find that General de Gaulle has any following of consequence in North Africa. I have no doubt there are a great many who listen to his broadcasts and cherish affection for him in their hearts; but I am speaking of organized support, anything that you can count on when it comes to action."

"That is what I have to be concerned with, Lanny."

"I bore your instructions in mind and kept before me the image of an army coming ashore. I found that of the people who exercise power of any sort, the greater number hate and fear De Gaulle and call him a puppet of Britain. Most of that, no doubt, is due to the fact that they have compromised, while he has stood out and is attacking them with bitterness. But allowing for that, there seems to be another factor: those who know him say that he is egotistical to the point of fantasy, that he is building himself into a cult, and will have nothing to do with anybody who does not make obeisance at the shrine. They say: 'He makes a fine propagandist, but he would make a wretched administrator.'"

"That is exactly the impression we have of him, Lanny. He is a stickler for punctilio, and does not know how to distinguish between things that are fundamental and those that are petty. He persists in acting as if France were the victor; as if he were doing us favors instead of asking them. He talks about liberty and democracy, but I get the impression that what he is really thinking about is *la gloire*, and that his point of view is fundamentally authoritarian and reactionary."

"Concerning that there is not the slightest doubt," said the P.A. "He was Pétain's Chief of Staff, and his point of view is that of St. Cyr plus the Catholic hierarchy. You do not like me to refer to the religious aspects of the matter, but it seems to me a fact of our world, which nobody can escape, that when you have a Church insisting that it has immutable law and authority handed down from on high, you have a force which cannot be excluded from politics. Whenever it is a question of fundamental social change, you will have the priests preaching against you from every pulpit in the land."

F.D.R. grinned. "I am never going to have them preaching against *me*, Lanny! Believe you me, I keep the Encyclicals of Leo XIII right handy on my desk, and when one of the archbishops starts pounding my desk, objecting to one of my New Deal measures, I read him the marked passages and make him listen."

Lanny would have liked to retort: "I said 'fundamental,' Governor," but he knew that would start an argument and take a lot of a busy man's time. At present there was only one thing fundamental in the world, and that was to unhorse the Axis dictators.

IV

Of the greatest importance to the Commander-in-Chief of an Army soon to land on foreign soil was to know how his agents were working and what success they were having. Lanny did not wait to be questioned, but said: "I avoided Robert Murphy, because I didn't want to attract his attention to myself, and I didn't want to be influenced by personal feelings. I gather that he is an easy fellow to like, and he has made many friends. I came on the trail of his agents in various places, and it is evident that they are doing a job of getting data of all sorts. I suppose that material is coming to the Army, and not to you personally."

"It is important for me to have your confirmation. Have you any suggestions to offer?"

"There is one thing I could not get out of my mind, and that is the question of what commitments Murphy is making with those *collaborateurs* who have already jumped onto his bandwagon, or are preparing to do so. I don't know whether you care to talk to me about that—"

"You have a right to know everything on the subject; you could not work intelligently otherwise."

"Well, I met a great number of Murphy's friends—a dozen at least. He seems to have picked out the big business people, the financial and social oligarchy. I don't know whether that is deliberate policy, or whether it is because he finds it easier to make headway with that sort. Certainly he has managed to please them. But I am wondering whether he is taking them into camp, or whether they are taking *him* into camp."

"It might be a bit of both, and still be of advantage to our cause when the showdown comes."

"These men, you understand, are the last in the world to yield to impulses of good fellowship, or to give something for nothing. They know what they want, and it isn't to be fed taffy."

"But they might want a lot of things and find that they aren't going to get them, Lanny."

"That is what I am wondering about—what commitments are being made."

"Nobody is authorized to make any commitments, except as regards the personal safety of these individuals, of course. Those who help us will escape with their necks—if we are able to arrange it."

"That's fair enough. But what is their political and financial position going to be?"

"The answer to that will be given by the people of France, who will determine the future of their country in a democratic election. That is our public commitment, and nobody is authorized to make any other."

"Let me give you a case, Governor. Does the name of Jacques Lemaigre-Dubreuil mean anything to you?"

"I have heard it, but I'm not sure if I can sort him out from Jacques Benoi-something."

"Benoist-Méchin is a journalist who has become a member of the Laval Cabinet. He is a small potato. But Lemaigre-Dubreuil is one of the most important of the big moneymakers of France. To give his American equivalent, let us say that he is Frank Gannett or Joe Patterson, or some such reactionary publisher; at the same time he is a member of the Federal Reserve Board, and his wife owns General Foods and he runs it; also he is president, or whoever it is behind the scenes who directs the propaganda, of the National Association of Manufacturers and directs its lobby in Washington."

"Quite a Frenchman, indeed!"

"I had a couple of long talks with him and I met him socially on several other occasions. He is in Algiers ostensibly to run his vegetable-oil business, but in reality to protect the interests of his associates of the Comité des Forges, both French and German, who are bringing their money to safety in North African banks and are preparing to follow the cat whichever way it jumps. As I told you before, I don't know what is in Murphy's mind, but I know that in Lemaigre's mind there is a clear conviction that he has got matters fixed up so that when our armies land he and his friends will have the inside track; that, in substance, they will be the government of North Africa, just as in the old days they used to be the government of France—operating, of course, behind a screen."

The President of the United States thought that over for a while before he spoke. "Put yourself in my place, Lanny. I lie here on a comfortable bed with an electric fan to cool me, and anything I choose to ask for is brought to me at the pressing of a button; and I have to speak the words that will send ten or twelve millions of our best young men overseas into jungle heat and arctic cold to fight and bleed and die. I want to save every life that I can, and every pang of agony that I can spare to any and every one of those boys. If I can save a million, or even a thousand, do you think I ought to worry about the fact that a few economic royalists of France will discover that they haven't got everything they thought they were going to get?"

"No, Governor, but that's not my point. What I don't want is for the economic royalists to fool *us*."

"Do you really think they can fool *me*, Lanny? I know them here, and I'm sure they are exactly the same in all other countries. If I have the power, I shall help to tame them there, just as I have tried to do in this country."

"If they are allowed to entrench themselves—"

"Listen, Lanny. You have been to that country, whereas I know it only from the map. I measured it with my pencil today. From the east corner of Algeria to the west corner of Morocco is about as far as from New York to Kansas City."

"If you travel by the coast it's almost as far as to San Francisco."

"A vast country, with poor communications. Somebody has to govern and police it. If we have to do this with our armies, it will take one or two hundred thousand men, and all the ships to supply them. If we can find Frenchmen who will do it for us—any sort of Frenchmen, so long as they know the job—we can save all those Americans and all those ships and supplies. What we want is to drive the Germans out, from North Africa, and from Italy, and from France. That's our job, and yours is to trust your country and trust me, and believe that when the war is won we shall know how to find out what the French people want, in the same way that we find out what the American people want, by letting them go to the polls and vote."

Lanny took it as a rebuke and said humbly: "Yes, Governor, I get the point. But you have to be forewarned that you're going to take an awful shellacking if you let men like Lemaigre-Dubreuil take charge of French North Africa."

"Don't worry about that either, Lanny. I've been in public life a long time and I've grown a tough hide. I'm going to win this war and pay what it costs—but no more than I have to! And anybody that doesn't like that program can lump it, as we used to say when we were boys."

V

F.D.R. paused to put a cigarette into that long thin holder which he liked to stick up in a jaunty manner, and which had become a symbol dear to the hearts of cartoonists along with "Winnie's" big dark cigar and "Uncle Joe's" pipe. (Hitler did not smoke, so all they had for him was a Charlie Chaplin mustache and a swastika.) F.D.R. lighted his cigarette and took a couple of puffs, then said: "The question of where the first landing is to be is still being argued, and with a great deal of heat. I am expecting Churchill here in a couple of days, and we shall go to it. You understand, of course, that this is strictly *entre nous*."

"You may be sure that I never speak about your affairs, Governor. I haven't told even my father or my wife that I am working for you."

"Winston, as I believe I told you, is hot for the Balkans. He insists that we can land there practically unopposed and have a clear road up the Vardar valley."

"I suspect that he has reasons in addition to military ones for that suggestion."

"Of course. He makes no secret of that. His 'Empah,' as he calls it, expects to be in that part of the world for a long time to come; whereas we cherish the hope that we can finish up the job and bring our boys back home. It may be a fond hope, but I'd hate to have to tell our mothers and wives and sweethearts that their boys will have to stay over there. What Winston wants, of course, is to get our armies into that part of the world so that we shall block off the Russians from the Balkans and the Dardanelles. That would be the best possible ending of a war from his point of view."

"Stalin is not so keen for the idea, I gathered."

"What Stalin wants is for us to come straight across the Channel and head for Berlin. From the military point of view that seems to me the only way to be considered. That is where we shall meet the bulk of the German armies, and they are what we have to beat."

"You can't do it without command of the air, Governor."

"That I know. And I think the British should be bombing German communications from now on, to prevent their moving reinforcements and supplies to the Channel. I've just been going over some of the data supplied by our General Staff. There's going to be a hot time in the old town when Winston arrives."

"It's a pretty hard strain on you," ventured the **P.A.** He had been watching this great man's face and noting the lines of care increasing and deepening. It had been only five years ago that Lanny had met him, but he seemed to have aged ten or more.

"Strictly between you and me, Winston as a guest is something of a trial. He has the habits of an owl, or perhaps a half-owl. He will come ambling into this room about midnight, full of ideas and conversation just when I am tired out and ready for sleep; he can sleep until late in the morning, while I have a schedule to keep." The tired man spoke as if it were a relief to have somebody's sympathy; but then in a moment the schoolboy grin came back to the mobile face. "Wouldn't you like to come and take him off my hands part of the time? You could listen, say, from midnight till three or four, and then go to your hotel room and hang out a 'Do not disturb' sign."

Lanny wasn't sure whether this was all jest or part serious. He grinned in return and said: "*Zu Befehl, Herr Kommandant*, as the German soldiers say."

"Joking aside," continued the President, "I think Winston would like to hear your report on North Africa. I could give him what you have sent me, but he'd probably put the papers aside and never find time to read them. If he talks to you, he'll have questions to ask. Can you stay a few days?"

"If you have nothing else in mind, I'd rather go up to New York and wait until you call me. I'll come at any hour of the day or night that you say. I'll motor or fly, according to how much time you allow me."

"Very good then. Give your address and telephone number to Baker and we'll arrange it."

"If I come to the White House openly, won't the reporters get hold of it?"

"I'll see that your name is not listed to the press; and for the White House staff we might change it a bit. Your middle name is Prescott? Then suppose you be Mr. Lanning Prescott? I'll give Winston your real name and explain matters to him."

"O.K. by me," said the P.A. "Let me remind you that you were going to fix it with him to have me taken off the British blacklist. It's important, because I can't fly through Bermuda. Also, I'd like to be able to stop off in England because I have important friends there, and a little daughter whom I haven't seen for more than a year."

"I'll make a note of it," said Roosevelt. "Remind me if I don't speak of it."

VI

Lanny spent the night in a hotel. Next morning he took a taxi to the old houses which had been converted into offices for the Co-ordinator of Information and his rapidly growing staff. They were down by the Potomac River, amid coal yards, behind an old brick brewery, and almost under the shadow of the gasworks; nobody objected, because office room was so scarce that you were lucky to get any sort of roof over your head. Armed guards kept watch, but the all-powerful Mr. Baker had telephoned, and Lanny was ushered in as soon as he had identified himself.

Colonel William J. Donovan was a short, somewhat plump Irishman who had commanded the famous 69th New York Regiment in World War I. He had earned all the decorations there were, and the sobriquet of "Wild Bill." He certainly gave no such impression in his office, for his voice was gentle and rather slow, and his manner lazy and easygoing. Sometime early in his life he must have kissed the Blarney stone, for in the first half hour he made Lanny think that they were old friends, and that the story Lanny had to tell was the most interesting the Colonel had ever heard. He seemed to have unlimited time, and it was only after he had heard Lanny all the way through that he thought to call in his confidential stenographer and a couple of department heads, to hear it again and take down the essential facts—names and addresses of Raoul Palma and Bernhardt Monck and Denis de Bruyne and General Béthouart, and what each of them wanted and what sort of person would be best to send them. Lanny got the impression that this amiable officer's organization was going to be somewhat loosely run; but, then, so was F.D.R.'s, and still we were going to lick the Nazis!

The Colonel gave his caller a pat on the shoulder, called him by his first name, thanked him with all the warmth of his Irish heart, and assured him that his secret would be kept and also those of his friends. He wound up by asking the son of Budd-Erling if he wouldn't like to come in and start another department and run it. Apparently there was room for an unlimited number of departments, and when the chiefs and directors and chairmen and what-nots began treading on one another's toes, the Colonel would pat them on their backs and give them a new title and some more assistants and secretaries to make them happy. That was apparently what it meant to be a "Co-ordinator" with a capital C.

Lanny spent most of that day and part of the evening in conference with various groups of the Colonel's administrators, telling them all he could about the old Continent which he knew so well and which most of them knew only from the newspapers; about Hitler and Göring and Hess and their subordinates, and the enormous military and governmental and propaganda machines they had built up; about their ideas and ways of life; how they had achieved power and how they were keeping it; about Pétain, Laval, Darlan and the rest of the French collaborators, and the underground which was opposing them, what sort of people they were, and how to reach them and win their trust; about the conditions they would find in Algeria and Morocco, and who would be their friends and who their enemies in those ancient, half-barbarous lands.

All these men of the C.O.I. agreed that this experienced man ought to join them, and he couldn't tell them frankly why he didn't. He just said: "I have been working independently for a long time, and I have some contacts that I am not free to reveal to anybody else. But I'll keep in touch with you, and maybe I'll meet some of you in the field." They all promised to keep his secret; they were going to send thousands of men and women into the enemy lands, and would keep the secrets of all of them. Very soon the name of their organization would be changed to the Office of Strategic Services, and the cocktail-party wits of Washington and New York would say that O.S.S. meant: "Oh, so secret!" But you could be sure that the men and women in the field didn't object to that secrecy nor to the armed guards keeping watch over the offices and the files at home.

VII

There is a midnight train to New York, and Lanny had asked Baker to make a reservation for him. He had just time to phone Laurel that he was coming; then he found himself in a compartment with two other men—for train space was beyond price. Washington had suddenly become the capital of the world, and New York had become a suburb, with big businessmen commuting, and sometimes sleeping, in limousines between the two cities at night.

It had been some time since Lanny had had a home of his own—indeed, had he ever had one? His father's home, his mother's home, his *amie's* home, his wife's home! When he had been Mister Irma

Barnes he had lived in Irma's palace on Long Island, and in one that she had rented in Paris, and it had all been the way Irma wanted it. When he had been married to Trudi Schultz he had visited her in a tenement room in Paris where she was hiding, carrying on her anti-Nazi activities; that had been her home, and only a stern sense of duty had made it tolerable to a reformed playboy.

He had said to Laurel: "Get a larger apartment so that you can have a room to work in and I can have one and Agnes can have one." She had told him that she wanted to pay her own way, even as a wife; she was a feminist. But now he pleaded: "Let me pay for it, please, *please!* It will be the first time in my life that I ever supplied a home for the woman I loved!"

That sounded strange, but he proved it to her concerning all the five love affairs which he had had, and about which he had told her truly. One of his wives had died, and another had left him to become a countess; oddly enough, the same thing had happened to two of his sweethearts—one had died and one had left him to become a countess. The third of this unlegitimized group had left him for a stage career, and that surely hadn't been the young Lanny's fault. "I never left a woman in my life," he insisted to his present one, and added: "And believe me, I never mean to."

The point was that all five of these ladies had had a home of one sort or another, and the only times when the grandson of Budd Gunmakers and son of Budd-Erling had been able to pay their bills had been when he had taken them traveling. So now Laurel had let him have his way, and the two women were established in an apartment house in the East Sixties, with three bedrooms and two baths. Servants were hard to obtain, but they had a woman who came in and cleaned up twice a week, and they had a kitchenette where light meals could be prepared when they did not feel like going out. It seemed to the economical Laurel a terribly expensive way to live, but New Yorkers took it for granted that you had to spend money in order to make it. Lanny had to have a room in which to type his mysterious reports, and certainly a woman who was carrying a baby and a novel at the same time had a right to comfort and convenience.

There she was when a taxi delivered him from the Pennsylvania Station at about seven-thirty in the morning. She had his orange juice cold and his toast hot, and Agnes Drury had gone to work early in order to take herself out of the way. Laurel was lovely in one of those dressing gowns with a big floral pattern. He could see at a glance that she was well, and her happiness was written on every feature and in every gesture and word. He caught her in his arms; time didn't matter—the orange juice would stay cold in the refrigerator and the toast could be reheated. He could say "I love you" as often as he pleased, and could make x-marks for kisses, and with no censor to question whether they were code. Parting might or might not be sweet sorrow, but certainly and without question coming home was sweet joy.

VIII

Meeting after two months' absence, they both had a lot of news. Because ladies like to talk and listening seems more polite, Lanny learned first what had happened to his wife. She had written two articles, one about their trip through China and one about what they had found at Yenan; both had been accepted and were soon to appear; he would read the manuscripts that day. Laurel was working on her novel about an American girl at a German university in the days of the Nazis, and there was a chunk of that awaiting his judgment. Her pregnancy had made no special difference in her work, she told him; she had kept her promise and not let herself get tired. Agnes had been lovely to her; she was a sensible, settled woman, who had great admiration for the art of writing and took many burdens from her friend's shoulders.

Then began a questioning of Lanny. How was Beauty, how was Parsifal, and the dear little boy? Lanny recounted what they had said and done and gave her the messages they had sent. He told about the refugees at Bienvenu and how they were getting along; the relationship of benefactor and beneficiary is seldom entirely satisfactory, and poor Beauty was finding this out. Lanny hadn't considered it his duty to take a hand; she had her own money, a thousand dollars a month that Robbie sent her, plus the large sums from the Detaze sales. He told about Marceline, whom Laurel had never met; a curious nature, quietly cold, pleasure-bent in a silent, incessant, almost vegetative way. Some day Laurel would meet her and probe her secret soul and put it into a story.

Then the other ladies. Sophie Timmons had obeyed her government and come back to her large hardware family in Cincinnati. Emily Chattersworth wasn't well enough to move, in fact she was all but bedridden. Lanny had been to call on her twice, and they had talked about the problems of their time. The chatelaine of Sept Chênes had lived too long, she thought; the world had taken on an aspect which she did not understand, and it terrified her; she could not imagine how social life could continue on such terms. Lanny had tried to tell her the basis of his faith, that they were in the midst of the birth pangs of a new social order. A birth is a messy thing, and if you had never seen one before, it would alarm you greatly; but when it is over, it is discovered to be a natural phenomenon.

Lanny told his wife what Emily had said, that she was going to leave part of her considerable fortune to her near-godson. Lanny had protested that he didn't want her to do that, that he had no need of more money; but she had answered that she had no special interest in her surviving relatives and thought that Lanny might find some way to put money to good use. He had asked what she wanted done with it, and she had said something to stop these cruel and dreadful wars. Lanny had decided that she was not long for this world and thought he ought to give her some hint that he was not just an ivory-tower dweller but was rendering service of importance to his government. She had told him: "I guessed that years ago. I have known you since you were a babe-in-arms, and I perceived that you were drawing out our near-Fascist friends. Don't worry, I have never spoken of it."

IX

It was Lanny's turn to ask questions of his wife. She had been down to visit the widow of Reverdy Holdenhurst, her aunt by marriage, to condole with her and tell her how it had happened that two passengers of the *Oriole* had been left behind in Hongkong and how the yacht had sailed away to its doom. "Poor soul!" Laurel said. "She was never able to forgive Uncle Reverdy's offense against her, but now she remembers only his good qualities and is a prey to remorse. She cannot make up her mind that he and Lizbeth are really gone. She studies the maps and speculates about what may happen to people on jungle islands, and whenever she reads in the papers a story about a sailor or a flyer who has come back to civilization, she starts hoping all over again."

"Did you tell her about your psychic experience?" Lanny asked.

"I told her, and it disturbed her greatly. You know, she is a devout Episcopalian, but she was educated in a Catholic convent, and I think she has the Catholic attitude deeply buried in her mind—the notion that there is something dangerous and even immoral in dabbling with 'spirits.' She came back to the subject again and again and cross-questioned me. I had brought the notes you had taken down and I read them to her. You remember, the spirit of Lizbeth, or whatever it was, said that her childhood rag doll in the old gray trunk in the attic had been used as a nest by mice. We went and found it was so, and I thought that Aunt Millicent was going to faint. An extraordinary thing, Lanny, and I don't know how to account for it."

"Let's give Lizbeth another chance to tell us," Lanny said, "if it isn't a strain on you."

"Not at all," she replied. "That is one of the things that surprise me; it seems to be a natural process, like falling asleep. I am puzzled as to how I manage to distinguish between going to sleep and going into a trance."

"I take it that you give an order to your subconscious mind. It is like what you do in breathing and swallowing food; you are using the same apparatus, and it is a question of which of two valves you close. Sometimes you make a mistake, and then you have a disagreeable choking spell."

"I must have made a mistake that day on the plane, flying to Ulan-Bator; I thought I was falling asleep, and instead I went into a trance."

"Possibly you do it often and never realize it. I shall have to practice listening while you are asleep." It reminded him of a story he had heard as a lad and had almost forgotten. It was told by a visitor at St. Thomas's Academy in Connecticut, which he had attended during World War I. It had been introduced playfully, as "a story that nobody can understand." A woman came into a grocery store and ordered a dozen boxes of matches. The grocer said: "But Mrs. Smith, you bought a dozen boxes of matches last week." The woman answered: "Yes, but you see, my husband is deaf and dumb and he talks in his sleep!"

X

They tried a séance that evening. A curious procedure, which would keep Lanny wondering as long as he lived on this earth. It disappointed him frequently, for these manifestations of the subconscious mind are vagarious and undependable, and the psychic prospector is like that other kind who goes wandering out into the desert with pick and shovel, blanket, food, and water, all loaded upon a patient burro; he may search for years and even for a lifetime and find no gold, but if he does find it—well, it is gold. Any chemist knows what gold is, but where is the soul chemist who can tell you where trance phenomena come from?—fragments of mentality that seem to be floating around loose in an infinite universe, and sometimes put themselves together in a fashion beyond the power of any conscious mind to explain.

Laurel's "control" was a personality whom she had met long ago, but only casually, and if she had been especially interested in him she had entirely forgotten it. The idea that he would some day decide to move in upon her subconscious mind and take his residence there would have sounded utterly crazy to her. But now, whenever she dropped into a trance, which she had discovered by accident, here he was, seemingly always at hand. She herself did not hear his voice, but whoever sat by and listened heard him speaking through her lips—or claiming that he did so, and what were you to make of the claim?

This "spirit" Otto Kahn chatted with urbanity, just as he would have done in life. He took it as a queer sort of joke, exactly as he would have taken it if anybody had presented him with such a proposition while he was alive. He was good company, and at the same time dignified, accustomed to be treated as a person of distinction. How he would have behaved if he had been treated otherwise Lanny had no means of knowing, for he had never tried it.

On this occasion Otto was in his best drawing-room mood. He responded to any playful remark about what was going on in the world, and especially in the great metropolis which had been his home. When asked if he had any messages for his family, he said No, they seemed to be getting along very well. When asked if he had any message for a certain operatic soprano, he said No with emphasis; she was married now, and he wouldn't take any chance of disturbing her tranquillity. When asked if there was any way he could find Reverdy Holdenhurst or his daughter Lizbeth, he replied that he was keeping away from the spirits, they bored him, and besides, he couldn't make up his mind that he believed in them. Then, somewhat incongruously, he added: "That old bore Zaharoff is here as usual. I don't suppose you are interested in him, Lanny?"

"Not especially," was the reply. "At least not until he can figure out some way for me to get that money he wants me to pay out for him."

Then—one of those unforeseeable developments—there came suddenly from Laurel's lips a different voice, surprisingly like that of the aged Sir Basil, Knight Commander of the Bath and Grand Officer of the Legion of Honor. "Go and see my niece in London, and she will give you the money."

"I'd be afraid to, Sir Basil," said the son of Budd-Erling, smiling. "She might have me arrested for attempted fraud."

"Tell her to consult a medium, and I will talk to her," commanded the voice of the Knight Commander.

"That would only make it a more elaborate fraud, Sir Basil. And besides, such things cannot be arranged nowadays. Don't you know there's a war on?" This was a stock formula of the time; it caused the former partner of Kuhn, Loeb and Company to break into laughter, and it brought the séance to a sudden end. There was a long silence.

"Did something go wrong?" asked Laurel when she opened her eyes. "I have a strange sort of feeling about it." When he told her, she said: "You offended the old man, and he took it out on me."

XI

Laurel told how she had been to call upon Mrs. Roosevelt, and what they had talked about. A truly great woman, she said, and one whose impress upon the country would not soon be erased. For the first time in our history there was in the White House a woman who was not merely a housekeeper or an ornament, but a democratic force. She was that in her own right, by the power of her own mind and heart. "She and her husband make a team," Laurel said. "He might not have the same steadfastness if he stood alone."

Lanny would have liked to say: "I was with him in Washington," but he didn't. It might seem strange that he had revealed his secret to friends such as Raoul and Monck, and would not reveal it to the woman of his heart. But those people in Europe needed the facts for the work they were doing; Laurel did not need them. She understood that and never asked. What she guessed was her own affair, of course.

He told her the details of his trip: the aspects of Vichy, the elderly roués being taken to the baths in wheel chairs, the half-starved poor standing patiently in front of half-empty foodshops. And then the Riviera, where the contrasts between the conditions of rich and poor were even greater; and then Switzerland, standing on guard day and night, making money, but having to spend most of it on defense preparations. He told about the paintings he had inspected and those he had bought; about North Africa and the mosaics, and the amusing process of bargaining; about the ruins of Timgad, the mosques and minarets and *marabouts* of Morocco, and the ten-course banquet he had tried so valiantly to eat. But nothing about the underground, nothing about the *collaborateurs* or the American vice-consuls. "Everybody is expecting something to happen, and everybody tries to guess what." That was as far as he would go.

Robbie sent a car down as usual, and Lanny took his wife driving and showed her the country in the luxurious robes of early summer. The first hot spell had come, and he worried about leaving her to be sometimes parboiled and sometimes baked in a vast stone oven—so impolitely did he describe Manhattan Island. But she assured him that it could be turned into an excellent summer resort for a writer who wanted to be let alone. She had a refrigerator well stocked with fruit juices and a room with an electric fan. In extreme cases she would work in the summer costume which nature had provided for her, and find it most comfortable. In the evenings she and Agnes would stroll on the edge of the park or go to an air-conditioned movie house if there was anything that wouldn't bore them too greatly. War pictures were dreadful, but Laurel said: "I want to face the facts of my time."

They drove out together to see the Budds of Newcastle. They were a philoprogenitive tribe and paid all honor to a bride as a guardian of their tribal future. They found it hard to understand that a woman left alone should refuse shelter and protection in Robbie's commodious villa on a hilltop overlooking the river and the distant Sound. But they had "queer" ones among them, and they accepted the fact that a literary lady might be another; some of them had read her stories and were a bit afraid of her, lest she some day make use of them as "copy." In this they had good reason.

Lanny hired a stenographer and dictated letters to his various clients. He prepared an elaborate dossier on the subject of the mosaics and the gateway he had purchased, with detail photographs of each and the history so far as he knew it. He drove out and presented these to the delighted Mr. Vernon, and told him the story of his travels, the sights he had seen, and the people he had met. When this wealthy gentleman realized how much trouble Lanny had taken and the expenses he had incurred, he said that ten per cent commission was not enough and insisted upon doubling it. He could not understand how a man had been able to travel to all these places in wartime, and Lanny attributed it to his father's influence, intimating that he had picked up a little information for his father on the side. It pleased a patron of the arts, of course, to have an expert who was not merely an employee, but a man of means, a social equal. That made it easier to believe what he said, and Mr. Vernon was pleased to put in an order for more art treasures which he could boast of being able to get from two continents at war. His fortune came out of a flour-milling empire, and the money poured in automatically, day and night, like the grain into storage bins and the flour into sacks.

XII

Lanny told his wife that he was expecting a call to Washington and might have to take off on another errand very soon. She did not utter a word of complaint, or even of sorrow; she knew now that men by the millions were going off to war. She was much in love with her man, and frank in showing it, but she would not add her grief to whatever burdens he was carrying. She set her teeth and said: "The job has to be done." She hated the Nazis almost as much as she loved her husband, and that made it easier for her.

She wanted to be with him every minute of this precious time, so she would dress and go out with him, in spite of being in a condition rather difficult to conceal. He took her to dinner in a chophouse in the theater district, where he knew that good cooking was to be had. It was his duty to feed her, so he ordered a green salad, which the dieticians recommend for her condition, and then she was going to have two freshly broiled lamb chops on buttered toast with green peas, and after that he would try to persuade her to find room for fresh strawberries and ice cream. He was watching over her, entertaining her, doing everything he knew to make her happy. He was going to leave her with the best possible memories, and the same sort of hopes for the future.

He meant to give her a peaceful evening, taking her up Riverside Drive where there would be a pleasant breeze, or at least there would be a breeze while driving. But this was wartime, and things didn't always happen according to schedule. A man came into the restaurant and took a seat at a table near by, not facing Lanny, but so that they were both facing in the same direction. It was by accident that Lanny happened to turn his head and see him: a well-dressed man in middle years, wearing a palm-beach suit. He had a light-colored mustache and a beard trimmed to a point, not usual in New York. The face was thin and rather dissipated looking, and something about it caught Lanny's attention in the first flash. He began looking out of the corner of his eye and presently said to Laurel in a low tone: "Don't turn to look. There's a man I think I know, and if so it's important. Go on talking, anything you please, but don't expect me to listen."

Laurel discussed the war news she had heard on the radio, while Lanny kept looking out of the corner of one eye while the man ordered his dinner. Once the man's eyes turned in Lanny's direction, and Lanny turned his head quickly. Presently he said: "I am pretty sure this man is an Englishman in the pay of the Nazis. I want to get a look at him from the front. Go on eating and don't pay any attention to him or to me."

He got up and went to the restroom. Through the partly open door he took a good look at the man, and when he came out he went down the other side of the room and passed behind the man, some distance away. Rejoining Laurel, he kept his head averted from his quarry and whispered: "Listen, darling, this is very, very urgent. I have to get the government agents to trail this man, and you have to help me."

"*I*, Lanny? How?"

"Don't look at him. Listen carefully. This won't be pleasant for you, but it may be the most important thing you've ever had to do. You have to keep him in this place until I give you a signal that I have him covered. I want you to strike up an acquaintance with him."

"Good gracious, Lanny! *How?*"

"After I'm gone, tell the waiter to bring you pencil and paper and write a note to the man. Ask him if you can have the pleasure of his company. Tell him you are in trouble. Offer to pay for his help—anything at all. Fold it up and tell the waiter to take it to him. Give the waiter a five-dollar bill at the same time and he won't find it too strange. When the man reads the note, give him your most heavenly smile. Don't be afraid, he can't carry you off."

"Does my figure look heavenly, Lanny?"

"He won't notice it, certainly not so long as you sit at the table. Once you have him here, keep him listening, entertained. Make up a story—your husband has just left you, he's no gentleman, you want to teach him a lesson. If I'm any judge of character, he's proud of his conquests and won't object to making another. Anything so long as you keep him busy."

"And then what?"

"When I've arranged for him to be trailed, I'll come back and stand in the door of the restroom until you see me. Then I'll step back out of sight, and you turn the whole thing into a joke—tell the man your nerve fails you, you're afraid your husband might be violent, arrange to meet him later in a park. When he's gone, you go to the women's room for a while and wait. Give me time to make sure the coast is clear. Then I'll tip the waiter again and he can take us out through the back door of the restaurant."

"Suppose the man doesn't accept my company."

"Keep after him. Use your wits and your sense of humor. At any cost, don't let him get away. If necessary, take his arm and go along with him. I'll be on watch outside, and I'll follow you at a distance. Don't let him take you in a cab, of course."

"Are you planning to have him arrested?"

"Only as a last resort. What I want is to have him followed and find out where he lives and what his connections are. For all we can know, he might be planning to have all the bridges around New York blown up tonight."

"I'll do my best," she said. She was a game person.

"You have what it takes," he answered gallantly. He got up quietly and slipped out, in the direction away from the bearded Englishman.

XIII

Outside the restaurant Lanny hurried to a near-by telephone booth and put in a call to the F.B.I. To the agent in charge he said: "My name is Lanning Prescott Budd. My father is Robert Budd, president of Budd-Erling Aircraft. I have been doing confidential work for the government, and am speaking on the basis of knowledge so acquired. Tonight, dining in Brown's Chophouse, I recognized a man whom I know to be a German agent. I can't go into details over the phone; he was connected with the flight of Rudolf Hess to Britain, and he is either a top man, or he deals with such. In London he was going by the name of Branscome. My wife is trying to hold him until your men come. Don't arrest him, but trail him and find out where he lives and what he is doing. It may lead to something of first-rate importance."

"O.K., Mr. Budd. We have a station in that neighborhood and should be able to get a couple of men there in a few minutes."

"This Branscome knows me, and I have to keep out of his sight. I will wait outside the restaurant, a little west of the entrance. I am wearing a panama hat with a black band. I will set it back on my head a little."

"Very good, Mr. Budd. Thanks a million. Will you drop in and see us in the morning?"

Lanny promised, and then hung up and hurried back to the restaurant. He was wise to the ways of the world and knew that establishments which aim at respectability do not relish having ladies "pick up" gentlemen at their meals; they might well invite such a lady to leave. Lanny put a dollar into the doorman's hand and instructed him to inform the head waiter that a gentleman outside wanted to speak to him about an urgent matter. To the head waiter Lanny quickly explained the situation and added: "It is possible that the F.B.I. may lose this man, so take a good look at him, and if you see him again, call the F.B.I. at once. He may be the most dangerous of enemies."

Lanny took up his post at one side, watching the restaurant door, prepared to turn away quickly if the suspect should emerge. After what seemed a long time but was less than a quarter of an hour, a young man who looked as if he had just come out of college approached him and said: "My name is Tulliver." Lanny replied: "Mine is Budd." The man flashed his badge, and Lanny described Branscome, also his wife, and told of the arrangements he had made. "I have told the head waiter the situation, and if you give him the high sign he will place you so that you can study this man."

"Very good, sir. There should be another man here any minute. Tell him how this man looks and tell him to wait here. Five minutes should be time enough for me to get the man fixed in mind; then you can come in and signal to your wife."

Lanny waited. Presently another man arrived, slightly older but equally dapper. Lanny told the story again, and after another while went into the restaurant. His wife was engaged in a vivacious conversation with the blond-bearded Englishman. Keeping as far away from them as he could, Lanny made his way to the men's room and stood in the doorway until Laurel's eyes met his; then he drew back into the room and stayed there for a considerable interval. When he took another peek he saw that Laurel was gone, Mr. Branscome was gone, and Mr. Tulliver was gone.

In a minute or two Laurel emerged from the women's room. She was flushed and excited, and didn't want any more dinner. She wanted to get out into the fresh air and away from a place where she had been making herself conspicuous, something most painful to ladies of her upbringing. She went outside to make sure the coast was clear. Meanwhile Lanny paid his bill and thanked the head waiter, warning him not to talk about the matter. The man said: "That party has been here several times before. I'll know him if he comes again."

XIV

Outside, there was nothing to be seen of either the man or his "shadows." Lanny took his wife to his car, and when they were under way she could at last relax. "I never did anything like that in all my life before!" she exclaimed; and Lanny had to stop his chuckling and assure her with all seriousness that he accepted her word on the point.

"Tell me all that happened," he said; "it may give us some clue."

She told him that Branscome was a man of education, and what she would have considered a gentleman if she had met him under normal circumstances. He had moved over to her table at once and showed himself ready to play the gallant. Laurel had exercised upon him those arts of pleasing which every lady in Baltimore acquires as second nature. He had ordered a bottle of wine and had pressed her to drink; he had asked her name and address and other questions about herself. She had stated that she was an actress out of employment at the moment, giving the names of a couple of plays in which she had had minor roles. "I don't know whether he believed me or not. He told me he was here with a mission from the British government. Do you suppose that could be true?"

"It might be, of course. A traitor may be deceiving his own government; he could hardly get here otherwise in wartime. I promised the F.B.I. man to come down in the morning and tell them what I know about him. They may never tell me what they learn—they don't do any superfluous talking. I'm not supposed to talk either, but I will tell you this much: when I met that man in London he had received a message from Rudolf Hess concerning Hess's intention to fly to Britain, and he was sending an answer back."

"Are you sure he's the right man, Lanny?"

"I only had a brief talk with him, but I made note of him for future reference. He has grown whiskers, but his eyes haven't changed. He was extremely nervous when he met me, and I suspected that he had been drinking, perhaps to keep his courage up. I suppose that with you he was at ease."

"He was greatly disappointed when I told him that I had made a mistake, that he was not the gentleman I had met. He said: 'You have met me now, so it's all right.' I had a hard time extricating myself. I told him that I had become frightened; that my husband might come back and that he was a very violent man."

"You did all right," the husband assured her. "If you weren't so worth-while a writer, I would introduce you to Colonel Donovan and let you take up a career with his organization."

"God forbid!" exclaimed the lady from Baltimore. "I am so exhausted from the strain of it, I believe I'd rather serve in the infantry!"

8

Much Depends on Dinner

I

IN THE morning Lanny went down to the offices of the Federal Bureau of Investigation and told them what he knew about the Englishman called Branscome. They revealed to him that they had followed the man to his apartment, and would keep after him and do a thorough job. They said also that they would get in touch with the British; so Lanny knew that they would learn that he himself had been blacklisted by the British because of his dealings with the Nazis. He told them to call the President's man, Baker, who would give him an O.K. They assured him that they were not unfamiliar with complications of this sort.

When the P.A. got back to his home there was a call for him from Washington, and when he called back he was told that he was invited to dinner at the White House that evening: "Seven-thirty, black tie." He answered that he would be on hand. His white evening jacket was hanging in his closet, freshly laundered, and now it was taken down and laid in a suitcase, all by itself. While he ate his lunch he told Laurel what the F.B.I. men had said; then he packed his bags, kissed her good-by, and went down to his car. Laurel herself would doubtless have been invited, but she had told the "First Lady" that she did not care to attend evening affairs in her present condition.

Across the park to the highway that runs alongside the Hudson, then by the tunnel which runs under the great river, then by the Skyway to Newark—that is the fast route out of the crowded metropolis. Highway Number 1 was crowded with wartime traffic; great heavy trucks loaded with oil, with pipe, with lumber, or mysterious crated boxes, were bringing supplies to the factories and taking finished products to the ports. Newark and Trenton and Philadelphia and Baltimore—Lanny was familiar with these cities and their fast-growing suburbs. He was a careful driver and enjoyed few things more. He watched the speedometer and the clock on his dashboard, and knew where he was and how long it would take him.

A room had been engaged, and he had time to bathe and put on his light-weight black trousers and cool white jacket. He took a taxi to the White House, so as not to be bothered with the problem of parking his car. When he told the driver "Pennsylvania entrance," he reflected that it was the first time that he had approached by that customary door. Since taxis were not admitted to the grounds in wartime, he got out by the curb. Soldiers with fixed bayonets were walking post in front of the fence that encircles the grounds. Inside the gate was a wooden sentry box, and in front of it stood a young Navy officer with a tommy gun over his arm. A second officer appeared as the visitor approached the gate.

"Good evening," said the visitor. "My name is Lanning Prescott. I am invited for dinner." They gave him a long look, then one of them said: "Proceed."

He walked up the curving drive to the portico of the mansion, where two Secret Service men stepped out from behind the tall columns and closed together in front of him. They were burly, tough-looking customers, with straw hats pulled low over their eyes. Lanny felt a bit uncomfortable, but said "Good evening" again. He could guess they had telephone connection with the gate, so he kept on coming and they kept on looking him over. Only when he was almost close enough to touch them did they step aside, and one signed for him to enter. Lanny knew that protecting the President's life was a Secret Service job both in war and peace, and he wished them success. He didn't think they were strict enough in his case.

II

The door was opened by a uniformed elderly Negro. He bowed slightly and said: "Good evening, sir," in a low, liquid voice. Lanny found himself in a spacious and brilliantly lighted hall, with many doors, a staircase, and several irregular rows of portraits and historical scenes on the walls. Another uniformed servant took his hat. Then came a slender man in formal attire, who announced himself as the chief usher. "Mr. Prescott" gave his name, and this official consulted a cardboard which he carried under his arm. "You will sit at Mrs. Adamic's right," he said. Lanny, who was used to these formal affairs, replied: "Thank you. I will remember."

He was escorted to a reception room and introduced to other guests:

a Mr. Robinson, tall and sunburned, a cousin of the "First Lady," as he learned later; two pretty girls of eighteen or twenty whose names he didn't get—they were English by their accent; finally a couple, Mr. and Mrs. Louis Adamic. Lanny recognized the name and knew the man as a writer, of Yugoslav descent, much interested in the problems of the foreign-born in his adopted country. He was about Lanny's age, and as tall, with thinning hair, gentle features, and a quiet voice. Lanny would have liked to talk to him, but circumstances did not permit. The two girls were worried because they were not wearing long dresses—they had been invited at the last moment and told to come as they were. Mr. Robinson was worried because the Allies were doing so badly in the war; he had just arrived from Peru and had got the full impact from the papers. How could it be that the Germans were able to have their way in the Crimea and North Africa, and the Japs all over the eastern world?

The usher appeared again and led them to a small elevator which took them to the second floor. Just as they emerged, Mrs. Roosevelt appeared from a door in the corridor. She wore a light blue gown in which Lanny thought she looked especially impressive; the upswept hairdress and long gown made her appear even taller than she was. She looked well and strong, but sad and harassed when her face was in repose. Now she was smiling, and stretched out her two hands to her women guests.

The English girls, having been the last to enter the elevator, were the first to emerge. She greeted them as friends of the family and motioned them to enter the Lincoln room. Then came her cousin; she revealed her affection for him and commented upon his sunburn acquired in high altitudes. Then came the Adamics—Lanny having lagged behind out of politeness. Mrs. Adamic, a tiny person, was enfolded in one of the First Lady's arms; the author's wife had just been told that she was to sit at the President's right hand, which could be expected to scare her. Then it was Lanny's turn, and the hostess shook hands with him warmly. "How do you do, Mr. Prescott?" she said distinctly, to let him know that she had been told and was not going to forget.

III

The Lincoln room contains fine old period pieces and chintz-covered armchairs; there are cheerful green-and-yellow drapes, and too many pictures and prints crowded onto its walls. Lanny had heard the tradition that sometimes late at night the residents of this mansion hear footsteps and see a very tall man clad in a long black frock coat. Certainly they could not be the steps of the present master of the household, who was taken everywhere about the building in a wheel chair. At present he was discovered seated at a desk halfway down the long wall of the room, amusing himself with a cocktail shaker, a bowl of crushed ice, and several bottles with fancy labels. If he had any worry about the state of the world, he wasn't going to let his wife's cousin see it. "Hello, Monroe," he called, and held out a firm strong hand. His face was ruddy and his close-set gray eyes flashed with a zest of living that infected everybody who came near him. When anything was going on he watched with his head cocked, ready for a bit of fun or a chance to start it ahead of the next fellow. He wore a well-fitted dinner jacket, soft white shirt, and natty black bow tie; his long broad-shouldered torso and powerful arms were so active that you lost all thought of his disability.

Mrs. Roosevelt brought up the other guests and introduced them, and he shook hands with each and had a friendly word. To Lanny he said: "Glad to see you, Prescott," putting emphasis on the name and grinning at the same time, a sort of half wink in his eyes. At this moment the President's little black Scottie appeared from somewhere and began sniffing at the visitor's shoes and the cuffs of his trousers; then, seeming satisfied, he sat back on his haunches. "You pass," said Roosevelt, laughing. "Do you have a dog?"

"My mother has too many at her home on the Riviera," Lanny replied. "You cannot give them away in wartime."

"For fear that someone might eat them?" And then, addressing the circle of guests: "Fala has been getting a very good press—much better than I. But nearly everybody misspells his name."

"It is an unusual name," remarked Mrs. Adamic.

The President reached down to pat the little dog's head. "One of my Scottish ancestors, away back, was Murray, the Outlaw of Fala Hill. No doubt he had a dog who thought his master was a great man."

Lanny thought: This is how he keeps sane in an insane world; calm in the dead center of a tornado. Even Cousin Monroe would have to put aside his worries and at least pretend to enjoy social life. It was as if the head of the state were saying: "I know things that you don't know. Trust me, as Fala does."

The President passed out the cocktails, one by one, then lifted his glass as a salutation to his guests and took a sip. "Orange Blossom," he said, and savored it. Mrs. Roosevelt set her glass down and went about with a tray of *hors d'oeuvres*. Lanny, knowing the customs of Europe, reflected that there a liveried servant, not the hostess, would have performed such a duty. The guests began drawing up chairs in a semi-circle in front of the host. There was a large armchair, and Lanny moved that, intending it for Mrs. Roosevelt; but when she saw his gesture, she said: "We will save that for the Prime Minister."

Lanny had been wondering if Churchill was coming to this affair. There hadn't been a line in the newspapers about his presence in Washington; it was a war secret. All the reporters must have known it, and the burden must have weighed heavily upon them. Later in the evening F.D.R. repeated, with one of his infectious grins, the remark which one of his secretaries had made at a press conference that day: "I am carrying two battleships around, one in each of my side pockets." He meant, of course, the President and the Prime Minister.

Roosevelt started talking and all the others listened. He wanted to know how Adamic's latest book had sold. Lanny hadn't read it, but gathered now that it was a proposal that immigrants and sons of immigrants in America should be used to help restore or set up democratic institutions in each of the Nazi-conquered lands; that a carefully selected and trained commission should be sent to each of these lands to give them material aid and political guidance. The President didn't say what he thought of the idea.

Said Mrs. Roosevelt: "It will interest you to know that the Prime Minister has had the book in his room four or five days."

The author's sunburned cheeks were flushed with pleasure. "I'd give anything to hear his reaction," he said.

"So would we," replied the First Lady with a laugh. "The President told Mr. Churchill he might not like the last part; so, no doubt, he read the last part first." For the benefit of the other guests she explained that the book concluded with an imaginary discussion between John Bull and Uncle Sam on board an American cruiser anchored in the fog off Iceland on a midsummer's day of the previous year. To Churchill that would mean himself and the President of the United States at the time they had agreed upon the Atlantic Charter; and naturally Adamic, an American liberal, not to say radical, had given the British Tory the worst of the discussion. "I am afraid he won't like it," said the author, in the tone of a man who has committed a faux pas. His hostess lifted her hands in a gesture which was equivalent to: "What can we do about that?"

IV

The company was seated; the President was tossing popcorn into his mouth; Fala was snoozing. Lanny was taking note of the technique whereby a shrewd and determined woman exercised influence upon public affairs. She had read a book which presented a program for democratizing Europe; she had had the same idea that her husband had expressed to his P.A., that the powerful and busy gentleman who governed the British Empire wouldn't read a book but could be made to listen to conversation; so she had invited the author and his wife to Washington and had added a couple of pretty English girls to "balance the table."

Lanny understood that this was no time for him to show off any of his social gifts; he was there to listen and learn how his country was being governed in this time of world crisis. He had been promised a talk with the Duke of Marlborough's descendant later in the evening— while the President of the United States was trying to get his beauty sleep!

Mrs. Roosevelt arose suddenly from her chair and hastened to the door. Here came John Bull himself, and she held out her hand and greeted him formally, respectfully: "Good evening, Mr. Prime Minister." The answer came in a close-lipped voice: "Good evening, Mrs. Roosevelt." The speaker held a fat, freshly lighted cigar in front of him, as if he were making sure that no evil should befall it.

Five years had passed since Lanny had met the Right Honourable Winston Spencer Churchill, who had grown even stouter in those years. He had a rotund dumpy figure with short, slight arms and legs, rather narrow in the shoulders; mostly girth, chest, and head; no neck. He had a pink-and-white baby face and light blue eyes. He advanced into the room with what seemed a semi-scowl on his face; he moved as though he were without joints, all of a piece; solid, unhurried, impervious to obstacles, like a tank or a bulldozer. Behind him came his personal secretary, a slight pale young man named Martin.

"Hello, Winston!" cried F.D.R., and extended his hand dramatically. The reply came through barely moving lips: "Good evening, Mr. President." It was the first time Lanny had heard them address each other—and what a world of information was in those greetings! Two civilizations meeting and establishing their agreements, but also their disagreements, once and for always! Lanny could imagine that at their first meeting the American had spoken first and had said in effect: "I call you by your first name because that is the American custom." To that the Englishman had replied in effect: "I address you by your title, because that is the English custom." Having begun that way, neither could yield with good grace. Having once said "Winston," F.D.R. couldn't very well take to saying "Prime Minister." On the other hand, for the Prime Minister to have said "Franklin" would have been a capitulation, and that was not his nature. So, in spite of all temptations to belong to other nations, he remained an Englishman!

For a longish moment these two gazed at each other, at once knowingly and quizzically. The President's expression mixed amusement and concern; the Prime Minister's large round phiz was perfectly smooth, and oh, so innocent!—except for the eyes which were shrewd and the mouth which was determined. The newspapers were making much of the fact that these men were friends; but they were not merely two human beings, they were two parties, two nations, and there were tensions between them.

No one knew this better than Lanny Budd, alias Prescott. Winston Churchill had adjusted himself to democracy in his own country, but he didn't want any of it in international affairs; he certainly wouldn't consider it a substitute for the divide-and-rule policy of the British Empire, politely known as the "Balance of Power" on the Continent of Europe. And here was a woman, as determined as he, scheming to force him to read a book and meet an author who was some sort of Pink and perhaps a Red—the Almighty alone could tell the difference. Had he and Roosevelt been arguing that day about it? Had they been at a deadlock over it ever since the two "battleships" had met? Was the democrat presuming to remind the imperialist who it was that had the money and was dispensing the lend-lease?

The democratic man put on one of those smiles which were at once sincere and an act. "Had a good nap, Winston?" he inquired. And at this perhaps undignified revelation the Prime Minister appeared to pout. He stuck his cigar into his mouth and mumbled something which Lanny couldn't catch although there was dead silence in the room except for that one sound.

V

The V.I.P.—Very Important Person—received his cocktail from the hand of his host; then he sat down in the armchair. Lanny was amused to notice that it had been contrived for the author of *Two-Way Pas-*

sage to be next to him. "Mr. Prime Minister," said the contriver, "Mr. Adamic is the author of the book I gave you."

"Yes, yes," was the reply, rather abruptly given. "I am reading it." But he didn't say what he thought of it. He deliberately dodged the subject by pulling from his pocket a letter from his wife. "She thanks you for your gift," he said to Mrs. Roosevelt, and put on his spectacles and read a paragraph. Then he added: "I have no words to express my appreciation of all the gifts that were sent to me the last time I was here. Someone sent me a corncob pipe!" He put the cigar in his mouth and made it glow.

"I get several every year," declared F.D.R.

"Are yours worm-eaten, too?" inquired Churchill.

The President grinned and offered him another "Orange Blossom," but Churchill declined. Meantime Mrs. Roosevelt took a tiny sausage impaled on a toothpick and held it up before Fala, who eagerly did his stunt of rolling over, and then sat up to get his reward. "Good boy, Fala!" said the President, and the little dog came and plopped down at his feet.

A butler appeared in the doorway, and the hostess rose. The others all followed suit, and in the momentary diversion the President quickly slid himself from his chair to his wheel chair. His wife wheeled him out to the hall and to the elevator, the ladies following her and the men following the ladies. Churchill and Adamic were last, and Lanny ventured to linger with them, for he was curious about the little drama.

Adamic said very politely: "It is a privilege to meet you, Mr. Prime Minister."

The reply was: "I am readin' your book. I find it int'restin' "—a strong accent on the first syllable of that word.

"Thank you, sir. How far have you got into it?"

"About halfway. Do you really think there is a problem there?"

"I do, sir. Unless we succeed in mustering our American idealism and putting it to work. . . ."

That was as far as this discourse got. They had come to the elevator, and the President, inside, was waiting. "Come on in, Winston," he called. "The rest of you boys walk down." On the way Lanny said to the author: "It looks as if he's not going to be drawn out." Adamic replied: "I am afraid so."

When they arrived at the lower floor a uniformed servant was wheeling the President into the dining-room. The First Lady paused and called the attention of the guests to a painting, and so, when they entered the room, the President had already been transferred to his high-backed chair at the large oval table. Lanny observed these deft proceedings; it was important that guests should be spared reminders of his physical handicaps, for the preservation both of his own dignity and the cheerfulness of the guests.

The table had as its centerpiece a silver bowl filled with roses, shining directly under the chandelier. The service began at once: a consommé, broiled fish, roast chicken, a salad, an English trifle, and a demitasse served at the table. Lanny had been placed between Mrs. Adamic and Mrs. Roosevelt's secretary; he understood that it was better for him to be inconspicuous, and he was glad to listen to what the great and famous had to say.

VI

The President of the United States rubbed his hands, grinned, and, looking over the centerpiece at his wife, remarked: "Well, we had a good day today."

"Indeed, Franklin?"

"I had a fine press conference. Our newsmen are pleased because I have combined all our information and publicity services into one organization and put Elmer Davis at the head."

Lanny was familiar with the voice of Elmer Davis, but it hadn't reached Cousin Monroe in Peru. He asked who this person was, and the President explained that he was a radio commentator so highly respected by his colleagues and by newspapermen that he would be able to put a stop to the bickering that had been going on among the various unco-ordinated bureaus. Having said this, F.D.R. beamed and took a spoonful of his consommé. Lanny thought: How much like Robbie, coming home in the evening and telling the family and guests what he had done that day, and what excellent judgment he had displayed!

"I hope you are not too optimistic," said the wife. "I am afraid he will find he has taken a very hot seat." Lanny said to himself: That might be Esther!

"Of course, the old crowd will fight him," replied the husband. "There are many who are afraid of having the government acquire any means of getting news to the public—and especially any ideas." Then, looking across the table: "Don't you find the same thing, Winston?"

"You forget," growled the Prime Minister, "that our government owns the B.B.C. and has from the beginning. We are far from being as reactionary as some people imagine." He went back to scooping up his consommé. Behind him was the concentrated knowledge which a statesman of Britain had acquired through a lifetime of observation and experience. He knew his half of the planet; and at present it was keeping him so busy that he had no time to bother with the other half. He sat calmly sure that he was wiser and more mature than anybody else in this room.

Perhaps the host felt the need of livening up the party; or perhaps he was tired and wanted to keep himself entertained. "Our enemies have got a new one on us," he announced. "They delight to keep track of the proliferating of our bureaucracy. At the press conference I was asked if it is true that we have a 'Biscuit, Cracker, and Pretzel Sub-committee of the Baking Industry of the Division of Industrial Operations of the War Production Board.'"

Everybody laughed, and someone asked: "What did you say, Mr. President?"

"I said I didn't know, but I hoped so, because I was very fond of biscuits, crackers, and pretzels."

"You get a lot of fun out of your job, Mr. President," remarked the author's bright little wife, having evidently made up her mind not to be scared.

"I take the fun as it comes. One of our O.P.A. men told me a good story this afternoon. It seems that somebody prepared a nine-page typewritten order on the subject of cotton duck, and it was passed around among the officials who had to do with it, prior to its being mimeographed and sent out to the industry. Each official had to sign it, and eight or ten did so before the discovery was made that it wasn't all about cotton duck—somebody had inserted a paragraph about Donald Duck!"

They all had another good laugh; and then the President, enjoying himself hugely, looked across the table at John Bull and said: "By the way, before I forget. Someone has sent me a painting of you. It's on my desk in the office; don't let me forget to show it to you. The man is a Canadian; Vancouver, I believe. He admits that he has never seen you, but I think he's got a pretty good likeness—except that he's given you a little more hair than you actually have."

The Prime Minister of Great Britain rubbed a gentle hand over his sparsely covered pate and grinned a little ruefully at his lack of immunity to the ravages of time. "Perhaps I have lost some since the painter started."

"There's a new portrait of me, too. Have you had a chance to take a look at it?"

"Which one, Mr. President?"

"Now see here, Winston! There are not so many portraits of me. There's a curious story about the one I refer to. The painter has a considerable reputation in his own country, which is not one of the lesser parts of the Western hemisphere. His country's ambassador requested three sittings, and I gave two of them, but then the Secret Service forbade me to sit any more for him. It turned out that the man was a two-time spy, working for a faction of his country's government and for the Germans at the same time!"

Everybody gasped; and F.D.R., waiting for the next course of his dinner, lighted a cigarette and waved it in the long holder, as if to say that he was still alive and it was all in a presidential day's work.

"What did the man do then?" inquired the Prime Minister.

"He finished the portrait without me, and it's quite good. I'm supposed to be making a fireside chat. The fireside is not shown, but one side of my face is flaming red. I thought I'd entitle the picture 'Roosevelt in Hell,' and offer it to somebody who might like to have me that way."

"Until recently the Wall Street boys would have been delighted to have it," remarked Churchill, and there was a gust of laughter.

VII

The situation which these statesmen confronted at this hour was perhaps the worst in the history of their countries. There had been a veritable deluge of bad news in the last few days. General Rommel had taken Tobruk, with more than twenty-five thousand British prisoners; his forces had advanced a hundred miles into Egypt, and the peril to Alexandria and the Suez Canal was extreme. The outer defenses of Sevastopol had been pierced. The submarines were sinking ships all up and down the Atlantic coast, a situation which could not be hidden by the strictest censors. At the same time the Japanese had taken nearly all of Burma and were threatening Calcutta and Ceylon; they had taken Kiska in the Aleutians and had shelled Vancouver and a point on the Oregon coast.

The President's cousin by marriage was worried about all these things and brought them up in the midst of a dinner party. F.D.R. refused to abate his cheerfulness, but said that measures were being taken and preparations being made. "We can't expect to make much of a showing as yet; but our boys in the air have shown the Japs what is in store for them. You perhaps don't realize the full significance of the victories we have won in the Coral Sea and at Midway."

"It has been hard for me to realize anything from so far away, Franklin."

"Well, we have shown the definite superiority of our carrier forces; and be sure that we are going to have plenty of them. The enemy is taking territory which he will not be able to hold."

The watchful hostess intervened. "Tell Franklin what you have observed of democracy in South America."

"I have heard much talk about it," was the dry reply.

The President took up the conversation: "I was down there and visited Vargas in Brazil. Wonderful people—they gave me a grand reception. In this country, when we make a to-do over a visitor, we throw confetti and ticker tape and torn telephone books. In South America they throw flowers, tons of them; roses, carnations, even orchids. Vargas met me at the quay in Rio and we got into an open car and drove through the city. For miles the streets were lined with people, and the windows and balconies were full—everybody throwing flowers and shouting *'Viva la democracia! Viva Roosevelt!'* as though the two were synonymous."

"Friend of the underdog!" rumbled Churchill.

Laughing, the other continued: "As we rode along, Vargas leaned over to me and said: 'Perhaps you have heard that I am a dictator.' I leaned over to him and said: 'Perhaps you have heard that *I* am one, too.'" Everybody laughed again, and then F.D.R. continued: "Vargas said to me: 'But I really *am.*'" There was another laugh, in which the narrator joined.

Said Adamic: "I recall that in your last re-election campaign you used that phrase *'Viva la democracia!'*"

"Yes," replied the President. "Those are about the only Spanish words I know. In Rio, of course, they were supposed to be Portuguese."

"In your Columbus Day speech," put in the author, "they were supposed to be Italian."

"I hope I did not mispronounce them," remarked the President, again joining in the laughter.

VIII

Did the First Lady make up her mind that this dinner party had given enough time to wisecracks and anecdotes? The main course had been served, which meant that the affair was half over; suddenly she remarked to her husband: "You know, Franklin, I am taking our guests to a concert, so we won't have time for a chat with you. I want you not to fail to talk to Mr. Adamic."

Never did the President fail to follow a lead from his wife. "By all means," he responded cordially. "I think it is important that people from overseas should understand that America is an amalgam of a great number of races and nations. Because we speak English and have so many Anglo-Saxon features in our culture, our British friends are apt to forget how many non-British people we have, and what an important part they play in our political and international decisions." The President was looking across the table as he spoke, and everyone at the table was listening to him. "It is a painful fact that distrust and dislike of the British Empire have been in our national tradition since the Revolution and the War of 1812; later there has been the Boer War, and India. Despite our intense admiration for a great statesman personally, these feelings remain, and anyone in our public life must reckon with them."

It was a little sermon, directed at the Right Honourable Winston Spencer Churchill, who sat as silent as a sphinx, holding a big cigar and looking at the long ash at the end.

"You, Mr. Adamic," continued the preacher, "remind us in your books that these foreign peoples, too, have their traditions, whether they are Yugoslavs or Irish, Germans or Italians, or Jews unhappy about what is happening to their fellows. The feelings of these people and of many old-time Americans about the British Empire may not seem very intelligent to the British, but they are natural enough, and justified from our different angles. The fact that they exist makes for all sorts of difficulties—all sorts—all sorts of—"

Had the President intended to go into details, and then thought better of it? He smiled suddenly and said: "I am English myself, but also I am Scotch and Dutch. That combination makes for a good bargainer." He was looking directly at his house guest. "I remember well," continued F.D.R., "when I was a boy of seven or so my mother took me to England, and I saw Queen Victoria being driven down the street, and I was quite sure that I disliked her greatly."

That was rather rubbing it in, and Lanny could only wonder what arguments had been going on and what tensions developing in the conferences between these two strong-willed men. Certain it was that the First Lady knew about them and was supporting her husband by bringing to Washington a writer who had put emphasis upon the non-Anglo-Saxon elements of the American community. She had tried to get the head of the Conservative party of Great Britain to read a book which said in substance that the peoples of Central Europe wanted democracy and not any kings; but Churchill, in the slang of his own land, "wasn't having any"! What a difference, Lanny thought, between him and the genial, overflowing conversationalist of five years ago! Also, Lanny wasn't forgetting that he was the man who had saved England and the world in 1940–41. Give him full credit.

IX

Mrs. Roosevelt spoke a few words to the butler, and the dessert and coffee were served quickly. "We must not be late for the concert," she said, "I dislike that because it makes people stare so." When she rose the others followed suit, and they went out into the hall, leaving the President to be transferred to his wheel chair. While they were saying their farewells, Lanny stood near Churchill, listening, while Adamic attempted to say a few words about Yugoslav affairs. The Prime Minister still wouldn't have it; he hadn't relished this dinner, and his disdain for a "Pinko" author was apparent in his face and in his grumbled words. To be sure, he was a guest in this household and had no right to be rude to any other guest; but he didn't have to talk unless he felt like it, and he played the role of his ancestor, the haughty duke.

As Adamic turned away, Lanny followed, and caught a glimpse of the President being wheeled to the elevator. It was as if a different man had been put into the chair. Gone was all the bonhomie, the laughter; his face was drawn and lined with care, perhaps with grief for the ten or twelve million boys whom he was getting ready to send into the inferno of war. Lanny remembered some history and knew that it was just so the tender-hearted Lincoln had grieved in these same rooms eighty years ago. That had been another black time for the Union; and the tall ungainly railsplitter from the West had done just what the Squire of Krum Elbow was doing—trying to keep himself cheerful by hearing and repeating funny stories.

Now the President's wife and her guests were going off to enjoy fine music, but there would be no such respite for the Chief. He was going up to his room to engage in a wrestling match with a stubborn British Tory, a match which might decide the future of the world for a long time to come. Lanny knew enough about the situation to be able to guess what the topics would be: Palestine and Egypt, India and Hongkong, the Ruhr and the Dardanelles, and what kind of government should be had by Yugoslavia and Rumania and Hungary and Bulgaria and Greece and Italy and Spain.

The guests and secretaries were to be driven to the concert in two limousines. In the first of these Mrs. Roosevelt sat in the back seat with Mrs. Adamic, while the author and the cousin sat in the two movable seats, facing the ladies. The obscure Mr. Prescott sat beside the chauffeur, and that suited him, because he didn't want to talk but to listen. Doing so, he discovered that his guesses about the evening's events had been correct.

Said Mrs. Roosevelt to the Adamics: "I can't tell you how grateful we are that you two came tonight. The President has been having considerable difficulty in getting the Prime Minister to grasp what kind of country we are. I've tried to help out. I talked with Mr. Churchill yesterday and again this afternoon. I explained that many of our Americans have strong ties with the countries from which they came, or from which their parents came. The Prime Minister was somewhat impatient, as I am afraid I was with him. He said he understood, but I don't think he does. Not *really*."

X

When they were getting out of the car the hostess said to Lanny: "You understand that I am taking you back to the White House after the concert." He thanked her and followed the rest of the party into the hall. It was a hot night, so although the hall was not very large, it was only partly filled. Lanny saw by the program that there were several performers, and he could guess what had happened—this kindhearted lady had been persuaded to further the careers of a group of aspiring young musicians. The first, a violinist, played the Mendelssohn concerto, and that is always pleasant to hear, even though it was not as well played as Lanny was accustomed to hear it from his brother-in-law Hansi Robin. The second artist, a young lady, played a Chopin étude, and Lanny thought that he could have done almost as well himself; so he took the liberty of losing himself in thought about what he was going to say to the Prime Minister of Great Britain.

Very certainly he wasn't going to take up the task of turning a rock-ribbed Tory into any sort of "friend of the underdog." No, indeed; it would be better to go back to his ivory-tower attitude and give the Duke of Marlborough's descendant to understand that the son of Budd-Erling was helping Roosevelt as an American patriot and not as any sort of New Dealer. Churchill would approve that, and Lanny would get what he wanted on that basis. He was invited, not as an adviser on policies, but as an expert on France and Germany, and especially, at this moment, on North Africa.

After the concert the other guests were delivered to their hotels, and then Lanny and the First Lady were taken back to the White House. With them rode a well-known columnist whom they had just met in the lobby; he was going in the same direction, and while they were driving he told a story which was going the rounds of Washington. It had to do with Churchill's previous visit. The President had then brought up the subject of Hongkong and the necessity of returning it to the Chinese. John Bull had declared: "You have nothing to do with Hongkong! I won't talk about Hongkong!" He wouldn't talk, but he had to listen, and the President had climaxed his efforts by saying: "Very well then, if you won't take my advice, I'm going to have to go over your head and appeal to the King."

That of course was a most horrible thing. The Prime Minister fairly shouted: "The King has nothing to say about the matter!"

"Maybe not, Winston," the tormentor continued, "but I am going to take a chance on it. I shall write him a letter, something like this: 'Dear King: Your Prime Minister is so stubborn that he will not listen to reason, so I am venturing to point out to you personally that we must have the continued help of our valiant and long-suffering allies, the Chinese people, and that they are in danger of falling into despair and giving up to their Japanese conquerors. I suggest that the way to hearten them is to make clear that in the peace settlement they will have all their territories returned to them, no matter by whom the territories are held.' Don't you think the King might be interested to read such a letter?"

"He would know that it would be unconstitutional for him to do so."

"At the same time I would write to Chiang Kai-shek, saying: 'I enclose a copy of the letter I am sending to the King of England, and I suggest that you might write him in return, assuring him that if Hongkong is returned to the Chinese people, their government will show its gratitude by guaranteeing to the British all trade rights and privileges which they have enjoyed in the past."

Such was the story. It was received with laughter, and then the columnist revealed why he had told it. Turning to the First Lady, he inquired: "Can you tell me if that really happened, Mrs. Roosevelt?"

Lanny, listening attentively, made note of social training in operation. With her most friendly smile the First Lady replied: "I was not there."

Inside the White House, Lanny had a few minutes with his hostess. All that evening he had been listening, saying very little, and now, with her customary graciousness, she asked his reaction to the principal topic of discussion. He told her: "I have an interest in Central Europe and its problems because I have visited Silesia, Poland, and Austria. The Germans, by a carefully thought-out policy, have integrated the whole industrial system of that region with their own, making it impossible for anyone to replace conditions as they were before the war. It seems to me that it would be folly to try. The thing to do is to turn the system into one public-service corporation under international control, and put it to work to restore the ruined cities and serve the welfare of all the people in that region."

"But what about the national boundaries, Mr. Budd?"

"The great cartels of Europe have shown us that boundaries need not interfere with the production and exchange of goods. The French and the German steel masters got along together before Hitler, and will do so again. Why cannot the consuming public do the same?"

Late as the hour was, the First Lady sat down to ask questions about that idea; and when she excused herself she said: "I will talk to the President about that. It is a service I am able to render—to bring him ideas which seem likely to be helpful."

XI

Left to his own devices, Lanny wandered about the ground-floor rooms, examining the many portraits which hung upon the walls. They were more interesting to him as a student of history than as an art expert. Having taken government by popular consent as his religion, he was concerned to see what sort of men the people of his fatherland had chosen as their guides and counselors. He stood in front of each, trying to recall what he had read about that statesman, and asking him mentally what advice he now had to give to the Republic, standing at bay against its foes on all the continents and all the seas of the world.

Well after midnight an usher came and escorted the patient guest to the second floor of the mansion, to the Prime Minister's room. He tapped, then opened the door, and found himself in the presence of the pale young secretary, Mr. Martin. "The Prime Minister is having a shower," said that functionary. "He will be out very soon."

Lanny had started looking at more portraits when the door of the bathroom was thrown open and there emerged what he found an extraordinary spectacle—the governing head of the British Empire, clad in the costume he had worn at the moment of his emergence upon earth and nothing else, not even a towel. Lanny had thought he looked like a large cherub in evening dress, and assuredly he looked still more like it when stark naked. His skin was white, slightly tinged with pink, and his flesh formed immense folds.

He didn't show any sign of embarrassment, but said a casual "Hello," and then to his secretary: "You may go to bed, Martin." The young man said: "Good night, sir," and departed, and Churchill addressed his visitor: "Take off your coat and make yourself as comfortable as you can in this damnable climate. Will you have a drink?"

"No, thanks," said Lanny. He took off his coat gladly.

"Make yourself at home," said the host. He had his own way of saying the last words—"a-tome." "I suppose a man can get used to this muggy weather, but I thank God I don't have to."

"You forget that I have recently come from Algiers."

"Oh, yes. I suppose that is worse. Well, Budd, I trust we don't have to go on with the 'Prescott' business while we are alone."

"I doubt that there are any dictaphones, Mr. Prime Minister."

The great man let his globular form down into a soft chair and remarked: "Let me see, how long since we had our talks at Maxine Elliott's house?"

"Five years and several months. You may not remember, but you were quite positive that you had been laid on the political shelf to stay."

"Yes, yes, to be sure! We seldom foresee what life is going to do with us. Did you?"

"Oh, God! Surely not!"

"The President tells me you have been doing very fine work for him. I congratulate you. Do you mind if I bother you with a lot of questions?"

"Not at all, Mr. Churchill." With Englishmen, you use the title once, and, if you are a social equal, once only.

XII

So began a merciless inquisition which lasted two hours. Churchill knew exactly what he wanted to ask, and it was everything concerning the enemies he was facing. Pétain, Laval, Darlan, Benoist-Méchin, Pierre Pucheu, Fernand de Brinon, Paul Marion, Joseph Barthélemy— he had met them just before the Franco-German armistice, when he had been trying to persuade them to hold out. What were they doing now and what was the state of their minds? And the people in North Africa—Lemaigre-Dubreuil and General Noguès and the rest of the Army crowd. And whether or not those who were in sympathy with the Allies dared reveal it. Lanny was free to tell about the vegetable-oil magnate and about General Béthouart and his group, and what the Arabs had said, and the Jews, and others he had met. He reported, without naming names, that he had friends from the old days who had whispered to him of the spread of the underground movements.

"Surely you don't think they can do anything against the German milit'ry power!" exclaimed the Prime Minister.

"Not at present. But if ever you put an army on those shores, you will find the partisans of great help in cutting communication lines and handicapping the enemy. The job at present is to get them organized and trained; to get the tools to them and teach them the know-how. Our own Army is doing that, and I suppose yours is also."

"Of a certainty; but that is some time in the future." He said it "few-chah," and went on to add that milit'ry hist'ry showed that a hostyle population could inflict much damage upon an invader.

Then he wanted to hear about Hitler and Göring and Hess. Lanny's knowledge was a year old, but even so it might be important, and he had to tell in detail how he had managed to keep the friendship and confidence of these Nazis. The Prime Minister called them "Nah-zies," and didn't care if they didn't like it. Lanny told how he and Hess had experimented with spiritualist mediums and astrologers, and how he had managed to persuade the Number Three Nazi that there was a large group of Englishmen sympathetic to the *Neue Ordnung* and making plans to oust Churchill and put in a Prime Minister willing to work out terms of peace. "Apparently," said the American, "your B4 was playing the same game with Hess."

"Quite so," said the cherub in the overstuffed chair. He had reached for one of his cigars and lighted it, and if there was any spectacle in the world more comical than an immense naked cherub puffing a big dark cigar, the son of Budd-Erling had never beheld it.

"I am told," continued Lanny, "that your B4 wrote letters in the name of Ivone Kirkpatrick and the Duke of Hamilton and others, and that Rudi fell for them completely. The Governor—I mean the President—told me that you gave them a good wigging for it."

There was a gleam in those bright blue eyes. "It was an outrageous violation of the rights of Englishmen."

"But it worked," said Lanny with a grin. "I rather guessed that B4 was paying the Germans off for those two agents of yours who were lured to the Dutch border and kidnaped just after the outbreak of the war. No doubt the Nazis would be glad to swap them for Hess."

The Prime Minister gave a grunt expressive of agreement. "The President tells me you got into a jam with our people over that episode. I'll be glad to straighten it out for you."

"Thank you, sir. You understand, I was under a pledge not to mention my connection with the President; so when your agents questioned me about my dealings with the enemy, I was helpless. They were perfectly right in their judgment that I knew too much."

"Or that you knew too many," chuckled the enemy of all collaborators.

"There is another detail about this Hess matter which may interest you, Mr. Churchill. The man who brought me a message from Hess just a few days before his flight to Scotland came to my London hotel and gave me the name Branscome. I suppose he made that name up for the occasion. Naturally I was interested in him and took a good look so that I'd know him the next time. And it happened. I saw him last night in a restaurant in New York."

"The devil you say! Did you speak to him?"

"I very carefully kept out of his sight and phoned the F.B.I. to get on his trail. This morning I went to see them and told them about the fellow. They've found out where he is staying and are keeping after him."

"Good for you! Your F.B.I. has been extraordinarily successful in preventing sabotage so far. Very capable men, and we give them all the help we can."

XIII

They talked about spies and saboteurs for a while, and then Lanny thought it a good occasion to bring up a subject he had thought of while motoring to Washington. Said he: "There is something I should like to suggest in connection with Hess, Mr. Churchill—if it's not too late in the night."

"By no means. What is it?"

"May I ask, did you get any important information out of him?"

"Not very much. He is a fanatic, and nothing could make him weaken. But we had already got together a pretty good dossier on all those blighters."

"This is what occurred to me: that it might be worth while to let me have a talk with him and see what I could get."

"You really think he would talk to you?"

"He made me his confidant in several important matters; and now he has been a prisoner for more than a year and must be pretty lonely. I can't doubt that he'd be glad to see an old friend."

"But he would know that we would never let you see him unless we were certain that you were against him."

"It would be my idea to frame up a little drama. Let me be taken to him in the middle of the night, in pretended secrecy. I'll tell him that I have bribed the jailer. I think I could get away with that. He knows that my father is a rich man, and he doubtless thinks that I am, too."

"By Jove! That might get us something! What would you give as your purpose in seeing him?"

"I could tell him that I have a message from the Führer. Bear in mind that I have a code that I use with these men. Hitler gave me the name 'Siegfried' to use if I wished to send him a secret message; and I gave Hess the name 'Kurvenal'—you may remember the character in *Tristan* who is called 'the truest of the true.' Imagine that I should have the jailer smuggle in to Hess a bit of tissue paper with the name 'Kurvenal' written on it, rolled, let us say, into a pellet and hidden in a slice of bread. Rudi would be thrown into a state of great excitement and would be ready for a frank talk when I came into his cell, or whatever he sleeps in."

"What would you expect to get from him? All his information is more than a year out of date."

"Even so there might be secrets that have not yet come to light. I have one idea that may sound fantastic, but I keep thinking about it in spite of myself—that I might get some message from Rudi to be delivered to the Führer, and by this device I might have another go in Germany."

"Would you dare try that?"

"The President thinks I should not. He has the idea that because I had an interview with Stalin the Nazis must surely have decided that I am a phony. I agreed with that for a time, but now I'm not so sure. Hitler's Intelligence service is by no means perfect. I have proved that more than once. And if I found that he had learned of my passing through Russia, I believe I could convince him that I had gone there in his interest, to pump Stalin and bring back a report on the possibility of a deal. Hitler made one in 1939, and why might he not consider another in 1942?"

"He'd jolly well be glad to in his present fix!"

"Exactly. Hitler gave me messages to take to the collaborators in Britain and France and America; and what more natural than that I should have been looking for some of the same stripe in Moscow? The Nazis must know of some, and I might find out from Hess who they are. Wouldn't that be worth while?"

"Good God, yes!"

"And that's only one of many possibilities. I am fascinated by the idea of coming to my old friend the Führer with a message from his *fidus Achates.*"

"My information is that Hitler raged at Hess for his folly in taking the flight—plain idiocy."

"I don't doubt that. But he must know perfectly well that no matter how misguided it was, Rudi had no thought but to serve his adored master and protect him from having to fight a war on two fronts. And now if I should come to him with a message from the friend's heart—and possibly with a talisman, or some password that Rudi would give me, something that would convince Hitler I had actually talked with him—wouldn't the Führer's heart be touched? It might even be possible for you to cause a rumor to start, after I had left England, that it had been discovered that I had bribed a jailer and had got in to talk with Hess. I wouldn't want it in the press, but you could find a way to let it become known in one of your prison camps for German officers. You may be sure that the Nazis have some spy lurking on the outside of such camps to pick up stories, and they wouldn't miss that one."

"Look here, Budd," said the Prime Minister. "Is this the scenario of a cinema you are telling me?"

The P.A. replied: "The whole war is the scenario of a cinema, Mr. Churchill. My guess is that it will furnish plots for many thousands of them before mankind loses interest in these events. And be sure that you will be in them."

"Get out!" exclaimed the pink-and-white cherub. "None of your treacle!" Then, as Lanny took the advice seriously and got up, he held out his hand and said cordially: "Come and see me when you find yourself in London. I'll think all this over in the meantime."

9

Treasons, Stratagems, and Spoils

I

FOR the first time Lanny exercised the privilege of calling his Chief on the telephone. He called the White House at eight in the morning, when he judged that F.D.R. would be having his breakfast in bed. He said to the operator: "I would like to speak to the President; the name is Traveler." He wondered what would happen next, and was taken by surprise when, a few seconds later, he heard the voice of his friend. "Hello, Presidential Substitute!"

"Did you have a good sleep?" ventured the caller.

"The best in some time. I wish you could keep it up."

"I will if you say the word."

"No, I'm afraid somebody might have his feelings hurt."

"What do you want me to do next, Governor?"

"Can you come back in a week or ten days?"

"With pleasure."

"It's a date. And by the way, Alston should be in New York in a day or two—he's been out West. Have a talk with him. He may have suggestions."

"I'll do it."

"So long, Traveler."

That was that; and Lanny, who was still in bed himself, had his bath and ate his breakfast, and then dressed and went down to his car. Such a pleasant thing to be a married man again, and to have somebody to come home to and to tell about your adventures, if only part of them! On that six-hour drive—heavy traffic slowed him up—Lanny thought about what he was going to say to Laurel, and then about what he was going to say to Rudolf Hess if he should meet him, and then, a truly serious question, what he would say to Adolf Hitler if he should meet *him*.

Lanny had phoned, and Laurel was awaiting him with happiness she did not try to hide. He was free to tell her about the dinner at the

White House, for there were no war secrets in that. Also he could tell about Churchill in the "altogether," though not about the topics they had discussed. He persuaded her to dress and have dinner out with him. He would take her to a roof garden and hope they wouldn't run into any more German spies. She protested that she looked too awful, and you couldn't hide anything in summer. But he insisted that women were getting bolder about such matters, and she, who called herself emancipated, could help to set the fashion.

II

Next morning he went down to the F.B.I. office and listened to a report on the mysterious Mr. Branscome, who was now bearing the name of Hartley. He had been watched closely and appeared to be just enjoying New York night life; he had only a few personal acquaintances, harmless persons so far as the watchers were able to learn. He had a three-room apartment and stayed in it most of the day, and what he was doing there was something the F.B.I. wanted very much to know. They were trying to find a plan to get him out of the way for a couple of hours so that they could enter the place and investigate. The agent, quiet in manner, but determined, fixed a pair of gray eyes upon his caller and said: "We are hoping, Mr. Budd, that you may be willing to give us a bit of help in this matter."

"What do you have in mind, Mr. Post?"

"We should like you to run into this man again—by accident, as you will pretend—and recognize him and renew the acquaintance and see if he will give you his confidence. At the least you could take him for a drive or something and keep him out of the way for a while."

Lanny did not answer at once; he was thinking what to say. The agent went on to point out that Branscome alias Hartley had every reason to assume that Lanny was a German agent or sympathizer, and he might be glad of someone to talk to. If he declined to renew the acquaintance, he might give some reason, and that might be a clue. If he showed fear or embarrassment, a desire to get away, it might indicate that he had dropped his treasonable activities; on the other hand, it might indicate that he was up to something especially dangerous.

Lanny said: "Your request embarrasses me, Mr. Post. I am not free to do what you ask, and I am not free to explain why. I can only tell you that when I met this German agent in England I was not just amusing myself. I was under orders, and I am still under them."

"Could you possibly get permission to do this?"

"I don't think I ought to ask permission, for it would indicate a lack of appreciation of the importance of my own work. I have connections which I am not at liberty to jeopardize. If I were to meet a German agent, and soon afterward he were to be arrested, I should be drawing suspicion upon myself. In certain contingencies that might cost me my life; and while a soldier is prepared to sacrifice his life in wartime, there are others who are ordered to stay alive."

"I can understand, Mr. Budd. Your position and your father's position make it possible for me to guess something about your work. But suppose I could pledge that under no circumstances will we arrest this Englishman?"

"But what good could it do you to find out about him if your hands were tied by such a promise?"

"One thing leads to another, and there might be many advantages we could gain. If the man is doing anything important, he will have associates, and we might be able to find out who these persons are. We might uncover a whole chain of activities so far away from the original clue that not even Hartley would suspect that he was involved. Another thing, we might make it possible for Hartley to make good money, so that he would be very well content with the results of his friendship with you."

"You mean trying to buy him?"

"No, that might give everything away. I mean that you might introduce him to certain persons of wealth who sympathize with his peculiar ideas, and he would know how to get money out of them without any more than a hint from you."

"How do you happen to know that I know such persons?" inquired the P.A.

The other smiled a quiet slow smile—he was from somewhere in the South, as his accent revealed. "You know this game very well, Mr. Budd, and you must not take offense that we made sure what sort of person we were dealing with."

Lanny smiled the quick smile which was characteristic of him. "Some day when the war is over, you must let me see that dossier. It would give me an amusing half hour."

III

The two of them spent the rest of the morning working out a program. When Mr. Hartley went out to dine, the agents would note where he went and then phone Lanny, who would be dressed for the occasion and who would stroll into the place and recognize the messenger of Rudolf Hess and greet him. He would try to soothe him down if he was scared, assure him of his high esteem, chat with him amiably, and take him for a drive. During that drive Lanny would assure him of his own devotion to the Nazi cause and would offer to introduce him to others of that way of thinking—first among them being Miss Cornelia van Zandt.

"You know this lady?" asked the P.A. The answer was: "We know her well, and all her friends. We even know the dates when you dined there with Forrest Quadratt, and again with Senator Reynolds and Mr. Harrison Dengue."

"I see you move in the best near-Fascist circles, Mr. Post. I trust you do not let yourselves be awed by big names."

"Not in the least, Mr. Budd. We don't arrest senators and congressmen, but naturally we know who their friends are."

"Let me ask you something especially confidential. Has your attention ever been called to the existence of a conspiracy to kidnap the President of the United States and hold him under the orders of a group of active and aggressive anti-New Dealers?"

"Indeed, yes, Mr. Budd, and I can assure you that the dossiers on those gentry fill a large cabinet."

"You wouldn't be surprised to hear that the name of the very wealthy and important Mr. Dengue is among them?"

"Not in the least, Mr. Budd."

"Nor that the names include several high officers in the United States Army?"

"Not the highest, we hope, Mr. Budd!"

"Not the highest, but still dangerously high."

"Some of them have been retired, and some, we are assured, are soon to be."

"Well, then, we understand each other, Mr. Post, and can talk as friends. I won't drop any hint to Hartley concerning this conspiracy, but I'll take him to dinner in Miss van Zandt's rather dingy old mansion, and maybe some day she will reveal the plot to him. What I will tell Hartley is that this is a slightly daffy old cow who gives the richest cream ever known, and whom all of us friends of Hitler and Mussolini have been milking for the last ten years or more."

"Twenty," said the F.B.I. man. "And one thing more. I hope it won't seem too risky if, while you are entertaining him, we take the chance to find out what is in his apartment."

"That is a pretty dangerous thing for my work, Mr. Post."

"I assure you it won't be. We have experts who know their business. They do not damage doors or locks and do not leave the smallest trace in the room. We can photostat documents at the rate of a few seconds each, and everything will be replaced exactly as it was. We rub out all fingerprints and dust that might tell tales."

"And how about the other people in the apartment house?"

"Everything has been taken care of. We have an apartment on the same floor, we have taken an impression of the lock and have a key to fit it. An hour will be the utmost that we need."

"You are tempting me unduly," said the P.A. "I ought to say no, but I don't!"

IV

Lanny went home and told his wife what he had learned and what he had promised to do. This was an adventure in which she could take no part, but she was an excellent adviser, and they discussed the psychology of an English Nazi and whether he was apt to be a fanatic or a crook or both, and how it might be possible to gain and keep his confidence. They agreed that he was certain to be a snob, and that Lanny's best bet would be his intimacy with Lord and Lady Wickthorpe. He would pose as a rich man's impecunious son and would suggest that Branscome might be introduced to the overpecunious Miss van Zandt, and the two men would divide whatever they could get from her.

At six in the evening Lanny was dressed in his elegant white jacket, soft white shirt, and black tie, and sat reading the evening paper, but rather inattentively. Before he had finished the phone rang. It was the F.B.I. man informing him that their quarry was settled in the Oak Room of the St. Regis Hotel, a place frequented by the richest refugees and therefore good for spies. Lanny's car was at the door and he hopped into it. Crowded traffic slowed him down, and it must have been fifteen minutes before he found a place to park his car near his destination. However, when he entered the room he was the picture of carefree grace. To the head waiter he said: "I am looking for a friend," and so he was left to stroll. When he saw the neat-whiskered Englishman he stopped in front of him, with a smile of pleasure on his face. "Well, well! What a happy coincidence!"—but no name, of course.

The victim looked up. He could not keep dismay from his features. Lanny made things easy for him, as any well-bred person does when he knows that he may not be remembered. "I am Lanny Budd," he said, "and we met in London." Then in a lower tone: "Kurvenal." That didn't relieve the tension, and Lanny realized that the man was greatly worried. It was the P.A.'s role to take the aggressive and keep it, so he continued: "I have been wishing very much that I might meet you again. May I join you?"

Branscome made a feeble attempt to get out of his predicament: "I am afraid you have me at a disadvantage, sir. I don't remember—"

"That's all right," said Lanny soothingly as he took the seat opposite—it was a table for two. "Let us wait until we are alone. I have something important to tell you; and be sure that I understand the situation."

The man was trapped. The waiter came, and Lanny ordered a small salad and a glass of iced tea; he wanted to be free to leave when his victim did, and without seeming hurried or importunate. His victim had a half-eaten mutton chop before him. "Beastly hot weather for June," Lanny remarked. "One doesn't feel like eating." And when the waiter had departed: "Don't be uneasy, my friend. You may count upon my discretion and good faith." Then, in the manner of casual conversation: "How long since you left London? I haven't been there for a year. Did you by any chance hear the funny story of my leaving?"

"I haven't heard anything," said the Englishman, not relaxing his uncordial manner. He was obviously in distress, and his eyes shifted from one part of the room to another, avoiding the other's steady gaze. His eyelids were red and the eyes slightly bleared, and Lanny thought: "He drinks." The man was somewhat stouter than he had been in London, and that was to be expected, since food wasn't so scarce in New York and rationing didn't seem to apply to restaurants.

The P.A. began making himself agreeable, an art which he had been practicing since early childhood. He must manage to interest this man, gain his confidence, or at the least awaken his curiosity, before that mutton chop was finished! "I have just come back from Unoccupied France and French North Africa. You know, my profession of art expert puts me in an especially fortunate position. I am able to travel, and people talk to me frankly because they assume that I am nonpolitical. In Vichy I had the pleasure of meeting Premier Laval and Admiral Darlan. I found they were getting along very well, far better than the newspapers had given me to expect."

Lanny paused for a moment to give the Englishman a chance to say how bad he thought American newspapers, but the Englishman did not take the chance. So Lanny went on to tell about his mother's home on the Riviera, and how he had found conditions there, especially how well the Italians were behaving in the tiny strip of France they had taken, and how little the armistice commissions were interfering with the daily lives of the French. "So different from what we hear!" said the art expert. Again he paused for a comment, and again the Englishman cut off another chunk of mutton chop.

Then to North Africa. The interior of that country is not often visited, and Lanny could tell interesting stories about ancient Roman ruins and mosaics and mosques and *marabouts* and Moorish banquets and veiled ladies in the casbahs. He told them; and in between times, when the waiter was gone and nobody near, he would say: "You may trust me, my dear sir; I am an entirely discreet person and I have something really worth while to tell you. I can show you a way to make quite a good sum of money."

When the waiter returned, or when others were passing, Lanny would talk about the great prosperity he had found in all North Africa, and how well affairs were being conducted; the French still had an army in Morocco, and General Noguès got along perfectly with the Germans. Having said this, Lanny would take another cautious glance about him, and add: "I have a car outside, and I hope that you will take a drive with me and give me an opportunity to put a business proposition before you. I have thought of you several times, and had the idea of looking you up the next time I was in London. I have friends there, you know, and I had the idea that I might find you through them."

That was a "lead," and took the conversation to a territory familiar to Branscome alias Hartley. He didn't have much to say about it, but Lanny had enough for two. He told how he had a little daughter there, and how his former wife was now the Countess of Wickthorpe, and they had remained friends in spite of a divorce. "Ceddy" Wickthorpe had been Lanny's friend from boyhood, and Lanny had been at the Castle at the time that a certain unnamed friend had made his surprise landing by parachute. "Some time I'll tell you a funny story about what happened at the Castle on that occasion," said the art expert.

With that hint, just enough to awaken curiosity, he passed on to Lord Londonderry and Lord Redesdale, whom he had known as ardent appeasers in the old days. Lord Redesdale was the father of Unity Mitford, and Lanny had met her in the mountain retreat of a Very Important Person who had to be nameless in a New York restaurant. That poor girl had apparently shot herself because of disappointment in her personal expectations. Did Mr. Branscome know what had happened? Mr. Branscome said he didn't, and Lanny went on to talk about the love life of the unnamable great one, saying only polite things, of course, and speaking with contempt of the slanders which were circulated by the kind of press, "well, you know the kind I refer to, both here and in England."

V

All this time Lanny was feeling somewhat queasy, thinking of what the F.B.I. men were doing. But he gave no outward sign, and by the time the meal had been eaten he had made himself so agreeable that his victim consented to walk to the car with him and be taken for a drive in Central Park. After the engine had been started and they were in the stream of traffic, Lanny said: "Now we can talk, and not be afraid to name names, Mr. Branscome."

"I am going by the name of Hartley in this country," replied the other. "As a matter of fact, that is my real name."

Lanny guessed that the fact was otherwise, but he wouldn't say so. "Thank you, Hartley. I don't want to ask any improper questions; but before I go into the details of my plan, tell me as much as you care to about who you are and what you are doing."

"To put it bluntly," said the Englishman, "I am keeping alive. I don't like the bombs."

"I can understand," replied Lanny. "I have been under them, too. You remember the Abbé Sieyès who was asked what he had done during the French Revolution, and he said: 'I survived.'"

"I want to tell you," continued Hartley, "I have dropped the sort of activity I was carrying on in London. I decided that it was inadvisable."

Lanny had expected just that and had planned in advance how to deal with it. "Surely, Hartley, you are not reconciled to turning the world over to the Reds!"

"No, but this war has become too big for anybody to control, and certainly for a man in my obscure position. I can't see how anybody can win it—except General Chaos."

Had the scamp lost his nerve or was it just that he wanted Lanny to think he had? It was up to the host, driving in the twilight of a warm evening near the end of June, to find cheerful things to say, cheerful from the point of view of Nazi-Fascism. Lanny expatiated upon the strong position of both Germany and Japan; many years would be required to drive them out of this position, and both Britain and America would be bankrupt before it could happen. Moreover, as one who had access to secret information, Lanny could say that the Nazis were working on new weapons which would make it impossible for Britain to stay in the war for another year. "You'll be even more glad to be out of London when those rocket bombs begin to fall, Mr. Hartley."

Thus discoursing, they drove through the park and over to Riverside Drive. The farther they went, the longer it would take to get back, and the more time the Federal agents would have to complete their work. Lanny didn't think that Branscome alias Hartley—or Hartley alias Branscome—really needed any reconversion to the Fascist cause; but the longer Lanny talked along that line, the more apparent he would make it that he was a genuine friend of this cause. He told so many inside facts and talked so freely about Berchtesgaden and Karinhall and the other shrines of Nazi glory that the Englishman could only conclude that this was a remarkable man, one of the insiders who were shaping the destiny of the world.

"Tell me frankly, Hartley," this insider opened up suddenly, "do you know Rudi personally?"

"Rudi?" replied the other. "What Rudi?"

"Rudolf Hess."

"Why should you think that I know him?"

"That message you brought me in London was from him. Didn't you know it?"

"I didn't know anything about it. I was told to give the password 'Kurvenal,' and take any message you might have."

Lanny was prepared for this answer; like all the others, it might or might not be true. He could see that Hartley was playing his cards close to his chest, and Lanny had to go on wooing him with facts and fancies, all having to do with the New Order of Adolf Hitler, the successes it had won so far and the fresh ones which were sure to follow. Lanny told about his friendship with the Führer's Number Three, his home, his wife and friends, and especially his interest in psychic phenomena, and how he and Lanny had consulted mediums and astrologers, and some of the curious things which had happened. Did Mr. Hartley know anything about this subject? Mr. Hartley replied that he had always supposed it was a lot of rubbish, and mostly fraud. Lanny said there was plenty of fraud in it, and unfortunately his friend Rudi wasn't very discriminating and had let himself be played for a sucker more than once.

VI

When you chat like that for hours you become friends, and when these two were far up through Yonkers and the villages beyond, Lanny decided that it was time to get down to business. "Listen, Hartley," he said. "I told you I had an idea of how you and I might make some easy money. Let me explain that I'm in a jam, because my father is making planes for the government, and I think it's a hellish thing to do, and I've told him so. The result is I can't expect money from him, and I can't make much at my profession in wartime, so I'm up against it. I have an idea, but it can't be worked by one man. I need a partner, somebody of the same way of thinking. I thought several times of you, and now I have the luck to run into you in the very place where I wanted to try out my idea."

"Tell me what it is," said the other.

"I don't know how much you know about America, and how easy it is to collect money here. There are so many people who are lousy with money and don't know what to do with it; they take up all sorts of 'causes' and put up sums that would startle you. I know an old lady who thinks nothing of writing a check for five or ten thousand dollars, just for the trouble of going to a dinner at her home and telling her what she wants to hear and offering her a new way to promote it."

"What is it she wants to promote?"

"I won't say that she has brains enough to understand the theories of National Socialism as it would be applied in America, or even that she would like it if she saw it applied; but she knows enough to be in terror of Bolshevism, and that's what you have to put up to her. You are an Englishman, so you have a new angle of approach. You tell her about the Labour Party and how it is riddled with Communism, how it is really nothing but a secret plot of the Reds to take over the country and align it with Russia. When this war is over, the Reds will be on top, and there will be no stopping them."

"That's really true, Budd."

"Of course it's true, and you know how to tell it with conviction, and to get her stirred up so that she won't be able to sleep at night. Tell her that you want to devote your life to putting these facts before the American public; you want to start a paper, put out leaflets, and get speeches into the *Congressional Record* and distribute them over the country, whatever we decide will be most effective. We'd have to do some of it, of course; the thing mustn't be a racket. We'd open an office and do real work, but the point is, we'd be able to pay ourselves good salaries, and we could travel and have expense accounts. We'd make it all perfectly respectable, and the money would keep pouring in. I've seen it done several times, and it can't fail if you have the brains to keep it on the right track."

"But I can't do things like that in America, Budd. I am a British subject, and the government would put me out."

"It wouldn't have to be done in your name. We'd find some Americans to serve as a front and carry the responsibility. I think I know one such man, a close friend, Forrest Quadratt, and Miss van Zandt knows him well. Perhaps you've heard of him."

"I have, of course. But he's been convicted of some war offense!"

"He's quite certain that his conviction will be reversed by a higher court. Meantime he's out on bail, and he's going right on with his work."

"But I couldn't afford to have anything to do with a man like that. He's bound to be watched by government spies, and a foreigner can't be put in that position."

"All right then, forget him. I might ask Miss van Zandt to suggest a man. That would help to give her confidence."

"You mean that she would put up money for a complete stranger, and an alien?"

"I would take you there and vouch for you. I know her well, and she knows I'm a rich man's son, so she thinks I'm above suspicion. She'll invite us to dinner, and all you have to do is to get ready your spiel, and make it good and hot, for there's nothing she won't swallow. She has a right to spend her money as she pleases, and, thank God, it's not yet against the law to tell the American people about the dangers of Red Communism. She owns an old brownstone mansion on lower Fifth Avenue, and she bears an old and honored name, so she's above suspicion and safe from any attack. If you're under her protection you'll be absolutely safe. You must understand, I can't do this alone, because I can't afford to let Miss van Zandt or any of my other rich friends know that I am broke; that would destroy my prestige. But here comes an Englishman with a load of new ideas, and I'll introduce you to one person after another and the money will come rolling in. You can insist that you need my guidance, and that I ought to have a salary, and I can reluctantly consent, and Miss van Zandt will agree, and maybe write another check."

Hartley alias Branscome hesitated for a while. He had other duties, he said, which he was afraid of jeopardizing. Lanny asked tactfully, might it be that these were dangerous? This plan had the advantage of being perfectly legal, and even honorific. "Don't forget that you'll meet tremendously important people who can be of use to you all the rest of your life. I can give you a string of names out of the Social Register, to say nothing of Dun and Bradstreet. And if it's a question of your time, this plan wouldn't take very much. All that you and I would have to do is the money-raising; for all the other work—the writing, printing, office management, and so on—we can hire. We don't have to worry about any of it. Let the others do that."

It just wasn't possible to turn down such an offer. After more hesitation the man of mystery said that he would go at least as far as to dine with the eccentric old lady and tell her his story and see how she reacted. Thereupon Lanny turned the car back to the city, and they arrived late in the evening. All the way he was shivering at the thought: Suppose the F.B.I. had run into trouble and hadn't finished yet! Or suppose they had left some clue and that Hartley alias Branscome discovered it and told his Nazi associates that the too plausible son of Budd-Erling had played this dirty trick upon him!

VII

Next morning Lanny wrote a note to the "angel" of the pro-Nazis, telling her about the remarkable Englishman he desired to introduce. He laid it on thick, for he didn't in the least mind if Hartley got some of her money—he told himself that if one rascal didn't get it, another would. He sent the note by messenger and then he went down to the F.B.I. office.

"I got what I wanted. Did you get yours?" he asked the competent Mr. Post.

"Indeed, yes," answered the agent. "If I tell you about it, you'll keep extra quiet?"

"I can't keep any quieter than I am," Lanny said. "I was learning to keep my father's secrets when I was four or five years old."

"Well, the man's room is lousy with diamonds. He has them hidden in at least half a dozen places."

"What on earth is he doing with diamonds?"

"He is part of a ring that is shipping them to Sweden, to be smuggled into Germany, we assume."

"That would be rather important, wouldn't it?"

"The German machine-tool industry depends upon them."

"Well, we've been lucky. Are you sure you left the place in order?"

"I went along myself to watch everything, and I was glad I did. We finished in less than the hour you allowed us."

Said Lanny: "I'm surprised that the fellow would come in on a scheme like mine if he has such an important matter already in hand."

"One thing you learn, no crook ever gets enough money. This one may be playing a minor role, the others getting a larger cut."

"I got the impression that he has a bad case of the jitters. So I put my proposition up to him as something within the law, and it may be he'll be glad to get out of the more dangerous racket. I hope you didn't take any of those diamonds, Mr. Post."

"Surely not. But we ought to get them before they disappear. That is going to be really difficult, because diamonds are so easy to move. We have to find a way to keep track of them without involving you."

"I have tried to make things easier," explained Lanny. "I suggested to Hartley that we might have to find another man, someone to carry the responsibility of our proposed organization. He had no objection, and he won't have any objection to a business manager and other people to do the work. You can surround him with your agents, both men and women, if you wish."

"If you don't mind," said Post, "let me introduce you to a chap who is working on this case, and if you approve you might tell your old lady about him and let him put up some of the money."

The agent pressed a button and told the secretary to send in "Cartier." A young man, slightly built, entered the room—Lanny learned later that he was twenty-one, but he might have been taken for a boy. He had a thin, eager face, bright blue eyes, and an expression of alertness, as if he were playing some game which required him to be on his toes every moment. "Mr. Budd," said the agent, "this is Tom Cartier. He has left the University of Virginia to help us out in this emergency. His conscience is troubled because he isn't in the Army, so we'll have to give him something dangerous to do."

Lanny shook hands with the youngster and promised to do his best. Cartier had evidently been told about the son of Budd-Erling and had conceived a great awe of him. The youngster knew German and had been "boning up" day and night on the subject of Nazi doctrines and practice. He had been working among the "Christian Mobilizers," the "Crusader Whiteshirts," and other fanatics who were trying to introduce the New Order into the sweet land of liberty. It amused Lanny vastly to hear the Nazi language with a Virginia accent.

He took a great shine to the youngster, and Post sent them off into a room where they could talk about the details of their scheme. Lanny was to tell both Hartley and Miss van Zandt about a capable young man who had some money and was eager to put it into the anti-Bolshevik cause. "I expect to find a note from the old lady when I get home," Lanny said. "She is always in a hurry, because she has visions of the Reds coming round the corner from Union Square and seizing her mansion."

"They would if they could," said the F.B.I. man, with a grin. "Some day she'll be asking us for help, and we'll have to give it to her."

VIII

Returning to the apartment, Lanny found the letter, as he had predicted. "Miss van Zandt requests the pleasure of Mr. Lanny Budd's company at dinner this evening. Seven o'clock. Black tie." There was a similar note which Lanny was supposed to deliver to Mr. Trescott Hartley, but he had no way to do that, for Mr. Hartley had not entrusted him with an address. He had said that he would telephone Lanny at four in the afternoon, so all Lanny could do was wait.

Meantime he went to call on his old friend and employer, Professor Alston, who had just arrived in New York from the Middle West. The presidential "fixer" had been trying to resolve what he called "an interdepartmental jurisdictional dispute." He didn't name names, or even departments, for he was the most discreet of counselors; but he was also a tired and overstrained old gentleman, who was glad to have a friendly ear into which to pour the story of human inadequacy in the giant crisis which was threatening the nation's existence.

Lanny drove him so that they could be alone, and took him to a roadside café where a "headliner" wasn't apt to meet a reporter and be asked for the name of his luncheon companion. So this ex-professor of geography with the little white beard and the gold pince-nez set forth his idea that the development of man's mechanical devices and economic organizations had outrun that of his moral codes. You could find men who were "big" enough to build colossal enterprises, but it was hard indeed to find those who were "big" enough not to quarrel with their associates and let personal antagonisms paralyze their usefulness in the public service.

"Here I am," said Charles T. Alston, "close to seventy and by no means a Hercules, and I have to spend my time being flown about the country and sitting in hotel rooms in stifling hot weather, administering paternal scoldings to schoolboys of anywhere between forty and eighty years. I have to get them together and plead and pray with them, threaten them with the Nazis, find slogans to inspire them, make them swear oaths of loyalty to their duty which they ought to have learned in school. I have to make them kiss and make up—"

"Actually kiss?" inquired Lanny, ready for a good laugh.

"No, that would be in France. Here they shake hands and get a soulful look in the eyes, or at any rate they refrain from punching each other in the nose. That may last for the duration, or it may not last till I get out of town."

"You should write a book called *The Memoirs of a Bureaucrat*, Professor."

"Don't fool yourself, my boy. Power is power, whether it is political or financial. It goes to men's heads and you see them swell up like bullfrogs, and it's just the same whether they are heads of alphabetical departments in the government or of coal or oil or steel combines. I go through the same ritual in Wall Street as in Washington, or out in the field, wherever jealousy and greed and self-will have taken root in the hearts of men."

"And women?" inquired the other.

"Women don't *do* so much, but they talk more, and oh, it's dreadful! Women take my suggestions more readily, I suppose, because I am a man. Sometimes when I'm dealing with the men I wish I could be a woman."

"A young one, perhaps?"

"Better a motherly one. I once had to call in the mother of one of our great big masterful men and tell her the situation. She gave her son a scolding that he wouldn't take from anybody else; and afterward he told me I had taken an unfair advantage of him! I said in his palatial office: 'Listen, man, you think that I enjoy giving you orders, as you call it? Let me try to set you straight. I am a geographer, and right now at my little place in the country I have on my table half a dozen books on exploration, and I'm counting the days till this damned war will be over and I can go home and lie in a hammock and read.'"

"And what did he say to that?"

"He said: 'I've got a trout stream on my place, Alston, and when it's over, come and we'll go fishing.'"

IX

Lanny underwent a thorough interrogation as to his recent trip. Vichy, Toulon, the Riviera, Switzerland, Algeria, and Morocco—Alston wanted to know about them all: what were the living conditions, what the people were saying about the war and about the Allies and the Germans. He explained: "The decision has not yet been taken where the first landing is to be made; and, of course, it makes a lot of difference whether we shall find ourselves among a friendly or an indifferent population."

"I should think," ventured the other, "that a decision will have to be taken soon if anything is to be done this year." When his friend nodded, Lanny went on: "Not meaning to fish, but just to guess, the longer they put it off, the more likely it is that it will be the Mediterranean rather than the Channel."

"It is hardly likely that the Germans will fail to make the same guess," smiled Alston. "Between you and me, the decision is to be taken at a conference of the military men in London very shortly. The President has indicated that he wishes me to attend."

"We may meet there, Professor. Churchill has promised to fix matters so that I can return to England. That is important to me because I haven't seen my little daughter for more than a year."

Lanny told of the interview in the White House, incidentally mentioning the odd detail of having met the Prime Minister of Great Britain freshly out of his bath. The ex-geographer remarked: "I had the same experience. He said to me: 'You see, Dr. Alston, I have absolutely nothing to conceal.'" They chuckled over this, and the older man added: "Has anybody told you what the Prime Minister's wife calls him? Her term of endearment is 'Porky'!"

Such are the delights of being among the "insiders"; you pick up amusing items of gossip and pass them on and feel proud of your privileged position—while hundreds of your fellow men are dying in agony and your civilization totters on the edge of an abyss. When Lanny's smile had died the ex-geographer remarked: "War makes strange bedfellows. If, while I was a humble instructor at a freshwater college, someone had told me that I should some day be hobnobbing with the Duke of Marlborough's seventh lineal descendant, I should have considered it extremely unlikely."

"He is good company," commented the younger man, "and a good ally in battle. But I'm afraid you'll have a hard time with him when it comes to setting up new governments in Europe."

"It is the people who are going to do that, Lanny. The British people will decide the destiny of Britain; and Churchill will submit to their will, I hope."

They talked about Lanny's plans, and he explained his idea of paying a visit to Rudolf Hess in pretended secrecy and getting from him a

message to be delivered to Hitler. Alston shook his head. "I don't
believe the Governor will want you to go into Germany again. He
told me definitely that he considered it too dangerous."

"What does he want me to do?"

"To go back to Vichy France and North Africa, especially if the
London conference decides upon an invasion there. We shall need
every scrap of information we can get, and the Governor counts on
you because you can meet the top people."

"If that's what he wants," Lanny said, "of course that's what I'll do.
Do you know the line of Dante, 'In la sua volontade è nostra pace'?"
When Alston said that he didn't know Italian, Lanny translated: "In
his will is our peace." It was a good wartime motto.

                                  X

The "fixer" had two matters of especial urgency on his mind and
proceeded to reveal them to his one-time secretary-translator. The first
was the problem of the rocket bomb, the jet-propelled missile reported
as capable of traveling as far as one or two hundred miles. If the
Germans should use this, they might be able to destroy London and
make it impossible for the British to be of any further use in the war.
"We know definitely that they have it," said Alston, "and we have
hints as to where and how they are working. The trouble is, we have
too many hints, and we strongly suspect that they are being 'planted'
for the purpose of confusing us. We have become convinced that the
Germans have one principal center of activity, and that is where their
best and most trusted scientists are to be found. We'd like to get that
place, and if possible the scientists, in one of our thousand-plane surprise raids. There is nothing more important in the whole war."

"I talked with my man in Geneva about it," reported the P.A. "He
promised to do his best. The arrangement was that Colonel Donovan's
office was to send a man to him, and I do not know what has come out
of that."

"I talked with the Colonel's office this morning over the phone—we
have a code name for the project, of course. They report that nothing
satisfactory has come in so far."

"I don't know what more I could do, Professor, unless it is to go into
Germany myself."

"Are you free to tell me more about this man of yours?"

"I think I am free to tell you everything. He has given me permission to trust our Intelligence organization, and you are surely a part

of that. His name is Bernhardt Monck, and he is an old-time German labor man and Social Democratic Party leader, one of those who did not turn patriotic in either the first World War or the second, so I suppose he should be classed as an Independent, though he sticks to the thesis that the party will arise out of the ashes of this calamity and lead the German people into Socialism. He went under the name of Capitán Herzog in the International Brigade in Spain, and now he calls himself Braun, or Brun when he writes to me in France."

"You are certain that he is trustworthy?"

"I trust him as I would trust you in the same circumstances. He was recommended to me by the woman who became my second wife. I told you about that marriage and its tragic end. She was in Paris, and the Nazis kidnaped her; I tried to save her and Monck helped me. He risked his life, and no man can do more; he didn't even want to let me pay him, although he knew I was what he would call a rich man. Now he is living the life of a student, pretending to be doing some historical work, and keeping his contacts with the anti-Nazi underground. Of course he has never told me what these are; but several times he has given me information as to German plans, which I have sent to the President, who has told me that it was useful."

"We cannot ask more than that. I think you should see this man again and impress upon him the urgency of the rocket-bomb matter. Give him whatever money he can use."

"I did that, and I assume that the new contact man will do the same. It may be that he will have some new lead that I can follow up. I'll ask him, of course."

"And now for the other matter, which is the problem of atomic fission and what progress the Germans have been making. Did you talk to your man about that?"

"No, because you didn't authorize me to. I asked him to find out where the Germans are making heavy water, that is all."

"I am quite sure they know we are working on atomic fission, so I don't see what harm it can do for you to mention the subject to your man. You should be guided by circumstances; if you find he has no contacts with that part of the scientific world, then there's no use telling him anything. But if he has a contact, tell him, not what we know, but only what we need to know."

"You forget, Professor, I am ten months behind the times on that subject, and that may mean ten years of ordinary times."

"That is true. Would you like to stop by and see Professor Einstein again?"

"Could anybody say no to that?"

"You remember his assistant, Dr. Braunschweig? He is kept up to date on the details and will tell you to what extent we are still in the dark about the Germans and their progress on the subject."

"You forget, Professor, a man doesn't just drop in and say to an atomic physicist: 'Tell me the most precious secrets of this war!' "

"I'm not forgetting. I'll make arrangements for you, and you phone and make a date before you go. It needn't be until you are ready to return to Europe. The old formula is reversed now, and a day may be as a thousand years. Good luck to you, Lanny, and see you in London!"

XI

Hartley phoned at the agreed hour, and Lanny made an appointment to meet him at once and brief him for the evening. They kept the car in movement while they laid out their plan of campaign. Lanny went into details about this old Knickerbocker lady who made no concessions to modern customs but lived as she had lived since girlhood, hating all the forces of change.

"Don't forget your glad rags," said the son of Budd-Erling, and the other said he had them. When Hartley showed up in front of the old mansion which remained stubbornly in a district of tall office buildings, he was in every way *en règle*.

Lanny had often wondered, did Miss van Zandt have one long black silk dress, carefully preserved through the decades, or did she have rows of them, and upon what system did she choose one each time? The cords in her thin neck were partly hidden by an old-fashioned "dog-collar" studded with diamonds; in addition she wore one string of pearls and a small tiara in her white hair. Her features were severe and pale—she scorned the use of rouge. She received her guests with stately courtesy. She served no cocktails, only a variety of wines at dinner. Hartley, forewarned, had got himself a drink or two in advance.

Whatever he was, he played the English gentleman acceptably. Lanny could understand Laurel's saying that she might have found him plausible if she had met him under normal circumstances. Hartley fully convinced his hostess that he was a person of conservative tastes, who had lived among the old "county families" and shared their ideas. When he turned loose upon the "Red peril" he became really eloquent and displayed a fund of knowledge which surprised his sponsor.

Yes, indeed, the world was in a desperate way, and unless it was

going entirely to pot at the end of this war, America must be prepared to take a firm stand against the Reds both at home and abroad.
The public must be awakened to the peril in advance, and Hartley
was the Englishman who knew how to do it. Before he was through,
he had the Jewish clothing workers, who walked up and down in front
of Miss van Zandt's mansion every weekday noon, exchanging their
cheese sandwiches and pickles for revolvers and hand grenades; and
there was Hartley himself, standing on the steps in shining armor, holding aloft the banner of the American Christian Union and sweeping
back the floods of blood and terror. The mixed metaphors were Hartley's own, and no more confused than the state of mind of an
economic-royalist spinster born half a century too late. The outcome
of the dinner party was that she wrote a check for five thousand dollars
to promote this righteous cause, but she wrote it to the order of
Lanning P. Budd and said in her royally firm way: "I am doing so
because I have known Mr. Budd longer and wish him to have the
handling of the money. I am sure that you, Mr. Hartley, will understand this decision."

"Certainly, certainly, Miss van Zandt," said the Englishman cordially. "Mr. Budd is my friend, and we are entirely in unison. I am
impressed by your clear insight and splendid courage in this matter."
Lanny wondered if the old lady's reason was that she had noted the
promptness with which Hartley had emptied his wine glass.

When they were outside, Lanny said: "I hope you understand, I
didn't have any idea the old bird would drop this thing into my lap."

"I take your word," replied the other. "But we don't have to take
her orders seriously, do we?"

"I promise to see that you get the better of every deal," was Lanny's
response. Which wasn't quite the same as saying: "I'll turn the money
over to you."

XII

It was late, and Lanny suggested that they should meet in the morning and work out the details of their plan. But Hartley wanted to know
if they couldn't take a drive now and settle the question of money.
He was obviously uneasy, having every reason to assume that Lanny
might be another such as himself. So they motored up to Central Park
and along its winding drives, all the way around, since Lanny had to
keep the man satisfied. He would surely not give him the money,
knowing that he might bolt with both it and the diamonds.

"You must understand, Hartley," said the P.A., "the last thing I was looking for was to get a business on my hands. But until we have raised more money I carry the responsibility for this check. Will it be satisfactory to you if I allow you three hundred a month out of it?"

"And how much will you take?"

"I'll be satisfied with two hundred at the start," Lanny said. He had to take something, because he was supposed to be hard up. "You should have more, Hartley, because you will be doing more work than I. You know more about the subject, and besides, I have to do some traveling to keep my art business going."

"That sounds fair," admitted the other, showing his relief.

"We shall have to pay office rent, and we must find an office with a telephone, because, as you know, new phones are practically unobtainable. Also, we must have a secretary, and I should think a business manager, since I don't suppose you want to bother with the details of getting literature printed and distributed."

"It seems to me," objected Hartley, "you'll be getting rid of the money in a very short time and leaving us on the rocks."

"We're only getting started, man. I'm going to introduce you to other people, and you'll raise a quarter of a million before you finish. Moreover, I have in mind a man who will work without salary, at least until we get going. It's quite likely that he'll put in a hunk of money when he sees what fine work we're doing."

Lanny told the wonderful story of his friend Tom Cartier, who hated this stupid war and had used his family influence to keep out of it. He was looking round for something to do that would satisfy his conscience, and he was ready to take Lanny's word for it that the American Christian Union represented the most worthy cause. Hartley, well fortified with wine, swallowed every word of it and exclaimed: "Righto! If you can produce a piece of magic like that, O.K."

Lanny said he could produce that magic the first thing in the morning. The agreeable young Virginian had a grandmother who owned the better part of a county down there, and she was much the same sort of person as Miss van Zandt; they might visit her before long and get another check. Also, Cartier had an uncle who owned a lot of real estate in New York and might be persuaded to rent them an office with a telephone, a treasure almost beyond price at the present moment. In short, Aladdin's lamp was at work and Lanny said: "Notice that everything has happened as I promised you!"

XIII

Next morning the pair met by appointment, and they picked up Cartier and drove into the park again. They stopped at a quiet place by the side of a drive, where they could talk for hours without interruption. Cartier surprised Lanny in much the same way that Hartley had done on the previous evening. Cartier had been studying the Communists; he had attended their meetings and even one of their conventions, and he said that they were planning the after-the-war conquest of the world. He had read a volume of Lenin and could quote verbatim what the master Bolshevik had said on the subject of revolutionary versus bourgeois morality: how the Communists must always think of themselves as soldiers in a war, using all the devices which soldiers use against enemies. "When there is need of it, we must know how to employ trickery, deceit, lawbreaking, withholding and concealing truths."

In short, the lively young Virginian was a perfect model of a crusader on behalf of the American system of private enterprise, slanderously called "capitalism" by the "Commies." He was as ready for a fight as they were, and wasn't going to be fooled by any of their camouflage. Hartley, who might or might not have believed what he said to Miss van Zandt, could hardly refuse to believe what Cartier said to him, and his rosy English complexion shone with pleasure when Cartier announced that he had already talked with his uncle, who would let them have a suite of three office rooms at the ceiling price and with no secret rake-off because of the two telephones.

Later on they went to inspect the place, which was everything the most fastidious propagandist could have desired. One of the rooms was to be Hartley's private office, and Lanny wondered, could it really be, as Post had told him, that the disk of the dictaphone was so hidden in the desk that nobody could find it without taking the desk apart, and the wires so wound in with the telephone wires that only an expert could have detected them, and then only by cutting into the wires. The dictaphone was legal, while telephone tapping was not. However, this was wartime, and against the enemies of the nation the F.B.I. would probably do what it pleased. Whether Branscome alias Hartley would be so indiscreet as to make appointments with his diamond smugglers over that phone, or to invite them into that office, were questions which only time could answer. Cartier felt quite certain that the blondined young lady whom he introduced as stenographer and secretary would be able to keep the susceptible Englishman busy at dinnertime whenever the government men desired to make another search of his apartment.

10

Man Is Born to Trouble

I

THERE came a call from Washington, and when Lanny called back it was Baker, telling him that an engagement had been made for him to meet Dr. Braunschweig in Princeton early the following afternoon. The day after that he would drive to the small town of Thurmont in the western part of Maryland, where he would find Baker and be taken to another appointment. "Both are for Mr. Prescott," said the President's man, and Lanny didn't have to ask for an explanation.

The much-traveled P.A. packed his bags again and said to his fore-warned wife: "It's a Number One matter, darling, so forgive me." She answered that she had a Number One matter, too, and he teased her, pretending not to know whether it was the baby or the book. She thought she was a feminist, but after all she was a woman in love. Millions of women were sending their men off to war, but they weren't enjoying it.

He had told her about developments in the Hartley matter, because that might fairly be considered hers; but he wasn't free to mention the awful subject of atom splitting, nor the town in the Catoctin Mountains, which he guessed contained the President's hideout. F.D.R. had dropped a hint that he had such a place, since the Secret Service and the Navy combined had refused to let him enjoy his former recreation of yachting. Not even Chesapeake Bay could be considered safe in these days of triumphant submarines.

Lanny took a bite of lunch early and set out. His route was the same as he had taken to Washington, and he had learned that you couldn't count upon making speed on Highway Number 1. He had been told to go to the Institute of Advanced Study, and just a few minutes before the hour specified he parked his car down the street from this new Gothic building. He announced himself as Mr. Prescott to see Dr. Braunschweig, and in a minute or two he was seated in the modest study of the learned scientist. He was perhaps ten years younger than Lanny, but what he knew about the universe was appalling to a mere art expert. Over a period of two months in the previous summer he had tutored Lanny for an hour or two every day, and most of the time Lanny had had to learn words and formulas like a parrot, without being able to understand at all what they meant. He had come away with the feeling that this dark-eyed, rather frail, and extremely serious young physicist possessed a brain of a type wholly beyond the imagining of the ordinary man. Sir James Jeans had written that "the universe appears to have been designed by a mathematician," and that sentence had stayed in Lanny's mind.

This time the tutoring wouldn't take so long, because Lanny would be free to make notes and carry them away with him. Alston had said that would be all right, provided he kept them pinned up in an inside pocket and destroyed them before he left the country. Dr. Braunschweig had a list of data which had come in during the past ten months concerning German progress in atomic research, and what particular details might be useful to the Americans. It was pleasant to hear him say that they believed the Germans were far behind, mainly because the Führer didn't believe in the possibility of atomic fission and had put his top physicists at other tasks. Lanny might have said: "He is concentrating on jet propulsion," but he didn't.

He listened with all the faculties he possessed, and when he did not understand he asked questions. He was embarrassed because he had forgotten so much of what he had previously learned. The physicist comforted him by saying that it was not to be expected that a man should remember so many details wholly outside the range of his own interests. Lanny had it all to do over again, but he didn't mind because he could tell himself that it was the most important subject in the world at this time. If he could gather the smallest mite of knowledge and have it passed on to the men who were working day and night in his country's laboratories—that might be the best contribution he had ever made to the cause of freedom.

II

This "advanced study" continued without interruption for a matter of four hours. Then the teacher said: "We will resume at eight o'clock, if that is agreeable." Lanny went out and telephoned his friend Alonzo Curtice, who had fed and sheltered him during the previous sojourn here. The art expert—so he was known here—explained that he was passing through and had a couple of hours. It meant inviting himself to dinner, but they had fed him something like a hundred and eighty times, and he was sure they wouldn't mind once more. He drove to the estate of this Wall Street investment banker and was welcomed by the owner and his wife. The story of his trip around the world was enough for anybody's dinnertime, and the couple could feel repaid for their hospitality.

Back to the advanced study, and time passed quickly, as it does when one is too busy to think about it. At about half-past ten there came a gentle tap on the study door, and there entered what to Lanny was a vision of delight—although entirely different from the one to which the poet Wordsworth had referred. It was a gentleman in his middle sixties, short and well filled out, with a rounded cherubic face, a small gray mustache, and a floating mist of uncontrollable white hair. He came in with that mischievous smile and two hands outstretched, and then appeared to change his mind and put his arms around the visitor and patted him on the back with both hands. "*Willkommen, Herr Budd!* It is good to see you still alive!"—which showed that somebody had told him about the accident. Then he turned to Dr. Braunschweig. "You are cheating me! You promised me time enough for three sonatas!"

The young assistant, who lacked a sense of humor, appeared flustered. "I am sorry, Dr. Einstein."

"I forgive you, but no more tonight! You must not cram this easygoing gentleman!" Then to the visitor: "You have a little time in the morning, *nicht wahr?* You can spend the night at my house, and we can play."

"That suits me fine," said Lanny, for he loved this warmhearted great man, one of the simplest and most genuine people he had ever met. Albert Einstein was comically out of place in this elegant university town, whose freedom and informality were of a conventional English sort. The wives of the faculty members must have had a hard time deciding how to deal with a German-Jewish scientist who forgot to keep his hair cut and went about the streets clad in a white shirt open at the throat, a pair of baggy pants, sandals, and no hat. In cold weather, when he had to be more warmly clad, he put on a celluloid collar, just about the most plebeian article of apparel that an academic hostess could imagine.

The two friends strolled over in the moonlight to the old and entirely unpretentious frame house which sheltered the discoverer of formulas which had changed the thinking and destiny of the human race. A wistaria vine, now loaded with blossoms, covered the front porch and filled the night air with scent. Apparently the door wasn't locked; the master just walked in and turned into the parlor, which had a piano and a good music stand, also a table and several chairs. "Any room will do to think in," he had told Lanny, and apparently any room would do to play the music of Mozart and Bach. The professor picked out the violin and piano scores of Mozart's sonatas and set the former on the music stand and the latter on the piano rack. He got out his fiddle, tuned it, and said: "*Also!* We played the first three. Shall we start with four?"

Lanny thought to himself: "My God! The greatest mathematician in the world has room in his head for the numbers we played nearly a year ago!"

They played Number Four, which is delightful, and then they played Number Five, which is also delightful. The old gentleman apparently knew the scores by heart, for he played with his eyes cast upward most of the time and an expression of heavenly bliss on the rounded, cherubic face. He played well, for this had been his form of recreation since early childhood. He had been very poor and had had a hard struggle to get along in the world and to win an education; he had been slaving for seven years as a clerk in the Swiss patent office when he had evolved the physical formulas which had revised the Newtonian conception of the universe.

They played the proper allowance of three sonatas; more would have been a dissipation—so the learned professor had said the first time and he repeated it. They sat for a while and talked about the bad state of the world, and then the Professor raided his pantry and made two cheese sandwiches, which they washed down with a pint bottle of beer divided between them. "Friendship is a delightful sentiment, and lends a glow to the most ordinary actions of life," thus spoke the author of *The General and the Special Theory of Relativity* as he escorted his friend upstairs to a modest chamber. In the morning, or rather, later the same morning, he fed the guest a light breakfast and then said: "It will be better if you walk alone to the office, for it happens, unfortunately, that I am an object of some curiosity. It is as if people came to see the giant panda"—this with his shy twinkle.

Lanny made his way back to the Gothic building and spent another three hours of the hardest kind of mental work. The lesson over, he said his thanks to the solemn young physicist. "You have taken a lot of trouble with me," he remarked. A shadow seemed to cross the teacher's dark eyes. "Mr. Budd," he replied, "I have a very special interest in what you are doing. The Nazi gangsters are every man's enemy. They are doubly mine. I am a Jew."

They both knew that they were playing with the fantastic notion of an atomic bomb, and the issue at stake was whether a missile of such destructive power should land on Berlin before it landed on New York or Washington.

The Professor wished to say good-by, so Lanny was taken into his office, or perhaps it was the seminar room, Lanny couldn't be sure. It had a large table in the center and several leather-seated chairs. As any room would do to think in, so any pencil would do to jot down a formula, and any piece of paper to receive it. Lanny knew that Einstein was now searching in the recesses of his unfathomable mind for the formula of what he called his Unified Field Theory, which would reconcile his Special Theory of Relativity with his extension of Max Planck's Quantum Theory, thus bringing all natural phenomena under one universal law. Recently he had thought that he had it, but it hadn't worked out, so he had told Lanny sadly.

Now he bade farewell to this agreeable guest. "*Glück auf, Herr Budd!* I know that what you are doing is dangerous, and I wish I had as much courage."

"Didn't it take courage to upset the entire scientific world?" inquired the P.A. mildly.

"Oh, that!" replied the Professor. "That is not so much. I have a mathematical mind and it will not rest. It goes its own way into the far reaches of this mysterious universe and I cannot hold it back. It finds harmony where chaos once seemed to reign." The great physicist said that, and then a shadow darkened his face. "It is a dreadful thing that we are doing now, trying to unlock the secrets of atomic power for purposes of war. The future will hold us responsible for the use we make of that knowledge if we get it! *Viel Glück, Herr Budd, und leben Sie recht wohl!*"

III

Lanny followed the highway as far as he could and then struck off to the west through the rolling farm country of Maryland. Fields and orchards and woodlots and farmhouses were rolling by, but he withheld the attention he ordinarily gave to such a panorama; his mind was absorbed with the subject of atomic fission and the means of producing it, and, more important yet, of controlling the process. It was something new and terrible in the world, and he never tired of speculating about the changes it might bring in human affairs.

Gradually the land rose, and there came into sight the beautiful Blue Ridge mountains. Here, so Alston had told the P.A., an area in one of the National Parks had been set aside for the use of a Chief Executive who could not walk and had been deprived of his recreations of fishing and swimming. Oddly enough it was the Navy which had taken charge of this forest preserve; the crew of the presidential yacht *Potomac* and its auxiliary tender and fishing boat had set to work, with the help of local mountain labor, and put in a paved road and a group of buildings for use as a rest camp. Now they guarded and ran it, and the President motored each week end from the capital, bringing officials and others with whom he desired to have conferences. Churchill had been here twice, and various generals and admirals, to consult with him; but not a line about it had appeared in any newspaper.

Lanny did not enter the little town of Thurmont, but telephoned from outside. He was told to be in front of the post office at eight o'clock that evening and he would be picked up in the usual way. Meantime he parked his car in a grove of chestnut trees alongside a little stream and sat and studied his atomic notes. Later he found a roadside inn and had a bit of supper, and then studied some more until it was time to drive into the town. Precisely on the minute he stepped into Baker's car and was driven up the new road, which climbed a couple of thousand feet to the camp. It was ten or twenty degrees cooler here than in the sweltering city of Washington; a gentle night breeze murmured through the trees, and fireflies showed their mysterious tiny lights. Lanny, who was worried about his great leader's health under the terrifying strain of war, thought this hideout the pleasantest discovery he had made in some time.

He felt free to ask questions on the three- or four-mile drive. Baker told him there was a massive lodge built of local timber, a number of smaller cabins, a swimming pool, and fine trout streams running through the area. One of these emptied into an abandoned quarry near the lodge, and this made a unique fishing place, well stocked with rainbow trout from the government's hatcheries. A feature of the main building was that one wall was on heavy hinges so that it could be let down like a drawbridge, making a ramp on which the President could be wheeled out in case of fire. Also, in the rear, there was a smaller lodge for the adoring Fala.

Lanny had seen mountain camps all the way from the Adirondacks to Bavaria, and many of them had cost more than the twenty-five thousand dollars this one represented. Also he was used to having flashlights turned upon his face, to make sure that he was the person expected. Baker had the right to bring anybody in, and no questions were asked. In the entrance hall, while they waited to be announced, Lanny surveyed a map of "Shangri-La," as this place was called. He noted that here, as everywhere, Americans had to have their fun. This building, the President's home, was labeled "The Bear's Den"; the laundry was "The Soap Dish"; the building set aside for the Filipino stewards was "Little Luzon." There was a row of cabins marked "Baker Street Urchins" on the map, and Lanny asked whether these were named after his escort. The reply was: "The Secret Service men get their names from Sherlock Holmes, not from me."

IV

A door was opened before Lanny, and he entered the President's room. Roosevelt was resting on a couch by an open window, wearing tan-colored linen trousers and a soft white shirt; he gave a welcoming hail, as always. Seated beside him was a man in his fifties whose features were familiar to all readers of newspapers. He was tall and thin, with deep-set, keen brown eyes, a sallow skin, hollow cheeks, and a prominent lower jaw. He was loosely put together, slouchy in his way of sitting, and informal in manner. He was a harnessmaker's son from Iowa who had gone through college in the American fashion, by working his way. He had devoted most of his life to social service, first for the Red Cross, then for the Tuberculosis and Health Association in New York, then as chairman of the New York State Temporary Emergency Relief Administration. When the newly elected President had been faced with the worst financial collapse in the world's history, he had given this man the enormous job of finding work for fifteen million unemployed. He was trusted by the President above all other men, and hated by the President's enemies to the same extent. In this war crisis he was working himself literally to death—he had had a perforated ulcer and now had a rare intestinal disease, and he looked rather ghastly as he lifted himself out of his chair to greet the new arrival.

"Lanny Budd, this is Harry Hopkins," said the President. And Lanny said: "I have never had the pleasure before, but I had plenty of time to look at you, something over a year ago, when we crossed on the same Clipper."

"I remember your face well," said "Harry the Hop," as his genial Boss called him.

"I didn't suppose you were seeing anything on board, Mr. Hopkins, except the papers in your portfolio. I took the liberty of guessing that they contained the lend-lease figures."

"You were correct, of course."

"Later on," added the ex-playboy with a grin, "I was told that you had landed with only one shirt and no hat, and that you had had to go to work without having time to shave."

"I see that you move in the best circles," was the dry reply.

"My father used to complain that you were spending more money than any one man in the world ever did before. That was in the old W.P.A. days. Now, doubtless, you are spending ten or twenty times as much, but my father doesn't seem to mind it at all."

"He is getting so much of it himself," put in the President, and all three of them enjoyed a laugh.

V

They got down to business quickly, there being little time for joking these days. "I want you to know Harry," said "the Boss," as Harry called him. "He will be in London while you are there, and I should like you to report to him anything interesting that you may come upon. The same goes for Alston, of course."

"Fine!" said Lanny.

"Churchill has told me about your idea of having a talk with Hess. That is interesting, and all right with me; but I don't want you to go into Germany. There are others we can send, and I can't spare *you*."

"All right, Governor. My wife will call that good news."

"There will be danger enough where you are going. I want you in Vichy France and North Africa. It may seem like treading in your old footsteps, but events are moving fast, and we need every item of information about the attitude of the big people there. Some of them are bound to be worried, and more so as the summer passes. Some will be ready to desert a sinking ship, and we want to know who they are and how we can use them. It's going to be a dirty business, and you may have your faith in human nature greatly tried. But keep your nerve, and never forget the one purpose we have in mind, which is to save the lives of American boys and win this war at the lowest price in blood."

"Yes, Governor," replied the P.A. meekly. He took it as an answer to the objections he had been raising, as to the wisdom of dealing with the rats deserting the Vichy ship.

"Remember our clear intention—the French people will decide the future of France, and we have no wish to do it for them. Our job is to put down the Nazis, and after that to see a free and fair election in every country we have entered."

"I get you, Governor." It was the nearest to an order the son of Budd-Erling had ever received, and it pleased him because it relieved him of responsibility. He added: "Professor Alston wants me to go to Switzerland and meet my old-time labor and Socialist friend there."

"That's all right; Switzerland, Spain, Portugal, wherever you think there is information to be had, but not into any German-held territory. It is possible you might get some of your Nazi friends to meet you in Switzerland. What is the name of that musician?"

"Kurt Meissner. He would come if I asked him, but I'd have to have something important to tell him, and something he could believe. It would be a dangerous game, because I'd be attracting attention to myself again, and they might comb the world to find out about me. It would be pretty hard for me then to continue as an art expert."

"Does anybody really accept that since we've entered the war?" It was Harry Hopkins, his questions always direct and to the point.

"I can never be entirely certain," replied Lanny. "I suppose it varies with different persons. The French are polite, and they pretend to believe it. Nobody has accused me to my face, except some of my friends of the underground, where I got into a jam. I suppose the *collabora- teurs* whisper about me behind my back and speculate. I spend money freely, and that helps."

The thin-faced chief of lend-lease nodded his head slightly. "That helps!" he echoed. "I know!"

Lanny took the opportunity to bring in a subject that lay close to his heart. "The last time I saw Kurt Meissner I told him about a plot of some of our high-up business tycoons and Army people to kidnap the President and make him obey their orders. That made a tremendous hit with Kurt, and later on with Hitler when I saw him. I think I could still use that story, but I'd have to report progress, and I might need to have some hint leak out here. But the Governor doesn't seem to want that to happen."

Lanny was speaking to Hopkins, as if answering his question. He took it for granted that F.D.R.'s best friend must know all about this affair, and Lanny wanted to know what the friend's attitude was. This was not difficult, for Hopkins was an outspoken person who said what he thought on any subject—unless it was a subject about which he didn't want to talk, and then nobody could get a word out of him. Now he said: "So far those bastards haven't done anything but talk, and it's one of the requirements of democracy that every bastard shall be free to shoot off his mouth."

"Even in wartime, Mr. Hopkins?"

"Even in wartime, Mr. Budd. The Nazis can liquidate people for talking, and so can the Communists; but if we do it, we have lost the war before we fight it."

"And more than that, Lanny," put in F.D.R., "you must admit that it wouldn't help morale either at home or abroad to let people know that such a junta exists in this country."

"You are the boss," replied Lanny. "I am just pointing out that this is the one way I can get any Nazi to warm up and talk to me as a friend. They would greatly like to get the Jewish-Democratic Herr Rosenfeld out of their path."

"You don't tell me!" responded Herr Rosenfeld with one of his infectious grins. "Do this, Lanny. Tell them anything that will help to loosen them up, and when you come back report to me about it, and I may figure out some way to give you a bit of support." Then, suddenly serious, he pointed to papers on a table beside him. "Here is a stack of orders that I must sign tonight; so you two fellows go into the next room and get acquainted."

VI

Lanny had read much about this chief boondoggler and leaf raker who now made his home in the White House; a greatly abused man, but he didn't seem to mind it—he had chosen his enemies carefully. He didn't believe in the system of monopoly capitalism any more than Lanny did, and he didn't care if his system of relief by public spending brought the profiteers nearer to their doom. He had been quoted as saying about the program of the New Deal: "We shall spend and spend, and tax and tax, and elect and elect." He had carried out this program to such good effect that his great friend and hero had become the first man ever to be elected President for a third term, and by all the political signs he might have a fourth term if he wanted it.

Now the harnessmaker's son had set out to put the Nazi-Fascists out of business by the same method of unlimited spending. Oddly enough, he had most of the big businessmen behind him in this, but that didn't either worry him or please him especially; he had only two-thirds of a stomach left, and no time or strength for a superfluous emotion. He had reports to study, orders to give, quarrels to abate. He had to fly to England with the President's instructions and guide the controversies of high-ranking British and American staff officers, bringing them to an agreement as near as possible to what the President desired. He needed all the help he could get, and when he had sunk into a chair in the next room, sliding down into it until he was sitting pretty nearly on the back of his neck, he opened up. "The Boss said to me: 'Lanny Budd is one of us.' And that is enough. I want to talk to you frankly. May I call you Lanny?"

"Indeed yes."

"Call me Harry; it comes easier. There's going to be what the English call a good show in London this month. We have to settle definitely upon the plan of campaign. The Boss wants very much to invade across the Channel this summer, but Churchill won't hear of it; he insists that we haven't the air power for anything but a defensive attitude, and he won't have anything to do with an invasion. But meantime the Russians are clamoring and, strictly between us, threatening to quit if we don't come to their help with a second front. So we have to do something. Churchill wants us to go up through the Balkans. I assume you understand what he has in his mind."

"Of course. He wants us to be in possession of that territory when the war ends, and to keep the Russians away from the Dardanelles."

"And of course our military men are not going to tie us up in any balance-of-power game between Britain and Russia. We want to beat the Nazis in the quickest way we can, and the cheapest with regard to the lives of our boys. So I think the decision will be for some action in North Africa this fall. That would cut Rommel off and be a minor disaster for the Germans. It would settle the control of the Mediterranean and save us the tonnage we waste carrying stuff around Africa. Also, it would enable us to take Sicily and Southern Italy."

"And have airfields from which to bomb the munitions plants of Austria and southern Germany," ventured the amateur strategist.

"I see that you have the picture in mind. I'm not saying that will be the final decision, but that's the way matters appear to be shaping up. If you are in London when the decision is taken, I'll tell you about it. You won't be free to tell anybody else, but it will guide you in your work."

"That suits me fine," replied the P.A. "I have a little daughter in England whom I'd like to see."

"I know about her. I met Irma Barnes once or twice in night clubs before you married her. I did a little playing round with the smart crowd in those days. I wanted to understand their minds. It helps me now."

"The same for me," replied Lanny with a smile. "But I liked some of them a bit too well."

They talked for a few minutes about people they knew; but the burdens of the time pressed upon them, and presently they were talking about the bleak outlook before the country. The Germans had taken Sevastopol, and their plunge into the Ukraine had reached the Don River. The British were making a stand at a place in the deserts of Egypt called El Alamein, but it was uncertain if their line would hold. Hopkins said: "If the enemy gets to Suez, it may set us back for a long time. But don't ever doubt it, Lanny, we are going to get the troops and the weapons and win this war!"

He wanted to question the son of Budd-Erling and proceeded to put him through the same sort of grilling as Alston had done. He desired to know everything there was to know about conditions in Unoccupied France and French North Africa. Not merely did he have to consider what materials must be allotted for a campaign there, but he had to start guessing what foodstuffs and other supplies might be required later. Lanny told him that the natives, who wore nothing but cotton sheeting, were pretty nearly in rags now, and what they would look like after the havoc of an invasion was beyond any P.A.'s power to guess. A curious whim of destiny, that a harnessmaker's son from a town of the corn-and-hog country should have the job of deciding what food should be eaten and what clothing worn by the people of Morocco and Dahomey and Iceland and Trinidad and China and the Solomon Islands and pretty nearly every other strange part of the world you could think of!

VII

The competent Baker came and took Lanny back to the town. On the way he said that he had been instructed to provide Mr. Budd with a properly visaed passport, and when would he want it? Lanny said in about a week, and Baker said he would have to be in New York before that and would deliver the document personally. Also he would provide a ticket for him on the Clipper. Lanny gave Baker his phone number, and that was that.

The sensible thing would have been to stop at a hotel for the night; but the breeze was cool, and the moonlight on this foothill country so lovely, that he decided he would rather drive and think out some of his problems on the way. How many things he had to think about! He had been born into a time of strain and suffering, but at least nobody could say that it lacked variety, nobody had a right to be bored! Lanny had identified himself with a cause, and he lived in that and for that, and it kept him busy most of the time. Only rarely did the thought occur to him that the cause might fail; and those were indeed uncomfortable moments. In that case, he reflected, he wouldn't want to survive—and probably would not be allowed to.

Back by the same road he had come, a dog's journey, as the saying goes. West of Wilmington he picked up Highway Number 1 again, and it wasn't so crowded at one o'clock in the morning. The great trucks were moving slowly; the factories were blacked out—but all of them full of activity. Night or day was the same in wartime, and Lanny knew that was the case all over this vast land. America was going into action, preparing to show the world what a free people could do in the machine age. The P.A. had been that night in the brain center where the whole project had been conceived and from which it was directed. His whole being was afire with the sense of living in a great period of history, of seeing the world's future in the making. With Tennyson's Ulysses he could say:

> Much have I seen and known; cities of men
> And manners, climates, councils, governments,
> Myself not least, but honor'd of them all.

It was after three o'clock when he arrived at the apartment. He had a key and let himself in quietly. He undressed in his own room, and the first awareness Laurel had of his presence was when he slid into bed beside her. He said: "Go to sleep again. I am tired." She complied, and when later on she opened her eyes at the normal hour she lay still so as not to disturb him. That was easy for one who had not made herself a slave of the coffee habit and who found this hour of fresh awakening a good time to plan the story she was going to write that day.

Later they prepared the combination meal known as "brunch," and afterward he told her the news that he was scheduled to leave in a week or so. She could not hide the look of distress which crossed her sensitive features, and he hastened to say: "I am one of the lucky ones, darling. I'm not going to be in any danger. I am only going where I have been before; first to London, where the bombing now amounts to almost nothing; then to Vichy France and Algiers, where there is no bombing at all."

"And when am I to expect you back, Lanny?"

"I can't be sure about that. It is usually two or three months. It will surely be before your confinement—if you take care of yourself and don't overwork."

She made the promise, but he wasn't sure that she would keep it. She, too, had a stern master, who went by the name of Art, and sometimes she couldn't be sure whether it was more important to produce a baby or a minor masterpiece. She was modest about her talents but quietly determined to make the most of them, and she was rebellious against the vegetative state her condition called for.

"Listen, dear," he said, to spare her feelings; "there are interesting things that I would give anything to be able to tell you; but I am under explicit orders. It appears that the military forces are especially afraid of wives."

This brought a sparkle of mischief into her brown eyes. "I grant you, I have known a few who would not be good keepers of secrets; but I have also known men of the same sort."

He answered: "Professor Alston tells me that in one single project with which I am concerned there are thousands of wives who have no slightest idea what their husbands are working on."

"Misery loves company," she said. "But, as a matter of fact, I have been putting two and two together—a good many twos. Be sure I'm not saying a word to Agnes or anybody else, and I'm not having my feelings hurt. Some day you will tell me all about it, and I promise to be interested." It was the sort of wife for a P.A. to have, and he put his arms about her and made plain with many kisses that he knew what a prize he had drawn in the marriage lottery.

VIII

Downtown there was the efficient Mr. Post, an executive with many problems on his mind, and just now a smile on his face after the fashion of the cat which has swallowed the canary. "Hartley has talked over the telephone," he said, "and has made appointments which he must have thought sounded innocent. We have picked up the people and I am awaiting more reports today. I think they are the men we are looking for."

Lanny said: "I have orders to leave for abroad in about a week; so anything you get from me will have to be within that limit."

"I think we have everything already, Mr. Budd. If you don't mind, it will be better if you don't say anything to Hartley until the day before you are going. No use to unsettle his mind."

"Quite so. I have a handy excuse—an important client who has given me a commission. I suppose it will be all right if I leave the propaganda business in charge of Cartier?"

"He is prepared to carry it on as long as necessary. Hartley won't like it, of course, but you can give him a raise in salary to salve his feelings."

"What troubles me, Mr. Post, is the fear that Hartley will get his mind fixed on me as being responsible for his betrayal. I don't see how that can fail to happen. And sooner or later he or his associates will make their suspicions known to the enemy world."

"We mean to take the greatest pains to avoid that, Mr. Budd. We shall not arrest any of these men until we are sure we have them all; then we shall carefully prepare a story of how we came to detect them, and it will be a story which has nothing to do with you."

"It will be bound to get into the papers, will it not?"

"Unfortunately we cannot avoid arraigning them in court, nor keep them from getting lawyers to represent them. But the account we give of the affair will reveal some clue which put us on their trail, one which will convince them and leave no reason for suspecting you."

"But if Cartier testifies against them, and I introduced Cartier to Hartley—"

"Cartier will never testify. He will be arrested with them and arraigned with them. He will be in a cell with Hartley and will pretend to be furious with Hartley for getting him into this jam. In the course of their arguments Hartley may reveal details of importance. If later on Cartier is released, it will seem natural to Hartley and his gang, for they know perfectly well that Cartier was not in the secret of the diamonds and that his propaganda efforts were no crime."

"All that sounds plausible enough. But can Cartier afford to have his family name dragged into such a mess?"

"Cartier is not his real name, Mr. Budd. I apologize for not telling you that, but you know how it is, the less a man knows, the less chance there is that he may let something slip by accident. Cartier is a name for the occasion; when he comes out of jail, he will be a martyr in the eyes of Miss van Zandt and people of her sort, and will be in an excellent position to keep contact with them and report on what they are doing."

"That sounds all right to me," declared Lanny. "I hope that among those who will appreciate his martyrdom will be Mr. Harrison Dengue and the rest of the group who think so ill of President Roosevelt."

"We are surely not forgetting them," declared the F.B.I. man with emphasis.

IX

Lanny went up to the newly established office of the American Christian League, which so far consisted of three men and a secretary, unless you counted one elderly spinster on Fifth Avenue and her secretary and companion. Things at the office were peaceful, but promised activity. Hartley had been to call on the spinster—without consulting Lanny—and had brought back with him a manuscript which had been composed by a member of the numerous retinue which surrounded this old lady and plied her with compliments day and night. It was entitled *The Red Nightmare*, and Hartley said that he had listened carefully to what Miss van Zandt thought of it, and then repeated it all to her in more vigorous words, thus confirming her opinion that he was a man of excellent judgment. He had asked if she did not think it would make a good opening shot for the new League, and she had assented.

Lanny read the article and found it a collection of all the most uncomplimentary things which had been said about the Soviet Union. It was old stuff, and he commented: "We could do better; but if this is what Queen Hortensia wants, it is a command performance." So they had something to do right away, and the efficient Tom Cartier had collected samples of other such propaganda literature and was in process of getting estimates for a first edition of ten thousand copies. Lanny said: "Let's go easy on this one, because it's really not very good, and if we send it to Miss van Zandt's mailing list and put it on sale at a few meetings, that is all she will ever hear about and it will satisfy her."

"But we ought to be doing something at the office to make things look right," said the Englishman.

"I'll make out a list of names and addresses of the right sort of people, and you and Cartier can get up a letter telling them about our work."

Lanny went back to the apartment where he had such a list, compiled during the years that he had been watching the Nazi-Fascist agents and their dupes. He didn't in the least care how much money Hartley might collect, especially since he was hoping that the F.B.I. would scoop it all up in a few days. He told Laurel what he was free to tell her about it, and she helped by typing out the list. He said: "They won't get very far with it, because most of these people have their own movements and won't want any rivals; but it will help to make it look like the real thing."

Next day Baker telephoned and brought the passport and the ticket for the Clipper, five days from date. Lanny took those precious documents and put them in his safety-deposit box at the bank; then he drove out to have lunch with his friend Mr. Vernon, who had just received the shipment of the first mosaic from Algiers and was as happy as a child with a new toy. In truth there could be no jigsaw puzzle so fascinating; all his friends had come in to see it, and it was that rare thing in the lives of the very rich, something entirely new. This country gentleman, who had already paid Lanny's bill in full, was now open to a proposition for a large and really beautiful Moorish fountain, used for ritual ablutions, which Lanny had observed on his last visit, but hadn't quite had the nerve to buy. Mr. Vernon supplied the necessary courage, and the art expert drove back to New York well content with his day. It wasn't that the money was so important, but he had a business letter to carry in his suitcase, to be read by all the spies and secret agents who would rummage through his belongings in the hotels of two continents.

X

To his wife he said: "I think you have a holiday coming to you. Let's have some fun before I leave." So they packed several suitcases and stowed them in the car and drove on a warm summer evening through a thunder shower to the town of Newcastle and had a reunion with the Budd tribe. They were begged to stay, but no, they were for the open road. Next morning they set out along the little Newcastle River and into the Berkshire Hills; from there northward to the foothills of the Green Mountains, and westward into the Adirondacks. Fine roads winding through endless pine forests, and vistas of mountains, tier behind tier, with rushing streams and blue lakes in the valleys—they were reminded continually of southern Bavaria where Hitler had his eyrie, and where they had had their first adventure together. They had been in fear at that time and hadn't been able to give much thought to scenery, but now by agreement they put all cares behind them and enjoyed their lives while still the little lamp shone. *Freut euch des Lebens weil noch das Lämpchen glüht!*

They had lunch at a summer-resort hotel, and Laurel slept for a couple of hours. Then they drove again, and toward evening came to the "camp" belonging to Lanny's old friends the Murchisons. He had telephoned to make sure Adella was there, and on the way he told Laurel about this couple, how Harry had wooed and not won Beauty Budd in the carefree days before World War I, and how he had married his secretary on the rebound, and how Adella had taken Goya for her hobby and purchased several examples with Lanny's advice. They had this comfortable camp on Saranac lake, and Adella was there with three women friends, enough to play bridge, but they were bored and glad to see company. In these days the men were all up to their ears in work in hot and smoky Pittsburgh; so were most of the women, but Adella had overworked and the doctor had ordered her away, and she had brought with her three members of the "younger set" who were "expecting" and therefore had an excuse. Now Lanny had brought a fourth, and they could have a pleasant time sympathizing with one another's symptoms while Lanny went fishing. In the course of his career he had caught a number of big political fish, but he didn't succeed in getting a single nibble from an Adirondack trout.

Laurel and Adella became friends at once, and Laurel was begged to stay and spend the summer in this cool delightful spot. But duty called her back to the sweltering city—she had to be near a library, so she declared. Adella said that Harry would be grieved at having missed them; he might not get here more than once or twice in the whole summer. He had given his plane to the government, and it wasn't considered patriotic to drive a car, and anyhow, you couldn't get the gas. They all wanted to know how Lanny had got it, and he explained that the car belonged to his father, and Lanny was using a couple of months' supply of ration coupons. Robbie, who had half a dozen cars, didn't have time to drive any of them except between his office and his home.

They stayed two days, and then set out again, through Keene valley and past Schroon Lake, and so out of the mountains and down along a little river to Albany. There was their old friend the Hudson River, where Henry had been so disappointed not to find the Northwest Passage. In a couple of hours they were passing Krum Elbow, and Lanny said: "The Squire doesn't have much time to look at his Christmas trees these days." He said nothing about "Shangri-La," and nothing about a P.A.'s duties; but Laurel knew well what he was thinking. Her lovely holiday was over, and she was coming back into the world of suffering and danger.

XI

That night, in their snug little nest, she said: "Let's try one more séance." They had held several, but always with disappointing results. Otto Kahn had talked only idle pleasantries and had reported that the "spirits" who made their appearance were persons of no social distinction, nor yet of intellectual; he kept insisting that he knew nothing about the Holdenhursts and did not have the honor of the acquaintance of Laurel Creston's grandmother. Now the time was growing short, for Lanny was to depart the day after next, and Laurel wouldn't dare to try a séance with anybody else. She had told her friend Agnes that sometimes she talked in her sleep, and not to worry about it if she heard it.

They tried again; and there was the genial banker, always on call. They could imagine him, dapper and elegant in his evening clothes, for surely he would not have appeared otherwise. He was ready to chat, but didn't have anything important to say. When they asked him to produce some of their friends in the spirit world he said that conditions here were difficult; but he didn't explain why. He said there was a spirit named Hodges, who had been one of his—Otto's—stockbrokers, but who wasn't a very talkative man, especially where there was no ticker and no quotation board. There was tiresome old Sir Basil, as always; and there was a lady who claimed that she had a special revelation from God. "You know how persistent these religious souls can be," said Otto.

"You haven't seen anything of God yourself?" inquired Lanny. And the reply was: "How would I know?" quite in the style of the New York sophisticates. When Lanny asked about Reverdy Holdenhurst and then about Lanny's former wife Trudi, the banker said that he was feeling under the weather that evening, and his voice faded away. It was for all the world like a phonograph running down.

Laurel came out of her trance and was told about all this. She asked, as she had asked before: "What can this fantastic thing mean?" Lanny's reply also had been heard before: "I'd give a good part of what I own to anybody who could find out."

It was difficult even to talk to the average person about these phenomena. You might explain ever so clearly that you didn't pretend to know what these entities really were; they called themselves "spirits," and that was as far as you could get. The person would say "Spirits!" and go off and report that you had "blown your top," and everybody to whom he mentioned the matter would agree. But that wouldn't stop the phenomena from continuing, everywhere, all over the world. There were thousands of persons who had this mediumistic gift, and many who never made money out of it, and gave no signs of being "cracked." The voices spoke and did their best to convince you that they were real, even to having their feelings hurt when they weren't believed.

Laurel said: "The most amazing thing is that my subconscious mind should be full of such fragments of human personality of whom my conscious mind never can get direct knowledge, and that they should use my voice without my ever hearing it. If it is Otto Kahn really, why can he not speak to me when I am awake?"

"Ask him," said Lanny, half seriously.

The wife replied: "All right." Then, after a moment's pause: "Mr. Kahn, won't you kindly use my voice now? I'll keep perfectly still and not interfere."

There followed a long silence; no sound whatever, and Laurel felt no power tugging at her vocal cords. No, she would have to go back into that other kind of sleep, which she knew was different, although she could not say in what the difference consisted or how she managed to turn the switch that brought one kind instead of the other. "I suppose it's a suggestion," she said, "but how I give it I could not say."

"Do you know how you tell your muscles to lift you up from your bed or to let you down again? You don't know that, and the wisest scientist in the world cannot tell you how a desire, or an act of will, can cause one of your muscles to contract."

XII

There was another aspect of this subject pressing upon her mind. "Lanny dear," she began, "there is something we ought to have an understanding about. You are going away, and I might never see you again."

"I am really not going into any danger, darling."

"I know you have to tell me that, but I don't want to fool myself. There isn't any safe place in Europe now, and everything will get worse before it gets better. What I want you to know is that if you should die, I won't be thinking about anything but trying to find you. Psychic research is just a curiosity now, but then it would become my life. Promise me you will try your best to come back to me!"

"Of course, Laurel!"

"I will go into a trance every night. Let us agree, exactly eight o'clock by New York time. You won't forget that?"

"Surely not."

"I will have Agnes sit by and tell me if you come. And if I don't hear from you that way, I'll go to other mediums and try. Don't tell me now, but think of things about yourself that I don't know, and tell them to me in the trance, so that later I can get Robbie or Beauty or others to verify them."

"Be sure that I'll think up plenty of evidence," he assured her, not without a smile. "Apparently I won't have much else to do. I can't find that the 'spirits' ever seem to have any work."

"It's curious; they appear to be wandering about in a void, lost and bewildered. What little they do, they don't seem to know how they do it. Let's promise that, if we ever find ourselves in that world, we shan't rest until we find each other."

"What else could interest us?"

"And when we do, we'll get busy with some medium and devise a way to convince our friends on earth that it really is Lanny and Laurel and not just 'that old telepathy.'"

"It's a bargain!" he said. "But I'm afraid it wouldn't do much good. Whatever the evidence might be, it would be embodied in one of the volumes of the Society for Psychical Research and gather dust on the library shelves." He had become discouraged about trying to interest people in another world. It would have to wait until this world was a more decent place to live in.

XIII

In the morning Lanny went to call at the F.B.I. offices. He found his reticent friend Mr. Post in a state bordering on complacency. "We have four men and one woman inside the trap at this moment and all we have to do is to shut the door. We are waiting for their chief, who is expected in the city tomorrow morning. Then we are ready to go into action."

"Good work!" said the P.A.

"Incidentally we have a story for the newspapers that will completely cover you and lead them off the track."

"I have been thinking that over," Lanny said. "I have a suggestion, if you don't mind."

"Surely not."

"Imagine this for the moment. As soon as you give me the signal tomorrow that everything is ready, I rush into the League office very much excited. I tell Hartley I have just learned from the janitor of my apartment building that Federal agents have been there and ransacked the rooms in my absence; that they have had my telephone wires tapped for weeks and have been getting the contents of my trash basket. I tell Hartley that I'm going to bolt, and he had better do the same. I give him half of what is left of the money—or a little more. When he comes out of the building, your men nab him at the street door. Wouldn't that leave me in the clear?"

"The trouble is, Mr. Budd, he wouldn't bolt until he had telephoned at least one of his gang and told that one to warn the others."

"I have thought of that, too. You might have the telephone wires cut, but that would excite suspicion. I am wondering if it might not be possible to have his wire diverted in the exchange, or perhaps on the roof of the office building, and have a woman answer his calls; and when he gives a number, sound the busy signal. That would make him try several different numbers, and it might be important for you, because it might provide fresh clues."

"Let me think about that, Mr. Budd." There was silence in the room for several minutes; then the man said: "I can't see any flaw in that, and, as you say, it might bring us something new. But suppose you didn't find Hartley in the office tomorrow morning?"

"I have promised him a check today, and I can phone him and say that I am very much rushed and will see him the first thing in the morning."

"What hour will suit you?"

"The earlier the better; I am taking the Clipper for England at noon. What time do you expect the man whom you call the chief to arrive?"

"He is not going to arrive in the city; we are going to take him off the train at a near-by stop, for fear that he may be intending to get off before he reaches the city and transfer his valuable baggage to somebody else. We can be ready for action at ten tomorrow, if that is agreeable to you."

"Exactly right," Lanny said. "I'll be packed and have my bags in the car."

"I will phone you at nine if all goes well. I will say your name three times—Budd, Budd, Budd. That will mean that arrangements are complete and that you are to proceed to the League office and carry out your part. If there is a delay, I won't phone; just wait at your place until I do."

"Don't make it too late," Lanny replied. "I have a really important mission and I can't afford to miss that Clipper."

"Don't worry," said the other. "In case of emergency I could call the airport and arrange to have the Clipper wait for you."

Lanny chuckled. "I have thought myself important sometimes, but never that much!"

XIV

The P.A. went home and from there telephoned Hartley. "I have good news for you," he said, "also some money. I've been out of town, and I'm crowded today, but I'll see you at the office in the morning without fail." That was that, and he set about writing letters to his clients and making business arrangements for his trip.

In the evening he took Laurel for a drive and told her what was in the wind. It was a relief to be able to tell her something, and this was an achievement in which she had a part. It seemed to her the height of melodrama—and so indeed was everything connected with this war. She was so excited that she wondered if she could sleep, so he took her to a roof garden and they had supper. They were spending every moment together that they could. When they came home, and she was undressed and ready for bed, she suggested: "Let's try one more séance."

She lay down and closed her eyes, and Lanny sat by the bedside, waiting for any voice that might speak. But there came no voice, only the sound of gentle breathing, and after a while he realized that his tired wife had made the wrong mental connection, had got aboard the wrong train. He lay beside her, speculating over the question of how this had happened and what it meant. Had there been spirits waiting to communicate, and were they now disappointed? Would they wake her up, or would they come to her in her dreams? Here was the thing called sleep, just ordinary sleep, and yet what a strange thing! In it his wife went off into a world of her own, often a completely crazy world of fears and adventures in which she was apart from her husband, in the company of fugitive and fantastic beings, "the fickle pensioners of Morpheus' train." Lanny was possessed by the thought of how little man knows of himself and his own mind.

XV

In the morning the P.A. finished his packing, and sat reading the papers, full of disturbing news which he could not think about consecutively. His wife's nerves were also on edge, for she had had bad dreams, she told him; she was becoming what the world called superstitious. The phone rang; it was Robbie to say good-by, and Lanny had to excuse himself: "I am expecting a call about an urgent matter. I'll call back before I leave."

Then silence again, and more waiting; until at last came another ring, and the voice of Post, giving the signal: "Budd, Budd, Budd." Lanny answered with "Roger," which was part of the lingo of the war. "Start now," said the voice.

His car was at the door, and he took his bags down. Laurel followed. She was going with him to the airport and would drive the car back to the garage. A girl from Robbie's office would come and get it there. Robbie had offered to leave the car, but Laurel didn't want it; she said that taxis were easier in big-city traffic.

Lanny drove to the neighborhood of the League office and managed to find a parking space on a side street some distance away. He walked to the office quickly, so that he might have color in his cheeks. Once, years ago, when his friend Rick had been writing and staging plays, he had watched an actor behind the scenes working up excitement preparatory to bursting in upon the stage. Now Lanny did the same, and found no great difficulty, for he really was nervous, having thought of so many things that might go wrong.

There was Hartley, waiting, and the little drama was played through convincingly enough. When Lanny told the bad news the Englishman leaped up, exclaiming "Good God!"—this, it appeared, was the standard exclamation for the English gentleman. He wanted to get out of there instantly; but then he thought of his confederates and said: "Wait a moment!" and took up the telephone, just as Post had predicted. He gave a number, and Lanny, standing near, could hear the busy signal. "Oh, hell!" the man exclaimed, and gave another number.

Lanny said: "I can't wait," and planked a roll of bills down on the table. "This will keep you going." And then: "When things have settled down you can write me in care of my father. Mark it personal." He turned and bolted out of the room.

And that was all there was to it. Lanny observed a dapper young man standing in the hallway, and two more down at the entrance of the building. He hoped they wouldn't mistake him for Hartley, and they didn't. He hurried to the car and drove to one of the East River bridges, and so to the airport, where the great seaplane was resting in the water basin. On the way he told his wife about what had happened, and when they reached the airport he called up his friend Post and said: "This is the man whose name is pronounced three times." The answer was: "Everything is jake, and we are everlastingly obliged to you." Lanny added: "If ever I want to take up a stage career, I'll come to you for a recommendation."

XVI

There was time to spare, so he showed his wife what a luxurious vehicle he was going to travel in. She did her best to pretend that it comforted her, but she had learned that he was flying north, by much the same route on which he had been wrecked before. Now and then her lips would tremble, but she said very bravely that she didn't want to make it hard for him and would go on and do her work, and learn to pray, after the fashion of his esteemed stepfather. He took her back to the solid concrete, and they strolled up and down until the last call came. Then he gave her a long kiss, and with tears running down her cheeks she said: "Don't forget, if anything goes wrong, I'll still be waiting for you."

"Eight P.M. on the dot," he answered, and forced a smile, because it is embarrassing to a man to have to wipe his eyes in public.

He went aboard, and the great seabird glided out into the Sound and rose into the air and away. It was a warm and quiet July day, and all the prognostications were favorable. Lanny had plenty of things to read, and a good appetite—he told himself that he had helped with an important job and might help with others, and he couldn't do any good to the Allied cause by worrying about it.

No voyage could have been pleasanter. He was flown to Newfoundland, this time to the seaplane base of Botwood on a clear blue sound. From there on to the ancient island of Iceland, with its many glaciers and boiling springs; now many Yanks were there—or "G.I.'s," as they were calling themselves, playing with the idea that they were "government issued," like everything else they touched. The Icelanders hadn't invited them and were making the best of a trying situation. Lanny saw few of them, for the plane paused only to refuel; it sped on through the unbroken daylight, and set its passengers down in the harbor of Prestwick in western Scotland, now a great airport. When he presented his credentials he was concerned lest the P.M.'s secretary might have overlooked the little matter of having a name taken off the blacklist; but evidently it had been done. The official, speaking with a strong Scottish burr, bade him welcome to the United Kingdom.

The first thing Lanny did was to borrow one of those little sheets, made up of four half-size pages, which passed for a newspaper in a nation under siege. There, under a modest headline and a New York dateline, he read a dispatch revealing that the Federal Bureau of Investigation had just arrested a group of five men and one woman charged with purchasing diamonds in America and smuggling them to Sweden, from there to be taken into Germany. Names of the gang were not given, but there was a dramatic story as to how the discovery of this conspiracy had happened to be made.

It was narrated that a man walking on Broadway had been observed to draw his handkerchief from his pocket, and from it had dropped a rough diamond. The man who saw the incident chanced to be himself a "diamond man," and he picked up the stone, intending to return it to the owner; but first it occurred to him to walk ahead and look at the man's face. Diamond men are a small group and rather clannish, and they know one another; but this man was a stranger. Realizing that it was wartime, and that diamonds were among the most important of war materials, the man had followed the stranger to his hotel, observed him get his key and go to his room, and then had called the F.B.I. There had followed a patient and careful job of detective work, continuing for several weeks. Lanny chuckled to himself as he reread the story; he didn't begrudge the hard-working agents the credit they had taken—he surely didn't want any share of it for the son of Budd-Erling. He thought that the story put him "in the clear."

BOOK FOUR

Still Point of the Turning World

11

Mother of the Free

I

LANNY'S first thought in England was of his little daughter. He had cabled Irma, and as soon as he reached London he telephoned the Castle to ask if it would be agreeable for him to call. It always had been, but he never neglected the formality. The relationship of a man to his ex-wife and her new husband is a difficult one at best, and the pair were trying to show what good manners could achieve in that field. Irma said: "Frances has asked about you every day for more than a year." Lanny might have made some joking remark about how trying that must have been; but he knew that a sense of humor was not Lady Wickthorpe's strong point, so he replied: "I appreciate your patience."

Gone were the good old days when Lanny had been able to step into his car and run out to Wickthorpe Castle in less than a couple of hours. Now he had to look up a timetable, and get to Paddington station on time, and be jostled by crowds that never failed to be there in spite of the government's efforts to reduce travel. When he stepped off the train he found that the child had come to meet him, driving her pony-cart, with a groom riding behind. Fourteen months had passed, and he was amazed when he saw her—this tall, long-legged girl! But when she flung her arms about him and kissed him, it was the same Frances, more demonstrative than her mother, more like her father in temperament, and having to be continually repressed. "Oh, Father, why did you take so long?" None of the business of calling her parents by their first names, of which Irma had always disapproved.

The groom touched his hat, and tucked two suitcases under his feet and the typewriter on his lap, and the pony trotted off—a properly trained English pony who knew that the right side of the road was the wrong side and that the left side was the right side. And while the well-trimmed hedges of an English village glided silently past them,

Frances plied this wonderful, rarely seen father with questions about where he had been and what had happened to him. Presently he told her that he would make a bedtime story of it; now she should tell him about herself and what she was studying and how the family was. So the floodgates were opened, and he learned the latest news about a castle which dated back to the time of Shakespeare and Sir Francis Drake, and which was an important factor in the life of this blessed isle, controlling the destinies of something like a thousand people.

The estate couldn't have been kept going if it hadn't been for the money which Irma Barnes had inherited from J. Paramount Barnes of Chicago, a disciple of Sir Francis Drake who had operated in the field of street-railway finance instead of on the high seas. The people of the estate knew all about her ladyship's fortune; the men all touched their hats and the women smiled and bowed to the little girl, and to her father, whom they knew at least by sight, for he had lived in a residence known as the Lodge years ago when he was still Irma's husband. These proper villagers tried their best not to think of this as a scandal, but as something exotic, characteristic of the wild and woolly West, which they took Chicago to be. After all, Britain was an empire, and might receive a visit from the King of Dahomey, or the Akhoond of Swat, bringing not one extra wife but four, the limit permitted to Mohammedans.

II

The Countess of Wickthorpe emerged from the "lift" which was a part of her modernization of the Castle. She wore a white housedress and looked vigorous and handsome with her crown of dark brown hair. Lanny's first thought was that the monster of *embonpoint* had been licked by the war; Irma appeared at least ten pounds lighter, and it became her well. She greeted him cordially, saying: "You have stayed away from us a long time!" Apparently she had never learned that he had been put on the blacklist by B4; he didn't tell her, for the less gossip there was on that subject the better. He told her that he had found travel less easy to arrange.

As on the last occasion, he was going to be put up in the cottage occupied by Mrs. Fanny Barnes, Irma's mother; and, as before, he said that would be perfectly agreeable. So many friends had fled the capital, Irma explained. Some of the refugee children had gone back to London, but they might be coming again any day—there were rumors of deadly new German weapons. Lanny said he had heard such rumors; and so they got to Irma's favorite topic, her hatred of this fratricidal conflict which was wrecking the modern world and could only end in the triumph of the Bolshevik terror. Conversation at Wickthorpe wasn't very entertaining these days, for all roads led to Moscow.

His Lordship came in from making the rounds of the estate. He was playing the role of country gentleman, having taken the increase of food production as the one rational thing a man could do in a mad world. He rode horseback, because petrol was so scarce. His erect figure looked well in a riding suit and his blond hair shone when he took off his hat in the sunshine. He shook hands cordially with his old friend Lanny, asked after his health and that of his father and mother, and then fell to talking casually about the state of his crops. Such was his manner, and whether you had come back after fourteen days or fourteen years wouldn't make much difference. Ceddy took life seriously, but rarely talked about it. The only place where he permitted the expression of emotions was on the stage, and not too much of it there.

He was deeply concerned about politics, both at home and abroad, but circumstances no longer permitted him to expound his ideas publicly. Once in the House of Lords, and then his duty was done; people knew what he thought, and some day he would have the melancholy satisfaction of saying: "You remember what I told you?" When he was among persons who agreed with him, he would speak freely, and few others were invited to the Castle nowadays. Lanny, in his role of near-Fascist, was one of these; and in the evening, seated outside in the cool twilight, the wife, the husband, and the ex-husband enjoyed the luxury of complete agreement.

Lanny, of course, was asked about his trip around the world and about his marriage in Hongkong. He said that his wife was a writer of magazine stories, but he didn't mention the character of her stories nor that her pen name was Mary Morrow. He answered questions about Hongkong and southern and central China, but didn't mention that he had visited "Red" China, and said only that he had been permitted to fly out through Russia, but had had no opportunity to make observations. Much more interesting to the earl and his countess were his more recent experiences in Vichy France and North Africa. Ceddy, until recently a Foreign Office man, knew most of the appeasers in France and had done everything in his power to further their program. Now, apparently, it was too late; Churchill was in the saddle, riding madly, and Britain was approaching a precipice, beyond which was the abyss of Bolshevism.

Lanny tried to be as cheering as he could. He said there was intense anti-Red feeling in America which was bound to produce a sharp reaction immediately after the war, however it ended. "How can it end," asked Ceddy, "save in the ruin of Western Europe? France will be a battlefield, and Germany completely exhausted." When Lanny said that Russia would be exhausted, too, the other answered: "Yes, but she will recover more quickly, because those people breed like rabbits. And she will have all the border states, and China, too, and how long will it take her agents to stir up revolution in India?"

Such were the ideas which Lanny had always heard in this ancient castle. They were the ideas of the privileged in all the countries he visited, the people to whom class was more than country. Lanny hated the ideas, but it was his job to express agreement and listen, and find out what powerful persons were still spending week ends at the Castle and voicing these ideas and the latest schemes for putting pressure on statesmen to bring about a compromise peace. Lanny would go back to London and type out a report and have it delivered to the American Ambassador. No doubt when F.D.R. received it he would tell some of it to Churchill over the transatlantic telephone, and sometimes it would be news to the anti-Nazi Prime Minister and sometimes not.

III

When Lanny returned to London he phoned Rick, who had taken to helping one of the labor papers for the duration. Once a successful playwright, able to entertain even the carriage trade, Eric Vivian Pomeroy-Neilson now couldn't think about anything except countering the intrigues of the Fascists and the near-Fascists all over the world. He despised the Cliveden and Wickthorpe sets and had been blasting them for years. For that reason Lanny no longer went to stay at The Reaches, Rick's home; the two men met in secret in a little hotel they had agreed upon. Lanny booked a room there, and the lame journalist and his sympathetic wife came and spent the day.

What a time they had, catching up with fourteen months of personal history of two families, indeed of several more, for Nina and Rick knew both Robbie and Beauty and had to be told about them, and still more important, about Lanny's marriage, and what sort of partner he had got. He had sent a photograph, and also the stories of Mary Morrow cut out of magazines; but that wasn't enough for Nina; she had to be told how they were getting along, and how Laurel was living, and how she took her husband's long absences.

Lanny had to recite once more the story of his year's adventures; and this time he didn't have to hide anything, save only the name of President Roosevelt. He could tell Rick about China, and especially Yenan; about Ulan-Bator and Kuibyshev and Moscow, and the two-hour interview with Stalin. Rick could make notes and could use this information in his writings, of course omitting anything that might point to Lanny as a source. The same was true for France and North Africa and other lands. For years before the war Lanny had been doing what he could to light the path of the British labor movement by bringing inside stories, forecasts, and warnings to this trusted friend, who would write them up and get them published, sometimes by a secret and indirect route.

In return Rick would tell all that he knew about the course of events; some of it inside stuff, for a baronet's son had access to important people, even to many who did not share his political coloration but who respected him for his integrity and believed that the people had a right to know what was going on behind the scenes. In spite of all the Nazi atrocities, there were still influential persons who wanted to beat Hitler but not too badly, and who were dreaming of an agreement which would prevent the Reds from breaking into the Balkans and gaining control of the Dardanelles. Lanny told what he had heard over the week end at Wickthorpe, and Rick told what his father had heard among his associates in the Athenaeum and the Carlton clubs. Rick said there was going to be a big military powwow of the Allied staffs, beginning in a week or so, and he might be in a position to get some of the inside stuff. Lanny didn't say that Harry Hopkins had promised to tip him off on the same subject; he just said: "Maybe I can learn something too."

IV

Lanny's arrangement with the Prime Minister had been that he was to drop a note, marked personal, to the unobtrusive young secretary, Mr. Martin. He did so, and received no direct answer, but next day was called to the telephone at his hotel, and a voice said: "Mr. Budd, this is Fordyce, whom you may possibly remember having met just before you left for home last year." Lanny replied promptly that he would never forget. When the voice asked if he might have the pleasure of seeing Mr. Budd again, Mr. Budd said yes, and agreed to await the arrival of this representative of B4, the ultra-secret British Intelligence department.

Lanny had acquired a great respect for this organization. They had done a perfect job on him, and as a professional he could appreciate it. When their representative was safely ensconced in his room and had started to present apologies, Lanny said: "Not at all, Mr. Fordyce; you were perfectly correct, on the basis of the evidence you had. You understand, I was not at liberty to reveal to you for whom I was working."

"Certainly, Mr. Budd. I had an uneasy suspicion about it. Also, I could guess that you might be on your way home, anyhow."

Lanny chuckled. "That guess was correct, and you saved me trouble by arranging for my prompt flight. So all is well, and we are friends, I trust."

"Righto! The Prime Minister has sent us a note, saying that you are to have everything you want. May I say, that is an unusual privilege in these times."

"The Prime Minister has his reasons, which some day I may be free to explain to you. Let me say straight off what I have in mind, and that is, to have a private talk with Rudolf Hess."

"I presume that might be arranged. You understand, he is an important prisoner of state, and especially guarded. He is a difficult prisoner and has to be treated to some extent as a mental patient. We use great care not to excite him."

"Knowing him well, I can readily believe that. You must know that he thinks of me as his devoted friend and sympathizer, and I wish to continue in that role. If you were to take me to him, he would know at once that I had gone over to your side, and so he would close his mouth, or possibly even break into bitter reproaches. It is my idea to make him think that I am coming to him clandestinely, and without the knowledge of his captors. I should like to have a jailer smuggle me into his room in the dead of night, and I'll tell Hess that I have paid that jailer, say, a hundred pounds. Hess is used to bribery and corruption himself and would have no difficulty in believing such a story."

"I see what you mean, Mr. Budd, and it seems to me a promising idea."

"You will naturally wish to know what I expect to get from the prisoner. I have no wish to keep matters secret from you, and if you have a dictaphone in his sleeping room it will be all right with me— rather better, in fact, because it will save me the task of having to remember what may be a long conversation. Rudi, who is supposed to be so reticent, is really a talkative fellow among his few intimates, and I don't suppose he has seen any of these in the past year."

"Indeed not; he is kept strictly, but he is fairly well informed as to the outside world, because he is permitted to have a radio set."

"You are indeed treating him well!"

"We are treating him according to his rank in Germany, and of course in strict accord with the Geneva Convention. We could not fail to do this, even if we wished otherwise, because they have many prisoners of ours upon whom they might retaliate. But of course Hess is not satisfied; he argues that he came as an ambassador and should enjoy diplomatic status; we consider him a military prisoner, because he is an officer of the Luftwaffe and came in uniform. Those in charge of him have had many wrangles with him on this subject."

"That I can imagine; no doubt I'll hear about it from him. You must understand that I have been posing as a Nazi sympathizer for many years, and have enjoyed the friendship of Hitler for about fifteen years, and of Hess about five. I cannot guess what I may find out from him, or rather, I could guess a great number of things which might or might not come out in our talk. One thing, I ought to be able to learn whether he has ever had any message from Germany or has been able to send one. That I am sure would be of interest to you."

"Indeed yes, Mr. Budd. And there might be one or two other things which we could suggest that you give him a chance to talk about."

V

The B4 man went on to reveal that the Number Three Nazi had recently been taken to the Maindiff Court Hospital, near the small town of Abergenny. Mr. Fordyce pronounced it so, with the accent on the third syllable; then he explained that it was spelled Abergavenny, with the accent on the fourth syllable. It was in the county of Monmouth, close to the border of Wales, and was an old town; near it was a twelfth-century Norman castle which appeared to exercise a spell upon the imagination of the unhappy prisoner. He was permitted to drive there, accompanied by an officer of the guard, and with other members of the guard following in the rear. He and his mongrel dog, called Hippo, would lie by the double moat of the ruined castle and watch the ducks on the surface of the water and the two golden carp which dwelt below.

"We'll be happy to motor you there," said the agreeable agent; and when Lanny objected that he didn't like to use up any of the nation's precious petrol, the man said that it wouldn't take much, only about fifteen gallons, and what they might get out of it was worth the price.

"You will be the guest of B4," he insisted. When Lanny had talked with this middle-aged gentleman a year ago, Fordyce had given the impression of being well filled out; now he was considerably slimmer, and his cheeks were not so rosy as they had been. That was the case with pretty nearly everybody in besieged London, and some of the people gave the same depressing effect as the ruins of the buildings.

Lanny said: "I hope that you will confine discussion of this project to as few persons as possible, for I am still playing a dangerous role, and you know that there are always possibilities of a leak."

"No one knows about it so far except my superior, who got the order directly from the Prime Minister. The only other person who needs to know is the medical superintendent in charge of the hospital. He carries the responsibility for Hess's welfare, and naturally we could not keep him in ignorance of a matter which will undoubtedly have an effect upon his patient, whether for the better or the worse we cannot be sure."

Lanny assented to that, and added: "Won't you also have to tell one or more of the jailers?"

"I don't see why they need know anything about it. If you are let into Hess's room in the middle of the night, he will not see who lets you in, and will have to accept what you tell him. It had better be the medical superintendent himself, and then none of the men will question what is going on."

"Fine!" exclaimed the P.A. He took out his billfold and from it extracted a folded sheet of paper which he opened. "Here is an idea," he said. "Here are four slips of flimsy. On each I have typed the names 'Kurvenal-Siegfried.' The first of these is the name of a character in Wagner's *Tristan*, who is described as 'the truest of the true.' It is the code name I gave to Hess so that he could communicate with me in England. Siegfried is the code name that Hitler gave me so that if I had anything to communicate to him I could be sure he would know where it came from."

"You have indeed been playing a difficult game, Mr. Budd."

"I have had special advantages, which were prepared a long time before this war. Now it is my idea to roll each of these slips into a little ball, and get it to Hess in his food. Such a pellet could be pressed into a chunk of bread, or into an apple, or a not-too-soft pudding. He might fail to notice one or two and swallow them; that is why I should try several times. It might be that he wouldn't eat that particular chunk of bread, and if so, we could put the pellet into another for the next meal. It wouldn't do any harm if he got several; they would all mean one thing to him and one only, that I was on the outside and planning to help him. He would be greatly excited, but would try to hide his excitement, and if this went on for several days, he would be prepared to have me appear in his room in the night, and to believe that I had really been corrupting his guards. We could talk in whispers and with all the atmosphere of melodrama."

"You Americans read detective stories, too!" was the Englishman's comment.

Lanny replied: "It was Sherlock Holmes who taught us most of what we know on the subject. And let me remind you that I watched the process by which you chaps lured Hess to Britain, and if there was ever a rawer piece of melodrama, I have never come upon it in any of our 'whodunits.' "

An Englishman's natural color came back into the B4 man's cheeks, and he beamed as he remarked: "It was rather good, we do admit." He couldn't refrain from adding: "Is 'whodunit' an American word, Mr. Budd? We are supposed to keep track of them, out of courtesy to your Armed Forces."

"It would pain you to mutilate the language in that fashion," replied the P.A. with his most amiable smile.

Said the Englishman: "I understand that our two armies are now in process of dividing up the burden of learning a new language. They are listing the objects which have different names and are going half-and-half on them. We are to agree that a spanner is a wrench, and you in turn are to agree that gas is petrol. So we hope to operate without confusion—except to the Hun."

VI

The program they agreed upon was that Mr. Fordyce was to drive that afternoon to the town with the abbreviated Welsh name and have a confidential talk with the medical superintendent. If he approved, the pellets would be fed to the patient one each day, and on the evening of the fourth day Lanny would be driven to the place early enough to confer with the superintendent. At midnight he would be escorted to the prisoner's room, and the guard who always slept in the room with him would be instructed to go outside until summoned again. Lanny said that was all O.K., and he would spend part of the interim making up his mind what he wanted to say to the prisoner and what he would try to get from him. If Mr. Fordyce had other suggestions, he might give them to Lanny on the drive.

So it was agreed, and the son of Budd-Erling went back to the job of renewing his acquaintances in London and picking up ideas and information. Rick had given him the address of his elder son, Alfy, who got leave and came to town. Alfy had been taken out of his fighting job and put to training younger flyers; that had come near to breaking his heart, but now that he was used to it, he had to admit that it was a better employment of his experience. The relief to his parents hadn't lasted long, for now his younger brother had been stationed at "Hell's Corner," down at the southeast point of this tight little island. He had got it rather badly a couple of months ago, but now was nearly all right again and ready for another go.

How different appeared the situation of England since Lanny had last talked with this young, old friend! Then it had been touch and go; now Alfy was quietly certain that they had got the Hun down. The new Budd-Erling pursuit plane was tops, as good as even the newest "Spit." That would tickle Robbie Budd, but unfortunately Lanny had no way to get the word to him until he, Lanny, got back home. The only thing that could change the situation now, said Alfy, was something completely new from the enemy. Lanny warned him about jet propulsion, and this slender, high-strung Englishman said maybe so, such bombs might make a bit of trouble, but before they could be produced in quantity the British would have them, too. "We're working on them, day and night, let me tell you."

Alfy revealed other secrets of his dangerous trade, for he had known Lanny from boyhood, and knew that Budd-Erling had a right to know everything. Blueprints and models and formulas of aerodynamics were all of first-rate importance, but nothing could take the place of actual combat experience, the things that men reported day after day as they came in from meetings with the enemy in which one or the other had to die. Alfy had had two full years of it, in addition to what he had learned in trying to help the Spanish Republic. He was only twenty-five, but had lines of care in his thin, sensitive features and a touch of gray in his hair. He slept very badly, but counted himself lucky to be alive and still to have something to give to his "Mother of the Free."

"We're going to hold the fort for you," Alfy declared. And his friend could assure him: "The Yanks are coming! We'll put enough weight on this little island to sink it!"

Said the airman with a smile: "We must get more barrage balloons to hold it up."

VII

The B4 agent had said: "When I call you on the telephone, I'll talk about a golf game." So, next day, he reported: "I have inspected the golf course and it's in good condition. I think we can have our round in three days." Two days later he called again: "Three of the four golf balls have been lost, and I think I know who found them." Lanny chuckled and said that he would be ready to play off the match on the morrow.

At two o'clock the next day Fordyce called for Lanny in one of those smallish Austin cars which were saving much precious petrol for Britain. Lanny, who had long legs, could just get them in. They drove by the road he had always taken to Wickthorpe Castle, and then on, slightly north of west, through Oxford and Gloucester, historic names. The Englishman told about his visit to the hospital and what he had found there. It was a fairly large place, new, and full of wounded men. Hess had a room at the extreme end of the "female wing," opening onto a small lawn with iron railings. He was never alone, day or night. He would stroll about the countryside on parole. Being a wealthy man, with money in several banks in neutral countries, he could indulge his whims and was permitted to do so within limits; he chose to dress himself in a blue sports coat, gray flannel trousers, and flaring yellow boots.

"That isn't like the Rudi I knew," said Lanny. "Then he wore a plain S.A. uniform."

"That was glory in those days," replied the other. "Now he chooses to be an English country squire—but yellow boots rather spoil the effect! The people of the neighborhood refer to him playfully as the Kaiser of Abergavenny. They are used to the sight of him on the roads, or sitting somewhere in the sunshine; he will stay for hours painting or sketching. Time hangs heavy on his hands, we may be sure."

"He is a military student, Mr. Fordyce, and must know that victory for his side is a long way off. No doubt he fights against the realization."

"He fights against everything and everybody. He frightens the nurses with his scowls. He cannot bear to take orders, and while he has never offered physical resistance, he has made it necessary to have a force of thirty men, mostly soldiers of the Welsh regiment, to guard him. I suppose that counts as a military gain for Germany."

They talked for a while about what Lanny might find out. It was of great importance to know if Hess had any way of communicating with the outside, and it would be a master stroke if he could be led to name any confederate or agent in Britain. It was entirely likely that the Nazis, who had apparently foreseen everything, had established a system for meeting just such contingencies as now confronted their *Nummer Drei*. B4 would have paid a small fortune for the information which Lanny was trying to get for them without charge.

VIII

They were winding through the hills of Monmouthshire, with its tree-shrouded country lanes and gray stone cottages. In the fields the old men, the women, and the children worked from dawn to dark, growing food for the workers and the soldiers.

They came to the town of Ross, and then by the "old road" to the small town of Abergavenny. "Aber" is Celtic for "mouth of," referring to a stream; there was an Abertillery and an Abersycha and others in the neighborhood. They were only a short drive from the great soft-coal centers of South Wales, where the miners were toiling long hours to provide fuel for the making of guns and shells. To the south lay the harbors of Swansea and Bristol, now crowded with war shipping.

They drove to the hospital, a modern building beautifully set among shade trees. The guards knew the B4 man and passed him and his guest without questioning. Lanny was taken to the home of the medical superintendent and whisked inside. This official's name was D. Ellis Jones; he was in his early forties, rather tall, smooth-shaven, and wore horn-rimmed glasses. He had the rank of major in the British Army.

Major Jones explained the peculiar responsibility which Rudolf Hess represented to his custodians. If Hess were to die, the Nazis would be certain to claim that it was the result of mistreatment, and they might take the lives of hundreds of the British officers whom they had at their mercy. Therefore the hospital was scrupulous in welcoming the Swiss Neutrality Commission which was charged with enforcing the Geneva Convention. They came whenever they wished and talked with the prisoner and made sure that he had everything to which he was entitled. Because of the fear that he might commit suicide in spite of the utmost watchfulness, the guardians babied him considerably, allowing him harmless little indulgences which were surely not in the convention. "As a rule he doesn't have much appetite, and he has lost weight in spite of our best efforts."

Said Lanny: "I can understand the extreme humiliation he feels. It is hard for me to imagine that he would want to live if the Nazi cause goes down."

"That is what we fear, Mr. Budd, and why we have to be so careful in handling him. He is liable to fits of depression which may last for weeks."

"You need not fear any result of that sort from my visit, Major. It has always been my role with the Nazis to be optimistic and admiring —that is how I have got them to trust me and to talk. You may be sure that your patient will have hope after our meeting. Of course, he will have disappointments later, but that is inevitable—since I am assuming that his cause will fail."

"It's damn well going to fail," said the medical man. He added that he thought Hess must have received at least one of the code messages, for he had shown signs of restlessness during the past two or three days. Of course he would not speak a word about the matter to any of his captors.

They discussed the program to be followed. There was no need to wait until midnight, for in order to save electricity they all went to bed with the chickens. After ten o'clock everything was as quiet as could be, and the Major would take Mr. Budd to the prisoner's bedroom and slip him inside without a sound. At the same time the guard who sat in the dimly lighted room all night would move out, as he always did when the Major entered.

That was all. The two secret agents drove to an inconspicuous inn and had supper, and then, since there was time to be passed, they paid a visit to the ancient Norman ruin called Whitecastle, of which Hess was so fond. He wasn't there now, so they got out and strolled around, and Lanny saw the ducks, and one of the two golden carp. A woman custodian showed them about. They climbed the well-worn stairs and inspected the defenses of the castle, which included many slits for bow and crossbow fire, planned in such a way as to give the maximum field of vision. "Herr Hess was greatly interested in this," remarked the custodian.

Later they sat by the double moat and watched the twilight settle over the beautiful scene. Fordyce told the inside story of how he and his fellow agents had lured Hess to England by getting up a conspiracy of pretended Nazi sympathizers. Lanny told how puzzled he had been when Hess had revealed this conspiracy to him, and for some time Lanny had been unable to decide whether or not it was real. He told stories about the secretary and disciple of the Nazi Führer who had risen to become a Reichsminister and party chief; about the country home he had maintained near Berlin, and Klara, the lean and by-no-means seductive lady he had married. She believed in psychic phe-nomena even more ardently than her husband, and had discoursed learnedly to Lanny about the mystical books of ancient India.

IX

Promptly at ten they returned to the hospital grounds. Lanny sat in the car until Major Jones came out and led him along a tree-shaded path to the "female wing" where the prisoner lived his strange solitary life. The medical man carried a small instrument case and requested Lanny to carry it into the room and out again; the guards were being told that he was making some observations of the prisoner during his sleep. The Major apparently had complete authority; he spoke a whis-pered word to the two soldiers at the door, and to the one who sat at the door of Hess's bedroom. The Major opened the door—it had no knob on the inside, so he had told Lanny. The latter stepped quietly in, and then moved out of the way of the man who had sat on duty inside, and who rose immediately and came to the open door and out.

Lanny stood in silence, looking about the room, which was plain, as became a hospital. There was a dim light burning, well shaded. There was a chest of drawers and a couple of chairs; by the starlight outside Lanny could see that the windows were not barred. On the bed lay the figure of a man wearing striped pajamas. Lanny waited until the door had been closed, then he stepped softly to the bedside and whispered: "Rudi."

Evidently the man had not been asleep. He sat up instantly. "Is it really you, Lanny?" he whispered.

"Yes, Rudi. You got my messages?"

"I got one, but could hardly believe it."

There was a chair by the bedside and Lanny slipped into it. The rest of the conversation was carried on in the lowest audible whispers; in English, which Hess knew as well as German, having been born in Alexandria and educated there.

"Lanny," he said in a tone of great stress, "have you turned against us?"

The P.A. was prepared for the question, and put pain into his reply. "Can you ask me that, Rudi, after all these years?"

"But how can you be admitted here?"

"That is a long story. The gist of it is a hundred pounds sterling, paid in cash this night."

"*Herrgott!* They are that venal?"

"A nation of shopkeepers, Rudi."

"Who has taken it?"

"I had to give my word not to tell. Suffice it that the right man got the money. It has taken me three weeks of making friends before I could drop a hint of what I wanted."

"And what do you want from me?"

"First of all, to see you, and to hear your voice. To let you know that you still have friends. How are they treating you?"

"Well enough, so far as food and shelter are concerned. But it is an outrage that I should be a prisoner. I came here in good faith, as a diplomatic representative. I am convinced now that I was trapped."

"I believe the same thing; but I did not find it out until it was too late. Did you get my messages?"

"I got only one, that everything was progressing satisfactorily."

"There it is! We cannot depend upon anybody! I sent you detailed accounts of my talks with the persons you had told me about. There was a man who gave me the name of Branscome, but I could never feel sure which side he was on. It has been very difficult for me to work in England."

"I can't see how you manage to do it!"

"I use my father's influence. I am supposed to be helping him. He used to be on our side, you know, until our government offered him so much money."

"American money is making it very hard for us, Lanny. Everything is going the way I feared and tried my best to prevent."

"You are not getting discouraged, I hope, *lieber* Rudi. Your armies hold all the vital points in Europe, and it would take decades of fighting to expel them."

"Do you really believe that? I try hard to hold to the idea; but it is not territory that will count in the long run, it will be air power, and you are building more of it."

"Don't say *me*, Rudi, say American big business. I have never been their man, not even in my boyhood."

"You are a true friend, Lanny, and I believe what you tell me. Have you been in Germany since you saw me last?"

"No, I have been crippled; I was in a plane wreck and had both legs broken. I have only recently been able to get about freely, and my first thought was of you. Tell me, is there anything I can do for you?"

"I don't know what it could be—unless you could figure out a way for me to escape."

"Believe me, I have been thinking about it day and night. There are many circumstances which might favor the plan. In Newport there is a large camp for German war prisoners. Many are bound to be seeking ways of escape, and I could get into touch with them and tell them where you are and how you are guarded."

"But what could they do in England, Lanny? The whole country-side would be up and after them."

"The action would have to be co-ordinated with what the British call a commando raid, say from Cherbourg. Later, when the nights are longer, there will be time for speedboats to come and go in the dark-ness. Parachutists might be dropped at this place, and bring you out, and the two forces might meet."

"That is possible, I suppose; but what could keep the British Navy from getting us on the return trip? They swarm in the Channel and claim it as their own."

"That would be a job for your airplanes. Surely they could provide a cover for the three or four hours it would take speedboats to get back to the French coast. Think what a colossal prestige stroke it would be to take you out of the hands of these insolent people! Surely the Führer wouldn't be in any doubt about that!"

"Yes, Lanny, but it would not have much military effect, and I am afraid that is what he is forced to concentrate on at present. I would fear to burden his mind and distract his attention for my benefit."

X

Lanny's eyes, growing used to the faint light, roamed over the features of this man leaning from the bed and not more than two feet away from him. A strange square face, with a stern mouth that made a straight line, and bushy black eyebrows making another. Lanny had known him at the height of his glory, a grim, implacable man in the service of his cause, but genial enough with the few friends he trusted, and oddly credulous when it came to the mysterious underworld of the "spirits." Now he was thinner; the bones stood out in his face, and the black hair was growing sparse. He suffered from gastritis; it might be due to British cooking, but more probably to worry. Lanny could see that his hands trembled when he made a gesture; he was obviously moved by this visitation out of his triumphant past.

"Listen, Rudi," began the solicitous friend. "You aren't by chance worrying over the idea that the Führer may have misunderstood your flight to Britain!"

"No, I am sure he knows me too well for that; he knows that I could never have any thought but to help him. All that troubles me is that I failed. It was an enterprise that had to succeed, or it was nothing."

"We can all fail, *lieber Freund*. Even the Führer has failed more than once. He hasn't been able to invade England, and he wasn't able to take Moscow last autumn."

"Yes, Lanny, but that is a cold sort of comfort. What tortures me is the bombing of our beautiful German cities, and the awful slaughter of our best youth. Day after day I listen to news of it, and while I know that the enemy newspapers and radio lie, I cannot suppose they invent whole campaigns."

"It is dreadful, and I share your heartache. I am troubled by the thought of your loneliness. Do you have no communications from the outside?"

"They permit me to receive letters from Klara, but of course if she said anything about political or military matters they would cut it out. There is not much else to say nowadays."

"You mean that you have not been able to get any communication from the Führer?"

"Not a word. I am far too carefully watched, and I have not the large sums of money that it would require to bribe anybody."

"It is dreadful that you should be so neglected, Rudi! Surely there must be many agents in this country!"

"Yes, but they have more important matters to work on than to bring birthday greetings to a prisoner of war."

"It is worse than I imagined. Would you not like to send a message to the Führer?"

"I would indeed."

"I was able to have Switzerland included in my passport. As you know, my mother lives in Unoccupied France, so that I have a good pretext for a trip. If I were to get word to the Führer that I had a message from you, he would surely send somebody to get it."

"He would do more than that; he would make it possible for you to come to him, if you were willing to take the risk of having the fact leak out."

"I cannot think of anything that would please me more. It might be that I could bring out some message to his friends abroad which would help to terminate this blind and cruel fratricide."

"I am afraid he has few friends in the so-called democracies now, Lanny."

"Many more than you think, take my word for that. But tell me, what message do you wish to send?"

"Tell him first of all of my undying love and devotion. Tell him that I have never wavered for one moment in that, and never shall."

"And what else?"

"I should have to think, Lanny. I am quite overwhelmed by the idea of being able to send word to him. I think of so many things that ought to be done, and that I might suggest to him if we could speak, but none that is important enough to send as a message. Quote him the English saying that the darkest hour is just before the dawn. Remind him of the glorious example of Frederick the Great, who was beaten more than once but refused to recognize it. Tell him that I lie here in the solitude and darkness and try to send him courage and hope by the secret channels of the subconscious."

"He will be deeply touched, Rudi, as I am. You have no concrete news of any sort for him?"

"What can a poor wretch in what is practically solitary confinement have to tell? Not a word! Describe how I exist, and how I wait for him to bring me deliverance. And of course if he can send me help without too great risk of loss to the Fatherland, I will do what I can to fight my way out."

XI

Lanny kept on giving leads and hints until he satisfied himself that he wasn't going to get any information of importance from this Number Three Nazi; either the Nazi didn't have it, or he was no longer trusting his American friend. Lanny had had no part in the scheme of B4 to lure Hess to Britain, but Hess, brooding over the matter in his too abundant leisure, was likely to have hit upon the possibility that Lanny might have been in on the plot. Or he might have decided that all Americans were enemies now. Anyhow, what he wanted was to get information, not to give. He wanted to ask about Lord Wickthorpe and others who were supposed to sympathize with his cause, and after that he wanted to tell his troubles, to repeat the complaints he had put before his jailers and before the Swiss commissioner who had visited him not long ago.

Lanny decided that the once vigorous master of the N.S.D.A.P.— National Socialist German Workers' Party—had become a querulous neurotic and a bore. He said: "Rudi, I am allowed only one hour here, and I promised not to overstay. Tell me frankly, do you want me to see the Führer for you?"

"Of course, Lanny."

"Well then, give me something to prove to the Führer that I was here. I hardly need to point out that he will not trust anyone from my part of the world." Lanny took from his coat pocket a small writing pad and pencil. "Will you write me a few words for him?" When Hess said "Surely," Lanny went on: "Write it as small as you can, in one corner of the paper, so that I can cut it off and conceal it in my clothing. If it were found, I should be turned over to the American Army and pretty certainly shot."

Hess wrote a few words in one corner of the paper. "This won't look much like my handwriting, written so small," he commented.

"Is there some talisman you could give me? Something the Führer would know?"

"I will give you my wedding ring." Hess took from his finger a plain gold band. "The Führer gave me this, and he will remember the inscription. To make it more sure, repeat to him what he told me when he put it into my hand: '*Dies wird das Lästermaul zum Schweigen bringen!*'"

Lanny knew what that referred to. In the old days of political strife the enemies of the Party had accused Adolf Hitler of improper intimacy with his devoted secretary, and they had had a nickname for the secretary, *Das Fräulein.* The story had it that Hitler therefore had ordered Hess to marry his Klara. "This will shut the mouths of the scandalmongers!"

Lanny took the ring. "You are doing me an honor, Rudi, and I appreciate it. I will put it into the Führer's hands, and when the victory has been won, he will return it to you. And now, *Lebewohl!* Take care of yourself, and keep up your courage. Every moment you give to doubt and worry is a moment wasted. Remember what Goethe said: '*Alles in der Welt lässt sich ertragen.*'"

They exchanged a firm handclasp, and Lanny picked up the Major's little bag and went to the door of the room and tapped gently upon it. Almost at once it opened, and Lanny stepped out and a guard stepped in. Lanny left the bungalow and walked to the Major's residence, in front of which Fordyce was waiting with the car; the B4 man offered to take the bag inside, which Lanny understood to mean that he wasn't expected to make any report there. "Tell him that everything went off well," said the P.A., and that was enough.

XII

They decided to drive home that night. On the way Lanny gave an account of the conversation, complete except that he said nothing about the scrap of writing and the ring. If B4 had had a recording device installed in the room there would be no harm done, but otherwise Lanny would keep that secret. He said he was sorry that he hadn't been able to get anything more important out of the prisoner. His guess was that Rudi had been telling the truth, that he didn't have any contacts with the outside world. The agent professed himself well pleased, but in his heart he must have been disappointed, for if he had helped to uncover a conspiracy it would have been a bright feather in his cap.

Churchill had suggested to Lanny that he would be interested to hear the outcome of the talk with Hess. But now Lanny told the agent: "I am guessing that I didn't get enough to make it worth the Prime Minister's while. Will you tell him, or shall I?"

"My senior will report to him," replied Fordyce. "His time is especially taken up at the moment."

"I have no doubt of that," said the other. "I understand that important decisions are being taken." That was as near as either of them would come to mentioning the fact that the top-flight American staff officers, the commanders of the Army, the Navy, and the Air Forces, had been flown to Britain a week or so previously.

When they got to London, Lanny bade good-by to his escort and went to his hotel room. There he took out the pad of paper. He read the fine script: "*Mein Führer: Ich bin es. Rudi.*" Literally translated the sentence means "I am it," but in English the words are reversed, and people say "It is I," or more commonly, "It's me," against which the grammarians fight in vain. Lanny took his nail scissors and cut off the bit of paper, about two square inches; he folded it once, and carefully sewed it into the lining of his coat—on the other side from Roosevelt's card. He put the ring on his finger—he, too, being a married man. It was his idea to go back to America soon and use these magical objects—the Ring and the Tarnhelm!—to persuade F.D.R. to let him go into Germany again.

XIII

The news of the military conference then going on was a closely guarded secret; but the newspapermen knew it, even though they could not give the least hint of it in print. Rick had told Lanny that the party included General Marshall, Chief of Staff, and Admiral King. Already in London was the newly appointed Commanding General of the American forces in the European Theater, whose name was Eisenhower. Lanny had never heard this name until the appointment was announced; he had to take it for granted that F.D.R. and his advisers knew their man.

"General Ike" had set up headquarters in some "flats" in Grosvenor Square, one of the fashionable districts of London, and the playful Americans had taken to calling it "Eisenhowerplatz." It seemed to them a charming stroke of fate that the new "C.G." should be of German ancestry and carry a German name. The words mean "iron hewer," and the word "iron" has been through the centuries a favorite of all military-minded German poets and orators. Now a hewer from the prairie state of Kansas had come to hew the German iron, beginning with the "blood and iron" of Bismarck and including the "iron soul" of Adolf Hitler.

Among the arrivals from Washington was Mr. Harry Hopkins, with the Army physician who labored to keep him alive through the strain of eighteen-hour-a-day conferring. The party had put up at the Dorchester, which was why Lanny hadn't been able to obtain a room there and had gone to the Savoy. After the trip to Abergavenny Lanny got some sleep, and then he called the Dorchester and asked for Mr. Hopkins's secretary. To that functionary he pronounced the magic word "Traveler," which had been given to Hopkins. It had the same effect as at the White House; Hopkins came to the phone.

"Are you going to be in town for the next three or four days?" he inquired, and Lanny answered that he had meant to spend the time with his little daughter at Wickthorpe Castle, but would come to town in response to either a telegram or telephone call. "Fine!" said Hopkins. "You'll hear from me."

Lanny called Rick, and they took a bus out to Hampstead Heath, and strolled by the ponds near the Vale of Health, where John Keats had lived; and then on to the ancient Spaniard's Inn, haunt of many poets. They had dinner in a place where no one knew them, and then sat out on the heath, discussing the future of the world, now being decided in town. Rick had attended a press conference given by the "C.G.," and reported him a straightforward and democratic fellow, a beneficent example to the brass hats of Britain. "The only thing is, I'm afraid he may be a little too kindhearted for a general."

"Don't worry," Lanny assured him. "Our fellows are really going to fight. I am told that our maneuvers in the Louisiana marshes were quite terrific."

"I know," agreed Rick. "They are drilling like all-possessed in North Ireland and practicing landings all round our coast. The Germans send in a tip-and-run plane now and then and get photographs. They can't find them very reassuring."

Lanny couldn't say "Roosevelt told me," but he could say: "I am told that Roosevelt is determined that American forces shall go into action somewhere this year. If it's not to be across the Channel, then it must be the Mediterranean, or we'll change our plans and concentrate first upon the Japanese. I don't suppose your people want that."

"Hardly," said the baronet's son. "But from all I hear Winnie is dead set against any more Channel crossings until we have overwhelming forces. So I suppose it will be the Mediterranean, and the farther east it is the better it will suit our Tory leader. If he could invade through the Balkans he would consider that he was killing two birds with one stone, winning two wars with one expedition."

"The Second World War and the Third," replied Lanny with a smile. They didn't need to say more, for they had both been in Paris early in the year 1919 when the descendant of the Duke of Marlborough had come there and labored mightily to persuade the Allies to undertake a holy crusade to crush the cockatrice of Bolshevism, just emerged from its egg and not yet having had time to develop its poison fangs.

"Winnie hasn't had a new idea in a quarter of a century," said the "Pink" journalist. "He wouldn't get another in the next quarter of a millennium."

Lanny thought that was extreme, and replied, "He was a consistent supporter of the League of Nations, and of collective security."

XIV

Lanny took an evening train to Wickthorpe and enjoyed a peaceful sleep, guarded by the elderly dragon lady who had once been his mother-in-law and now was his co-parent, so to speak—he an ordinary parent and she a grand one. She was a grand lady in her own estimation, also in physical aspect. Lanny had no doubt that in her secret heart she disliked him; how could she have any other attitude to a man who had failed to appreciate the magnificent Irma and the equally magnificent Barnes fortune? But he had over her a terrible power; at any time he might choose to take the little Frances away for a holiday, even to America, and if he chose to keep her there, who could guess what the law might say about it?

The result was that Fanny Barnes the haughty was polite to the point of obsequiousness. Lanny's room in her cottage was kept inviolate, and the place was silent while he slept or read or pecked on his typewriter. Poor old Uncle Horace, ex-manipulator of Wall Street securities, was rudely forbidden to bore him, and Fanny herself didn't even invite him to make a bridge four, but left it for him to confer that favor if he chose.

So Lanny lived a life of ease, roamed the estate, played tennis and bowls with the little one, played the piano for her, and danced with her to the music of radio or phonograph. They lunched with the grandmother, and dined at the Castle with mother and stepfather and whatever guests might be on hand. The child was old enough for that now; she was perfectly behaved; her mother was a strict disciplinarian, and Lanny could find no fault with the upbringing of a future heiress and bride of some British nobleman. He would have liked to teach her some of his ideas, but his role forbade that. He could only hope that events might do it for him.

He lived this elegant and expensive life, in which even the play was formalized, and all the time he was thinking: "The future of the world is being decided!" Not a line about it in the newspapers, not a word over the radio—you couldn't have dreamed that the directing brains of the American Armed Forces were in London. But the Earl of Wickthorpe and his countess knew it, and imparted it to Lanny as a state secret, and he was duly grateful for the favor. The guests speculated as to the probable decisions, and of course they expected to hear what a much-traveled art expert thought. Lanny could make a good guess, and did so, for it was important to him to keep the respect of the "Wickthorpe set." He might have need of it again!

Early on the morning of the twenty-fifth of July there came a telegram reading: "Can see you this afternoon. Urgent. Harry." So Lanny bade farewell to this life of a country gentleman, and to his dear little daughter, who could not be told why her father had to leave so soon and never knew when he would return. Always a new heartache, wherever he was, in Connecticut or New York, in Buckinghamshire or Provence! He was sure that he'd be leaving Britain in a few days, but all he could say was: "I'll write you, darling; and I'll come back as soon as I can."

XV

The President's right-hand man, clad in a pair of shorts on a hot summer afternoon, looked like a very sick man indeed; but apparently he had learned to live with his diseases, and they did not inhibit his cheerful manner. He offered his visitor a drink, and when it was declined, remarked: "I am on a schedule, too." Then: "Excuse me if I stretch out," and let himself down on the bed. He signed Lanny to a chair alongside.

"You won't mind if I come right to the point, Lanny. These have been strenuous days for all of us."

"Indeed, I am surprised that you remembered me."

"The Boss told me to remember you. This is the result of the conference. The British refused positively to go in with us on a cross-Channel invasion this year. They say we couldn't force the Germans to divert anything from Russia, because the Germans have enough forces in France to withstand anything we could put ashore this year. And another defeat would be a catastrophe."

"That's about what you expected, isn't it?"

"Yes, but we had hopes. Now we have to change all our plans. It's to be the Mediterranean. Churchill, of course, wants it to be the Balkans; he fought like a tiger for that. You should have been there—it was quite a drama. The first time he saw me he gave me the devil because I had talked to some of the generals before I talked to him. That's not protocol, it seems. He gave me to understand that he was the master of the British Empire, and that he, not any of the generals, is running the British part of this war. He grabbed the law book in which this is written and read me the passages in the same tone as if he were making a speech in Parliament; when he finished each passage he ripped the page out of the book and threw it on the floor. A good show, as they say."

"I hope you stood up to him, Harry," ventured the P.A.

The harnessmaker's son looked intently at his visitor. "Listen, brother," he said. "You are a plutocrat, I take it, and Churchill is an aristocrat; I'm only a democrat, and with a small 'd.' But I had to learn to stand up to our business tycoons in the old W.P.A. days, and even before that, in Albany. They want the earth with a blue ribbon tied round it, and when they can't have it they roar you down. The Boss told me to talk back to Churchill from the beginning, and I did, and he took it like a good sport."

"There is a thing that he calls 'lease-lend,' " remarked Lanny. "Who pays the piper calls the tune."

"Not in this case. We can't go it alone, or even threaten to. We agreed to compromise. We gave up the Channel and the P.M. gave up the Balkans. We're going to invade through French North Africa and put Rommel into a sack."

"Oh, good! That's been my hope from the beginning."

"You understand, this is top secret, and for your own use only."

"The Governor seemed to mean that I would be free to share it with one or two persons who are working on the spot."

"If he said that, it goes, of course. But be sure they are persons you can trust to the death. You know what it means to be caught spying on the Nazis."

"Indeed I know. I have visited their dungeons; and Göring once put me in one. It was his idea of a joke, but I got all the feelings."

"The name of the operation is Torch. Eisenhower will command; it's to be kept an American show, with the idea of riding easier with the French. The coast is long, as you know, a couple of thousand miles. We may take Dakar or Casablanca on the Atlantic, or Oran or Algiers on the Mediterranean. We leave the enemy to guess. Between you and me, it will be all, or most of, those ports."

"I see. And the time?"

"Nobody knows the time yet. We have to change a million details, and it depends on when we can be ready. But it will be this year—that is the agreement. You will be going there immediately?"

"Vichy is my first goal."

"You have transportation arranged?"

"I have to cable Baker."

"That is not necessary. Let me attend to it for you."

"I don't want to put any burden upon you, Harry, I—"

"I have secretaries. You'll take a Clipper to Lisbon and fly by way of Madrid?"

"That will be fine."

"O.K., I'll see that you get a seat on the first plane. You travel under your own name?"

"Always. I am an art expert, you know. I have commissions to buy paintings in Vichy France, also a very fine fountain for ablutions in Algeria."

"Harry the Hop" broke into a grin. He started to get up, but Lanny saw that it was an effort and said: "Stay where you are. Thanks, as ever."

"I have to get up. Our train is leaving tonight. You may be interested to know that I am flying back to Washington to be married in the White House."

"You don't say! Congratulations!"

"I have found a woman who is willing to take care of these tired bones. I understand that you have recently been married also. Good luck to you and yours, old man."

They exchanged a handclasp and a smile. So men parted in wartime, knowing well that they might never see each other again. Very often they didn't, and then they were not supposed to wreck themselves with grief. As Goethe had said more than a century ago: "Everything on the earth can be endured." Lanny had quoted it to Hess.

1 2

Lull before Storm

I

LISBON was still in its safe berth by the River Tagus, and still pleasanter from the air than from the ground. Portugal was making money out of both sides in the war, and, as always, the rich were adding to their hoards while the poor discovered the meaning of inflation and that wages never kept up with the stealthy increase in the cost of food. The city was so full of spies that they tried to work on one another, and, of course, the arrival of an American art expert via London was not overlooked. Lanny was glad that he had to spend only a few hours telling ladies and gentlemen with assorted foreign accents that he was an esthete, entirely aloof from the hateful intrigues of politics; also, that he never lent money, no matter how sad the story.

In Madrid he had to stay over until the next day, and he didn't mind that, for he could spend the evening at the home of his elderly friend General Aguilar, and be internally drenched with *copitas de manzanilla—* in English, cups of camomile tea. This white-whiskered old aristocrat with the many medals, which he wore even at home, was one of the few Spanish Fascists who were interested in the outside world and made a pretense of culture—meaning, of course, the kind that cost money and was elegant and exclusive. He listened with interest to Lanny's account of the wonderful art collection which Reichsmarschall Göring was assembling in Germany. "A man out of the old times!" he exclaimed admiringly, and went on to reveal the fact that a year or two ago this conquistador had assembled more than three hundred of the largest guns ever made in the world, with the intention of taking Gibraltar. The fact that the elaborate emplacements had been constructed on the soil of Spain, which was supposed to be a neutral country, and that they were aimed at the property of Britain, which was supposed to be a friendly country, troubled the military commander of Madrid so little that he didn't mention it and probably didn't think of it.

"I suppose those guns have been taken to the eastern front now," remarked the art expert casually.

"No, they are still there," said the General, who was in a mellow mood, having listened to much flattery. "They serve a useful purpose in protecting the neutrality of Morocco."

He didn't say Spanish Morocco, but Lanny knew he meant that; he was refusing to acknowledge the existence of French Morocco. "Do you mean," asked the American, "the guns are powerful enough to be effective across the Strait?"

"They might be; but I mean that our ability to take Gibraltar will exercise a restraining influence upon hostile forces that might wish to land on the other side."

"I keep hearing talk of such expeditions," remarked Lanny, "but of course a civilian never knows whether it is something real or just a smoke screen. From what I can gather, the most likely place for a landing appears to be the Vardar valley in Greece."

Said the Spaniard: "It is a never-ending source of wonder to me, how you Americans continue to let yourselves be persuaded to pull chestnuts out of the fire for the British."

"I don't think it is going to go on much longer, my General. There are signs of an awakening. Just before I left New York I had a part in the founding of a new organization called the American Christian League. I was amazed by the extent of the public response." Lanny reached into his pocket and took out one of the leaflets which he had taken off Hartley's desk. *The Red Nightmare*—he translated, *Le Cauchemar Rouge*, for they were speaking French. The document suited the old General's ideology, and he was glad to hear about the sums of money that had been collected and the mass meetings that had been held. In return he talked freely about the "Blue Division," which represented the first installment of El Caudillo's promised million men to help the Führer put down the Red demon. These "Blues" were volunteers, in the same sense that the Germans and Italians who had come to fight in Spain had been—that is, they could volunteer or be shot. They had been meeting with heavy losses in Russia, but now the Axis armies were advancing rapidly toward the oil of the Caucasus, and it looked as if the dawn were breaking at last.

Too bad this victory could not have been won by Christian armies, instead of by the Nazis, who were not exactly cordial to Holy Mother Church! But Marshal Pétain had the word of the Führer that the Church would be restored in France as a bulwark against the Reds. They talked about the old Marshal for a while; Aguilar had come to know him intimately while Pétain had been French Ambassador to Madrid during the period of the *Sitzkrieg,* before the German invasion of France. The fact that Lanny had been received by Pétain here at that time, and had been able to visit him in Vichy, was one of the reasons that the commandant of the Madrid district trusted him completely and talked to him freely. Lanny wasn't a Catholic and couldn't pose as one, but he could cite the names of wealthy Americans who recognized the Hierarchy as the chief means of holding down the labor unions and keeping the Reds and the Pinks out of power. Lanny had discussed this subject with Mr. Hearst and Mr. Henry Ford, and what these great men had said on the subject was heard gladly by generals and admirals as well as cardinals and archbishops throughout Europe.

II

In Vichy a free-spending American was an old friend by now. A landlord would vacate his own room for him, and *maîtres-d'hôtel* would greet him by name. He could look up important ministers of state and tell them what their friends in Washington and London and North Africa were doing, and promise to take them messages in the course of his travels. To M. Benoist-Méchin and others of his set Lanny could explain that the present depreciation of the franc offered unusual opportunities to do business in old masters. American collectors were attracted by the prices which Lanny reported to them; and while this would represent a loss to French culture, the French might consent to look at it from the international point of view and be willing to assist in uplifting the American hinterland. When the matter was put thus tactfully, any statesman could agree, and would tell friends who needed ready cash, and Lanny would be invited to inspect art works in elegant country villas; mostly they were third-rate, but it cost him nothing to say: "Very interesting, and I'll be happy to report it to my clients."

Meantime he invited important persons to lunch or dine, and was invited to soirees where the elite of this miserable government displayed their shoddy splendor. "A banana republic without any bananas," some wit had called it, and yet, the smaller the prizes, the more bitterly men fought for them. Intrigue, jealousy, and hatred appeared to be staple foods at Vichy buffets. Lanny had never been in any place where secrets were so ill kept; you could hear all the crimes of all the world, except of the person who was talking to you, and you might hear about him from any of his associates. Bourgeois France was falling to pieces, and Vichy was the garbage can.

First of all Lanny sought out his friend Charlot de Bruyne. Here was one man who still believed in his creed and was willing to make sacrifices for it. Lanny felt pity for him and would have liked to say: "Wake up, *jeune homme!* You are in the middle of the twentieth century, not the eighteenth." But of course he couldn't speak such words; he had to go on with his role of superspy, which he had not chosen, but which had chosen him.

What he did, the first thing, was to tell Charlot about his older brother. Denis was well, he was doing his duty as an officer, and he had received Charlot's messages of love with the same affection that had prompted them. "But so far as concerns his political opinions, I'm afraid there's nothing to be done, Charlot. I argued with him, but it was useless; he is not to be moved from what he believes."

"What does he believe, Lanny?"

"He believes that General de Gaulle is a great man, a prophet and all that sort of thing. And of course it's a very dangerous opinion for an officer to hold; it won't further his career. All we can do is to recognize the fact that he is sincere, and respect him for it."

But the younger brother couldn't leave it there. The times were too critical, the feelings too intense. Men were killing each other, and not even brothers could be spared. Lanny had to take refuge in his ivory tower, the stairs of which were getting badly worn with his footprints running up and down. "You know, Charlot, you mustn't expect an American to take part in French politics."

"But your President is doing just that, Lanny! He made a radio speech in the French language, denouncing our present government!"

"It was in very crude schoolboy French, Charlot, and can hardly have made any impression on your intelligent public. Don't blame this old friend for anything that any politician does. Let me stay *au-dessus de la mêlée*, and continue to work at my profession."

Lanny asked about Charlot himself and what he was doing. He was working hard at organizing and training his Légion Tricolore, for the purpose of repressing the traitor enemies here in France; they were expecting an Allied landing somewhere and planning to aid it, and Charlot was planning to put them down—yes, even if it proved to be his own brother! There was no keeping away from subject of Denis, and Lanny saw that there couldn't be any peace or reconciliation between them, only a war to the cruel death.

III

The P.A. followed his practice of not seeking out the higher-ups but letting them seek him. This increased his importance and at the same time laid him less open to suspicion. What Lanny did was to tell Monsieur le Ministre Jacques Benoist-Méchin that he had recently come from New York, where he had been instrumental in organizing the American Christian League, and what great encouragement this group would offer to Christian France. Later on, he asked after the health of Admiral Darlan, and expressed his great admiration for that sailor-statesman, knowing that Benoist-Méchin was the Admiral's man, or had been until lately. The next time Lanny met the ex-journalist he was told that the Admiral had expressed the hope of seeing M. Budd before he departed. Lanny telephoned promptly and an appointment was made.

What did this pipe-smoking Commander of the French Fleet want of an American dilettante and playboy grown up? First, to offer him some of his favorite Pernod Fils brandy; then to chat politely, asking about the visitor's mother and father, and where he had been and what he had seen; then to state how deeply he had been hurt by the American attitude toward Unoccupied France since the formation of the Laval government. He wanted Lanny to tell his father and his influential friends how Frenchmen had been compelled to choose between Red anarchy and White law and order. Also, he had felt his personal honor impugned by the suspicion, so generally expressed in America, that he, Commander of the French Fleet, might somehow be persuaded or intimidated into letting that Fleet come into the possession of the Germans. "*Jamais, jamais, jamais!*" exclaimed Jean Louis Xavier

François Darlan, and he said it several times more in his discourse. It just wasn't going to happen. But of course if the Americans should be so misguided as to put troops ashore upon the soil of France, the French would have no choice but to defend their *patrie* and their *honneur*.

Did Lanny think the Americans were preparing to do this? The Frenchman had heard rumors and was greatly worried. Lanny said: "Believe me, *mon Amiral*, if I knew I would tell you. I hear this and hear that, and I wonder, does anybody really know? This I can tell you: My father expects it will be Salonika and the Vardar River. He talks learnedly about reaching the Germans in their unarmored back, and I get the impression that he has got it from some of the military men who come to Newcastle to supervise the fabricating of fighter planes. I can tell you only of my sincere hope that none of those planes will ever be flying over French soil."

"The British have flown over it, as you know. They recently bombed the Renault plant, near Paris, and I think the bitterest experience of my life has been the discovery that there are Frenchmen depraved enough to have rejoiced in that bombing, and to welcome the murder of their fellow citizens."

"I have never met any such, *mon Amiral*, but I have heard that it is so. I am told there are clandestine papers being published and circulated, but I have not come upon one."

That was true at the time, but it didn't remain true. That very evening, strolling to his room after a soiree, Lanny was passed on a dark street by a man wearing the blouse and cap of a workingman. This man put out a hand to him, saying: "*Pour la France!*" Lanny saw that he had a leaflet and took it automatically. He hadn't far to go, so he ventured to keep it till he got to his room, and to read it by the dim light that was permitted. A leaflet, entitled *Le Témoignage Chrétien*— The Christian Witness—it gave the text of a manifesto issued by a group of Catholic priests and Protestant pastors who had come together to protest against Fascism and Nazism in the name of freedom and the dignity of the individual human soul. This discovery warmed Lanny's heart, for he knew that there was another side to Christianity than the defense of capitalist property rights, and he was glad to know that there were humble priests who did not share the political attitudes of the Hierarchy. He mentioned this leaflet in the report to his Chief, which he wrote and sent through the Embassy.

IV

Darlan was important because he commanded the Fleet, and the Fleet might command the Mediterranean. Of second importance was Pierre Laval, who would hardly have dared to interfere with the Admiral. He, the *fripon mongol*, commanded the Army; but if the Allies could keep their hold on the Mediterranean they could deal with whatever army the Germans had allowed to the French in North Africa. With the Premier, Lanny pursued the same waiting tactics; an American art expert went about his business, while the word spread among members of the government that he had been to London and met the "Wickthorpe set," and to New York, where he had founded a powerful new organization in support of the Axis.

Just as he was making his plans to leave, there came to his humble lodgings one of the Premier's undersecretaries, bidding him welcome to Vichy and saying that the Premier would be pleased if he would call at *quinze heures* that day. Such an invitation was a command, and Lanny said it was also a pleasure. He took an ancient horse-drawn cab—taxis being nonexistent—and drove to the Hotel du Parc, where the Mongolian rascal had the royal suite. It was, Lanny thought, the hottest day he had ever known in France, and he found the head of the state in his undershirt amid the best French gilt and rococo. The visitor was invited to take off his coat, and did so, hanging it carefully on the back of his chair and never forgetting it. There were two treasures hidden in it, one of which would have lifted him to glory, and the other of which might have caused him to be hanged.

The son of Budd-Erling wasn't going to be taken out to Châteldon this trip; relations with his country were too bad, and it wouldn't do for the head of the State to exhibit too much intimacy with an American. But in the privacy of his office was another matter, and the butcher's son spoke as if the son of Budd-Erling were an ambassador, able to swing the destiny of nations. Pierre Laval said that he was desolated by the situation between the two countries, and by the blind, unreasoning prejudice which President Roosevelt and Secretary Hull showed to his harmless self. He said that he was firmly resolved never to break relations with America; if that calamity occurred, it would be Washington's act, not his.

Having said this, Pierre proceeded to "fish." What was Lanny's own attitude in the present calamitous situation? Surely he could not have weakened in his abhorrence of the Red Terrorists! When Lanny said that he was the same friend of order and property rights that he had always been, Pierre appealed to him as a personal friend to tell him what he knew about the *méchanceté* which the Allies were preparing to inflict upon Europe. Lanny in reply explained that he was not well informed, for the reason that the ruling people in America knew his sentiments, and the only place where he heard frank talk was in his father's home. There the opinion seemed to be that the Allies were planning an invasion through the Vardar valley. "A safe distance from France," he commented.

"*Vraiment*," said the Premier, "*mais quelle ivresse!* They really imagine they can conquer the whole of Europe? They will make a shambles of it, and what they leave the Reds will finish!"

"Perfectly true, *cher Maître*. The only question is whether our people can be awakened in time."

"Look at the situation, M. Budd! The Germans are almost at the Volga and the Caspian Sea. When they have reached those goals they will have cut Russia in half, and will stop her oil supply and bring all her machinery to a halt. And Rommel is at the gates of Alexandria and Suez, and then of what use will the Mediterranean be to the Allies? They will have to go all the way around Africa, and what means will they have to keep the Panzer forces from penetrating to India and meeting with the Japanese?"

"I agree with you altogether, *cher Maître;* the situation is the most encouraging we have yet seen."

"May I talk to you in confidence, *mon ami?*"

"Indeed so; I shall feel honored."

"As you must know, I have never had any heart for this or any war. I am a man of peace, a lawyer and no killer—even my worst enemies will tell you that. As a French statesman, I am by no means pleased that one nation should be gaining too great power on this old Continent where we all have to live."

"I understand that, and you are right."

"What I desire to know is whether, when Russia has been forced out of this war, Britain and America cannot be persuaded to listen to reason, and to make a settlement with Herr Hitler and myself, whereby a peace can be established in Europe that will last for the lifetimes of our grandchildren. All that any of us want is to keep what we have, and to unite in establishing and maintaining a government in Russia that will respect the rights of private property and will not carry on propaganda of social revolution throughout the rest of the world. I have the personal word of Herr Hitler that that is all he desires, and that he is willing to respect and to guarantee the rights of both the British Empire and of the United States. Surely that is statesmanship, M. Budd!"

"It is, and also it is what I have been urging upon my friends."

"Here is what I have in mind, *mon ami:* would you be willing to take that message to the public men of Britain and America for me?"

"*Hélas, cher Maître,* I do not have access to such persons; nor do I have confidence in my own ability as an envoy."

"That last statement is surely a mistake; you have the ability, and I should be glad to give you a note stating that I have authorized you to speak for me. The time to act is now, before the German victories have become too great, and before their armies have advanced into territory which they might not be so willing to give up."

"Everything you say is wise, *cher Maître;* and I promise you this—I will do my best to make contact with men of influence and present your views to them."

"When do you intend to return?"

"I wish to see my mother on the Riviera, and then I have several art commissions to carry out, one of them in North Africa. I hope to return to New York by way of Britain, where I have a little daughter whom I try to see as often as I can."

"If it is because of business reasons that you do this work, M. Budd, let me make it possible for you to postpone it, and attend to this far more important commission for my government."

"Thank you for the kind offer, but I do not need money, and would not consent to take the money of the people of France in this tragic hour."

"Let me assure you, *cher ami,* there is no service that would be worth so much to the people of France as to get them peace and national unity once more. For that they would authorize the payment of half the contents of our treasury."

The pair had a little debate over this proposal. Pierre Laval simply couldn't believe that any man was actually turning down money; it was contrary to human nature, and to good manners if not good morals. He was sure that the son of Budd-Erling was holding out for a high price, and first he offered half a million francs and then he offered a round million, to be paid in dollars in New York, and strictly on the quiet. "We know how to handle money, M. Budd."

Lanny saw that the matter was serious, and he had to be careful or he might awaken suspicions. He said that he had lived most of his life in France, and that Marianne was his fostermother; he would do everything he could to help her, and some day he might receive a medal for it, but no money. He would be willing to drop everything and go to her aid, but his recent talks with British and Americans of his way of thinking and Laval's convinced him that the time was not yet. Let the Germans get to the Volga and across it, let them actually divert the oil of the Caucasus into the tanks of their Panzers, and then there might be a chance of putting some sense into the heads of Roosevelt and Churchill—or possibly of replacing them. Lanny brought encouragement to the soul of Vichy's Premier by telling of the conspiracy of high-up Americans to do just that, and the pair shook hands warmly and parted on the basis of friendship and trust. Of course the *fripon mongol* wouldn't really trust anybody, but he would tell them that he did, and with the manner which the French call *empressé*.

V

A train which needed repairs and did not run on time conveyed the P.A. to Cannes. At the station he was met by the "Bienvenu local," as he had dubbed the family buggy. The steed was thinner, it seemed to him, and so was the driver; he congratulated her as he kissed her, and she said: "I am getting so that I cannot eat when I know that so many other people are hungry." He assured her that it was the way to live longer, and she answered that it was the way to make wrinkles deeper, and to shudder every time you caught a glimpse of your own throat.

At home everything was peaceful, as much so as was possible with a World War in the newspapers and radio waves, and in the atmosphere, too, for guns were heard out at sea now and then, and military planes large and small passed overhead. Parsifal Dingle refused to let himself be troubled by the war; it was God's plan, otherwise it could not have been. Beauty insisted that whether it was God's plan or Satan's, the lovely little Marcel wasn't allowed to hear anything about it, and that had become one of the rules of the household.

One of the first items of news Lanny got was that his half-sister had gone back to Berlin. "Oskar crooked his finger, and she went," said Beauty. "He wrote her, and she wouldn't even show me the letter."

"Perhaps he neglected to be polite," ventured Lanny. "Or maybe he was a little too frank as to the nature of his interest. The Nazis are that way."

"Love is a terrible thing to a woman, Lanny. Marceline does not trust her man, I don't think she even respects him; and yet she goes to him."

"My guess is that snobbery has much to do with it. Oskar is an aristocrat, and she takes him at his own valuation. The more arrogant he is, the more she admires him in her secret heart, even when she herself is the victim. You brought her up wrong, Beauty."

"What can you do?" demanded the mother, making a French gesture with the shoulders. "The world is more powerful than any person in it, and what the world admires is what a child desires. I must admit that I have looked at Marceline with surprise most of her life; she is so self-centered, and so quietly determined."

"Why not start over again with this new one? Let him set out to be useful at once, and let him understand that all his life he is never going to get anything without earning it."

"What strange ideas you have, Lanny! I believe you are just as much a radical in your heart as when you were young!"

"Say that to me, but never to anybody else," replied the son.

He listened to his mother's account of what Marceline had been doing before her departure. She had got an engagement to dance at the International Sporting Club in Monte Carlo. A fantastic story. The Italian Army was respecting the independence of that tiny principality, and the hotels, *pensions*, and villas were packed with wealthy refugees from every country in Europe. Gambling at the Casino was going on from noon till daybreak, and hundreds of millions of francs changed hands every evening. Marceline had been paid a hundred and fifty thousand francs per week, but she hadn't been happy because of the crowding—people sleeping even in the chairs and on the sofas of the world's most famous gambling palace. To Lanny the place meant Sir Basil Zaharoff, who had owned it, and whom Lanny had met there as a small boy. He was moved now to try another séance with Madame, and heard the old munitions king of Europe lamenting the breakdown of the world, especially those parts of it which he had possessed and had been reluctant to leave behind him!

VI

The Golfe Juan was still blue in the deeps and green in the shallows, and the sun set each night in glory behind the red Esterel Mountains. The oleanders along the hedge were masses of white blossoms or pink, and the scarlet hibiscus were small flaming suns. In the court the bees made an endless humming in the flowers, and a new half-grown puppy tumbled over himself trying to follow Marcel about. The Midi displayed all its midsummer lusciousness, and the playfolk, as distinguished from the working folk, went about in bathing suits all day. If anybody wept for the million and a quarter young Frenchmen who were prisoners of war in Germany and were being worked as slave labor, they did their weeping alone and kept a face of courage in public.

Of old, Lanny had come here to rest and to refresh himself with happy memories. But this time he came as a disturber, a herald of bad tidings. A day or two after his arrival he went into his mother's room and shut the door. "Old darling," he began, "we have to have a confidential talk, the most important ever."

"Yes, Lanny?" she said, and a scared look came upon her face, for his tone was even more grave than his words. She was sitting at her dressing table, doing her best to repair the ravages of time. Now she put down her tools, and he seated himself on the side of the bed, facing her.

"You must have been doing a lot of guessing about your son during the last few years, and you have been very good about not talking—or so I have believed."

"Never a word to anyone, Lanny."

"This time is the most important of all. Here is something about which you are not to breathe the faintest hint to anybody on earth. It might cost me my life, and more important yet, it might cost the lives of a great many American boys. I really haven't the right even to speak of the matter, but I am trusting to your tact and good sense. You have to take yourself and Parsifal and the child away from Bienvenu."

"Oh, *mon Dieu!*" she exclaimed. "The war is coming here?"

"You must never breathe such words, nor even think the thought. You are a lady of the leisure class, and you haven't had any sort of trip or vacation for many years. You have a whim to see some new part of the world, some place where food is not rationed."

"Where is the place?"

"I have been trying to think of one that isn't too far away or too difficult to reach. I have decided that French Morocco would be highly suitable."

"But Lanny! such a fantastic place! And I keep hearing that the war may come there!"

"Trust my judgment, dear mother. Marrakech is one of the most fascinating spots I ever visited. It is high up and reasonably cool in summer. There are elegant villas there, and you might find one to rent, and play the social queen if you have a mind to. Also, there are good hotels. It will be expensive, but don't try to save money at this time."

"And when do we have to go, Lanny?"

"I don't know the date, and if I did I wouldn't be free to tell it. But you have time to make your plans and build up a propaganda among your friends. It will be O.K. if you are out of France by a month from now."

"It is going to be so hard to make anybody believe that I am really interested in a trip to Morocco!"

"Put it on my account if you like. I have been there, and am going to be there again, perhaps for months. I have found a gold mine there—I mean, figuratively speaking. I have interested American millionaires in the marvelous fountains and floor mosaics which are in that country; they have become quite a fad in New York, as fascinating as jigsaw puzzles. You can say that I made several thousand dollars in a single month out of them, and that I want you to help me, inspecting and overseeing the packing and shipping. That's business, and you know how to talk about it as well as the next person. I have a book about Moroccan art, and you can pick up a few phrases and become an expert. I have photographs you can show to friends, and a letter from a millionaire ordering a fountain. With a little practice you can get yourself all steamed up."

"I suppose I could. What shall I do with Bienvenu?"

"Pick out some trustworthy French couple and put them in charge; pay them to take care of the place."

"And the paintings, and your library?"

"We just have to take our chances with all those things. If you started packing them it would certainly look like a flight, and that would be absolutely fatal. People would say, I have just been here and have told you something to frighten you. Don't take anything but what you would naturally take on a trip. Be a tourist, think like a tourist."

"What shall I tell Parsifal?"

"Tell him what you tell the others. It makes no difference to him where he is. There are many mosques in Marrakech, and he will study the Mohammedan religion and find out if they have any psychic experiences and what they make of them. Tell Parsifal that you have seen so little of me during the past few years, and I am going to be there off and on during the next few months."

"Shall we take Madame with us?"

"That would be too much of a burden. No one will harm an old woman here. But take a maid, of course."

"And what about Emily? Should we not warn her?"

"That is a painful decision. I simply dare not take the chance of having her leave at the same time that we do. Emily is an old woman, all but bedridden; the worst that can happen is that her home will be taken by the military and she moved into one of her cottages. I am sure she would not be interned."

"Oh, then it is the Germans who are coming here!"

"Nobody can say who is coming, dear. Only a foolish person would attempt to guess the result of the clash of forces. What I have tried to do is think of some place where there is little chance of your being caught in any fighting, or of being shut up in a concentration camp for the duration—and this war may have a dreadful lot of duration! It happens that I have special knowledge, and you must trust me. Play the game according to my rules."

"All right, I will take your word. One question more. What am I to do about that money I buried in the garden?"

"The best thing will be for me to dig it up and use it, and send a check for your account in your New York bank. It so happens that I have use for a lot of money in small bills, which cannot be traced because of being new and having consecutive serial numbers."

"Lanny, I have felt for a long time that you were doing something frightfully dangerous!"

"Others are doing far more dangerous things, Mother dear. Let it rest here, that I am doing something that counts, and that some day I'll tell you a lot of interesting stories!"

VII

Next morning the P.A. called his old friend Jerry Pendleton on the telephone. First he inquired: "How's business?" and when Jerry gave the expected reply: "Rotten!" Lanny said: "I have to go to Geneva to get a painting. Can you fix me up for the train tomorrow night?" The travel bureau man promised to attend to it, and Lanny added: "How would you like to play some tennis this afternoon?"

They played three sets, and then went for a swim from the rocks below the estate. Sitting in the hot sunshine, with the insurgent waves drowning his low voice, Lanny opened up: "Do you suppose your wife could run the bureau for a while, Jerry?"

"A child could run it," said the other. He was what the French call a *petit bourgeois*, and the Americans a small businessman; by either name his situation was unpromising.

Lanny looked at this good fellow who had once been his tutor, although only half a dozen years older. The Army had claimed him in World War I, and he had risen to be a lieutenant; but he hadn't bothered to come home, he had stayed and married a French girl and a *pension*, or so he had said, in his playful fashion. Now Lanny observed that Jerry's hair was turning gray. He remarked: "You are worrying, aren't you?"

"Well," was the reply, "it's hard to run a travel bureau when people can't travel and to run a *pension* when the cost of food goes up faster than the boarders' incomes."

"Have you thought about the danger of staying on here?"

"Of course; but what can I do? I can't afford to drop everything and take Cerise and the kids to America."

"I have an idea to suggest. I have come onto a fairly prosperous business, buying mosaics in Morocco and shipping them to New York. I told Beauty about it, and she has taken a notion to go in with me. She thinks she'd like to see Marrakech, and Parsifal wants to study the Mohammedan religion."

"Jeepers!" exclaimed the ex-tutor. "Isn't that a sort of dangerous place to be in? I keep hearing talk about our Army coming to Casablanca."

"Well, suppose they do? The fighting will be at the coast, and Marrakech is a hundred miles or so in the interior. From what I've learned of the French Army there they couldn't stand up against us very long even if they wanted to, which I don't think they will. And when they give up, any Americans who are there will be in America, and without the expense of crossing the ocean."

"You know the situation better than I, Lanny."

"I'd a lot rather be there than here when the fighting starts; for it's certain that if we invade any French territory, the Germans will move here. They have to do it, not merely to keep us from landing here, but to keep the French from helping us."

"Yes, and their first move will be to intern all the Americans, especially the able-bodied men."

"This is what has occurred to me, Jerry. You know Beauty—she has all the social gifts and can help by getting introductions and oiling the machinery, but she's not much good at the details of a business. I thought you might travel with the party as a sort of secretary, and when you get there, I could put you to work for a while and pay you enough to get along and have a bit to send back home."

"That's very handsome of you, Lanny. What is it, just kindness?"

"Not at all. I'll promise you plenty of work, maybe more than you want. I put only one condition on it, that you don't say a word about it until I tell you to come, and then you just tell Cerise that you are helping Beauty on the trip. When you're safe in Morocco, you can write her that you're staying a while longer. You understand, Cerise won't be in any danger here because she's French, and the Germans are behaving correctly. But if you were to tell her about it now she might be tempted to tell her aunt, or one of the servants might overhear, and I can't afford to have my name talked about in this connection."

"Mum's the word," replied this dependable friend. And then with a grin: "I wonder who Mum was."

VIII

The art expert was retracing his footsteps of the previous spring, except that he visited Geneva ahead of Toulon. Among the conservative disciples of John Calvin he set to work to make his presence known to art dealers and collectors; also he dropped a postcard to "M. Philippe Brun" at the address which he had stowed away carefully in his memory. "Just a line to let you know I'm in town. Bienvenu." He went to the public library next afternoon and made connections with Monck in the usual cautious way. In the evening they took a long walk, and rested as before on the steps of the League of Nations building, a mausoleum to them, the tomb of their hopes of past years.

The German had a lot to report. Colonel Donovan's organization had sent a man to him, a young college instructor of German descent, a man of keen intelligence with whom Monck was especially well pleased. The agent had given him money, and later had produced some apparatus. Monck didn't say what it was, but Lanny could guess that it was a radio-sending outfit. There were hints that several other people had gone to work; Monck didn't know the details, but he said that it was encouraging to have such competent support. The anti-Nazi movement of Germany was like a reservoir that had been drained almost dry; but now a new aqueduct was being constructed, and soon a mighty new stream would be flowing in.

Monck talked more freely than he had done before; it was as if he were preparing to come out from underground. Lanny had to warn him not to become too confident; it would be a long time yet before an American army could enter Germany. But they would be fighting somewhere before this year was over, that much a P.A. was free to tell his friend in confidence. Fresh from a visit to the Budd-Erling plant, and from driving on Highway Number 1, he could testify that the sleeping giant overseas was stirring his limbs and getting to his feet. "As sure as tomorrow's sunrise, the Nazis are going to be knocked out." The old-time labor man and Social Democrat replied that these were the most pleasant words he had ever heard.

He reported on the results of his own inquiries. His "contact" had been in touch with a physicist, and it was true that Germany was making or preparing to make *schweres Wasser*. Indeed, the physicist had seen the blueprints of a very elaborate plant, but unfortunately he had never been told where the plant was to be located. "It is dangerous to ask questions in Germany nowadays, even of one's intimate friends." Oddly enough, the man went on to say, he had got some information about conditions in America, where there existed only a few quarts of "heavy water"; it was one of the scarcest products of the new physics.

The question of jet propulsion was not so ultra-secret, not because the Nazis didn't want it so, but because the job was far advanced and therefore had to have workers sharing the secret. There were a number, both Communists and Socialists, who had joined the Nazi party as a means of surviving, but who still kept the old faith buried in their hearts. Every day it became plainer to the workers that they were going to have to face a long war, and against fresh forces from the New World; if only the Russians could hold out through this summer and autumn, many of the German workers would become desperate and would risk their lives to tell what they knew. Said Monck: "I have sent out the call, and I'm waiting for echoes to come back. It isn't something that can be done in a few days. I hope and trust that people are working on it, and that some day I'll get answers, and possibly even the blueprints."

Lanny had no right to complain. He wasn't risking anything, but was staying in a palace hotel, the Beau Rivage, and strolling about looking at *objets d'art*. In the lining of his coat was a tiny oblong of paper with six words written on it, and this burned inward all the way to his heart; he longed so to use it, and was sure that if he were to address a note to Führer Adolf Hitler at the New Chancellery in Berlin, a telegram would come at once, followed by a courier and a plane, to bring him to the *Hauptstadt*, or to the Führer's *Hauptquartier*, wherever it might be. But what could Lanny accomplish, so far as concerned either atomic fission or jet propulsion? He was an enemy alien now, and would be watched every moment, no matter how plausible his story and how charming his manners; very certainly he would not be permitted to chat with any nuclear physicists or designers of supersonic projectiles. And anyhow, F.D.R. had said no, and until he said yes, Lanny would have to go on traveling *en prince* in neutral lands.

The best he could do was to pump this ex-sailor and ex-*capitán* completely dry of information concerning conditions in Germany and Switzerland. It was a mild night, and they were in an open place where no one could steal up behind them. They kept their voices low. Monck told about some of the comrades who had been helping him and who now were gone—these were the only ones he could mention. Some of them had been Trudi's friends whom Lanny had known in the old days that now seemed a hundred years past. "What fools we were!" remarked the Social Democratic leader. "We actually believed that the great cartelmasters would let us organize and vote them out of power!"

"And we thought the workers would stand by us when it came to a showdown!" responded the American. "We gave them credit for too much intelligence, Monck, and the capitalists for too little."

"Hitler is a cunning knave, you must remember."

"Part knave and part genius, *Genosse*."

"I suppose we have to admit that. It would seem as if some devil had constructed him especially to hoodwink the German folk and lead them to utter ruin and despair."

"The Pied Piper of Hamelin town!" said Lanny.

IX

Just before leaving Bienvenu the P.A. had stopped in Cannes and rented a typewriter of German make; at home he had spent several hours producing a document labeled: "Professor Zimmermann's Examination Questions." These questions, twenty-three in all, covered the points on which Lanny had received instructions from the young Jewish doctor of science. They represented the matters concerning which American physicists wished to ascertain how far the German physicists were informed; each question was one which Lanny had learned by heart and had kept reciting to himself ever since leaving the Institute of Advanced Study at Princeton. Several of the questions read: "What is the significance of the formula"—and then followed. one of those assemblages of mathematical symbols which, so far as the layman was concerned, might as well have been ancient Hittite or modern Gujerati. Each formula contained carefully studied errors which would lead the German scientists astray if it fell into the wrong hands; but any scientist who really knew the advanced steps toward atomic fission would correct the errors. Dr. Braunschweig's last words had been: "Do not tell even your trusted agent that the formulas are wrong. The errors are a means of testing what comes back to us."

Coming from Bienvenu, Lanny had carried this document pinned to his undershirt, and he had slept with it. Now he unpinned it and laid it in Monck's hands, also the pin, and saw the German make it safe in the same manner. Lanny explained: "Professor Zimmermann is a top-flight physicist who happens to be an especially ardent Nazi. If this paper should come into possession of the Gestapo, they would call upon this learned gentleman to explain for whom his examination questions were intended, and this might cause at least a temporary slowing up of German progress in nuclear science."

Monck said: "I will put my man to work on it."

Lanny gave his comrade some of the money he had dug up from under Beauty's yellow oleander; after which he went to his hotel room and slept well. In the morning he typed out a report on what he had learned and took it out and dropped it into a postbox—he wasn't afraid to trust the mails in this six-hundred-year-old republic. He spent the day visiting his art friends, and purchased a portrait by Mary Cassatt of a charming tiny girl, intending it as a present to old Mrs. Fotheringay, his client in Chicago who had a mansion full of painted babies. Having thus established himself as an art expert and no spy, Lanny took the night train back to the Riviera.

He had only a few duties left: the first, to pay a call upon Emily Chattersworth and do what he could to cheer her up. This wasn't easy, for she said that her world had come to an end. And indeed it was so, the world that she had known and enjoyed was gone, probably forever. Beauty hadn't yet told her about the harebrained plan of buying mosaics in Morocco; Lanny didn't want to have to discuss the idea with Emily; he wasn't sure he could make it sound plausible to her shrewd mind. To flee and leave this old friend behind seemed cruel; but, on the other hand, to take a semi-invalid with them would be telling the world that Lanny had special information about events in the making.

He visited several persons on the Riviera who owned paintings and were living on the proceeds of their sale. Sooner or later the funds would be running low; and this was a cruel world, in which, when your funds were gone, nobody brought you any food, nobody prepared it for you or served it to you, and your friends had a tendency to cross to the other side of the street, for fear that you might start trying to borrow from them. But Lanny would be on hand and would say tactfully: "If you would care to put a price on that Ingres, I know a gentleman in New York who might be interested." Then he would say, even more tactfully: "I am sorry, but I fear that is much too high. I don't think I could advise my client to pay more than half the sum."

X

Lanny had written to "M. Guillaume Bruges" at Toulon, saying that he would soon arrive to inspect the sketches about which M. Bruges had informed him. There was a train that ran along this rockbound Coast of Pleasure, sometimes passing so close to the villas that you feared it was going to hit them. If you were rich and could afford *première classe*, you could be comfortable. Lanny with his carefully packed suitcases and little portable typewriter boarded the morning train, and a couple of hours later descended in Toulon and was driven in an old-style *fiacre* to the Grand Hotel.

All hotels were crowded, but there was always room for a gentleman who was known to be a friend of the military commandant of the port. Lanny made it a point to inquire of the hotel clerk what sort of transportation he could get to the mansion of the D'Avrienne family in the suburbs; he had come, so he said, for the purpose of giving further study to an art collection of which the city was proud. He had dropped a note, requesting permission, and now there was a reply awaiting him at the hotel, and he did not fail to refer to it.

Also, he asked whether any new art dealers had set themselves up in business since his last visit. He went out to look for them; and it was pure chance that he happened to be passing the bookstore of Armand Mercier. It was chance, also, that he happened to see on the stall in front of the shop a book that interested him. It was natural for a clerk to come out to see if he wished to make a purchase; and nobody heard the words which the clerk murmured: "Twenty hours, at the statue of the Genius of Navigation."

Lanny moved on, and inspected paintings in the shops, and admired them even though he found them commonplace. He inquired about old masters and made note of where some might be found; he did all this, knowing that rumors would spread and help to make him *persona grata*. The law required all foreigners to register with the police, and Lanny went and reported himself as on the way to Algiers; he was stopping by for a couple of days to find out if there was a possibility of obtaining examples of the art of painting, in which it was well known that the French excel all the rest of the world. The statement that "fine words butter no parsnips" had originated in England and would surely never have occurred to anyone who had been raised in the Midi!

XI

Promptly at the hour set, Lanny made contact with his friend, and they strolled in obscure streets, taking pains to make certain that no one was following. Their destination was the beautiful gardens of the hospital, out on Cap Cépet which forms one arm of the harbor. They found a quiet spot, in the open, there being sufficient moonlight so that no one could approach without detection. Speaking in low murmurs the ex-schoolman revealed that a man had come from Colonel Donovan's office, and that the little group of the underground were well pleased with what he had brought them and had promised.

Raoul himself hadn't met the man. "You know, Lanny, the fact that I am a Spaniard and worked for the Republican government makes me vulnerable. If ever the *flics* should take my fingerprints they would spot me, so I stick to my job and avoid the *rafles*, the round-ups in which they collect slave workers for Germany. I make friends among the workers, and listen, and try to pick out the honest comrades from the police agents and spies. It is dreadfully difficult these days; you have to guard every word you say, every gesture, and every expression of your face."

"I know," Lanny answered. "I worry about you; but we greatly need your help."

"You want to know about the Fleet. There is a civil war here, as everywhere in France. Partly it is the class war—three-quarters of the *marins* are for the Allies, whereas three-quarters of the officers are for tradition, that is to say, for obeying orders whatever they may be. Of course the situation is complicated by what the British did at Mersel-Kébir; a good part of the men hate them heartily for that; but few hate the Americans, and if the common sailors could have their way, the Fleet would sail out tomorrow and put itself under American command."

"That is unlikely, of course. The question is, whether they will let themselves be put under German command."

"That surely cannot happen, Lanny. There would be a mutiny on every ship."

"What is the truth about the Germans being taught how to run the machinery?"

"That is being done to some extent. The officers claim they cannot refuse to comply with German demands. There is an underground war going on over the issue. Wherever the Germans come, our *marins* of course know it, and they get together and agree to teach them wrongly as far as possible. They know what the Nazis want and hate their very guts. Naturally we make the most of the situation. I have written three leaflets that have been printed; many of the men have had a chance to read them. That is one of the ways your Intelligence man has been able to help us, with money, and now he has promised to get paper. That is scarce."

"Do you yourself need money, Raoul?"

"I can use some always; and so can Julie. She, being French, is not in as much danger as I. Believe me, I remember the months I spent in a concentration camp. The French are a grand people in many ways, but their treatment of the politically suspect—well, I'd get out of this country if I didn't see so much to be done."

"The critical time is near, Raoul. I don't know the day or the place, but I can tell you this much; the Americans are coming to the Mediterranean, and it will be this year."

"That is great news, of course; but it won't satisfy our little group; they want to see the Army here tomorrow! The fortifications of Toulon are powerful, but they don't extend very far to the east or the west, and landings could be made and the port surrounded."

"No doubt our military men have maps, Raoul. What you and your friends have to do is to save the Fleet, or at any rate keep it out of German hands. No one could exaggerate the importance of that. So long as the Germans don't have it, we can command the Mediterranean and can land at any place we select. The day we land on French territory, you can be sure the Germans will come down here in force, and they will use every stratagem they know to get the ships. That is when you must act, and put in everything you have. I probably won't be here, so I'm telling you now: get ready for the day. The fate of the war might depend upon it—at least for years."

XII

Raoul urged his friend to tell these things directly to the leaders of his group. There were differences of opinion, he explained, but all three had been tremendously impressed by that little engraved visiting card with the name of President Roosevelt on it. Lanny said: "I'm still carrying it." At the same time he wondered, what would they make of the other bit of paper which was sewed up in his coat? An appointment was made for the following evening, and Lanny returned to his hotel. He discovered that his baggage had been gone through, not very skillfully. He had left his correspondence conveniently on top, his address list and his data on Moorish and Arab art. Nothing had been taken.

In the morning he inspected the D'Avrienne treasures again, and visited more art dealers, and took the trouble to get permission to see another collection about which he had been informed. In the evening he dined upon fish, newly caught in that old sea which had fed so many human tribes for so many thousands of years. Then he went for a "constitutional," and stopped to look in shop windows, and out of the corner of his eye made certain that nobody else was stopping at the same time. When at last he picked up his Spanish friend, they walked separately around a couple of blocks in the Old Town before at last they dived into the dark alleyway.

In the same dingy room were the three comrades to whom Lanny had told his life story: Jean Catroux, the Communist, who wished to be known as Zed; Soulay, the docker, tough and weatherbeaten; and the mysterious young woman who had first been Mlle. Richard and now was Mlle. Bléret. Zed was either the leader, or else the more talkative; he said: "*Bonsoir, Camarade Zhone. Asseyez-vous, s'il vous plaît.*" Comrade Jones took a vacant chair, and the spokesman continued: "We have met the agent you sent to us, and everything is satisfactory. We don't know whether you know this man, or wish to know about him."

Lanny's reply was: "I do not know him, and I much prefer not to share any secret that is not necessary to my work. I only want to be sure you have got what you want."

"We have, and we thank you."

"I have already told Comrade Bruges, but I will repeat for your benefit, that there is to be an American invasion of the Mediterranean area before the end of the present year. There was a conference of the general staffs of Britain and America last month, and that was the decision. I have it upon the highest authority, and you may accept it as settled. The exact place and date are still to be determined, but your duties are the same in any case. You are asked to do everything in your power to make certain that the French Fleet does not fall into the hands of the Germans. That is the one absolutely vital thing that is within the field of your efforts."

"We have been told that, Comrade Jones, and we are doing our best and hope to do more."

"You should try to win the confidence of individual sailors and persuade them to organize so far as it can be done; you should also try to win officers; there are many who understand the principles of the Revolution, and are not under the Vichy spell. And not merely the sailors, but the arsenal workers, the dockers, the whole labor force of this port must be prepared to rise in a mass movement, to seize arms, and to make every building at the harbor a fortress to keep the Germans away from the ships."

"You are perhaps aware, Comrade Jones, that the Germans have compelled our commanders to reduce the fuel in the tanks, so that the ships cannot make their escape."

"I have been told that, and if that is the situation when the crisis comes, it will be necessary to sink the vessels. Men must be found with courage enough to open the seacocks, and then stand by and defend the ships while they sink. There have been such heroes in French history, I know, because my stepfather, the painter Marcel Detaze, was shot down in an observation balloon and had his face burned off; nevertheless, in the last desperate days of the second battle of the Marne, he took a gun and went into the fighting and gave his life."

"We know that story, comrade." It was the woman speaking, and Lanny turned toward her. She had been gazing at him intently out of her fine brown eyes, something he had observed on the previous occasions when they had met. She was an extremely attractive young woman, so Lanny had thought at the beginning, and he still thought it: slender and graceful, with sensitive features and an ardent expression. He had been interested to make her acquaintance; but now the circumstances had changed and he was a bit afraid of her. All his life he had been made aware that ladies "fell for him" easily, and he knew the world well enough not to attribute it altogether to his personal charms. He hadn't been more than six years old when Robbie had pointed out to him that he was the grandson of an American millionaire and might some day be the son of such a godlike being; the ladies would find that out, somehow or other, and for the rest of his days—young, middle-aged, or old—he would have to be aware of that special danger. Now, desiring no entanglements, he remarked:

"Let me tell you, comrades, that a few years ago I was married to a German artist of talent, a Socialist who did not give way to the Nazis.

She was seized by them and tortured to death, but she did not betray any of the secrets with which she had been entrusted. She used to quote to me the words of a German poem, supposed to be spoken by the Tirolese hero, Andreas Hofer: '*Wir sind all des Todes eigen*,' that is to say, '*Nous appartenons tous à la mort*.' Such is the spirit in which we have to work in these tragic days, men, women, and even children; we all belong to death. That is true of me, and also of my wife, for I have recently been married to an ardent comrade who would be here with me tonight, except that she is expecting a baby soon."

Without waiting to observe the effect of this statement upon the mademoiselle, Lanny turned his eyes to the sturdy dockworker with the well-browned skin and leathery hands. "It would be well, Comrade Soulay, if a few of you *enfants de la patrie* could get hold of some sticks of dynamite and plant them under the vital machinery of the arsenal before the Germans arrive. It would be better yet if you would study some of the bridges and tunnels and wreck them to delay the enemy's approach. This one thing you have to get clear, and don't let anybody persuade you otherwise—the instant they get word that an American soldier has set foot upon French soil, whether here or in North Africa, the Panzers and the parachutists will set out for Toulon. So don't let anything delay you; be ready to act the first night, because that may be the only night you have."

"*Que vous avez raison!*" said the horny-handed *enfant*.

13

The Yanks Are Coming

I

FROM Toulon to Marseille is another short train journey, and there the Pendleton Agence de Voyage had engaged passage for M. Budd on the same steamer which had carried him to Algiers the previous time. The great "midland sea" was still and the air was hot in midsummer, and again Lanny spent the night on deck. Late the next afternoon there loomed up that shining white city on the steep hillslopes, and once more a bus took him on the boulevard which runs along the shore, ascending slowly, and then turns and comes back in the opposite direction, still ascending. The bus continued into the suburbs until it came to a high, level spot which had been made into a beautiful garden, and here was a hotel prepared to provide a collector of mosaics with every comfort, provided that he could pay the high price.

The faithful Hajek had been notified and was on hand. He had been seeking new art treasures, and soon the visitor was immersed in those elaborate negotiations which he found amusing. They were the custom of the country, made him a great gentleman, and provided protection against espionage. Just as by going into a French café and ordering a cup of coffee or a glass of wine you had the right to sit and read all the newspapers in the place, so by bargaining over several fountains for ablutions and buying one of them Lanny could have the right to hold secret conferences with as many conspirators as he could find in Algiers.

Capitaine Denis de Bruyne came to the hotel and they sat under an arbor, conversing in low tones. Lanny told about his meeting with Charlot, and it was sad. Denis was not so bitter against his brother as the brother was against him. Denis took the position that Charlot was a strayed lamb whom he yearned to bring back into the fold. But Lanny couldn't hold out any hope; he had to report that Charlot had completely committed himself to the *collaborateurs* and could not be brought to hear reason. The older brother sat with his lips pressed together and the knuckles showing white in his clenched hands. "If only I could talk to him!" he lamented.

Lanny replied: "It would only add to the bitterness between you. You will have to leave it to events to change his mind."

"What events will do is to get him shot!" exclaimed the brother.

II

Lanny gave an account of his visits to Washington and London, and of the decision taken by the Allied Combined Chiefs of Staff. Denis, a man of honor, could be trusted with the great secret. Lanny told him that it was certain to be North Africa, and hardly possible that Algiers should not be one of the first ports taken. It was to be an invasion in force, and the troops would come to stay.

"It is most important for us to be sure of that," said the younger man. "We shall be staking our lives upon it. Our friends have been terribly discouraged by Dieppe."

He was referring to an event which had just been reported, of course with the high coloring the collaborationist press gave to all German successes. Some five thousand troops, mostly Canadians, had been thrown against Dieppe, and had managed to hold portions of the harbor for half a day. They had been forced to retire, and if you could believe the Algiers papers, they had lost several vessels of war, a great fleet of planes, and more than half the men who had taken part. The Germans had given them a bloody lesson and vindicated the claim that the Channel coast was invulnerable.

Lanny said: "It was a commando raid, Denis; a big one, but still a raid. It had to be undertaken because the Canadians were so impatient. What I am talking about is an invasion, with force enough to take and hold all French North Africa. You know how the Americans came last time, and the job they did; they are coming again, and in far greater force. We are building an army of eight million men, and the decision has been taken to open up the Mediterranean, destroy Rommel's army, and build air bases to put Italy out of the war. That is going to happen, and the Germans can no more stop it than they can stop tomorrow's sunrise."

The other replied: "I am ready to stake my life on my faith in you, Lanny; but you can understand how hard it is for a Frenchman to believe in success any more. For almost three years we have seen nothing but defeats, all over the world, and we have got the habit of despair."

"That is because you have to see the war through the enemy's spectacles. We in the outside world see it differently. The siege of London has certainly not been a defeat for Britain, and the sieges of Leningrad and Moscow have not been defeats for the Soviet Union. I am told by friends at home who are close to sources of information that we destroyed something more than a third of Japan's most highly trained flyers at the Battle of Midway, and we are destroying more every day in the struggle for the Solomons. Those things don't show up in the daily reports, but they are bound to have an effect in the long run."

"All that seems far off to us, Lanny. Here in North Africa we contemplate the fact that Rommel is only seventy miles from Alexandria, and that reinforcements and supplies are being poured in by way of Tunis and the other ports so close to Italy. I have been told that in Cairo there is a *trac*, a panic. The well-to-do residents are packing their belongings into their cars and preparing to flee to Palestine or to wherever they can go."

"That may be, Denis; but it is not the well-to-do residents who fight battles, and it may be they are encouraged to take themselves away and relieve the food situation by that much. What you do not hear about are the convoys we have been sending around South Africa and up through the Suez Canal. We have a new tank called the General Sherman that is believed to be good, and we have a self-propelled anti-tank gun that the Desert Fox isn't going to like a bit when he hears it go off. Don't forget, too, we have an airplane route established across the middle of Africa, and we are sending all kinds and sizes of planes to Cairo. I have no idea when the British will feel strong enough to attack, but I do know that they have been bringing up forces from all over the Middle East, and you can be sure that Rommel will have to do a lot more fighting before he gets to Alexandria, to say nothing of Suez."

III

Lanny was taken again to the apartment of Professor Aboulker, and had another session with him and the two Royalists, D'Astier de la Vigerie and the Jesuit Father Cordier. Lanny did not reveal to these three that he was positive about the Allied decision; he contented himself with saying that he had checked upon and verified his previous information, which was that the big attack was to come by way of the Mediterranean and was to be this year. Since Algiers was the most important French city in North Africa, it was fair to assume that it would be included in the program. Lanny was told that a represent-ative of Colonel Donovan's organization had made contact with this group; the news pleased him greatly, for it meant that "Wild Bill" and his miscellaneous crowd were missing no openings. The Frenchmen professed to be satisfied with what they had got; the Americans were a wonderful people.

When this group learned that Lanny had been in London, they wanted to know if he had visited General de Gaulle. The truth was that he had kept as far from the French Joan of Arc as possible, for he had got the impression both in London and New York that the headquarters of this movement was beset with spies, intriguers, and publicity seekers. But he couldn't say this to Frenchmen in exile, who knew the General only by his radio eloquence. When they asked why President Roosevelt did not at once espouse this great leader's cause and place him at the head of the expedition, Lanny answered tactfully that the President was doing his best to distinguish between the win-ning of the war, which was the American task, and the future of *la patrie*, which was a problem for Frenchmen, and in which Americans had to exercise care to avoid even seeming to interfere. France was an ally, and all Frenchmen would be friends, save only those who had chosen to be friends of the Nazis. This statement pleased the group, and Lanny could only hope that when the Army came it would have some advisers who understood this touchy people.

Here in this apartment were five Frenchmen determined to work like all possessed for the occasion which the Americans oddly called "D-day." Their movement was spreading rapidly, and the different groups were at one in their desire to make as much trouble as possible for the enemy. Lanny promised to let them know what was coming and when; but they must understand that the Germans had many submarines, to say nothing of dive-bombing planes, and these constituted greater menaces than anything likely to be encountered on shore. Therefore every effort must be made to deceive the enemy as to the destination of the great convoy, and the friends of the cause must not expect definite information until the vessels were immediately at hand.

That didn't sound so good to the conspirators, and M. d'Astier remarked: "If our Chantiers de la Jeunesse take the key points of Algiers and then your troops don't come ashore, hundreds of French lads and all their leaders will be shot."

Lanny replied: "I will explain the situation to Washington, and no doubt Mr. Murphy will do it also. A code must be arranged, and you must know exactly what steps to take at every stage of the landing."

IV

The visitor inspected several fountains and made himself conspicuous as an art expert, telling about his achievement in starting a new fad among the American rich. This would have the effect of increasing the prices of what he hoped to buy, but under the circumstances he didn't mind that; his client, Mr. Vernon, would be making a contribution toward saving the lives of American soldiers. In the salons of the Algerian nabobs, in their town houses and their magnificent estates at the foot of the mountain range, Lanny discoursed upon the fact that they had treasures of art which they failed to appreciate; he rallied them because they were content with butchers' calendars for paintings, while the wealthy of New York were sending an agent to North Africa to snatch ancient Moroccan masterpieces from under their noses.

In one of these soirees he ran into the vegetable-oil king, and that gentleman, professing friendship, was hurt because M. Budd hadn't looked him up. Lanny went to lunch again at the Golf Club, and let himself be pumped dry concerning what was going on in New York and Washington, London and Madrid, Vichy and Cannes. He didn't mind it, for he told only what could do no harm, and he charged a good price for the service. M. Lemaigre-Dubreuil was a fountainhead of information about the leading personalities of Algeria, both French and German, to say nothing of American. He was a man to encourage, for he had great power and was ready and eager to make a deal for his own safety.

The son of Budd-Erling was the sort of person he could understand, and he asked anxiously what would be the policy of the American Army and administration to French capital in these colonial lands. He had heard so much about "That Man," and his dangerous prejudices against all "economic royalists." Lanny explained that F.D.R. was doing what he could to cut the ground from under the Communists by persuading the super-rich to part with some of their excessive gains. His New Deal was a milder set of measures than the British Tories had introduced two or three decades ago. This statement comforted the representative of the "two hundred families," now preparing to seek shelter under the Stars and Stripes.

Members of the *haute bourgeoisie* of Algiers were making money fast. They had found secret ways to undermine the Nazi system, by bribing individual officials of the Reichswehr, the *Partei*, or the various commissions which were looking out for German interests. "Some day the war will be over," a French high bourgeois would say to a Nazi big or little wig, "and then you will have nothing but your salary. Wouldn't it be the part of common sense to lay a little by?" This would enable the Frenchman to get hold of a block of stock in some bank or industry that was being acquired by the Germans, and then to transfer the shares to a newly organized holding concern in Switzerland or Sweden, Spain or the Argentine.

They whispered about these stratagems among themselves, and when they had come to know the son of Budd-Erling well enough they let him hear the whispers. They even offered to let him in on some of the good things, going fifty-fifty, of course. Lanny would smile amiably and say that whenever he had any money to spare he put it into his father's business; and he offered to let them in on that without any commission whatever. Some took him seriously and asked questions about Budd-Erling stocks; they had the most exaggerated ideas about the earnings of airplane shares, and equally exaggerated fears as to what would happen to such shares when the fighting stopped!

Lanny listened attentively and learned new things about both France and Germany. There were more tricks than you could shake a stick at, or even a whole bundle of sticks tied together with a cord and with an ax in the middle of them. Such had been the symbol carried before the ancient Roman lictors, proclaiming to the world their authority to flog backs and to chop off heads. The fasces, the bundle was called, and Mussolini and his gang had taken it over and used its name and its threat. Now Il Duce's sticks were falling apart, and if you could believe the big-business *émigrés* of North Africa, the Führer was struggling in vain against the same forces of disintegration. Every American knows the phrase, "Business is business," and every Frenchman knows *"Les affaires sont les affaires."* The Germans had their version: *"Geschäft ist Geschäft"!*

V

A rather amusing episode arose out of Lanny's dealings with the vegetable-oil king. The latter said: "I mentioned you to Mr. Robert Murphy, and he expressed a desire to meet you. What do you say?"

Lanny had been carefully keeping away from the Counselor and his twelve vice-consuls—one of whom, according to the gossip now going the rounds, had fallen under the spell of a French woman who was revealed to be a Nazi spy! Lanny, a spy himself, didn't want to have anything to do with any of his fellow workers, whether German, French, or American. But he couldn't very well say that he was unwilling to make the acquaintance of the man who was his country's ambassador to this colonial world. He told Lemaigre that such a meeting would give him pleasure, and Lemaigre offered to arrange another luncheon. Lanny protested that it ought to be his turn, but the other answered that it was such a small matter they surely didn't have to talk about it; some day they would meet in America, and then it would be the American's turn to feed the Frenchman.

Lanny gave thought to this meeting in advance. He had heard about Mr. Murphy wherever he went, among rich and poor, for Mr. Murphy was a super-important person. Many of the farseeing French were looking upon him as soon to be consul, not in the modern commercial sense, but in the ancient Roman sense, the civil governor of a province. He was a person acceptable to the French because he was a Catholic, and also because he was genial and friendly, a democrat in the human sense of that word. The Americans had sent such a representative to France in the days when the young nation was striving to be born;

his name was Benjamin Franklin, and he had made a hit with the liberal elements of France both rich and poor. It was very probable that Mr. Murphy had read about this eminent predecessor, and would try in a modest way to follow his footsteps.

Lanny was bound to assume that Mr. Murphy, a career diplomat in Paris prior to the war, was nobody's fool. He could hardly have failed to have suspicions concerning a fellow countryman who traveled about so freely in wartime. Mr. Murphy received mysterious missives marked "Personal to the President, from Traveler," and he had orders to forward these promptly in the diplomatic pouches, which couriers bore by way of Tangier, the Azores, and Brazil. Could the Counselor have failed to note the fact that these letters ceased when Mr. Budd left North Africa and were resumed when he came back? Could the thought have failed to occur to him that his Chief had set somebody to watching him and his twelve subordinates? Mr. Murphy would have been less than human if he had not been curious about such a person; and he would have been less than a shrewd diplomat if he had not "pumped" the vegetable-oil king on the subject and hinted that a meeting might be brought about in a way that would not seem too obvious.

Lanny had been told by Roosevelt that he might reveal himself to the Counselor if he saw fit, but he had decided not to see fit just now. What the P.A. had on his mind were those six words which Hess had written on a scrap of paper, and the hope he was cherishing of taking them into Germany. If that should come about, the less he had had to do with American agents in North Africa, the better for him. He knew that the place was swarming with agents of the enemy's Armistice Commission. Now and then one of them sought out Herr Budd, who talked volubly about the charms of Arab and Moroccan architecture, and the wonders of Timgad which he had seen and of Volubilis about which he had been told. He expressed also the conviction that war was a sad and cruel thing, with which an art lover could not possibly have anything to do. And he was careful not to let any one of them get him alone in a dark alley.

VI

The career diplomat came to the Golf Club; tall, handsome, comfortably dressed, but not at all "high-hat." He was an agreeable talker, and Lanny liked to listen, but knew that he had not been invited there for this purpose. Presently the Counselor mentioned having been told that Mr. Budd had had the advantage of knowing some of the Nazi leaders. That was an invitation, and Lanny talked about the personal characteristics of Numbers One, Two, and Three, and told illustrative anecdotes. Mr. Murphy asked the art expert's guess as to the circumstances under which the war might end. When and how would the Nazis give up? To this Lanny said that Hitler was a fanatic and would die fighting like a rat in a corner; Göring, on the other hand, was a practical man and had sound military judgment; he would know when victory was no longer possible. Lanny smiled as he said: "I think he would be willing to surrender all Germany, provided that he was allowed to keep his castles, and the money he has deposited abroad, and above all, his art collection."

They commented upon that curious psychological complexity, a genuine love of beauty combined with monstrous greed. The Frenchman told a story about a refugee of his acquaintance, a German Jew who had been a great capitalist and had owned fine paintings. For a moment Lanny thought he might be talking about Johannes Robin, but no, it was another man, who had lived in Nürnberg. He had been put under house arrest, for his own good, he was told, to protect him against the anti-Semitic mobsters. The person who came to give him advice and to aid his exit from Germany was none other than the fat Marshal's wife.

"Emmy Sonnemann, the actress," Lanny remarked. "I had the pleasure of meeting her several times. She is a really kindhearted person and tried to help a number of the Jews."

"Maybe so," replied the vegetable-oil man. "The way she helped this particular Jew was by telling him that he had to sell his art works, his palace, and his shares in several big German companies, all for a few thousand marks. Emmy's husband was the buyer, and I have often wondered if Emmy got a commission on the deal."

"My God!" exclaimed Lanny. He was astounded, for he had thought that this stage star was really a kindly creature. Millions of Germans had thought so, too; she was built on a generous scale, the very archetype of Nordic blond beauty, praised by Hitler under the name of "Aryan." Lanny said: "I didn't think there was anything more for me to learn about the Nazis, but I see I was naïve." In his mind was the night which he and his father had spent in Karinhall, and in their bedroom Robbie had written on a scrap of paper, being afraid that the room might be "wired," a warning to his son not to be too cordial in manner to the Reichsmarschall's wife. Göring was known to be of a jealous temperament, and Robbie was afraid that he might resent even the ordinary social courtesies.

When the time came for the luncheon party to break up Lanny decided to make a brief "pass" at the Counselor. He remarked: "My mother is living on the Riviera, and she is talking about coming to Morocco this fall to help me in selecting some works of art for which I have orders. I don't know what to advise her. Can you tell me whether it is likely to be safe?"

There were only three in the private room, and certainly there wasn't any reason for caution in the presence of the vegetable-oil king. In his talks with Lanny this man of great affairs had made plain that he knew what was coming, and Lanny suspected that he had got it from his Irish-American friend. But perhaps Mr. Murphy didn't realize that Lanny had got that far with the French collaborator. What he answered was: "I wish I could tell you. I hear many reports, but I really couldn't say."

Lanny recognized this as the kind of skillful answer he had been taught to cultivate from his youth on. Mr. Robert Murphy hadn't made any false statement. No doubt he "wished" that he could tell, just as he wished many other good things—that the war was over, and that the world was a better place, with no gangsters and no gangsters' molls in it. Also, he heard many reports and read many, and he "couldn't" say—because he had been told not to. (He had just come back from a flying visit to Washington and London.)

VII

Lanny took a plane to Casablanca, leaving the faithful but too talkative Hajek to follow by the slower method of the rundown railroad. The P.A. had already written a note to General Béthouart, at military headquarters, saying that he was coming and hoped to have a chance to inspect the especially fine mosaic which the General had told him about. The General hadn't told any such thing, but Lanny guessed that he wouldn't be too dumb, and he wasn't. There came to the hotel a note making an appointment for the next day; and when the pair met they didn't talk about *objets d'art*, but about the American agents who were now at work in "Casa," and when was the Army coming, and in what force? There were several key persons whom the General could name, in the strictest confidence: persons whose help would be invaluable, but who would not move until they were certain that the great Army overseas was no dream. They were ready to climb onto the bandwagon, but not until they heard the music!

Beauty had written to Algiers, and now she wrote to Morocco.

Lanny had warned her not to say a word about her reasons for coming, or to ask any questions, and to this she carefully conformed. She said that good old Jerry had offered to escort them, not even asking for his expenses. Of course she was insisting upon paying these. "As you know," wrote this playful mother, "I have never failed to have a man to 'lean on' if I could get him, and usually I could. Parsifal, I fear, will not be much good for travel, because he is absent-minded and is apt to be 'saying his prayers' while the train conductor is asking for his tickets, or while the cusstoms man is 'going through' his bagage." It was a peculiarity of Beauty's epistolary style that she used a great many quotation marks, seeming to have the idea that they served for emphasis. Also, she was not strong on spelling, and the small dictionary which Lanny had bought for her always got covered up by other things. When he called her attention to errors, her answer would be: "Gertrude Stein writes as she pleases and gets away with it, so why shouldn't I?"

Anyhow, she was coming, and on a baking hot day Lanny went by the four-hour, overcrowded, dusty train to Marrakech and made hotel arrangements for the party. Incidentally he renewed acquaintance with the Moorish *caid* who owned an oasis and had presented him with a mosaic. Lanny had sent him in return a snappy chiming clock with bright-colored figures which came out and danced the hours. This gift was appreciated immensely, so Lanny had to attend another of those overwhelming banquets. He couldn't mention to this host that he was seeking a fountain, lest it be taken for a hint.

He put Hajek on the job, and very soon the word spread throughout the city, small in population but large in acreage. Partly it was an "old town," and partly a retreat for the rich, both native and foreign, with large estates planted in orange trees and date palms. They had very little interest in their native art and spent immense sums of money upon the crudest and gaudiest objects produced in Europe and America for colonial markets.

In this great center of Mohammedan piety, ritual ablutions were common, and fountains for that purpose were everywhere. Lanny inspected many and picked out one he wanted. He directed Hajek to start negotiations for half a dozen, and didn't tell the paynim Sancho Panza which one he really meant to purchase. The elaborate negotiations went on day and night, and meantime Lanny collected military information and stowed it away in his mind, for he would never trust the mails of French North Africa. When the negotiations were completed, the fountain had to be taken apart and boxed piece by piece, an elaborate task, and Lanny would be glad when the family arrived so that the efficient Jerry could replace the somewhat bungling Mohammedan at this job.

VIII

The family arrived, decidedly worn after four days and nights on three trains and one steamship in hot weather. Beauty had brought her Provençal maid, grandniece of her old-time cook, to take care of little Marcel; she had also brought Madame Zyszynski, which had not been according to plan. "I just couldn't bear to leave her," the mother explained. "The Nazis have been so cruel to the Poles. It wasn't such a difficult trip after I had once made up my mind to it. But the visas were hard to get. It took a lot of 'drag.'" Lanny told the old woman he was delighted to see her, for to have done otherwise would have broken her heart. And besides, he could try some more experiments.

Living here was going to cost the family dear, but Lanny hoped it needn't be for too long, and, as he told his mother, it was no time to save when you might lose your life. Beauty had a thousand dollars a month which Robbie's secretary mailed to her New York bank account on the first day of every month unless it was Sunday; and she had sums which Lanny's colleague, Zoltan Kertezsi, kept adding to that same account for the Detaze paintings he was authorized to sell. Also, her man of God had a small income from investments he had made back in the State of Iowa; God had protected them as per request. So they could afford four thousand francs a day at the Hotel Mamounia, and the incidental expenses which were necessary to the happiness of a one-time "professional beauty."

It didn't take them long to get settled. Beauty had never failed to find people she knew in whatever part of the world she visited, and soon she was in the "social swim," which wouldn't completely stop its splashing for any wars. She was delighted with this unique Mohammedan city: the mud walls, the tall towers, the great market place with snake charmers and dancing boys from the Atlas Mountains. It was cold at night and hot by day; and strolling on its streets you saw not merely all the tribes of North Africa, but refugees from all Europe, French Syria, and even Indo-China.

As for Parsifal Dingle, he sat in his elegant room, sipping tea with various Mohammedan devotees who came to call, astonished and delighted to find an American gentleman taking a genuine interest in the technicalities of their Prophet's faith. So the two parents both had what they wanted; and Lanny could only hope that his judgment had been correct, and that Marrakech was a safer place for Americans than Juan-les-Pins. He believed that the fighting in North Africa would be on the beaches, and he knew that this city of mosques and millionaires was not equipped to stand a siege, even if the French had been minded for it. Of course if the "Yanks" were repelled, the Wehrmacht would come here, but the situation would be no worse than on the Riviera.

IX

Lanny put Jerry in charge of the packing of the fountain and left himself free to continue the gathering of information. Also, he had a little time for play, and took Madame to his room and seated her in a well-stuffed chair, where she could rest her head back and go into one of her trances. He had decided that her powers were waning, if not entirely gone, but he had to indulge her once in a while because she had adopted him in her heart as a son and must not be made to feel that she was put away on the shelf.

Perhaps it was that travel had stirred up her faculty. Whatever the reason, she gave a demonstration that reminded him of the old days. There came the familiar voice of Tecumseh, the Amerindian chieftain who said he had been an Iroquois, and much superior to the one known to history. What he actually was Lanny had never been able to decide, but he talked in character and his voice was sometimes like Madame's, sometimes not. For thirteen years the Polish ex-servant had assured the Budds that she knew about this voice only what other people had told her; she had never heard it in her life.

"So here you are again, young man!" boomed the "spirit." "Where have you been keeping yourself?" That a man of stone-age culture two centuries dead should be using modern slang was something you just had to guess about.

"You ought to know as well as I," bantered Lanny. They had treated each other in this fashion through the years.

"I am not nearly so much interested in you as you are in yourself. What is it you are looking for?"

"Nothing in particular, Tecumseh. Just the pleasure of a chat with you."

"You know you don't believe in me and never will. You just want to sit and make a lot of notes, and then what do you do with them?"

"I study them diligently, old friend."

"To what purpose? A ten-year-old child would know more. He would understand simple facts and wouldn't need such long words." Then, abruptly: "There is a man here, a foreign fellow. He speaks English badly, word by word. Why can't people learn a sensible language? I am tired of these queer ones who come crowding around you, always in trouble."

"I have lived most of my life in Europe, Tecumseh, and met all sorts of people. Ask the man his name."

"He says it is Hoo-go. Is that right?"

"I knew a man by that name."

"Is he an Indian? He gives the name Bear."

"He is a German. They spell it B-E-H-R. I remember him well. Ask him how long he has been in the spirit world."

"He says eight years. He says he went suddenly."

"No man could go more suddenly," declared Lanny, who held the event as one of the most vivid memories in his life. He had been driving the young Nazi in his car, and two Schutzstaffel men had driven up from behind, ordered Hugo out of the car, and shot him in the face, scattering his blood and brains over the pavement of a Munich street. Such things had been going on all over that city and also Berlin —it was part of the dreadful Blood Purge at the end of June and the beginning of July 1934. Adolf Hitler had become Chancellor upon a program of fundamental economic reforms, and after a year and a half his most sincere followers had realized that he had sold out to the cartelmasters and had no idea of abolishing "interest slavery" or breaking up the great landed estates. Adolf Hitler was getting ready for war, and the first thing he had to do was to rid himself of those "old companions," the *Sturmabteilung* men who had helped him to power and were clamoring for their reward. "National Socialists," they had called themselves, and they wanted the "Socialist" part, while their "Adi" was going to give them only the "Nationalist" part.

X

That was how Hugo Behr had been hurled suddenly into the spirit world; and now here he was, stammering poor English, trying to find out if Lanny Budd remembered and understood what had befallen him. Lanny answered yes to both questions, for somehow he didn't feel it necessary to continue his P.A. role in this strange limbo. Tecumseh said there were tears running down the German's cheeks as he lamented what was happening at present; the spirits were arriving by the thousand every day, and it was a most dreadful calamity, the murder of a whole race, the best in the world. It was that two-front war which all the military men had held to be the one inexcusable blunder; but Adolf Hitler, the ex-corporal or less, thought he knew more than all the trained minds of the *Generalstab*. "Send him over here, Lanny!" exclaimed the SA man.

"What would you do with him?" inquired Lanny, ever curious about this mysterious half-world.

But Hugo was vague, like all the others in that world. "Some still love him and some hate him," he declared. Apparently the German limbo was one vast clamor of controversy; all the spirits who hadn't been allowed to say what they thought on earth went at it eagerly now, and the German colony was what Germany itself might be expected to be when the Germans had been beaten—as Hugo said they were surely going to be.

When Lanny asked how he knew this, Hugo said, painfully through the mind and lips of Tecumseh, that his world was full of mentality in the same way that radio waves filled all space on earth. When Lanny asked why Hugo hadn't come to him before, he said it was like the problem of finding a receiving set on earth. He said that Madame was a battery that ran down quickly, and then there was no more power. He said it two or three times: *"Keine Kraft mehr,"* his voice dying away. There came silence, and then a sigh from the medium, and little moans as she came out of her trance.

"Was it good?" she asked, and Lanny told her it had been wonderful. He went off by himself to speculate, as he had been doing for years. Was there a fragment of the Hugo Behr personality floating about somewhere in space or out of space, in some universe of consciousness of which all our minds are part? Or was this an elaborate process of fictional creation which went on in the subconscious minds of some living persons, perhaps of all? Lanny hadn't thought of Hugo Behr for a long time, and there was no special circumstance connecting him with North Africa or with Lanny's present activities. Was this interview the product of Lanny's own subconscious fictionizing, and had some force in the mind of Madame dipped into his mind and taken this story, which surely he had never told to her or in her presence? Madame's mind had tied it up with her own subconscious fictionizing, which had to do with a stone-age man from North America. Was that man made out of some story told to her as a child, or picked up in some medium parlor which she had visited while in process of discovering her own gift?

This much could be certain, and only this: there were forces in our minds of which we had only the vaguest notion, and these forces went on creating mindstuff, in the same way that plants went on creating plants and animals creating animals. The process never ceased while life lasted; and whether it ceased then was a problem about which we had better keep our minds open—while life lasted.

XI

When the fountain had been packed and shipped, Lanny took his old friend Jerry for a walk and revealed to him the carefully guarded secret that for the past five years he had been working as a secret agent of the United States government. He was prepared to be told that his ex-tutor had guessed it, and this proved to be the case. "I never for a moment thought that you had lost interest in everything but buying paintings, Lanny. I knew it must be something serious so I never spoke of it even to my wife."

"That's fine, Jerry. And now here is the situation. The American Army is coming to North Africa before the end of the year, and it seems to me most unlikely that the Germans will fail to move into the Riviera. I was pretty sure you'd rather be in American hands than in those of the Nazis."

"I guessed that, too, and I'm very much obliged. I take it that Cerise and the children won't be in too great danger, for the Germans have shown that they want to conciliate the French. They've confined their murdering and raping to the eastern front."

"Exactly so. And here's the point: I have been authorized to pay out money to persons who are worthy of trust; and that means you. You know the French, and you can do first-rate work as an Intelligence man. You will have to keep up the pretense that you are working for me, and I have figured it out that it will be fair if I pay half your salary out of my own funds and half out of the government's. I don't know what Intelligence is paying, but I can find out. Meantime, would ten dollars a day and expenses seem right to you?"

"Very handsome, indeed; but I've no idea how to earn it. You'll have to tell me that."

"Don't worry; you'll be kept busy. The word is that the invasion is to be this year, and we have only three months before bad weather. I will tell you as much as I have already learned, and you can start from there. It will be your job to meet people who have information, and find ways to get it out of them. Of course if you have to pay them, that is O.K., and I will honor your account. My basic instruction is that we are trying to save the lives of our boys, and not to save money. The Nazis are printing it wholesale, or making the French do it. We want maps, we want photographs, everything of that sort. We want to know where military goods are stored, where the big guns are and their caliber, where the Germans have built their flak towers, every sort of military data. We want to know what is in the minds of the men, of the officers, the dockers, everybody."

"I'll do my best, Lanny, but I'm utterly lacking in experience."

"Nearly all our people are lacking, Jerry. We have to start from scratch. There will be other fellows working, and more and more of them coming. No doubt there will be a lot of duplication, but that's all right; what one man reports will check the next man's. And don't forget that wherever you go you are looking for mosaics and fountains and beautifully carved doorways—you are really looking for them, just as I am really buying them. If ever it happens that you get caught and questioned, whether it's by the French or whomever, you must swear that I employed you in good faith in connection with my art business, and that I haven't the slightest idea that you have been thinking about anything else."

"Sure thing, Lanny. All that goes without saying. Wild horses won't drag anything out of me."

"And one thing more, old man. Keep watch who is walking behind you at night, and don't let anybody lure you into a dark alley."

XII

So there was another secret agent, and it didn't take him long to get the hang of the job. A couple of hours questioning Lanny, and he was ready to go out and talk with Frenchmen and French-speaking natives, first about art works, then about politics and about the defenses of Casablanca. He would come back to his boss to report, and it wasn't many days before he had an interesting story. "Have you been to Volubilis?" he inquired.

"No," replied Lanny. "I saw the ruins of Timgad, and I imagine they are much the same."

"I've met a chap who has been studying Volubilis. He calls himself an archeologist and comes from Chicago."

"Name Faulkner?" inquired the other.

"Oh, then you know him!"

"I came over in the plane with him, the trip before last. Nice chap, I thought."

"Funny about him, Lanny. He's been to Volubilis, all right, and knows all about some new excavating the French did just before the war; but he isn't doing anything with his information so far as I can make out. What he does is to hang around and gossip with dock-workers and fishermen and people like that. He seems to have no end of time to make friends."

"I guessed that he was an O.S.S. man, Jerry. Our State Department isn't letting anybody over to study ancient ruins these days."

"He picked on me because he found I had lived half my life in France and knew the people. I've an idea he doesn't trust himself any too well. Seems shy."

"Another one who's lacking in experience!" remarked Lanny with a chuckle.

"He's been trying to find out everything I know, and of course I've been trying to find out everything he knows. We had a fine time taking in each other's washing."

"Well, you might combine forces, once you've made sure he's all right. He struck me as being very much the gentleman and scholar."

"I've a feeling that he's about ready to open up and propose something of the sort. I wondered what I should say."

"Let him do the talking. Tell him you're a patriot, of course, and would be glad to help in any way you can. But don't tell him you're an agent till you're absolutely certain of him, and don't ever let on that I know about it. Let it be that you're using my business as a camouflage. It might be that you could turn in your information through him, or he could put you in touch with his superior. I have to go back to New York very soon, and while I'm gone you might come on something that was too hot to keep."

"Just what I have been worrying about!" said Jerry Pendleton.

XIII

Once a week Lanny had been writing a letter to his wife. He told her about the art works he had inspected and about the scenery and the weather; he said that he was well, and so were the other members of the family, and that he loved her, and thought about her often, and hoped that her literary work was progressing, and that she wasn't over-doing it. All that, but not a word about the war, or politics, or anything approaching thereto; nor any strange words or mysterious statements which might excite the suspicion of a censor. Laurel, carefully warned, did the same; she informed him that she was well and moderately active, though she had come to a state where she moved slowly; she said that the weather was not troubling her; that she had been to visit his family, and also her own people in Baltimore; that the book was not so good as she had hoped, but she was trying to improve it. Assuming that the anonymous censor would be a human being, she had the boldness to add: "Marriage is a dreadfully bad habit; I miss you so!"

By the beginning of October Lanny felt that he had got as heavy a load of information as he could carry in one head. It was a question of flying back to Algiers and having it delivered to the office of Mr. Robert Murphy or of taking a trip home. Really there wasn't much difference, or so he told himself, and added that he could do better work if he had a chance to bring his mind up to date with that of his Chief. In the back of his head was the notion that he might win the Chief's permission to go to Switzerland and write a letter to Adolf Hitler, offering to bring him a message from his most loyal secretary and friend. In addition to all this was the desire to see Laurel, although he sternly told himself that the service of the country must come first and that his personal interest must never take precedence. Of course, if he could manage to make the two kinds of interest coincide, he would be glad to see a wife whom he missed as much as she missed him.

Things had worked out neatly in the matter of Jerry Pendleton. He had had a showdown with his Dr. Faulkner. (The archeologist had a Ph.D. from the University of Chicago, but was thinking of dropping it in Morocco because the natives knew the meaning of the word "doctor," or thought they did, and while he was measuring the dimensions of ancient Roman dwellings they would bring him cases of trachoma to be treated and tumors to be cut out.) Jerry had told this earnest scholar-turned-spy that he had a good salary as assistant to an art expert and had time to spare and would be glad to help him in the collecting of data useful to an army. So now Jerry had a way to turn in information and have it reach headquarters promptly, for Faulkner reported to one of the vice-consuls who had a concealed radio-sending set. Lanny gave Jerry several items which might be urgent, and Faulkner would get the credit for these and of course be made happy. This arrangement set Lanny free to take wing with a good conscience.

His procedure was to cable Robbie that he was ready to come home. A message to his father on such a subject would seem natural to any enemy agent who might have bought or exacted the right to inspect cablegrams out of French Morocco. Robbie would pass on the word to a man in Washington, about whom he knew nothing except the name, Baker, and a telephone number. The result was that a couple of days later a messenger from the consulate called at Lanny's hotel, informing him that a place had been reserved for him on the plane from Tangier to Lisbon, and from there on the Clipper to New York by way of the Azores and Bermuda.

XIV

So "Traveler" packed his belongings, leaving a bundle of summer clothing in his mother's care, it being no longer summer in New York. He wrote a few letters having to do with the business of art, letters which he wanted to come from Marrakech for the effect upon the clients, and also because he wanted censors and enemy agents to have a chance to read them. He bade good-by to the friends he had made and took a dilapidated train into Spanish Morocco. Two days later he went on board one of those luxurious flying boats that have nearly all the American comforts. It was shoved off from the Lisbon pier, its propellers began to whirl, and it went racing down the River Tagus. The waves slapped its underside, shaking it, and presently there were no more slaps and it was airborne, heading into the west, a crossing which in 1492 had taken the little caravels of Columbus a matter of seventy days, and which in 1942 could be made, without stops, in half a day. Such a difference when two numbers exchanged positions!

This flying boat was playing safe, and stopped at the Islands of the Green Cape, which the bold navigators of Portugal had taken long ago and which now the timid dictator of Portugal had rented to the Allies for a high price to save them the embarrassment of having to seize them. From there on to the still-vexed Bermoothes, which now had become an American naval and air station, to the embarrassment of staid citizens who had hitherto refused to recognize the existence of motorcars. Lanny's baggage was politely searched by the British authorities, also his clothing. He held his breath, wondering if they were going to find those two scraps of paper sewed up in the lining of his coat, scraps which were so oddly contradictory in their content! But the search was not that thorough, and whatever the name of Budd meant to the officials they gave no sign.

The Clipper was put down on the water of Long Island Sound, and after another customs investigation Lanny was free. His first act was to step into a telephone booth. He had been debating, in the words of a poem which schoolchildren learn: "Which shall it be? Which shall it be?" He had decided for duty instead of love; but as it happened, duty's telephone line was busy, so love had its chance. He heard the dear familiar voice and said: "Here I am, safe and sound!" She cried: "Oh, Lanny! Lanny!" There was a catch in her voice.

"Everything's jake!" he told her, "and I'll be home in an hour. Don't make any preparations, for I may be flying to Washington today." Such was the fate of a P.A.'s wife, who didn't even know what a P.A. was!

He telephoned Baker and was told as usual to call back in three hours for an appointment. Then to a taxi, and in due course he greeted the familiar elevator girl—all operators were women or old men now— and gave her a dollar bill so that she would be as glad to see him as he was to see her. He had left his key to the apartment with Laurel, so he had to ring the bell. Here she came, and what a spectacle! The bright eager face was the same, but the rest of her so different! He took her gently in his arms and told her it was grand and that he was tickled to death, and so on, and of course he was.

Thirteen years had passed since he had been through this same experience. Irma had been brought up in smart society, where the young women of the twenties had done what they damn pleased and said it in that and other four-letter words. But Laurel had come of a Southern family and was old-fashioned in spite of calling herself a Socialist and feminist. She blushed when she saw her husband glance at that large protuberance, and as they sat on the couch, his arms about her, old-fashioned tears of happiness ran down her cheeks. What she said was: "Oh, do for God's sake get this awful war over! I can't stand it much longer!"

She had almost three years more of it yet to stand; but her husband didn't know that and couldn't tell her. The wisest men in the world could have given her only their guesses—"all different and no two alike!"

BOOK FIVE

Time by the Forelock

14

Able for Thine Enemy

I

ROOSEVELT was at "Shangri-La," and Lanny was told to be there the following evening. This suited him well, giving him a chance to see his wife, and also to have Robbie send in a car. He had a lot of fun preparing a supper in that "kitchenette," smaller than anything he had seen in his amply spaced life. The process was retarded by his stopping every two or three minutes to kiss his wife, and tell her how glad he was to get home, and how he hoped to stay at least a week. A woman expecting the ordeal of motherhood has to be absolutely certain that her man is going to stand by her and not show any signs of irritation or impatience or other characteristics which the male animal so distressingly develops. Lanny laughed a lot and romped a little and cheered her up before the meal, and while they were eating he told her stories about a strange part of the world which she had never seen. Afterward he settled down in an easy chair to read three months' production of manuscript—another kind of baby in process of gestation. It was a much better baby than she had led him to expect, so he was able to tell her, and that made his homecoming a complete success.

In the morning he went down to see Mr. Post, to make sure whether or not any of those German agents in the hoosegow had given any indication of laying the blame upon the son of Budd-Erling. He was assured that they had not; they had swallowed the story of the diamond dropped in the street, and since they had no chance to communicate one with another, they were left to lay the blame each upon all the others. Branscome alias Hartley had been turned over to his own government, and what they had done with him was something that might not be known till the end of the war. The son of Budd-Erling said: "O.K. by me!"

The car was brought to the door, and Lanny packed a bag and took his warm overcoat, prepared for an October evening in the Catoctin Mountains. He drove the familiar hundred miles on crowded Highway Number 1, and then the same distance through the lovely farmlands of Maryland, where all the trees by the roadside and along the hill-slopes had put on their brightest autumn colors, which were really a burial shroud for that year's departing glory. Sudden gusts of wind brought the leaves down upon the car and over the roadway. "O wild West Wind, thou breath of Autumn's being"!

Toward sundown, approaching the little town of Thurmont, Lanny stopped and got supper, then drove into the town, parked and locked his car, and was picked up by Baker in the usual way. They had come to be friends in the course of the years, and winding up the mountain road with the car lights wandering here and there over vistas of trees, they talked about the war, the past, not the future. They agreed that the Russians were fighting like tigers, and the Americans were holding on marvelously in the Solomons. "How they can hit a ship ten miles away in darkness is certainly a miracle," said Baker, and Lanny contented himself with commenting: "It must be a new invention." Maybe the President's man had heard the magic word radar and maybe he hadn't; in any case, Lanny wouldn't speak it.

Some of the "brass" had been consulting with the President, and they had stayed for dinner, so Lanny had to wait. He sat in the entrance hall and chatted with a young lieutenant; neither of them said what he was there for, but they talked about the war in the quiet professional way of men who were taking part in a job and neither hated nor loved it, but did their duty as a matter of course. Nobody would show fear, nobody would show horror, and grief only in extreme cases, and for a few moments. Millions of men were trying to live up to those standards, and most of them succeeded; the few who couldn't were no longer called white-livered cowards, but were spoken of professionally as "shock" cases.

II

F.D.R. was sitting in an easy chair in front of a log fire, welcome in this mountain climate. His wheel chair had been placed out of sight, and when he desired to move he pressed a button attached to a cord and hung on the arm of his chair; the attendant would bring up the wheel chair, and the President with his powerful arms and shoulders would lift himself from one to the other. That was the way he got about, except when he wore the steel leg braces, which were heavy and which hurt. With such a handicap, he carried the burden of a nation's destiny—indeed it would not be too much to say the destiny of the democratic world.

His face never failed to light up when he saw a friend; he made every friend feel, just as Lanny felt, that it was a special happiness. Few men gave themselves more freely to friends, or got so much from them. "Welcome, world traveler!" he exclaimed, and with his large hand outstretched he shook Lanny's hand and then sort of guided him to a chair alongside. "I received all your reports, and read them, and they helped me."

"That's what a P.A. lives by," returned Lanny. "I had an easy time. I took your advice and kept out of danger. My conscience troubles me, Governor."

"Don't let it. You are under orders, and that is enough for you."

" 'Theirs not to reason why!' " quoted the agent.

"You are to do but not to die," retorted the Boss, who was quick on the uptake. "Now tell me, what is going to happen to our forces when they come ashore?"

"They will get a mixed reception, Governor, different in different places, depending on the commanding officer, and on subordinates who may or may not obey completely. Some will join us, others will wait to see what happens; some will fight, at least until their sense of honor is satisfied. That means a great deal to a Frenchman, you know."

"How many of their men have to be killed before their honor feels satisfied?"

"There seems to be no schedule set. General Noguès, in Morocco, is more determined on resistance than any of the officers in Algiers, many of whom have been deprived of command and are out of uniform. You understand, there are such things as salaries and pensions, and army officers have to eat like all other men."

"That is why we are sending seven divisions, Lanny."

"If you send that many, and if the officers know it for sure, their honor will be satisfied more quickly. I might add that the Navy will fight harder than the Army. You know that their officers are as a rule much more conservative; they have their own little world, and they rule it by divine authority."

"Indeed I know it, Lanny. I have some Navy officers of my own, and you should hear the ideas they put before me!"

III

The confidential agent was subjected to a long inquisition as to Vichy and Toulon, Switzerland and Germany. There were many things that Lanny hadn't been willing to put on paper, and now he told

them. In general he had only good things to report about American
officials abroad, and an overworked administrator was glad to hear
that; he received mostly complaints, he said, and it was so hard to find
competent men for unfamiliar jobs. So many thousands of things to be
administered and to think about and try to understand! The lines of
care showed in the once-so-jovial face; his hair was growing thinner,
and age was creeping on him noticeably. But the smile came back
when he told a story, or heard one, such as that about the stage queen
of Germany manifesting her tender sympathy for a Jew in distress.

Lanny had not written an account of his interview with Hess, for
there was no war information in it. But it was the kind of story that
gave Roosevelt delight, and Lanny had a purpose in telling it fully. He
showed the ring and the scrap of paper, which he had unsewed from
his coat for this occasion. He left it for the other to ask: "What do
you expect to do with that?"

"I am hoping, Governor, that I can persuade you to let me go into
Germany. If I should write Hitler from Switzerland that I have had
an interview with his most trusted friend, he would surely invite me
to come and would probably send a plane to Friedrichshafen or some
other place at the Swiss border to take me."

The President's face became suddenly grave. "What would you expect to get out of such a venture, Lanny?"

"It's hard to know in advance. I have a feeling that I can tell a lot by
looking at Hitler, listening to his voice, and watching his manner. He
is a reckless talker, and when he gets going, nobody can predict what
he will say. He will ask me what I have been doing to help him bring
peace to Europe, and I will tell him, and he will tell me what proposals
he wants me to take to the Wickthorpe set and to Henry Ford and
Mr. Hearst and the others he believes are his friends here."

"But we don't care a damn about any of that, Lanny. We are going
to knock him out and not argue with him."

"Yes, Governor, but you say you want to save lives; and if you
know what is in your opponent's mind, it is easier to figure out how to
break him. I have never met Hitler that I didn't come away with valuable information, and I think that will be truer than ever now when we
no longer have any contacts with him and hardly know what anybody
in Germany is thinking."

"But they would watch you like a skyful of buzzards. Nobody
would talk frankly to you on peril of his life. Do you imagine for a
moment that you could go about in Germany as you used to do?

What's in the back of your mind, to make contact with some atomic physicist?"

"I just can't be sure, Governor. I would have to watch for my chances and take them."

"And walk into some trap they had set for you! If any person came to you, even an old friend, pretending to be a sympathizer, that would certainly be a plant." There was a moment's pause, and then the President burst out: "I don't want you to do it, Lanny! I need your services too much to risk them in harebrained adventures. And besides, I have something else for you to do. I had made up my mind to get into touch with your father and have him cable you to return."

"Well, of course, Governor, if that's the situation, there's nothing for me to do but forget my little scheme."

"Our North Africa expedition is all but ready. I don't know the exact date—it depends upon winds and other factors—but our armada should be at sea in a fortnight or so."

"That's big news indeed, Governor!"

"You bet your life! And behind it is the biggest story of human labor in all this world, I believe. Some day when we have more time, remind me and I'll tell you what was going on the last time you were in this building. Winston had just told me the terrible news that Rommel had succeeded in trapping and destroying the greater part of the British tank forces at El Alamein, and the British were almost helpless to defend Alexandria and Cairo. It was just a question of days before Rommel would realize the situation and begin an advance. Winston asked: 'What could we do?'"

"What *did* we do?" Lanny knew this overworked great man, who was still part boy; he wanted to tell a story, even though there wasn't time.

"We had just got our new tank-killer in production, a 105 mm. gun, self-propelled, mounted on an M-3 tank chassis; it can do thirty-five miles an hour and hit a target at seven miles. We sent out telegrams to plants all over this land where guns and carriages and engines and parts were being made, and men and women gave up their Fourth of July week end and worked ten-hour shifts, two a day, and foremen and superintendents worked eighteen-hour shifts, living on sandwiches and soda pop and sleeping in the plants. Believe it or not, in nine days we had enough destroyers and tanks at the docks to fill a whole convoy, and the stevedores worked day and night to load them. Those vessels sailed around South Africa and the subs got only one of them. Since that happened to be the most important of all, we sent more telegrams and the factories duplicated their feat; we put the stuff on a fast vessel that traveled alone and reached the convoy before it got round the Cape of Good Hope. General Alexander has everything he needs now, and if you're watching the news you know that Rommel is a cooked goose."

"I'm glad to hear you say it, Governor. Remember, I've been getting mostly Axis news."

"People for the most part judge military situations by advances and retreats. But in that Egyptian desert there has been desperate fighting for weeks, and we are satisfied with the fact that Rommel has been nailed down. We are pouring more stuff to the Eighth Army all the time, and we don't know when Alexander will be ready for his push, but I'll bet on his not waiting after we land in the west."

I V

Lanny had come to understand this genial man well after five years of service. It was possible to divert him and to have a good time at his expense. Lanny might have heard a collection of inside stories, just by dropping hints; for example, by saying a word or two in praise of American labor. F.D.R., an aristocrat by upbringing and temperament, loved labor, and it wasn't just politics; he idealized labor, imagined the best about it, called for the best from it, and got that. Lanny had the same attitude, and would have enjoyed an evening hearing about miracles being wrought by miners and steelworkers, builders of ships and guns and planes and every one of the quarter-million items which were on the purchasing lists of the U.S.A., the U.S.N., and the U.S.M.C.

But one of the ways by which the son of Budd-Erling had kept his favor at this court was by being considerate and never wearing out his welcome. So now he said: "Governor, I have no right to keep you from your job. Tell me what mine is."

"We are going to send out the greatest flotilla of ships in all history. It will be something close to one thousand of all kinds, some of them never seen in the world before, built especially for this occasion. We are going to take Casablanca on the Atlantic coast and Oran and Algiers on the Mediterranean. We would like to take Tunis, but we are afraid to come that close to Italy and the German airfleets. Our ships of all sorts will have to lie off the ports for several days while men and cargo are being put ashore; and we won't have any land-based aviation, with the single exception of one base at Gibraltar which the enemy could knock out in an hour if they knew what we were doing. It's a tough situation, and I lie awake nights thinking about the German U-boats. You know how they will gather, a hundred of them at least, and with all the defenses we can muster we shan't be able to keep them from getting at our ships."

"I'm afraid not, Governor."

"A horrible thing to think of those loaded transports being torpedoed, and its being impossible to save more than a small part of the troops. My heart aches for those boys, Lanny, and I have racked my brains trying to figure out a way to protect them. I have discussed it with everybody who might have suggestions, and it comes down to this: we have to find a way to make the enemy think we are coming to Dakar. That is the one port we are not coming to, because it is too far away from the Mediterranean; but it should be easy to make the Germans think its our objective because it's nearest to us and would be impossible for them to reinforce. They are very contemptuous of us and would expect us to distrust our own powers."

"Yes, Governor. I have heard much talk of Dakar among the French and reports of it among the Germans."

"All right. We want to have their wolfpacks gathering off the peanut coast, while our armada is a couple of thousand miles to the north. I won't be satisfied with planting rumors; we have to fix a definite certainty in the minds of the German command that Dakar is our goal. I've tried to recall all the spy stories I've ever read, and I've invented some new ones, but none is good enough. Somebody will have to get some German drunk—what's the fellow's name, their head diplomatic agent?"

"Theodor Auer."

"Do you know him?"

"I have seen him. He's somewhat halfhearted about the Nazis, I'm told. He not only gets drunk, but he's a homo."

"Well, some American might get drunk with him and spill the secret. Somebody might be selling out, or some document might be stolen; somehow or other Herr Auer must be convinced that he has the inside dope, that Dakar is the goal. Of course the Germans know that we are preparing a fleet, and we can hardly hope to keep their spies from finding out that it is sailing and then their getting a wireless message across."

"You are right in that," opined Lanny. There was quailing in his heart, but he wouldn't for the whole world have let any sign of it appear. Keep a stiff upper lip!

"I discussed the matter with Alston a few days ago, and he suggested it might be a job for you. I don't mean that you personally should do it, but find the right man and work out the right device. You know the Germans better than we do, and you know the ground."

Lanny was thinking hard. "Listen, Governor," he said; "why cannot your plan be dovetailed into mine? What's the matter with my going into Germany right quick and telling Adi himself what I have learned?"

"Would he believe you?"

"I can't be sure, but I have managed to make him believe everything I have told him so far."

F.D.R. knitted his brows over that one. "I thought you told me he was bound to have heard about your interview with Stalin?"

"That is true. But after my talk with Hess I believe I could get away with anything. I could tell the Führer that I talked with Stalin in order to come and report to him what Stalin said. Hitler has known for many years that I have an uncle who is a Communist, and it would be a conceivable thing for me to use that Red connection as a part of my service to the Nazi cause. He knows who my father is, too, but that has not kept him from believing that I am a Nazi devotee."

"And how would you get out of Germany?"

"I would get out the same way I had got in; Hitler would send me, with important messages for this one and that."

"But suppose he had his doubts, and suppose he were to offer some polite pretext for keeping you in Germany until after the landings in North Africa had taken place?"

"That would be awkward, I admit."

"You would die by torture."

"Well, I could have one of those tiny glass capsules which Professor Alston gave me the last time he ordered me into Germany. It would be one life for many thousands, and, as wars go, that's a good bargain."

"It just so happens that I want to keep you, Lanny. I need you in North Africa after the invasion, to watch how things are going and give me the straight dope. Later on, perhaps, I'll be willing to consider your idea, but now I want you to return, as fast as you can, to Casablanca, or to Algiers as you think best. And I want you to find some way to get this job done without risking your life. There are plenty of men to do the fighting and dying; when I have one whom I have tried and tested, who has special knowledge and whose judgment I trust, such a man is not expendable. Your orders are to take care of your life and your health, and come back here every two or three months for consultation."

"O.K., Governor," said the P.A., "and thanks for the compliment. My wife will appreciate it even more than I do!"

V

Lanny drove to Washington that night, and when he tried to find a hotel he was told that people were sleeping in the chairs of the lobbies, and he could see it. Simpler to him appeared to be a parking lot for his car; he locked himself in and slept fairly well. The war was doing a lot of things to America. Families by the million were being uprooted or lured away to new places—the shipyards, the airplane plants, the factories where the war goods were being made and the big wages paid. People were living in their cars, in trailers, in made-over sheds and chickenhouses, anything that would keep off the rain. They were eating whatever they could find. Meats and fats, canned goods and sugar, were rationed. You went shopping with little books, one for each member of the family; you paid little square stamps and got change in the form of tiny red and blue disks.

F.D.R. had suggested that Lanny should consult with Colonel Donovan, and so he spent the morning with that outfit. C.O.I. had been their initials, but now they were O.S.S.—Office of Strategic Services. They had a wonderful machine that made a record of what you said on a thin wire which rolled off one spool and onto another; that could be run again and again, without limit. Lanny told them all he had learned in the places he had visited, and answered half a hundred questions. In return he asked a few, and one had to do with that young Dr. Faulkner. In the public library in New York, Lanny had looked in the Chicago University catalogue and had found him there; now the O.S.S. men said that he was all right and a capable fellow. They offered Lanny a letter to him, but Lanny said he didn't carry letters and was sure that he could arrange what he wanted, or rather, what the President wanted. He told them the ideas he had worked out, and they fell in therewith. They all showed respect for the son of Budd-Erling, for most of them were tyros, whereas Lanny had been on the job for years.

All the way to Washington he had been making up spy stories, and all the way to New York he was trying them out in his mind. Always the villain of the story was Herr Theodor Auer, and the hero was sometimes Lanny himself, sometimes the director of a travel bureau in Cannes, and sometimes an innocent-appearing archeologist from the Windy City, the Hog Butcher of the World. Many of them were fantastic stories; but, try as he might, their creator would never produce one too fantastic to happen since the rise of Nazi-Fascism. The quarter century between the years 1920 and 1945 would become the reservoir and repository of all melodramas and movie plots, spy stories, murder mysteries, crime-and-punishment fiction, to the end of time. "Cloak and dagger boys," the wits of New York had dubbed the Donovan outfit, and the outfit took an apologetic attitude toward itself. They had all read and written so many stories that it was hard for them to believe that fiction had suddenly become reality, and that they were in it. Lanny told them: "The first one of you who falls into hands of the Nazis will learn that there is nothing funny about it."

They answered gravely: "It has already happened, Budd."

VI

Back in the great crowded city, Lanny told his wife the bad news. He had only two days and a half with her; his plane reservation had been made and his ticket and passport would be delivered to him. He saw Laurel go pale and then clench her hands and set her lips together. She had promised him, and promised herself, that she would never make things harder for him. Over and over again, she repeated it.

"Darling," he said, "I truly wanted to be with you at your confinement, but I have no choice in the matter. I have a positive order. Important events are impending."

"I can guess it," she replied. "All I can do is to hope and pray for you."

"It will comfort you to know that one of my orders is to live. When the shooting starts, I am to be in the background. I am one of those important persons who are not 'expendable.'"

"Well, Lanny"—she tried to force a smile—"do your best to obey that order. If I get a telegram, my heart will stop beating."

"You have your job, dear, a double one. Don't you think you had better go and let Robbie and Esther take care of you while you have the baby?"

"I have my doctor, and my hospital arrangements are made. Agnes will be here to take care of me when I come home, and the baby will have your room until you come home again. How long will it be?"

"My orders are to return every two or three months and report. I'll do my best to make it two. It depends upon events of which nobody in the world can know the outcome. You will read it in the papers."

"I have my guesses, Lanny, but I know that it wouldn't be proper to ask. I want you to know that I haven't any trace of hurt feelings; I realize fully that if all the wives knew, the enemy would know a lot more quickly. Be sure that I am with you heart and soul. I know that this Nazi horror has to be destroyed, and I would risk my life for the task if it would do any good."

"You did risk it, dear," he told her. "And don't forget that your stories about the Nazis have been read by hundreds of thousands of people, and they now have a better understanding of the enemy as a result, and are more willing to stand by the government and make the necessary sacrifices. Knowledge has its way of spreading in a free society; the movements of the public mind are slow, but they happen, and we wake up and discover that we are in a new era before we thought possible."

"God grant that we get out of this one quickly!" exclaimed the author of *The Herrenvolk*.

VII

She was in her last month and had made up her mind not to go out in public any more except for a stroll with her woman friend in the evening. But now her time with Lanny was so short that she decided to throw out her old-fashioned notions and permit small portions of mankind to see her in what was known as an "interesting condition." She put a maternity cape about her and went down to the car. She let Lanny drive her to Newcastle, where they had dinner with members of the family. Lanny spent an evening talking with his father and his two half-brothers, telling them things that would be useful to them in the turning out of faster and more deadly fighter planes. Meantime Laurel absorbed the wisdom of the Budd ladies; three had been through it all and told their experiences and conclusions, but unfortunately they did not agree.

The couple spent the night in the Budd home, and in the morning drove to the estate of Lanny's client Mr. Vernon. It was always important to have more commissions and keep up his camouflage. When the client learned that the wife was sitting in the car, he of course wanted her to come in, but Lanny explained that her condition was too interesting; so a well-bred gentleman kept away and parted with his art expert inside the house. Thus people of the old school avoided getting uncomfortably close to the facts of life and left it for the younger generation to work out a better technique if it could.

They had lunch in a roadside tavern, and afterward the wife had a nap in the car while the husband read. Then they drove to Mr. Winstead's place, and Lanny reported to him on art works he had come upon. They saw beautiful country estates, which gave the impression that America was a most delightful place to live in. Great numbers of persons all over the world had that impression from the cinema screen, and dreamed of some day coming to this land of peace and plenty. The couple knew that there was another side to the picture, but on this brief holiday they were content to feast their eyes upon the colors of October landscapes, and the hedgerows and beautifully tended lawns of "show places."

Laurel had been hoping to finish her novel before the baby's arrival, but the work had grown beyond her original conception. She was telling the story of an American girl, daughter of a college professor who had received his Ph.D. in Germany, and the daughter went there to follow in his footsteps. She became a boarder in the home of a German professor whose son and daughter had been brought up in the Hitler Youth movement. The drama of the story lay in the contrast between the old Germany and the new, as it was revealed bit by bit to an American girl.

The German lad fell in love with her and expected her to behave according to the code of the Hitler *Mädchen*, but she didn't; instead she argued with him, and not merely about sex, but about the true meaning of freedom and about the dignity of the individual soul. The Nazi had never heard of such ideas, but was tempted by them, and the result was a split personality; he was no longer sure what he believed, or what he wished to do with his life. His sister, a Hitler fanatic, raged at the American, and the father looked upon this domestic strife with only one thought in his mind, that if he were to speak some indiscreet word, his daughter might betray him and he would lose his position, to say nothing of being shipped to a concentration camp.

The end of all this would be the tragic breakdown and suicide of the German lad. It would be a grueling thing to write, and Lanny, who was no artist himself but had watched Rick in the throes of creation, tried to persuade his wife that the baby came first, not merely chronologically but morally. Let the story rest until she had fully recovered, and by that time she might find that she had a clearer vision of it and new forces to record it. Meanwhile they spent their spare time going over the manuscript. There was nobody Laurel could find who knew the Nazi system—body, soul, and mind—better than her husband, and he answered her questions and gave her the little details which are revealing and are not always easy to find in the books. It was going to be a real novel when it was done.

VIII

The holiday was over, and the P.A. boarded another Clipper. Men were flying back and forth across all the oceans and the continents, and no longer thought anything of it; they read the papers, played pinochle, or swapped stories. Lanny looked out of the window, to where the wrinkled sea beneath him crawled; he thought again what a great quantity there was of it, and how in this war crisis men were beginning to take the mineral treasures out of it. He thought about the wonders of flying, and about Professor Langley of the Smithsonian Institution, who a half century ago had worked out the mathematical problems of flight and had constructed a machine in conformity therewith; something had gone wrong with the launching, and the machine had plunged into the Potomac River amid the laughter of the world. Some six years ago Alfred Pomeroy-Nielson had been learning to fly, and had mentioned how monotonous it was, going round and round in the air to make up his required number of hours; his father had been moved to construct a couplet addressed to Samuel Langley:

A mighty dream you dreamed, your hopes were mocked by a swinish crew;
And now young men of fashion are bored, aloft with nothing to do.

There came a cry from one of the passengers who was looking down toward the sea and pointing. Everybody rushed to the windows of the plane, and there on the wrinkled sunlit sea was a long thin shape, longer and thinner than any cigar ever made. Great excitement, for it was bound to be an enemy vessel. The Clipper carried no weapons, but the U-boat was taking no chances on that; already it was diving, and in a fraction of a minute there was nothing but a streak of foam on the water. The apparition caused much excitement, and the passengers talked subs, the damage they were doing and the remedies against them, for hours thereafter. The Clipper would radio the position of the sub, but no one on board would know the outcome.

Most of the time Lanny Budd sat with his eyes shut, pretending to be sleeping, but thinking spy stories as hard as he could. There were so many, and each might succeed, but again it might fail, and to estimate the chances of them all would have required the services of

Samuel Langley or perhaps of Albert Einstein. Lanny wanted help, and when he arrived at "Casa" by train from Tangier, he got a hotel room and set out without an hour's delay to find the dependable Pendleton.

IX

They took a walk into the suburbs, and sat on a beach where before the passage of a month the G.I.'s would ·be swarming. Lanny said: "I promised to keep you busy, Jerry, and here it is." He told the story from beginning to end, because the time was short and somebody had to be trusted. "This comes straight from the President, and he told me it would be the most important thing he had ever put up to me. I don't want to appear in connection with it, because I have an idea of getting permission to go into Germany later on, and I don't want the Germans here to spot me as an agent. I was told to find somebody, and tag, you're it!"

Lanny began telling one of the spy stories he had thought up all the way from Shangri-La to Washington to New York to Casablanca. In the first place, Jerry was to go to Dr. Faulkner and speak the word "Tutor." Lanny had fixed it up with the right man in O.S.S. that Faulkner was to get a radio message through the vice-consul in Casablanca, telling him that when "Tutor" appeared, he was to drop his other work and follow orders. The next thing, Faulkner was to arrange with the vice-consul to fire him, Faulkner, in disgrace; the vice-consul would tell his friends that the Chicago doctor was no better than a Nazi, that he had spoken with contempt of the New Deal and its founder, and had declared that the American agents in North Africa were a bunch of Communists and Jews. Faulkner would make such statements to the people he knew, and would move into a cheap lodging, saying that he was broke and that he had been shamefully mistreated.

"What I am figuring," explained Lanny, "is that before many hours have passed the Germans will have this story, and somebody will approach Faulkner and sound him out. He will be in the dumps, and will pretend to get drunk with the German—"

"Look, Lanny," put in the other. "This is a very moral young man; he comes of an old Methodist family and I doubt if he has ever been drunk in his life. He would pass out cold before one of the Germans got started."

"All right, let him do what he can; let him be on the verge of suicide, and some Nazi will come to cheer him up."

"They have already made his acquaintance, and he has a couple who try to pump him now and then."

"All right then, that is time saved. We have only two or three weeks to work in. But wait for them to come to Faulkner; don't let him go after them. They give him money and he starts giving them secrets. We'll have to work this out carefully, because they must be real things he gives, things that won't do us too much harm, but that will convince the enemy he still has a pipeline into the consulate. He will have an old codebook that he will sell to the Germans, and the vice-consul will send some messages in that code; the Germans will pick them up and decipher them, and they will be in heaven."

"For Pete's sake, Lanny," said the ex-tutor, "did you dream this, or did you get it out of E. Phillips Oppenheim or Sherlock Holmes?"

"That's what the cloak-and-dagger boys are forever asking themselves. They say: 'Is this Washington, or is it Ruritania?' The joke of it is, they really are working a number of schemes that came out of spy stories. And why not? The mystery writers spend a lot of brainwork thinking up devices, and they have to be plausible or the editor would say 'N.G.' I've no doubt that some crime editor will say that this one of mine is an old one. All I know is, I thought it up driving to Washington just after my talk with F.D.R. If you can think of a better one, I'll be glad. Meantime I told the O.S.S. that if the vice-consul radios the words: 'Send transfer,' they will send him a couple of old and well-worn codebooks, and Faulkner will sell one of them to the Germans at a good price. The vice-consul will send some messages in that code, and the O.S.S. will understand that these messages are phony. They will mention things that the Germans already know, and a lot of other things that would do harm, only they will deal with the future and won't come off. Does this sound too crazy to you, Jerry?"

"No, but it's complicated, and will take a gosh-awful lot of planning."

"Well, you asked for it. Everything in war takes planning, and we have to do more of it and better than the enemy. The O.S.S. fellows gave it their O.K., but it's understood that you and Faulkner are to do the job, and you're to be guided by circumstances always. That's the way they're working, each team is an individual unit and has a code name. This is Operation Tutor; I figured that nobody would know that you had once been my tutor, and anyhow, I'm hoping to keep out of it. I'll probably be in Algiers when the invasion comes off. I told the O.S.S. people what I knew about you, and they are taking my word."

"Thanks, Lanny, and I'll try my best not to let you down. Do I understand that we're to plant the Dakar idea by means of these radio messages?"

"I would say that you should be guided by circumstances. You can begin to talk about Dakar, orders for Dakar, secret agents to be sent to Dakar, and so on. Or maybe that would be too obvious, the Germans would think that we would never name the place, even in code. The real name of the operation is Torch; but let us invent an imaginary name, say, Operation Cornucopia. Let's talk about that in the fake code; keep talking about it, and the Nazis will all be saying: 'Cornucopia, what is Cornucopia?' They will come to Faulkner and urge him to find out. He will charge them a good price, so that they'll think they are getting something, and he will come to them in triumph, telling them that Cornucopia is the invasion of Dakar. He will offer to find out the sailing date, and when he gives it to them it will be the correct date. It will have to be, not merely because we couldn't keep secret the sailing of such an immense convoy, but because we want their U-boats to be gathering near Dakar at the very time that we are making our landings. The distances from our ports are about the same."

"Lanny, I believe you have it!" exclaimed the ex-tutor. "I'll get after Faulkner right away. Do you want to meet him?"

"Not if I can avoid it. And it will be better if you are not seen in public with Faulkner, because you are known as my man. You may be one of those who tell the world that you are through with the fellow, he is too much of a Nazi for your taste."

"If he stands for that he'll be a game kid," opined Jerry Pendleton.

X

As it turned out, the young archeologist was game. He was, according to the travel-bureau man, a sensitive and romantic soul, scared to death by the job into which he had been dropped, but at the same time thrilled to death by the excitement of it. How he would manage to survive this double death was a problem, said Jerry with a grin. "When I said to him, 'I am Tutor,' it was as if I had said, 'I am Jesus Christ,' or at the very least 'General Marshall.' He listened to the program as if he were four years old and it was the story of the Three Bears. He has a capable mind; I made him recite it all over to me, and he didn't miss any details. He's gone to talk it over with the new vice-consul."

"Is there a new one?"

"His name is Strickland."

"But Strickland has been here for some time!"

"He's still called 'new.' There's a funny situation here, as Faulkner explains it. There was a complete consular outfit in Casablanca, under the jurisdiction of the American Legation in the international zone of Tangier. They were all career men, and did the regular things that consuls and their clerks do—issuing visas, putting stamps on bills of lading, telling unfortunate refugees why they can't get into America. Then we made a deal with Vichy France to let French North Africa have a certain minimum of oil and other supplies. You know about that, no doubt?"

"There's bitter criticism of it at home, I found."

"People don't understand; the agreement gives us the right to oversee the distribution of the stuff, and so the gates are wide open to our underground work. During the past year all kinds of mysterious new consular employees have been appearing, not taking orders from the old vice-consuls, but traveling over the country and doing things that scare their nominal superiors out of their wits. Faulkner says the old vice-consul begs him to keep quiet, to keep out of sight, not to let the Germans get any idea of what they are up to. He's afraid the Germans will demand that the French order us out of the country. General Noguès sends for the chargé d'affaires at Tangier and complains, and how can a mere chargé stand up to a general with a front covering of medals?"

"How does he?"

"He promises, but can't keep the promises, because the agents have their orders from higher up. Under the trade agreement they have a right to go anywhere in the country; and besides that, under the treaty between the French government and the Moors, the Sultan has a semi-independent status and he can let us in here if he wishes."

"I know about that, Jerry. But take my advice and don't trust any of the Moors. They are for the side that is going to come out on top."

"Quite so; but recently it has begun to get through their heads that that might be us. I have been surprised at how the news seems to be spreading; everybody has heard that the Americans are coming, and soon. The Germans are bound to know it."

"Yes, Jerry, but they have no means of being sure. They know what rumors are, they have been in the business of spreading them wholesale years before the war actually started. They would take it for granted that if we meant to take Dakar, we would be doing everything in our power to spread the idea that we were coming to Casablanca and Algiers."

"On that theory it might be well for me to talk Casablanca out loud."

"Why not?" replied the P.A. "The more openly they hear it talked, the more certain they will be that the truth must be something different."

XI

Lanny spent the next three days with Hajek, looking at mosaics, of which, to tell the truth, he had become rather tired. Now and then he would excuse himself—he had told the Mohammedan scholar that he had a lady friend, and this gave him the right to be secretive. The "lady" wore trousers, American fashion, and Lanny would go to her room, making sure that he was not being followed, and Jerry Pendleton would lock the door and tell him in whispers the latest developments in their conspiracy. The call for the codebooks had been sent and acknowledged, and Mr. Strickland, the "new" vice-consul, would get these by air pouch. Meantime the young archeologist had retired to his "doghouse," where Jerry saw him only by night, and after the most elaborate precautions. The story of his disgrace was all over the bazaars. Hajek brought it to Lanny, and that was one of the tests.

Lanny played the role of incredulity, and the dark brown man assured him solemnly that "all Morocco" knew it. Then Hajek wanted to know if there were really many Americans who hated the Jews; the Moors had got along very well with the large Jewish population along the North African coast, and only now, under the steady pressure of Nazi propaganda, were beginning to realize that the Jews were much better traders than the Moors, and had perhaps been accumulating more than their share of money, land, and business. Lanny said, as he had said a thousand times during his secret career: "Such matters do not concern me. I am interested in art values, which are not subject to the influence of wars and political changes."

Lanny's guess that the Germans would not overlook the bait which Faulkner had set before them proved to be correct. First to come to the disgraced archeologist was an Austrian refugee artist who had struck up an acquaintance with him some time ago. Now he came as to a friend in misfortune, and it speedily developed that he wasn't a refugee at all, that was camouflage. He fished around to find out how bitter Herr Faulkner was, and Herr Faulkner was as bitter as gall. Before they parted he had made an offer to relieve the American's financial distress, and next day he brought a bull-necked and shaven-headed

Prussian with him to the "doghouse," obviously so that an important Nazi might sound out the American renegade and judge what he was worth. Faulkner told some of the secrets of the consulate, and his offer to furnish one of the codebooks, now being used, for the sum of fifty thousand francs, less than five hundred dollars, certainly seemed moderate.

The books had come promptly, and Jerry brought Lanny a list of messages which were to be sent to Washington in this stolen code. Jerry, Faulkner, and the vice-consul had worked out the messages, and some were true and some false. For example, they would say that the freighter *Lucy J* which had just sailed for Halifax was in reality bound for Sydney; that wasn't so, but the Germans wouldn't have any way of knowing it for a couple of weeks. On the other hand, the statement that the consulate was spending a great deal of money and must have more at once was true, and must have been known to the enemy without any code. The statement that the agent Faulkner had been discharged for insubordination and indiscreet talk, and that he was now being closely watched to find out the reason for his meeting with Germans, would afford the Germans some amusement, and they would warn Faulkner and thus provide a check on the code. Every word of these messages had to be studied carefully, and every item of information given to the enemy had to be weighed for its cost as against the greater gain hoped to be collected.

There was a lot in the messages about Operation Cornet (the name had had to be changed because there was no "Cornucopia" in the code book). The town was full of rumors about Operation Cornet, the Germans were doing their best to find out about Operation Cornet and had tried to get consulate clerks in their pay—and this was all true. The consulate begged to be informed of the date of Operation Cornet at the earliest possible moment. A military traveler recently returned from the site of Operation Cornet expressed the opinion that it would cost a full division in casualties, and that it could not be undertaken with fewer than four divisions; and so on.

XII

The conspiracy was going smoothly, and Lanny thought that the farther away from it he was, the better. The longer he stayed in Casablanca, now a spy center almost as active as Lisbon, the more he would draw attention to himself and cause the Germans to wonder if he had anything to do with this and that. So he hired the same charcoal-powered car as before, and had himself and his Hajek driven to Marrakech. Delightful weather there, with sunshine rarely ceasing, and the immensely high Atlas Mountains making a snow-white background to brick-red mosques and marabouts. Plenty of mosaics, fountains, and doorways to be looked at, and therefore plenty of camouflage for a secret agent.

Lanny found a room at the elegant Hotel Mamounia, on the same floor with his family. He met Parsifal's Mohammedan friends, and listened while Parsifal explained at length that their religion was another form of the Semitic revelation, strictly monotheistic and fundamentally spiritual; it had fallen victim to various forms of corruption, just as Judaism and Christianity had done, but in its pristine form it was worthy of respect. From this discourse Lanny would go to drink tea—real tea, brought in from Tangier—and chat with some of Beauty's ultra-smart friends. There were wealthy refugees from many parts of Europe, and regardless of their political views they were polite to one another. The war would be over some day, and then they would play together again and consider that they were helping to rebuild civilization. This suited Lanny's role, to be everybody's friend, provided that it was some person of the "right" sort.

They tried not to talk about the war, but of course that was the subject uppermost in everyone's mind. There were people who liked to pose as being on the "inside," and who could not resist the desire to show their superiority. This appeared to be especially true of "the sex," and so, as Laurel had said in New York, when the wives knew it, the enemy knew it soon. The Hotel Mamounia had become a spy center, just as were the *souks*, and, in Casablanca, the walled restricted quarter outside the city. It was one world, for the rich had servants, and these knew what the ladies were doing; they reported it in the underworld, and brought back to their mistresses the gossip of the underworld, and the gossip about other ladies.

So Lanny in Marrakech was interested to learn that in Casablanca one of the American secret agents had been fired because he had been discovered to be in secret league with the Germans. Some said that he had had a wireless set and had been reporting the sailing of Allied vessels; others said that he had been shot, and others that he had been deported to the States. In fact, you could hear almost anything about him, including the fact that he was drunk most of the time. The idea of corruption among the Americans pleased the Germans, because it fitted in with what they had been taught about democracy. What interested Lanny especially was to hear fashionable people, including

Americans, whispering to one another that the obvious invasion place was Casablanca, and that it was Dakar, and then Tunis, and then the Vardar valley.

Beauty Budd, wealthy widow of a famous French painter, had been a social success in Berlin during the twenties; and now came her urbane and cultured son, who had traveled all over Germany since childhood and knew "everybody." Among the Germans here were half a dozen of the old kind, who had been good Europeans in the past and who looked forward to the return of those more tolerant and agreeable days. They couldn't do anything about it, but they would talk about it in low tones when they were in the right company. Some of them would tell you that they had come to French Morocco because it was a way to get as far as possible from the disagreeable Nazis.

XIII

The most curious experience to Lanny was his meeting with Herr Theodor Auer, the German political agent in Morocco. Herr Auer was an important person in his country's diplomatic world, and also in its industrial world, being the fortunate heir of the great Auer Chemical Works in Cologne. In North Africa he had under his command a couple of hundred Reichswehr men, many in uniform. It was their business to make sure that the French Army was properly disarmed and stayed that way; also, of course, they had an elaborate spy system, watching everybody and everything that might threaten German power. Lanny met a young officer of the very stiff and *korrekt* sort at one of the tea parties in the hotel, an officer who reminded him of General Emil Meissner as he had been in the old days. He mentioned this, and Leutnant Schindler was pleased. He invited Lanny to meet the Chief, and Lanny said he was honored, and was taken upstairs to the great man's suite.

Red-faced and blond-haired, Herr Theodor Auer looked like an Englishman. Lanny had been told that he was one of those upper-class Germans who, before the war, and still more in the days of Kaiser Wilhelm II, had aped the British aristocracy and aspired to an alliance with them. Unfortunately King Edward VII hadn't liked his German nephew, who was jealous of him, so there had been a French alliance instead. The greatest war in the world's history up to that time had been partly due to the fact that two chartered libertines with enormously inflated egos had been unwilling to yield precedence to each other.

Here was the son of a great chemical magnate, also with an inflated ego; and like so many of the Kaiser's intimates, he was a homosexual. For some reason he was choosing to be cordial to the American art expert, son of a man who was making deadly weapons to be used against Herr Auer's fellow countrymen. Lanny was invited to have a drink; and immediately afterward Herr Schindler pleaded that he had an urgent engagement and discreetly disappeared. Lanny wondered if this had been fixed up, and presently he was sure that it had.

The German began asking questions about where Herr Budd had been in the Fatherland, and whom he had met. So Herr Budd knew Kurt Meissner, the great *Komponist,* and his older brother, General Emil Meissner! A wise and really competent professional soldier, and it was Germany's tragedy that the advice of such men had not been taken during this war, and even before it, by keeping out of the war. And Herr Budd knew Hilde, Fürstin Donnerstein! She was an old friend of the Auer family. The tragic death of her son at the hands of Russian partisans had broken her heart and she was said to be in poor health now. But what a delightful companion, so full of wit and charm in the old days! And Graf Stubendorf—he had been wounded two or three times; Auer had not seen him for years, but of old they had been fellow members of the Herrenklub and the Kaiserliche Automobil Klub. Had Lanny visited the *Schloss?* Lanny said yes indeed, many times, beginning when he was a small boy. That was when he had learned to love Germany; he had gone there one Christmas after another, and two dreadful wars between Germany and France, which had been his home, had cast a black shadow over most of his life.

That was the right sort of talk, and presently Herr Auer asked to be allowed to speak in friendly confidence. When Lanny said that he might, he proceeded to explain that he was no Nazi and never had been, but what could a German diplomat and businessman have done when that storm of madness swept over the Fatherland? Now he was in a devilish position, because he was supposed to direct this Armistice Commission, but he was not a free agent; the Nazis, distrusting him, had an SS agent watching his every move and the moves of all his subordinates, many of whom felt as he did and not as the Nazis. Herr Budd could be assured that there were many Germans of the better class, men of culture and humanity, who did not approve the path their country had taken and were anxious to save it from the ruin which was now falling upon it out of the skies.

XIV

The son of Budd-Erling had to be extremely careful in meeting such an approach as this, for he had no means of knowing whether the speeches were genuine or just a subtle scheme to trap an enemy agent. Lanny said that as a lover of art he hated all war and did his best to keep aloof from it. This satisfied the talkative German, and he went on to explain that he had become sure the Americans were coming to North Africa, and what he wanted was to unbosom himself to some reputable citizen of that country, who would testify to the fact that he, Herr Auer, was no Nazi, but a friend of law and order in Europe. This friend even hinted that when the Germans here fell captive to the American Army, their head would like to be recognized as a supporter and given his passports so that he could go to America to live the rest of his days in peace. He knew that Herr Budd's father, an industrialist like himself and a man of influence, would understand such a situation; and so on.

Lanny explained with the utmost tact that his father had no influence, having been a vehement political opponent of the Administration. As for Lanny himself, he had never had anything to do with politics, because his clients belonged to various nations and schools of thought. "Of course in the event you anticipate, I'll be glad to do anything in my power. I have cherished all my German friends, and I hope to number you among them, and you may be sure that what you have revealed to me will never be mentioned except as you may request it."

They parted with mutual protestations of esteem. But, as fate willed it, they never laid eyes on each other again. When the Americans took Morocco General Noguès smuggled most of the Armistice Commission into Spanish Morocco, and Herr Auer was flown to Berlin. Lanny heard a grim story of how the Nazis put him on trial for incompetence and treason as well. They found him guilty, and took him out into the courtyard of the building, removed his coat, tied his hands behind him, and made him kneel down and place his head on a large wooden block. A sturdy *Henker*, dressed in ceremonial black swallow-tailed coat and top hat, took a large broad-bladed double-bit ax, and with one swift stroke chopped off that well-shaped head with the rosy cheeks and the crown of properly barbered blond hair. This spoiled forever Herr Auer's idea of escaping to the peace and quiet of the Western world; but it also spared him many worries which the fates were preparing for his countrymen during the next decade and perhaps longer.

15

Rattling Good History

I

LANNY received a letter from Jerry, saying: "I have come upon an especially fine old mosaic, which you ought to see as soon as convenient." This was code, and Lanny packed his few belongings and had himself transported back to Casablanca. His Moor followed, since the French did not permit their traveling together. Lanny made a rendezvous with his "lady friend," and was informed that the plot was succeeding well. Items of information had been deliberately planted, and these had been mentioned by the German who was dealing with Faulkner. Jerry said: "They are all hopped up over the mystery of Operation Cornet, and they have offered Faulkner two hundred and fifty thousand francs if he will find out about it."

"Well," said Lanny, "let him tell them that he has got it and that the price is five hundred thousand. They will appreciate it more."

"That part is all right; but I don't see how we can go ahead without having some idea as to the date of the invasion. The thing is apt to go stale; the Germans will become suspicious, they may find ways to check on the story, and anyhow they'll no longer feel sure. Can you imagine a pack of U-boats lying off Dakar for a month?"

To this Lanny could only reply: "All I have been told is that the move will come this year." It was then mid-October.

"I have been listening to some of the fishermen and others who know this coast," added his friend. "They say that the swells from the Atlantic make it impossible to land most of the time. They say it would be only by a fluke that we could have several days of good weather, and that after the middle of November it would be impossible. Nobody but a bunch of amateurs would try it."

"Well, we have plenty of amateurs in the Army, Jerry, but I think our weather men and our Planning Board know their business. There's always an element of luck, and we shall have to take our chances."

Jerry had learned through Faulkner and the vice-consul about Mr.

325

Robert Murphy's recent air journey to Washington and from there to London; he had returned to Algiers, and all the Americans were agog, believing that this meant action—and oh, how tired they were of waiting! The British forces in Egypt were beginning a huge bombing campaign against Rommel's forces, an indication that there also an attack was impending.

Lanny came to a decision: "I have several matters to attend to in Algiers, and I will put the situation before Murphy and see what he advises. I will write you a letter from there, saying that you may expect me back in Casablanca to look at a mosaic on such and such a date. That will be the date which Faulkner is to give the Germans as the date when the convoys will be leaving the United States. If I say that I have already seen the mosaic in question, it will mean that the sailings have begun."

"I'll remember," promised the ex-tutor. He repeated the words, to make sure.

II

In Algiers it was still summer, hot and sultry; the rainy season was soon due, but it was hard to see how the air could carry any more moisture. The white office buildings and apartment houses on the hill slopes gleamed in the sunshine, and were pretty to look at from the air or the sea, but not so pleasant when the hot pavements and walls were giving you a perpetual Turkish bath.

Lanny shut himself up in a hotel room and typed out a report about conditions in Morocco. He addressed an envelope: "To the President. Personal from Traveler," and put the report in the envelope, but did not seal it. Instead he went outside to a telephone and called the American Counselor. When he heard the friendly Irish-American voice he said: "This is the party whom you met at lunch with Lemaigre-Dubreuil. I have something of first-rate importance to tell you, but there are reasons why I should not come to your office. Would you be willing to come to my room in the St. George Hotel."

"Why certainly, Mr.—" the Counselor stopped just in time.

"I'll be sitting in the lobby waiting, and if you will follow me into the elevator, the visit will not attract any attention. I will explain this to you."

Mr. Murphy said that he would come at once, and Lanny went back and waited. When the pair were safely shut up in his room, Lanny took the envelope from his pocket and put it into the other's hands. The Counselor glanced at it, then stared at the giver. "Where did you get this?"

"I wrote it," Lanny said.

"Well, I'll be damned!" exclaimed the other. "So you are 'Traveler'?"

"Didn't you have any idea of it?" inquired Lanny with a grin.

"To be frank, I did; but I could never feel sure. Why are you telling me now?"

"The President left me free to tell you some time ago, but I make it a rule never to tell anything unless it is necessary. Even my parents and my wife have not been told."

Lanny took from his pocket the visiting card which he had unsewed for the occasion. Murphy took it and read: "My friend Lanny Budd is worthy of all trust. F.D.R." He handed the card back, remarking: "Of course that settles it. What can I do for you?"

"First, transmit this report to the President. I have left it open so that you may read it."

"There is no need to do that."

"There are items in it which may be of use to you, and anyhow, I wish you to know what I am saying. I have to explain that the President sent me here to do one particular job. Did he say anything to you about it?"

"He didn't mention you."

"I'm not sure whether you saw him after I did, or before. Anyhow, here is the story." Lanny told about Jerry Pendleton and Dr. Faulkner and the stolen codebooks and other devices.

Murphy listened attentively, and when he had heard it all he said: "Very ingenious, and of course if we can succeed it will be tremendously important. I heard about this Faulkner matter while I was in London, but nobody has taken the trouble to report the truth to me."

"I doubt if anybody in Algiers knows the facts, and it isn't a matter to be entrusted to a letter. I hope you won't feel that I have been butting in on your vice-consuls. At the President's suggestion, I talked it over with the O.S.S. outfit in Washington, and they gave their approval."

The Counselor held out his hand and shook Lanny's. "Here is a bargain," he said. "You need never worry about protocol. What I want is to lick the Nazis, and everybody who can help is my friend. Keep me informed as much as you can, so that we won't be treading on each other's toes."

III

It was by dealing with men on this heartwarming basis that Robert Daniel Murphy had risen from a humble post-office clerk to a position of responsibility for his country's affairs in a territory of nearly two million square miles and containing some seventeen million inhabitants. He had no jealousy or pettiness, and he really believed in his job. Lanny was prepared to be fond of him, and he in turn did his best to make this possible. They agreed that for reasons of secrecy they had better not adopt the American custom of addressing each other by their first names. Each would trust the other with the information necessary to success, and if either had any fault to find with what the other was doing, he would have it out face to face and not behind the other's back.

This career diplomat had come up the hard way; he had been born in Milwaukee, and his father had been a railroad sectionhand; he was, as he told Lanny, "sod" Irish, not "lace-curtain." He had worked his way through college and law school, an experience which fills some youths with rebellious egalitarian feelings, and others with respect for the privileged classes and a desire to join them. Lanny had already made up his mind that the genial Bob Murphy belonged in the latter group; it was obvious that he could not have had a career in the most snobbish branch of the United States government on any other basis.

Lanny had had opportunity to watch this phenomenon from boyhood. Whenever he had met an American diplomat or consular official he had found a gentleman who called himself "conservative," and believed wholeheartedly in the "free enterprise" system, as it had come to be called; to Lanny it was the "capitalist" system, but that was a term rarely heard among respectable people. Under that system America had become the richest and most prosperous country in the world, and when a diplomat talked about making the world safe for democracy, he meant safe for that system, and was certain that it was the destiny of his country, under God, to establish and maintain it throughout the world. That was why Robert Murphy could get so much help from Lemaigre-Dubreuil and others of that sort; Lemaigre was capable, he was accustomed to command, and he was quite sure that men like himself would be restored to their property and power when the victory was won.

Lanny guessed that some day he would find himself in opposition to Robert Murphy's policies in North Africa and elsewhere; but that time was not now. First, the Nazis had to be licked, and for that purpose this genial yet determined Counselor was a tower of strength. What the diplomat's heart was set upon was keeping the French Army and Navy from fighting the Americans, and for this purpose he needed the support of the "best" people, the people who had influence in a colonial community, those who could entertain Army and Navy officers and persuade them that the Nazi-Fascists were not the only people who knew how to hold down the Reds, that the Americans had a method at once more polite and more permanent. Look at Mr. Murphy and his twelve vice-consuls, such fine gentlemanly fellows, all of them admirers of French culture, and surely not one of them offering any threat to the established social order!

The railroad sectionhand's son talked frankly about these matters with the son of Budd-Erling Aircraft. It never occurred to him that this scion of wealth might have any views different from his own; and of course Lanny gave him no reason for questioning. Lanny was a lover of the *beaux arts*, who had been picked up by the President of the United States and put to work for his country, just as thousands of others, indeed millions, had been picked up and given jobs in this desperate emergency. Lanny was "right" in every way; he knew the "right" people, and could be trusted to say the "right" word and do the "right" thing, whether it was winning a war or merely holding a knife and fork.

IV

The problem they had to settle at present was what Faulkner was to tell the Germans. Murphy said: "The date of D-day is the most precious secret in the world. We aren't telling it even to the Frenchmen who are helping us. Surely we can't give it to the Germans!"

Lanny countered: "On the other hand, the President has given me a commission to try to get the U-boats to Dakar. And I have to tell them some date to be there. We can't just say, go and stay until something comes along."

They discussed this dilemma from various angles. Lanny admitted that he should have thought to put this question to the President; he wondered now if he would have to fly back to Washington and have instructions sent to the Counselor in code. He was afraid to let Murphy cable the details and ask for instructions.

Roosevelt had mentioned to Lanny that the expeditions to Mediterranean ports were sailing from Scotland, while those to the Atlantic ports were sailing from America. "I suppose that means New York,

Boston, Baltimore," Lanny said, and Murphy replied that it might also mean Savannah and New Orleans, the railroads were heavily taxed. Lanny added: "I suppose they will have different sailing dates and meet at sea. Does it seem possible that all those convoys can sail without the German agents getting some message through by way of Spain or Sweden or Switzerland?" When the Counselor admitted that this seemed hardly likely, Lanny continued: "Then suppose we give the Germans an approximate sailing date. I don't mean necessarily the correct one, but one which would put the convoy close to Dakar at the time we want the subs to be there."

But, really, it would be the date! Distances from American ports to Dakar and to Casablanca were not so different—about four thousand miles—and the speed of convoys could be estimated; it was always, of necessity, the speed of the slowest vessel. Lanny was prepared to have Murphy give a flat no to his suggestion. After all, it would be possible for a crook to have a visiting card engraved with the name "Mr. Franklin Delano Roosevelt," and to imitate that important person's handwriting. But Lanny was a "gentleman," and the genial Bob assumed that he was behaving as one; the Counselor assumed the same thing about Jacques Lemaigre-Dubreuil, and about that gentleman's Man Friday, who had been notorious in Paris as a member of the Cagoule. Lanny had met in Algiers a score of men who had records as partisans of the cartels, the Two Hundred Families, the royalist pretender—and all looking to Mr. Murphy for their future. Lanny wanted to say: "Watch your step, Bob!"

V

Lanny sent the code letter to Jerry, giving him the date. Then he dropped a note to young Denis de Bruyne, and they had one of their quiet meetings and long talks. Lanny told about his visit to the States and about his father and his mother, both of them known to the Frenchman from boyhood. Lanny couldn't say anything about the scheme he had cooked up, but he could say that the Yanks were coming, and before the end of the year. Denis said: "I hear a lot of talk about Dakar, Lanny, and that worries me; it is too far away to do us any good." Lanny could only answer: "It might be that we would feel it necessary to keep the Germans from getting that port, so close to South America."

The *capitaine* also had news. He and his group had been diligently working and had made a great deal of headway. Many officers, as well as many influential civilians, were coming to the opinion that things would be better if the Americans came; this was true even from the business point of view, for, while the Germans took all the products of French North Africa and paid high prices for them, what could you buy with the money? The Germans sent no goods, and very little could be sent from France because the Germans bought the French goods, too. People were beginning to say that if the Americans came, trade would be open, and the soldiers would spend money—no French man or woman would ever forget those wonderful free-spenders of World War I.

The really important news was about the French officers. The continued killing of hostages by the Nazis in France was troubling their consciences, while the stand the Russians were making at Stalingrad was impressing their professional minds. A deadly battle had been waged on the banks of the Volga for weeks, and the Germans could not keep the truth about it from spreading. If now the British could actually drive Rommel out of Egypt, and if the Americans would actually come and not talk just about it, Frenchmen might be able to hope again. General Juin, commander of what was left of the French Army in North Africa, and General Mast, who commanded under Juin in the region of Algiers, were both now committed to welcoming the promised invasion. Denis was exultant about this, because he had been working on these top men. "You understand, Lanny," he explained modestly, "in military terms I am a mere *capitaine*, but because of my father's position I enjoy a sort of civilian rank."

The art expert was again invited to the home of Professor Aboulker, and here he found the same atmosphere of eagerness mixed with anxiety. There was a half-open conspiracy to turn Algiers over to the gay legions of the New World; but it was a tremulous conspiracy, for if the Vichy elements became sufficiently aroused, they might recall Juin and Mast, as in the past they had recalled Weygand; they might send some of their terrorists over to take charge and jail all the disaffected ones and submit them to torture. "Sister Anne, Sister Anne, do you see anybody coming?" had been the cry of Bluebeard's wife in the fairytale, and that was the mood of the anti-Nazis in Algiers. What were the Americans waiting for, and why would nobody set a date so that people here could make plans? And what was this talk about Dakar, and how did they expect to get to any place from a peanut port down near the equator?

All that M. Budd could say was: "You will have to believe, gentlemen, that the Joint Chiefs of Staff know what they are doing, and that it takes time to turn peacetime industry to war production."

VI

Lanny received a note from Jerry, saying that he looked forward with pleasure to showing his friend the wonderful mosaic on the twenty-first inst. That meant that the plot was going according to schedule, and that Lanny had nothing to do but wait. He was by this time so tired of mosaics that he wished never to see another; but he had to go and view some in Algiers, and to start Hajek at some negotiations, even though he had no more purchasers in sight. He devoted a couple of days to this, and then came a note from Denis requesting to see him. The arrangement there was that Lanny would be at a retired spot in the showy gardens of the hotel, and Denis would stroll through, first having made sure that he was not being followed. In such a spy center as this it was likely to happen at any time, and Lanny had thought once or twice that it was happening to him.

Denis had a lot to report about the success of the underground work that he and his friends were doing. He said that everyone he talked to kept repeating one word: "When? When? When?" Saying it in French, "*Quand? Quand? Quand?*" with the nasal "n" and the "qu" pronounced as "k," it sounded exactly like the cawing of crows; but Lanny had no food for these hungry crows and could only say: "I wish I knew."

The *capitaine* had one truly exciting bit of information. Said he: "Here is something you must keep absolutely to yourself. Some of your top Army officers are coming secretly to meet Juin and Mast in the next day or two, to work out plans for letting the Army in without resistance."

"That is indeed news," replied the P.A. "How did you come to hear it?"

"In a very simple way. It is D'Astier de la Vigerie who was asked to arrange a meeting place. He recalled a house on the coast, beyond the town of Cherchell, a lonely spot. One of our friends, an ardent Gaullist and former mayor of Algiers, owns the house; it is off the highway, on a bluff almost over the sea, and it is an ideal place for such a meeting. This will show you that our officers really mean to coöperate. You see, they are afraid that the Germans may come first, and that Franco may help them. Also, I think it means that your Army must be coming soon, or they wouldn't take such a risk. It would certainly mean shooting for our Army friends if the Laval gang should get wind of the meeting here."

"Do you know who the American officers are, Denis?"

"We have not been told that. We only know that they are coming in a submarine, which will surface after dark and put them ashore. The water is deep in front of the house I speak of, and I suppose the sub will bring little boats."

"That is surely an important story if it is true," said Lanny. His old friend assured him that there could be no doubt about it, the French generals had this appointment and were going to this rendezvous. Whether the Americans would show up was of course another matter. Presumably they would fly to Gibraltar and board the submarine there.

VII

Lanny prepared another report for F.D.R., this time on conditions he had observed in Algiers. He left it unsealed, as before, and called the Counselor's office. He had another *nom de guerre* now, "Mr. Merriweather"; Murphy, who liked to make jokes as much as the President of the United States, had assigned this name on a particularly hot and muggy day. He would instruct his secretary that when Mr. Merriweather telephoned, the call was to be put through to him at once. Lanny would say: "I have some cigars," and Murphy would come to the hotel. Since his car was so well known in the city he would park some distance away, take a stroll, enter the hotel by an inconspicuous door, and come up the stairs, not using the elevator; he would come directly to Lanny's room and enter unannounced, and he would leave in the same quiet way.

The relationship between these two men was a delicate one; they were rivals for the favor of a prince, and that through all history has been a cause of poisonings and the play of rapiers and daggers. Lanny didn't want any such play, and had been relieved to discover that the genial Bob was not of a jealous and suspicious nature. Lanny had the advantage in the relationship, in that he dealt directly with the President, whereas Murphy dealt through the State Department, which meant the aged and tired Mr. Hull; Lanny could go to see the President at any time, whereas Murphy had gone only when he was summoned. Lanny had descended upon the Counselor, literally out of the clouds, and he might fly away again to his home on Mount Olympus, and who could say what thunderbolts he might cause to be hurled down upon a helpless mortal known as a career diplomat?

There was a still more embarrassing element in the relationship, the deadly thing known as snobbery. Lanny was to the manner born, while

Bob was the son of a railroad sectionhand; could it be that in his secret heart he was awed by the elegance and serenity which inherited wealth confers? Lanny had observed this phenomenon in the case of Charlie Alston, who had been a "barb" at Yale, earning his living by waiting table, while Robbie Budd had been a splendid aristocrat, a shining football hero. All his life that attitude had lingered, deep in Alston's soul; he had told Lanny about it in a laughing way. When the time had come that his official duty had required him to browbeat Robbie, he had done it, but it had taken greater moral effort than if he had been born to wealth and had learned to browbeat people from infancy.

So, naturally, Lanny wondered whether that same situation might exist here. Did Robert Murphy consider the son of Budd-Erling a socially superior person? Lanny was embarrassed to have such an advantage over any man; but he couldn't say it to this one, because it might sound like Pink doctrine, or even outright Red. All he could do was be as friendly as possible, and at the same time wonder whether this might wear the appearance of condescension. He would have liked to say "Call me Lanny," but they had agreed that that would be dangerous. So they would just go on doing their job, and Budd would convince Murphy that he, too, had only one thought in the world, to knock out the hateful Nazis.

VIII

Lanny handed his report to Murphy, who read it and said he had no changes to suggest. Looking at him with a slight quizzical expression, the P.A. remarked: "I don't suppose you want me to put in anything about the Cherchell meeting."

Utter consternation on the other man's face. "What the dickens!" he exclaimed.

"Don't blame me," smiled Lanny. "It is my business to find out things."

"Would you mind telling me what you know?"

"Surely not. I am told that several top American officers are coming in a sub from Gibraltar, and that Juin and Mast and some of their staff are to meet them in a house on the coast a few miles beyond Cherchell."

"Well, Budd, you have me down. Understand, I don't object to your knowing, but who told you? I am terrified at the thought that others may be talking about this ultra-secret matter."

"Don't worry, my friend. The person who told me will not tell anyone else."

The amiable Irishman got over his panic, and the blood came back to his usually rosy cheeks. He studied the son of Budd-Erling through a pair of bright blue eyes, and suddenly he opened up: "See here, Budd; since you know about this, how would you like to come along?"

It was Lanny's turn to be taken aback. "I hadn't thought of the possibility. How could I take the risk of meeting a bunch of French officers? I have carefully caused them to think of me as an itinerant art expert."

"You wouldn't need to meet them, nor the Americans either. I wouldn't propose to introduce you."

"What use would I be, then?"

"Let me explain. You may have difficulty in believing this—"

"I am going to believe anything you tell me, Murphy," Lanny put in quickly.

The other flushed with pleasure. "Thank you. I thought several times of the idea of inviting you. The only person who will ride with me is Knight, one of our vice-consuls, a man of integrity and discretion. If I told him that you were my friend, and that your name was not to be mentioned, now or later, he would obey orders, I am certain."

"That I don't doubt. But what good could I do?"

"You must understand that we are going into a really dangerous adventure. I don't want to sound stagy, but we are in the enemy's country; the Vichy crowd command here, and they would like nothing better than to shoot a few Frenchmen whom they would call traitors. What they would do to Americans and British whom they would call spies I cannot be sure, but it would make a terrific international scandal."

"I had not been told that any British were coming."

"The party will come in a British submarine, because there is no other available. As a concession to French feelings, an American will command it, but it will be British commando officers who will put the party ashore, and they will have to stay in the house while the conference goes on. It might happen that they will stay for some time, if a storm should come up and they could not launch the boats. You can see that all this presents a lot of worries to a civilian official who has never played a part in a melodrama and thought that all spy stories were made in Hollywood."

"I can understand that, Murphy. And if I could help without jeopardizing my own position—"

"This is what has crossed my mind. Both Knight and I will have to sit in at the conference to answer questions; and we ought to be free to have our minds on that. If in the meantime I were sure that there was someone keeping watch outside who would know how to handle any situation which might arise, it would be a great load off my mind. Understand, I don't mean that you should serve as an armed guard or anything of that sort; if it comes to a fight the commando men and the American officers will not need any help. The head of the expedition will be General Mark Clark, who is General Eisenhower's next in command, and is to head all our invasion forces in North Africa. You will not need be told of my intense anxiety to protect such a man."

"Indeed yes, Murphy. I am surprised that he should be taking this chance, or series of chances. Tell me exactly what you imagine I could do."

"You know French, Budd, and you know the French people. You understand the situation in this part of the world, and you possess that happy gift called savoir-faire. I can't imagine that you would lose your head in any emergency. I would tell both the Americans and the French that I had brought a personal friend, who was going to keep watch, and you could stay out in the darkness, unidentified. If any persons approached the house you would know how to greet them and answer their questions and allay any suspicions they might have. I hope and pray that nothing of the sort will happen, but there are many things that *might* happen, and I would be grateful to be relieved of anxiety so that I could put my mind on the problems of the conference."

"What story would I tell anyone who came?"

"We should have to talk that out. There are many details I would need to tell you, but there is no use bothering your mind unless you mean to come. What do you say?"

"What I say, Murphy, is that this isn't the job I was sent here to do; but I appreciate that it is an emergency, and if you feel that you need me, I won't say no. I put it up to you, however: you have to take the responsibility of asking me to come."

"I ask you," said the Counselor decisively.

"All right, then," said the P.A. "I will come."

IX

The meeting was set for the day after next, or rather for one o'clock in the morning of the day after that. Meantime Lanny attended a session with Murphy and the vice-consul named Knight, an American who had been a wine salesman in France for so long that his English had a French accent. These two had already visited the house, and they described it as extensive, of Moorish construction, two-storied, and white, like most houses here. It stood out conspicuously, the only building for several miles of the coast; at the hour appointed there would be a light burning in a second-story window facing the sea, which would make it easy to identify from the submarine. There were woods on the property, which might serve as a place of escape in case of emergency. There were two Moorish families who farmed the land, and the owner had arranged to pay these and let them take a holiday during the time of the conference.

The three conspirators set their wits to work to imagine all the things which might go wrong, and it was astonishing how capable their imaginations proved. The submarine might be sighted by somebody, or the trail of the boats when dragged ashore might be noticed. The plan might have been betrayed by one of the French officers, or by a wife or a mistress. Spies might follow them, or observe them as they entered from the highway. Someone on the highway might have a flat tire, or get into a wreck and come to the house to use the telephone. The Moorish families might have had their curiosity excited, or they might take some whim to come home—they were an undependable people. And so on and so on. What Lanny, the guardian of the gate, would have to say in each of these situations had to be thought out and discussed.

The most serious possibility was that something might bring the French police. Murphy said it was a safe guess that American staff men and British commando men would not let themselves be taken without a fight; if there were any prisoners, it would be the French, and there would be a jolly time getting them out to the sub in the sort of tiny boats that a sub could carry. And always hanging over everything was the possibility of a storm, or even an ordinary wind from the north, that might keep the invaders helpless on the shore for a week; also the fact that the place was only about seventy-five miles from Algiers, not much more than an hour's drive in a fast car. Yes, there were plenty of troubles to be imagined!

The host was to provide food and wine, to be paid for by the consulate; undoubtedly the French would bring wine, and the men who came ashore might be expected to have pocket flasks at least. If all that were set up on a table it would make quite a show of liquor, and possibly it wouldn't be long before some of the bottles were empty.

Murphy said: "If the police should come, I think our best story would be that I am giving a wild party for some of my friends, and it would be very rude of the police to interrupt. Unfortunately I'm not sure that I know just how to give a wild party. Do you, Mr. Budd?"

Lanny answered: "I once got two Nazi officers drunk and got some information out of them; so I could play a part in such a scene. But I haven't the right to, for reasons that you know."

The Counselor agreed that Lanny was not to come into the house under any circumstances. Lanny's job was to stay outside and use his savoir-faire, his bonhomie, his insouciance, his *bel esprit*—all the social qualities which the French have been cultivating through the centuries—to try to dissuade anybody from approaching the house. If the person insisted, Lanny was to let him come, and the Counselor would be the one to deal with him. There was a courtyard and a gate, and Lanny's post would be just outside; in the daytime he could sleep in the servants' quarters, or hide himself in the woods and read a book; Knight would see that he got food and whatever liquid he voted for.

Lanny said: "I suppose it wouldn't do any harm if during the day I strolled out toward the highway, and if I saw a car turning in, I might stop it and put my arts to work out there." This permission being given, a man who was expecting his forty-third birthday in less than a month, and who had been playing the role of Prince Charming since the age of three or four, spent a good part of the next two days imagining all the different kinds of people who might turn off a *route nationale* in Algeria, and what might be said to them to persuade them to turn back. Before he got through he decided that he had invented a new kind of parlor game.

X

On the appointed evening, which happened to be the twenty-first of October—the day when the Germans had been told that the convoys would be sailing—the consulate car was loaded, and Lanny Budd was picked up while strolling on the street at twilight. A beautiful drive, because French roads are always good, and mountains looming into a starlit sky make a landscape that affects the subconscious mind with a sense of awe, even while the conscious mind is occupied with treason and stratagems. As the car sped into its own bright beam the three men rehearsed their little dramas. They knew they were heading into adventure, and might be making history.

The house was not far from the highway, but was hidden by pine trees. The elderly French owner welcomed them; all his servants had been sent away, so they carried their belongings themselves. The owner showed them around again, so that they might know their way in the dark. There was a good path down to the beach, impossible to miss. The place seemed made to order for smugglers, and in past times it had been used for that purpose. Lanny, introduced under the name of Merriweather, was shown a place where he could sleep, and Murphy suggested that he should sleep now if he could. His vigil would not begin until the submarine gave a signal; after that it might be long.

Lanny slept, and the fleas were not too bad—he could tell himself that it was wartime and the G.I.'s would have far worse to endure. He did not waken till dawn, and then sat up with a start, wondering if he had been failing in his duty. But no, the others told him that they had lighted the window on time and had kept alternating vigils, but there had come no signal from the sea and no boats. What had happened was beyond guessing, but now, obviously, it was too late, and they would have to wait until night returned. Lanny might sleep some more, or have his breakfast and take a walk. The French officers were expected by motorcar at seven in the morning. After they had arrived, he might keep watch out near the road if he didn't mind—thus the polite and considerate Bob Murphy.

Lanny didn't mind at all. He had picked up in a bookstall a well-thumbed and marked-up copy of Palgrave's *Golden Treasury*, which some tourist had left behind. In boyhood Lanny had learned a good deal of it by heart, and now to reread it was to relive the happiest of his days. In between Sir Philip Sidney and Thomas Campion he would take glances at the highway, on which very few cars passed, only patiently plodding donkeys, overloaded and cruelly mistreated, in Mediterranean fashion. None of this traffic showed any wish to turn toward the lonely house on the bluff, and none paid any attention to an American gentleman sitting in the shade of an acacia tree, reading a small book bound in dark blue cloth.

XI

What had happened to the submarine? Later on Lanny learned that it had arrived at four o'clock in the morning, and those on board had seen the light; but it was judged too late to get ashore and hide the boats, and anyhow, there had been a misunderstanding as to the date. Now the sub was out there under the water, and for a while it poked its periscope up so that one of the commandos could make sketches of the shoreline, something that would be useful to them later. Then it went down again, and all on board were in a miserable situation, for there were eight extra men on board and that was an overload; the air became so foul that a struck match would not burn. Everybody had a headache, but they stuck it out until dark, and then the little vessel surfaced and came as close to the shore as it dared.

They had four tiny collapsible boats on board, called kayaks, after the craft of the Eskimos. They were made of board and waterproof canvas, shaped something like a bird bathtub, and just big enough for two men, facing each other and curling up their legs. It was a beautiful clear night, but a high sea was running, and it was a job to get those little walnut shells off. One capsized and had to be pulled on board and started again, badly cracked; but all four made the beach, and five Americans and three Britishers stepped ashore. The first was Colonel Julius Holmes, who was General Eisenhower's Political Adviser on French Affairs; stumbling up the path in the darkness, he was pleased to hear the voice of Vice-Consul Knight, and to learn that they had found the right place.

Lanny stood on the bluff at one side of the path, out of sight in the darkness, and learned that all was well. Then he went back to his post at the gate and stayed there all through the night, which seemed abnormally long. Sometimes he paced up and down, sentry fashion, and sometimes he sat propped against a tree, reciting to himself the great poetry of England which he had been reading all day. The soul of Britain seemed near and dear to him in these days when the Mother of the Free was being tried as never before in her long history. Her fate was bound up with that of all her children, including her wayward and overgrown child across the Atlantic.

Now and then the watcher dozed. There was no harm in that, because he was sure that no one could approach the gate without his awakening, and his job was not military but diplomatic. Neither friend nor foe appeared, and when daylight came, Knight, who brought him breakfast, reported that the French and the Americans were still in unbroken conference; the three Britons were asleep in an upstairs room, making themselves inconspicuous to the resentful French. The vice-consul added with a chuckle that their pants were still wet and wet pants were uncomfortable.

XII

Lanny's imagination was busy with what was going on inside that house. He could guess that the French generals had not summoned the

Americans unless they meant business, and he could be sure that the Americans had come for no other reason. Later on, when Murphy told him what had happened, he knew that they had really been making history. The new allies had given data beyond the dreams of any superspy: a complete set of military maps of all French North Africa, showing the ground, the elevations, the beaches, the airfields; charts of the waters, with soundings, and facts concerning military installations, fortifications, storerooms, and supplies; figures as to the airports, the length of the runways and materials of construction; figures concerning transportation, the number of engines and cars. Most important of all were complete plans for an invading army, including the various forms of co-operation the French might be able to give—the blocking of fortifications from the rear, the seizure of radio stations and airports, newspapers, public buildings, and records, and the protection of water power and transmission lines in Morocco.

All that was surely worth collecting, and a solitary watcher sitting out by the highway could be sure that his time was not being misspent. He read more British poetry; and whenever a car came along, which was rarely, he watched it, prepared to step out if it should turn in toward the house. Shortly after Lanny finished the box lunch that was brought to him, there came a peasant cart, hauled by one forlorn donkey, which turned into the road. Lanny hailed the man, and discovered that he knew only a few words of French. But one of these was *poulets*, and he drew back a cover and revealed sixteen dressed chickens, undoubtedly intended for the visitors' dinner. Lanny would get his share and be pleased; but orders were orders, so he walked beside the cart to the gate and called the master, the proper one to handle this situation.

The P.A. returned to his post. In the middle of the afternoon came another interruption of Wordsworth and Shelley. This time it was a large cart drawn by two mules and containing an assortment of Moors of both sexes and all sizes. One middle-aged man spoke a voluble if confusing French, and appeared to be annoyed at being stopped by a stranger. These were the farmers who lived here and had been sent away for a holiday; they had come back early because they were worried about the care of their stock. This was an emergency which had been foreseen by the Americans, and Lanny faithfully tried all the diplomacy, all the arguments, everything that had been planned, and more. But the Moors were as stubborn as the mules they drove; this was their home, they didn't want any more holidays, they didn't want any more money, they wanted to come home and make sure their livestock was not suffering neglect.

Lanny followed them up to the gate and called the owner. There was a delay in finding him, and meantime two of the younger fellows leaped off the cart and started toward the tenant houses. Lanny called to them, but they started to run and he had no way to stop them. Presumably their curiosity had been aroused, for one of them went to the edge of the bluff and looked down. Lanny could only pray that the submarine was not in sight. Later on he learned that there had been something else in sight. The British officers, who had hidden the boats in the brush, had brought up the damaged boat and repaired it, and then had decided that it would be wise to bring the others up into the ample kitchen and dry them and make sure there were no cracks.

The owner came out, and he had authority; also, he could speak Moorish. He gave each of the farmers money, and the cart was turned about; the two youths were called, and the whole outfit drove away again, but not without grumbling. What the master had told them Lanny didn't know, but he could guess that the town of Cherchell didn't offer much in the way of recreation, and that an undesired holiday paid for with unaccustomed sums of money must have seemed a strange phenomenon to primitive-minded peasants, whose cows and ducks and chickens were the most important things in the world to them.

Lanny called Murphy out and warned him that the situation did not look good. Murphy replied that the Americans would go as soon as it was dark. Lanny added: "If they can." Heavy swells were rolling in from the sea and pounding on the beach; the chances of launching those tiny kayaks in such a surf appeared extremely slim to a man who had lived a good part of his life on Mediterranean shores and had played in boats of all sizes.

XIII

Back to his post of duty. Lanny was worried now, and did not think about poetry. The Counselor had said exultantly: "We have got treasures beyond price!" And Lanny didn't have to be told how important it was to get those treasures on board the submarine. He watched the highway to the east, from which trouble was to be feared. Meantime the sun sank lower behind the hills to the west. Being no more than human, he thought occasionally of roast chicken, and wondered who was going to cook it. The three Englishmen, who had nothing else to do? And would Lanny's share be brought out to him, or would he have to wait until darkness had fallen and he returned to the gate?

The alarm, when it came, was not from the highway, but from the house. There was a telephone line to it, and Lanny could guess that somebody had called and given warning. He heard loud voices from the courtyard, and a minute or so later the gates were thrown open and two cars came roaring out without lights. It took them but a few seconds to reach the highway; there they had to slow up to make the turn, and in one quick glimpse Lanny saw that the occupants were French officers, one of them, a gray-mustached and pudgy person in his underwear. Lanny was later told that in the excitement the old gentleman had taken off his uniform and rolled it into a bundle, thinking thus to escape recognition. But he was riding in a car with other officers who had their uniforms on!

The cars turned to the west, which told Lanny that the alarm had come from the direction of Algiers. Somebody, whether police or military, was coming from the capital, and the officers were getting away. Where the officers would go was their problem; where Lanny went was to the house, as fast as he could run, and through the open gate. The courtyard was empty, the front door open, and lights burned brightly.

He had been forbidden to enter, but he knew that the French were gone, and he was willing in an emergency to be known to the Americans and the British. So he went to the doorway and looked in. There were Murphy, Knight, and two young French lieutenants in uniform; in one glance Lanny took in a large living-room, with several tables put together in the center. No doubt they had been covered with maps and papers, but these had been swept up and put away, and now there were bottles of all kinds and sizes, empty or full.

"Murphy!" Lanny called, and the Counselor came quickly. He was in a state of agitation; his skin had the peculiar whiteness which so many Celts show. "Come outside," Murphy whispered, and they moved out of the light. "A terrible thing! A telephone call to the owner, the police will be here any minute."

"Where are the Americans and the British?" asked the P.A.

"We have put them down in the wine cellar, and we must keep the police from lifting the trapdoor. The boats are in the kitchen and that is locked; we must keep them out of there also. Remember, it's a wild party, and it has to seem real."

"I'll do my best," Lanny promised, and Murphy went back into the house and closed the door. Lanny went to the gate, drew it shut, and took his stand in front of it, not without palpitations of the heart. He had faced many dangers and difficulties in his career, but at the moment this seemed to top them all. Mentally he rehearsed his lessons, and incidentally got his breath back. He was going to need a lot of it this time!

XIV

Car lights appeared on the highway to the east, speeding rapidly. When they came to the entrance road, they slowed up and turned, and the two lights made a wide quarter-circle and came to rest, both of them precisely on Lanny Budd's face, or so it seemed to him. They became larger and larger, brighter and brighter, and he faced them as if they were the eyes of all the world, or at any rate of all Nazidom and all Vichy *collaboratisme*. He stood his ground, and the car stopped within a few feet of him. From it descended a *commissaire de police* and a couple of his men. The driver remained in the car.

They would be armed, Lanny knew; but he was pleased to notice that what they had in their hands were flashlight torches. With the politeness acquired in the best social circles Lanny said: "*Bonsoir, Messieurs.*" The official replied with the same politeness, and added a question, which when literally translated reads: "What is it that it is that is going on here?"

So began the long duel of wits which had been so carefully prepared. Lanny explained first that he was a friend of Counselor Robert Murphy, and that this American official had leased this house for the purpose of giving a party to his friends. "It happens unfortunately, Monsieur, that my countrymen do not always content themselves with the good wines of this district; they have to have distilled liquors, and they get into a state of frenzy. It happens that I prefer good wines, and I don't like to stupefy myself, so I came out to get a little fresh air and look at the stars which should make all drunkards ashamed of themselves."

This with Lanny Budd's best drawing-room grace, and a *commissaire de police* could have no doubt that he was in the presence of a gentleman of elegance and wealth, even if his linen suit had been rumpled by sitting out under trees.

"So it is that that is going on," said the officer, and Lanny replied that that was precisely what it was.

"It causes me regret to say," announced the official, "that it has been reported to us there has been black-marketing going on here."

"Black-marketing, Monsieur? But it must be that some enemy is telling you the tale. The American Counselor and staff are surely not black-marketeers."

"It is reported that men have been seen carrying heavy bundles up the path from the sea."

"*Oh, ça!*" exclaimed the gentleman, hardly able to keep from bursting with laughter. "That is a tale which you will enjoy telling to your grandchildren. There were three of the guests at the party whose drinking was not to be controlled, and for fear that they would kill themselves we carried them down to the sea and doused them in the water. It had an excellent effect and they are now peacefully sleeping. I am sure that if you had seen us struggling to get them up the path, you would have agreed that they were heavy bundles."

For some reason the officer was not eager to share this merriment. "Is this party still continuing?" he demanded.

"It is our very bad rule that parties go on so long as anybody wants to drink. Most of the guests now are sleeping, and I trust that you will not have to disturb them. But, of course, if you wish to join the party, we should be most happy."

"I am on duty, Monsieur."

"We have good wine, as well as English whisky, and it is no violation of duty to enjoy one glass. I am sure that if you care to come, the Counselor will welcome you. I am happy to tell you that the etiquette of American parties requires the host to remain in possession of his senses."

X V

It would have been bad tactics to try to keep the men from entering, and much better to invite them than to wait for them to make a demand. Lanny pushed back the gate and the party entered and flashed the torches around. Perhaps they noticed that there was only one car; if they had commented on it, Lanny was prepared to explain that the guests had come to stay for some time. This was a wild party to end all wild parties.

Lanny led them to the front door and opened it, and there was a sight to shock the eyes of any guardian of public morality: a long table with plates and remnants of food, and not fewer than thirty bottles of every description, some of them empty and some full, some upset and dripping. Many glasses, some broken, and a dozen or more ash trays, full of ashes and cigar and cigarette stubs. At the table sat Vice-Consul Knight and the two French lieutenants in uniform. These latter were risking their lives to play this part; they had taken the decision on the spur of the moment, and were now doing it very well; their eyes were half shut and their heads were drooping and they were singing "Madelon" in droning voices.

In the center of the room stood the Counselor, tall, slightly stoop-shouldered, a man close to fifty and with thinning hair—surely he ought to have known better than to conduct such an affair as this. Lanny, who had made up on the spur of the moment the story about the dousing of the drunks, wanted his friend to be prepared, so he entered the room laughing gaily and explaining: "These gentlemen have come to investigate the place. It has been reported to them that we have been engaged in black-marketing. The men we doused in the sea and carried up to the house were taken for heavy bundles. You can certify how heavy they were!"

The three drunks at the table broke into maudlin laughter, and Murphy, suave and dignified, smiled pleasantly and assured the *commissaire* that neither he nor his government were engaged in cheating the government of France. The inquisition began all over again, and the *commissaire* revealed that he considered it his duty to search the house. At this the diplomatic official became very dignified and insisted that he would consider this an act of extreme discourtesy. He was greatly embarrassed because his guests had drunk too much, but now he had got them to bed, and he would certainly resent having them disturbed.

XVI

During the time of this ceremonious discussion the eight raiders were crowded into an ancient winecellar, dry in two senses of the word. Everything was covered with dust, and they had disturbed it. The dust got into the throat of a British captain, and he had to struggle with the impulse to cough. In his desperation he all but choked himself, and he gasped a request to General Clark for a piece of chewing gum. Clark gave him a piece, and he chewed it and managed to suppress the cough. Later Clark whispered to him, asking if the gum had helped, and the Briton replied that it hadn't much flavor. Clark said: "I had been chewing it for an hour." This was considered to be hilariously funny, but not until later.

They could hear the voices overhead, but could not make out anything. They had all been ordered to crouch close against the walls, with the idea that if the trapdoor were lifted they might escape notice. Clark had whispered the order: "If we have to fight, shoot to kill." But they all knew that that would be a calamity and might entirely defeat the purpose of their visit. They could only sit still, and pray if they knew how.

Up in the main room the controversy had reached a point where Lanny judged it advisable to point out to the *commissaire* that American wild parties sometimes involved the presence of ladies, and it would be extremely embarrassing to these to have their privacy disturbed by a police search. The Counselor inquired: "What would you think if you were to read in the newspapers that Frenchmen in America, giving a private party, had had their home invaded and searched?"

"But this is not your home, Monsieur," objected the official.

"When I have leased it, it becomes legally my home," was the reply. "And moreover it becomes diplomatic premises. You apparently do not realize that I enjoy diplomatic immunity, and that you are standing upon the soil of the United States of America."

"But this is wartime, Monsieur!"

"It is not wartime between my government and yours. My government is doing everything in its power to preserve peace and friendship with your government, and it is you who have committed a hostile act."

That rather stumped the police official; at any rate, he didn't know what to answer, and Lanny, with his best society smile, took the chance to intervene again. "Come, come, *Monsieur le Commissaire*, let us not prolong the argument unduly. You have the word of honor of the representative of the American government that there has been no black-marketing or smuggling here. You have my word, and you might have the word of these French officers."

The two lieutenants had sunk their heads in their arms on the table and were supposed to be in a stupor. Lanny went over to one of them and shook him. "*Monsieur le Lieutenant*, tell the *commissaire* that there have been no *contrebandiers* here."

"*Contrebandiers?*" echoed the other. He started up, swaying slightly and looking dazed. "*Où sont les contrebandiers?*"

Lanny said: "They think that *we* are *contrebandiers*."

"Who thinks that we are *contrebandiers?*" The young officer was ready for combat.

"Tell the *commissaire* that there have been no *contrebandiers* here."

"*Non! Pas de contrebandiers.*" The officer was as emphatic as could be desired.

"You see, *Monsieur le Commissaire*. These gentlemen are officers in your country's Army. Surely you cannot wish to push this matter further."

"I am not sure that I have the authority, Monsieur. I shall report the matter to my superiors."

"And so shall we, Monsieur. In the meantime, let us drink to the welfare and friendship of our two countries."

He went to the table and picked out a bottle of burgundy. There were clean glasses on the buffet, and he poured one and handed it ceremoniously to the *commissaire*. He poured for the others, and proposed a toast, and they all drank. After that there could be no more argument, and the three policemen retired to their car. In the doorway the reluctant official served warning: "My superiors will come, Messieurs." He didn't have to say that, and the thought flashed through Lanny's mind: Can it be that he has guessed correctly, and that he is on our side in the situation?

XVII

The car turned, and drove to the highway, and its lights disappeared to the east. Lanny didn't wait to see the raiders come out of their hiding-place, but closed the gate and resumed his vigil outside. He stayed there, a faithful Cerberus, the whole night long, and this time did not sleep. Afterward he learned what had been happening. The raiders had wanted to get away with their precious freight at the earliest moment, and had lugged their collapsible boats down to the shore, where the heavy surf was still pounding. They had a powerful blue torch with which they signaled the submarine, and the order was: "Come as close to the shore as possible. We are in trouble."

The first to make a try was General Clark. He took off his outer clothing and rolled it into a bundle, and he and a British commando captain walked out into the surf. Clark, a powerful man, six-feet-three, got into the frail walnut shell; the other man followed, and they began paddling like mad. A tall comber came sweeping in, seized the tiny boat, turned it up on end, threw it over and back toward the beach.

"Save the General's pants!" somebody shouted, and the reply was: "Hell, no, save the paddles!" This they managed to do; but the pants were gone, and somewhere in the boiling surf was a musette bag containing six hundred dollars in gold. When this story reached the newspapers, the amount had been increased to eighteen thousand dollars—apparently nobody stopped to figure that such a quantity of gold would weigh about sixty pounds and would have been rather difficult to transport in a kayak.

They saw that nothing could be done with that surf. Clark decided that they would not trap themselves in a cellar again; they would hide the boats in the underbrush and themselves in the woods. There was a new problem in military etiquette: the commanding officer couldn't be left without pants, so the next in rank gave up his, and this politeness ran down the line until there was left a forlorn lieutenant who had to wrap himself in a blanket. The night was chilly, and now they were hungry and longed for the chickens. They sat in the darkness with carbines or tommy guns on their knees and debated what to do next.

At eleven o'clock came the lights of another car, and Lanny gave the alarm. This time higher officials had come, and the whole farce comedy was played over again. In spite of all protests, they insisted upon searching the house. The remains of the wild party had been left, but the wine cellar was found empty and there were no boats in the kitchen. Murphy stated that his guests had departed, and that was all there was to that. The police, of course, knew that there were woods close by, but they couldn't have done much searching at night. They stated that they would return in the morning; and again Lanny wondered, did this mean that they didn't want to find out too much?

Anyhow, it was notice to get out before day, and the raiders hiding in the woods were shivering with more than cold. One of the Britishers, trained to amphibious operations, roamed the beach and found a spot where there appeared to be a riptide, and he persuaded General Clark that an attempt might succeed there. So once more the tiny boats were made ready; the submarine was ordered to come still closer, and this time the commandos tried the method of posting themselves one on each side of the General's kayak, running it out as far as they could go in the water, and then giving it a parting shove. By this means the little craft got enough headway to surmount the first comber, and it disappeared into the darkness. The second boat was overturned, but it got away on the next try, and the other two managed it with the help of Knight and the young Frenchmen.

Out by the submarine one boat was smashed to bits against the side. This presented a new problem, for it had contained uniforms and a bag with papers, and when these and the boat fragments were washed ashore it would be a dead giveaway. The sub signaled to Murphy to clean up the beach, and he and the vice-consul got the boat fragments and other debris, tore them to pieces, and buried them in the sand. They did not find the gold, but they did find General Clark's pants, and wrung them out and wrapped them up and locked them in the trunk of the consulate car. When they climbed the bluff, Murphy was exhausted and deathly pale, and Knight's feet were full of thorns and cuts.

They were just in time, for Lanny gave the alarm again; there were cars coming, two of them this time. The Americans had done their job, and a high diplomatic official felt justified in standing upon the dignity of his office. "Gentlemen," he said, "since I am not free to entertain my friends without repeated annoyance, I retire from the field. The house is yours, and I am going back to Algiers." The other two Americans were already in the car. The French lieutenants had betaken themselves to the woods.

Once out on the highway, Robert Murphy wiped from his forehead the mixture of perspiration and sea salt. A religious man, he permitted himself to exclaim: "Thank God!" As for Lanny Budd, he could hardly keep awake, but he ventured the opinion that what had been done in the last two nights would be told in the history books along with Paul Revere's ride and that of General Sheridan. He added: "But leave me out of it!"

16

Thrice Is He Armed

I

LANNY wrote a report to the Chief about French co-operation and the various details that he had picked up in Algiers. He told him that the general belief was that there would be an expedition to Dakar; also, that the Vichy-controlled newspapers were predicting a Mediterranean expedition, having as its aim the taking of Crete. There was also a lot of talk about Norway, and what purported to be an inside story, that newspaper correspondents in London were providing themselves with fur coats and mittens. When Murphy read that he smiled and said: "They really are, you know. They have been told it's Norway!"

Lanny added in his report that the French had apparently settled in their minds that D-day was to be the end of November. When

Murphy read that he remarked: "Nobody here knows the date but myself, and I am under orders not to tell anyone until the proper time." Lanny's reply was: "I much prefer not to know any fact that I am not supposed to make use of."

The Counselor asked what Lanny was intending to do now, and the P.A. said that he had in mind to fly to Casablanca and ascertain how his Dakar scheme was going. He said: "I'll have to come back here to file a report, as I don't care to trust the mails. How long shall I stay?"

That was a "leading" question, and the other might have said that it was for Lanny to decide. Instead he smiled and replied: "I wouldn't stay more than a week or ten days if I were you." Lanny did not fail to make note of both the words and the manner.

"I'll tell you something interesting," the other continued. "The plans which the French had prepared for a proposed invasion of their territory correspond almost exactly with those which our Allied Combined Chiefs of Staff had worked out. General Clark didn't tell them that, of course. There was only one important difference: they don't think we can take Casablanca, and their plan was to take Oran, and then backtrack on land."

"That is exactly what General Béthouart suggested to me," replied the P.A. "I find very few who think that we can land on the Atlantic coast, because of the surf."

"They don't know the new devices we have prepared. They will be surprised, and so will the Germans."

"I was told about the landing craft by my half-brothers, back in Connecticut," said Lanny. "I am waiting on pins and needles."

"We have all been waiting more than three years," remarked the Counselor. And Lanny exclaimed: "I have been waiting ever since the day Hitler took power, and that lacks only a couple of months of being ten years. I am indignant when I think how that man has dominated my life!"

II

The plane to Morocco went via Oran, and it flew along the coast, over the town of Cherchell, and almost directly over the house where the "wild party" had been given. Lanny saw it as if it were a map, one drawn in indelible ink on the tablets of his memory. He looked down on the gray thread which was the *route nationale*, and in his mind were yet other images, stamped by that faculty known as imagination. He saw that sixteen-foot-wide highway crowded with tanks and trucks, and with long thin files of G.I.'s marching at the side. And they weren't backtracking to Casablanca, no indeed! On all the roads of French North Africa their faces were turned toward the rising sun. They wouldn't be aiming to occupy two million square miles of territory; they would be heading for Tunis, the great German supply base, and for the armies of General Rommel, intending to smash them and surround them and force them to surrender. Lanny didn't need to ask any military man about that; he had learned the technique of war by watching the Germans, who had done it in a couple of months in France, and had been doing it continuously for sixteen months in Russia—only now they had come to Stalingrad!

In Casablanca, Lanny sat down with his old friend Jerry, who was in a state of delight over the job he was doing. He had disliked the "Heinies" in World War I and now he heartily loathed the "Krauts" and enjoyed a chance to thwart them. He reported that the Chicago archeologist had done a perfect job; he had been accepted as a Nazi sympathizer and spy, and was feeding them whatever the vice-consuls wanted them to get. "Of course there's no telling till the showdown comes, but if the German wolfpacks aren't heading for Dakar I'm a lobster and ready to be boiled."

Jerry had a mass of information which he himself had collected; most of it had been turned over to the vice-consuls and had gone to Washington by the diplomatic pouches. The conscientious Lanny made mental note of a few items which he thought might be of special interest to the Governor. Lanny had adopted the practice of numbering the items, and every night before he went to sleep he would go over them in his mind. If he forgot one he would be greatly distressed, and would give powerful commands to his subconscious mind to return it to him.

Hajek always followed, for the Moor was not only perfect camouflage, but also an errand boy and a fountain of gossip. It was permissible for an American gentleman of wealth and nothing special on his mind to be interested in all the rumors that were circulating in the *souks*. Not all of them were true, but a large percentage were, and the rest were what the different governments were giving out; it was important to see what effect they were having. Everybody "knew" that the Americans were heading for Dakar, and it was generally expected that the U-boats would sink most of their ships; everybody "knew" about the Sahara railroad heading for that port, and "knew" that it was about three times as near to completion as it actually was. Everybody "knew" that the British and American warships were already at Gibraltar for this expedition, and no doubt they were.

The pair were driven up to Marrakech, and Lanny made sure that his family was getting along contentedly. Beauty, too, had heard about Dakar, but she wasn't so sure, having lived through some seven years of war and forty years of propaganda on the old Continent of Europe. She wanted Lanny to tell her, but he said that he didn't know, and if he did he wouldn't be free to say. He had a séance with Madame, to see if the "spirits" had anything to contribute; but the only "spirit" was old Zaharoff, getting the two World Wars mixed in his mind and being blamed for them both. Lanny looked at some mosaics and some fountains, and had another private chat with Herr Theodor Auer and a couple of his friends. Oddly enough, he discovered that the *souks* knew that this gentleman was at odds with his own government and was not averse to being captured by the Americans if they didn't delay too long.

Lanny played a few sets of tennis to keep in condition, and played the piano for some of Beauty's friends who enjoyed it. With his Moorish friends he drank many more cups of mint tea, which most white people considered a horrid concoction. Then he went back to Casablanca, and after another conference with General Béthouart, returned to Algiers. He wrote his report, and the Counselor came as usual to read it.

Lanny said: "Murphy, I am thinking of following this report personally. I am supposed to return every two or three months. And I have a personal reason, too: my wife is expecting a baby, and I'd like to be at her side."

"Of course you are the one to decide," replied the nervous and overstrained official. "But you will want to consider the news which I am now free to tell a few of our most trusted people: D-day for Operation Torch is next Sunday, and H-hour is one A.M."

Lanny said: "Holy smoke!" Of course the news knocked his little plan completely out, and he could do nothing but write a letter of apology to Laurel.

III

That was Thursday afternoon, so Lanny had some fifty-six hours of suspense to pass. He was told the names of the men who had so far been trusted with the secret: General Juin, and his subordinate Mast, who, because he was very thin, was known in the American code as "Flagpole." Lemaigre was "Crusoe," and his henchman Rigault was "Friday." Lanny was told that he might impart the secret to his friend Denis de Bruyne. It was being released to persons who had specific jobs to do in advance. One of the vice-consuls, Kenneth Pendar, had set out on an automobile expedition through French Morocco to impart it to officers of the French Army and Navy who were known to be on the Allied side. Murphy said: "We figure there won't be time for submarines to come up from Dakar now."

"Don't forget the planes," warned Lanny, and the other exclaimed: "Surely not! The Germans sent a thousand over our last convoy to Malta. But fortunately their bases are not so near to our landing points."

"Unless they fly from Spain," warned the P.A.

He had an interesting contribution on that subject. Just before leaving Casablanca he had got into a chat with a Spanish consular official who was obviously desirous of pumping him. Lanny had taken his pose of old-time Fascist sympathizer, a friend of General Aguilar; so the Spaniard had talked and revealed that El Caudillo was being pulled this way and that by his advisers, as to whether the Spanish armies should seize the moment to march into French Morocco, block off the Allies, and take the rich territory for their own. So simple it seemed, and then they could take the Rock, with German help if necessary. Some of those magnificent big guns which Marshal Göring had set up had been sitting there idle for more than a year, covered with grease and with their muzzles plugged!

"What have they decided?" inquired the anxious Counselor; and the answer was: "My Spanish informant felt certain that they will wait and see the result of our efforts. If we are thrown back, it will be the chance of a lifetime for them."

"We are not going to be thrown back," declared Murphy. He was an American, and so was Lanny, and Americans have the habit of thinking that their country can never fail in what it sets out to do. Battles can be lost, mistakes can be made, long delays can occur, but once America gets going she will not be stopped. Once that huge armada had set out from her many ports, once the sealed orders had been opened and read, the tremendous job would be put through, in spite of everything that Vichy French and Nazi Germans and Franco Spaniards could do.

IV

The turn of the tide was beginning, and not only in Algeria. Murphy confirmed the fact that the British had won a tremendous victory at El Alamein. Lanny had been afraid to believe it; he had been disappointed so many times in that three-year seesawing back and forth along a thousand miles of African coastline. But the new tank-killers had really killed; the German armies had been routed and were in full retreat out of Egypt, harried day and night by swarms of British and American planes. The Desert Fox himself wasn't there; he had gone to Berlin to be feted and have decorations pinned on him. By the time he got back, he would have only part of an army. The P.A. heard with delight about the war bulletin which the Nazis had published, stating that "Rommel's forces are advancing *westward* according to plan and without opposition"!

Also, the Russians were holding at Stalingrad; they had been backed up against the Volga on a long front, and were clinging there desperately, reinforced and supplied across the river by night. The city and its giant factories were one vast line of ruins, extending for twenty miles along the west bank of the Volga. The discovery had been made in this war that concrete and steel buildings, hammered into ruins, become fortifications. Men can hide in cellars and shell holes while bombardment is going on, and when it stops they come up and hide behind steel girders and concrete blocks and defend their fortress with rifles and machine guns and grenades.

They can fight in tropical jungles, too, in a tangle of vegetation so dense and so full of thorns and diseases and poisonous insects and snakes that it had been thought no man could penetrate it. But soldiers could camouflage their clothing and faces and hide there and fight. The Americans were proving it in New Guinea, which was a way of defending Australia; the handful of marines that had been put ashore on terrible Guadalcanal were holding on in spite of Japanese bombing every night. Lanny had been there, just a year ago, and had learned about "Solomon sores," which were all but impossible to heal; half of the G.I.'s had them, but they were sticking it out, and the ships in "the Slot" and the flyers overhead were fighting deadly duels night after night.

In short, it was the turning point of this dreadful war. Now the greatest assemblage of ships in the world's history was approaching the shores of Africa, to establish bases for an attack upon the "soft underbelly" of Europe. The Russians declared that they would refuse to consider this a "second front," and that was their privilege; to the Americans it was a "first front," the first American front. It was their first large-scale action, and they would learn here, and making their mistakes in places where they would not be so costly. By the time they had conquered North Africa they would be veterans and would no longer make mistakes. That had been the decision, the result of the meeting of many minds, both British and American. Now came the time for action, for the carrying out of the unimaginably elaborate plans. The Americans who shared the secret were like children who can hardly bear to wait for Christmas morning.

V

Lanny would have liked nothing better than to throw off his camouflage and take part in this high adventure in Algiers. But that wasn't his job; he had to keep out of the way, and meet secretly with his friend Denis and learn from him what the conspirators were doing. Denis would pop in like a jack-in-the-box, so excited that French words rolled off his tongue like bullets out of a tommy gun. He wanted advice, because he had looked up to Lanny from boyhood, and besides, Lanny knew the Americans and what they would be apt to do in this or that contingency.

The center of the intrigue was the home of the Jewish professor-doctor on the Rue Michelet. He was seventy-eight, a big man, with a leg hurt in World War I; he could not get about without a cane. He was wise, and had money, and also courage, so the others listened to him. Robert Murphy had come there and imparted the secret to a dependable half-dozen, and they had agreed upon all the things that were to be done on the Saturday night before D-day. As it turned out, a great part of the program was dependent upon the Jews; they were the people who hated Vichy to the point where they were willing to risk their lives to get rid of it. The reason was the odious anti-Semitic laws which the Nazis had forced upon Vichy and which Vichy had forced upon all France, including the colonies.

Professor Aboulker was President of the Jewish Federation of Algeria and also a professor of medicine at the university; he was allowed to continue at this post because he was a wounded veteran, and therefore was exempt from the laws which excluded Jews from the professions. Prominent also in the movement were Aboulker's sons, the sons' cousins, and a *couturier* by the name of Cohen, who in business used the name Elie Calvet; short, dark, and energetic, he owned a dressmaking establishment in Paris, and had shops in the four principal cities of French North Africa where he sold his products. So far he had been able to hold onto the business; he was counting the days before he would have it safe under American protection.

Denis, wearing civilian clothes, could slip up to Lanny's hotel room without attracting attention. He was in touch with the French officers, and reported that Admiral Darlan had arrived unexpectedly in Algiers.

The stocky commander of both Navy and Army forces—under Pétain, but no one else—had made an inspection trip throughout North Africa, including Dakar, which all Vichy now expected to be attacked. He had returned to Vichy, but because of the serious illness of his son he had been flown back to Algiers. Lanny wondered, had he been "tipped off" to what was coming? Denis didn't think that was the case.

Another item of information: the Americans were planning to use General Giraud in their efforts to avoid bloodshed here. This aged hero of both world wars had escaped from a German fortress into Vichy France; then he had gone to the Riviera, and from there had been taken in a submarine to Gibraltar. As soon as the Americans were ashore he would be flown to Algiers, and would invite the French to accept him as their leader. "Will they do it?" Lanny asked; and the reply was: "It seems to me a bad guess."

Lanny didn't ask any further, for he knew that Denis, a Gaullist, would not accept anybody but his Joan of Arc. The *capitaine* was greatly upset because the Americans were not bringing De Gaulle from London; but when Lanny pinned him down he admitted that the tall radio orator had very little following in North Africa, and that most of the French military regarded him as a British tool. Lanny considered De Gaulle a Jesuit imperialist, but all he could say was: "You know, Denis, I am no politician, and I'm not in the confidence of our military men. I can only guess their attitude, that they will do anything on earth to avoid having to shed French blood. Whoever can best help them in that may become civil governor of French Africa."

VI

The actors in the coup for Algiers were for the most part the Chantiers de la Jeunesse, and they were preparing to make good the jest that Robert Murphy would take Algiers with the boy scouts. These youths—up to the age of eighteen—had been provided with American small arms and had buried them. Now they were told to dig them up and to report at their assembly places at eleven o'clock on Saturday night. Lanny went out to see the show, and discovered that the people of this "African Paris" were enjoying themselves after the fashion of all Mediterranean peoples, who turn night into day as far as they can. The radio had reported an immense Allied convoy, first leaving Gibraltar, and then moving eastward through the middle of the Mediterranean, the established route to Malta and the strait of Sicily. It was assumed that this meant another effort to reinforce the most bomb-battered spot in the world. No one could observe in the darkness that this convoy, due north of Algiers, made a right-angled turn to starboard and was now heading straight for the city, whose harbor and beaches had been photographed and reproduced in replica and studied until everyone on board knew them as well as he knew his own back yard.

The band was playing in the park down by the waterfront, and the Rue Michelet, the principal street, was thronged with sightseers. All the shops were open, and there were lines in front of the movie houses; American pictures were barred, of course, but the crowds took what they could get. Here, as all over the world, any movie was better than no movie. Groups of the Chantiers in their green trousers strolled past, but nobody paid any special attention to them.

H-hour was one in the morning. At that time the ships were supposed to be as close to the shore as possible, the landing craft launched, the men on board, and the craft with engines idling, ready on the second to begin the race to the shore. Ten thousand men were coming, not into the harbor, but to beaches just west of the city; they would march in by the roads. Some of the conspirators were at the beaches, ready to welcome them and guide them in; others were in front of all the important points of the city: the post office, which contained the telegraph and telephone offices; the power stations, the radio stations, the Préfecture de Police. They were to hold these and permit nobody to come or go until the American forces arrived.

Lanny stood in the crowd outside this last all-important place and watched what was happening. He learned once more the lesson that events of historic moment are frequently poor shows to the spectator. He watched, and nothing happened, except that young men with revolvers in their hands stood in the doorway, looking very solemn and determined. He did not learn until later that inside the building the chief of the secret police was down on his knees, trembling and pleading with tears in his eyes that he should not be shot. He well knew what he deserved to get from anti-Fascists and Jews. All kinds of political opinions were represented in these groups, but they all hated Germans and friends of Germans.

Lanny strolled from one place to another, and realized that the whole city was in the hands of the pro-Allies. Planes flew close overhead, and showers of leaflets came fluttering down; Lanny picked one up and found that it had the American flag on it, but was printed in Arabic. Shortly afterward he stood in a crowd and listened while a man read aloud one that was printed in French; it was a proclamation by General Giraud, calling upon the Army to make no resistance to their American allies.

A little later the P.A. had the strange experience, while walking on the Rue Michelet, of hearing from an open café the sound of a familiar voice, booming with tremendous volume from a radio set. All activity had come to a halt, and the Algerians listened to Franklin D. Roosevelt, assuring them in careful college French that the sole purpose of the American Army was "to liberate France and the French Empire from the Axis yoke" and to "bring about the early destruction of our common enemy." This was from a recording, and Lanny heard it more than once during the next days. He also heard an address by General Eisenhower. That, too, sounded strangely familiar, and he realized that it was a voice he had heard from the underbrush near Cherchell. It was Colonel Julius Holmes, doubling for his overworked commander!

But where were the Americans? He was told later that there had been a mistake, and that in the darkness the landing craft had hit some beaches farther away from town. Maybe that was true; anyhow, some of the officials who hadn't been caught in the coup had warned the French troops in the suburbs, and these troops now came rushing in with motor transport. In the next hour or two several of the pro-Allied groups were under siege in the buildings they had taken. They were outnumbered, and the troops had artillery, so a few of the insurgents were killed and others had to surrender.

So much for amateur war-making! It wasn't quite as bad as it appeared that morning, but Lanny was greatly upset. There was nothing he could do about it, of course. He had been told that the people at the consulate had been burning confidential records and codebooks all day Friday and Saturday, as a precaution against just such a mishap. Sooner or later the Army would get here, and if there was fighting to be done, the Army would know how to do it. Meantime the one clear duty of a P.A. was to keep out of sight and out of range.

VII

An exhausted art expert went back to his hotel and fell asleep to the sound of several kinds of gun fire. That was just before dawn, and he slept for two or three hours. He was awakened by a tap upon his door, and when he opened it, there was Denis de Bruyne, haggard, red-eyed, and in a terrible state of depression. He had been in the battle at the Préfecture, and had made his escape by jumping out of a back window. Since then he had been roaming the streets, not daring to go to his home. So many of his friends were in the hands of the enemy, the Vichy gangsters, and Denis could see no possibility save that they would all be shot.

Lanny brought him inside and locked the door, and they discussed the situation in low tones. Lanny didn't think it could be as bad as his friend feared. "They know the Americans are coming, Denis."

"But where *are* the Americans?" burst out the other.

"You haven't seen any of them?"

"Nobody has seen them that I can find out. They are shooting some guns, but they don't march."

"You may be sure they have their orders, Denis. Their first objectives would be the airports, and the installations of heavy guns. As a military man, you know that they would make certain of such objectives before they started marching down a city boulevard at night."

"That may be true; but then, they should not have told us to go into action at midnight."

"Murphy told you; and Murphy is not a military man. The commanders will necessarily be guided by what they find ashore. I thought I heard shooting from the direction of Maison Blanche." This was the larger of the two airports of Algiers.

"I heard it also from the Blida airport. I suppose the defenders would have to fire a few volleys to satisfy their sense of honor."

"How many Americans do you think they will have to kill in order to satisfy their honor, Denis?"

It was an unkind question. The *capitaine*, in a state of extreme exhaustion, made no attempt to wipe away the tears which welled into his eyes. "Lanny, you know how I feel about it. I am in despair, because I am so impotent. Several times I have been on the verge of going to the authorities and pleading with them. Every decent Frenchman has a love for America buried somewhere in his heart, ever since your war with England when we helped you in good friendship. But these Vichy people have the hearts of rats, and they would probably throw me into jail."

"Whom did you think of going to, Denis?"

"To Darlan."

"Darlan!" echoed the astonished P.A. "Of all men!"

"He is the one who can prevent a war, or stop it if it has started."

"You don't think Giraud can do it?"

"Not a chance in this world. I have talked about him with scores of our officers, and they all say they would pay no attention to him."

"And Juin cannot control them?"

"Juin would never dare to give an order contrary to Darlan's. Darlan is his superior."

"It goes entirely by rank, then?"

"It goes by rank in every army, Lanny. If a man defies his superior officer, he is a mutineer and he is shot."

"But you, Denis, you are a Gaullist! Is that mutiny?"

"It is revolution, at least, and De Gaulle would be shot by the Vichy crowd if they could get him."

"He would be shot by Darlan, would he not?"

"Certainly."

"And yet you would appeal to Darlan!"

"I would be appealing for the Americans, Lanny. You don't have to deal with the question of French legitimacy, you only have to consider American lives and how to save them. What I am trying to do is to save the lives of those Chantiers who are now in the hands of the Garde Mobile. Tomorrow may be too late."

"You understand, Denis, if we were to make terms with Darlan he would certainly demand control. He would remain at the head of the French Army and might even dominate the civil government."

"I wouldn't worry about any of that. Once the Americans have their armies in here and are firmly settled, they could give orders to Darlan, and if he didn't obey them they could kick him out."

Lanny found this one of the strangest developments in this complexity of greeds and jealousies and fears. A fighting Gaullist recommending one of the fighting Vichyites! But when he voiced this, Denis exclaimed: "Darlan is not for Vichy. Darlan is for Darlan! If you brought him such an offer, he would think of just one thing, what forces you were bringing and what chance you had of staying. If you stay, and he is against you, he is a prisoner of war; but if he helps you, he becomes the governor of an immense province, and perhaps— who can say?—of all France."

"And you are willing to take that chance?"

"What I wanted, Lanny, was for you to bring General de Gaulle here with your armies and put him in authority. But for some reason your President does not understand our great General and does not trust him. Even so, I trust your President. If the selfish and cynical Darlan can bring it about that the American Army will fight Germans instead of Frenchmen—all right, I am willing, and I will take my chances that in the end the people of France will be permitted to decide who shall govern them. I know that will be De Gaulle!"

The P.A. thought that over for a while, and then said: "I'll go and talk with Robert Murphy." He bade his friend to lock himself in this room and have a sleep. Lanny would hang the "Do Not Disturb" sign outside the door and Denis would be all right, even with the headquarters of French Naval Intelligence in this same hotel!

VIII

The P.A. went out on the streets of Algiers on a beautiful Sunday morning. The European shops were closed, but you couldn't exactly say that it was quiet, with guns large and small going off at the harbor and now and then in the suburbs. Crowds of people, both white and brown, had come out to see what was happening, and there were swarms of soldiers of the Garde Mobile. Lanny observed that they were still besieging the post office, which had refused to surrender. A small British war vessel had forced its way in during the night, and some sixty men had been killed. Then, coming up from the harbor, he saw the first of the long-awaited American troops, a company of commando men, making their toilsome way up one of the steep streets. All of them were heavily camouflaged, with hands and faces black except around the eyes. The Moors stared at them in wonder, no doubt taking them for some new and strange kind of savages.

Soon afterward Lanny saw a column of infantry marching in from the west. They had had difficulty in getting ashore in rough water, and they looked exhausted after a long march with heavy packs. They plodded along, manifesting little interest in the sights of a strange city. Few cheered them, for who could know if it was safe to do so? Frenchmen remembered Dieppe, and before that St. Nazaire. High and low had the same idea: better to wait and see how things turned out!

Lanny went to the home of Professor Aboulker; he found nobody there except one American official who had imbibed too heavily amid the excitement of the night and had passed out. There was an American soldier guarding him, and claiming to have been the first soldier to enter the city. Lanny used the telephone to call the Counselor's home, but Murphy wasn't there; he tried the British Consulate, which was opposite the Admiralty building, but Murphy wasn't at that place either. Lanny spent a lot of time looking for him; and in that time he saw three Allied planes bombing targets in the harbor, and large fires starting up. It was all very confusing to him, and even more so to other people. Certainly that was true of the G.I.'s with whom he chatted as they rested in the park. "Some frog soldiers give us wine, some give us black looks, and some shoot at us. Tell me, Mister, is this a war or what is it?"

IX

Toward noon Lanny decided to see what was going on at the Préfecture, so he strolled on the Boulevard Boudin. There he happened to see a parked automobile which he recognized—there were few but official cars out on this dangerous day. He waited, and presently from the building came Vice-Consul Pendar, a Harvard man whom Lanny had met at a social affair, and with whom he had got along very well because of Pendar's interest in art. Now Lanny greeted him, saying: "How are things going?" The answer was: "I would tell you if I knew." When Lanny said that he couldn't make heads or tails of it, the vice-consul replied that it appeared to be mostly tail and very little head.

Lanny explained that he had been trying to get in touch with Murphy, and the other's response took him by surprise: "Murphy is a prisoner of General Juin."

"*Prisoner!*" Lanny exclaimed. "In heaven's name!"

"Don't take it too seriously. The town is a madhouse. When the French think that our troops are delaying they arrest us, and when they hear that our troops are ashore they turn us loose, and we arrest them for a change. I myself have been arrested three times since midnight. Just now I have a pass from Commandant d'Orange, Juin's aide-de-camp, but I don't know how long it will be good."

When Lanny said that he had a message for the Counselor that might be important, the other said: "Why not telephone him at Juin's villa?" When Lanny expressed surprise at this suggestion, he was told that the diplomatic head was busily carrying on negotiations, just as Juin had been carrying on negotiations while he was Murphy's prisoner. An odd melodrama indeed!

The vice-consul explained that he couldn't stop for a chat as he was on an important errand. "You might ride with me if you like. I'll be seeing Murphy in the next hour or two, if that's not too late."

Lanny stepped into the car, and as he drove Pendar explained the errand on which he had been hurrying about town; he was trying to find Admiral Battet, who had been taken prisoner by the insurgents during the night. "Battet is Darlan's friend and adviser," said the vice-consul, "and Darlan refuses to negotiate without him."

"Oh! You are negotiating with Darlan?" inquired the P.A.

"Naturally. He is in our hands and he knows it. At least, he's coming to know it."

Lanny didn't say: "That is what I wanted to talk to Murphy about." He had long ago learned to let the other fellow talk when the other fellow was willing. Said he: "Do you think that the Admiral came to Algiers for that purpose?"

"I don't know. He is supposed to be here on account of his sick son, but it is possible for a man to have more than one motive. He must be aware that the Vichy ship is foundering. Murphy has been arguing with him until both of them are worn ragged. All this shooting is because he can't make up his mind which way the cat is going to jump."

"He has power to stop the shooting?"

"There's no question about that. All the French officers consider him their military chief. He is Pétain's deputy, and they are prepared to be told that Pétain is Hitler's prisoner and is not a free agent. Darlan's word will stop the resistance, not merely here but at Oran and Casablanca, and it might even get us Dakar and the French Fleet."

"You are indeed playing for high stakes, Mr. Pendar."

"Indeed yes," said the vice-consul. "Bob Murphy never asked for this and he wasn't trained for it; he's been dropped into the middle of a cyclone. He'll tell you he's scared stiff, but so far he's handled himself very well. He acts as if placing admirals and generals under house arrest was an everyday affair in the lives of American career diplomats."

X

In the course of this drive Lanny heard the story of what had been happening to the American diplomatic corps that night. They had been dealing with French officers whom they thought they knew, but whose conduct in the crisis appeared to be hysterical. General Juin, for example, commander of the troops in all North Africa, had promised solemnly to support the landing; but he was also under oath to the Germans not to bear arms against them; and suddenly Darlan had appeared, and a mind trained to authority was paralyzed by the fact that Darlan was his superior and a representative of the revered old Maréchal.

Moreover every French officer quailed at the thought of another commando raid; the raiders would depart in their ships and leave their friends on shore to lose, not merely their jobs, not merely their necks, but their military honor. The Americans had kept the time of their coming a secret, very unfair indeed; and who could know how many ships they had, how many men, and how serious was their purpose? No doubt they were exaggerating their forces. Pendar smiled as he admitted: "We are exaggerating them not more than three times." The bewildered Frenchmen argued and changed their minds and then changed back again, and with every hour they became more nervous. They scolded and screamed and even wept—behavior that Anglo-Saxons were supposed never to indulge in.

Soon after midnight Murphy and Pendar had gone to Juin's home, the Villa des Oliviers, in a high suburb of the city, called El-Biar. Pendar was sent to bring Admirals Darlan and Battet, who were staying at the home of Admiral Fenard. This he did, and then stayed out in the garden, keeping watch. Presently there arrived a troop of insurgents, sent by someone, Pendar didn't know whom. They posted themselves about the house and announced that nobody would be allowed to leave, save only Pendar, whom they knew. When the mighty admirals and generals made this discovery they were naturally indignant and unwilling to accept the word of Murphy and Pendar that they had no idea who had sent these gun-toters.

When the American troops did not show up, the same thing happened at this villa as in town; members of the Garde Mobile rushed into the garden and captured the insurgents. Murphy and Pendar were lined up in the porter's lodge with their hands in the air and were thoroughly searched and had their papers taken. They were rescued by Commandant d'Orange, and General Juin ordered them brought back into the villa where the debate was resumed.

Admiral Darlan had written a telegram which he wanted sent to Pétain, and Pendar was assigned to take it to the Admiralty. Members of the Garde Mobile escorted him there, and on the way he made the extraordinary discovery that the guards had been told that it was Germans who had surrounded the villa and Germans who were attacking Algiers. At the Admiralty another admiral, Leclerc, refused to believe that the signature was Darlan's, so Pendar was a prisoner again while Leclerc sent to the Villa des Oliviers to make sure.

The Admiralty is down near the harbor, so the young gentleman out of Harvard spent the next hour and a half listening to guns being fired at the British commando ship. When he was released, he drove away in Murphy's car, and he was arrested again by the Garde Mobile who were defending their city—against the Germans! This time he landed in the barracks of the Fifth Regiment of the Chasseurs d'Afrique. There he sat and drank coffee while tanks rumbled by and ack-ack banged in the vicinity; when his story had been verified they gave him a pass and he went back to Murphy, who was still arguing with the admirals and generals at Juin's villa.

Such a night had never been known in Cambridge, Massachusetts, even after a football victory. The Harvard art lover was sent out again, this time to find Admiral Battet, who had got himself arrested again by the underground. Pendar was taken to Fort l'Empereur, General Juin's headquarters, to get a really valid pass, and there he had the strange experience of sitting and listening to French generals and colonels getting telephone reports of the fighting in the west. This had been only a short while ago, and was the latest news that anybody had. The French were having a hard time on the outskirts of Oran, but in the town itself all was going well. The Americans had been driven off at Safi beach, near Casablanca, but were attacking violently at Port Lyautey near by, and at the city itself. Pendar said to Lanny: "H-hour at Casablanca wasn't until four A.M., and it was a blunder to release the President's radio talk before that time. We gave them notice!"

XI

There was no finding Admiral Battet, and Pendar mentioned to his guest that the officers at Fort l'Empereur had urged him to find the American commander so that an armistice could be arranged. Again he said: "Would you like to go along?" And Lanny replied that he couldn't think of anything that would please him more. They drove to the Villa Sinetti, where the Americans had their secret radio sender. Here Pendar was told that the commanding general of the American forces was at the little harbor of Cheragas. They drove by an inconspicuous back road and came out to the sea to confront a marvelous sight—hundreds of gray-painted vessels of all sizes, and the roads filled with marching men, jeeps and trucks and light tanks, all eastward bound. Here Lanny had his first glimpse of those new landing craft about which he had heard whispers; they were like great scows, with high walls, and in front was a sort of drawbridge which was let down with chains when the craft had been grounded, making a ramp on which all kinds of heavy vehicles could roll down. Lanny asked: "How do they get the craft off the shore?" and the other told him that they had heavy anchors which they dropped when nearing the shore, and that winches wound up the anchor chains and pulled the craft back.

The American commander had his headquarters under a tree by the road, on what must have seemed to him an especially delightful Sunday morning. Ryder was his name, and he was unusually tall, and thin as if he had been drawn out in the process. Lanny sat in the car. He could see General Mast there, one Frenchman who had gone over to the Allies without any hesitation; "Flagpole" was his code name and he was thin but not tall. Lanny observed also a British Army captain, and was told later that it was Winston Churchill's son. General Ryder gave Pendar two sets of terms for the surrender of Algiers, one easy if they quit at once, and the other tough if they delayed.

The vice-consul drove back to town with his guest, and just before they got to Juin's villa they met Murphy, setting out to find General Ryder himself. They all drove to Fort l'Empereur, where the ceremony of surrender took place. It was, as Pendar remarked, "wonderfully French, like a historical painting in some museum." Six French soldiers lined up in arrow shape, and in front of them stood Commandant d'Orange, extending his sword by the point and letting General Ryder take the hilt. The Commandant announced that with the sword he surrendered Fort l'Empereur and the city of Algiers to the American General. The cease-fire signal was sounded by the French with trumpets. The French officers were sad because they had been defeated, but they were happy because their honor had been preserved.

It had been a confusing day; but now people knew what it was permitted to feel and do and say. The word spread quickly that Algiers was in the hands of the American soldiers, and by nightfall the crowds turned out to welcome them. No more shooting, no more black looks —save from persons whose premises were commandeered for army purposes. Lanny went back to the St. George and released Denis from his imprisonment. They both had a bath and a shave, and then went out to see the mad excitement in the streets. Lanny, who looked like an American, had a hard time getting along; so many persons, male and female, wanted to welcome him and tell him that he was a deliverer and that they had known all along that he would come.

XII

Just after the ceremony of surrender Lanny had a few moments with the Counselor and said: "I think I told you that I know Darlan, and I wondered if it might not be a good thing for me to talk with him." Murphy exclaimed: "Oh, *would you?*" Evidently this overworked man was glad to have someone to share even a small portion of the responsibility.

Lanny continued: "It might be better if I sought the appointment myself, so that it will be a social matter and not official."

"Fine!" agreed the other. "You know where Juin's villa is?" When Lanny said that he could find it, the other added: "Keep clear of Madame Juin if you can. She is an Algerian heiress, very set in her opinions—and they are not ours."

"Don't worry," smiled Lanny. "I was once married to an heiress, and I know how they behave."

So, fairly early on Monday morning, Lanny tried to telephone, and discovered that the line to the villa was continuously "busy." He went out and tried to find a taxi, but in vain, so he enjoyed the pleasure of a walk in weather which had a touch of chill. He was in the midst of fine scenery, and there was one aspect he observed with special pleasure—a line of gray-painted ships of many kinds and sizes filing past the breakwater into the crowded harbor of Algiers.

He came to the Villa des Oliviers, an estate of magnificence suited to an Algerian heiress. At the elaborate iron gates he addressed himself with his best society manner to a *sous-officier* in the Garde Mobile, saying that he was a friend of Admiral Darlan and would be pleased to have his name sent to that august person. Members of the privileged classes have their clothing cut and pressed in exactly the proper way so as to indicate that they have a right to have their names submitted to admirals. The officer answered: "*Bien, Monsieur,*" and went into the porter's lodge, presumably to telephone. Lanny reflected that this was the building in which, some twenty-four hours ago, Murphy and Pendar had been stood against the mantelpiece with their hands in the air.

The officer came out, a member of the guard opened the gates, and Lanny walked up the drive. Ordinarily it would have been bad form to approach such a place on foot, but now even the rich sometimes had to walk—you couldn't come up into these hills on a bicycle. A servant escorted M. Budd upstairs to the great man's bedroom; he had apparently just finished shaving, and was buttoning up his shirt. Lanny saw that he was pale and had dark rings under his eyes; no man plays the rude game of power politics without paying a price.

He greeted his visitor cordially, and Lanny explained that he had developed an interest in Algerian mosaics and fountains for ablutions and had been caught here by an astonishing series of military events. The commander of all the military forces of Unoccupied France took up this lead and plunged into the subject of how completely astounded *he* had been by the rude and unceremonious intrusion of the American armies. Lanny listened to all that the astounded gentleman had to say, now and then nodding and putting in a sympathetic murmur. Yes, it

was most distressing, and so different from what the French had a right
to expect in view of a century and three-quarters of unbroken friendship between the two countries.

There came a time when the stocky man of affairs had said his say;
then Lanny began: "*Voyez, mon Amiral!* You know that I am a lover
of art, and no politician, and I have no control over the movements of
armies. When I heard this distressing news, I thought at once of you,
and the problems that would confront you. Since I am an American,
you can hardly consider me a disinterested observer; but truly I am
that. I have no thought but of friendship between our countries, and
the preservation of our social order, which seems to me in grave peril."

"*Vraiment, Monsieur Budd;* but it is your country and not mine
which is in alliance with the Red terrorists and is supplying them with
arms."

"So it seems, *mon Amiral;* but it is necessary to take the long view.
You must know that America is the strongest bulwark of the private
enterprise system, and offers the best hope of holding down the Reds
when this hurricane has blown over."

"You feel so sure of that, Monsieur Budd?"

"It is my firm conclusion. The changes which the so-called New
Deal is making are purely superficial; they are small concessions made
to keep the masses contented. Basically the system in which we both
believe stands unimpaired. You will have an opportunity to observe
that where the American armies come, no property rights are inter-
fered with, and everything that is commandeered is liberally paid for.
I have heard those policies stated to my father by some of our highest
officers, and you may be sure that my father is not supporting a program without knowing its ultimate purposes."

That was the sort of reassurance a French authoritarian would
value, and when Lanny perceived that his bait was being taken he
went on to sing the praises of America as the classic land of big business, where every worker had been persuaded that he was soon to become a capitalist, or that, at the least, his children would. American
armies were disciplined, and American officers knew gentlemen when
they met them. It seemed to the son of Budd-Erling that all believers
in law and order ought to welcome such an army, and that Admiral
Darlan owed it not merely to himself, but to his class, to his friends,
and to the best interests of the traditional France, to realize that the
Americans came as conservators of the established order. The Catholic
Church throve mightily in America, growing rich both in numbers and
possessions; French industry, producing mostly luxury goods, found

its best market in America; the two countries had no rivalries, no memories of ancient antagonisms. And so on and on.

XIII

Shrewd as Darlan was, he must have known that this was no mere social call. But what Lanny told him was what he wanted very much to hear just now. It was a fact that he was in Algiers, not in Vichy or anywhere else; he had to deal with what he found here, and it was obvious that if he stood out against the Americans and they stayed on, he would become one of those pitiful refugees of which Europe was full, frustrated and helpless people without property or functions. On the other hand, if he could make a satisfactory deal with them—!

The son of a great airplane manufacturer was in a position to tell him that the Americans were here in force and meant to win this war. "I have seen the preparations at home with my own eyes, *mon Amiral*. I was not told where the forces were coming, but I know that they are being brought into existence, on a scale never equaled in this world. What you see here is just a beginning."

Events timed themselves conveniently to support these arguments. There came the sound of heavy firing from the sky, and the pair went out to the balcony to see what was happening. A notable war game was playing itself out. At the hour which under the American system was described as H-plus 3 or thereabouts, American commando teams had rushed to the great Maison Blanche airport and seized it and cleared the field. With a matter of only a few minutes to spare there had appeared a fleet of British and American fighter planes, coming from Gibraltar, having fuel enough for a one-way flight, but not for a return. The field had to be ready for them, and it was. For thirty hours thereafter the pilots had been on tiptoe, waiting for the enemy to make a try.

Now, at H-plus 33, the Junkers and other bombers made their appearance, coming presumably from Sicily. They could have no idea that pursuit planes were already at Algiers, and, warned by the wonderful new radar, would be waiting high up in the "wild blue yonder." The Americans came diving down, and there occurred one of those battles which Lanny had watched over London, but which the Admiral had perhaps never had a chance to see. Lanny had the satisfaction of counting, one after another, eighteen German bombers tumbling out of the sky in flames; and he was in a position to remark casually: "I don't know whether you are familiar with the Budd-Erling plane, *mon Amiral.* I should say that about one in four of those fighters is from my father's plant. The rest are Spitfires and a few Hurricanes."

Coming out from that villa, Lanny had the good fortune to encounter Robert Murphy on his way in. "Be tough with him," Lanny whispered. "Demand what you want. You have all the high cards."

XIV

The P.A. went back to his hotel, and there discovered that he had troubles of a private nature. The Army had commandeered the old St. George Hotel! It was to become the headquarters of important officers, and Lanny could guess who they were. He went hunting a room, and it wasn't easy to find because the city was so crowded with refugees. Finally he had to appeal to Denis, who undertook to find some officer family which could crowd itself together and make room for a paying guest. Lanny had to insist that it must be a non-political family, for he knew that Algiers, suddenly liberated from the Nazi yoke, was seething with every sort of intrigue, some of it violent and dangerous. Already Denis's friends D'Astier de la Vigerie and the Abbé Cordier were busy arranging for the coming of the Count of Paris from Spanish Morocco, and were printing secret literature in his behalf. Lanny didn't want to be in any household where that was going on.

That afternoon General Mark Clark and his staff arrived by plane from Gibraltar—right in the midst of another air battle over Maison Blanche. They went to those rooms which Lanny and other guests of the St. George had vacated, and there began the final duel of wits with Admiral Darlan and his military staff. The Americans at this time had only about thirty-five hundred men ashore, with a few guns and small tanks; but Clark had to talk big and look big. The latter was easy, as Lanny knew, having seen him in the twilight at Cherchell; six-feet three, lanky and rawboned, with an unusually prominent nose that gave him a hawklike appearance. He could be very emphatic when he had to be, and this was one of the times.

Murphy told Lanny about it afterward. The General's demand was that all fighting should cease throughout all North Africa. Darlan, of course, wanted to wait and see how the fight was going, so he would do nothing but stall; he had sent cablegrams to Pétain, and insisted that he could not act without Pétain's authority. They met a second time next morning, and then Clark cut short the debate by telling Darlan that Pétain had that day broken relations with the United States and had declared the landing a hostile act. "You're the man in authority," said Clark, and gave him half an hour to decide. When he couldn't make up his mind, Clark ordered his arrest; but General Juin, sitting beside Clark, laid his hand, maimed in war against the Germans, on Clark's arm. "Five minutes, please," he pleaded. Clark said: "O.K., five minutes."

He gave them eight minutes, during which he and his staff could hear the hysterical arguments going on in the next room. Then Admiral Fenard, a champion quick-change artist, rushed out with the news that Darlan had given way. Clark re-entered the room, and watched while Darlan wrote with a trembling hand the order that all French forces were to cease combat. "I take authority over North Africa in the name of the Marshal," he wrote. "Present military leaders will retain their command, and the political and administrative structure will remain intact. No changes will take place until new orders from me. Prisoners on each side will be exchanged."

That ought to have ended it, and for a while everybody thought that it had. Darlan made a radio address that afternoon, telling all French North Africa what he had done. But next day came the news that the revered old Marshal had repudiated both Darlan and the armistice, and had put General Noguès at Morocco in command, with orders to the troops to fight to the death. That bowled the Admiral over, and he wanted to revoke his previous orders. Clark thereupon placed him under arrest; but the French still wouldn't obey anybody but Darlan, and there was a pretty mess.

The only person who could solve that problem, it appeared, was Adolf Hitler; he broadcast an announcement that the German armies were occupying all southern France; and with this as a club, the American commander started beating Darlan once more. They argued back and forth for two days and nights, with Clark threatening to set up a military government and treat North Africa as conquered territory. Reinforcements were coming in, and the French could see them. In the end the matter was settled by General Noguès' being flown from Morocco and formally handing back his authority to Darlan. Then they all embraced and kissed one another on both cheeks, and at last were ready to welcome *les Américains bien aimés* and join with them in making war upon *les Boches maudits*.

17

Honey from the Weed

I

LANNY BUDD had had a vision of swarms of brown-clad men moving eastward over the roads of North Africa, and now that vision had become reality in a most satisfactory way. New convoys of transports came crowding into the ports; the men poured out of them, and stopped only long enough to get their equipment, and then were loaded into jeeps and trucks and started on their way. Always east, a river of men, a flood spreading over the landscape! The British took a small port called Bougie, a hundred miles or so beyond Algiers—far enough away to spare the feelings of the French officials. From there they moved to the larger port called Bône, still farther eastward. They put their own small army ashore and set out for Tunis, another hundred and fifty miles along the coast.

The Americans moved by the inland routes. All those youngsters who had bivouacked in the parks and had roamed about staring at Moors clad in ragged white robes and at women invisible except for a pair of mysterious dark eyes—those boys had only a day or two for sightseeing, and then they were started toward Tunisia. They had the lame railroads and all the facilities, for, once the French had signed the armistice, they cast in their lot with the Americans, and there was nothing to be done but to go after the Germans.

A heavy load off the minds of the American officers, to have this vast country and all its administrative machinery on their side; to know that they were among friends, and that there would be no sabotage and no underground resistance. The entire land, a shelf between high mountains and the sea, was furrowed by a cross-hatching of gullies, called *wadis*, and this meant that every road was a series of bridges. The destruction of any of them might have delayed the advance, and to protect them would have required an army; but the French took care of them all, and the Americans raced over them; the French, too, as quickly as they could be equipped.

That was, to Lanny, the most interesting result of the deal with Darlan: the rank and file of the French Army and the sailors of the Navy got a chance to fight the Germans, and it turned out to be what they had all been waiting for. Under the armistice with the Germans, the French had been limited to a hundred thousand troops in North Africa; but they had managed to evade this limit, and they had hidden considerable quantities of munitions. Now all this came out of hiding, and with the promise of American supplies, a draft was ordered and the various populations of the territory accepted it willingly.

The streets of Algiers in these days looked like the stage setting of a comic opera. In addition to the regular Army, there were Spahis in long red cloaks riding white horses; Goums in their brown *galabiehs;* the Chantiers in their short green trousers; the Foreign Legion wearing pantaloons and cloaks, and various kinds of kepis and berets; and many sorts of native battalions. There were French sailors in blue uniforms and little round blue caps with red pompons, British sailors in blue and gold and white, and all the different British and American Army uniforms. The streets, which had been so bare of traffic that the crowds walked in them instead of on the sidewalks, were now so crowded with vehicles that it was difficult to get across.

II

The intriguing and wire-pulling among the politicians continued, and it was a P.A.'s duty to linger on the scene, repugnant as he found it. Who among the French had burned their bridges behind them, and who were still trying to keep a way of retreat back to Vichy? It seemed to Lanny that Algiers was the most depraved city he had ever dwelt in: its rich the most greedy and reactionary, its governing group the most treacherous and corrupt. It was as if the scum of Paris had been swept off to Vichy, and then the scum of Vichy swept off to North Africa. There was no faith or honor, save among the fighting troops; among the politicians there were jealousy and greed, childish vanity, raging spite, murder barely repressed.

With this the Americans had to deal as best they could; they had to get what they needed, first by bluffing, and later, when they really had the power, by threats to use it. They tried to get Tunis, and hounded Darlan until he ordered the French general in command there to resist the entrance of the Germans; but Vichy sent an agent to persuade him otherwise, and the agent had a good argument, for the Germans were just across the narrow sea in Sicily, some eighty miles, while the Americans were several hundred miles away.

Then there was Dakar. The governor-general there was Pierre Boisson, a staunch Vichyite who had resisted De Gaulle's ill-starred expedition and driven it off. Now, receiving Darlan's order, Boisson sent a delegation of three officers to investigate the situation at the capital. Later he came himself and talked with Darlan and then with Clark. After long negotiations he decided to come over to the Allies. It was a tremendous gain, for Dakar was a great naval base, as well as an airport from which to hunt submarines trying to blockade the British lines to South Africa and the Near East; also there were three French cruisers, three destroyers, and thirteen submarines, plus the great battleship *Richelieu*, damaged but capable of being quickly repaired.

Most important of all was the main Fleet at Toulon. The Americans wanted it to sail and join them, but they couldn't persuade Darlan to order that move; instead he "suggested" it. Hitler had sent his troops down to the French Riviera, but solemnly promised not to enter Toulon. Of course the whole world knew by now what Hitler's word was worth, and the Allies waited in suspense to learn whether the French naval men were going to believe him, or pretend to believe him and let him get that Fleet.

Several days after D-day Lanny had received a postcard from Toulon, signed Bruges. It had been sent to Bienvenu and forwarded from there. "I am glad to hear that you have found some good art works. Congratulations. I am looking for the paintings you want and feel sure I can find them." Lanny didn't need any codebook to understand that Raoul was referring to the invasion, and was telling him that the Fleet would be saved. A couple of days later the German Army arrived, and Lanny would get no more news by that route.

He wasn't sure whether mails would still come through from Switzerland. A week or so previously he had got a card from Brun—cards were safer because they tended to disarm the censor. This one said that Brun had not heard from him, but had made some new friends and was doing very well in a business way. The "friends," of course meant the O.S.S., and the message told Lanny that Monck had nothing special for him at present; otherwise he would have said: "I have a painting for you."

III

Lanny asked Robert Murphy what damage had been done to the convoys by enemy submarines, a subject that was never reported or publicly discussed. The Counselor replied that the losses had been trifling. "Your little scheme evidently worked," he said, and this pleased Lanny, needless to say. He wrote the words to Jerry Pendleton, and added: "I expect to have some news for you soon."

Lanny told Murphy about this one-time tutor and long-time friend. Jerry had a black mark against him in the records of the United States Army. He had been a lieutenant in World War I, and had fought all the way through the Argonne; but during the long-drawn-out Peace Conference he had become disgusted with hanging round in barracks and had gone off to the Riviera and married his French girl and her mother and her aunt and her *pension* full of boarders. Thousands of men had quit the Army thus unceremoniously, and the Army had decided to forget them. Lanny thought that what Jerry had done entitled him to another chance, and Murphy agreed. He knew the right officer to speak to, and so, when Lanny saw his friend again, he was in the employ of Army Intelligence, helping to keep track of the enemy spies who swarmed across the border from Spanish Morocco.

Another person who received his reward was Denis de Bruyne. What he wanted was liberty to sing out loud the praises of General Charles de Gaulle, and this liberty, under the protection of the American Army, he proceeded to take. Over in London this six-and-a-half-foot Jeanne d'Arc in striped trousers was using British liberty to denounce the Allied occupation and to dissociate himself explicitly and completely from it. Then he proceeded to send several agents to Algiers, well provided with funds, who began a propaganda to the effect that De Gaulle was the first and only choice of the French people to protect the glory and honor of *la patrie*.

At the same time Denis's friends, D'Astier de la Vigerie and the Abbé Cordier, also well provided with funds, took up the cause of *their* favorite, the Comte de Paris, darling of the Royalists. He had been raising pigs in Spanish Morocco, but now he moved into French territory and began raising ructions. His followers were getting ready a coup—that ended in the murder of Darlan. One of their steps was to have printed a quantity of manifestos and newspapers explaining their reasons for the murder and setting forth the claims of their pig raiser.

One day Lanny read in the *Dépêche Algérienne* of the death of Eugène Schneider in Paris. Seventy-two years he had lived, carrying on the tradition of his father and grandfather, and had made himself the successor to Zaharoff as the "munitions king of Europe." He had lived just long enough to confront the calamities that his policies had brought to his country and to the whole of Europe. To Lanny it was one more of those "sad stories of the death of kings." He had seen this cultivated and agreeable French monarch in his home, and knew that he was one of those many who had adopted the motto "Better Hitler than Blum." He had got his Hitler, and Lanny could guess that he had died of humiliation.

IV

Lanny was of the opinion that he, the son of Budd-Erling, had witnessed a decidedly precarious military adventure, and that it had met with extraordinary success. Newspapers from America were slow in arriving, but from a chance meeting with Pendar he learned that there had arisen at home a storm of criticism of the deal with Darlan, which was considered a betrayal of all the war aims we had put forward in the Atlantic Charter and elsewhere. Darlan was a Fascist and Vichy tool or worse, and now we had put him at the head of the first government we set up in the course of our military advance. What would that mean to all the peoples of Europe who were expecting our arrival?

Lanny, who had helped to make the deal, was inclined to brush off the complaints, saying that the critics hadn't been on the ground and couldn't know the circumstances. But he learned that the storm was continuing to increase, and that Murphy was greatly troubled by it; General Eisenhower, who had come to Algiers, and who wanted to devote all his attention to the race for Tunis, had to divert his mind to answering questions from the State Department and objections from the swarm of newspaper correspondents who had come with the Army.

There were even people who thought that we should have brought De Gaulle in with us, and put him at the head of the French Army and government. To Lanny it was obvious that this would have meant upsetting the entire administrative machinery of the territory, and would have required a war with the French, who considered De Gaulle a British stooge and would have fought him to the death. We might have spent six months fighting the French instead of the Germans, and we might have needed a hundred thousand men to hold the territory.

Lanny read articles in which it was maintained that no fighting had been stopped by the "Darlan deal." He knew that at the moment the armistice was signed, our fleet was about to start a bombardment of Casablanca, which would certainly have wrecked that port and delayed our progress there for weeks. As a result of the deal we got Dakar intact with all its installations, including nineteen vessels of war ready for action, and great airfields which provided the shortest route for our planes flying from America to North Africa. Furthermore we got the loyal services of a French Army, which was to suffer heavy casualties before the fighting in North Africa was over.

V

But there were two sides to this question, as to most others, and as the days passed Lanny was forced to see the other side. Just as one could not touch pitch without being defiled, so one could not deal with Vichyites without giving aid to reaction. Darlan and his crowd were helping the American Army, but they were also helping to keep themselves in power, and they were using the chance to punish their political enemies. Some of those fellows who had been too eager to help the Americans ashore, and the ten thousand political prisoners who were in concentration camps, under truly infamous conditions—these people were going to stay where they were because they were dangerous to Darlan and his crowd. Many were fighters from the Spanish civil war; they had come into France to escape the Franco murderers, and the French reactionaries had thrown them into jail and now were afraid to turn them loose. Also, they were afraid to repeal the laws which the Nazis had forced them to pass against the Jews; by two years of propaganda they had made the people of North Africa fear the Jews, and it would be unpopular to tell them to stop fearing the Jews!

Lanny went to call on the aged Professor of Medicine who had done so much to assist the American landing. He discovered that this lame Jew, and all his friends who had helped in a war for freedom and democracy, had now discovered that the victors had no use for them. On the hatrack in the hallway of the Aboulker apartment there hung a black homburg hat of the latest design and most elegant make. "We are keeping it as a souvenir," explained one of the family. "That is Mr. Murphy's hat. He wore it the night of the landing when he came and told us how to risk our lives for the cause of freedom and democracy. In the excitement he went off without it. When somebody told him about it he said that he would get it the next time he came. But there has never been any next time. Three weeks have passed and he has not been near us."

Lanny had to exercise tact and caution in dealing with that situation. He was posing as a friend of the reactionaries, and could not afford to appear tinged with any trace of Pink. But when he took his next report to Murphy, and heard Murphy's complaints about the "raspberry" he was getting from home, Lanny ventured several mild suggestions as to how the violence of the storm might be reduced. Americans who didn't understand the situation here would naturally expect the anti-Jewish laws to be promptly repealed and the political prisoners to be released. Might it not be good tactics to advise Darlan to take these steps, regardless of his own wishes?

In reply Lanny listened to a long explanation about the difference between America and Africa, and the special dangers of wartime. The public at home had been given very little idea of the hard fighting that had gone on here; they didn't realize the vital importance of the race for Tunis, and the fact that the Germans were bombing our airports every night, and that it was the rainy season, and that on the way to Tunis we had only dirt airfields that were turned into mudholes, while the enemy had hard-surfaced fields at Tunis and Bizerte and in Sicily. Surely this was no time for us to be meddling in the political squabbles of the French, and perhaps inciting anti-Jewish riots, and turning loose a lot of Communists and Anarchists to make trouble for the French authorities who were co-operating with us so amicably.

President Roosevelt, back in Washington, had trimmed his sails to the blast of protest. He had issued a statement to the effect that our agreement with Darlan was "a temporary expedient, justified solely by the stress of battle." This, naturally, upset Darlan, and caused him to protest: "I see they are going to treat me like a lemon, to be squeezed and then thrown away." Murphy had had a hard time pacifying him and didn't want any more of it. He had to be careful in hinting a criticism of the head of his own government, but he made it plain to Lanny that he thought this was a bad time to be trying to apply the New Deal in Africa, and that he hoped Lanny would support the Army's policy of leaving French politics *in statu quo* until after the German Army had been licked.

VI

The struggle over the French Fleet was settled when the Germans tried to rush Toulon, and the French scuttled the ships, in many cases standing on guard while the ships filled and sank. A few smaller vessels got away to the Allies, but all the large ones went down. This was a tragedy to those who were thinking about the future of France, but it was all right with the Allies because it made certain that the vessels would not be used by the Germans. To raise them would take a year, and then their machinery would be found damaged by salt water and their elaborate electrical installations completely ruined. Lanny wondered what had happened to Raoul Palma and his little group of friends, but there was no way to find out at present. One thing was certain: they had done their job.

In the midst of these events arrived a cablegram for Lanny, several days delayed. It was from Robbie, informing him that he had an eight-pound son, and that both mother and child were well; Esther was with Laurel in New York. This excited Lanny so that he had to do something to celebrate, and after sending a message of love and devotion to his wife he invited Denis to a dinner in the fashionable Restaurant de Paris. They did their best to be cheerful, but Denis had to wipe the tears out of his eyes once or twice. Lanny knew that he was thinking about his own wife and little ones, whom he had not seen for more than two years, since he had fled the Château de Bruyne where he had been recovering from his war wounds. Under the pressure of defeat and suffering this *capitaine* had become reserved and rather severe in manner, but underneath he was still the tenderhearted boy whom Lanny had loved; he had a Frenchman's devotion to family, and being separated from them all, and politically estranged from his father and brother, was pain from which he was never free.

This news from home brought Lanny to a decision that it was time to return. He had been told to come every two or three months, and he had stayed four because of the pressure of events. Now it was time to make a personal report to his Boss, and say things that he was not free to say to Robert Murphy. He paid off the faithful Hajek and said good-by to his friends and took the train to Casablanca. From there he cabled Robbie, according to their arrangement, and while waiting for the reply he had a sit-down with Jerry Pendleton and heard the story of days and nights as full of events as those which Lanny had spent in Algiers.

Things hadn't been so easy in Morocco, for the stubborn General Noguès had stood out against the Americans, and General Béthouart in Rabat had been unable to accomplish anything except to get himself in jail, where he still was. An amazing thing, the Americans who were so brave in battle seemed to be paralyzed when it came to any political struggle, and they didn't have the courage to stand by their friends. This from a travel-bureau agent who was not at all a political person. Lanny said it was too bad; he didn't attempt to explain it, but made a mental note that Béthouart would be one of the subjects he would surely bring up to F.D.R. The P.A. had become quite fond of the amiable French officer with the round face and prominent eyes and small mustache; he held more liberal views than most career soldiers.

The "iron coast" of Morocco was extremely unfavorable to landing parties. There were few beaches, great numbers of treacherous rocks, and ocean swells high beyond belief; the invaders had had to be prepared to lose many of their fine new landing craft, and also many of their fine young men. The only air cover was from carriers, vulnerable to submarines; and the troops defending the shore were natives who enjoyed fighting, and did not have ideas, like, the French troops at Oran and Algiers. General Mast and the other officers at Cherchell had given their opinion that Casablanca could not be taken from the sea, and the Americans had assigned to the job their toughest fighting man, "Old Blood and Guts" Patton, who carried two pearl-handled revolvers and exploded into an oath with every other sentence. He gave his troops a directive: "We shall attack and attack, and when we are exhausted we shall attack again."

Three landing places had been chosen: the shore at a town called Safi, some distance south of Casablanca; the beach at Fedala, a resort known as the "African Riviera," immediately above Casablanca; and Port Lyautey, a harbor on a river close to the border of Spanish Morocco. At Safi two of those old four-stacker destroyers were sacrificed; one of them rushed the beach, loaded with troops, and these troops got ashore and proceeded to clean out the town. The other landed at the pier and took possession of the loading facilities; other troops could then come ashore, and they started a march to Casablanca, resisted fiercely all the way. At Fedala the first wave got ashore in the darkness, but then enemy searchlights were turned on and enemy batteries opened fire; these were manned by French marines, and they fought off all land attacks until their batteries were knocked out by the ships. At Port Lyautey fast launches dashed in, defying heavy machine-gun fire, and cut the net which blocked the river; a destroyer then brought in raiders, and they seized the airport, making it possible for planes from the carriers to land, and more planes to come quickly from Gibraltar.

But the heaviest fighting was at Casablanca, where Jerry had witnessed it. He and the other agents had a secret radio sender and had been in communication with the ships before H-hour, reporting damage to the enemy and movements of enemy troops. A dangerous job, but they had many French helpers; the most efficient had been those of the left wing, and Jerry Pendleton, a conventional American businessman, said: "Damn them, I don't like them, but they know what they want and they work like the devil."

There had been two light cruisers in the harbor and several destroyers. These had sallied out to meet the invaders—everybody had warned the Americans that the Navy would fight. The French vessels were knocked out and beached. Also there was an almost completed battleship, the *Jean Bart*, and its heavy guns went on firing even after it had been hit ten times by sixteen-inch shells and airplane bombs. That went on for two days and nights, and by that time Algiers and Oran had surrendered, and Old Blood and Guts was the only one behind schedule.

A bombardment of Casablanca was ordered for seven o'clock on the morning of the 11th—which was Armistice Day of World War I. The agents were ordered to get out, and Jerry and Faulkner took their overcoats and blankets and went back into the hills—it was bitterly cold everywhere in North Africa at night. They hid out and in the morning they stood on a height and waited for the firing to begin. But it didn't, and when they saw the American ships coming into the harbor, they knew that the town must have surrendered. They went down and saw the crowds welcoming the landing parties with wild cheering. This was the phenomenon which so greatly puzzled the G.I.'s; first they were killed and then they were cheered. The G.I.'s had been well trained in shooting, but nobody had troubled to explain to them the class struggle which existed in France; how the great mass of the people wanted peace and bread, while the higher officers of Army and Navy wanted *la gloire* and *l'honneur*.

VII

Vice-Consul Pendar had come to Casablanca, and Lanny met him there and heard a frank account of what was going on behind the scenes in this center of gossip and intrigue. The consequences of the deal with the Darlan-Noguès outfit were the same here as in Algiers; perhaps even a little worse, because of General Patton, himself a reactionary martinet. The deal had saved many American lives, but it imperiled American principles and exposed American officers to temptations against which they had no weapons. Pendar said that he had talked with many of them soon after the invasion and found that they saw the Vichy crowd in their true colors; but after a dinner at the Residency, where they were received with a fanfare of Moroccan trumpets and given a welcoming escort of Spahi guards, they would come away dazzled and with a different point of view about Noguès.

Pendar told an amusing story about the American commander. The vice-consul had been sent to find out what had happened to a letter that President Roosevelt had written to the Sultan of Morocco, telling him the purposes of the Americans in coming to that country and saluting him as the head of a friendly state. This letter was supposed to have been delivered by General Noguès to the Sultan on D-day, but of course Noguès hadn't delivered it; Pendar had a copy and took it to General Patton, who had set up his headquarters in the very sumptuous offices of the Shell Oil Company. Patton took the letter and read it, said he didn't like it, and proceeded to make alterations.

After he had finished he read the letter aloud and asked if he hadn't improved it. Pendar, a petty civilian official in the presence of a bloodthirsty warrior, muttered something about not being sure that anybody had a right to revise a letter of the President without his knowledge. Whereupon the General banged his desk and exclaimed: "God damn it, I'll take full responsibility for the letter." To this Pendar replied: "Very well, sir, I shall tell Mr. Murphy when I telephone him tonight." The old warrior glowered and shouted in his strange high-pitched voice: "God damn it, I won't have you or any other God-damned fool talking about this letter over the telephone. Don't you know the wires are tapped?" The vice-consul replied: "Yes, sir, they've been tapped for a year and a half."

"The old boy's curses are not to be taken personally," explained Pendar. "We had a talk about conditions here, and I told him about the situation of General Béthouart and the other French officers who had failed in their efforts to help us. Noguès was actually proposing to ship them to Algiers by airplane to be tried for treason and was only deterred from it by the protest of French patriots. Patton's answer to me was: 'General Noguès and I have a perfect understanding, and I have left all these problems of personnel up to him. Morocco is an extremely difficult country to manage.' And then he started talking about the Jewish problem. You see how it stands—Noguès has used one of the Fascists' favorite devices to distract Patton's attention from the fate of our brave friends."

Lanny said very mildly: "I suppose the General has his mind centered on getting his troops off to Tunis."

VIII

Lanny received his instructions about returning; he was to be flown back in an Army transport plane from Marrakech. Specialists of many sorts were being rushed to North Africa by this route, and the planes carried lightly wounded men back. Marrakech had been chosen as the landing place because of its almost perpetual sunshine, and a thousand-year-old oasis had suddenly become the busiest air center in this part of the world. When Lanny told Pendar that he was to fly from there in three days, the vice-consul offered to drive him; he had business in the town. They drove southward, through rolling country covered with broom sage, and looking very much like southern California desert.

On this drive Lanny absorbed a mass of information about an ancient land, so suddenly and startlingly brought into the spotlight of history. He had never told Pendar that he was reporting directly to the President, but it must have been evident to the alert young Harvard man that his fellow traveler was fulfilling some important function. Civilians didn't fly back home in Army planes unless that was the case, and Pendar had a lot of things on his mind that he thought needed to be known in Washington. He wasn't a regular State Department career man and therefore was free to think for himself and to judge his superiors as if he had been their equal.

In Marrakech this vice-consul dwelt in a splendor which impressed both French and natives. It happened that a wealthy widow who had moved to America had let him have the use of the most elaborate and most famous villa in the province. Lanny was invited to this home, and didn't have to waste his time hunting hotel accommodations in a small city which had suddenly become one of the world's great traffic centers.

The villa La Saadia was soon to have the spotlight of history turned upon it; but Lanny Budd, not being psychic, had no intimation of that fact. The villa was built in imitation of an ancient South Moroccan *casbah,* or castle, with pinkish walls of great thickness; one story high, it had a tower of six stories from which there was a marvelous view of the town and its environs, with a background of the snowy Atlas range. There was a high wall about the estate, and two inner court-yards with orange trees, geraniums, and bougainvillaea around black marble fountains which an art expert might have been glad to buy. Everything was indirectly lighted by electricity, giving an undersea effect. The grounds spread out in gardens full of flowers, with rivulets running through them and a large pool with many strange fishes. An immense terrace led down to the pool, and the vice-consul, telling Lanny about it, said: "You will think you are in the Arabian Nights."

The son of Budd-Erling had seen many kinds of showplaces, on Long Island and in California, in England and France and Germany, and he knew that there is a ritual to be gone through in all cases. The host or hostess will take you about, or perhaps assign the steward or some friend of the family to this duty. You will gaze and do your best to express admiration—new words are not necessary, all possible words having been heard before. Unless the owner is a vulgar person, he will never mention what anything has cost; but sooner or later some fellow guest will whisper it to you with awe in his voice, and you will reply in the same spirit. Never by chance will you say anything about there being starvation outside the gates; and if the owner takes you to the Episcopal Church or the Catholic, you will not quote what you hear about laying up for yourselves treasures on earth, or about how "the Lord hath put down the mighty from their seats and exalted them of low degree. He hath filled the hungry with good things; and the rich he hath sent empty away."

> 'Tis well that such seditious songs are sung
> Only by priests, and in the Latin tongue!

IX

Lanny went promptly to see his family at the Hotel Mamounia, and found them well and contented with their fate. Beauty wouldn't have been Beauty if her first words hadn't dealt with the telegram Lanny had sent her, announcing that she was a grandmother for the third time. She wanted more information, but Lanny hadn't any. He told her that he was going home, and she made him swear to write her all those details with which men seldom care to bother: the color of the baby's hair if he had any, and which of his parents or grandparents he most "favored." Laurel had stood far down on the list of Beauty's choices for a daughter-in-law, but now that Lanny had made the choice Beauty wanted it to stick, and no nonsense about it. The arrival of a son would be a bond, and Lanny assured her that he felt all the proper thrills, and there surely wasn't going to be any "nonsense."

In the matter of the move from Bienvenu, Beauty understood now a lot of things about which she had been guessing hitherto. "You were wise," she declared; "we are in exactly the right place." It was a certainty that if they had remained in Juan, they would now be in a German internment camp, and on a very restricted diet; whereas here they enjoyed everything, as at Bienvenu in the old days of peace and plenty. Only one matter troubled Beauty, and that was that they had left Emily Chattersworth behind. Lanny explained why he had not been at liberty to suggest bringing her. As they learned later, there was no need to worry; their old and best friend had passed away several days before D-day of Operation Torch. More than two years were to elapse before Lanny received word that his near-fostermother had bequeathed to him securities of more than a million dollars' value, with the direction that he was to use them in the effort to prevent another World War.

Parsifal Dingle had been busily proving his thesis that God is everywhere, and that He is in all the religions. One of Parsifal's Mohammedan friends had brought him a sick child and Parsifal had healed it, or at any rate, the child had recovered. That was enough, and great numbers of brown-skinned people, most of them poor and ragged, desired to visit this miracle man from overseas. It was hardly the proper thing for the ultra-fashionable hotel, now the playground of American and French generals, so the man of God had established a sort of spiritual clinic in the courtyard of one of the Mohammedan scholars.

He went there every morning, and had a hard time getting away, because so many people came with dreadful diseases, all the way from trachoma of the eyes down to sores which made their ankle bones break through the skin. Not all got well, but some did, and it was enough to excite the displeasure of zealots of the Prophet, who insisted that it didn't count unless you did it in the Prophet's name. The onetime realtor from the corn and hog country of the Middle West was thinking seriously of becoming a convert to this faith. He believed in all the religions, and why shouldn't he join them all?

He never missed his daily session with Madame; and a curious development had come. Parsifal had had to move to the French Riviera in order to get communications from India, and now he had had to move to Morocco to get communications from Connecticut. Lanny's greatuncle, Eli Budd, had taken to sending messages through Tecumseh, and Lanny spent an afternoon reading a mass of notes which his stepfather had accumulated. It was for the most part not very convincing, for the former Unitarian clergyman spent most of his time discussing metaphysical matters. But then, those were the matters which the old gentleman had discussed with the adolescent Lanny Budd, and the library he had willed to Lanny contained hundreds of books on the subject. Parsifal had studied these books, including marginal notes written by the ex-preacher; so the skeptic found it perfectly natural that Parsifal's mind should be full of the ex-preacher's personality. But how had a Polish ex-servant got hold of all this?

Lanny had time for a séance himself. He had managed to make peace with Tecumseh by being very respectful, even reverent; and now as a reward the ancient Amerindian reported that there was a spirit present who said he was Lanny's Uncle Phil. At first Lanny said that he had no such uncle, but the spirit insisted, and a vague memory stirred; there had been a younger brother of Jesse and Mabel, alias Beauty Budd. In childhood Lanny had heard his name mentioned, and that he was "no good," and had gone off to the South Seas.

Now the "spirit" said that he had lived in the Philippines, had been captured by the Japanese, and had died in a concentration camp. Uncle Phil described his physical appearance, and when Lanny told his mother about it, she said it was right, and it gave her a jolt. Immediately she wanted to try a séance herself; but all she got was that little daughter of hers which she had not permitted to be born. That gave her an even worse jolt, and renewed her conviction that this frightening underworld of the mind was not made for her entertainment.

X

The airport at Marrakech was large, and gangs of Moors were working day and night to make it still larger. Lanny boarded the olive-drab aluminum transport which was to take him home, and found it like the one on which he had attempted to fly by way of Greenland and Iceland, and which had dumped him into the sea. He resolved to keep his fingers crossed this time, but he didn't, because he found work to do. The floor of the transport was covered with little thin mattresses called "pads," and on these lay men with bandaged arms, feet, or heads. There was only one nurse to attend them, a young man who, as Lanny learned, was a "C.O.," a conscientious objector who had accepted this unpleasant sort of duty. Lanny saw many chances to help and took them all.

He was deeply interested in these boys, whose war experience had been so brief and so lacking in glamour. They had come ashore in the darkness of a rainy night or early morning. They had been wounded in the surf or on the beach and had lain for hours and then been carried to a hotel which had been turned into a hospital. Then they had been put into trucks and carried to Marrakech, and now they were going home, at least for a time. Lanny didn't hear a single complaint; they had been luckier than a lot of other guys, they said. The Army had got ashore, and it was going to stay, wasn't it? Lanny could tell them: "It sure is, soldier!"

He thought it was a good thing for himself to make friends with some of these "guys," to remind him that war wasn't all pomp and parade, trumpets blowing and flags waving. He had seen that showy side, and so far had escaped the other; as it chanced, he hadn't seen a single dead body in North Africa. He had seen politicians pulling wires in their struggle for position and power, and he thought he preferred these simple, straightforward fellows who did their duty and took it for granted that there was nothing else to be thought of.

The trip was without incident; warm sunshine outside and no wind to be noticed—it was like being ferried across the Mississippi River, as one G.I. said who lived upon its banks. The engines roared and never stopped until they were set down in the gigantic new airport of Belém in Brazil. There they stopped only long enough for Lanny to stretch his legs, and incidentally for the plane to renew its fuel and food and to take on some mail. Then off they went to Puerto Rico for another stop, and then to Washington, where these boys would rest in a hospital, and then have a brief furlough before they went back to General Patton's hard-fighting command.

Lanny's first duty was, of course, to phone Baker; and then, while waiting for his appointment, he called the apartment in New York. He had cabled that he was coming, but in these times there could be no certainty that any message would arrive. This one hadn't, and his announcement that he was in Washington all but took Laurel's breath away. "Oh, Lanny! Lanny!" was all she could say, and he heard a little sob of joy. He told her that he was safe and well and would be with her in a day or two. First she laughed a little, and then she said: "I am nursing the baby; perhaps he will talk to you." She must have put the baby's lips close to the receiver, for the father heard a little gurgling sound such as babies make when they are pleased with what is being done to them. He took it for a greeting and said: "Hello, Buster!"

Then he added: "I promised to cable Beauty about my arrival, and she wants to know the color of the baby's hair." When Laurel answered: "It is brown, like ours," he said: "She will be satisfied."

"Is she satisfied with me?" asked the wife.

"She is tickled to death," he told her. "She says that I am to stick this time and I promised that I would."

"Oh, please do!" cried Laurel.

XI

Lanny's appointment was made for that evening, and Baker took him into the White House in the customary way. It was a cold and rainy night, and Lanny found a warm grate fire in that large bedroom; the Chief had on his warm blue cape, for one of his weaknesses was a susceptibility to what he called "the sniffles." He was just getting over some of them now and looked worn; but nothing could have been more cordial than his greeting, and he proclaimed himself the happiest man in the land. "We've really done it!" he exclaimed. "And nobody on this earth will ever know what a responsibility I carried and what fears have tormented me."

"I have tried to imagine it, Governor," replied the caller.

"The first time sets the pattern; and, by golly, we got away with it! There is going to be a tide of vehicles and men rolling across that land. No doubt you have seen the beginning."

Indeed yes! Lanny told what he had witnessed. This man of eager curiosity had the figures before him in reports, but he wanted to see the thing as a show. There was a boy in him that had never died, and how he would have enjoyed being thirty years younger, sound of limb and free of responsibilities, so that he could take an active part in this war, as his four tall sons were doing! He listened to the story of the Cherchell adventure, the first eyewitness account he had had; and to the intrigues in Algiers on D-day, or rather D-night. What melodrama, mixed with *opéra bouffe!* And yet every detail had happened, just as Lanny told it. F.D.R. slapped the bedcover with delight when Lanny told about Juin and Darlan spending the night arresting Murphy and being arrested in turn. When Lanny told about Kenneth Pendar's three arrests in a twelve-hour period, the President burst into a guffaw—you would have thought he was the most carefree gentleman who had ever been graduated from Harvard University.

But of course it wasn't all fun. Lanny had to tell about the other side of that seemingly-good coin, the Darlan deal: the wire-pulling, the betrayals, the vengeance on political opponents. When Lanny mentioned that some of the men who had done most to help the Americans were now in jail, his Boss exclaimed: "You don't tell me!"—one of his favorite exclamations. When Lanny told about General Béthouart being under arrest and about his interviews with that officer before D-day, F.D.R. exclaimed: "Something must be done about that!"

Lanny ventured to explain: "Murphy is in a difficult position because he has made promises to Darlan and Lemaigre and others of that ex-Vichy gang. Also, the British agents work on him incessantly for their own purposes, which of course are imperialist."

"I know, Lanny; it's the old story. Where can I find men who know the business of diplomacy and will carry out my policies?"

Lanny didn't try to answer that. He said: "I don't want to say anything against Bob Murphy; he's been doing a good job. The thing is to tell him to be tough with that Vichy crowd. Give him explicit orders."

"I am planning to make him our Minister, with the idea of giving him more prestige."

"That will help, certainly. But somehow the striped-pants boys in that old building across the street here will have to have some starch put into their spines. Nobody can do it but you."

"What specific measures have you in mind, Lanny?"

"First of all, the Darlan outfit must restore to the Jews their civil rights in North Africa. Everybody took that for granted, and is puzzled that we don't do it. The Jews were active in the crowd that kept the Vichyites busy on D-day, so busy that they had no time to resist us. And of course now the Vichyites are paying the Jews back in every way, both open and secret."

"Check," said the Governor. "And what else?"

"Almost as important is the release of political prisoners. There are about ten thousand in concentration camps, under shocking conditions. They include Jews, and of course Communists. That could be understood in 1939, when the Reds were opposing the war, but what sense does it make now, when they are all for the war and ready to work as hard as anybody? Many of the prisoners are liberals and democrats like you and me, and many have only one black mark against them, that they fought against Franco in Spain. I don't need to tell you, Governor, that Franco and Laval are two worms out of the same apple."

"Check," said the Governor a second time.

XII

Lanny knew better than to argue or insist. He could foresee easily enough what reasons the reactionaries in the Administration and the Army would present for not taking this step or that to trouble the

French administration of North Africa during the advance into Tunis. He could imagine that an overworked executive might hesitate and postpone. The thing to do was to give him more facts; to tell him Pendar's story about how Old Blood and Guts had refused to send the President's letter to the Sultan of Morocco as the President had written it. F.D.R.'s brow darkened, and Lanny could be sure he wasn't going to forget *that* bit of warning.

The question period continued. A bearer of grave responsibilities wanted to have the different personalities put before him, their connections, their functions, their ideas. What was the North African reaction to General Giraud, and to De Gaulle? Who were the fanatics promoting the Comte de Paris, pretender to the French throne? What was the attitude of the French Navy, and could we depend upon its officers now? How were the roads across the Algerian plain, and would they stand military traffic, and how soon would our boys hit the mountains on the way eastward? How heavy were the rains, and what did the French think of the chances of our taking Tunis before the Germans had reinforced it?

Lanny mentioned his friend Jerry Pendleton, and how they had worked to get the U-boats to Dakar. The President gave the figures as to ship losses, and said there was no doubt that the Nazis had been fooled. "I can't thank you enough," he said, and Lanny answered: "You know how I feel, Governor. All I want is another chance to be of use. How about that little scheme of mine to visit Hitler?"

The great man looked at his faithful servant, who was so much like himself, and his lips twitched into a chuckle. "It's hard to give up, isn't it?" he said. "I am going to give you a military order."

"Yes, sir," said Lanny in military fashion.

"Forget that little scheme. Don't let it keep worrying your mind. I have told you that I need you in North Africa, and later in France. I want you to go back there and keep track of those Vichy so-and-so's, and give me the inside dope, week by week."

"All right, Governor, if that's it, that's it."

"I'll prove my trust in you by telling you a top secret. Instead of your having to come to see me, there's a chance that I may be coming to see you."

"Indeed, sir? The latchstring will be out!"

"You know that Churchill has paid me two visits, and it won't seem courteous if I make him come a third time."

"I can understand that he might feel so."

"Well, keep it under your hat. It will depend upon events, and probably won't be till after Christmas. I suppose you'll be wanting to see your wife for a while?"

"I have just had word that we have a son."

"You don't say! Congratulations! Take a furlough until New Year's and then let me see you again. Take the precaution to tell Baker your whereabouts so that I could reach you in case of emergency."

"Sure thing, Governor. I'll be in New York, or perhaps at my father's in Newcastle. I have to tell him how his planes behaved over the Maison Blanche airport at Algiers. An odd coincidence, Governor; you plan a campaign in the White House, and you capture a town called White House in Spanish and an airport named White House in French."

"Capital!" exclaimed the President, who nearly always had time for a joke. "See if there is a place in Germany called Weisses Haus!" Then, as happened so often, this busy man's mood changed suddenly. "Lanny," he remarked, "you have earned an honor. I pay it to you because it may give you courage for your work. It is for yourself and no other person on this earth."

"Yes, Governor?"

"A new era in human affairs has begun. The first uranium pile has started operation; we are making the fissionable material at last."

"That is indeed extraordinary news, Governor!"

"It is at one of our great universities, I won't tell you which. Suffice it that the operation was started early this month; so this year may be known as A.A.1—the first year of the Atomic Age. That is worth having lived to see."

"And to have helped in," ventured the P.A. "What you have done along that line may dwarf this war."

XIII

Baker had reserved a berth for Lanny on the midnight train to New York, so at breakfast time next morning the traveler stepped into the apartment and surprised his wife, who was sitting up in bed. What an exciting homecoming, with that small bundle of life that gurgled and winked and made strange faces! "Bundle from heaven" was the popular phrase; but where was heaven? Not where the prophets and the saints had imagined it, up in the sky. No, there had to be a new set of ideas to account for this creature, which, during a period of nine months, had been repeating the history of life on this planet over a period of many millions of years. It had consciousness, and had—or was—what people called a "soul." It would go on expanding and would become what it was now fashionable to call a "personality." Lanny and Laurel together had made this mite of being, or, at any rate, it wouldn't have been if they hadn't caused it to be.

Lanny would sit and study it. A scattering of light brown hair, finer than any silk he had ever seen; he had promised to wire Beauty about this, and he did so. The lips kept moving; the creature was reaching out for food, the thing of greatest importance to him. Sometimes he smiled, and Lanny could think only of Wordsworth's ode:

> Not in entire forgetfulness, . . .
> But trailing clouds of glory do we come.

Lanny knew that Freud had a different opinion, and so did the evolutionists. Where was the philosopher who would reconcile these contrary sets of ideas?

Lanny thought about the psychic experience he had had in Marrakech, only a few days ago. Wherever souls, or personalities, came from, did they return to that same place? Was the universe full of souls, or personalities, some waiting to be born, others coming back from having lived? Did they come into the world more than once, as the reincarnationists imagined? Or were they broken up and shaped into new forms every time, like the dust of which their earthly bodies had been made? And were there traces of them left over, psychic bones in the void, as it were?

A crazy lot of speculations, a materialist would say. And yet, think what the materialist was so blandly imagining inside his own head! Millions of memories stored away in brain cells and kept at call as long as life lasted, although nobody had ever seen a memory in a cell or anywhere else. Millions of ideas, constantly changing and shifting, drifting into consciousness and out again, and all supposedly at random, with no "soul" to direct them! No purpose, no goal, though every materialist was a living determination to destroy the idea of a soul, and of a God who had anything to do with a purely accidental universe! What a strange accident, that men should labor so purposefully to destroy the idea of purpose!

BOOK SIX

Doors That Lead to Death

18

'Twas the Night before Christmas

I

LANNY'S furlough centered on a baby, whose name already stood on the city's records as Lanny Creston-Budd. The very determined mother said, not Lanning, but Lanny; she didn't know any Lanning, but she had met a man named Lanny whom she liked fairly well. The hyphen was to call attention to the fact that she, Laurel Creston, was just as important as any of the self-important Budds; at any rate, she had had as much to do with this baby as all of them put together. Lanning Prescott Budd in his usual amiable fashion remarked: "O.K. by me."

Laurel had developed emphatic ideas on the subject of motherhood and the care of infants. She had read books, and had made up her mind that her child was going to be a model specimen. In the first place, it was going to be breast-fed, and the nonsense called "social life" was never going to interfere. Literary life was another matter; a woman could hit the typewriter keys in between her maternal duties, and the baby would learn to accept the sound as a phenomenon of nature. In the next place, there was never to be any fondling or dandling or rocking to sleep; the baby would be laid in its crib, modern style. The precious mite of life was never going down into the dust- and germ-laden atmosphere of megalopolis; it was going to stay in a high-up room where the air was pure, and several times a day it would be covered warmly and the room would be thoroughly aired. When the child was fed and when it was bathed, it would be brought into a warm room, but it would sleep in winter air. Nobody who had a cold would ever come near it, and any person who kissed it would be executed on the spot.

Laurel would bundle herself in the wonderful fur coat which the Russians had insisted upon giving her, and her husband would take her for a drive, first into Central Park and up Riverside Drive, and later into the country—anywhere, so long as she could be sure of returning home within the four-hour schedule which the pediatrician recommended. It was almost unimaginable luxury, Laurel said, to have a fur coat and a car and a husband all at the same time. But for how long a time?

She had produced another quantity of manuscript, and Lanny read it, absorbed; here was the same sly satire and shrewd characterization which he had been admiring for years. Laurel told that she had put off the tragic concluding chapters until after her confinement. She would soon be ready to tackle them; she went over the story with her husband and he answered her questions about Nazi psychology, doctrines, practices, and vocabulary. What a busy brain there was inside that small head! They even took time off to try a few experiments in mediumship, but not much came of them. "I am too contented," she said. "Cows do not develop psychic phenomena."

II

The routine for Baby Lanny had been laid out on scientific principles and was supposed to be like the law of the Medes and Persians, which altereth not. But, alas, it is one thing to make laws, and another to enforce them. There came that medieval institution known as Christmas, and there were two grandparents and a host of greatuncles and greataunts clamoring against what they called modern innovations. It was just impossible that Lanny shouldn't see his relatives at Christmas time, and everybody's feelings would be hurt if his wife didn't come along. Esther telephoned and proposed a compromise; she would provide a room for the baby, where everything might be exactly as in the baby's home. Esther would personally see that nobody who had a cold entered the room, and that nobody touched the baby except Laurel and the well-trained nurse whom Esther would provide.

So the car was brought to the door, and Lanny carried the precious bundle down and laid it in the mother's arms; she held it while he drove—carefully, because there was snow and sleet on the highway. The infant was established in another upstairs room, and had no idea of the difference; the mother appeared at the proper times, and her soft warm breasts were made available. No one was allowed into the room who had not passed a hygienic inspection; Laurel herself held the little one, and there was no fondling or dandling or kissing. The female cousins and the aunts and greataunts were allowed to witness the suckling, a procedure which had become practically obsolete among fashionable folk; the elders watched it with approbation and the youngers with awe.

Exactly a quarter century had passed since Lanny had first spent a Christmas in the home of his father and stepmother. That had been time enough for the two sons of this marriage to grow up and produce children of their own. The house had had wings added on both sides, so it was now a mansion, with room enough for all of the clan that chose to come. It was a bigger party than Lanny remembered from his youth, but otherwise it was exactly the same. Everybody was kind, everybody was cheerful, but it seemed to the man from overseas that there was an undercurrent of boredom which even the children shared. Nobody believed in Santa Claus any more, and nobody had made the effort or done the work which are necessary to real enjoyment of play.

There was an immense tree standing by the circular staircase which went up to the third story of the house. Under it was a great pile of packages, all wrapped in fancy paper and tied with bright red ribbons. There were presents to everybody and from everybody, including the servants. The country was at war, the whole world was at war, just as it had been at Lanny's first visit. Goods were supposed to be scarce; yet somehow it seemed always possible for the rich to get what they wanted.

The problem was to find presents which might give pleasure to people who already had everything they needed and a lot more. When the packages were opened, a boy just home from boarding school might find himself with three sweaters, and he had several perfectly good sweaters from last Christmas. The same applied to dressing gowns, to bedroom slippers for the old, and to neckties for all ages; indeed, neckties seemed to be the bane of life at Christmas parties. The colors didn't please people, and Lanny guessed that most of the Budds were secretly busy with the question of to whom they would give this superfluous merchandise.

Lanny's memory went back to his childhood on the Cap d'Antibes, when he had taken a present to the child of one of the poor fisher families. The present was a cheap valentine, saved over from that season; but it was covered with paper lace, tinsel, and gold, and had a brightly colored picture in the center. The rapture which had come upon the face of the child who received this gift was something Lanny had never seen upon the face of any grandchild of Robbie Budd, president of Budd-Erling Aircraft.

Still, nobody could deny that it was a proper family party in the dignified New England way. Nobody drank too much punch, and nobody was rude to any of his in-laws. They all talked about family affairs, and took Laurel into their secrets. Upstairs in their own room Lanny told her with a grin that she was a novelist, and some day might be moved to write a story about the American rich. "They are the ones who buy the novels," he said, "and novels about them are the ones that sell."

There was talk about the war, too. These Budds knew that Lanny had just come back from Europe, and they asked questions about how things were going; he noticed that no one asked him what he personally had been doing, or even where he had been. He wondered: Had the rumor spread among the tribe that he was doing work of a confidential nature? Or was it just that reticence which was a part of their good breeding? In any case it was convenient, and he had to admit that there was something to be said for that stiffness and personal pride which was the mark of caste in this region, called "New" England even after it was three centuries old.

III

The celebration was brought to an end for Lanny by an item of news which came over the radio on Christmas eve. Startling news, wholly unforeseen and preceded by no omens: Admiral Darlan had been shot by an assassin in Algiers! A couple of hours later it was reported that he was dead. The P.A. said: "Darling, I'm afraid that ends my furlough. It will change everything over there and will certainly mean that I have to go and report."

He had been able to tell his wife much more about his work, for now the great secret of Operation Torch was known to all the world, and to the world's wives. Thus Laurel could understand why the head of the French government in North Africa was such an important factor in her husband's life. "Who do you think has done it?" she asked.

"I can't guess," he told her. "There are so many factions, pulling and hauling."

"Do you suppose it's the Leftists?" That seemed probable to her because most of the criticism of the Darlan deal which she had been reading in New York emanated from that side of the political house.

"I don't know," he answered; "but if it is, it will be terrible, because the Jews will be blamed."

He shut himself in his father's study and put in a call for Baker. It wasn't easy to find him—no doubt the President's man also was having his family celebration. Lanny waited up late Christmas eve, but no call came. He stayed near the house on Christmas morning, helping the children celebrate and playing the piano for them to dance; but still no call. Dinner was in midafternoon: turkey with chestnut dressing, cranberry sauce, roast sweet potatoes, asparagus, mince pie and plum pudding, every sort of goodies, and a California wine which they were learning to appreciate in wartime. And just as they had all started to sing carols and songs, there was a call for Lanny, and he went into the study. Baker said: "The Boss would like to see you tomorrow evening. Can you meet me at the usual place at nine?" Lanny said: "Make me a reservation on a plane from New York tomorrow noon, and phone me at my apartment tomorrow morning."

The family begged Laurel to stay, but she said that if Lanny was going she would rather be settled in her small nest; so Lanny drove her and the baby home on Christmas night, keeping a careful lookout for the drunks. In the morning Baker called about the reservation. Lanny bought the newspapers and read all there was about Darlan. The Admiral had been shot several times by a seventeen-year-old youth who had waited for him at his office. Bonnier de la Chapelle was his name, and there was much speculation but no information as to his motive. It was obviously a political crime, and there was believed to be a group behind the youth, but no one could be sure which of the many political factions he represented.

In the morning Lanny drove with his wife to the airport, and in the back seat was Robbie's office girl, who had come down on a morning train for the purpose of taking the car back. Lanny expected to be ordered to fly from Washington to Algiers and had his bags packed for that trip. This time he had told Laurel what he was doing, for there no longer seemed any sense in trying to keep the secret. She would not talk about it, not even to her friend Agnes, who had turned herself into an infant's nurse and "mother's helper" for the duration. Lanny had said, in the munificent way which he had learned from his father long ago: "Pay her what she can earn anywhere else and then double it." He had put ten thousand dollars in Laurel's bank account, for he could never be sure what might happen to her husband; he didn't say this, but told her that money was flowing like water in New York and that Zoltan Kertezsi was selling Detaze paintings at fancy prices. Of course Laurel knew what was really in his mind, and she could never keep the tears out of her eyes when they parted.

IV

It was Saturday night, and a movie was being run in the projection room upstairs in the White House. Lanny sat in a small reception room and waited; he didn't mind, because he had time to think about what he wanted to say and what not. If there was anything made in Hollywood that would divert that overburdened mind, the adoring P.A. was glad.

When the visitor was brought into the bedroom, the President had already retired, wearing his pongee pajamas and his sweater. Nobody but the attendants ever saw him transferred to the bed. A strange thing to realize, that this man with the large head and the torso of a shotputter or a weightlifter had legs of no more thickness than an ordinary man's wrists. That handicap he had carried for some twenty years, and all the processes of his physical handling had been studied like a military campaign: this not merely to save his own time and comfort, but in order to keep his public appearances from being painful to the spectators. Press photographers were permitted to take him in his wheel chair, but always under the rule that the pictures must be cut off at his waistline before they were used.

Now this lover of life was in a relaxed mood, for he had seen a film which had amused him, and he took several minutes to tell Lanny about it. His eyes sparkled with fun, and his laugh was that of a schoolboy. But then, as quickly as you could wink your eye, his mood changed, and he was the grave, even worried, statesman. "Lanny, can you tell me what this murder means?"

"I was hoping that you might tell *me*, Governor. It is evident that the press correspondents don't know, or haven't been allowed to tell."

"The State Department doesn't know. Either the French authorities don't know, or they are keeping the secret."

"More likely the latter, I should guess. There are many factions, each enraged against all the others. Darlan was hated because he was a Vichyite, and because he was an enemy of the Reds, and of De Gaulle, and of the Comte de Paris, and again just because he was in power. Any of those might have been the reason. If the assassin had been a Red or a Jew, the world would surely have been informed at once."

"I am told that he was a member of the Chantiers de la Jeunesse."

"Well, that tells a lot. That is a French organization, Fascist but anti-German, if you can imagine that combination. You see, the French reactionaries preferred Hitler to Blum, but they didn't want either then, and they don't want either now. Two brothers whom I have known since their boyhood, Denis and Charlot de Bruyne, are at daggers' points because one wants to collaborate with the Germans, à la Vichy, and one wants to fight Germans, à la De Gaulle. There is another reactionary faction which wishes to fight Germans, but which hates both the others; they are the backers of the Royalist pretender, the Comte de Paris."

"I am thinking of having that fellow shipped back to Spanish Morocco."

"Perhaps somebody heard of it, and blamed Darlan. The leader of the Chantiers is a fanatical person named D'Astier de la Vigerie, and his aide is a Jesuit priest, Abbé Cordier. They are Royalists, and many of this group are capable of any violence, for they have been raised in the school of Charles Maurras, the editor of *L'Action Française.*"

"I know about him, from of old."

"It is hard to know about him unless you have actually read the paper. The ferocity of Maurras' writing really seems insane. There is no crime he does not advocate. He is a madman out of the sixteenth century, the days of the St. Bartholomew massacre. My guess is that some of that crowd put this schoolboy up to shooting Darlan, and that the government is hushing it up because some of its members are compromised, or because the instigators are too rich and too important to be punished."

V

This was what it meant to be President of the United States, in charge of a world war, and obliged to carry in your head the political movements and factions in a score of countries, and the greedy and vain and jealous personalities whom these movements had thrown up to the surface of history. A few heroes, very few statesmen, and no saints, but hundreds of persons who wished to be taken for one of these and perhaps all three! The squire of Krum Elbow had to remember them and sort them out and decide about them, sometimes at very short notice. He might be awakened from his sleep and asked to give a decision over the telephone.

"We have to put somebody in Darlan's place," he remarked. "Giraud looks like the man. What do you think?"

"I suppose that's all you can do—if you can do it! Six weeks ago I would have said, 'Impossible.' But he's been head of the Army that long and the fact may give him legitimacy. Does Murphy think he can get away with it?"

"He thinks, as all the others do, that there's no one else. De Gaulle, I take it, is out of the question."

"The people might accept him, but the Army and the ruling group—never!"

"Well, I want you to go over there right away. Listen to what people say, but don't tell them you are reporting to me, and don't show your reports to anyone. I want to hear from you as soon as possible as to what is being done and what you think I can do. Remember, we don't want to favor any group in French politics; we want to get our armies into Tunis before Rommel gets there in his grand backtrack."

"Governor, I know how tired you must be of hearing it, but I have to say it again: the French politicians won't be satisfied to be put in storage until the war is won. They have their careers to think about; they know that the war is going to leave some group in control of the police and the machinery of government. They all want to be that group."

"We'll still have an Army there, Lanny, and we can supervise an honest election, if they won't. Surely the French people have enough political intelligence to want that, and to know if they are getting it."

"I must repeat, Governor—the people won't have much political intelligence if most of those who have political intelligence are shut up in concentration camps and starved into impotence."

The weary great man forced a smile. "I get you, Lanny, and I'll do the best I can for your political prisoners. But we *must* get Tunis and Bizerte."

That wasn't quite the same as Lanny had been told some two weeks earlier; so he had to assume that the Boss had been hearing from the brass hats or the striped-pants boys on the subject. He gave up, and the President turned quickly to a different matter. "I have definitely decided to meet Churchill in Morocco. I am going to fly there, and it will be two or three weeks from now. I want you to meet me when I arrive; you may have something important to report, and I may have some instructions to give."

"I'll sure be on hand, Governor. How shall I get to you?"

"Baker will be with me. I am not certain yet whether it will be Casablanca or Marrakech. Which would you recommend?"

"The climate of Marrakech is better; also, you will be a little farther from German planes."

"We have thought of both; but the Army seems to think they can protect us better at Casablanca. You understand, the whole thing is secret to the uttermost degree. Not a line will be published until I am back in the United States."

"I understand, sir. Am I to assume that Murphy will know about it?"

"He will know, and you can get the date from him, and Baker's address. Baker doesn't know he is going yet; nobody will know an hour sooner than necessary."

"O.K., Governor. My lips are sealed."

"Baker tells me he's made a plane reservation for you early tomorrow morning. I hope that is not too sudden."

"Not at all. I guessed the situation as soon as I heard about Darlan. I'll collect what facts I can and send them to you as quickly as possible. I'll get the date of your departure from Murphy, and hold everything that wouldn't get here before you leave. Good-by, sir."

"Good luck to you, Lanny!" A firm handclasp, and they parted.

VI

The P.A. traveled on a Clipper this time, by way of Bermuda and the Azores. He came ashore at Casablanca and sent a cablegram to Robbie—it was agreed that he should always cable Robbie and not Laurel, because the name of Budd-Erling Aircraft would have magic with the censors. He wrote a postcard to his mother, and then spent the evening hearing the latest news that Jerry Pendleton had collected. In the morning he was flown to Algiers, that, too, having been arranged by the all-powerful Baker. He reported to Murphy, as a matter of courtesy, and heard what the Counselor had been able to learn about the Darlan killing. Then he had a session with Denis de Bruyne, who really knew the inside story and would tell Lanny what he wouldn't tell any other American.

This was what had happened. A handful of lads of the "Workshops of Youth," ardent Royalists, had been told that it was their duty to rid French North Africa of the double-dyed traitor Admiral. No doubt they had been prompted by older persons, but they wouldn't name them. They had drawn lots, and the first who had been drawn refused the task. Bonnier de la Chapelle had accepted, and had greeted the Admiral in the corridor of his office and put four bullets into his chest. In jail, a police officer had offered him his life if he would confess; this he had done, but no one had seen that confession, and it was possible that the officer had put it away to use for purposes of blackmail.

The youth had been tried by a court-martial and taken out that night and shot. There were two stories of his end, and you might take your choice. One "insider" told Denis a pitiful tale of the terrified boy screaming and crying on the way to his execution; another declared that he had been assured that blank cartridges would be used, and had gone quietly, relying upon this promise. That is how it was in this vast gossip factory of Algiers; one person made up a tale, and a thousand others repeated it eagerly. What was certain was that Darlan and his assailant both were dead, and that the government was in the hands of an elderly general who held the same reactionary views as his old Marshal, but who despised politics and had only one real interest in life, which was to destroy the German Army.

General Giraud would leave the administration to Lemaigre-Dubreuil, the vegetable-oil king, whose code name was "Robinson Crusoe," and his man Rigault, whose code name was "Friday." Rigault, once associated with the Cagoule, was Minister of the Interior, in charge of police work. No American could penetrate all these labyrinths of intrigue, but this much was certain; the boy's mouth had been shut forever, and the Jewish doctor Aboulker and his son and several others who had been most active in aiding the Americans were shipped off to southern Algeria and put under what the French politely called *résidence forcée*. Lanny had to see that, and report it to Roosevelt, and then wait for something to happen.

Robert Murphy at this time was a desperately tired man, and greatly worried; but it seemed to Lanny that this worry was because of the storm of criticism from home, and not from Murphy's own doubts as to the wisdom of his course. It surely wasn't his fault that the government of French North Africa had been in the hands of greedy politicians for a long time, and that the only men who had experience in administration were men of reactionary views. Nor was it his fault that they had elegant manners, and luxurious villas in which they knew how to entertain charmingly. It had been a Counselor's job to make friends with them and get their help; now he was under social obligations to them, and how could he kick them out and put untried and unknown men in their places? How could he recommend such a course to his superiors in the State Department, who were divided into warring factions, or to the heads of the United States Army, who didn't care a profane damn about Frenchmen and their political squabbles but were hell-bent on getting after the Germans?

VII

It was a trying time in Tunisia, and so many things were going wrong. The British and American forces were rushed eastward, and there weren't enough of them; they had had to be supplied by narrow roads winding through mountain passes and over bridges not strong enough to carry tanks and artillery. It was the rainy season, and the landing fields were turned into bogs. The Germans, on the other hand, had excellent hard-surfaced airfields in Tunis and Bizerte, the great French naval base; also in Sicily and southern Italy, from which they could bomb incessantly. American boys were rushed into places from which they had to back out again. The Army was like a young and inexperienced boxer who comes dancing into the ring, full of assurance, and gets a bloody nose in the first minute. He is staggered, and realizes all of a sudden that a fight is not the same as a picnic.

It was bitterly cold in those mountains, and the G.I.'s were lying in trenches and foxholes, half frozen and entirely forgotten, so it seemed to them. They were bombed incessantly, and where were their own planes? They had to hold on, while the engineers did their work; the roadbuilders and the bridge strengtheners, the bulldozers that extended airfields and the men who laid steel mats upon them. The S.O.S., the Services of Supply, had to load and transport the quarter of a million different kinds of articles which an American Army requires. Ships had to bring them, and port facilities had to be set up to handle them, and trucks had to carry them over the freshly repaired roads. Millions of men were working at these tasks, day and night, at home and all along the route—four thousand miles of water and one or two thousand miles of land, according to which of the various ports you were using. All that vast machinery had been set into motion by the decision that had been taken in London five months ago. A presidential agent, along with the rest of his countrymen, had to learn the painful lesson that waiting constitutes a larger part of war than any of its other ingredients.

Next among the ingredients is pain; and Lanny, who had never willfully caused pain to any living creature, saw the wounded men being brought in from the not-so-distant front, and renewed his hatred of the cruel and barbarous monster which has tormented the human race from the beginning of time. It had been Lanny's fate to live through two world wars, although he had been too young for the first and too old for the second; but he had wanted the second war, helped bring it on, and carried the moral responsibility for it in his soul. He had to learn to think straight about it, and to be sure that he was doing everything in one man's power to make certain that this war would be the last.

Among the Pinks whom the grandson of Budd Gunmakers had cultivated in his youth and early manhood had been some outright pacifists; people who said that war was morally wrong, and that the way to end it was to have nothing to do with it. "Wars never settled anything," so Lanny had heard them say a hundred times. But reading the history of his country, he thought that the Revolutionary War had settled the question of American independence, and that the Civil War had settled the question of chattel slavery in America, and also of the right of a state to secede from the Union. What any war settled was a question of statesmanship after it; and Lanny, who had centered his hopes upon Woodrow Wilson and his League of Nations, was now living in the faith that Franklin D. Roosevelt would be able to reap where Woodrow Wilson had sown, and that this time there would be an international police force with real power to enforce international

VIII

Lanny had a little fun with Robert Murphy when he met him. He said: "I understand that you are expecting some V.I.P.'s." Murphy, of course, couldn't be sure whether Lanny had been told or was only guessing. At last Lanny told him what instructions F.D.R. had given, and then the Counselor opened up. The Conference was to take place the second week in January, and was to be the most secret thing in the whole world. The President supposedly would be having a vacation in the South, and Churchill would just disappear from London. The meeting place was a suburb above Casablanca, known as Anfa, a group of fourteen luxurious villas centering on the Anfa Hotel. This great structure would be commandeered, and the district would be surrounded with a high fence of barbed wire. The Army would be in charge, but the Secret Service would have a hand, as it did wherever the President's protection was concerned.

Baker was already in Casablanca, and Lanny returned there. The faithful Hajek came, too, and the American art expert resumed the business of inspecting mosaics and fountains and listening to the talk in the *souks*. The town was as full of rumors as a vacuum tube is of electrons, and flying as fast. Stalin was coming, the King of England was coming, the Sultan of Morocco was invited—this dignitary lived in Rabat, the capital, and of course wanted to be more important than the French would let him be. Lanny found that his friend Jerry had heard all the rumors but didn't know what to believe. He came to Lanny's hotel room and said: "There's something big going on here, and the enemy knows about it."

Lanny didn't have to be urged to take an interest in that remark. "Why do you think that, Jerry?"

"Their agents are swarming over the border. You know, they come and go freely, because Spanish Morocco is supposed to be neutral. But of course it's the same as Nazi territory."

Lanny was prepared to hear that it was an effort to murder somebody; but no, Jerry said it was a "peace offensive." He went on: "You know that Juan March has a villa here in Casablanca, something *très snob.* I was introduced to his steward in a café, and it seems the old man himself is here. I gave the steward a line of talk about how this war is going to lay Europe at the mercy of the Bolsheviks, and so he opened up. I think he guessed that I'm an American agent and he wanted to know how it was possible for Murphy, a Catholic, to fail to realize that danger. How could our military men fail to see it? I said that when people get to fighting they get blinded with anger, and their minds close up. We talked on quite a high moral plane, you see."

"And then?"

"Oh, he gave me all the bull, about Franco being anxious to mediate, and how Señor Juan was all hopped up about it, and making headway with American Army and Navy officers who were entertained at his home. They are making a sort of club of it."

"He will have plenty of good food and liquor," Lanny remarked.

"It was the steward's idea that I should help the Señor to make friends with some of the higher-ups. He assured me that the old man was generous with those who helped him to get his way. I was being offered a tip."

"Use a dignified word," said Lanny with a smile. "It would be a retaining fee. If you don't mind, let me try out the Señor. I know him rather well, and it happens that there is something urgent under way. Time is of the essence!"

IX

Lanny wrote a note on the stationery of the fashionable Hotel Transatlantique where he was staying, telling the ex-tobacco smuggler who had become the financial master of Spain that he had just returned from America and had information that might be of interest. In reply a note was brought by a liveried servant, inviting Lanny to lunch next day and saying that a car would call for him—a necessary favor in these times.

Lanny was driven to a sumptuous estate and greeted with cordiality by Señor Juan, less than two years older than when Lanny had lunched with him last, but he looked ten years older. He was losing his hair, and the strange rubbery appearance of his complexion was more striking because it was full of wrinkles. Juan March was what the Spaniards call a *Xueta*, that is, a Jew who has been a Spaniard for so long that he is not a Jew but "a descendant of Jews." Of course, one who was so rich, and whose money had made a humble army officer into a Caudillo and Generalissimo, such a man could have become an "honorary Aryan" if he had cared to; but apparently he thought it the greatest of honors to be plain Señor Juan, owner of several of the big business monopolies of his native land.

He had not forgotten the son of Budd-Erling, and was fully informed as to the part this son's father was playing in the war. Lanny had a special "line" reserved for Fascist industrialists—his father was distressed by having to see his planes used on the wrong side of the world's great struggle, and had authorized his son to tell this to his old friends on the Continent. Lanny himself was in distress of mind over the prolongation of this blind conflict, in which the propertied classes of Europe were laying themselves at the mercy of the *sans-culottes*. Not even the most elegant luncheon, served by a liveried butler, could calm his soul; not even reclining in a well-padded chaise longue on a loggia looking out over the blue harbor of Casablanca, now crowded with gray-painted warships, transports, and freighters.

This "line" pleased Señor Juan, and while he puffed a long dark Havana cigar, he disclosed what was in the mind of those who controlled Axis policy. The Señor didn't know who was coming to the conference at Anfa, but thought it was the military leaders, gathering to decide what to do about the grave check they had sustained in Tunis. Also, he had been told that Robert Murphy would be present. Lanny said that he knew Murphy well, and the Señor agreed with his steward, that it was inconceivable to Catholics how any man of that faith could be supporting the policy of turning Europe over to the Bolsheviks.

Yes, it was another "peace offensive." Señor Juan wanted Lanny to drop the business of buying mosaics and fountains for ablutions, and begin a crusade to persuade the American leaders to work out a compromise with the Axis before it was too late. He had the complete Hitler line of talk: *Der Führer* would guarantee the integrity of the British Empire forever, and would let America have all South America and all the Japanese Empire. What he wanted was Russia, Central Europe, and the Balkans, so that he could wipe out Bolshevism there for good and all. As a special concession he would let Britain and America assist him in this and have a share in the spoils of these conquered provinces.

This last was something new, a sign of how the Stalingrad collapse and the defeat of Rommel had frightened the Nazi leaders. Lanny didn't say anything so impolite as that; he said it sounded to him like common sense, and he would transmit it to his father, and to Mr. Hearst and Mr. Henry Ford and other powerful friends of his. He said that he found it a very good sign that the American Army was show-ing its conservative tendencies in this province; there surely wasn't any Bolshevism in General Patton, for example. And Señor Juan was pleased to agree; he had been delightfully impressed by the American officers who had been his guests, and was agreeably surprised to learn how many of them shared his outlook. They just hadn't understood the Spanish situation; they had been fooled by the wrong labels which cunning enemies had put on El Caudillo and the Falange.

Lanny mentioned the French administration in North Africa, and the Señor admitted that he had been agreeably surprised by this, too. He knew Lemaigre and what he stood for; also, he had a high opinion of Marcel Peyrouton, who was coming. Lanny hadn't heard about that, and March was pleased to tell him that this one-time Minister of the Interior in the Pétain cabinet was flying from the Argentine, where he had been the Vichy Ambassador. Prior to Darlan's death he had de-clared his support of the Admiral, and now he was invited to become Governor-General of Algiers. Lanny was staggered by this news, for he had met Peyrouton in Vichy and knew him to be one of the most determined anti-democrats in the Pétain outfit.

What he said was: "A capable administrator, and we can all feel safe in his hands." He added: "What my father says, Señor Juan, is that the people who ought to put through a peace deal are the German in-dustrialists; they and the Comité des Forges ought to reach an under-standing and work out the details of a settlement over the heads of the politicians. Hitler's greatest blunder has been his unwillingness to heed the advice of these men. Now he must see that he is nowhere near to winning this war, and he should let the men of affairs take control."

The tobacco king replied: "That is exactly what is going on. It has to be very secret, because the Germans who are taking the initiative are incurring extremely grave risks. But our French associates, who have represented the Comité from the earliest days, know how to get word to their German friends and gain and hold their confidence. I don't mind telling you, Señor Budd, that I myself have been in communication with some of the masters of the steel and coal interests of Germany, and that in my opinion the only thing that stands in the way of European peace at present is the stubbornness of Churchill and Roosevelt."

Lanny promised that he would see what could be done about that!

19

Old Men for Counsel

I

THE last time the Prime Minister and the President had met, six months previously, had been the darkest period of the whole war. Then it had seemed likely that the Germans would take Cairo, and that the German armies far to the north would take Stalingrad and cut Russia into halves. But now had come the sunrise, and all the clouds were aglow with promise. The Germans had exhausted themselves in the ruins of that mile-long tractor plant, and their armies of some three hundred thousand men were surrounded and being chopped to pieces. As for Rommel, the Desert Fox, he had about run his legs off. Something like twelve hundred miles his armies had fled, westward along the Mediterranean shore. By now he was out of the desert and almost to Tripoli, the pride of Mussolini's African Empire. The British meant to keep him moving, all the way to Tunis, and there to bottle him up, along with General von Arnim's Tunis army of a hundred thousand men. That was the first of the problems these warmakers had to solve.

A flight of Navy seaplanes set the presidential party down in the crowded harbor of Casablanca. Another flight brought the Churchill party, and the military and naval staffs. An interesting development at the very outset—the Nazi radios, beamed all over the world, began reporting that the British Prime Minister was at the White House in Washington for the third time. They kept this up for two weeks without let-up, pointing out how the once-proud Empire had now become the lackey of Yankee imperialism. The Americans in the listening post in the Hotel Anfa chuckled and felt very clever; they wondered if somebody had translated Casablanca into White House, and if this had caused the error. While it continued, no German bombers would appear over the Anfa Hotel, and statesmen and generals inside their barbed-wire enclosure might study their maps and carry on their discussions in security.

Lanny told Baker that he had something important for the Chief, and on the second night of the Conference the P.A. was taken to the enclosure up on the hill of Anfa. He was amused to notice that the heavy barbed wire was decorated with festoons of tin cans, the idea being that if any strand was cut it would make a clatter and give the alarm. Silent Moors stood in long lines to stare at this spectacle and wonder what would be the next fantastic thing these white magicians from overseas would be up to. They had all seen the movies in days before the war, and knew that America was a land fabulous beyond anything in their own Arabian Nights: a land where plain workingmen lived in palaces, where motorcars were as thick as fleas in Morocco, and where custard pies were made to be thrown into people's faces.

The soldiers on duty at the gate were ill pleased by the idea of letting in a strange man on the mere say-so of Baker. Lanny was willing to be searched for arms, but he refused to have his papers examined, not only because of his name, but because of that Hess document sewed up in his coat lining. They flashed a torch in his face, and sent for a higher officer, who in turn sent for a Secret Service man. Lanny had to stand there and wait on a freezing cold night until this man had phoned up to the apartment and received the President's personal order that Baker was to bring in any man he pleased, and the man's name was not to be asked nor was his face to be studied. Very bewildering indeed, and it was almost, but not quite, one of those rare cases when the Secret Service insisted upon giving orders to the President. Something like a doctor!

II

Here was a modern "palace" hotel, in the standard European style, extremely ornate and florid; you paid for the thrill of being able to imagine that you were Louis Quinze or Seize. What the Army had paid for the place Lanny never heard, but doubtless it was enough to keep everybody happy. The Chief was in Villa Number 2, known as "Dar es Saadia," and he had an air-raid shelter in a swimming pool only ten feet from the house. He was settled in bed, with his Negro attendant Prettyman at the door as always. He had a cheerful grin for the caller, and a "Welcome to our city!"—a sort of double entendre which would not have pleased the French. Lanny knew that Roosevelt enjoyed travel, and no doubt had got a kick out of coming down into a harbor full of ships which had carefully cleared a way for him.

"Well, Lanny, what do you hear?" and the secret agent started on a thousand-and-second Arabian Nights' tale. It had to do with a tobacco smuggler who was reputed to be the richest man in Europe—unless Göring had surpassed him. Anyhow, he had been rich enough to destroy the People's Republic of Spain, and to put his little private murderer in its place. Now he was in league with the chiefs of the steel and munitions cartels of France and Germany and was all ready to put through a peace offensive; he was waiting only for the son of Budd-Erling to convert the two stubborns, Churchill and Roosevelt, to the program.

"Good for you!" chuckled the object of this conspiracy. "And are you going to do it?"

"I decided I'd better ask your consent," said Lanny, who also enjoyed "kidding." "What do you think my chances of success are?"

"I'll tell you, provided you'll keep it under your hat."

"Always, Governor."

"Well, do you know what General Grant said at Fort Donelson?"

"I'm sorry, Governor. I know Europe better than I do my own country."

"He was asked for an armistice, and be replied: 'No terms except unconditional surrender can be accepted. I propose to move immediately upon your works.'"

"Is that the answer this time?"

"It's what I plan to announce as the outcome of this Conference, and I don't think Winston will have any objection. But it's confidential for the present."

III

Lanny mentioned what Juan March had said about Peyrouton, and learned that it was true—this eminent Pétainist was on his way from the Argentine to run Algiers for the Allies. F.D.R. said he wondered how March had learned about it; the P.A. reminded him that the Argentine was the Nazi propaganda center for all South America and that Peyrouton had been sent from Vichy to do his share. "It's as bad as that?" asked the President, and the other replied: "Listen, Governor. I don't want to be in the position of nagging you. The bearer of bad news is never popular."

"Go ahead and shoot the works, Lanny. I have to hear the worst, but you mustn't be disappointed if I can't always see my way to do what you want. Sometimes I have to use indirect ways, sometimes I have to wait for a situation to come to a head, or for public opinion to change."

"Unless I am mistaken, Governor, you won't have to wait long to hear from public opinion on Peyrouton. He is the perfect type of political servant for those greedy and cynical old families who have ruled France for a century and brought her to her present plight." Lanny went on to describe this former Minister of the Interior, urbane and agreeable, round-faced, comfortable, and completely anti-democratic; as head of the Vichy police he had been responsible for carrying out the orders of the Nazis.

"They tell me he is a good administrator, Lanny."

"I don't doubt that. He is a good judge of his kind of men, but he wouldn't have any understanding of your kind."

"Here is the problem: we have to find a man whom the French officers will accept in the place of Darlan. Giraud is no administrator, he is a soldier and he wants to fight the war. Murphy is our man there, and I either have to give him support or replace him, and who else knows that field? Murphy has confidence in Lemaigre, and Lemaigre says that Peyrouton is the best man available."

"That I can understand readily. Politically speaking, those two are twins."

"This will sound cynical to our liberal friends; but I am in the midst of a war, and I can't run everything personally. Here is a Frenchman who sees that we are going to come out on top and he deserts the sinking ship. He is ready to sell us his services, his knowledge of all the other rats who are coming over in swarms. He has the prestige, and can make all the others obey us and do our work. Am I not to use him?"

"Yes, Governor; but the question is, will he do your work, or will he work against you secretly, and how will you watch him and make sure?"

"That's easy, Lanny. It happens that I have a friend whom I trust and who knows the French. He's going into the rat cage and watch what goes on and tell me about it. He's going to be patient with me and not expect me to change everything at once. He's going to be sure that in the end I'll bring it about that the people of France have a government which they themselves have chosen in a free and fair election. From that time on it will be up to them, and we can bow ourselves gracefully out."

The President began this speech with the familiar little grin. But halfway through he became serious. "Listen, man," he said; "this is a subject so delicate that I have to walk on eggs when I approach it. These wealthy Frenchmen are all Catholics. I don't see how they can do the dirty work they do and still think they have any religion, but they do, and they are very determined and bitter about it. I explained to you a long time ago how it is in the Democratic Party at home: Irish, Italians, Poles, French, Germans, Mexicans—there is simply no carrying an election in any of our big cities if you antagonize the Catholic vote. Here in France—of course I know of the long fight against clericalism, a century at least, isn't it?"

"Three centuries, I'd say. It goes back to Molière's *Tartuffe*, and perhaps to the Gallican movement of the fourteenth and fifteenth centuries."

"Well, it may have succeeded among the workers, but so far as concerns the governing and big business class, you simply have to make terms with the Catholic system if you want to get anywhere. Murphy is a Catholic and he understands how to deal with them. I am a Protestant, and so, as I say, I have to walk on eggs. We in America have educated a generation of Catholics to the idea of free democratic elections. Whatever the hierarchy may wish, the Catholic masses accept that principle at home; and it seems to me that our technique is to bring American Catholics over here and let them teach it to European Catholics. It can't be done all at once, but only with patience and tact, and if we stand by and don't seem to be dictating or interfering. Believe me, if I could have my way I would sweep the whole Vichy gang out of the way overnight; but then I would find myself having to govern a Catholic country, and maybe to conquer it first. Surely it is better to let the politicians alone and have their help in knocking out the Nazis."

Lanny had heard this before, and had wrestled over it in his own mind. Now he knew that he was taking up the time of a fearfully busy man. He said: "Just one thing, Governor. You know the old doctrine that the end justifies the means. I was reading some modern philosopher the other day and noted the statement that it is the means that determine the end."

The busy man sat in silence, pondering that one. At last he said: "I don't think that Vichy is going to determine our ends in this war, Lanny. If ever you think you see it happening, come and tell me."

IV

The P.A. offered to leave, as he made a point of doing now and then. But Roosevelt said: "Wait a moment." This, too, happened frequently. Perhaps he wasn't satisfied with the argument he had made; he wanted the faith and friendship of the liberals, and even of the Pinks. "There is something you ought to know," he said. "I have brought about the setting up of a Joint Commission to deal with the question of political prisoners here, and I am assured that virtually all of them have now been released."

Lanny replied: "Oh, gosh! I hate to be a wet blanket, Governor. You are an old hand at politics and you know the tricks in America; but here they have new ones. Has anybody pointed out to you that the Vichyites have their definition of 'political prisoners'? They mean only those who have been charged as such, and that is less than a thousand out of the ten thousand they have in jail. The other nine thousand are 'criminals' of one sort or another, or else they are in jail without any charges whatever, and of course that keeps them from being 'political prisoners.' Do you realize that it's a crime to be a Freemason here?"

The President sat with knitted brows. "Oh, what a mess!" he exclaimed.

"Indeed yes! Just the other day General Giraud announced at a press conference that some decrees against the Jews would be rescinded. For example, he said that Jewish children would be allowed to go to school again; but then he added, it would have to be done 'gradually,' which of course means that he takes it all back."

"Lanny, the State Department people swear to me that Giraud is not anti-Semitic."

"Maybe he isn't, personally, or consciously. He is a man who has been trained from boyhood to fight Germans, and his whole being is centered on that. His dream is of the day when he will march into the fortress of Metz under a French flag. For the rest, he lets the politicians run things, and fusses because he has to be bothered with their problems."

"We have got to get this government on a firm basis, Lanny. We have invited De Gaulle here to work out some kind of compromise with Giraud. We simply must get the French together, so that we can all keep our minds on the war."

"I wish you luck, Governor. It was the inability of the French to get together that caused their collapse."

"I mean to pound that fact into their leaders' heads. I am thinking about the masses of the French people, who want freedom and then peace. I refuse to believe that they are as stubborn and bigoted and vain as their head men have shown themselves in this crisis."

Lanny said amen to that, and wished that he could help in some more effective way than he was doing. But Roosevelt said that his P.A. was doing what nobody else could do, and that he was to go on doing it. "Come to me whenever you have news," he said. "I'll find time to squeeze you in."

Lanny went away with an aching heart. He did not see how a human body and mind could survive under the burdens which this man was carrying, certainly the heaviest that any public man had borne in his country's history. Washington had had to deal with thirteen little colonies; Lincoln had had to deal for the most part with domestic problems; but Franklin Roosevelt had to deal with pretty nearly the whole world, and with a war that included all the continents and the seas.

V

"Stick around," the Boss had said, so Lanny stuck. He paid another visit to Señor Juan, and told that gentleman that he had sent the valuable peace proposal to his father by a secret route, and was hoping for results. He met several of the friends of this *Xueta*, all of them men without a country, unless you counted big business as international. One and all, they were certain that there was a conference of military leaders going on at the Hotel Anfa, and scouted the idea of the natives that other potentates were present. Wealthy refugees who had had the forethought to get their money and themselves to a safe retreat, they were now "on the hills like gods together, careless of mankind."

But they still listened to the radio and discussed what they heard, thinking of the new chances of profit in the confusion of the war's end. From their conversation a P.A. could pick up many tidbits, and among other things he verified a fact which he had reported to Roosevelt, that Göring had been all set to take Gibraltar in the spring of the previous year. Lanny hadn't realized how close to action *Der Dicke* had come; he had had his three hundred giant cannon all uncovered and aimed, and four divisions of paratroopers all set to fly. With *Der Tag* only one week ahead, Hitler had sent for him and informed him that he had decided to take Russia instead. The fat Reichsmarschall had been almost beside himself with vexation, and had spoken so plainly that his Führer had never forgiven him, and since then they communicated only in writing.

The Number One Nazi had set one month, or two at the outset, for the taking of Russia; nineteen months had passed, and those four divisions of magnificent paratroopers were dead in the snows of Russia or prisoners in Russian labor camps. Their Führer had just proclaimed three days of mourning for the three hundred thousand heroes who had been cut to pieces in front of Stalingrad—after he had forbidden them to surrender. Also, Rommel had had to abandon Tripoli without attempting to defend it. Señor Juan took his American guest aside and confided that he thought things looked very black indeed for the Axis, and that he had sent word to El Caudillo that he must abandon any thought of a surprise attack upon the American armies.

This was an important item of information, and a P.A. did not fail to make note of it. He had taken for granted that Franco had such a thought, and so had the American military leaders. If now he had given the thought up, that would enable the Americans to reduce the number of troops they would keep along the border of Spanish Morocco, guarding the railroad and the highway which ran past that territory. So, after the dinner party, Lanny went straight to Baker, and was taken to the President's room.

When F.D.R. heard the news he chuckled delightedly and exclaimed: "Wise guy!" He told Lanny that the Army had received the same information from its agents in Madrid, but they couldn't be sure whether it was planted by the Spaniards. "Obviously," said the President, "if Franco had an attack in mind, he would do everything possible to make us feel secure."

"One other matter," Lanny continued. "There's an old fellow named Salzgutter whom I met at March's. He's one of those Sudeten Germans, but he rates as a Czech citizen, so I suppose that technically he's a neutral. He was one of the owners of the Skoda munitions plant, and I don't know whether Göring has expropriated him or bought him out or what. He has manifested a liking for me, and I'm not sure whether he's trying to pump me, or whether he's just an old boy who is bored and likes to chat. From one or two of his remarks I got the impression that he knows something about the subject of jet propulsion, and I'm wondering if he'll talk about it. You remember, you put that on my list."

"Yes indeed. Does he want money?"

"I can't say. Here is the point: I find that the way to get men to talk is to tell them things. Then they feel that you are friends with them, and not just trying to use them. I have picked up a few notions about jet propulsion, but I'm afraid to talk because I don't know what is secret and what is already known to the Germans. I need some information, not a great deal, say, half a dozen technicalities that will sound right. They might even be things that we have tried and dropped; that would mislead the Germans into thinking we are on the wrong track."

"That ought to be easy to arrange. We have a man here, Major Dowie, who is reporting on the subject. Tell Baker to go to him and get you what you want. Baker should not give your name, of course, but just say that an agent needs this information in his work. Let Dowie write out half a dozen statements, and then you can learn them and destroy the paper."

"Thanks as ever," said the P.A.

VI

It was after midnight, and Lanny felt that he ought to be going. But the Boss began to chuckle, and the visitor knew that he had something else on his mind. "The funniest adventure we've been having! I suppose you know that De Gaulle is here?"

"I've heard it."

"Winston and I have been devoting a lot of time, together and separately, to trying to make friends with him; but I'm afraid we lost out by failing to let him know in advance that we were proposing to invade the sacred soil of France. We just couldn't tell him, because we had learned that there are leaks in his London headquarters. There are honorable Frenchmen among them, but there are also spies."

"I don't have any trouble believing that, Governor."

"Well, here we are, on the sacred soil, and we want to get on with the war. But the first question is, who owns the villa in which the General is to reside? If it belongs to a Frenchman, he won't enter it, because he doesn't admit the right of our Army to commandeer a French home, even though we pay ample rental for it. Fortunately it turns out that the home belongs to a Swiss, so that issue does not have to be fought out."

"I've heard that Giraud is rather touchy, too, Governor."

"Oh, *my!* We brought that old gentleman to Gibraltar in a British sub because it was all we had; but there had to be an American officer in command before he would step on board. When he arrived, his first demand was that he should be in full command of all troops which invaded French North Africa. Imagine Old Blood and Guts taking his orders from an elderly Frenchman whom he had never seen before and whose language he is supposed to know but doesn't!"

"And who always speaks of himself in the third person, or so I am told. Giraud thinks this, and Giraud requires that!"

"The strangest thing—these two Frenchmen hate each other so bitterly, and yet they are so much alike!"

"I don't think I would say that, Governor. Giraud is dull, and De Gaulle is smart. When Giraud found that his orders were not obeyed, he asked us to replace him. But De Gaulle will never do that!"

"Charlie lost a war," said F.D.R., "and now he won't let us win it for him. His terms are fixed and final: We must oust every former Vichyite from the government, and we must rescind all the Vichy decrees on the instant. When we point out that there just wouldn't be any government left if we started such a purge, and that all the energies of everybody would go into the question of who was to be purged and who not, there is no answer except: 'That is my will.' And meantime the Germans are pouring troops into Tunisia and getting ready for a long campaign!"

"Does De Gaulle want control for himself, Governor?"

"I asked him if he was prepared to take control, and he admitted that he couldn't; the officers would not support him. I told him that our estimate of his strength here is fifteen per cent of the population, and his answer was that he has had no opportunity to conduct a plebiscite, so he cannot discuss the question. But he demands that Giraud shall co-operate on De Gaulle's terms, and Giraud answers that he is nearly twice De Gaulle's age and several grades higher in rank. He offers De Gaulle joint command, but De Gaulle will not accept that."

"What are you going to do?"

"Keep on arguing, I suppose. I've watched roosters in the barnyard and it's exactly like that. Both of this pair are extremely tall, and they look at each other from under their ornate military caps exactly as if they were going to peck. But the funniest thing was when we persuaded them to have their pictures taken with us, sitting outdoors, among the flowerbeds: Churchill and myself, and me between Giraud and De Gaulle for safety! When that was taken, we sprang it on them to be taken shaking hands, for the sake of the morale effect upon the French all over the world. They couldn't quite bring themselves to say no in the presence of the photographers, so they held each other's hands—very gingerly, and I'm afraid the public will observe the fact that there is not much love between them."

Lanny joined in the smile; then he got up suddenly. "Governor," he said, "you ought to be asleep. I know that Churchill keeps you awake half the night, and you don't like it. I don't want to be in the same box."

"When this war is over," the other said, grinning, "I'll take you on as my caretaker and nurse!"

VII

Lanny conceived a great respect for the efficiency of the Army. The information from Major Dowie was in his hands at lunchtime the next day, and he at once phoned to the retired Sudeten industrialist, inviting him to dinner at the Transatlantique. The old gentleman replied that it would be much more convenient if M. Budd would come to dinner at his villa; so Lanny took a long walk in a showy Moroccan sunset, learning his jet-propulsion lesson on the way. He was treated to some good black-market food, and afterward sat before a log fire, chatting in German with a large and florid "merchant of death" who had known Zaharoff and Hugo Stinnes in the old days, and had managed to take care of himself through all the kaleidoscopic changes of Europe during the past half century. Before the talk was over Lanny decided that he was no spy or German agent, just an old man who didn't know what to do with himself in Casablanca, and enjoyed exchanging reminiscences with a younger man who had been all over Europe and knew the right people.

Lanny's role was that of the art expert who hated war and refused to take part in this one; whose only concern was to see it ended without turning Europe over to the Reds. His position as the son of Budd-Erling made him a social equal, entitled to share confidences. They discussed the war, and the various ways it might come to a halt. Herr Salzgutter admitted that things looked bad for the Germans now, but he remarked that they were developing new weapons which might be the means of turning the tide. Lanny said yes, but would these weapons be ready in time, and might it not be that the Allies were ahead in that race? "If what you have in mind is jet propulsion," he added, "I happen to know that both Britain and America are working at it, and making great progress."

"That is what I had in mind," responded Herr Salzgutter; "rockets and rocket bombs."

Lanny stated that his father had built a laboratory in the Far West for experiments in that field. The subject was extremely technical, and

Lanny, a mere esthete, wasn't sure that he understood any of it, and was afraid that perhaps it would bore Herr Salzgutter. But the other said: "Not at all, not at all," and Lanny proceeded to reel off the stuff he had learned by heart that afternoon.

The old gentleman seemed greatly impressed and said it was a branch of research with enormous possibilities; we might some day be flying to the moon, or to some of the other planets, as H. G. Wells had imagined. He said he was especially interested in the subject because he had a nephew who had been playing with it for years and urging him to go in for it as a business venture. Herr Salzgutter did Lanny the honor to say that he must have the right sort of mind for the subject, for what he had said was very much to the point.

VIII

The Sudeten capitalist wandered on, and Lanny sat, shivering inwardly, having a hard time to keep his tension from showing. He knew that he was at the very door of the treasure chamber, he almost had the key in his hand. It was like the old story of "Open sesame"; he wanted one word, just one German word! He would, quite literally, have been willing to give his life for that word; indeed, he had for months been planning to risk his life by going into Germany in an effort to get it. Lanny was certain that this old man knew that word; and could he be lured, or trapped, or bribed, or otherwise caused to speak it?

He rambled on and on, playing all around the subject, and Lanny thought that these were the most tantalizing minutes of his life. Herr Salzgutter said that German physical research at the present time was the world's miracle of efficiency. You might say what you pleased against the idea of state supremacy, but it certainly was the instrument for getting practical things done. A definite goal was set, and every resource of the nation was concentrated upon it. Money was no consideration, the scientists in charge had only to say what they wanted, and presto, it was at hand!

Lanny said: "Yes, but it isn't necessary to have a dictatorship for that. My father has everything that he requests for his project. There is a staff of Army officers observing the work, and anything that he needs has number one priority. Money is no object there, either."

"It is the pressure of war, of course," said the garrulous old man. "It is too bad that the same efficiency cannot be obtained for the needs of peace."

"Indeed yes," replied Lanny. "But we have to take this world as we find it. Some day, I hope, the walls between the nations will be broken down again, and scientists will be free to share their secrets. It might be that at this very moment, if the Americans and the British and the Germans were to pool what they know, all the problems would be solved and we could fly to the moon before the end of this year."

This sparring went on for what must have been an hour; the perspiration would come out on Lanny's forehead, and then be dried by the heat of a log fire! He couldn't be sure that it was sparring on the old man's part; he might just be chatting, and without the idea of getting or giving any secrets. Perhaps he didn't notice that this genial and well-mannered American was making one leading remark after another; he had no idea that Lanny's mind was working with the speed of a dynamo, inventing new remarks, new schemes, new questions. Or could it be that this elderly man of great affairs was short of funds, and was waiting for a chance to come out frankly and say: "What are you prepared to pay me for the secret I possess?" Lanny would reply: "Would twenty-five thousand dollars be enough?" And then: "Fifty thousand?" And then: "A hundred thousand?"

But no, it wasn't that way. Quite casually, and as if he had been commenting on the weather, the old gentleman remarked: "My nephew had to sign an agreement to stay on this research job until the war is over. Even his letters are not mailed from Peenemünde, but are taken to Berlin, and of course strictly censored."

There it was, and to Lanny it was like a flash of lightning in his brain. Peenemünde! Peenemünde! He had never heard the name before, but it was etched on his memory by that lightning stroke. Peenemünde! Like the well-trained man of the world that he was, the son of Budd-Erling remarked: "Yes, it is the same with the work at my father's place. He tells me a little about it, but never where the place is, not even the name of the state."

IX

The Sudeten industrialist-gentleman had his guest driven back to town in a renovated old buggy—even the very rich were reduced to such means. Lanny looked up Baker, and was taken into the villa and to the President at once. The light had just been switched off in the room, and the Negro, Prettyman, was coming out and closing the door. There was a soldier with a tommy gun on guard, but he had been told that what Baker did was O.K.

Baker tapped on the door, and the light was turned on again, and he went in and reported that Mr. Budd had something of special importance. When Lanny and F.D.R. were alone, Lanny said in a low voice: "I got the secret out of the old Czech. The place where the Germans are carrying on their rocket research is called Peenemünde."

"Well, I'll be switched!" said the President. "It's the old saying, it never rains but it pours. Not two hours ago I got that word in a code message from the O.S.S. in Washington."

"I'm sorry to have come in second, Governor—"

"Don't worry!" broke in the other. "Your report is confirmation, and that is hardly less important. I turned the first report over to Tedder, and I'll tell him in the morning that it has been confirmed."

Air Chief Marshal Sir Arthur William Tedder was the air commander under Eisenhower, and Lanny knew what that meant. "I think I heard the name right," he said, "but I can't recall that I ever heard of the place before."

"It's a small island near the west end of the Baltic. We're probably getting photos of it tonight."

"Photos at night?" echoed Lanny involuntarily.

The other grinned. "Infra-red rays. Keep them under your hat, too!"

This man of great kindness knew that his secret agent had worked faithfully at a difficult assignment, and might be feeling chagrin through having "come in second." It was with special cordiality that he said: "I'm telling you another secret, Lanny. We're breaking up this Conference in a day or two, and Winston and I are going to Marrakech to have a look at it. I believe you said your mother was there."

"My mother and stepfather."

"We are to be put up at the Villa La Saadia. Probably you know it."

"I was a guest there recently. A wonderful place."

"I understand there's a wall around it."

"A high pink wall, and you'll be well hidden."

"I wonder if you couldn't be smuggled in there without attracting too much attention? I want to have a real talk with you before I leave. I have a major project to suggest."

"I should think it could be managed, Governor. Is Kenneth Pendar there?"

"Yes, he will act as our host."

"All right, then, I'll go at once and fix it up. Good night, Governor, and good hunting to Marshal Tedder!"

X

Lanny went to Marrakech again, and found the villa in a state of excitement, getting ready to be put on the map of the world. For the past two or three weeks the White House and Secret Service people had been going over the place with a fine-tooth comb, investigating the origin and habits of every one of the numerous servants, looking for secret chambers and dictaphones and bombs, installing ramps for the President's wheel chair and railings so that he could walk. It had just been decided that the entire staff of servants must leave the estate, and now squads of G.I.'s were being taught how to wait table in proper state, how to make beds for high dignitaries, and so on through a long list. The young Army officer in charge of these preparations was on the verge of nervous breakdown and was shut up in his room with a bottle of whisky.

Lanny told Pendar the instructions he had received; he had a visiting card reading: "Admit L.B. to La Saadia. F.D.R." It was agreed that he was to come back on Sunday morning, before the visitors arrived, and to stay in his room and read until the President sent for him, or decided whom he was to meet. Lanny went off to the Hotel Mamounia and saw his family. The great hotel was packed and he had to sleep on a cot in his stepfather's room. He had to answer a string of his mother's questions about Little Lanny—what a very nice name! she said. He had to tell all about Robbie and Esther, and who had been at the Christmas party, and even what the presents had been.

Also, he had to undergo questioning about the business of the visiting potentates. Operation Torch had been nothing to this—it was an Operation Thermite that had set the whole community aflame! The Provençal maid who was Marcel's nurse of course had met the other servants, and they had all the rulers of the world at Casablanca, and most of them coming to La Saadia. It was known all over town that the villa's staff had been ordered out; and what could that mean? The King of England and the King of Egypt, Marshal Pétain and Marshal Stalin, Mahatma Gandhi and Generalissimo Chiang Kai-shek—everybody except Hitler, Mussolini, and Franco! There were people who swore that passengers arriving at the new Casablanca airport were carried to Anfa in limousines of which the windows had been carefully spattered with mud; you might see American soldiers engaged in making mud like school kids, or like the drillers of oil wells! There were people who declared that President Roosevelt had driven in an open car to Rabat, where he had reviewed the American troops, all other persons being excluded from the encampment grounds. And the provoking Lanny wouldn't say a word!

When he told his mother that he was going to spend the next night elsewhere, she looked worried. They had always dealt on a basis of frankness, and she said: "What is this, Lanny, another *affaire?*" He told her: "Don't be silly, old goose. I adore my wife, and there will be nothing of that sort ever. This is business. By-and-by, when you find out about it, you may talk about it like everybody else—but don't mention my name."

XI

Lanny was ensconced in one of the numerous servants' rooms of the villa—there being only six master bedrooms. It was a plain room, but clean, and he could get along without ornate carvings and sunken marble bathtubs. He was absorbed in a volume of Taine's *English Literature* from the villa's library; and meantime the Roosevelt and Churchill party were traveling in a large Daimler limousine, painted olive-drab like all the Army vehicles. The hundred-mile road was guarded all the way by the Army, and the party stopped off on the way for a picnic lunch. A beautiful drive, the latter half with the Atlas Mountains for a background, snow-white almost to their bases.

The first thing on his arrival, Winston Churchill wanted to climb to the top of the tower; and when he saw the magnificent view, he wanted Roosevelt carried up to observe the sunset. The stairs were not wide enough for a chair, but two husky Secret Service men made what children call a chair by putting their hands and wrists together. The President sat on this and put his arms about the men's shoulders—he was no small load. They carried him up sixty steps without a stop, he joking with them all the way. The pudgy Prime Minister toiled behind, out of breath but panting the song: "Oh, there ain't no war, there ain't no war!"

The mountains are more than two miles high, and the sun, going down behind an oasis of palm trees, turned their whiteness first to pink and then to purple. At the moment of sunset it was the solemn duty of every devout Moslem to take off his shoes, kneel, facing toward the Holy City of Mecca, and murmur his prayers. Of old the muezzins had summoned them to this duty, but in these modern days there was an electric light on top of the tower in every mosque, and these lights all flashed on at the same instant. The camel trains stopped and the bells fell silent and even the infidels felt like prayer. The mosques and most of the other buildings of Marrakech were a deep rose, and in the sunset their colors gleamed and then slowly died.

Lanny had his dinner brought to his room by Prettyman, who knew him well by sight but had never heard his name. A wonderful experience for an American Negro servant, to be flown overseas and find himself in a land of dark-skinned men who dressed like the Ku Klux and didn't understand a word he spoke! Prettyman was agrin with pleasure, and said: "Yes, sir, the President is comfortable, and his room is fancy." The Negro knew that Lanny hadn't been sent off to his room because he had been a bad boy, but because he was "a very confidential gentleman." Said he: "The Secret Service gentlemen don't quite know what to make of it, and I don't think they likes it, sir." Lanny replied: "I won't do any harm."

After dinner Harry Hopkins came to Lanny's room for a while; he looked more gaunt than ever. He wanted to chat about Lanny's interview with Stalin; that had taken place some ten months ago, but apparently he didn't consider it out of date. Harry revealed that he and Averell Harriman were there to assist in drafting a summary of the results of the Conference, also letters of transmission to Stalin and Chiang Kai-shek. There were no work tables in Villa La Saadia, and Harry the Hop smiled as he expressed a doubt that anybody had ever worked in this place since it was built. He added that Stalin had refused to come to Casablanca, or to any other place outside of Russia, and he was believed to be "sore" because the Allies wanted him to accept the invasion of North Africa as a substitute for the "second front" for which he was clamoring. Would Lanny care to read the various drafts of the letter? Lanny replied that nothing would give him more pleasure. Harry remarked: "Put your mind on Uncle Joe and try to think up something that will salve his wounds."

So the P.A. knew that nobody was going to get much sleep that night in the soft beds of this millionaire's playground. The system of working appeared to be that Harry and Harriman made drafts, and then, after they were criticized, went off to their own rooms and rewrote them. Each time Harry the Hop would stop at Lanny's room and leave a copy of the latest draft, and on his way back to the big chiefs he would stop to see if Lanny had any suggestion. Since the P.A. had been through China, he had suggestions for the letter to the Gissimo, and he was shown the drafts of the Conference summary. He didn't get very much of Hippolyte Taine's opinion of the English poets that night.

XII

It was three in the morning before this labor was completed; and Lanny had been told that the President was scheduled to fly from the airport at eight. He didn't expect to have any interview, and perhaps not even to see his Boss. But that showed that he still didn't know Roosevelt. Pendar came and took him to the President's room, which opened upon the court—the Secret Service had refused to let him have a room with outside windows. Lanny discovered that F.D.R. hadn't even been put to bed; he was lying on a very elegant divan with all the appurtenances of silken pillows and drapes. Extending his hand to the P.A. he said in languid tones: "You may kiss my hand. I am the Pasha." Never while he lived would the impulse to fun die in him.

When they were alone he said: "I meant to give you more time, Lanny. I am sorry it didn't work out."

"Never mind, Governor. There'll be other times, I hope."

"I'll come to the point. I want you to go to Moscow for me and have a talk with Stalin. Are you in a position to do it?"

"Why, of course, Governor, but—"

"I suppose you know that we invited him to this Conference, and that he turned us down. He was too busy with his winter campaign, he said, and all we had to do was to decide to open the second front—'as you have promised,' were his words. That means that he is angry, and I feel that at all hazards we must persuade him to have a meeting with us, and both put our cards on the table."

"You think I am the man for that?"

"I would send Harry, but the trip in midwinter would be a severe strain upon his health."

"That part doesn't worry me. But what can I say to Stalin?"

"Talk to him as a friend and make him understand our position. Tell him about me and my intense desire for real friendship between our two countries. Make him understand that I am doing everything in my power to get help to him. Some of our military men thought we could get across the Channel last fall and hold on; we had all our plans made for a try, as you know. But the British disagreed with us flatly. Winston put his foot down; he wouldn't take any part in the venture, and we couldn't possibly have done it alone. Winston wanted to force us over to the eastern Mediterranean, and of course you know that Stalin doesn't want that. The decision is for Sicily and Italy this spring, and that's a sort of compromise we hope Stalin will accept. We simply *must* keep Russia from giving up!"

"You think there's any chance of that, Governor?"

"We can't any of us be sure. You know that Hitler is making desperate efforts to get out of his predicament. He makes offers to us, and he's bound to be making them to Russia. My heart is set on talking to Stalin personally, and making him realize that he can trust me—as he surely cannot trust Hitler."

XIII

Lanny was fairly staggered by this proposal, but he said: "Of course I'll go, and I'll do my best. But don't you think it might be wise if I came back to Washington and got your instructions in detail?"

"I don't believe that is necessary. I want just one thing: for Stalin to set a time and place for a conference with Churchill and myself. You realize the importance of it without any further elaboration. You know me and my ideas, you know Stalin; you told me the details of your talk with him, and what you said was exactly what I would have said if I had been there. You told Harry about it, and he agrees. You understand the Communists, and the Socialists, too; you have lived among them for long periods, and you don't need me to tell you how to deal with them."

"You compliment me, Governor; but I beg you, don't expect too much. They are difficult groups to deal with, the Commies especially. They change their Party line overnight, as fast as one of our PT boats dodging a submarine."

"Do you think I am ill advised, trusting Stalin in this crisis?"

"I can't see that you have any choice in the matter. The Axis attacked us, and on the battlefield we take such Allies as we find there. What will happen after the battle is any man's guess."

"I have to try to guess, Lanny. The future depends upon it. Will the Reds be exhausted and want peace and reconstruction, or will they want to take the whole of Central Europe?"

To the P.A. it seemed infinitely pathetic that this overdriven statesman should be bringing up such a topic at half-past three in the morning. There was a look of tragedy upon his face, the expression of a man who was carrying the burden of the world upon his shoulders. Was some inner voice telling him that his strength was no longer equal to the strain?

Lanny answered in the same mood. "God knows I would like to say what you want to hear, Governor; but only God can tell what will happen under a dictatorship."

"Surely the Russian people will be demanding peace—world peace—after their frightful losses!"

"No question about that. But how much will the Russian people have to say? In a country where public opinion rules, you can form some idea of the way it will swing; but when you have a Party dictatorship embodied in a Politburo of thirteen men, who can guess what the next turn will be? There will be a struggle for power, and maybe a purge—there is always a purge, whichever faction wins out."

"I know there is a strong element that favors understanding with the West, and is willing to take a chance on winning by persuasion. Litvinov, for example."

"Quite so," agreed Lanny. "Unless I am mistaken, Litvinov is now Molotov's deputy in Narkomindel, the Foreign Office. If I were to hear that he had been set aside, then I would put my money on the guess that the strict Leninists have won, and that the Party is going to have its way by force wherever it dares."

"We must do everything in our power to prevent that, Lanny. I have lost much sleep thinking about it."

"Well, you need sleep now, Governor. I'll say just one thing more about the way to prevent it. We must handle our own affairs, and those of Europe, in such a way as to convince the people that we are not asking them to return to the old system of exploitation. We must offer them democracy in industry as well as in politics. That is the only method by which we can get them behind us and make headway against dictatorships, whether Left or Right."

"In other words, get rid of the Vichy crowd here in North Africa!" The tired man made an effort to smile, but it was a feeble one. Then he added: "You will go for me. There is no immediate haste—I mean, you can take a week or two to make your plans. Go to Algiers and send me a report from there."

"And how am I to travel to Russia?"

"I have spoken to Murphy about it, and he will arrange for the Army to fly you, first to Cairo and from there to Teheran. The Russians are flying our planes in from there. I understood from you that Stalin asked you to call again."

"That is correct."

"You can wire him from Teheran; or if there is any hitch you can wire me, and I will endeavor to arrange it."

"All right, Governor. You know the story of Isaiah, how he heard the voice of the Lord, saying, 'Whom shall I send, and who will go for us?' And Isaiah said: 'Here am I; send me!'"

Lanny received a strong handclasp, and a smile, and went out of the room, wondering if that overburdened great man was going to lie down and sleep his two or three hours without the labor of undressing.

20

The Great Divide

I

LANNY sent a cablegram to his father, telling him that he was taking a considerable journey and might not be heard from for some time. "No dangerous place," he added, and "love to all"—hoping that would not sound too mysterious to the censor. Laurel would understand that he could not say more; she would have the whole world, except the Axis part, to speculate about. He called off his negotiations over Moorish fountains, greatly to the distress of Hajek, who was on the verge of successes. "Orders have been changed," Lanny said, and that was true enough.

He flew to Algiers, put up at his old lodgings, and went about meeting his friends and listening to their talk about what was going on under the administration of Marcel Peyrouton: not much headway being made in the canceling of Nazi-inspired policies, but some headway in getting rid of persons who expressed disapproval of these policies. Denis de Bruyne was well content, Lanny found, because the De Gaulle agents had won the right to work freely with both propaganda and money; they were setting up recruiting offices close to the barracks of Giraud's Army, to lure both officers and men away to join the De Gaulle forces in French West Africa. Lanny had been told that De Gaulle himself had promised to moderate his criticisms of the American campaign, but this apparently did not extend to his representatives.

These details Lanny duly incorporated in a report which he delivered to Robert Murphy. It was sealed, because the President had ordered that no one else should see it. No doubt this would make the new Minister uneasy, but he said nothing, and was extremely polite, though possibly a bit more formal. Could it be that in spite of a P.A.'s most careful efforts the other had come to realize that there existed some difference between their points of view? Could it be that Murphy suspected Lanny of having influenced, not merely the Boss, but also some of the newspaper correspondents who were "panning" the Minister's policies by touches subtle enough to elude the strict censorship? Several of these men had gone home and had fed the fires of dissatisfaction in liberal circles. Lanny had had nothing to do with this, but it was hardly possible that Murphy should not suspect him of it.

The Minister said: "A letter came for you several days ago. I was sure you'd be coming here, and I wasn't sure what day, so I held it."

"Thanks," Lanny said, and glanced at the envelope. A fraction of a second sufficed him to recognize the writing of Raoul Palma, alias Bruges. He put the letter into his pocket without a word, and finished the conversation, which consisted for the most part of hearing the Minister's complaints concerning the lack of information on the North African situation in the United States. Lanny said very mildly that he had done what he could to make certain that the President understood it. Then he discussed the arrangements for his flight to Teheran; Murphy had spoken to General Clark about it and said that the Army was flying planes to Cairo daily, veering to the south to avoid what was left of enemy territory. Lanny might be flown any time at a day's notice or less. He promised to set the date.

II

Outside the office Lanny opened the letter and read:

Dear Monsieur Budd: This is to let you know that I am in a concentration camp at Bou Arfa. Nobody has told me the charge, but as I have not committed any crime it can be only that I am suspected of improper political activities. I have a chance to smuggle this letter out, but do not know if it will ever reach you. If it does, please note that I have located some paintings which I am sure would interest your American clients.

Respectfully,
Raoul Palma

Lanny understood at once that the signature to this note was no oversight on the part of his Spanish friend. By signing his own name instead of the alias he had been using, Raoul was telling the P.A. that the French had discovered his identity. Doubtless that was the reason for his incarceration. Raoul must have escaped from Toulon and come to Algeria; and now he was in one of the desert concentration camps where the Vichyites were holding those thousands of men whose political activities they feared.

Lanny went back to the Minister's office and asked to see him again. He put the letter in Murphy's hands and explained: "This is a man whom I have known for something like twenty years. He is an American secret agent, who has been working under the direction of the O.S.S."

"Do you know that positively, Budd?" inquired the other.

"He has worked under my personal direction for several years. I gave him money and sent him to Toulon, and told the President about him. I sent the information he gave me to the President through Admiral Leahy. Later he gave me permission to give his name to Colonel Donovan. The last time I saw him, which was in Toulon last summer, he had been contacted by an O.S.S. man and received orders from him. His assignment was to make friends with the sailors and spread propaganda to see that the Germans did not get hold of the Fleet. A dangerous assignment, at which he has been working for the past couple of years on money which I gave him, first my own money, and then some which the President gave me out of his secret funds."

"Why in the world do you suppose he didn't make himself known to the French?"

"I suppose because he didn't trust them; he would think that they would probably take him out into the desert and shoot him."

"But surely they wouldn't, Budd! An agent of ours!"

"They might choose not to believe him. It happens that he has what they would consider a very bad record—he was with the Spanish Republican government, in their press department. I don't know whether the French have discovered that, and so I ask you not to mention it. It may be that all they have against Raoul is that he is using forged papers. He was going under the name of Bruges in Toulon. I suppose he may have been helping to resist the Germans there, and somehow got himself smuggled over here."

"Do you suppose our O.S.S. people here would know about him?" inquired Murphy.

"I doubt that very much. They work in teams, and the teams have their contact with the home office, but seldom with one another. You can inquire about him from Colonel Donovan if you think it necessary."

"Not at all, Budd, your word is sufficient. I'll get busy at once."

"I should like very much to see the man and send a report to the President before I take off on my journey. You understand, what he writes about paintings is camouflage; he means that he has something to tell me. You might, if you don't mind, be a little indignant when you talk with Peyrouton or whomever you speak to, and ask that the man be flown here. It will be a long journey otherwise."

"Certainly, Budd," replied the Minister, who surely didn't want to be reported as being indifferent to the fate of an O.S.S. man.

Said Lanny, with studied mildness: "It might be that this would be a favorable opportunity to call the government's attention to the distressing consequences of throwing people into concentration camps without charges or hearing. It was, as you can see, only by accident that this valuable man was able to get word to me."

III

So it came about that Lanny sat in an obscure waterside café and listened to the tale of his old friend's misadventures. Raoul was half starved, and his olive complexion was blanched; however, he didn't want to talk about his own troubles, but about the thousands of captives in that desert hellhole called Bou Arfa. Raoul was one of the most selfless men that Lanny had ever known, and no amount of injustice had ever been enough to make him cynical; he said that the worst shock of his life had been the discovery that the Americans didn't care enough about their friends here in North Africa to protect them against the scoundrels and traitors who had been shooting at American soldiers less than three months ago. Persons who had risked their lives to help in the landings had been picked up on the streets of Algiers by the pro-Vichy police agents and shipped off to be half baked by day and half frozen by night in the Sahara desert. And not a voice raised in protest, not a chance of any help for such victims!

Lanny could only repeat the excuses which had been made to him: the weakness of our Army, the dangers of taking over the government of a vast province, the ignorance of many of our officials, the desperate need of getting into Tunis, the impossibility of thinking of everything at once, to say nothing of doing it. Here was Lanny, under orders to take a long journey on behalf of the President, and how could he stop to carry out a crusade against the French system of concentration camps? And if he did it, what would be left of his camouflage as a collector of Arabic mosaics and Moorish fountains for ablutions? "We just have to do first things first, Raoul, and the first of all is to knock out the Nazis."

The Spanish Socialist told the story of his efforts to awaken the sailors of the Fleet to the danger of losing it to the enemy. "Cells" had been established and literature had been distributed under the noses of the Vichy authorities. Three days after the Americans had landed in Africa, the Germans had moved into Unoccupied France; they had pledged themselves not to enter Toulon, but Raoul and his friends had realized that this was nothing but an effort to gain time, so as to get airplane bases established on both sides of the harbor, to be in position to bomb the Fleet if it tried to escape. A strange situation, with the city and its semicircle of forts completely surrounded by the silent and unmoving German Army for nearly two weeks.

"We did our best to persuade the sailors of the Fleet to make a try at escape," said Raoul, "but the officers were divided among themselves and unable to do anything but argue and scold one another; and it's hard for seamen to take action against officers whom they have been trained to respect. What we anti-Nazis did was to concentrate on watching the enemy and spreading the alarm the moment he showed signs of moving in."

Raoul described the wild scenes when the German advance began. "It was at four o'clock in the morning, nineteen days after your D-day. They came in by the Castigneau gate, and their planes dropped flares to illuminate the warships, and magnetic mines to block the entrance to the roadstead. We learned afterward that there were German and Italian subs outside, ready to torpedo any vessels that got out. The enemy headed for the arsenal, where the headquarters were; others had pontoons to take them out to the ships. But a signal gun was fired and it brought the whole Fleet into action."

A strange story this observer narrated about the order to sink the Fleet. It had been given more than two years ago, and all plans had been made. Now, when the Germans were ready to move, Hitler sent a letter to Pétain, demanding that the Fleet be surrendered, and threatening dire penalties if it resisted. The poor old Maréchal gave way and countermanded the order; but the stupid Germans had cut all the telephone and telegraph lines into the city, and there was no way for the countermand to reach the Fleet in time.

Said the Spanish eyewitness: "It was a scene like nothing this side of hell. All the magazines on seventy war vessels began to explode. I was on top of the Grand Hotel, with Catroux and Mlle. Bléret, and we though we were going to be knocked off by the concussion. The first to go was the battleship *Strasbourg*, and after that there was a roar every minute or so. The sky was like the inside of a steel furnace. Many of the sailors stayed with the Fleet, to make sure the Germans didn't get aboard to stop the sinking. Some turned machine guns on the German planes, and others fired big guns at the arsenal, to wreck that for the enemy. We succeeded in setting off its huge store of explosives, and the wreckage rained all over the city. There were ammunition dumps burning and exploding all the way around the port, at Cépet, at Sicié, over the Saron, at Cap Brun, Carqueiranne—everywhere you looked; all the big guns and mortars were destroyed, and their ammunition, too. When the Fleet officers had once made up their minds they did their duty, and stayed on the bridges of their ships until they rolled over or went down; some fought off the Germans while the job was being done. By ten o'clock in the morning all the big ships were sunk and only half a dozen small ones afloat. The whole harbor was a mass of black smoke, and you could hardly find your way about in town. Burning oil almost suffocated people."

"Well, we could have used those ships," Lanny said; "but so long as we know the Germans won't get them, we can rest." He asked about their friends, and Raoul said they were hiding in the city. He himself had made his way down the coast at night and found a sailor-comrade who helped him to stow away and get to Algiers.

"I wanted to see you," he explained, "and to make contact with the O.S.S. again. I didn't know where you were, but I thought a letter in care of Mr. Murphy would reach you. Before I had a chance to write it I was picked up by the *flics*, and of course my papers were wrong. I suppose they had a complete set of fingerprints from France."

"Your letter came just in time," Lanny told him. "Mr. Murphy will introduce you to the O.S.S. men here. What do you have in mind for the future?"

"What I want is to get back into France and rejoin our friends, but of course with the backing of the Americans, so that we can get weapons and supplies. I suppose your armies will be coming very soon now, won't they, Lanny?"

The P.A. had to reply: "I don't know, Raoul, and I couldn't tell you if I did. The military will keep that a secret until D-day, just as they did here."

I V

All the spare time that Lanny had in Algiers, he thought about Stalin. He remembered everything the Red Marshal had said to him in a two-hour conference, and he tried to imagine everything the Red Marshal might say now, after nearly a year. Still more important, he imagined what a presidential agent might, could, and should say to a Red Marshal—a vast anthology of military and political facts and philosophy. He weighed each item, and compared it with others; he selected the best, and then polished it diligently upon his mental emery wheel. Whenever the machinery threatened to slow down, he lubricated it with the thought that the future of the world might depend upon what an American Democrat said to a Russian Leninist. Peace, understanding, friendship—these were the key words his Big Boss had given him.

He reported to Murphy that he was ready, and was told to be at the Maison Blanche airport at eight the next morning. Transportation to the airport, twenty miles from the city, was difficult to obtain, so the Minister offered the use of his car; Lanny would have to go early so that Murphy would have the car in time to get from his villa to his office. So it came about that at dawn Lanny was sitting on a bench at the completely blacked-out air base which the Americans had been running for nearly three months—it was now the beginning of February. He had twenty ten-thousand-franc banknotes sewed up in the lining of his coat, and some of smaller denominations in his billfold. He could not know how long his journey might be, or what part of it he might have to pay for.

When daylight came the passenger saw that the field was so crowded with planes of every sort that they were parked wing to wing: British Spitfires and Warhawks, Blenheims and Wellingtons, American Lightnings and Mitchells, Bostons and Flying Fortresses; also Douglas and other kinds of transport planes, affectionately dubbed "flying boxcars." A new one was coming or going every minute or two, and the speed and precision with which the jobs were handled were heartening to a man who had been watching more than three years of world-wide defeat.

This was "American efficiency"—thousands of men, all young, and all on their toes. Apparently they knew everything there was to know about airplanes, and they signaled them in, ran them to one side, serviced them, repaired them if need be, and waved them on their way again, all with the speed and snap of football squads practicing. Jeeps and trucks were rolling here and there, distributing supplies. Negro labor groups were digging slit trenches, placing anti-aircraft guns on the heights near by, building new hangars and storerooms. Bulldozers and cement mixers were making the field bigger and widening the roads. "This is the Army"—so ran the words of a song, and it was much pleasanter watching it than listening to the wrangling of politicians.

The morning was bitterly cold, and in spite of having his winter overcoat, Lanny had to get up and move about now and then. The circumstances reminded him inevitably of a previous time when he had sat at a military airport awaiting transportation. That had been seventeen months before, and the place had been a long way off, the Gander airport in Newfoundland. The Army had undertaken to deliver him to Scotland by way of Iceland or Greenland, depending upon the weather. Their calculations had failed, and they had plunged him into the Atlantic Ocean. A most unpleasant experience, and Lanny couldn't help recalling it every time he stepped into a plane.

While grounded in Newfoundland he had chatted with a pilot who had told him about the art of navigating in fogs and storms, and then with a fellow passenger who had had a premonitory dream and had been so frightened that he ran away and didn't continue on the trip. Lanny hadn't had any dream, but Laurel had had a warning in one of her trances; Lanny wondered if she had had anything of the sort now, and if there might by any chance be a cablegram awaiting him at Murphy's office. He tried to comfort himself with the old adage that lightning never strikes twice in the same place; but he knew that wasn't so—there were exposed points such as trees and crags and steeples that were struck by lightning over and over again. His thoughts moved on to an item he had read in *Le Soir* of Algiers, that one of the planes carrying the military conferees from Casablanca had crashed at Gibraltar, and Brigadier Dykes, a British officer, had been killed.

V

The son of Budd-Erling knew a lot about planes, and he watched them and was pleased to see Budd-Erling pursuits of the newest type. He would have liked to ask how they were doing, but he didn't want to attract attention to himself, and anyhow, nobody here had time for chatting. He observed American bombers going out, and British bombers coming in—the Americans took the day missions and left the night missions to their allies. There were fighters "revved up" and ready at all hours; but the Army's warning system was well established now, and the Germans did not venture into this territory so freely as they had done at the outset. "We are pushing them back," remarked the young officer who had charge of Lanny's departure.

The passenger had observed a light two-seater plane being made ready. It was a British reconnaissance plane, what they called a "recce." Lanny was led to it, and introduced to Flight Lieutenant Weybridge—leftenant, he called it himself, but he had become used to American-isms. He was a short, bright-eyed lad, a blond who evidently didn't take to hot climates, for the end of his nose was red and peeling. He was a Londoner, and his accent betrayed the fact that he did not wear the old-school tie. The caste system in the Royal Air Force was gone—forever, Lanny hoped. His first question was whether the young man knew either of the Pomeroy-Nielsons. The reply was: "No, there are too many of us these days." Lanny said: "The more the merrier."

This plane had no armament and no photographic apparatus. Lanny observed several small bags, of the size and shape of mailbags, stowed here and there in the cockpit, and others were brought and piled around him after he had climbed in. Evidently it was a mail and dis-patch plane; but Lanny made no comment and asked no questions—it is not good form in wartime. He himself was one more piece of bag-gage, a hundred-and-sixty-pound package, to be delivered at Cairo. They put a flying suit on him, and a parachute on top of that, and they strapped him with a heavy leather belt. The American officer who had him in charge remarked: "This belt is not to be unstrapped while you are in the air, unless you are bailing out. Are you familiar with the use of a parachute?"

"I have been told that you must count ten before you pull the rip-cord."

"Do not fail to count, and don't count too fast. As you leave the plane, throw yourself as far from it as possible. In landing, try to land feet first and backward, and roll with the chute. In the left breast pocket of the flying suit is a leaflet in the Arabic language. It asks the natives to take care of you and promises them a liberal reward if they deliver you to an American or British military post."

"I have seen one of these circulars," Lanny said, and added with a grin, "but I have not read it."

"I hope you won't need to," replied the other. "Happy landing, sir."

"Thank you, sir," replied the passenger. The blocks were drawn from under the wheels of the plane, the engine began to roar, and the plane rolled down the field, faster and faster, then lifted itself into the air and swung away into the newly risen sun.

VI

Two men sitting side by side didn't have to turn and shout into each other's ears; they had an "intercom," with earphones, and while the engine roared they chatted as comfortably as if they had been drinking tea in a London drawing-room. They were climbing high, swinging toward the south, over the mountains. The young R.A.F. lieutenant explained: "We give a wide berth to Tunisia, to keep out of Jerry's way."

"Jerry doesn't patrol to the south?" inquired the passenger.

"We are keeping him busy trying to protect his airfields and munitions dumps. The only time he goes afield is when the Long Range Desert Group drive him crazy and he takes out after them."

Lanny had heard talk about this new kind of warfare which had been invented by the Eighth Army, and in which both British and Americans had been taking part. Land commandos, they might be called; they operated with jeeps and trucks, carrying their own water, petrol, and food. They would travel through the wastes of the interior, hiding in the *wadis*, and come out to the coast at night to surprise the Italian and German airfields, military posts, and truck convoys. They would kill everybody in sight, wreck planes, set fire to stores and ammunition dumps, and then disappear into the recesses of the Sahara. "Plenty of room there," commented the flight officer.

"About three and a half million square miles, I have read," responded Lanny. "It extends farther than most people realize, from the Atlantic Ocean all the way to Mesopotamia."

"I have flown over pretty nearly all of it. They sent me to Bagdad once with some emergency stuff."

This young flyer had seen only about four months of service, but what months they had been! He had been flown in an American transport plane from England to Cairo by way of the Cape Verde Islands, the Gold Coast, and the heart of Africa. He had been one of that freshly trained R.A.F. group which had made possible the victory at El Alamein by knocking out the Luftwaffe and keeping it out; a desperate battle, like that over Britain, lasting for several weeks. When the advance of the Eighth Army had begun, it had been his job to fly ahead and wreck enemy transport and airfields. He had hoped to keep this up for the whole fifteen-hundred-mile anabasis across the top of Africa; but a bullet had gone through his shoulder, and after he had been patched up he had been used as a sort of office boy of the air. He didn't say any more than that about his duties.

Lanny listened to stories of the fighting, and in fair exchange told the flight officer about his friend Rick, who had had one knee damaged in a crash during World War I, and about the two sons who had become flyers in the present war, and what had happened to them. Lanny didn't say anything about having been in Germany and seen the Nazi Air Marshal decorating German flyers; for that might have taken a lot of explaining, and he was traveling as an art expert, and no questions asked. The battle with the Luftwaffe over three continents provided subjects enough for friendly intercourse.

The distance they had to fly was about two thousand miles, and they were going straight through, the young pilot said. After they were in Tripolitania they would veer northeastward toward the coast, where they would have fields to land in should need arise. At this time the British had driven Rommel clean into Tunisia, where he was now digging in for his last stand. They talked about this for a while, and how long it might be before the Allies would have forces enough to break in from the west. Sooner or later there would be a grand assault all along the line, and the Desert Fox and his once-proud army would be bottled up and forced to surrender. "This spring, for sure," ventured the passenger.

VII

They were over the Sahara, about due south of Bizerte, the pilot said. A completely uninhabited country, except that here and there a shepherd kept his flock by some ancient well, no longer dependable. There were none of the "lone and level sands" of Shelley's sonnet; in fact, you rarely find these in the Sahara, because there are terrific windstorms which pile the sands into dunes and high ridges. In many parts there are only wastes of rock, with the remains of old watercourses. So it was beneath them now, said the pilot; but from the height of a mile only deep depressions showed. No longer were there oases, spots of bright green; from here eastward everything was brown or gray. It was an unmapped region, given up to the jackal and the wild camel. Weybridge remarked that if you flew low you might see a few stones, one on top of another, revealing the fact that people had once lived here. "Maybe hundreds, maybe thousands of years ago," said he, and added: "Hot as all hell, it is."

It was cold up in the air, and Lanny was glad of his cumbersome flying suit. Both heat and cold are inimical to man, and he exists precariously balanced between them. Lanny reflected upon those forces of nature, which are crude, but cannot be called cruel, because they do not know man and have no interest in him. It is up to man to master them if he can. Here, in freezing air, looking down upon a furnace of blazing sunshine unprotected by any trace of cloud, Lanny contemplated one of his familiar ideas, the feebleness of man confronting these natural forces, and the tragedy of the fact that he cannot concentrate upon overcoming them, but has to devote the greater part of his attention to conflicts with his fellow men.

Lanny Budd was the son and grandson and great-grandson of merchants of death; he had been born and reared and educated on money made by the manufacture and sale of instruments of death; he was flying now in a warplane, upon an errand of war, even though he persuaded himself, as men do, that it was one of peace. He asked himself whether man was doomed because he could not deliver himself from the curse of war. Lanny's was a mind that was not content to contemplate landscapes in desert sunshine, to converse about airplanes and their speeds and ranges and various gadgets, about military events and their prospects; it was a mind that kept asking itself fundamental questions: What am I here for? What am I doing? Why can it not be brought about that men will live in peace and safety, with dignity and mutual consideration, instead of turning every new discovery to the art of destruction, and raising one generation after another to commit mass suicide?

VIII

While the philosopher reflected, the engine of the military plane roared on, the propeller whirled, and the war vehicle was drawn through the air at a speed of a mile every twelve or fifteen seconds. Until suddenly—military events were becoming more and more sudden—there was a series of tearing, splintering sounds. Lanny looked at the young Londoner, intending to ask what it was, and was horrified to observe that the man had fallen forward upon the steering wheel, and that his gray brains and bright red blood were pouring out of a gaping hole in the back of his head. The windshield in front of him was shattered, and the instrument board wrecked. Lanny looked out in front and saw an enemy fighter plane, a little above and streaking ahead; he knew that this plane had dived upon them and machine-gunned them without the sounds being heard above the roar of their own propeller.

And there in a fast-speeding plane was the son of Budd-Erling, who had never flown a plane or tried to fly one, and knew only what he had learned from the conversation of his father and friends. In front of him was a second steering wheel, a stick, an instrument board, intended for the use of a co-pilot, but surely not of an art expert. He knew that the stabilizer was set, the automatic device which the Americans called the "iron Mike" and the British called "George"; the plane would go on flying, level and straight ahead. But how would he divert it to Tripoli or one of those other airfields which lined the coast? And how would he land it?

Then, looking ahead, he guessed that he wasn't going to have to bother with those problems. The enemy plane had started to climb again, and to turn, and he knew that it was coming back for another attack; there wasn't a thing he could do to get out of the way of another burst of heavy slugs. He could only sit there, helpless as a rabbit gazing at a snake. He watched the other plane, and suddenly saw it change course again and start off to the north. For a moment he felt relief, but then he noticed a smell of smoke. He turned and saw a mass of black and red streaming behind; he knew then why the enemy was no longer bothering about him.

The plane was on fire, and Lanny had a matter of seconds to get out of it alive. He unstrapped the belt which held him to his seat. Fortunately he knew the lever which threw off the stabilizer; the young Englishman had talked about it, and Lanny had seen it in other planes. He threw it off and gave the steering wheel of the plane a sharp turn to the left; that would create a centrifugal force to help him get out, and it might also help him to dodge the sheet of flame behind. Without a moment's hesitation he opened the door and threw himself out. He felt a touch of fierce heat, but couldn't know whether his clothing or parachute had caught fire. At least he couldn't know for a few seconds.

Count ten, and don't count too fast; count as a clock counts, regularly, without emotion; to make sure, you say "thousand" between each number. Such was the British practice, as Alfy had told it to him. The count must begin with "nought." So you say: "Nought thousand—one thousand—two thousand"—and all the time you are dropping like a lump of lead toward the earth. "Three thousand—four thousand"—and through Lanny's mind flashed the remark he had heard a flying man make: "You never have to worry when you jump. If your parachute opens you have nothing to worry about, and if it don't open it's no use to worry"— "Six thousand—seven thousand—eight thousand—nine thousand—ten thousand." Lanny had his finger in the ring at the end of the ripcord and he gave it a tug. The next instant it was as if all his insides were torn loose and thrust down to the bottom of the cavity in which they were contained. The blow threw his lower teeth up against his uppers, and for a moment he was staggered; then he realized that his parachute was open, and that he was safe for the times.

He looked up and saw it, a great umbrella made of seventy yards of silk, yellowish in color, between him and the desert sun. There was a wind blowing which he hadn't noticed in the plane; now he was swaying and swinging in it. "Rock-a-bye, baby! When the wind blows, the cradle will rock!" He wondered if the enemy plane would return to machine-gun him; they did that sometimes, he knew. But he never saw that plane again. He saw his own plane, far below him, plunging like a comet, flaming fire and smoke. It would reach the earth long before he did, and he would never see that one either.

IX

Far below was the Sahara Desert, and it was coming closer, slowly, slowly, or so it seemed from high up. And it was drifting by, southward, and that was to the good, because Lanny wanted to go north. More than once he had stood on land and watched parachutists on their way down and had tried to imagine what it would be like up there. Now that he was there, he found that he had but one thought: what am I going to hit? He remembered what the American officer had said: "Try to land feet first and backward, and roll with the chute." Elsewhere Lanny had heard argument as to whether it was better to have your feet apart or together. He had read that the Army considered it a good record if no more than one per cent of parachutists were killed; and that was comforting to all but the one per cent.

The ground was coming nearer, and now Lanny discovered that the rate was alarmingly fast. He had heard that it was twenty miles per hour, and he was going to have a collision at that rate, and no way to lower it. If he hit a rock, he would surely be crippled, and if he were crippled in this desert land he would die a miserable death. He looked, and it seemed to him that the terrain below was all rocks; hardly a trace of sand in this unmapped border between Tripolitania and Tunisia. There were a few patches of what appeared to be bare earth; and one of these lay ahead, slightly to one side. Fortunately for the son of Budd-Erling, he had been listening to the talk of flying men off and on for many years, and he knew that if you pulled on the shroud lines at one side the chute would slide to that side. He tried the trick, aiming himself straight at the bare patch.

Holding onto the shroud lines, he could turn. When he was a few feet from the uprushing earth he turned his back to the direction of the drift, and when he felt the ground he rolled backward, making himself into a ball. The result was that he got himself tied up in a dozen silken cords, each sixty feet long, and was dragged until he was stopped by a large rock. The blow wasn't as hard as if he had been falling, and the rock held him against the pull of the parachute in the wind. He disentangled himself, and pulled the three rings which released the shrouds from his harness. Then, gingerly, he got to his feet, tested his arms and legs and back, and found that they all worked. He was safe, with nothing worse than a few bruises.

The first thing he became aware of in his new environment was the suffocating heat. He took off his parachute harness, then his flying suit, then his winter overcoat, which had been intended for Moscow, not for the Sahara. He sat on them, because the earth was hot and the stones like so many stove lids. He rested, and let the pounding of his heart die down, and meantime he thought. No use to do anything in a rush; the chances appeared to be very much against him, and his life might depend upon choosing the wisest course.

He could be sure that search planes would be sent out to look for him; but he wouldn't be missed until late afternoon, and nothing could be done till next day. They would know the route that Weybridge would follow; but what a vast area they would have to search—a two-thousand-mile journey—and who could guess how far the pilot might have chosen to veer to the south? Assuming that the veering was no more than a hundred miles, that would be two hundred thousand square miles of desert to be searched for the remains of one wrecked plane and one parachute spread out on the ground. A man might perish of thirst many times over while such a search was going on.

Lanny examined the flying suit, which had been put on him in a hurry. He made the pleasant discovery that the United States Army Air Corps had given thought to the exigencies of desert flying. The suit was heavily padded, and instead of hanging things onto the outside, where they would get banged about and might be torn off in a parachute jump, the objects had been fitted into depressions of the suit and buttoned fast. Marvelous beyond belief, there was a flat canvas bag filled with water, so full that it was solid and did not gurgle when you shook it. There was a flat packet of food—K-rations they were called; there was a small first-aid kit, and a sheath knife, and even a tiny compass. Lanny recalled Christmas morning at Newcastle—but this time be sure that the recipient of the gifts appreciated them!

Important also was that leaflet in the Arabic language which the American officer had mentioned. He had hoped that the passenger wouldn't need it; but now the passenger might need it urgently, and he put it away safely in the jacket he was wearing. He hoped that the language was eloquent and the reward adequate.

X

The first thing the castaway used was the sheath knife. He cut some chunks out of the beautiful silk parachute and made himself a four-ply hood to go over his head and hang down over his shoulders and back. Made fast with silken shroud lines, it would protect his head and spine from this burning sun—and he took it that the dark men of the desert had not been thinking entirely of ornament when they designed their elaborate headdress. With other cords he tied the Christmas gifts about his waist. He spread out the parachute on the ground, with its cords pointing toward the north, and put rocks on it to hold it in place. To accentuate the arrow effect he spread the flying suit farther north, and the harness still farther; he could figure that if any search plane came gliding down to inspect that array, they would understand that the parachutist was heading for the Mediterranean on foot.

That was what Lanny had decided to do, and without delay. Along the coast of Tunisia the great midland sea makes a dip far to the south, and as well as Lanny could figure the course of the plane, he ought to be within a hundred miles of that coast. It was his guess that he might make his water bottle last for that long a walk, and he would be within the "search belt" most of the distance. His last action was to cut a silken flag from the parachute, about four feet by six; the material was light, and if he saw a plane in the sky he would wave it. It caused him a pang to leave his elegant brown tweed overcoat there on the desert floor, to be covered with windblown dust and buried forever; but he knew that he couldn't walk in it, and the effort to carry it might be just the margin between life and death.

Fortunately he was a good walker, and had had practice in Casablanca and Algiers, due to the shortage of vehicles. He made one last examination of the flying suit and the pockets of his overcoat; he held the little compass in his hand, picked out a distant ridge of rock as his landmark, and then set out. He had no thermometer, but he knew that the heat was greater than anything he had ever endured before in his life. He didn't know how long he could walk in it, but there was nothing to do but try. It would bake the moisture out of his body, and he would have to replace it from the precious bottle, one sip at a time, and only when the need was extreme.

He walked, dodging the big rocks and stepping over the small ones. When he saw a level place he headed for it; but always he kept the guiding ridge in view. He tried not to think about the heat; the Arabs lived in it, and Doughty and Lawrence and other Englishmen had proved that they could do the same. An interesting fact, he did not perspire; at least no perspiration formed, and he knew that the tiny fountains were evaporated the instant they were pumped out of his body. With every step he took he was drying up, and there was nothing but the contents of a canvas bag between him and being turned into a bundle of bones covered by parchment. What became of the soul of a man when that happened?

XI

He walked until the sun went down, a huge pulsating red ball. The twilight was brief, and after that he had to stop. There was no moon, and the ground had depressions full of boulders; a man might sprain his ankle, or even break his neck, and the latter would be the more merciful. Lanny lay on the bare ground; it was hot, but he doubted if it would stay that way. He knew that on the heights the nights became bitterly cold; he wasn't sure how it would be here on the flat. He was not impressed by the immensity of the vault above him, with stars brighter and more numerous than he had ever seen before. He was a poor insect, struggling to survive against natural forces wholly beyond his control. He took a sip of water, and gave himself suggestions of peace and safety—what Parsifal Dingle called saying prayers. But unfortunately this reminded him of home and started a painful train of ideas. Would he be reported as missing, and would the newspapers carry the story? Would his wife, and his families on three continents, have the pain of waiting and hoping and despairing, the fate of so many millions of families on every part of those continents?

At last he fell asleep. When the air grew chill, as it did before many hours, he crept into a nest of boulders, which held their heat longer. Propped against these, he slept again. He was tormented by both hunger and thirst, for he was stingy with his supplies and took only enough to keep him going. At the first streak of dawn he was up and ready to travel, for these were the best hours, and he would walk for his life. He picked out one landmark after another, always due north, having learned that a straight line is the shortest distance between two points and wanting very much to get to the other point.

No trace of a cloud, no mercy from the sun's heat. By noon the traveler could no longer stand it; his tongue was swelling up and threatening to choke him. He crawled into a steep *wadi*, whose walls offered a bit of shade, and lay there gasping for a couple of hours. He dozed, and was haunted by dreams of the aqueducts of Marrakech, the half-dozen clear cool streams running through the grounds of La Saadia, and the fountains for ablutions for which he had been bargaining. What a price he would have paid for one of them now, with water supply included!

He crawled out again, for every moment of daylight was precious. He toiled onward, now and then stopping to look up at the sky, in any direction but that toward the blazing murderous sun. Now was the time for the search planes to be out; Lanny saw a plane, high up and far away, bound eastward. Surely a search plane didn't behave like that! Perhaps it was another dispatch plane, carrying duplicates of the documents which had been lost. The war had to go on, no matter who was missing—even a V.I.P. like the son of Budd-Erling! Lanny waved his yellow-white flag, but the plane gave no sign of interest in that microscopic object.

XII

On the second night the traveler lay down again, picking out a deep *wadi* to shelter him from the wind, which was hot now but would be cold before daylight. He had to take sip after sip of his precious water before he could nibble his food. Of the two the water rated higher, for a man can fast and keep walking for a long time, but he cannot walk when the moisture has been dried out of his body cells. Lanny had kept count of the number of hours he had walked, but as he didn't know how far he had to go it did him little good. He slept between extreme heat and extreme cold, and waited as best he could for the dawn. Then he took another sip of water and started again.

The desert had become black volcanic rock, alternating with patches of soft sand into which his feet sank. The sun came up, a great round copper ball; as it mounted in the sky it seemed to quiver more than ever. Lanny couldn't be sure whether this was because of heat waves in the air, or whether he was becoming dizzy. Ahead of him he saw a tree, and his heart began to pound with excitement. He veered off his course toward it, thinking it must mean water, but he found that it was a tree skeleton, and whatever moisture there had been must have sunk deep into the sand. If he had had a spade he might have dug to it, but the efforts with his sheath knife revealed no trace of moisture. He picked out another landmark and toiled on toward the north. His endurance gave out sooner now, and he sought a rock shelter, gasping, and in between gasps straining his ears for the sound of an airplane engine in the sky. He imagined that he heard one several times, but he was no longer sure if he could trust his senses.

Twice he noticed wild camels on the desert horizon, and once a small antelope galloped away from him. A jackal followed him for a while, and he wondered if this creature would reappear when his strength began to wane. The presence of these animals indicated that water must be somewhere available, but he had no way to get the secret from them. Staggering onward, he watched for the faintest sign of moisture, and nature played a cruel joke upon him. He saw a level place, shining with what appeared to be water. He wondered: Could this be the mirage of the desert, about which he had read so often? He came nearer and decided that it really was water; he hastened to it with pounding heart; he splashed into it, stooped and scooped up a handful of it and put it into his mouth, then spat it out quickly. It was bitter alkaline; he had come to one of those salt marshes, called *shotts*, of which he had been told that this locality was full. He was ready to weep with despair.

He found himself a rock shelter for the night; he ate the last morsels of his food and drained the last drops of water from the bag. He told himself that he would be good for one more effort in the morning; if he did not come to an oasis, he would be done for; he would fall somewhere on this oven floor and hide his face from the sun and give up the struggle. He passed a fevered night, and rose at the first glimpse of dawn. He saw that the way to the north was level before him—perhaps more *shotts*. His tongue was so swollen that it was hard to breathe, and his eyes were so burned that he kept them closed most of the time, taking a peek only now and then to be sure of his path. When the heat grew too intense for endurance, he slid under the edge of a rock and lay there, gasping, resisting an impulse to give up and say that he would not try to rise again. There was nothing before him any different from what was behind him, and what was the use?

His heart was pounding, fighting for its life and his. He could hear it, and he could hear something, perhaps his own blood, making a dull murmur in his ears. Listening, he began after a while to imagine that he heard another sound—of bells. He was prepared to believe that he was becoming delirious; he had every right to expect that, and didn't want it to happen. He said: "I am dreaming," but the sound continued, a clear continuous jangling, and suddenly an idea struck him: Sheep bells. Or camel bells. A nomadic shepherd, or a native caravan!

He started up and gazed to the north, where his route lay. There on the horizon was a line of perhaps a dozen camels, a couple of hundred yards away; they were moving slowly, and were already half past him. It took him only a fraction of a second to unfurl his silken flag and start waving; he began running toward the caravan, shouting in a cracked and feeble voice. Soon he realized that they wouldn't hear him, on account of the bells; he saved his energy to put into running.

The next minute was one of desperate bodily effort and agony of mind. They were going by, paying no heed; and he knew that if they passed he wouldn't have strength enough to overtake them. He could see them so plainly, and was gripped by such a nightmare sense of impotence. There were half a dozen men in the caravan, each riding a loaded camel and leading by a rope a second and still more heavily loaded camel. They were Bedouin Arabs, wrapped in their long robes which had once been white but now were the color of desert dust. Voluminous hoods over their heads, covering their ears and sometimes even their eyes; they were rocking back and forth with the swaying motion of the steeds—something that was their life for all the hours of daylight, day after day, week after week. Perhaps they were asleep, dreaming as Lanny had dreamed, of oases with running water and green date palms, or perhaps their special Mohammedan dream of a heaven full of houris.

The last one was passing, and Lanny had covered less than half the distance to their trail. Again he shouted—but how feebly against the racket of a dozen bells! In desperation he stopped, picked up a stone, and threw it with all the strength he could muster. It went no more than half the distance, but it hit the ground and kicked up the dust, and perhaps caused the camel to start, and so caused the driver to sit up and look. He saw a man, not white, but wearing white man's clothes, staggering toward him waving a yellowish flag. The driver shouted, the caravan came to a halt, and all the others turned to look. The once-white man staggered and fell forward with his face upon the hot ground.

XIII

Desert men didn't have to be told what was the matter, or what this stranger wanted. They lifted him to a sitting position and put a bottle of blessed water to his lips. Then they picked him up and set him on one of the camels, in front of the driver, so that the driver could hold him in place. The caravan set forward again, and to the jangling of bells and a rocking motion like that of a small boat on the ocean, Lanny Budd came back to consciousness and life. He needed only one thing, water and more water, not merely to keep his blood normal, but to make perspiration to cool his body. The Arab apparently didn't know a word of either French or English, but he understood pointing to the mouth and lent his bottle again and again.

When they halted for a midday rest, one of the camels was milked, and a cup of the warm milk was passed to the white man—they would call him that even though he had a four-day growth of beard on his face and a four-day increment of dust all over him. The odor and taste of camel's milk is strong, but Lanny sipped it as nectar from Olympus. When they gave him a handful of sticky fresh dates he did not worry because neither their hands nor his own had been washed; he ate the sweet fruit, and thought of Jerusalem the golden, with milk and honey blest.

He had noted the route of this caravan, which was northwest, and he tried to guess what this would mean. He knew there were caravan routes cutting the Sahara in all directions; Bedouin traders brought in the products of the oases, and ivory and other valuable products from the lands to the south. Those who came from the French part of the desert preferred to deal with the French; others had found that they could get high prices from the Germans in Tunisia, and no doubt there were some who were spies in German pay and others ready to sell to whoever was in power. What were the white men's wars to brown men who came out of the wilds, stayed just long enough to trade their loads for almost unobtainable cotton cloth, for scissors, knives, needles, drugs, and other products of the machines?

Soon after regaining his wits Lanny had taken one precaution: removing from his finger the gold ring which Rudolf Hess had given him, and slipping it into his mouth. To get it down his half-dry throat was no easy task, but he had gulped and gulped, and now it was safe for a while. He didn't worry about his money—he would give his rescuers all of that, if necessary—but the ring was irreplaceable, and he might need it badly. When he regained it he might swallow it again, depending upon where he was. For the present he was only concerned that when he stretched out his hand for food, these desert men should not see a valuable gold ring on his finger.

The leader of the expedition, a middle-aged, black-bearded man who rode in front and carried a hunting rifle, knew only enough French for trading purposes. When Lanny was helped down from the camel, he took out the precious Arabic leaflet and handed it to this man, who examined it carefully, but in such a way as to reveal that he didn't know how to read. Lanny explained to him, in careful child's primer French, what the leaflet asked and promised. *"Je suis américain,"* he said, pointing to himself. *"Menez-moi aux français,"* again with point-ting, to where Lanny imagined the *français* to be.

Most of Lanny's money was sewed up in the lining of his coat and he hoped they wouldn't search him. He took out his billfold, and let them see what he had in it—a couple of thousand-franc notes and a number of hundred-franc notes. With this most amiable smile he pre-sented the two large notes to the leader, and a couple of the smaller notes to each of the men. That left him only two of the smaller notes, and he kept these, to make it seem plausible; he pointed to himself, say-ing: *"Pour moi,"* and their grins showed that they appreciated the humor if they did not understand the words.

"The Americans will pay more," Lanny assured the leader; and the Arab, a glum-appearing and not talkative person, accepted the gift, saying only: *"Oui, oui."* Lanny did not press for assurance, for he knew that the man would do what he wanted to do, regardless of arguments or pleas. He had been well paid, but it might be that the Italians or the Germans, or both, were outbidding the Allies in everything.

XIV

The journey was resumed, on the same trail. Lanny could be sure that these nomads knew the route, and their camels also. The passenger would meet whatever happened to be at the end of the journey, and match it with the best wits he could summon. Using his wits now, he began to work with his fingernails at the inside lining of his coat where he had two precious pieces of paper carefully sewed: one, the visiting card of Franklin D. Roosevelt, certifying that Lanny Budd was his friend and worthy of trust; the other, the scrap of paper on which Rudi Hess had scribbled *"Lieber Führer: Ich bin es."* Lanny might need either of those scraps, but under no circumstances would he need both, and it might be that to have both would be fatal. He must be able to get at either one quickly and repeat his swallowing act. He worked at the fine threads until he had them loose. If the man riding behind him became aware of the motion he would assume that the fellow traveler was scratching himself, an action familiar among all nomadic peoples.

At sundown the caravan halted, and the men with one accord went through the Moslem prayer ritual: they stood upright, then bowed, then knelt, then touched their foreheads to the ground, and repeated their Arabic prayers. Lanny felt embarrassed to stand indifferent to this custom, so he, too, followed the ritual, to let them know that he worshiped the same God. He knew that they called him a Nasrany, that is, a Nazarene, or Christian; the fanatics among them would hate him and perhaps wish to plunder and kill him.

The men arose, and gave their camels a scanty allowance of fodder. Evidently the journey had been long, for the ribs of these ungainly beasts stood out. They must be the most unhappy creatures on earth, Lanny thought, for all their doings were accompanied by rumbles and groans of protest. The driver made a sort of hissing sound, which was a signal for the beast to totter forward upon his knees, then to sink back upon his hind legs, and finally to come to rest with all his four legs under him. In that seemingly miserable position he would spend the entire night, noisily chewing his cud, apparently while asleep.

The passenger lay down and slept the sleep of exhaustion; but later, when the cold awakened him, he lay and thought about his strange plight. He had seen mountains ahead on the trail, and this puzzled him greatly, because, according to his idea of the map, the Mediterranean should have been where the mountains were. Apparently his plane must have been veering more to the south than he had realized, and had fallen on the Tunisian side of the border. He decided that on his walk he must have been on the way to the Mareth line, which Rommel was supposed to be fortifying against the British Eighth Army; that now he was heading into southwestern Tunisia, a no-man's-land at the moment, where one might meet Americans, Germans, or Italians, according to the fortunes of war. Very probably these Bedouin would know nothing about military events; they wouldn't be concerned, for both sides in the war were eager to get goods and to promote trade with them.

Lanny's position reminded him of a story which his father had told him as a boy. It had to do with a stretch of land, perhaps only an inch or two wide and a thousand miles long, known to Americans as "the

Great Divide." Robbie had stood upon it once, when he had been hunting Rocky Mountain sheep in Montana. He and his guide were out upon a ridge of rocks, looking over forest-clad valleys both behind and before. Rain had begun to fall, and the guide had taken him to a certain spot and told him to watch. Striking the rocks, the raindrops splashed, part in one direction and part in the opposite. Said the man: "That which splashes this way runs to the west, and finds its way into the Columbia River, and so into the Pacific Ocean. The part which splashes the other way runs to the east, and will find its way into the Missouri River, then into the Missisippi, and from there into the Gulf of Mexico. You are on the continental divide."

Just so Lanny thought: "I will go into a village and there will be French and Americans, or maybe Italians and Germans. If it is the former, I go to Cairo and Moscow; if it is the latter, I go to Berlin, or perhaps first to Rome!"

XV

The caravan plodded on, to the jangling of bells and the shuffling of broad, padded feet in sand. There were more *shotts*, and the trail wound between them, marked here and there by heaps of stones. More hills, also, and it seemed to Lanny not quite so hot, though perhaps it was just that he had more water in his system. His strength came back; a diet of camel's milk and dates, upon which the Bedouin Arabs have existed for thousands of years, proved an ideal restorative. His mind became more active, and he tried, as was his fashion, to imagine every possible development, and plan how to meet it. With the Germans he had no cause to worry, for he possessed the Ring and Tarnhelm of the Nibelungen; but with the Italians it would not be so easy, for he had a black mark against his name in their books. Nineteen years had passed, but fingerprints do not change and police records are not destroyed, at least not among the Fascisti.

The driver who rode behind Lanny grunted a word or two now and then, and so the traveler learned some Arabic. He learned that a camel driver is a *jemmal*, and that dates are *tamr*; they were no less sweet by that name. He learned that the favorite exclamation of the Bedouin is "*Wellah!*" but he never found out exactly what it means. Now the *jemmal* spoke excited words and pointed ahead; the passenger looked, and on the dim horizon saw what appeared to be a bluish-green rim. He could guess that it was an oasis and the goal of this expedition. The man was perhaps giving it a name, but Lanny had never heard it before. Rocking backward and forward was a kind of motion to which he was not accustomed, and it seemed to him that whatever might be ahead, he would welcome it.

You do not come gradually out of this desert; at one moment you are amid rose-brown rocks and yellow sand, and at the next you are in an oasis, the village and farms grouped about it. Clear cold water comes up out of the hot sands and is led in trenches. Here were many kinds of fruit trees, and what seemed to the traveler the most beautiful green patches of vegetables he had ever beheld. Most common of all were groves of date palms, each tree a giant centerpiece with graceful curving branches marking a perfect circle. From such trees the natives took beams to support their huts, branches for walls and roofs, shade for their heads, and food for their stomachs. And still another use: they had pegged the branches to the ground to make barriers, holding the shifting desert sand back from their crops.

Startling to a wanderer, a paved road ran northward from this oasis. Lanny looked for road signs but found none, and could guess that they had been taken down as a war measure. He liked the appearance of this spot, and especially the fact that there were no soldiers in sight. It might be a good place to rest for a while and ask questions. When he saw that the caravan was going through without stopping, except to let the thirsty animals drink, he decided to part with his rescuers. He said: *"Pardonnez-moi"*—it seemed more polite to say something, even though it was not understood. He started to slip from the camel's back; but at once he felt a strong grip upon his arm and heard an outburst of angry protest; so he gave up. He could understand that these men wanted their promised reward; more important yet, he knew that the leader had a rifle and doubtless would use it.

XVI

Soon came another oasis, and then another, but still no road signs. The caravan plodded by the side of the road, and suddenly there was a honking behind them and a motor-car sped by. In it were four men in uniform, and so at last Lanny's great question was answered. There was a swastika on the car, and the helmets of the men were of the German pattern. Lanny could know that he was going to Berlin!

It was what he had been secretly desiring ever since the previous summer. Roosevelt's veto had compelled him to give up the project, but it hadn't kept him from wishing and imagining. And now not even Roosevelt could stop him; he couldn't even stop himself! He had no anxiety about his position, for he had joined the Wehrmacht once before, at Dunkerque, and had "got away with it"—that is, he had been taken to Hitler and received as a friend and guest. And this time he had the magic Tarnhelm and Ring.

Also, he had a little visiting card from the President of the United States, something he surely wasn't going to need! He slid his fingers into the recess in his coat lining, took out that once-precious card, and moving his two hands close against his body he tore it into tiny bits. He was afraid to drop even one piece at a time, so he got the whole lump between his fingertips and pushed them into his mouth. He didn't know what ink was made of, but hoped there wasn't enough on that card to do him harm. While the camels plodded and the bells jangled and the riders rocked like so many Chinese mandarins made of porcelain, Lanny chewed and chewed, and little by little the pulpy mass went down to a place beyond the reach of the Gestapo.

Again date orchards and farms, this time extensive, surrounding a mud and tile village. The Arab driver said "Nefta," and this was a name Lanny had heard; it was a small town near the southwestern border of Tunisia. He learned later that if he had arrived two weeks earlier he would have fallen into the hands of the Italians. If he had come only a week earlier it would have been the Americans. If he had come a week later it would have been Americans again, so sudden were the shifts of war in this no-man's-land. At the moment the Nazis were holding it with a handful of men, and a dozen or so had set up a roadblock at the southern entrance to the town.

Lanny knew by the darker shade of green uniform and the black collars that they were a Waffen SS division, and he knew how to handle them. The moment the caravan halted, he slid down off the camel's back—he was no longer afraid of Arab weapons. He advanced toward the *Feldwebel* in command of the roadblock, shot out his right hand, straight before him and upward, and cried: "*Heil Hitler!*" The salute was obligatory, and all the Germans leaped to attention and returned it.

Then this stranger with a five-day growth of brown beard and a five-day layer of gray dust slapped his hand to his side and introduced himself: "*Lanning Prescott Budd, amerikanischer Kunstsachverständiger, persönlicher Freund und geheimer Agent des Führers! Wo ist Ihr Kommandant?*"

If an art expert had descended from heaven in a golden chariot with fire-breathing steeds, a humble *Feldwebel* couldn't have been more awe-stricken. He clicked his heels, saluted all over again, and exclaimed: "*Ja, ja, mein Herr. Bitte, kommen Sie mit mir.*" He had a motorcycle with a sidecar, and Lanny stepped into it, and into the town of Nefta they went in a cloud of desert dust.

BOOK SEVEN

More Deadly
Than a Mad Dog's Tooth

21

'Tis Time to Fear

I

"*A*BER, HERR BUDD*,*" said the young officer, "you must admit that this is a very unusual story you are telling me."

"*Gewiss, Herr Leutnant,*" replied the traveler, "you must be aware that many unusual things have been happening in the last few years. It is possible that you yourself did not expect to be spending a winter on the edge of the Sahara Desert."

"*Allerdings,*" admitted the Nazi. He was a Waffen SS lieutenant, wearing on his sleeve the silver initials made in imitation of lightning, with the idea of intimidating the beholder. It had taken him only a few minutes to realize that this American who had appeared so suddenly out of the wilderness was not to be intimidated. "Could you supply me with some verification of your story?"

"I could supply it, *mein Herr*, but it is of a highly confidential nature. I trust you will not take it as a discourtesy if I say that I should reveal it only to the person who has the authority to send me to the Führer."

"*Unglücklicherweise, Herr Budd,* I doubt if there is any such person to be found in Nefta."

"Then, shall I say, to a person who would have the authority to notify the Führer that his confidential agent is awaiting his summons."

"That may be done, I suppose. Let me be sure that I have the facts correct." He took pencil and paper and wrote: "Lanning Prescott Budd, son of Robert Budd of Budd-Erling Aircraft Corporation, Newcastle, Connecticut, U.S.A.; profession *Kunstsachverständiger*, left Algiers by plane five days ago intending to join General Rommel's army, shot down over desert, brought in by camel caravan, is personal friend and secret agent of Führer, has important information, requests that Führer or Reichsmarschall Göring be notified at once of his presence." Having read this aloud to check it, the officer turned to a telephone—Lanny could guess that it was a field instrument, because the cord ran out at the window of this small hotel which the Army had commandeered. The speaker asked for "Oberst Vogel," and presently began dictating the information. Then he reported to Lanny: "The *Oberst* will receive the information."

"In the meantime, *Herr Leutnant*," said Lanny, "would it be possible for me to have soap and water, and perhaps the use of a razor, so that I may appear a little more like an art expert and less like a bandit?"

The officer called one of his men, and Lanny cleaned himself up, at least so far as his visible skin was concerned. Very soon he was informed that the *Oberst* had sent for him, and that, most regrettably, it would be necessary for him to be blindfolded on the way. "*Befehl des Kommandten*," said the *Leutnant*, and Lanny said that it was perfectly all right, the same thing had been done to him when he had been flown to Reichsmarschall Göring's *Gefechtsstand* somewhere in Belgium nearly two years ago. The Waffen SS man was duly awed, and did not fail to shake the hand which had shaken the hands of so many august personalities.

II

A hotel towel was tied over Lanny's eyes, and he was led to a car and driven at high speed to a town which he later discovered to be Tozeur, the railhead to northern and northeastern Tunisia. There in another hotel he met the commander of an SS regiment, a rawboned and red-faced man who had been sent into a precarious position and was preoccupied with his dangers. These officers of the Schutzstaffel were for the most part different from the Wehrmacht men, the regular Army; they had come from the people, chosen because of their loyalty to Nazi principles, and lacked European culture and interest in it. They were Hitler's own police force, brought into being to protect him and his Party and his National Socialist movement. For that reason the SS divisions were precious, and the fact that some of them were holding this line in remote North Africa was proof of the anxiety in their Führer's heart. The first American attacks had been repelled, but more were coming, and at all hazards the new enemy must be shown the invincibility of German arms.

Lanny understood that the way to deal with Oberst Vogel was not to display any social graces, but to be precise and even a bit severe. The names he used so casually would be to this regimental commander at least semidivine; he would know the persons only as voices over the radio and as figures on a platform, usually a long way off. He would not know whether to credit the statements of an enemy civilian who had appeared so mysteriously on his front line; but the intruder would surely be shot if his tale was not verified, so why should he come?

"*Herr Oberst*," said the visitor, "I have been your Führer's personal friend for some fifteen years—the only American friend he has, so far as I know. I have been a guest in his home at Berchtesgaden frequently. I have carried messages to important personalities in France, Britain, and America, and brought the replies. I have information for him now, so important that I risked my life in order to bring it to him."

"May I ask, could you not have come into Germany by way of Sweden?"

"I was unable to get passports to Sweden, and I did not have the information at the time I was last in America. I am not at liberty to discuss the nature of the information; it is for the Führer alone. The moment he learns that I am here, he will order me flown to him. If he is not accessible, then notify Reichsmarschall Göring."

"You understand, Herr Budd, a mere field officer does not have access to such high personages."

"It will suffice if you notify the Führer's secretary, or the Reichsmarschall's aide, General-Major Furtwaengler, who happens to be a dear friend of mine. I assume that you have established telephone connections across Sicily; if so, you may call the Führer's private number and speak my name."

"You possess the Führer's telephone number, Herr Budd?"

"I do, and I have his authorization to use it in case of need. I have never given it to anyone, but if it is absolutely necessary, I will give it in confidence to you."

"I would rather not carry such a responsibility. My duty is to refer the matter to my superiors. In case they ask me, will you tell me when you last saw the Führer?"

"I visited him in his New Chancellery office in April of 1941. I went into Germany by way of Unoccupied France and Switzerland. Now, as you know, that route is no longer open to one who is technically an American citizen. To make my position clearer, let me add that while my father is an American, I was born in Switzerland and raised on the French Riviera. I have spent far more time in Germany than in the United States. I have been a National Socialist ever since I learned the Führer's ideas, which was about twenty years ago."

Said the *Oberst:* "I will transmit your statement. I trust you understand that in the meantime I shall have to ask you to remain under detention in this hotel until the orders come."

"Certainly, *Herr Oberst*, I could not expect anything else. There is only one problem to be mentioned. When I set out on this trip I had a warm woolen overcoat, but I had to leave it in the desert; I did not dare to carry an extra burden. When I am called to Berlin, I know that it will be a rush order, and I would hate to arrive there in the month of February with the inadequate clothing I have. I have plenty of French money. Would it be possible for one of your men to take my measure and go shopping for me?"

A tactful proposal. The man out of the desert did not ask to be allowed to go around looking at German defenses in an important railhead; also, he implied that he was so sure of the Führer's response that he was willing to throw his money onto the gaming table. The officer replied: "Make a list of what you need, and if the goods are obtainable they will be brought for your inspection."

"*Besten Dank*," said the polite art expert.

III

As it turned out, the black market of Tozeur was unable to produce a suitable overcoat or warm underwear, but the traveler was provided with a small bag containing a toothbrush, a comb, and other necessities of civilization. Guarded by a sergeant and a *Gefreiter*, he was escorted to the railroad station, or what a bomb had left of it. He spent the night sitting up in a train which bumped, but even so was more comfortable than desert rocks. In the morning the sergeant, with due apologies, put a blindfold over his eyes, escorted him from the train, and drove him to what Lanny judged from the sounds to be a large military encampment. Soon afterward he was ascending the steps of what he guessed was a country villa; when the blindfold was whisked off he found himself in a billiard room, in the presence of a monocled Wehrmacht officer, who clicked his heels, bowed correctly, and introduced himself as Major von Dozer of the staff of Marshal von Arnim, commander of all the Axis forces in Tunisia.

Lanny was invited to a seat, and his two-man escort was ordered out. The Prussian officer first apologized to his guest for the temporary necessity of treating him like a prisoner; Lanny replied that he had come prepared for this. The same thing had happened when he had met the German Army at Dunkerque, and had introduced himself as a friend of the Führer's; he had stayed at the corps headquarters until a message had come from the Führer, and then he had been taken to the great man's headquarters on the western front. "I found it easier to join the Wehrmacht then than now, Herr Major," said Lanny with his most agreeable smile.

Naturally the staff officer wanted to hear that entertaining tale having to do with the greatest days of his country's history, the conquest of France. Lanny told how he had spent his time with Kurt Meissner, the *Komponist,* at Godesberg, and how they had traveled to Paris as the Führer's guests, to witness the march of the German armies up the Champs Elysées. Lanny put in so many personal and human touches that it was difficult for a Wehrmacht officer to doubt the truth of his statements.

"You have known the Führer for a long time, then?" said he. And Lanny told how as a lad he had come to Schloss Stubendorf to spend Christmas with Kurt Meissner, whose father was manager of this large estate. After World War I Lanny had come again, and the son of the head forester there, Heinrich Jung, had talked incessantly about a great new leader who had arisen in Germany; Heinrich had visited this leader in prison, and in later years took both Lanny and Kurt to meet him. Lanny had become convinced that National Socialism was the means of freedom for the world, and had visited the Führer off and on and brought him information which he said was of help to him.

"The Führer many times offered to take me into his paid service, and General Göring, as he then was, did the same; but I always declined because I have been able to earn what I need by my profession of art expert. I have bought and sold many paintings, both for Göring and for the Führer. I gave them the same service and at the same commission as for my various clients in America. Have you ever visited the Berghof, Herr Major?"

"*Leider*, I have not had that honor, Herr Budd."

"I had the idea that I might tell you some of the details, so to convince you that I have been there. I happened to be visiting the Führer on the day that Chancellor Schuschnigg of Austria was brought there, just before the Anschluss, and I heard the Führer give him what we in America call a 'bawling out.' A great many people heard it, for when the Führer becomes excited he does not care who hears. His study is on the second floor, and it was observed that a great number of the Chancellery men and the military went up to their rooms and left their doors open. Perhaps you know some of them," and Lanny named a number whom he recalled. The Major knew a couple of them, but not well enough to have shared their confidence.

He would have liked very much to "pump" this mysterious personage of the information which had brought him here; but Lanny had to tell him that his orders from the Führer were strict, that the information was for the Führer alone. "I can say that it is of a diplomatic nature and would be of no help to you in the local situation."

"You have been in North Africa for some time, Herr Budd?"

"Coming and going. I must explain to you that I employ a double camouflage. Locally, I am an art expert, engaged in purchasing Arab mosaics and Moorish fountains for my American clients. This is a genuine business and I have had a number of these items shipped home. Naturally I could not get passports for such private business, therefore the War and State Departments are given to understand that I am aiding my father by observing the performance of Budd-Erling planes and reporting to him."

"Your father is sympathetic to the ideals of National Socialism?"

"Many of our leading businessmen are, and see clearly that we are on the wrong side in this war. My father is a great admirer of Hermann Göring, with whom he did business, and whom he visited at Karinhall several times. My father's position is one of extreme painfulness; he is, to all intents and purposes, a prisoner of the War Department. He has to do what they tell him, and he knows that if he fails his plant will be taken over."

"You have a complicated career," commented the officer, and added a subtle touch: "I hope you do not ever get your various roles confused."

Lanny was *Weltmann* enough to get the meaning of this remark, and he reacted with a touch of severity. "Concerning that, *mein lieber Herr Major*, there is only one judge, our Führer. He has seen fit to approve my services, and to urge me to come more frequently to see him."

IV

Lanny repeated his statement concerning the need of warm clothing, and gave the Major one of the ten-thousand-franc notes which he had sewed up in his coat lining. The resources of this place proved to be better, and he found himself equipped with an overcoat and woolen underwear, together with a suitcase in which to carry it. In this villa he found a shelf or two of French books, and ventured to borrow a copy of *La Chartreuse de Parme*. Nothing pleased him more than to stretch out on a bed and reread a good novel, while his muscles and bones got over the effects of parachuting and cameleering. The Wehrmacht fed its officers well, and the semiprisoner had an ample tray brought to him.

Most of all he enjoyed having the ramrod-stiff aide-de-camp come to him next day, bend himself in half, and announce: *"Ich freue mich, Herr Budd.* The Führer has instructed us that you are his guest, and are to be flown to him at once. Will it be agreeable to you to depart at about midnight?"

"Whatever seems best to you, Herr Major."

"It will be advisable to make a wide detour from Tunis, because enemy planes are active over all the routes to the north. As you doubtless know, they have a device they call radar, which enables them to find our planes at night."

"I have heard of it, Herr Major, and am glad to hear that you also have heard of it."

"We have various devices to counter it. You will be flown toward the northeast, and then veer toward Rome. The plane will refuel and then fly to Nürnberg, and from there to the Führer's field headquarters. I do not need to tell you that that place is ultra-secret, and it will be necessary for you to be blindfolded on the final lap."

"Herr Major, I should have been troubled if you had told me otherwise, for I would not wish to be the sharer of such a secret. It has always been my motto never to hear any confidential statements unless they are necessary to my own errand."

"There is no reason why you should not know that you will be flying from Tunis. As both the airport and the harbor are being frequently attacked, we shall not take you there until the moment for your departure."

"Thank you, Herr Major. It would be most annoying to have come so far and endured so many discomforts to no purpose."

"Is there anything else I can do for you, Herr Budd?"

"You might tell me if it would be considered looting if I should take this paper-back Stendhal novel on my journey."

The Wehrmacht officer was glad of a chance to unbend. He smiled broadly and replied: "Under the terms of the armistice, we are well supplied with French francs, and shall include the price of the book in what we pay for the use of this establishment."

V

While Lanny was being driven to the Tunis airport, there was a bombing raid; he heard the crumping sounds, and when he arrived at the field he saw a hangar and several planes burning. He hoped that his wasn't among them, and it proved not to be; but he had to sit and wait while craters in the field were filled up. Meantime he chatted with the officer who had accompanied him; they were all very cordial now, and ready to absorb the wisdom which fell from the lips of the Führer's secret friend. He told them that the Americans could send few fighter planes because the near-by fields were of such a poor character; but the long-range bombers could operate from Algiers, and numbers of these were coming in to Casablanca by way of Brazil. One of this P.A.'s established practices was to reveal things which he could be quite sure the directing heads of the enemy already knew.

In a fast two-seater plane, not so different from the one in which he had been shot down, Lanny was lifted from the great Tunis airfield and carried across the Mediterranean and around the heel of the Italian boot. There was no "intercom," so he didn't do much talking. He dozed part of the time, and employed the rest to go over in his mind what he meant to say to the genius-madman upon whom his safety now depended. It wouldn't be so easy this time, Lanny could guess; he could hear the Führer's raucous tones, scolding at Lanny's homeland, and it would be strange indeed if he did not vent at least a part of his irritation upon the one member of that evil Judeo-pluto-democratic monstrosity which he had in reach of his voice. Lanny rehearsed a score of speeches which he would try to make, but he had little hope of completing any of them.

Daylight had come when the traveler was set down at the Rome airfield, and he could see the familiar architectural landmarks upon the seven hills. Nearly two decades had passed since he had been here with Marie de Bruyne, adored *amie* whose memory would never grow dim in his mind. He hoped there wouldn't be any Fascist official at the landing field carrying a briefcase with a dossier in it—and there wasn't. It was rarely now that Italians ventured to interfere with, or even to question, anything the German military did in Il Duce's realm.

The plane stopped only to refuel, and then sped away to the north. Over the mountains, one range after another, all covered with snow and dazzling to the eyes even at a distance. A Franco-American playboy had motored through most of these passes in the good old days, and had picnicked on the shores of some of these tiny lakes, which were hard to distinguish now because they, too, were snow-covered. First the Italian Alps, then the Austrian Alps, then the Bavarian Alps, and at last he was set down on the airport of Nürnberg, the town of the Meistersinger; the Nazis had chosen it for their patriotic shrine. Lanny had attended their *Parteitag*, a "day" that lasted a whole week; it had been the final one of these celebrations before the war. He had been Hitler's guest, and had moved among the throngs of fanatics roaring their war songs and proclaiming their intention to take possession of the world. *"Heute gehört uns Deutschland, Morgen die ganze Welt!"* It had taken the "whole world" a long time to realize what was being prepared for it, and Lanny had grown sick at heart with waiting and fearing. Now the Allied planes were finding their way to this Nazi shrine city, and not all the evidence of their visits could be hidden from the traveler.

The plane was again refueled, and with many apologies the aviator tied a black silk bandage about his passenger's eyes and asked his word not to remove it until he was inside the Führer's headquarters. *Befehl,* which means an order, or command, is a sacred word to every German, and a sufficient excuse for anything and everything he may do. Lanny promised cheerfully, for he had looked at enough mountain scenery by now and was well content to relax in his seat and rehearse dramatic scenes with the new master of this obedient race. In the course of nature, Lanny's magic gold ring had made its reappearance and had been put back on his finger; now he could turn it, and recall the various melodies with which Wagner had associated the Ring of the Nibelungs, so full of wondrous powers. Adolf Hitler, an ardent adorer of Wagner's music, had taken the Ring cycle as an expression of his own *Weltanschauung;* in his own mind he was completely identified with Siegfried—always with the qualification that he had been forewarned and would avoid the spear in the back.

Lanny couldn't help speculating as to his destination. If it had been Berchtesgaden, he would have been flown directly to the airfield there. Undoubtedly the commander of all the German armies would be somewhere near the eastern front, where the winter campaign of the Russians presented such a terrible menace. Not too near, of course, for it was no part of a Führer's program to be captured or killed. His headquarters would be in some building not too conspicuous, preferably in a forest, and perhaps especially constructed for the purpose. An airfield would be near, and the location would be the most closely guarded secret in all the Axis realm. Lanny's guess was the western part of the Ukraine.

VI

The plane turned, its engine slowed, and presently it touched the ground—a perfect landing. The blindfolded passenger was helped out, escorted to a car, and driven away. Nobody spoke—that, too, no doubt, was *Befehl*. When the eyes are closed the ears get more attention, and Lanny became aware that he was being driven on a snow-covered road; the echoes from the engine told him that he was in a thick forest, as he had expected. Then the car slowed up and stopped, and he was helped out and led up three or four steps—wooden steps, so it was not a *Schloss*, but a hunting lodge, or else a hideaway newly built for the world conqueror and his staff. There would be many tele-graph and telephone wires, a large switchboard, and a radio aerial raised above the treetops. There would be more than one barricade of barbed wire about the spot, and sentries with watchdogs would pace at all hours of the day and night.

The visitor was escorted to a reception-room, and the blindfold was taken off in the presence of two SS officers. They asked if he had any weapons upon him; when he said no, he was told politely that it had now become the requirement that all persons who entered the Führer's presence must be searched. He answered with equal politeness: he was glad to know that those charged with the safety of the greatest man in the world were not neglectful of their duty.

This fine speech didn't save him from a minute search, including even his fountain pen and the inside of his watch. In the course of the search the men discovered the tiny scrap of paper sewed up in the lining of his coat; on the camel ride he had pulled loose some of the threads, and had not sought an opportunity to resew them, because he did not have a needle or the right color thread. Knowing that he was in German hands, he no longer had any fear concerning this paper, and he told the SS officers that it was a secret message for the Führer, and was a part of Lanny's reason for coming; the Führer would be ex-tremely angry if anyone were to read it but himself, so the searchers contented themselves with feeling all around the paper, and did not remove it from its hiding place.

The search included the new overcoat and the contents of the two bags which had been purchased for him in North Africa. He explained about these, and said that if there was anything wrong with them it would not be his fault. The Führer's guardians did not respond to his smile, and their eyes had a steely look. Lanny had known in the old days that there were members of the Führer's household who did not approve of his intimacy with an American, and that attitude would be intensified many times now that America had become the newest and deadliest of the Fatherland's enemies, a people whose Jew-loving leader was ceaselessly proclaiming to the world his intention to thwart and abort the hope of National Socialism. Members of the Reichsführer's own SS Leibstandarte could not understand the incursion of this bland and easygoing American; they would be polite to him, because that was *Befehl*, but they certainly didn't have to smile at him, and would certainly make sure that he had no new kind of deadly weapon or poison concealed on his person or in his belongings.

While this investigation was in process, there entered another personage, this time not military but domestic; a rosy and rolypoly Bavarian—but less so, Lanny thought, than the last time they had met. From him there was no lack of cordiality, for that was his stock in trade as well as his nature. "*Welche Überraschung, Herr Budd!*" he cried, and held out a fat hand, which Lanny promptly took. "*Grüss Gott, Herr Kannenberg!*" It was the one-time *Kellner* of Munich who had been for years his Führer's steward and official greeter; Lanny suspected that he came now on purpose to make sure that the visitor was actually the right person and no impostor. For a certainty Lanny Budd was Lanny Budd, and so the bundle of *Gemütlichkeit* wrung his hand warmly and asked why he had delayed so long to visit them. Just as if it were an everyday affair for American tourists to come strolling into Hitlerland and be received at the military headquarters of their country's Number One foe!

VII

Lanny Budd was going into the ogre's den. He was going with his usual air of bonhomie, but not without quailing inwardly. There was a vast difference in the state of the world since the last meeting of this pair, almost two years ago. Then Adi Schicklgruber had been at the height of his fortunes, and had had no doubt that the world was his. Now had come the dreadful calamity of Stalingrad, and his armies were retreating in midwinter all the way along the Russian front; his African desert armies had been reduced by half and driven halfway across that immense continent; the Americans had a secure foothold and were preparing a heavy attack. Surely no sane man could any longer believe that Adi was going to win this war; some of his generals must have told him so, and he could not demote or liquidate them all.

"*Bitte, kommen Sie mit, Herr Budd,*" said the older of the SS men. Lanny followed him out of the room and down a hallway; the man knocked upon a door, then opened it. Lanny entered a large room, and there was the Führer of the Germans.

He was dressed in that simple soldier's uniform which he had promised never to take off until victory was won. He was standing in front of a fireplace, warming his back before some burning logs. Before he could speak a word, the young officer announced: "*Mein Führer*, it is my duty to report that in searching this gentleman we found what appeared to be a small piece of paper concealed in the lining of his coat. He states that it is intended for your eyes alone, therefore we have not touched it."

"Bring it to me," said Hitler promptly.

The officer turned to Lanny and extracted the two-inch square of paper from its hiding place. Holding it in the palm of one hand and covering it with the other hand, he made certain that he would not see its contents. While this was happening Lanny spoke: "*Mein Führer*, I make one request. Do not speak about this paper until we are alone. There are reasons which I will explain to you."

"*Gut*," replied the other. There was no cordiality in his tone, only a businesslike precision.

Lanny, observing everything, thought: He has gained weight; his face is pudgier, especially his nose, and his complexion is more pasty than ever. He is worried, and must be taking more of his benzedrine pills. He intends to be cold and stern. He does not know what to make of the paper, and he stares at it. "*Lieber Führer: Ich bin es. Rudi.*" He would like to be able to guess about it without asking me. He does not mean to trust me if he can help it.

"You may go, Franz," said the Führer, addressing the officer, and the man clicked his heels, bowed, straightened himself, turned on his heel as if it were a parade maneuver, and went out, closing the door.

VIII

"*Bitte, kommen Sie, Herr Budd.*"

Lanny advanced to the fireplace and took one of the seats in front of it. On previous occasions the Führer had come halfway to meet him and had cordially shaken his hand. Evidently it was going to make a difference that the two countries were at war. "What is this paper that you have brought me?" demanded the German.

"It is a note from Rudi's hand, written in my presence."

"The British permitted you to see him?"

"Only one Britisher, *mein Führer*. I was able to find a pretext, in connection with my art business, for staying in Rudi's neighborhood for a couple of weeks. I made the acquaintance of one of the guards, and paid him a hundred pounds to take me into the hospital at night."

"What was your purpose in incurring such a risk?"

"First, because Rudi is my friend, and I thought I might comfort him by telling him good news, and by enabling him to send a message to you. Naturally I could not know whether he had been able to establish contact with you."

"There has been no contact between us, and I have sought none. His action was that of a mentally unbalanced man, and has been most damaging to our cause. For him to take it without consulting me was an act of presumption, not to say of insubordination."

"You must understand, *mein Führer*, that I had no means of knowing that this would be your attitude. I knew only that Rudi was the best friend you had, the most devoted to your cause. I had called him *Kurvenal, der treueste der Treuen*. I took it for granted that you must have known of his action, or that, at any rate, he felt sure of your approval."

"In times like these, Herr Budd, a German soldier takes his life in his hands when he acts without my authority. For me, Rudolf Hess no longer exists."

"That is indeed sad news for me, *Exzellenz*, and I am sure that it would kill Rudi if he heard it. His whole being is centered about you and the cause which you are defending. He thinks you the greatest man that ever lived upon earth, and he charged me to deliver messages of love and devotion, and to tell you that he lives only for the day when your forces will come and rescue him. He outlined to me detailed plans by which this might be accomplished—and surely you cannot fail to realize what a tremendous stroke of prestige it would be if you were to take him out of British hands."

This gave the Führer something to think about, as Lanny knew it would; prestige was his specialty, and never since his days as a prisoner in Landsberg fortress twenty years ago had he stood more in need of it. Lanny waited respectfully, for it was his role never to urge, nor even to advise, but merely to bring information and answer questions.

"I was told that Rudi was being held near London, Herr Budd."

"That may have been the case previously. When I talked with him, which was last July, he had just been moved to a hospital in Monmouthshire, and I have every reason to think that the arrangement was permanent. The town of Abergavenny is near the Welsh border, and less than fifty kilometers from the harbor of Newport, where there is a large German prisoner-of-war camp. Rudi's plan calls for a combined expedition of parachute troops and fast speedboats, something like what the British did at St. Nazaire. The prisoners could be freed and

armed, and the parachutists could seize the hospital and carry Rudi
to the port."

Again there was a silence. Then Hitler remarked: "It is something
to be considered; but how can I know that this is not a British trap,
like the one by which they lured him into their clutches?"

"It is Rudi's own idea, and no Briton has heard anything about it.
We conversed in whispers at night, and Rudi was quite certain that
there was no apparatus in his small room."

"Nevertheless it is possible that our enemies have deceived him.
They have everything in their hands and their malice is diabolical.
Also—I must state it frankly—I am forced to bear in mind that the situation between you and me can no longer be what it was. Your country
has made a shameless attack upon mine. Your President has constituted
himself the world's Number One public enemy, by allying himself
with the rapacious British and the barbarian Russians. Your planes are
systematically wrecking our beautiful cities and mangling and maiming
thousands of innocent German women and children. Such crimes
against civilization constitute a blot upon the pages of history, a shame
that will cause the American name to be execrated for the rest of
time."

The son of Budd-Erling appeared greatly shocked. "Surely, *mein
Führer,* you do not hold *me*—of all persons in the world—responsible
for such events!"

"You are an American, and I no longer know how to distinguish
among them. I am beset by enemies who employ every form of intrigue and treachery, and how is it possible for me to trust anyone of
your nation, or even of your Anglo-Saxon race? It would seem that
the poison of Jewish pluto-democracy has permeated your entire culture, so that there are no longer any Americans or Englishmen who
know what human decency is. I see you arming the hordes of Asiatic
devils, helping them to overwhelm the one truly civilized nation in
Europe; and I see so clearly the punishment which this malignancy
will bring down on the whole world. What mercy can you hope to
find, or what salvation, when the Bolshevik terror sweeps over Western Europe, as surely it will if you succeed in breaking down the
barriers of sturdy German bodies and heroic German souls?"

IX

Lanny knew that he wasn't supposed to answer that question; he
wasn't supposed to say anything, or even to try. He was there to listen

to one of the Führer's tirades, which might last an hour, two hours, three hours, according to circumstances. The master of Germany would work himself into a frenzy; he would slap his thighs, he would pound his knees, he would get up and pace the room, back and forth, turning his head to face the person he was addressing. Some people said that he would fall down and chew the rug, but Lanny had never seen him do that. What Lanny had seen and listened to with amazement had been the delivery of an oration as violent and prolonged as if the Führer had been addressing the whole Nazi Party at the Nürnberg annual assembly. He would go on and on, pouring out his vexation, his rage, his sorrow for a world that had not the wisdom to hearken to his words and conform to his demands. Lanny would have to listen, not trying to argue, but exhibiting humiliation and shame for the crimes his fatherland was committing against mankind.

And then, just when the auditor was beginning to fear that the orator might be working himself into some kind of convulsion or fainting fit, there would come a transformation as surprising as the tirade itself. The Führer would remark: "Enough of that," or some phrase of the sort. He would wipe the froth of spittle from his lips, return to his chair, and in a perfectly quiet and rational voice resume the conversation. In this case he said: "Will you tell me where you have been during the past two years, Herr Budd?"

Lanny grabbed the occasion. *"Dazu bin ich hergekommen, mein Führer.* I have been risking my life several times in the effort to serve you. I conceived the plan of getting into touch with Rudi and possibly helping in his rescue. In September of the year before last I set out by airplane for that purpose, but the plane was wrecked in a storm on the way to Iceland, and I was thrown into the sea, with both legs broken. I was picked up by a flying boat, and for weeks it was questionable whether or not I would survive. This took nearly a year out of my life, and it was last June before I was able to come to England again. I had hoped to get passports to Sweden, but I could not satisfy our State Department that I had any legitimate reason for visiting that country; they have become suspicious of me, and cannot understand why I visit Mr. Hearst and Mr. Ford and the other 'appeasers,' as our friends in America are called."

"Are there still any such, Herr Budd?"

"Many, as I hope to show you. I returned to America and persuaded my father that I could help him by observing the performance of the Budd-Erling plane in North Africa. So I came, and I collected information that I thought so important that I could no longer endure not to see you. I found a young aviator who had been reading the Hearst newspapers, and who said to me that he could not see why, when Japan attacked us, we proceeded to fight Germany. I paid him to take me with him on one of his flights and permit me to parachute down near your lines. Unfortunately the plan went wrong, because one of your planes attacked our plane and the young aviator was killed. I had to parachute far out in the desert, and nearly perished of thirst before I encountered a camel caravan. Fortunately I was brought into the German lines, and was able to persuade your SS officers to notify you of my presence. All this I have risked out of my friendship for you, and with no thought of anything but to help you."

"A very unusual story, Herr Budd. But put yourself in my position, and see if it might not occur to you that the British could have had the handwriting of Rudi imitated on this scrap of paper."

"As it happens, *Exzellenz*"—Lanny became formal when his honor was doubted—"that is exactly the difficulty I put before Rudi when he wrote the message. I said: 'Can you not give me some talisman?' He replied by taking this ring from his finger and handing it to me."

Thereupon Lanny did the same thing for Hitler, who took the ring and examined it. The visitor continued: "I asked Rudi if there was something connected with the ring that he could tell me, and he said that you had given it to him as a wedding gift, and had spoken a sentence which you would surely recall. I hope that you do."

"What was the sentence, Herr Budd?"

"*Dies wird das Lästermaul zum Schweigen bringen.*"

Adi Schicklgruber stared at his visitor, and his face betrayed deep emotion. Was he shocked to have those old ugly rumors lift their heads out of the grave of the past? Could he have imagined that this elegant American would never have heard the jokes about the founder of the National Socialist movement and his one-time secretary, called "*Das Fräulein*"?

When Hitler spoke, it was not of these unpleasant matters. "Herr Budd, I see that it is all right, and that you have actually talked with Rudi." He had never been known to apologize to any man.

"*Mein Führer*," said Lanny, returning to his place among the worshiping congregation, "let me remind you for how many years I have been coming to you, bringing such reports as I could gather. All that time I religiously refrained from asking you any questions, save only about matters which you yourself asked me to report to persons abroad. This I did in every case, and brought you back the replies as promptly as I could. You assured me that this service was valuable in the past, and, relying on that statement, many times repeated, I risked my life to come to you now. You should hear what I have to tell you, and then you will be better able to judge whether it was worth my trouble and your time."

"You are right, Herr Budd. Tell me, if you will, everything you can recall concerning your talk with Rudi."

X

So Lanny began. He described the place where the *Nummer Drei* was confined, how he spent his time, what he ate, what he had said about the people who had charge of him. "The British are polite to him, in order that you may have reason to be the same to the many British officers whom you hold. Rudi smiled as he told me how careful they were not to excite him, because, if he were judged insane, it would be necessary under the Geneva convention to return him to Germany. Of course he is not in the least insane, but is very unhappy because of being separated from his friends, especially yourself."

Lanny went on to tell what the faithful Parteiführer had said about his adored Reichsführer. Older, with thinning hair and features lined by grief, Rudi had wept as he talked about the old days, the days of ideological war, when he had had his scalp split by a beer mug thrown in one of the *Saalschlachten*, the battles of the beerhall. He had mentioned old Nazi companions, some long since departed, and others of whose fate in the present war he could only guess. Lanny made a good part of this up, and he pulled all the tremolo stops, for he knew that Adi had a sentimental streak, the German *Schwärmerei*, and saw these old days as it were under a rainbow of glory.

And who had done more to help create this glory than Walther Richard Rudolf Hess? He had come out of World War I an aviator, while Adi had been a mere *Gefreiter*, a subcorporal, the next in rank to a common soldier—and how common these were in Germany, in every sense of that word! Rudi had been an educated man, the son of a well-to-do merchant, while Adi had been a street waif, trying to survive by painting little picture postcards and sleeping in the shelter for the unemployed of Vienna. They had kicked him out because he wouldn't stop his soap-boxing!

And yet Rudi had recognized his genius, and had become his faithful secretary and friend, had marched with him in the futile Beerhall Putsch in Munich, and had gone to prison with him. In that prison he had taken Adi's rambling and ridiculous notes, and had put them in order and made a book called *Mein Kampf*. He had fought in the ten-year battle for power, and when it had been won he had become the head of the Party, taking Hitler's orders with never a doubt or a qualm. That he had dreamed of inducing perfidious Albion to assist in the putting down of Bolshevism—well, it had been a mad dream, *ein toller Traum*, but surely not a disloyal one!

XI

The question of whether to attempt to rescue this "old companion" was one which would call for much investigation and study, said the Führer; the trouble was that the Luftwaffe was so badly needed on the Russian front, and in North Africa, where the Americans were building up their strength so rapidly. The harassed man's brow darkened, and Lanny was afraid he was going to start on another tirade; but no, he had been impressed with the American's statement about information concerning North Africa, and he asked what it was. Lanny told many facts—all of which he could be quite certain that Spanish agents had long ago picked up in Morocco and Algiers: how the bombers were being flown across from Brazil and the fighters brought on carriers and flown ashore; what divisions had arrived and who commanded them; how the ports were being repaired and the airfields made over; what Vichy politicians had sold out to the Jewish democracies and what they were doing.

And then, of course, the Casablanca Conference. Its secrets had begun to leak out, and really were secrets no longer. The son of Budd-Erling had hung around on the outskirts and had wined and dined a number of the Army and Navy officers; more than one of them had drunk too much and talked freely. Lanny made a funny story out of the two French fighting cocks, De Gaulle and Giraud, and the amount of time that Churchill and Roosevelt had spent trying to get them to agree. "The Allies expect to take Tunis this spring," he said, "and then, of course, they will move across to Sicily." He was afraid to say more, not because it was a secret, but because it might drive Adi into another tantrum.

The visitor talked about the Jewish-plutocrat-democrat Rosenfeld and his overwhelming ego, which desired to do all those evil things it accused Hitler of doing. A terrible calamity, that the destiny of a powerful nation should rest in the hands of this crippled and abnormal personality! Lanny said: "I don't know if it has come to your ears, *mein Führer*, but I have it on first-rate authority that the man has taken up the notion that our scientists can solve the problem of developing power from the splitting of the atom. You may not believe it, but he has diverted considerably over a billion dollars from war manufacturing to this purpose. Huge plants are being erected, purely on mathematical theory, to carry out processes which have not even been tested in the laboratory. We have a saying, 'putting the cart before the horse'; this time we are putting a million carts where there is no horse visible. I doubt if there has been such madness in the world since King Canute set his throne on the sand and ordered the tide not to advance."

"I have heard about the atom splitting," replied the Führer, "and I am well pleased to have our enemies spending their money that way. Some of our own scientists have been playing with the same idea, and have tried to persuade me, even to frighten me, into taking up the same projects. But I am not an easy man to frighten, as you may realize, Herr Budd."

"*Ja, sicherlich, mein Führer.*"

"I have my own plans, and my way of winning this war. I have told the German people that we are creating new weapons, and believe me, I was not telling them fairy tales. What is coming to the British before this year has passed will knock some of the 'ginger' out of them."

"You may be interested to know that the news has already reached them. I have had it revealed to me in England that you are developing jet propulsion. The people who are in the know expect what they call rocket bombs to be falling upon them before this year is over. They are working hard on the project themselves, but they know that you are ahead. The Americans are even further behind, mainly because of Roosevelt's fantastic idea of nuclear fission."

"I am glad to have this reassurance, Herr Budd."

"As it happens, my father is in touch with many technical men, and he talks to me freely. I do my best to remember what I hear, but you will understand that I am only an amateur, and for obvious reasons I dare not make notes. There are a few things I can tell you about what our own people have discovered on the subject of jet propulsion. I cannot be sure that it will help you, but I offer it for what it may be worth."

"*Ich verstehe, Herr Budd.* Tell me, by all means."

So Lanny proceeded to repeat that list of details which he had been furnished by Major Dowie, technical details likely to impress the Germans without doing any harm to the Allies. The P.A. had learned these sentences by heart and had been careful not to let them grow dim in his memory. As he recited them to the Führer, he could see that that emotional person was enormously impressed. Whatever doubts he may have had in his mind were shoved into the background as he heard this supposed-to-be traitor reeling off a list of American achievements and objectives in the new and vitally important science of jet propulsion. Hitler wasn't a technical man himself, but he thought he was, and that made him an easy mark. "I must let you discuss these matters with some of our own specialists," he said. And this, of course, was one of the hopes that had lured Lanny into the ogre's den.

XII

The conference proved the longest a wandering art expert had ever had with the commander-in-chief of an empire at war. Hitler wanted to ask questions about one after another of the important persons this friend had met, in America, in Britain, in Vichy France, in North Africa. Lanny was expecting at every moment to have him ask: "What is this I hear about your having been through Russia and talked with Stalin?" He was prepared to answer that he had been forced to take this trip to escape from the Japanese, and that he had used his father's position to meet the Red dictator and find out his idea of peace terms in order to bring them to Hitler. But apparently there had been a slip of the Brown dictator's secret service; the Führer mentioned no rumor about Lanny's having been in the Soviet Union.

Just as there had been men in prewar France who preferred Hitler to Blum, so in America there were men who would have preferred Hitler to Roosevelt. Lanny had talked with some of these men, and now he told Hitler what they had said and were publishing in their great newspaper chains. The Führer found this agreeable listening. In particular he was interested in the little group of "economic royalists" and their military friends who were so embittered against a Judeo-pluto-democratic President that they had been discussing the idea of seizing his person, holding him incommunicado, and issuing decrees in his name. Lanny had reported this on his last visit to Hitler, and since then he had got from Roosevelt's friend Jim Stotzlmann a lot of new details concerning the junta. He didn't mind embellishing them, for he could be sure that Hitler had no way of checking at present. There was nothing that pleased Adi more, and he found no slightest difficulty in believing the story, for that was the way he had treated his own rivals, and he had no doubt that these rivals would be eagerly seeking a chance to do the same thing or worse to him.

Lanny outlined the program which these men intended to put through in the name of a captive President. America was to cease making war upon Germany, and this would force Britain to do the same. America would concentrate upon defeating Japan, and in return for this service to civilization would take the empire which Japan held at present, including the control of China; also, of course, of Central and South America, and Mexico. The United States and the Führer would jointly guarantee the integrity of the British Empire forever. The Führer would hold what he had at present, and would concentrate upon defeating Russia, something he could easily do if his western front were relieved from pressure. Such a settlement would preserve the peace of the world for a thousand years.

It was Hitler's own formula, exactly what he wanted, and he rubbed his hands with satisfaction; every trace of vexation, every trace of melancholy, disappeared from his flabby features. "*Sehr richtig, Herr Budd!*" he exclaimed. "I will promise to liquidate every Bolshevik man and whore on my part of the earth! Tell me, why cannot this be brought about? Why does it take so long? My heroic German youths are pouring out their blood on the snows of that barbarous land, while I wait for your Western Powers to come to their senses. *Warum? Warum?*"

So simple it seemed to him, a little matter of kidnaping a crippled President and keeping him safe from harm! The great newspaper proprietors of America, the great industrialists, the great bankers—they were men of such enterprise and initiative, they had built up a vast empire, and were they now going to surrender it without a struggle? Surely they could see that if the Bolsheviks were permitted to destroy Germany, there would be no stopping them anywhere short of the Atlantic Ocean on the west and the Indian Ocean on the southeast. And how long would it take their expert agitators to eat their way into the heart of the American labor movement?

A wise P.A. didn't say anything to break the spell of this *Führertraum*. He didn't point out that the President was especially well guarded in wartime, and that the effort to depose him might result in a civil war; on the contrary, he gave the explanation: the economic masters of America had believed that Germany was going to win the war singlehanded, and only now was it becoming clear to them that this was less than certain, and that more positive action might be called for. Lanny didn't have to put words into the mouths of the American business potentates—he had only to repeat what he had heard them say at their own dinner tables and on their private golf courses, and in the locker-rooms of the Newcastle Country Club. Hitler rubbed his hands still more gleefully, and was ready to send Lanny back to the United States at once, to organize these gentry and put them to work.

XIII

"What are your plans, Herr Budd?" the future world master inquired; and Lanny replied worshipfully that he had no plans except to carry out the Führer's wishes. His suggestion would be for him to return to America by way of Spain and Portugal to make the Führer's terms clear to the key persons upon whom the project depended.

"If you don't mind," he added, "I might be of use to several of your people before I go. For example, Hermann Göring. I have heard the report that you are not on the same intimate terms as formerly, so naturally I consult your wishes."

"Hermann set himself against my policies in a way that I considered presumptuous; but even so, he is the Commander of the Luftwaffe, and in that capacity he is indispensable to me."

"It was my idea that he might like to hear some of the technical details concerning the Budd-Erling plane and others that I have been able to watch in North Africa. Of course I would not dream of seeing him unless it was in accord with your wishes."

"It is quite all right and a good idea. I also want you to talk to some of our jet-propulsion people; Professor Salzmann, I think, would be a good choice."

"I'll be happy to meet him. And then I should like to renew one or two old friendships: Heinrich Jung, for example—how is he?"

"He has an important position now in the Hitler-Jugend, and is rendering his usual devoted service. He and his family are well, so far as I know. I rarely see any of my old friends these days; I am a prisoner of the war. I am afraid you will find Berlin a far from pleasant place to visit this winter."

"I will get along, *mein Führer*. I have become so used to the bombs that I miss them. One more question, if I may—Kurt Meissner?"

"Kurt insisted upon going back into the Army; but before he could go to the front he was injured by a falling building in one of the night raids to which the *Hauptstadt* is subjected. I am told that he may never be able to play the piano again."

"Oh, how tragic!"

"The Fatherland is full of tragedy, so full that I cannot spare the time to think about my friends. I was told that Kurt had returned to his family in Stubendorf."

"As you know, he is my oldest and dearest friend. Would it be possible for me to see him?"

"Certainly. I will have you flown there if you wish."

"There may be some difficulty about my traveling in Germany under present conditions, *mein Führer*."

"I will give you my personal *Erlaubniss-schein*, which will protect you from embarrassment. You speak German so well that no one but the police and the military will pay attention to you. Will a period of three weeks suffice?"

"That will be more than ample, I am sure."

"When you are ready to leave, notify either Hermann or myself, and arrangements will be made for you to fly to Stockholm or Lisbon."

"My passport does not cover Sweden. If I may make a suggestion, it will suffice if I am flown to Madrid. I can consult with some of your friends there, and then in a day or two make my own way to Lisbon. My arrival there in a German plane might attract undesirable attention."

"*Ganz richtig, Herr Budd.* You will spend the night here as my guest, and fly early in the morning, if weather permits. In case we do not have a chance for further talk, let me say now that I appreciate the devotion you have shown to our cause, and that it will surely not go unrewarded."

"There is nothing I want for myself, *mein Führer;* only that thousand-year peace you have promised the world, so that I can go back to playing the piano and looking at beautiful paintings."

"Hermann has collected ten thousand old masters," said the Führer of the Germans. "He will have them all assembled in one place and you can spend the rest of your life studying them."

22

The Mighty Scourge of War

I

"*BITTE um Verzeihung, Herr Budd*," said Arthur Kannenberg, coming into the little reception room to which Lanny had been escorted, and in which he was comfortably ensconced in a wicker *chaise-à-deux* before a grate fire. A wind had arisen outside, and snowflakes were lodging on the windowpanes. The rolypoly little ex-*Kellner* was now comical in a Bavarian suit, with black leather short pants and a brightly embroidered short jacket; Lanny knew it was his equivalent of "formal dress," and he carried his accordion as a sign that he was ready to entertain if requested, and would be hurt if he was not.

"The Führer has asked me to explain," continued this professionally jolly soul, seating himself beside the guest. "He dines with his military staff, and they discuss the news of the day and the strategy of tomorrow. They would not understand having an *Ausländer* present."

"*Sicher nicht, Herr Kannenberg*. It would be embarrassing to me, and I appreciate being spared the ordeal. Am I to have the pleasure of your company?"

"You are kind, Herr Budd. We are to dine here."

"Let us pretend that we are in the old days," said Lanny with his best smile. "*Un cabinet particulier*, if you recollect."

"We always use French when we think of elegance," sighed the ex-*Kellner*.

"Even Frederick the Great did that," replied the other, "so it should be *en règle*."

So these two made friends; and a soldier in uniform brought them cabbage soup and rye bread on trays. This was followed by a chicken, which had been sacrificed for their pleasure, divided in half, and roasted with potatoes, the principal food of the German *Volk*. The deputy-host apologized for the lack of variety in this repast, but Lanny said: "I spent five days all but starving in the Sahara Desert and I have not yet made up my weight. I assure you this food has a most delicious flavor. When I think of what your people are enduring, I feel myself a sybarite."

II

A former beerhall impresario found this a highly intellectual conversation, and he drank to the long life of the mysterious *Führerfreund*. They talked about the good old days, to which good old Bavarians looked back with melancholy. They had accepted their Air Marshal's word that no enemy bombs would ever fall on German soil; they had thought they were safe from the war, snuggled up against the Swiss border; but now it was coming to them, and their sufferings were multiplied by their fears. Herr Kannenberg drank a draught of *Liebfraumilch*—which is wine, not milk; he looked at the snow coating the windowpane, he listened to the wind howling in the small chimney, and tears came into his eyes. "I think of our *Jungens*, out there in the frightful Russian winter, on those plains that have no end!"

The *Weltmann* said tactfully: "All wars come to an end, Herr Kannenberg. Some day we shall be back at Berchtesgaden, and there will be a crop of new songs about the heroes who won this war. Do you remember the first time we met there, and how you played and sang, and I played the *Moonlight Sonata* for the Führer?"

"I remember it well. It must have been—how long ago?"

"Some seven years."

"You had your wife with you, I recall."

"I have a new wife now. Irma Barnes, whom you met, was immensely rich, and I was obliged to live in palaces and to behave accordingly. I found that I tired of it quickly. The richest people are not always the best company."

"They expect a great deal of one. *Glauben Sie mir, Herr Budd*, I have had opportunity to observe them in the course of my business."

"You have had an extraordinary career, Herr Kannenberg, and some time you should set it down on paper. Think what a book! *Die Grössen Die Ich Kannte!* Indeed, you might say *Die Grössten*, for you have known the greatest of our time. Shakespeare tells us that 'All the world's a stage, and all the men and women merely players.' The public has an irresistible desire to go behind the scenes and into the dressing-rooms of these players."

"The public would find it a complicated and confusing kind of life. Believe me, *lieber Herr*, the person who serves *Majestät* sleeps in no bed of roses."

Lanny wondered: Had this combination steward and court jester been getting into trouble of late, and was he longing for an opportunity to pour out his soul? The grown-up playboy smiled his most genial smile and remarked: "You may always have the assurance that you are rendering a service to the German *Volk*, preserving for them the man upon whom their destiny depends. It is surely not to be expected that the man who carries such responsibilities as *unser Führer* should not have his whims indulged, his human failings made allowance for. Surely it cannot be any great trouble to prepare his vegetable plate with a poached egg on top, even here in this remote land in wartime!"

"It is not that which troubles me, Herr Budd; it is the fact that I am not allowed to do more for him in the line of nutrition. The Führer suffers from incessant stomach trouble, as you no doubt know."

"He gives many evidences of it."

"*Leider!* And if only I could persuade him to try a good *Bratwurst* now and then! Surely it was not intended that the human stomach should be loaded with the fodder of rabbits and cows, even when it has been well boiled! For what did man tame the rabbits and the cows, except that they should digest all this spinach and carrots and turn it into more concentrated food?"

"I am afraid you are coming into conflict with the Führer's religious convictions, Herr Kannenberg."

"I ventured to protest to him in the old days, and he used to make a joke of it; but now my remarks annoy him, and I no longer dare open my mouth. I don't know whether you are aware of it, but of late Adi has become convinced that he suffers from a stomach cancer."

"*Gott behüte!* I trust that is not true!"

"Doktor Morell, Doktor von Hasselbach, his surgeon, and Doktor Karl Brandt, who is our Reichs Commissioner for Health, all have solemnly assured him that this is a mistake on his part, but nothing can take the idea from his mind. It has very important political consequences. Pray do not ever quote me—"

"*Ach, gewiss niemals, Herr Kannenberg!*"

"I have heard from his own lips his statement that the attack upon Russia was caused by his belief that the time is short, and he felt that was the one task which no one else was adequate to perform. 'If God will give me two months,' he said. God has given him nearly two years, but the end is not yet; and how can it end if we lose each winter the half of what we have gained in the summer?"

"It must be a frightful strain upon our friend's mind, I fear."

"It would be enough to destroy any man's digestive system, even without the rabbit-and-squirrel-fodder diet. You may have noticed that the Führer's left hand trembles, and that he drags his left leg slightly. This embarrasses him greatly, so that he never signs his name in front of others—you see, he would have to hold the paper still with his left hand, and he cannot do it. This is a result of the grippe he suffered last year in the Ukraine. Doktor von Hasselbach calls it Parkinson's disease, and says that its cause might be mental—the dreadful strain and worry, the sleepless nights, the bad news breaking in all the time. We who love him and who would like so to save him stand helplessly by and dare not even speak."

"Who is his physician now, Herr Kannenberg?"

"Oh, it has been Doktor Morell for years. Adi swears by him and obeys him as religiously as he requires others to obey the Führer himself."

"Who is this Doktor Morell?"

"He was a venereal-disease specialist to Berlin actors and gay blades. He is about fifty-five, and gray-haired; a very positive and convincing person, and, of course, high-priced. He fills his patient full of strange drugs for strange purposes, and by strange methods. Even by enemas—do you believe in enemas, Herr Budd?"

"I have never had occasion to try them."

"Nor I either. Nature does not seem to have made me the right shape for such a proceeding. It is called 'colonic irrigation,' and I believe it came from America, perhaps by way of India or some other place where strange ideas have prevailed for thousands of years. No one would dare to ask the Herr Doktor such questions. He comes with new remedies; he shoots glucose into the patient's muscles to give him energy, and a stuff called orchikrin to relieve his fatigue. It is one of a steward's duties to see that the supply of these substances is kept up, so I know them all by heart: euflat pills, which combine pancreas extract and charcoal, and intelan, which combines vitamins A and D. He takes ultra septyl tablets for his catarrhal condition, and omnadin, a protein and gall mixture, to keep away colds. He relies on cardiazol to increase his circulation, and now he is beginning to receive intravenously another preparation—I have not yet been told the name, but it is supposed to check his arteriosclerosis."

"*Um Gottes Willen!*" said the art expert. "Is there no chance that some of these substances might combine to make something poisonous?"

"Or explosive," replied the faithful steward. "And all this would be unnecessary if only our dear Adi would permit us to prepare him a simple *Weisswurst* one day, and a *Leberknödel* the next! Look at me and see for yourself!"

III

The trays were removed, and the pair sat before the fire. The *Ausländer* told how much he loved this greatest man in the world, and the oft-told story of how an American playboy came to find out about him and to know him. When a household, great or small, has a master, everybody talks about that master, and everybody knows everything about him. Lanny emphasized how important it was to preserve and protect this Führer of the Germans from any sort of harm, and the steward told of the extraordinary care that was taken with the purchasing of food, all brought from Germany, because they would not trust any Ukrainian— The ex-*Kellner* stopped in the midst of his sentence and flushed with embarrassment. "*Ach!* I have said something that I should not, Herr Budd. Be so good as to forget it."

"Certainly, *lieber Freund*. I have no interest in such matters; and besides, I could be a good guesser if I wished to."

His smile was reassuring, and the other went on: "There is no one in this household who would not gladly die to help our Führer. We do everything in our power. Eva is here now, and he is always quieter for a while after she comes."

"I do not think I have ever met Eva," said Lanny, always quick on the uptake.

"She does not meet many persons. She is a simple Bavarian *Mädel*, without much conversation; that helps the Führer, because he likes to have someone to listen to him."

"I do my best to fill that need when I am here," smiled the visitor.

"*Ja, Herr Budd*, but men such as you stimulate him, because you have ideas. Eva has none, so she is restful. There have been other women, but she is his permanent friend. She exacts nothing from him and does not complain of long absences. You, I am sure, are not one to heed the hateful gossip about Adi; his sex life is rather deficient, because he is so much wrapped up in his cause, and as a rule more interested in trying to convert a woman than to take possession of her."

"Quite so, Herr Kannenberg," assented Lanny. At the same time he wondered if the ex-*Kellner* had failed to hear, or had managed to forget, the experience of the psychic medium who was now Lanny's wife, and whom Lanny had taken to Berchtesgaden as a guest.

IV

The court musician took his accordion. "What did I sing at Berchtesgaden?" he asked, and Lanny said that he had sung *"Tiroler sind lustig."* So he sang: *"Tiroler sind lustig, so lustig und froh,"* very softly, so as not to disturb anybody. Then he asked: "What else?" And Lanny said: *"Z'Lauterbach hab' i' mein' Strumpf verlor'n."* He sang that. He was just starting on *"O, du lieber Augustin,"* when there came a roar from outside in the hallway, a familiar and terrifying voice bellowing: "What fool is that making a racket at such a time? *Maul halten!"*

The rosy accordionist turned almost yellow with fright. He sat as if frozen, holding the instrument in mid-air; his eyes looked as if they were about to emerge entirely from their sockets. His mouth dropped open, and he stayed that way, like a statue of terror, a living proof of the truth of his statement, that the person who serves *Majestät* sleeps in no bed of roses!

The screaming continued: *"Fäulniss! Verdammte Scheissdreck!"*—a torrent of the language which Adi Schicklgruber had picked up in the gutters of Vienna, some of them words that Lanny had never heard before. Deeply shocked, he thought: The man is really beside himself. And there goes my chance of an *Erlaubniss-schein!* It was hard to imagine such a tirade because of the simple offense of singing in low tones the songs which were native to Adi's homeland and which he dearly loved.

Gradually both auditors came to realize that only the opening words had been meant for them. Out in that hallway some other person was getting the dressing down of his life. *"So ein grenzenloser Blödsinn, in eine Irrenanstalt sollte ich Sie schicken!"* In German it is the custom to address a single individual with the plural, *Sie,* and so Lanny never did know whether there was one general out there or a whole company of them. Adi called him or them *Teufelsdreck*—devil's dung—and threatened him or them with confinement, not merely in a lunatic asylum, but in a *Konzentrationslager,* and again in *die Hölle,* even harder to get out of. "For what do I pay salaries to generals? If my troops are to run away, can they not do it by themselves? I send you fresh divisions, and no sooner do they arrive than they have to retreat. I send you guns, tanks, trucks, and you present them to the enemy, and come home and tell me that it was impossible to bring them out. *Ihr Hurensöhne,* I did not send them to be brought out, I sent them to be used to fight and to win victories—*um zu kämpfen und zu siegen!*"

The voice receded, because the Führer was walking down the hall-way. A door slammed, and there was silence. Even then it took some time for the terrified *Kellner* to be able to move and to use his voice. "*Gott erbarm' dich unser!*" he exclaimed, for most Bavarians had been brought up pious and remembered the phrases even when they became Nazis. "We have had another defeat!"

"*Leider, leider!*" responded the sympathetic visitor. "Too bad!"

"Almost every day now we retire from places. The day before yes-terday it was Rostov that was taken from us, and a few hours later it was Voroshilovgrad. What disagreeable names those Russians do give to places!"

"I suppose they don't sound so bad to them," ventured the other.

"If you will excuse me, Herr Budd, I will go out and see what has happened. Do not think that it is too bad, because Adi behaves this way all the time now. Since Stalingrad he has never had any peace of mind."

The faithful steward went out, and while he was gone Lanny's face assumed the expression of the cat that had swallowed the canary. He tried to guess what the defeat might be; he knew the battle line as it had been the day before he left Algiers, and he hoped it might be Kharkov, the second greatest city of the Ukraine. He knew that the Germans had been diligently restoring it ever since they had taken it, early in their attack on the Soviet Union.

Kannenberg came back, and his face was that of the canary which has been swallowed by the cat. "It is Kharkov," he said. "It is awful, awful! Who can stand against these Russian hordes? We kill a million, and there is another million treading in their footsteps."

Lanny assumed the manner and tone of a high-priced undertaker—or "mortician," as they were asking to be called in the land of his fathers. "Often a retreat is preliminary to another advance, Herr Kan-nenberg. The Russian boots can march in deep snow, but when the ground is hard, the German Panzers roll over them."

"So we have been told, Herr Budd. But this second winter is worse than the first. If we retreat much farther, it will be necessary to aban-don this headquarters; and moving in the month of February will be miserably uncomfortable!" *Der arme Dicke* was thinking about him-self.

V

In the morning the storm had ceased, and Lanny was told that the snow was not too deep for his departure. He packed his few belongings, and a young officer of the household staff first came and asked his wishes about money and other matters, and then placed in his hands the promised permit, on the Führer's official stationery and signed with his own hand. "The bearer of this letter, Herr Lanning Prescott Budd, American, has my permission to travel in German territory for a period of three weeks. Police and military authorities are instructed to treat him with all courtesy and to afford him such travel facilities as he requests. He is authorized to leave Germany at any time within the period stated, and to exchange his French money for German, or take it out with him. Adolf Hitler." No explanations or qualifications—it was the Führer's will, and no laws would stand in the way.

The blindfold was put over the visitor's eyes and he gave his word not to remove it. He was escorted from the building and into a waiting car. It was a freezing morning, and he was glad of the woolen underwear and overcoat. He was driven to the airport and put on board a plane. "*Sie fliegen nach Stubendorf, Herr Budd,*" said the young officer, and Lanny replied: "*Richtig. Danke schön.*" The officer said: "*Gut Rutsch*"—it was the fighting pilots' phrase.

The plane rose and flew steadily. The pilot did not speak; he may have been told not to, or he may not have relished carrying an enemy passenger. Lanny knew that they were starting from the western Ukraine and flying to Upper Silesia, so he could guess the course as slightly north of west and the distance as some four hundred miles. He would be over Poland nearly all the way. The cold outside would be deadly, but in the enclosed cabin it was comfortable enough. He occupied his mind with sorting out what he had learned in the ogre's den and memorizing the important points; he could not make a single note.

At last the crackling in the passenger's ears told him that he was coming down; the leaning of his body told him that they were turning. Presently he felt the plane touch the ground; the engines died and the plane came to a halt. The pilot said: "You may remove the blindfold," and Lanny did so. The door was opened, and he thanked the pilot, and stepped out upon the snow-covered field. Airfield guards were running toward them, and Lanny took out his *Erlaubniss-schein.* They had never seen anything like it, and he realized that he was going to make his progress through Germany over the awed and stunned bodies of Nazi *Beamten* of all ranks.

They told him that Herr Kurt Meissner's home was a couple of miles away, in the forest near the *Schloss;* Kurt had no telephone, but a sleigh could be hired. An officer ordered one of the men to carry the visitor's bags, and presently he was bundled in a sleigh, with a venerable livery-stable horse taking him toward the five-story stone castle on the height. When Lanny had first come here, at the age of fourteen, the road had seemed steep and the *Schloss* magnificent; now everything seemed smaller, but still precious to his memory. He liked most non-Nazi Germans, and even a few of the Nazis; he was ready to like the whole nation whenever they would stop trying to conquer their neighbors.

VI

Kurt's home on the edge of the great forest had been built for him by the "Old Graf," long since deceased. Kurt was to have the use of it during his lifetime, and his widow after him: this because he was a great *Komponist* and had brought new glory to *Seine Hochgeboren's* ancient name, though, of course, that haughty personage wouldn't have put it that way. The house had had to be added to as Kurt's blue-eyed and buxom wife had performed her duty of making up for the destruction of German manpower. There were three little ones playing about the place, and five others at school, the visitor was told. They all knew this munificent American, for he had never failed to send them presents at Christmas, that is, until the last two Christmases.

A truly fairy-story occasion when a sleigh stopped before the door and this Prince Charming from overseas stepped out unannounced. The children, shy little creatures with flaxen hair and blue eyes, stood staring, speechless. Lanny lifted and dropped the knocker on the door, and there came the plump matron—her name was Lisa, but Lanny chose to call her Dorothea, after the *gute verständige Mutter* of Goethe's poem. Fifteen or sixteen years had passed since Kurt had left the soft warm love nest which Beauty Budd had provided for him at Bienvenu. If he had delayed any longer to marry he would have broken his parents' hearts, and Kurt was a dutiful *Deutscher*. Now he had a dutiful wife and eight little ones who would surely not fail in this virtue, for Kurt was a stern disciplinarian.

Here he came, and Lanny was shocked by his aspect. His long face was longer than ever, pale and deeply lined; his hair was gray and thinning. He was less than two years older than Lanny, but you would have taken him for a man of sixty. His left arm hung limp at his side, and Lanny was told that it was due to a spinal injury. He could never play the piano again, but fortunately he could write and compose.

The coming of this guest was like a burst of sunshine in a storm-bound land. These two had been united by ties of deep affection, and if Kurt had ever had any doubts of Lanny's loyalty to the Nazi cause, these doubts must have been dissipated now. Lanny had come from the Führer, whom Kurt had not seen for more than a year. How was he, and what had he said? Lanny made it as cheerful as possible, saying nothing about Rostov and Voroshilovgrad and Kharkov, and surely nothing about the Vienna gutter talk. The Führer was close to the battlefield, and standing firm with heroic courage. The winter was bad, but mighty forces were being built up in the rear, and in another three months the march to victory would begin.

Did Kurt believe this? Lanny didn't know, and surely wouldn't ask. He told about the strange route by which he had come, and that indeed was a winter's tale, lending color to an afternoon of cold gray clouds. This land lay open to the Baltic winds, and to those from the Arctic beyond. It was frozen hard and blanketed with snow for half the year; and here came a man who said that less than a week ago he had been in a place where there was no drop of water for hundreds of miles, and where the sun's glare was so terrible that you could not bear to touch your hand to the rocks. The older children came home from school and sat in a circle, drinking in this story, wide-eyed and as still as so many mice.

VII

Later, in Kurt's tiny study, Lanny told the story he had told the Führer, for Kurt had been a secret agent himself and held his great master's confidence. He wanted to know what was going on in North Africa, and what opinion was in London and Washington and New York. He was deeply moved by the Hess story, and the means by which Lanny had convinced the Führer of its truth. Was he cheered by Lanny's optimism? Or did he think of his friend as an amiable playboy and dreamer, as in past years? The two-thousand-mile battle line, from the White Sea down to the Black, must have looked pretty grim to an old-time Wehrmacht artillery captain. If the Russians could fight their way into Poland they might be able to fight through it, and Stubendorf was right at the border, indeed, it had been made a part of Poland according to the Versailles Treaty. For twenty years the Graf and his friends and retainers had suffered that indignity. The Führer had won them back—but suppose he were to lose them again!

Kurt had just completed a composition, he told his friend, and of course Lanny was interested. When the masterpiece was produced, it proved to be a Nazi fighting song, the words written by one of their bellowing verse writers. To this depth had the man fallen, whom

Lanny had once compared with Beethoven! But Kurt took the work with complete seriousness—it was a crippled man's effort to save the Fatherland. Lanny ran his eyes over the composition; he knew Kurt's music script well and could play it at sight. Of course he had to do so, while Kurt sang in a voice that had never been more than moderately good.

Lanny burst into praise of the song, but in his heart was the thought: What an insult to art, and what a betrayal of life! Kurt had abandoned all those ideas of brotherhood and humanity which he had taught to Lanny in their boyhood; Kurt, who had repeated the noble saying of Goethe: *"Im Ganzen, Guten, Wahren, resolut zu leben."* Now Kurt's "whole" had become the narrow dogmas of National Socialist racism, his "good" had become the plundering and enslavement of Germany's neighbor nations, and his "true" had become the product of Doktor "Jüppchen" Goebbels' lie factory!

Lanny had to lie to Kurt, to cheat him and thwart him in every way possible; but even while he did it he was sick at heart and wished that he was elsewhere. Here in Stubendorf the P.A.'s soul was torn in halves, because the old affection was still there, and pity for the hard-working devoted wife and the innocent little children. Over and over again Lanny recalled the saying of Trudi, also a German, that he and she and all of them had chosen a bad time to be born.

Lanny couldn't do anything to save this family either from the Russians or from the network of lies in which were enveloped. All that he could do was to get from Kurt what information Kurt possessed. That wasn't easy, for the *Komponist* was no free-spoken person like his Führer and the Führer's steward and clown. When Lanny asked after Emil, Kurt's oldest brother, the reply was that he had recovered from his wound and now commanded an Army corps; when Lanny asked where he was, the reply was: "On the eastern front." An inquiry about *Seine Hochgeboren* brought the reply that Kurt believed him to be in Berlin at present.

Only once did the older man break loose, and that was when Lanny quoted the Führer concerning the traitors who were plotting to kill him; the Führer hadn't said this, but Lanny was sure there were such persons, and that the Führer knew it. Now he discovered that Kurt knew it also. Kurt didn't say "on the authority of Emil," but Lanny could guess it was so. He remarked that there were dissident generals in the Wehrmacht, men who were embittered because the Führer pre-ferred his own ideas of strategy to theirs, and who blamed Germany's defeats upon his bad judgment. Those men whispered among themselves and were ready for anything. "You know," said Kurt, "the Wehrmacht is old and haughty, while National Socialism is new, and its men are looked upon as upstarts. Our *Generalstab* has been the real ruler of Germany for generations, and they do not easily surrender to newcomers. That is the great danger to our national unity."

"You are the man who ought to do something about that," ventured the art expert. "You could get the confidence of those men, and keep the Führer informed."

"I have many times thought of it," was the reply. "I would be willing to sacrifice my art. But Emil tells me that there are others keeping watch, and he is quite sure the Führer knows who his enemies are."

VIII

The next day Lanny took the local train to Breslau, and from there the night train to Berlin. Germany's railroad system was run down; the cars needed paint, and the broken windows had been replaced with wooden boards; the trains were irregular and crowded, but a man with a letter from the Führer in his pocket could always get on board. He had changed some of his French money for German at the Führer's headquarters, so he traveled *erste Klasse,* and had the good fortune to have a *Halb Abteil* to himself. He would have been glad to hear the Germans talking, and he might have passed for a citizen of Geneva, or even of Paris; but he was afraid to make such a statement, lest some official might come through and ask to see his papers.

When the art expert got off at the Friedrichstrasse Station, he was only a few blocks from his old haunt, the Adlon; but he wasn't going there. The registration of an American would have caused a sensation, and it wouldn't have been diminished by the presentation of a *Führer-erläubniss-schein*—quite the contrary. The hotel had been "the Club" of American correspondents, and now it must be "the Club" of Swedish, Swiss, Spanish, and Balkan correspondents; they would surely send stories about the presence in Berlin of the mysterious son of Budd-Erling. Was he a peace emissary? Was America at last getting ready to shift her position and take the anti-Communist side? For what other conceivable purpose would the son of an American airplane manufacturer be in the capital of his country's chief enemy? The American State Department would have to say that it knew nothing about him, and the War Department might state that he would be arrested if and when he returned. A P.A. wanted no such publicity.

Where to go, then? Any *pension* would be a hothouse of gossip, he knew. It must be with some friend, but whom? Heinrich Jung had a large family in a small house; moreover he lived in the suburbs and transportation was difficult. Graf Stubendorf? He was a formal person, and staying with him would be a burden—much deferential conversation, and the impossibility of getting any "clothes," in the meaning of that word used by *die grosse Welt*. General-Major Furtwaengler of Göring's staff? He was a bore, and his wife even worse, a Nazi snob and toady. Lanny would want to bite her!

He bethought himself of the Fürstin Donnerstein; *gute alte Hilde;* she wasn't as old as Lanny, but that was the smart way of hailing your women friends. She was the best source of gossip in Berlin, and always good fun. She lived in a white marble palace, but even so she might be glad of a little ready cash, for the taxes were frightful, with Hitler's financial wizards doing their best to make it impossible for anybody in his Third Reich to get more than the absolute necessities of life.

IX

Lanny went to the telephone in the station, and presently heard her eager voice. Usually Hilde spoke all the cultured languages mixed up in a potpourri, but now it was *"polizeilich verboten"* to speak anything but German over the phone. *"Ach, Lanny!"* she cried. *"Wie schön! Wie wunderschön!"* And then, apparently realizing all at once that it was an enemy alien she was talking to: *"Aber, was—?"*

"It's all right," he said. "I want to see you."

"Can you come for coffee this afternoon? That is, it is called coffee."

"I'd like to see you now. It's rather important."

"Lanny! You are not in any trouble?"

"Not at all. Quite otherwise. I'll explain."

"Well, come by all means."

Outside the station—it was snowing again—he found a hack that must have been forty years old and a horse of about half that age, with a driver older than the two put together. Lanny put in his two bags and was driven down Unter den Linden and through the Tiergarten, a park full of so many memories—of plottings against the Nazi regime, with Trudi, with Monck, with Laurel, but alas, he couldn't see that he had accomplished very much so far. He looked for the signs of bombing destruction, and he saw some buildings missing, but not much debris, for the Nazis considered the sight bad for morale and they cleaned up quickly. He realized with sinking heart that an empire's capital is a big place and takes a lot of destroying.

X

Inside the palace, here was the princess, very thin, pale, nervous, and dressed entirely in black. "What is this, Hilde?" he asked, for he knew that nearly two years had passed since her son had been killed in Poland. She told him that her husband had died of a heart attack a couple of months ago. "Oh, I am so sorry!" he said. He knew that the Fürst had been an old man, and it had been a *mariage de convenance*, but he spoke the proper words even so.

"We are a sad family," she told him. "My older sister is here, and she has lost her husband and her two sons. My mother, also here, is a widow, and has lost all her grandsons as well as her two sons-in-law. We are three lonely and hopeless old women, so you must not expect the good conversation you used to hear in this house."

"Oh, my dear, you have my sympathy! Perhaps you do not want to see visitors now?"

"On the contrary, it is a relief. There are so few Germans who are not sad in these cruel days. But how is it possible that you, an American, can come to Berlin?"

"It's a long story, and unfortunately I'm not free to tell it. What I can tell is confidential to the utmost degree—you must swear to me that you will not talk about it even to your family. I am here on an errand having to do with peace."

"Oh, Lanny! How amazing! But do the authorities—?"

"I have in my pocket a letter from Hitler, authorizing me to be in Germany for three weeks. I have just come from his headquarters."

"*Épatant!* Lanny, you do the most extraordinary things! I have always had the certainty that you were not just a collector of paintings."

"Whatever you think, keep it locked in your heart. Sooner or later, you know, this war has to come to an end."

"It is too late for me and mine, but I can think of the other women of Germany. I will keep the secret." And then, with a trace of the old Hilde: "It is not the first time that I have made such a promise, but it may be the first time I have kept it."

"I have just stepped off the train, and I came to you at once. If an American should go to a hotel it would surely attract attention. I have to stay with some friend, and I thought of you because you have so many rooms."

"I have the rooms, but no way to heat them. We live as if in a tenement."

"I can get along in a cold room. It will be a matter only of ten days or so, and you will not have to be bothered with meals, because I'll pretty surely be dining with others, or in restaurants. All I want is a bed to crawl into, and an address to give to the police."

"That would be all right, Lanny; but I must have your word that there is nothing illegal about it, because I haven't the right to involve my mother and sister in any trouble of that sort. We are, as you know, a class of people liable to fall under suspicion with this *Regierung*."

"You may have more than my word, Hilde. You may see with your own eyes." He took out the Hitler letter and handed it to her.

After she had studied it she said: "It is the first time I have ever seen his handwriting. You will have to register at the *Polizeiamt* within twenty-four hours, you know; it will be better if you go at once, so then I shall be able to tell two frightened women that they are not harboring an enemy spy. You understand how it is, I am sure."

"Certainly, Hilde."

"I must tell you," she added, "that my mother is hopelessly grief-stricken, and I fear is close to the borderline of sanity. She sits in a chair and does not move for hours; sometimes she falls to groaning softly to herself. Now and then she asks: 'What was I born for?' And I must confess that I do not know what to answer. She has only one thought, to join her loved ones in the next world, but she is only half assured that that world exists, or will prove to be any kinder."

"My dear friend," he said, "you provide me with one more reason for working at my task. Believe me, America also is having losses, and the British—you can imagine about them."

"Tell me, how is Irma?" she inquired, for she was still a *Weltdame*, and in the happy old days had lived half her life abroad.

Lanny told her that he had seen Irma the previous summer, and that she was well. He took the occasion to add: "I have married again. My wife is in New York and we have an infant son."

"Oh, how nice!" she said. She wanted to know all about this wife, and Lanny said that her name was Ada, and that she was young—just out of finishing school—and very devoted to him. Surely he couldn't give Laurel's name, for she had lived in a Berlin *pension* under that name and the Gestapo were no doubt still looking for her—they never gave up. He couldn't say she was a writer, for at once Hilde would have exclaimed: "*Ach, wie schön!* What does she write?" It was as the poet had said: "Oh, what a tangled web we weave, when first we practice to deceive!"

One thing more. The scion of a millionaire family remarked: "I know how hellish money conditions must be here in Berlin. I have a bundle of French ten-thousand-franc notes, and, as you see, the Führer has given me permission to exchange them. You must let me be a paying guest, and leave you the proceeds of one of them. I should have to pay more at the Adlon."

"You would get much more there, Lanny; but I will be honest and tell you that we have only two servants now, and we have difficulty in getting the money to pay them each month. I receive only half my husband's pension."

"I should have some change left over for them," he answered with a smile. "I'll tell them to take good care of you, because it is a great honor to be working for the Donnerstein family." Lanny always knew exactly what to say.

XI

He went to the nearest police station, as the law required, and presented his Hitler letter. They were awe-stricken, and at the same time frightened, for they had never seen such a document before, and a German *Beamter* is helpless without a precedent. They bowed and begged a thousand pardons, but they must ask the American visitor to wait while they telephoned headquarters. There being no precedent there either, headquarters had to phone the Führer's secretary at the Chancellery.

Meantime Lanny sat on a bench and examined a copy of the small four-page sheet which he had purchased at a kiosk on the way; the *Völkischer Beobachter*, edited by the Nazi Reichsminister of People's Enlightenment and Propaganda, Herr Doktor Josef Goebbels. It was the Berliner's principal newspaper, their source of information about the outside world. Under bold headlines Lanny read that the American forces had sustained a bloody and decisive defeat at Kasserine Pass in Tunisia; also, in smaller headlines, the statement that the German forces had victoriously withdrawn from several more Russian towns, after inflicting heavy losses upon the enemy.

Lanny wasn't sure if it was good form to be reading such war news in a *Polizeiamt*, so he turned to the back page of the paper, which was given up to classified advertisements. This afforded a visiting stranger as it were a mental map of the Nazi capital and its inhabitants. One part consisted of death notices, each with a little black border; only a limited number of such were allowed to be published each day, so you had to wait your turn. He read:

IN THE BATTLE for Germany's future, for Führer, people, and Fatherland, in a heroic fight against the Asiatic world enemy, who broke into our quiet fields nefariously, our unforgettable husband and father was killed at Stalingrad: Pg. Hanns Mjoelnir Hartmann, SA-Oberscharführer, Storm-troop "Walhall/IV." company sergeant-major in an armored grenadier-regiment, decorated with the Iron Cross I and II. Sleep well, dear husband, your boys are already playing soldier. In proud grief: Sieglinde Hartmann née Eder, proprietress of a grocer's shop, and children Hunebald Ethelwulf, Rautgundis, and Gerhilde.

When the visitor had finished such death notices, he turned to the column in which the maidens of Germany competed for the attentions of the Fatherland's heroes. These latter were growing more scarce, and the bidders were hard pressed. All were racially patriotic, sober, and submissive, but now and then one attempted a note of originality:

BLOND BDM-GIRL, believing in God, of peasant kin, conscious of race, likes children; with big hips, 1.68 meters tall, would like to be gleeful manageress of the progeny of a real German young man. (Low heels, no lipstick!) Only marriage because of affection is in question with smart wearer of uniform! Offers to "Wigalaweia," 3807 B, will be forwarded by this newspaper. ·

And then another column, full of miscellaneous offers and cries for help, such as this:

WHO WILL take a woman, who has suffered heavy damage by bombs, with three small children into their house? Empty room would suffice, since some furniture salvaged. Return service: housework, can wash, iron, sew, etc. Schindler, air-raid bunker, Müllerstr. by gas works.

XII

The Führer's secretary at the military headquarters had thoughtfully notified Berlin that this mysterious Herr Budd was on his way, and so Lanny didn't have to wait too long. The police officials apologized and assured him that the *Hauptstadt* was his. They gave him a proper identification card and a food card, without which he could not have eaten in any restaurant. They offered to drive him back to the Fürstin Donnerstein's palace, or anywhere else that he pleased; but he assured them that it gave him pleasure to walk in falling Berlin snow—not too deep as yet.

His way led through the Siegesallee, with its familiar double row of marble statues of old-time German rulers and heroes, each now with a snowcap on his head and a snowcape on his shoulders; Lanny hoped that before this war ended the Allies might have a separate bomb for each of these Prussian grotesques. He came to the fire-gutted Reichstag building, now hit also by bombs. Across the street was the official *Residenz* of the *Reichsluftmarschall, Der Dicke.*

Lanny ascended the steps and informed the SS men on guard that he desired to call upon General-Major Furtwaengler. Informed that this officer was not in Berlin, he said he would see the Reichsmarschall's secretary, and one of the men took him inside to make sure he was all right. Göring's secretary knew him well, for Lanny had been coming here off and on for ten years and was the Reichsmarschall's art expert as well as friend. The secretary was not permitted to say where the great man was, but would try to get him on the telephone; so presently Lanny heard that bellowing voice which made the receiver jangle: "Lanny Budd! *Was zum Teufel!*" And then: "*Woher kommen Sie?*" and "*Was treiben Sie?*" and "*Wie lang bleiben Sie?*"

"I'll tell you all that when I see you," replied the visitor. "I have just come from the Führer and he told me to talk with you. Do you expect to be in town?"

"I'll be there in a couple of days. I am going to Karinhall over the week end with friends. Will you come?"

"*Herrlich!* I'll leave my address with your secretary and he can call me. I have a lot of news for you."

"And I have ten thousand four hundred and seventy-one master-pieces of painting. I have just been looking over a list of them."

"*Wundervoll!*" exclaimed Lanny; and the pleased fat man replied: "*Auf Wiedersehen!*"

The American strolled, found an inconspicuous restaurant, and bought himself the first meal on his new food card. If you had the price you could get a perfectly good meal, a soup, an entree, two vegetables, a dessert, and ersatz coffee. There was white bread and butter, and, if you cared for it, a foaming stein of beer. Eggs and citrus fruit alone were scarce. The restaurant patrons appeared in all ways like the prewar Berliners; if they had lost weight it did not show, and the women had presumably taken good care of the French silk stockings they had purchased two and a half years ago. Hitler had promised that all the other peoples of Europe would starve before they did, and this was one promise he was making good. Lanny did not enter into any conversation, for he knew that by now Americans were the most hated of all peoples in Germany; the Germans attributed the defeats in Russia solely to American aid.

The *Ausländer* strolled again, up the familiar Wilhelmstrasse, to that immense and ugly building that Adi had donated to himself at the expense of the German *Volk*. The New Chancellery, made of granite, resembled a huge barracks, and in its top story the Führer had shown his friend an elaborate set of miniatures of other magnificent structures which he had dreamed up. Adi's sycophants called him the greatest architect in Germany, and to him that meant the greatest in the world. He was building for a thousand years, not merely architecturally, but constitutionally, educationally, morally—in all ways known to men.

Again Lanny parleyed with SS guards, and one of them accompanied him into the building and down the long red marble corridor to the bronze doors with the Führer's monogram, "AH." The Führer's secretary had been told to make arrangements for him to meet Professor Salzmann, a name that Lanny had never heard until the Führer had spoken it. Asked when it would be convenient for him, he said the sooner the better, and then sat and read more *Völkischer* while the secretary telephoned. He was informed that the professor would receive him at the Institute on the following afternoon; he made note of the address and promised to be there.

XIII

Lanny's experience in the Sahara had not caused him to lose interest in walking, and two long plane rides and two train trips had rested him fully. His next destination was the great Staatsbibliothek. This elaborate rococo structure, often compared to a chest of drawers, had its windows boarded up and its base protected by sandbags. No doubt its rare volumes had been carried away and hidden, but its reading-room was still open to the public for limited hours. Lanny consulted the reference work called *Minerva, Jahrbuch der Gelehrten Welt*, to find out what he could about the important person whom he was to meet next day: a leading physicist, a professor at the University of Berlin, and a research authority at the great Kaiser Wilhelm Institute.

Seeking to learn more about the learned gentleman, Lanny was informed that his technical publications were on a severely restricted list. The visitor drew out the magic letter which he carried, and was amused to see the excitement it produced. To the head of the library staff he explained that at the Führer's request he was to interview Professor Salzmann, and thought it a matter of courtesy to know something about his work. The librarian explained that the results of recent research in jet propulsion were never supplied to libraries, they were circulated only among the top persons in that *Fach;* but such material as was in periodicals prior to the war would be placed at Herr Budd's disposal.

Lanny had become expert at learning scientific formulas and principles by heart without understanding the half of them; he could still recite enough about nuclear physics to have filled a small textbook. The "recoil principle," upon which rockets are based, is easier to understand, and he spent the rest of that afternoon and evening learning about compressors, combustion chambers, fuels, turbines, and the cone-shaped jets of which rockets and rocket motors were, or might be, composed. Most of the professor's learned articles were of a speculative nature, setting forth what, in 1939 and earlier, he believed to be possible. Lanny could guess that this material would be in American laboratories, and he wasn't learning it with the idea of carrying it home; he thought that by telling it back to the professor he might impress that gentleman with American backwardness and tempt him to let slip some details about German progress.

When the library closed, the visitor walked back through the Berlin blackout to the Donnerstein "tenement." He might have taken a hack, but walking was warmer, and on the way he could recite his lessons. In a freezing cold chamber inside marble walls he spread his coat, trousers, and overcoat on top of the bedcovers, put his shoes where he could reach them in the dark, and then crawled into bed in his underwear and lay shivering until the heat of his body warmed the bed and bedding.

He had barely fallen asleep, or so it seemed, before he heard the air-raid sirens. He had been told to hurry down to the second basement of this building, on the theory that it was better to be buried alive down there than to be crushed at once by a falling roof; but he was so sleepy and so warm that he decided to take a chance this once. He lay and listened to the almost incessant banging of the ack-ack, and then the dull "crumping" of the bombs. He could imagine the sky full of searchlights, a very picturesque sight, but he had seen enough of it in London. Presently a blessed silence fell, and tormented Berlin slept again—all save those who had been buried under debris and those who were trying to dig them out.

XIV

Next morning Lanny breakfasted with his hostess by special invitation, of course giving up food tickets to cover what he would consume. Present also was the older sister, the Frau von Ehrenberg, a faded blond lady who looked much older than she was. She had lived in Dresden and Lanny had never met her. She also was in mourning, and listened in silence while her sister asked questions. Lanny could guess that she had her doubts concerning an alien enemy myteriously appearing in the Fatherland. Lanny chatted about the Countess of Wickthorpe and her friends, about Beauty Budd in Marrakech, about Mr. Ford and his wife in Detroit, and Mr. Hearst and his movie lady in California. It was indisputably chic conversation, and you might have heard it without ever suspecting that this world of elegance and fashion was now engaged in tearing itself to pieces.

The researcher returned to the library and spent the morning at work, stopping only to telephone Heinrich Jung and invite him to lunch. Heinrich was Lanny's second oldest friend in Germany. Son of the *Oberförster* of Stubendorf, Heinrich had climbed step by step up the Nazi ladder, until now, in his early forties, he was halfway to the top. In the N.S.D.A.P. he had been a *Gruppenführer*, a *Staffelführer*, a *Scharführer*, a *Standartenführer*, a *Rottenführer*, a *Sturmbannführer*, an *Oberführer;* in the *Reichsjugendführung* he had commanded first a *Kameradschaft*, then a *Schar*, then a *Gefolgschaft*, then an *Unterbann*, then a *Bann*, then an *Oberbann*, then a *Gebiet*, and now an *Obergebiet*, this last composed of 375,000 youths. He sat in an office full of push-buttons and gadgets, and read reports and dictated instructions to all the lesser Führers of the vast organization which was preparing the young people of Germany to march cheerfully into the slaughterpit. Heinrich saw that they received the proper quotas of inspirational literature, and sometimes he took a trip to various districts and let them hear the living voice of one who had been the Führer's friend from youth up, had actually visited him in prison at the Fortress of Landsberg, and had once had in his hands some of the original manuscript of *Mein Kampf*. It was as if Lanny had been able to tell those camelmen in the Sahara that he had trimmed the beard of the living Prophet!

Heinrich had long seemed to Lanny a dull person, but he was useful because he was a mirror of the Nazi mind. He knew nothing about the outside world but what Doktor Goebbels told him, either through the *Völkischer*, the radio, or the special bulletins prepared for his organization. A faithful believer, he would never dream of listening to a foreign radio, and all he wanted to hear about the Allied lands was that discontent was spreading, and that the U-boats were sinking half the vessels which set out from America. Lanny said that was why the Americans had been repelled in Tunisia, and he had no doubt that when the SS men had gone into action, the invaders would be forced to withdraw at least as far as Algiers.

Heinrich admitted that the German people had been terribly depressed by the Stalingrad defeat. "It is hard for them to understand that in winter our transport is helpless, but that we shall make it all up in the spring. I wish that you could tell our *Jugend* how it all appears to you. Could you not talk to them just once?"

"Thanks for the compliment, Heinrich; but if I should go around meeting Germans promiscuously, news about me would spread and I couldn't go back to America."

Heinrich had just returned from a visit to one of the so-called *Ordensburgen,* the schools where young Führers were being trained. "The most marvelous places, Lanny, where you meet the cream of our movement, the lads who are going to run the new Germany, and indeed the new Europe. We shall of course have to do that for many years, perhaps a generation, until we can educate enough National Socialist Frenchmen and Dutchmen and so on."

Lanny had heard of these schools, but little was known about them in America, so he said: "Tell me what you saw, Heinrich."

Thus for the rest of the meal he listened to enraptured details about Ordensburg-Vogelsang, a combination university and military school. It had dozens of magnificent buildings, designed by the Führer, with walls of reinforced concrete four feet thick and covered with brownstone. It was in the region east of the Rhine, where the legions of the Roman general Varus had been slaughtered by the wild Germans of the forest; a land held sacred by all the devotees of *Blut und Boden;* the land of Siegfried and Brünnhilde, of Nibelungs and giants and dragons. When the stormwinds blew the mountain mists across the moon, all good Wagnerians saw the Valkyries riding, and hummed a melody that to the skeptical outsider was more suggestive of rockinghorses than of war steeds.

Lanny knew this region, having motored through it with Laurel Creston at the time when the Gestapo was looking for her, and Lanny was trying to figure a way to get her out of the country. But the P.A. didn't say anything about that; he learned about a place where the Nazi *Mystik* was being taught to two thousand super-Aryan youths, and where new buildings were going up even in the midst of war. The institution stood on the slope of a mountain, arranged in vast terraces; the administration buildings, the guest house, and the mess hall stood on the highest level, forming a court and enclosing a fountain flanked by German war eagles and a circle of sculptured heroes with big muscles and horses with even bigger ones. Having just walked down the Siegesallee, Lanny could have no trouble in imagining these.

Broad steps led down the slope to classrooms and dormitories; still farther down were drill grounds and game fields, gymnasiums, open-air theater, and swimming pool; below these was the cold black Urfstausee, a mountain lake, where young Nazi heroes might look for the Rhine maidens. They wouldn't be maidens much longer, for the Hitler religion was a fertility cult, and it was considered disloyal and decadent for any German female of the proper age to refuse herself to heroes. The world could be possessed only by a race that reproduced quickly and replaced the losses of war. This was part of the lore for which Adi had erected a "Tower of Wisdom" at Ordensburg-Vogelsang, and all the elite students were thrilled by the promise he had made, that he would deposit in this tower the original manuscript of the sequel to *Mein Kampf*, embodying the wisdom that was to guide his thousand-year Reich.

"*Eine frohe Botschaft!*" exclaimed the admiring Lanny; and the worshipful Heinrich asked, not without bitterness: "How can it be possible for intelligent people to fail to understand what we are doing, and combine with us to save the world from the Asiatic hordes? Has America gone entirely Bolshevik, Lanny?"

23

Enemy within the Gates

I

THE new Physics Building of the world-famed Kaiser Wilhelm Institute was situated in the Dahlem district, near the other Institutes. Oddly enough, it had been paid for with Rockefeller money. It was on a corner, an impressive structure with a rounded entrance, a tall tower above, and many small dormer windows. As Lanny Budd walked by its semibasement windows, he saw that he was under the observation of guards with tommy guns, and realized that he was approaching one of the most carefully guarded buildings in Germany.

But when he gave his name at the window of the booking-room, he discovered that the way had been prepared for him. A polite SS man escorted him to the private office of the Herr Professor Doktor Salzmann, who proved to be an old-style stoutish Prussian with white military mustaches and scanty close-cropped hair; he was clad in black broadcloth and wore gold pince-nez. He must have been surprised by the order to meet an American, but he had had time to prepare, and no doubt had looked up Robert Budd in *Who's Who in America*, and the Budd-Erling Aircraft Corporation in *Moody's Manual*. He was polite, but reserved, and his manner said: "I am here to listen."

Lanny's first move was to show his letter. Then he told his story, so well rehearsed, his stock in trade in Naziland for almot ten years: how he had come to know Kurt Meissner and Heinrich Jung nearly thirty years ago, how he had come to know the Führer nearly twenty years ago, and Göring and so many others nearly ten years ago; how he had become a convert to National Socialism and had labored to explain it to his British and French and American friends; how through the years the Führer had asked him to take messages to this and that sympathizer abroad; and how recently, being in possession of what he believed to be important diplomatic information, he had found a way to get into Germany and had been flown to the Führer's headquarters on the eastern front.

Lanny was aware that many of Germany's top scientists were not Nazis at heart; but nearly all of them were Germans before they were scientists, and if the head of their government told them to believe a certain story, they would believe it. When Lanny explained that his father was in a position of great delicacy, being held as it were in bondage by his government, the Herr Professor Doktor could understand perfectly, because he, too, did research according to order, and if he had any private wishes or even thoughts he would reserve them for his wife and one or two trusted friends. When Herr Budd said: "You understand that I am in position to hear my father's conversation with those technical men whom the government has assigned to his plant," the Professor nodded and said: "*Ja, ja.*" When Lanny said: "I have to ask you to give me your word that you will never name me or my father as the source of any information," the Professor replied: "*Auf mein Ehrenwort, Herr Budd.*"

"One thing more," added this modest American. "You must understand that in me you have a rank amateur on all these difficult subjects. I am by profession a *Kunstsachverständiger*, and what I know about jet propulsion and wind stresses and air-cooled motors I have learned through the skin, as it were, by constantly hearing talk about airplanes, and prior to that, oil, and prior to that, gun-making and explosives. I will tell you to the best of my recollection what I have heard, and if it does not quite make sense you will have to forgive me. I took the trouble to visit the library yesterday and this morning, to learn as much as I could about your own work, so that I might not appear too completely an ignoramus." Lanny said this on chance that the Professor might have been told of his visits.

The elderly scientist assured him that this had not been necessary, that it was surely not to be expected that an authority on old masters should understand the principles of the recoil and all its corollaries. Lanny, reassured, proceeded to repeat one by one those statements and formulas which he had carried in his head during a month of turbulent events, including a parachute landing which might well have knocked all ideas out of any head. The statements were correct, but they were things the Germans were almost certain to know already, and this proved to be the case. The severe old Prussian, mollified by Lanny's extreme humility, and perhaps hoping to encourage him to speak freely, would remark: "*Ja, Herr Budd*, that is important, but we have been familiar with it for some time." Once he went so far as to say: "Your people will not get very far along that line; we tried it out and it proved a false lead."

Lanny talked about rocket cannon. He had seen a British creation, a fantastic thing that looked like a church organ, with twenty big barrels; it was mounted near the coast for the purpose of protecting ships in the Channel against dive bombers, by roofing them over with salvos of rockets. Lanny could be sure that the Germans knew all about this, for they had a six-barreled mortar which was fired like the chambers of a revolver and could shoot fifty-pound rockets at the rate of one every second. Lanny added: "I have heard my father talk about what is called a 'Katyusha,' a Russian device that is carried on a truck; they have a larger one with thirty barrels, so arranged as to cover an area where there are tanks."

"*Ja*," replied the other, "we have captured many of them; but we were unable to get across the Volga, where the enemy had them lined up on the far bank, under the trees."

"*Wie Schade!*" said Lanny.

II

All this was preliminary so far as the P.A. was concerned. He was letting the somewhat grim old man get used to the sound of his voice and come to like him a bit if such a thing were possible. Then, with the utmost casualness, the P.A. remarked: "Another thing that might interest you—they are trying to apply the rocket principle to airplanes."

It was comical to observe the Professor's efforts to gather information about this matter without revealing his great concern. Lanny deliberately teased him by talking generalities, many of them collected from the Professor's own published papers. He explained in his father's words the difficulty of planes, that it took twice as much power to get into the air as it took to stay there; and this had suggested the idea of auxiliary rockets, called "boosters," to aid the take-off. This would have been a dreadful thing to reveal—but for the fact that the learned Prussian had written a paper about it in 1938. Lanny said that his father had an experimental plant where he was trying out such ideas. "Somewhere in the deserts of the Far West, Nevada, I believe." The last two words were for Lanny's protection, the plant being in New Mexico.

"Do you know whether they are doing anything with the idea of jet-propulsion planes?" inquired the Professor. He tried his best to appear casual, but Lanny thought that as an actor he was a great physicist.

"I know that they have passed the 'mockup' stage, if you know what our airplane men mean by that term."

"I do, Herr Budd."

"Whether they have a practical prototype, I do not know."

"Do you know what speeds they are hoping to attain?"

"I have heard them talk about five hundred miles an hour. They talk about supersonic speeds, but only as a speculation. The difficulty there will be the air friction, and the blacking out of the pilot on even the slightest change of direction. As you no doubt know, Professor, the British are far ahead of us Americans on this subject. Some British engineers arrived at my father's plant just before I left. I could easily make friends with them and bring you a report on what they are doing."

"That might be extremely useful, Herr Budd. You expect to return to us?"

"The Führer has given me a commission to carry out. I cannot be sure how long it will take, but I hope to return and make a report to him, say, in a couple of months."

This friendly chat continued for some time, but without Lanny's getting what he wanted. The elderly Prussian was like most of his tribe; he held to the belief that it was more blessed to receive than to give. He seemed to Lanny the perfect type of the hard materialist who was a military man regardless of whether he called himself a politician, a diplomat, a historian, a scientist, a philosopher. Their favorite theoretician, Clausewitz, had said that war was diplomacy carried on by other means; and now here was science, using the same means. In Lanny's mind, as he chatted so urbanely, was an image of the horror that these world-famous gentlemen were bringing into the world; long and thin like a lead pencil, with a point as sharp as a needle, a warhead filled with high-powered explosives, and a tail that spit the flames and fumes of hell. It would be thirty or forty feet long and of the thickness of a barrel or perhaps a hogshead, and would be installed on a launching platform hidden in a forest, or in the mouth of a cave, or a sloping tunnel with an entrance well camouflaged. Always these platforms would be aimed at the vast sprawling city of London, with its more than eight million inhabitants. A button would be pressed, and the demon thing would shoot out a blast of flame from its rear and leap into the sky at a speed of a thousand miles an hour or even more—who could guess?

III

The visitor satisfied himself that this man of scientific murder did not take any pleasure in talking. So Lanny tried one last device, which had worked in other cases. "Professor Salzmann," he remarked, "it might be a good idea if you would tell me exactly what you would like me to find out for you. You understand, I am sure, that I dare not bring any notes into Germany. Whatever I bring has to be memorized, and there is a limit to what my untrained mind can retain."

The Prussian took a few moments to think about this. Obviously he couldn't ask questions without revealing what he didn't know, and that might be telling a lot. Here sat this mysterious American, a traitor according to his own country's standards and a novice according to the Professor's. He had notepaper and a pencil poised—for it was all right for him to have notes in Germany, he explained; he would learn them by heart and destroy them before he went out. The Professor might well have reflected that if he failed to show proper co-operation with this stranger, he might be reported to the Führer and become the target for one of those fearful tirades, which every person of importance in Naziland knew about and dreaded.

The way out of this dilemma was to confine the questions to the subject of American and British progress. What fuels were they using, what type of combustion chamber, what size of projectile, what speeds, what possibility of radio control? The visitor, disappointed but not showing it, wrote these down and promised to do his best to obtain the answers. Then he added: "I don't want to take any more of your time, Professor, but there is one other matter that the Führer showed interest in: our American researches into atomic fission. He told me that he had declined to take this matter seriously, but he appeared to waver when I told him of the immense sum, more than a billion dollars, that Roosevelt has set aside for the project."

"You are informed about nuclear researches then, Herr Budd?"

"It so happens that I have an art client in Princeton, New Jersey, Mr. Alonzo Curtice, who has a valuable collection of paintings, and invited me to visit his home and prepare a catalogue for him. While there I heard a good deal of discussion among the research professors— this before they were taken into the government project, and so they talked freely. Afterward I told my father about it, and listened to discussions with some of his technical men. The Führer seemed to think it might be a good idea if I talked with one of your people; he mentioned Professor Walter Gerlach." This wasn't so, but Lanny was taking the chance that Hitler wouldn't remember every word he had spoken at a crowded and anxious time.

"Professor Gerlach is out of the city at present, Herr Budd; but Professor Plötzen, who directs our theoretical work on such projects, is available, and I am sure would be happy to meet you. When would be convenient for you?"

"The sooner the better, because Reichsmarschall Göring told me over the telephone that he expects to arrive in town and wishes me to spend the week end at Karinhall."

That was the way to impress the mind of a Nazi *Fachgelehrter!* Salzmann took up the house telephone and gave a room number and asked for Professor Plötzen. Then he said: "Get him at his home," and talked with Lanny for a minute or so until the phone rang. "Plötzen, this is Salzmann," he announced. "There is a gentleman in my office with whom I think you should talk. Oh, I am sorry! Yes, I will ask him." Then to Lanny: "The Professor says he is not feeling well, but if you would be good enough to go to his home this evening—"

"Certainly, Professor Salzmann."

"The gentleman will come. Eight o'clock? Very well. His name is Budd—bay-oo-day-day. He will show you a letter of introduction from a person of importance. *Heil Hitler!*"

Lanny jotted down the address on his notepaper. Then he said:

"Unless I am mistaken, I have met Professor Plötzen somewhere. I think it may have been at the home of General Graf Stubendorf, or possibly at the Fürstin Donnerstein's. Both are old friends of mine."

"It might be," said Salzmann—and could it be that there was a little more cordiality in his cold tone? "Plötzen goes into society occasionally. He is one of those cases of a man of means who takes scientific learning seriously, and works at it as hard as if he were obliged to. I hope that his indisposition will not prove serious."

IV

The two men parted with expressions of high esteem, and Lanny went out and found himself a restaurant and ate a meal. He read in the *Völkischer* that there was bitter fighting on the soggy-wet plains in front of Kasserine Pass, and also on the snowbound plains of the Ukraine. He studied a pocket map of Berlin, and then went out and groped his way through the blackout to the Underground. He prayed that there wouldn't be an air raid while he was down there, because then the stations filled up with mobs of people, so that you couldn't get out until some time after the raid was over. So far the Allies had been considerate of this P.A.; there had been only two raids, and neither had touched him! He crossed the fingers of the elegant fur-lined gloves which had belonged to Hilde's son, and which she had lent to her guest with tears in her eyes.

Emerging from the Underground, Lanny felt his way along a slippery street, thinking that he could share the feelings of a blind man; thinking how cruel it was that men should be using their powers to make other men miserable. Two lines of poetry haunted his mind:

> Where savage beasts in forest midnight roam,
> Seeking in sorrow for each other's joy.

Even while he was helping to win a war, Lanny hated that war and all others; he hated the lies he had to tell fully as much as those he had to hear. He was a man with a divided mind, and this put him at a disadvantage with men like these Nazis, who were never troubled with doubts and had consigned all scruples to the dustbin of history.

The P.A. was going into another adventure, one of the strangest; but he had no idea of it, and thought it would be just one more duel of wits such as he had come from in the Kaiser Wilhelm Institute. He made his way slowly along a fashionable street, stopping at corners to listen carefully before he ventured across. He found the right number

without striking any matches, something that was *strengstens verboten*.
He went up a flight of steps, evidently belonging to a fine home; he
groped and found a button and pressed it. A door was opened, and
revealed a darkened interior, for it was also *verboten* to open a door
while lights were burning inside. He asked: "Is this the home of Professor Doktor Plötzen?" And a voice replied: "*Ja, mein Herr.*"

It flashed over the caller that the voice had a familiar sound, and his
thought was that it must be the Herr Professor whom he had once met.
The next moment the light was turned on, and Lanny was half blinded
because he had been so long in the dark. He stared, and couldn't credit
what he saw; he all but took a step backward. The man confronting
him, in the black costume of a butler, was Bernhardt Monck!

"Herr Budd?" inquired the familiar voice. Lanny was able to make
himself say: "*Ja.*"

Like a proper butler, the man stepped toward him to take his coat
and hat; then, in a voice barely audible, he whispered: "Message in
your overcoat when you leave."

Lanny nodded slightly, took off his overcoat and hat, gave them to
Monck, and then obeyed his sign to ascend the stairs. Monck followed,
and at the head of the stairs bowed the caller into a room. "Herr
Budd," he announced, and promptly departed.

V

The presidential agent found himself in a moderate-sized, tastefully
furnished drawing-room, confronting a gentleman who afforded a
curious contrast to his colleague Salzmann. He was tall and slender,
obviously something of a dandy, though his present costume consisted
of a brown silk dressing gown and a pair of gold-embroidered bedroom slippers. He had been lying on a couch, and sat up to greet his
visitor, apologizing for his indisposition. He was a man of forty or so,
urbane and sensitive, and his conversation soon revealed that he was
interested in all the cultures of Europe; he was pleased to meet an
American and to hear what was going on in the outside world. He
remembered having met Lanny at one of the *Abende* of General Graf
Stubendorf, and of course Lanny politely pretended to remember him.
They talked about their mutual friends at home and abroad, and it was
more like something out of the *Almanach de Gotha* than a conference
on nuclear fission.

Lanny had begun to wonder: Could it be that this was a secret anti-
Nazi, and that he was in league with Monck? But no, the man suddenly

remarked: "We are playing truant and must get down to business. Salzmann tells me that you are one who is not willing to turn Europe over to the Russians."

So Salzmann had telephoned again! Lanny wondered: What had he said? Perhaps: "You can trust this man." Or perhaps: "Watch out for him." It might take some time for Lanny to find out which, for Plötzen would be a better actor than the crusty old Prussian.

Anti-Bolshevism was Lanny's cue. He said that he had been something of a "Pink" in his early days. ("Most generous-minded young men are, Herr Budd," put in the host.) But soon he had come to realize what was behind the storm clouds in the east: not a new birth of freedom, but the old Tartar despotism. He and his father had tried in every way to keep their country out of the war, and now that it was in on the wrong side, Lanny was doing what one man could to correct the error. "I have been carrying diplomatic messages for the Führer; you understand this is confidential in the extreme."

"Oh, surely, Herr Budd."

"I came upon some information regarding the progress of what is called atom splitting in America. Immense sums are being devoted to it, the idea being that the nuclear forces may be used to make a bomb. Also, they and the British are working on jet propulsion. I mentioned these matters to the Führer, and he sent me to see Professor Salzmann."

Lanny gave his elaborate explanation about being a rank amateur, able to do nothing but repeat phrases and sentences which he had heard. The other replied, as courtesy required, that he would make all allowances for this. Then Lanny said: "One thing I understood clearly. It has been found necessary to discover a substance which will retard the chain reaction and thus make possible its control. It has been found that deuterium oxide will do this."

"*Ach, ja, schweres Wasser,*" said the German. "We are acquainted with the principle."

Lanny had known as much, and one of his assignments had been to find out where and to what extent the Germans were making heavy water. The Americans were using graphite, and this was a secret that all the torture instruments of the Gestapo could not have dragged out of the P.A. Said he: "The trouble with heavy water is that it is so difficult to make, and so costly."

"That is a problem we have solved," replied this gentleman turned scientist and smiled indulgently. "Perhaps it may be that German science will keep in advance, even without billion-dollar appropriations."

"I sincerely hope so, Professor. I was shocked to hear the Führer reveal his indifference to this important subject. I did what I could to bring him to a realization of the danger; but it appears that he has convinced himself that rockets and jet-propulsion planes will win this war."

"We are making great progress there; but I consider it a calamity that we cannot spare enough for a real program of nuclear fission. I have put up small sums from my own purse, in spite of having suffered great reductions of income. The trouble is that no money can buy the things we need. The approved war programs take all the materials."

VI

This pair chatted on, but with one lobe of his brain Lanny was trying to think about Monck, and what his presence in this house might mean. The sight of an O.S.S. agent—for such Monck had become—made a great difference in Lanny's procedure with the master of the household. Lanny had understood from Monck's whispered words that they were to meet, and Lanny would find out what Monck was doing, and what he knew. There was no use in Lanny's trying to get information which Monck might already possess. To meet this genial "atom splitter" a second time would be easy enough if it proved necessary. The art expert would please him and be his friend.

The principal reason for which Lanny had come here was to find out about a certain Professor Schilling, who was an authority on nuclear physics and at the same time a hater of the Nazis and a secret informant against them. He was the goal for which the P.A. had tried to reach Germany a year and a half ago. Where was Schilling now, and what was he doing? No one had mentioned him; for all Lanny knew he might have been uncovered and "liquidated" as a traitor. To name him might bring suspicion on a visiting American. Obviously the proper course was to wait.

Lanny devoted himself to being agreeable, and occasionally he dropped some fresh item of information, something that he knew was not vital, and that the Germans were sure to know already. This was all the easier, because Professor Plötzen himself liked to talk, and his conversation had a tendency to wander from the technical details of atomic fission to its possible effects upon the future. Power would be practically free; and what would that do to the coal and oil industries? Lanny said that his father had talked about that, and believed it would make a new civilization. Plötzen said: "What a shame that mankind cannot exploit such a discovery for the creation of wealth instead of for its destruction!" Lanny replied: "I see that you are a man after my own heart."

So when they parted they were friends. "I am afraid I haven't been able to tell you very much," the visitor apologized. The other replied that the subject of nuclear physics was a frightfully complicated one; a man had to study for years even to understand its language, and Herr Budd must be considered to have done very well to remember what he had and to repeat it so accurately.

Lanny shook hands with the gentleman on the couch and wished him a speedy recovery. He went downstairs, and there was the polite butler, ready to help him on with his overcoat and to hand him his hat. Lanny did not speak a word, for there were portieres in the doorways and someone might easily have been listening. But there was no reason why a gentleman before departing should not put his hands into the different pockets of his overcoat. In the pocket on the right side, there were the fur-lined gloves, and he took them out. In the pocket on the left side was a handkerchief. The outside breast pocket was empty, and that was as it had been. Lanny was beginning to feel worried; but he reached into the inner breast pocket, and touched a piece of paper which he knew had not been there before. So everything was all right.

He took his hat and put it on his head; he put on his fur-lined gloves, one after the other, in the manner of a person who has enjoyed leisure all his life. The polite butler said: "Pardon me, *mein Herr*, if I turn off the lights." Lanny replied: "Certainly."

The lights went off, as the law required, and the door was opened, letting in a blast of wintry air. As the visitor started out, the butler said, in a voice for all to hear: "Be careful of the steps, Herr Budd; they may be slippery."

"*Danke schön*," replied the guest. "*Gute Nacht.*"

Lanny groped his way through the blackout to the *Unterbahn;* and there, in the bowels of Berlin, for the first time was a light. He took the paper from his overcoat pocket and read: "*NW Ecke Strom- und Huttenturm-Strasse, Moabit, 9 Uhr morgens.*" Monck had arranged for a meeting at once, on the chance that Lanny might be leaving the city. He had made a morning appointment, when it was unlikely that Lanny would have anything scheduled. The P.A. learned the directions, and when he had left the train and was walking to the Donnerstein palace, he tore the scrap of paper into tiny bits and dropped a few here and a few there. The winds which blew from the Brandenburg plains would scatter them still more widely before daylight.

VII

In these tragic days even the smart people of Berlin went to bed early, because fuel was so scarce and getting about so difficult. When the traveler reached his night abode and was ascending the stairs to his second-story room, he was surprised to have Hilde open one of the other doors and invite him in. It was a small sitting-room, where these bereaved ladies had installed a tiny gas heater without any vent, an extremely unhygienic device. That was a part of what the Fürstin had meant when she said they were living "as if in a tenement." Now she invited Lanny to have some coffee—she always said "so-called coffee," in bitter determination to be honest. She had bought some *Kuchen* as a further lure, and Lanny knew that she wanted to chat. The other ladies had gone to bed in another room, and this one had been tidied up, sewing baskets put aside, and everything swept and dusted for a visitor out of a so-much-better world.

Lanny sat and sipped a drink that had the virtue of being hot, even though it had little flavor. He knew what Hilde wanted, to talk about old times and old friends. Dante has said that there is no greater grief than to remember happy times in the midst of misery; it may have been true of an Italian poet, but it wasn't true of a Prussian princess, for to remember happy times was the only happiness she had left. She wanted to hear about the sumptuous hotel in which Beauty Budd was staying in sun-drenched Marrakech. How fortunate she had been, to anticipate where the American Army was to be, and yet far enough away to miss the bombs! After three and a half years of war, Hilde Donnerstein's desires had become very restricted; she asked only to be where there were no bombs.

Lanny suggested: "Why don't you go to your place on the Obersalzberg?" She answered that they were planning to go there as soon as the snow was out of the mountains. Her place there was a summer "camp," but it was substantially built, and by doubling the windows they could make one or two rooms warm enough in winter. She had received notice that the Berlin palace was required for a hospital; she would be paid a rental for it, and on that they could live comfortably in the Bavarian Alps. She wanted Lanny to tell her whether the war might come there, but he wouldn't have been free to tell even if he had known. "Anyhow," he said, "our Army won't bomb summer residences."

He told her about Irma and life at Wickthorpe Castle; the bombs had not come there, at least not up to the time of his last visit. Through this winter the Germans had been making only sporadic fire raids on London and other cities, but Hilde didn't know that—she read the *Völkischer*. Lanny didn't contradict any of her ideas, for he thought that one secret was enough for her to keep. He told her what he had told Hitler, that there was a strong peace movement in Britain, and that "Ceddy" was active in it; he had resigned from the Foreign Office so as to be free from Churchill's control. Hilde said in a tone of bewilderment: "Imagine that there is a place where a man can oppose his government in wartime!"

She wanted to know more about that "Ada" whom Lanny had married. Where had she come from and what was her family, rich, poor, or medium? What did she look like, tall or thin, blond or brunette? How old was she, and what had she been doing when he met her? Hilde was one of these modern ladies who have a smattering of feminist ideas, and have applied them to their personal selves, or, at the utmost, to their own set, their own circle of friends. Freedom for women? Yes, of course! Freedom to do what you please, to say what you think, to ask what you want to know! She had known Lanny for close to two decades, and especially well because she had picked his heiress wife for her "pal." She knew about him, not merely what a man will tell a woman friend in these modern days, but what a man's wife will tell about him.

Now Lanny was in a pickle and had to think fast and talk slowly. He had to grab in his mind for an imaginary woman, and he chose Lizbeth Holdenhurst, who had gone down on board the yacht *Oriole*, escaping from Singapore, and who therefore could never appear to confront either Lanny or Hilde. He grabbed in his mind for a family name, and the one that came was "Harkness." He placed this Ada Harkness in Pittsburgh, a city that he knew fairly well because of his friends the Murchisons. He gave her a "steel" family, because he knew there were a lot of them in Pittsburgh and he could only hope there was no Harkness among them. He described Lizbeth in this environment; and when he was through, the shrewd woman of the world remarked: "Lanny, I don't believe you love her very much."

"Why not?" he asked, taken aback.

"You don't want to talk about her. When a man is very much in love, he doesn't want to talk about anything else."

"I assure you, I love her, Hilde; and we have a little son, a treasure in our lives. As you know, these are not happy times, and a man's thoughts are preoccupied with what may happen to the world his child is to grow up in."

"Tell me," persisted the other. "Did your mother know Ada?"

"Yes, quite well."

"And did she make the match?"

"No, but she approved it."

"Did you marry for money a second time, Lanny? You will never be happy that way!"

"Take my word for it, Hilde; that isn't the case with this marriage. I have all the money I need, and Ada is well satisfied with an apartment in New York."

"And a husband who goes away most of the time? Don't tell me any such tale!"

VIII

The P.A. went up to his icy chamber. He put his clothes on top of the bed, as before, and climbed in. He had just about got warm when he heard the knob of his door turned; the darkness was complete and he could not see, but he heard faint sounds of an approach, and then a voice whispered: "Lanny, may I come in?" The voice was close, so evidently it was the bed and not the room that was referred to.

"*Um Gottes Willen, nein!*" he exclaimed. "I am a married man."

"Lanny, I am so lonely and so miserable!"

"I am sorry for you, Hilde; but I have pledged my faith and I mean to keep it."

"No one will ever know, Lanny."

"I will know, and my honor is involved."

"You know I have always loved you; and now I am the most desolate of women."

Poor soul! He had always been sorry for her; and a poet had told him that pity moves the mind to love. She had made what New Yorkers called a "pass" at him some years ago; she had indicated a willingness to become his *amie*. He hadn't known quite how to get out of it, and had intimated tactfully that there was something wrong with him. Now, since he was married and had a newborn son, he could hardly expect that excuse to stick. Hilde was a widow, and empty-hearted; it was the state of so many women of Germany, and indeed of all Europe; their husbands, their lovers, their sons—all their men were gone, and millions would never come back.

"Lanny," she pleaded, "I am freezing, standing here."

He might have said: "Go to your own room." But she was his hostess as well as his friend, and he was sorry for her. When she pleaded: "Let me get into the bed," he answered: "You may have half of it, for friendship's sake, but nothing else." He moved over and gave her a generous half.

There they lay and talked; a strange procedure, but one that has happened to more men than have told about it. Lanny didn't rebuke her or lecture her; he had no such feelings, for he had been sorry for women all his life, considering that they got the worst of things. The war had broken down most of the barriers in civilized life, and the scarcity of men would prevent their restoration. Lanny told her that, but said that in his case a promise had been made and he had to keep it. "Do you think your wife will keep it?" she asked. He replied: "I am absolutely certain that she will."

He talked further about the imaginary Ada, and this time he took the trouble to put in some of the real feelings he had for his real wife. He lay there, a safe distance away, and presently he realized that the woman was sobbing gently to herself. He knew enough about love not to let that move him to any response; he did not even touch her hand, and there remained a foot of space between them. When she said: "How few German men have such ideas!" he agreed with her, and added: "Especially among the Nazis."

She answered: "I mean the aristocracy, the businessmen. They keep mistresses, nearly all!" Then, after a pause: "How I wish I had known you when I was young, Lanny." He was being as tactful and as kind as possible, so he replied that that might have been fortunate for both of them.

IX

It was as pleasant a place for conversation as any; and Lanny, knowing that philosophical disquisitions do *not* move the mind to love, talked freely about his ideas as to the origin and destiny of man. He couldn't discuss his ideas about economic affairs, for that would have stamped him as a Socialist, and surely not of the "National" variety. But he could talk about his belief in the possibility of a world government to keep the unruly tribes in order, and to guarantee the peace that all decent and intelligent people desired. He had to be a little vague about how to get this blessed state, for he was supposed to be depending upon a German to lead them there, and he must say nothing to contradict that.

How long this informal *entretien* might have continued, and how Lanny would have got out of the predicament, there can be no telling. The matter was taken in hand by a flight of British Lancasters and Wellingtons, far out over the North Sea; they turned in the direction of Berlin, and kept on coming. Suddenly the sirens began to scream, and Hilde behaved as if she had received an electric shock. "I must go!" she exclaimed and leaped out of bed. Her house guest suspected that she might be more afraid of being discovered by her mother and sister than of being hit by a bomb.

A mansion just up the street had been shattered in broad daylight by an American bomb only the previous day, and Hilde had begged Lanny not to take the risk of staying in his room during raids. So he hurriedly donned his clothes and groped his way down to the sub-cellar of this large building. He had been shown how to get there, and presently was sitting in an empty winecellar, full of dust and odors reminiscent of past delights. There were the three ladies and the two servants, one an old man and the other an old woman. All sat hunched and shivering, for it was cold as a tomb and there were no extra blankets; everything had been collected the previous winter for the Army that had been trapped in the Russian snows without proper equipment—because Adi Schicklgruber had been so certain that he was going to finish off the Reds in six weeks from the twenty-second of June!

With bombs crashing in the distance and shaking the foundation walls of the house, Lanny sat reflecting upon the strange series of adventures he was having that night. He wondered: Did the mother and sister know where Hilde had been when the sirens had started? He would never know the answer to that question; and he made up his mind that there was one other person who would never know anything about it. Laurel already had reasons enough for not wanting him to come to Germany, and for being worried when he did come! Poor soul, he thought, another woman to be sorry for! She must be certain that he was dead in the Sahara Desert at this moment. How puzzled she would be if word should come out that he had been found buried in a cellar of the Donnerstein palace on the Bismarckstrasse in Berlin-Charlottenburg!

X

Lanny awakened soon after daylight, jumped into his clothes, and went shivering out into the bitter cold. He ran, to get his blood circulating, and dived down into the Underground. What a difference in the traveling public at that hour of the morning! His fellow travelers were not the well-to-do, but the workers, who showed the tragical effects of overwork and undernourishment. The Nazis were driving their wage slaves without mercy, and the newspapers were full of demands for still greater sacrifices. Those who showed unwillingness to make them were scolded. People who had lost half their night's sleep were told that the Fatherland needed them to work faster, and to report their fellows who neglected to do so.

The German people had always been a clean people, and Lanny was touched to observe that they were clean now, in spite of all difficulties. Clothing was neatly patched, and the workers did not smell too bad, even when packed together in a subway car. Lanny knew what that cost, for he wasn't clean himself, and was trying to figure out a way to get his underwear washed and dried while he waited. Impossible to buy more, and even getting himself clean would mean a trip to some sort of bathhouse, for he had no right to impose upon the kindness of his hostess.

He glanced at a morning paper. It reported a public address by Jüppchen Goebbels, a furious tirade against those who were not making proper sacrifices for the country's safety. Mostly it was against the rich, who were objecting to the new "all-out" war demands. Lanny knew what that meant, coming from this unscrupulous demagogue: the workers were discontented, and the Herr Doktor was trying to please them, talking the kind of "Socialist" talk which the "National Socialists" had used in order to get power but had long since forgotten.

Sure enough, in another column there were accounts of "disturbances," protests against the new draft procedures. In their frantic efforts to get new troops for the Russian front, the Army was conducting a proceeding known as *eine Razzia machen*, swooping down upon public places where men were gathered and sorting them out and carrying them off regardless of health, occupation, or previous claim to exemption. Oddly enough, the officer in command of this campaign was named General von Unruh and his adjutant was General von Wirbel; the former name means "unrest" or "anxiety," and the latter means "whirlwind," so the wits in night clubs and cafés were afforded opportunity for all sorts of innuendoes. Perhaps that was why these places had just been ordered closed, and with them the luxury shops of all sorts.

Lanny watched the row of faces in this car, the weary, anxiety-driven faces of both men and women. Most of the men were old, and others crippled. He wondered: Did they still love their Führer? And were they still thrilled by the glory of belonging to a master race? In the days when they had been free men, great numbers of them had been Social Democrats, and others Communists. Had they all forgotten what they had been taught?

His question was answered as he was leaving the train. Others were behind him, and he was jostled at the exit. As he passed through the gate something was shoved into his hand, and a voice muttered: *"Neh-men Sie's"*—take it. The man walked quickly off, and Lanny stuffed a bit of paper into his pocket.

He knew better than to look at it there; he walked on until he found a small café, where he got his breakfast—a cup of *Ersatzkaffee*, bread with imitation butter, and a bit of sausage, composed largely of flour, that tasted like sawdust. While eating this he kept his overcoat over the back of his chair, sitting on part of it for safety. He made so bold as to take out the bit of paper, and found it a small six-page folder. On both its outside covers was an advertisement: "Wagon-Lits Cook: World Organization for Tours, 350 Branch Offices, Information and Advice Free of Charge." There was a map showing the railroads of Germany, Belgium, Holland, Switzerland, and parts of France, Italy, and England, which, assuredly, no tourists from Berlin were visiting at present. This might have puzzled you, until you turned inside and discovered, neatly sandwiched in between half a dozen little labels of "Wagon-Lits Cook," an article in small print entitled: *"Wehrt Euch, von Heinrich Mann."* Defend yourselves! There followed the text of a speech delivered by the well-known anti-Nazi refugee at an "International Conference for the Defense of Democracy, Peace, and Human Rights, attended by six hundred delegates from thirty-six lands."

Lanny thought that he didn't need to read it and knew that he had no business to have it on his person, for he might run into one of those round-ups directed by the General of Anxiety and the General of Whirlwind, and no place more likely than in Moabit, a workers' district of the *Hauptstadt*. He called for an ash tray and matches and carefully lighted the leaflet and held it by one corner while it burned. He mashed the black remains with his fingers, lest anybody's curiosity might have been excited by his behavior. But apparently in these days all Germans were too tired to have any curiosity. No one showed the least interest in his odd performance.

XI

Lanny knew this poverty-stricken district well, for he had come here in the days when he had helped to support a workers' school in

Berlin. It was here that he had met Käthe Kollwitz, artist of the poor, who had devoted her whole life to pleading their cause. It was here that he had discovered Trudi Schultz, also an artist, working in a tailor-shop and hiding from the Nazis; it was from here that he had picked her up in his car and got her out of Hitlerland, just in time. He had no car now, and had to go on foot; he wondered what he would do if Bernardt Monck were to get into trouble and call for help. For all that Lanny knew, he might be in trouble right now!

The P.A. walked around a block a couple of times, to be sure that no one was trailing him. He came to the corner appointed exactly on the second; he didn't want to have to linger or to come a second time. And sure enough, here came the ex-sailor, ex-*capitán*, now butler. He saw Lanny and did not come to the corner, but turned on his heel and walked slowly in the opposite direction. Lanny followed, not catching up, and looking over his shoulder now and then to be sure that no one was following. Monck disappeared into a narrow alley between two tenements.

He was out of sight when Lanny got there; but the American entered, and came into a small court having several doors. One was partly open, and as Lanny came near it a hand beckoned him in. Monck whispered: "Follow me," and they went through a passage in semidarkness, and into what was apparently a storeroom with a small gas taper burning. There were trunks piled against the wall, and some boxes. Monck took a seat on one and signed Lanny to another beside it.

The first time this pair had met, in London almost ten years ago, the man from Germany had said: "*Besser wir sprechen Deutsch.*" Now, in Berlin, he said: "Better we speak English. There are friends here, but no one can say when there may be an enemy. Speak low; and let us be brief, because both of us are too important to be caught together."

"Right," said Lanny.

"Tell me first, are you in any danger?"

"None whatever."

"You are using your own name?"

"Yes. The Number One has given me a letter."

"*Herrgott!*" exclaimed the butler, forgetting that that wasn't English. He began: "What—" and then remembered that he didn't ask questions. "I am here under the name of Konrad Kraft, and I'm a real butler, doing my best to make good. It is not so easy getting off this morning, because the master is sick and that is the time he needs attention."

"He has no idea that you are—different?"

"Not the slightest. He's an easygoing person and not keen about extra-scientific activities. He had no idea that the friend who recommended me is—well, extra-scientific."

"I get you, Konrad."

"There are coming to be more and more such persons. Events are making them. Stalingrad was, I believe, the Gettysburg of this war."

"I agree with you."

"It is amazing what one hears people say, quite openly; and the jokes by the night-club entertainers."

"Perhaps that is why they have shut them up."

"No doubt of it. But literature gets circulated, and by people we have never heard of."

"A sample of it was put into my hands on my way here."

"So it goes. You may say outside that the German people are waking up."

"Have you anything you want me to take out for you?"

"It is not necessary; there seems to be an excellent courier service. Sometimes it breaks down, but at present it is working. There was, I am told, a cell of opposition in the censorship office; eight people were shot. You wouldn't find anything about that in the papers, of course. Nor the fact that when Admiral Doenitz took Raeder's place at the head of the Navy, more than eighty officers were shot for 'treasonable activities.' "

"And yet there are persons at home who blame the German people for this war!" exclaimed the P.A. Then, remembering that the time was short: "Tell me a little of what you have done, so that I will know what I don't have to do."

"I take the master's papers in the night and copy essential parts. Twice he has entrusted me with secret documents to be delivered, and these have been photographed. Also, I have had chances to listen to conversations, but that is not so easy because I don't know the technical terms."

"What you have sent has to do with your employer's subject entirely?"

"For the most part, yes; but other chances are coming into sight now. Day before yesterday I got hold of one of Salzmann's reports. The Germans have more than a hundred types of guided missiles in or near production, using every type of remote control—radar, radio, continuous wave, infra-red, light beams, magnetics."

"I congratulate you. An extraordinary feat!"

"Another matter: I don't want to use names, but you remember the learned Austrian coin?"

"I remember it."

"That party has been visited. Everything he can furnish has been sent out."

"I am relieved to hear it. I have been giving a lot of thought to the problem of meeting him. I was afraid it might be dangerous even to mention him—dangerous for me, or for him."

"He has escaped suspicion, so far as we know, or as he knows."

Ever since the summer of 1941, Lanny's mind had been obsessed with Professor Schilling, the "Austrian coin"; Lanny had come near to death several times in the effort to get to him. It had been in the hope of hearing his name that he visited Plötzen; and now to be told that he could forget him was like coughing up the traditional alligator.

"One thing more," said Konrad Kraft. "You remember that you asked about the location of a place where very important experiments were being tried?"

"I remember." The reference, of course, was to Peenemünde.

"That name has been sent out, also."

"It may interest you to know, Konrad, that I learned that name and gave it to our Number One about a month ago. Has anything happened to the place that you know of?"

"Nothing. If it had, I would surely have known about it."

"I can guess that somebody is waiting for developments to occur, for processes to be completed and so on. There is a precise hour to strike; before that would be premature, and after it might be too late."

"I will try to learn more on the subject and send it out. You talked with a very important man yesterday afternoon, and one difficult to reach. I don't ask what luck you had. How long do you plan to be here?"

"A week or ten days more. I am expecting to keep an important engagement in a day or two. Then I will return to this city. I am staying at the palace of Fürstin Donnerstein, on Bismarckstrasse in Charlottenburg. You telephone me there if you should have anything important. Use my name."

"I cannot give mine."

"Surely not. Choose another."

In the course of ten years Lanny had learned half a dozen names for this man of many roles. Now Monck said: "I'll be Vetterl." And Lanny replied in the best American: "Okeydoky."

There was nothing more to be said. He rose, and they shook hands.

The German said: "I'll go out first and have a look. If I don't come back, it means trouble, and you find your way upstairs in this house and go out by the front door if you can." Such was the life of an O.S.S. man in the Nazi *Hauptstadt*.

But it was all right. Monck returned and whispered: "The coast seems to be clear." Lanny went out into the court, and from there to the street. No one paid any heed to him, but he decided that Roosevelt had been right, and that he ought to get out of this dangerous position without delay. He wasn't needed here any longer.

BOOK EIGHT

The Devil Is Diligent

24

In Fair Round Belly

I

ON A MORNING of feeble sunshine in late February, the P.A. enjoyed a walk to the official *Residenz* of the *Nazi Nummer Zwei, Der Dicke,* who had so many titles that his own secretaries couldn't remember them, and so many decorations that he had no room for them on his vast expanse of chest. The traveler inquired for General-Major Furtwaengler, and this aide-de-camp, whose career Lanny had followed from *Oberleutnant* up, came out with a mixture of delight and amazement. How in the devil's name could it be that an American art expert was traveling about Germany?

Lanny said: "I came to see *Seine Exzellenz.* I hope he won't mind." This by way of diversion, for of course the dear friend had to reply that *Seine Exzellenz* would be delighted. "*Aber, wie? Aber, wie?*" he persisted; and Lanny said that the Führer had arranged matters for him. This wasn't very satisfactory, but a mere staff officer knew that he had no right to ask questions about the doings and motives of exalted personages and their intimates.

Lanny asked about Furtwaengler's own family, as he was in friendship bound to do. He listened to a recital, name by name, for there were a lot of them, as with all good Nazi families; Furtwaengler, like his Chief, was a blond Aryan, and it was his duty to provide for the Fatherland's future. When that subject was exhausted, he reported that the Chief was arriving by air that morning—he didn't say from where, of course—and he would surely want Lanny to lunch. The tactful caller replied that he had some work to do in the Staatsbibliothek, and he would phone just before noon, because it might well be that so busy a man had other engagements and plans.

So Lanny went over and read more about jet propulsion, in the light of what Professor Salzmann had revealed. When he phoned Furtwaengler, he was told that he was wanted at the *Residenz* at once. He came; and there was that bundle of avoirdupois and energy, clad in a uniform of pale blue broadcloth with white stripes down the sides of the trousers. He was only five-foot-five, but even so it took a lot of cloth to cover that frame; he had tried reducing, but it had weakened his heart and almost killed him, he said, and from now on he would be the way nature intended him and the way he liked himself. So he weighed some two hundred and eighty pounds, and bellowed like a bull, and roared with laughter over his own jokes; if he was the least bit worried about the thousands of his best-trained young flyers who had gone down over Germany and the North Sea and the British Isles, he kept that fact hidden until he was alone, or at least until he thought that nobody was looking at him.

He received his guest in that sumptuous study with the big black table in the center and the golden curtains at the tall windows—but no lion cub in these more serious days! Lanny told the story of his coming to Germany, the same story that he had told to the Führer. It was received differently here, for this old-time German robber baron was only about half grown up in his mind; he delighted in adventure for adventure's sake, and this was the sort of thing he would have loved to do, and indeed had tried to do in the days toward the end of World War I when he had been a dashing guerrilla of the air. *"Herrlich! Famos!"* he cried.

He asked a score of questions about Rudi Hess in England. *"Der Mann ist toll!"* he declared, but that was meant for a sort of compliment, for Göring was mad also, and his conduct of the air war had been mad, and for that matter the war was mad, too. The Führer was mad, the Party he had created was mad, and they were all trying to drive the world mad—or so thought the son of Budd-Erling.

The visitor was interested to note that the thing which interested *Hermann der Dicke* most of all to hear was what the Führer had said about *Hermann der Dicke*. When Lanny said the Führer still loved him and considered his help indispensable, the Reichsmarschall beamed like a schoolboy who had just received a medal. Then he frowned and added: "But his strategy has been wrong, Lanny, tragically wrong! Just think, if only I had been permitted to march through Spain and take Gibraltar, as I could have done in a couple of weeks and at almost no cost—then we should have been able to close the Strait, and to keep *Euch verdammte Yankees* out of North Africa, and our armies would have bottled up the British instead of theirs threatening to bottle up ours. *Nicht wahr, mein Alter?"*

Lanny said: "My opinion about military strategy isn't worth the hole in a doughnut, Hermann; but certainly I should have liked to see it tried. For one thing, it would have saved me a lot of trouble. I could have just walked into your office in Tangier and asked if you had any paintings you wanted me to dispose of, say in the Argentine!"

II

That was a "lead," of course. *Der Dicke* talked for a while about the art treasures he was accumulating, and the troubles he was having with other greedy leaders who thought they ought to be allowed to immortalize their names by being associated with Rembrandt and Rubens and Cranach and Holbein, and who could say, perhaps some day Turner and Sir Joshua! There was, for example, Reichsleiter Alfred Rosenberg, that irresponsible depredator—so Göring called him—who had managed to persuade the Führer to let him set up a so-called *Einsatzstab*, which had taken possession of no less than two hundred and three French collections, a total of some twenty-one thousand works of art—"cultural goods that appear valuable to him," was the phrase.

So it had come about that many treasures that otherwise would have been at Karinhall were missing. This had become so intolerable that Göring had been unable to forget it, even while the tragic failure and breakdown of his beloved Luftwaffe had been going on; he had managed to persuade the harassed Führer to give him the right to make selections from the *Einsatzstab* collections, and had flown to Paris no less than twenty-one times in the past year and a half. He would order the choicest works set up in the Musée du Jeu de Paume, the building that had been the handball court of the old Bourbon kings. Göring would stroll through and select the works he wanted, and his secretaries would make a note of them and check their arrival at Karinhall.

Lanny got exact information about all this, because, when he reached the hunting estate, *Der Dicke* showed him the lists of these treasures, and there were twenty-one folders, each with the date of the visit on it. Lanny saw that the Chief of the Luftwaffe had made such a visit one week before his airmen had raided Coventry; again three days before the Japanese had attacked Pearl Harbor; again two weeks after the Americans had invaded North Africa; again while Lanny had been in Casablanca, awaiting the beginning of the great Conference. It had always been Göring's boast that he had so systematized his job that he could take time off for play, and he had proved it even during this calamitous campaign.

A tough old Teutonic plunderer, in very truth; Lanny, a gentle soul by nature and by choice, looked at him with awe. Impossible to understand him, impossible to imagine such a being—yet here he was, a phenomenon, and a menace to the future of mankind. Deep in his own consciousness, what was he? An incarnation of greed, a creature so swept away by its impulses that reason had no power to check him, that facts had no significance for him? One of his lion cubs would be like that; no matter how kindly you treated it, no matter how tame you thought it, the day would come when it was mature; the hunting impulse would possess it and it would leap upon its benefactor. Göring had known that, and so his lion cubs, now grown, were all behind bars. Would Lanny ever live to see the Göring lion himself behind bars?

This explanation only half satisfied the amateur psychologist. Göring was so intelligent, so capable, and he had such a delightful sense of humor! In so many different ways he was a civilized man! His love of art was one such way; his taste was crude and flamboyant, yet he did appreciate true greatness in many cases, and showed it by his comments. His mind was top-grade; he knew not merely military science and the technicalities of airplane construction and operation; he knew the international situation, the personalities of the opposing statesmen, the character of their populations—ten thousand details of which Hitler was ignorant. He knew Hitler, too, and how to manage him—much better than Hitler did! He considered his Führer an erratic genius, yet a real one; with all Göring's braggadocio, with all his absurd vanity, he knew that the Führer could dominate and inspire the German *Volk* in a way that Göring never could.

No, there was more to the man than crude animal greeds; there was training, there was culture. Lanny's thoughts moved on to the Prussian spirit, with its *Ordnung und Zucht*. A hard, grim people, living on a not-too-fertile plain, with no natural defenses against enemies—such as the English had, and the Swiss—they had to depend through the centuries upon their stout hearts and keen, strong swords: *Blut und Eisen*, as they called it. They were the Spartans of this modern world; the Bavarians and other Germans were the Athenians of the same period, and the Prussian Bismarck had welded them into one empire and started them off at world conquest. They wanted to do what the English had done three centuries ago, and they refused to listen to any argument that the times had changed and that the nations now must stay as they were put.

That was the way to explain Hermann Wilhelm Göring, Field Marshal, Air Minister, Commander-in-Chief of the Air Force, Head of the State Secret Police, President of the Reichstag, Prime Minister of

Prussia, Chief Forester of the Reich, *und so weiter*, as the Germans say. He was a social product, a child of Prussian *Kultur*, of the German *Weltanschauung*, their way of looking at the world. The natural greeds of childhood, instead of being restrained and disciplined, had been cultivated and encouraged, sanctified under the name of patriotism and pride of race. Acquisitiveness had become the fulfillment of destiny; jealousy had become protest against *die Einkreisung*, the restraints imposed by neighboring peoples; vanity had become the glory of a master race, destined by nature to subject all others to its will. Lanny would have enjoyed sitting down with the fat Hermann in some hour of leisure and tackling him on this thesis. But instead, it was his job to feed these fires of greed, and to call their victim *alter Wunderknabe* and *Urdeutscher*—original German, founder-German, German from way back! This crude American jesting gave Hermann delight, and even *Rauberritter* wouldn't annoy him too much. He would take a lot of "kidding" from an American that no German would ever have tried twice.

III

Der Dicke pressed a button and roared for his lunch. Lanny guessed that he was roaring louder because there was company; he was acting the part of Hermann Göring, the world's terror, the German Falstaff, *Unser Hermann der Bauch*, the darling of all hearty feeders in the Nazi realm. Liveried servants came running, cleared the center table, and presently appeared a little wheeled cart with silver dishes and cutlery, and a steaming silver tureen full of chicken noodle soup. The host beamed, spread a large napkin over his decorated bosom, and went to work on the food; he sounded like a suction pump emptying an oil sump.

It was the first square meal that Lanny had had in Berlin, and there was no reason why he should not gratify his host as well as himself. He wasn't doing any work for the German *Volk*, but there was no chance that the *Volk* would get any of this food if he passed it up. So he enjoyed a platter of boiled turbot and potatoes with cream sauce, and then as much of a *Rebhuhn mit Specklinsen* as he had room for. "These come from Rominten," said *Der Dicke*, and added: "I have the head of the stag that you shot there, and some day I'll send it to wherever you are living."

"I hope it may be here," replied Lanny. "I have my eye on a little place in the Danzig district, but I decided to wait until the war is over."

The guest had to decline a second helping of fruit pudding. He had emptied two glasses of wine and refused any more, and now he turned down his *Branntwein* glass before it was filled. "I cannot compete with you, Hermann," he said. "I should have to be carried out." It was the robber baron's idea of a fine compliment.

After the table had been cleared, the guest mentioned that he had a lot of news that the Führer told him to pass on. The Reichsmarschall replied that he had a staff conference now due. "But tomorrow morning I am taking you to Karinhall, and there we'll have plenty of time. Arrange with Furtwaengler and I'll send my car for you." Then he added: "Have you been having a pleasant time in Berlin?"

This may have been ironical, and Lanny replied: "How can I, when you have closed all the good cafés and night clubs?"

"I have insisted that one be kept open for my officers. Tell Furtwaengler to take you to it."

"Do you think your officers would relish the company of an American?"

"You won't have to be introduced. I'd like you to be able to tell the outside world that we have not been intimidated by their bombings."

Apparently *Der Dicke* meant that seriously, for when the General-Major came into the room he said: "Take Herr Budd to the Fledermaus tonight, and put it on your expense account."

"I had been intending to invite Furtwaengler," put in Lanny, "and introduce his wife to the Fürstin Donnerstein, who is my hostess."

"Bring them both along," ordered the commander. "What you have been doing for the German people is worth a lot of money which you have never taken. Surely they can entertain you once."

Lanny was taken to the General-Major's office, and made two appointments, one for a staff car to call at seven that evening, and the other for Göring's own car at ten the next morning. He telephoned Hilde and told her to put on her gladdest rags. Furtwaengler said he would phone his wife; and Lanny could imagine the heart palpitations of that lady, the most ardent social climber he had met in Berlin, and that was saying a great deal.

IV

Die Fledermaus is the title not only of an operetta but of a very expensive night club, with scarlet and golden bats all over the ceiling and walls. Here came what elegance and fashion was left in a *Haupt-*

stadt under bombs. It was perhaps the only place that was warm in all the town that night, excepting, of course, government offices and the residences of high Nazis. The ladies wore their evening gowns, revealing lovely shoulders and bosoms not suffering from undernourishment. Many of the escorts wore uniforms, but by no means all, and Lanny realized that this place must represent a black-market deal. Somebody had presented Emmy Sonnemann, Göring's actress wife, with a diamond bracelet, or perhaps a whole stomacher of diamonds, and so this club was allowed to keep open, and Göring could whisper to his officers that it was a special favor he was doing for them. Lanny wondered if the venison he ate was from the fat Marshal's hunting estate in Silesia, the Reichsjägerhof Rominten, which had once belonged to the Kaiser. *Der Dicke* had taken it over without a by-your-leave to anybody, unless possibly his old friend and Führer.

The General-Major, in dress uniform, played host, and his wife, oh, such glory and such gorgeousness! Lanny wondered if she had borrowed these jewels from her relatives and friends, or if they were paste. She was entertaining a *Fürstin*, and while the Nazis publicly scorned and humiliated the old aristocracy, it was different when they met these exalted creatures socially. Hilde still had the "glad rags," but no jewels—Lanny could guess that she thought it imprudent to let one of Göring's henchmen see what she owned. She had put off her mourning, for it was *polizeilich verboten* in public, as being bad for morale. She had confided to Lanny that she would have preferred not to come; but she knew that he was doing her a favor, and perhaps— well, who could guess when anybody might need a friend among the *Regierung?* To have declined an invitation would have constituted an affront and made an enemy.

So here was this haughty *Dame*, feeling as if she were attending a party given by her butler, or perhaps by the police captain of her district. "What on earth shall we talk about?" she had asked, and Lanny had told her to tell about her family and ask about Frau Furtwaengler's; also, to ask about Frau Göring, whom Frau Furtwaengler had met once or twice, and about whom she would be delighted to talk. So there was no lack of elegant conversation, and presently Hilde was repeating stories about her fashionable smart friends just as if Frau Furtwaengler had "belonged" and had the right to know these intimate and sometimes risqué details.

V

There was a floor show, with singing and dancing, sexy but not too crude. The orchestra played no jazz, and Lanny gave the Nazis their due meed of credit; it was the one completely good thing he knew about them. What astounded him were the comedians and their jokes, most of which were topical, and so many critical of the regime. For the past ten years there had existed in Germany a phenomenon known as the *Flüsterwitz*, the joke that no one dared tell publicly, but everyone whispered it to a friend whom he trusted, and thus it attained a circulation of tens of millions. Was there anyone in any German town who did not know the definition of the perfect Aryan, that he was as blond as Hitler, as slender as Göring, as handsome as Goebbels, and so on and on? Was there anyone who had not heard the story of the left-handed teacups—how Göring had told Hitler how much smarter the Jews were than the Germans, and had proved it by taking him into one china store after another, asking for a set of left-handed teacups. All the Aryans said they had never heard of such a thing; but the first Jew they applied to went into the back of the store, took a set of teacups and set them on a tray with all the handles turned to the left, and then produced them as a special treasure at a high price. Going out of the store, Göring remarked: "You see how much smarter the Jew was?" Hitler replied: "I don't see that he was smart at all; he was just lucky to have that kind of set."

Now it seemed to Lanny that under the pressure of misfortune the *Flüsterwitz* had come out into the open, or at any rate, onto the floor of a leisure-class night club. There were no gibes at the Führer, but there were plenty at Göring and at Goebbels, and apparently nobody took it for *Majestätsbeleidigung*, not even the Number Two's staff member and his super-elegant Frau. Werner Finck, the favorite comedian of this floor show, told how Göring and Goebbels were sent to Purgatory, where special punishments had been prepared for them. *Die Nummer Zwei* was handed one thousand new bright-colored uniforms, but no mirror; the Minister of Popular Enlightenment and Propaganda was presented with a thousand broadcasting stations, but no microphone.

Then presently the comedian was telling about his side partner, who had been sent to prison for telling jokes about the *Regierung;* the judge had sentenced him to stay in prison until he had told all such jokes that he knew. "He has been there three months, and he's still going strong." The laughter of this audience revealed that they, too, knew many of the *Flüsterwitze!*

So it went, about one aspect of the Nazi system after another. It was told that Foreign Minister von Ribbentrop's idea of happiness was to have a suit of genuine English wool, and to be able to rub a real grease spot out of it! And then the story about the tiger that escaped from a traveling circus, and everybody was told to shoot the tiger at sight. One Jew remarked to another: "We had better get out of here!" When the other replied: "Why? We are not tigers," the gag was: "Yes, but can we prove it to them?" And presently there were four comedians sitting at a table, presenting in pantomime an elaborate picture of grief and despair. One sighed, one groaned loudly, a third wiped the tears from his eyes; the fourth remarked: "Be careful, my friends, I beg you. It is not proper to discuss politics in this public place."

VI

There came strolling into the Fledermaus a tall, solidly built Teuton in civilian dress, with a red face and a shaved head. He wore a collar that was a sort of trademark, at least, Lanny Budd knew nobody else in the world who wore one like it: round, smooth, and about four inches high, it caused the wearer to hold his chin high up, and gave the square head and knobby face the appearance of a rooster with his neck-feathers picked off. He saw Lanny and stared for a moment or two through his watery blue eyes; then he came over, bowing from the waist, something he couldn't have done from the neck. "I beg pardon, isn't this Herr Budd?"

No chance to deny it; and anyhow, Lanny was curious about this old rooster, over whom he and his father had had many a good laugh. Lanny rose, saying: "How do you do, Dr. Schacht? Won't you join us?"

The one-time head of the Reichsbank was willing, so Lanny introduced him to the others, and a place was set for him. He ordered a meal—Lanny was amused to observe later on that he allowed the General-Major to take the check, and without much protest. Oddly enough, this great financier, who had shown Adi Schicklgruber how to manufacture several times as many marks as anybody had dreamed that Germany possessed, had himself a reputation for penuriousness, which had made him a target for the *Flüsterwitze*. He had been raised in Brooklyn, and his father, an admirer of America, had named him Hjalmar Horace Greeley Schacht. A charming person of no scruples whatever, he had climbed to the top of the country's financial ladder; then he had been tumbled off, and when Lanny and Robbie had met him four years ago in Berlin, he had inquired as to the possibility of getting a chance to manage one of the big banks in New York.

How he stood now Lanny had no idea, and surely wasn't going to try to find out in a night club and in the presence of one of Göring's aides. Nor did the American offer any hint as to the wherefore of his presence in Berlin, though he could be sure that the old rooster must have been puzzled about it. They listened to the floor show, laughed at the jokes, and made a few of their own. The ex-banker had a plate of ham with pickles and potato salad, and while he gobbled it greedily he remarked: "This may be some of my own; I am raising pigs now." Lanny said: "It appears to be a favorite occupation of retired statesmen; Prime Minister Baldwin did it, I remember." The money wizard replied: "It is obligatory upon all good Prussians."

When the party broke up, the Herr Doktor remarked: "If you have time to spare, Herr Budd, you might lunch with me." Lanny explained that he was going out to Karinhall, but that when he returned he would telephone. To Furtwaengler, as they were being driven home, he remarked: "My father did business with him in the old days, and he came to New York frequently. Have you any idea what he's doing now?" This, because in Naziland the Lord alone could know what any man's status might be, or who was trying to cut whose throat.

In the hallway of her palace, Hilde said: "I have had a delightful evening, Lanny; and I want to tell you that I am not going to spoil it by repeating my mistake of last night."

He answered as kindly as was safe: "Don't worry about that, Hilde. It didn't happen." He didn't make the mistake of touching her hand; instead, he remarked: "We have a saying in English that there is many a true word spoken in jest. Listening to those comedians, I kept wondering if that is the way they really feel. And the audience, that laughed so freely."

She answered with bitterness: "I won't tell you how *I* feel. It would be putting a responsibility upon you."

He realized that this remark, made to a man who had a letter from Adolf Hitler in his pocket, was grim indeed. Not wanting to carry any such responsibility, he dropped the subject. "Get out of Berlin as soon as you can," he advised. "It would be better in the Obersalzberg; you won't freeze to death there, and you can meet terrible things here." On that note he went to bed, and the Allies and the ladies mercifully allowed him a night's sleep.

VII

Great day in the morning! Lanny opened his eyes to note sunshine streaming into his room; it was a fraud, however, without any warmth, and he dressed in record time and fled to the kitchen. There he had a hot drink, but he wouldn't eat the food of these women; he knew, and so did they, that he was going to a house of abundance, and also of warmth. To the old servants, of course, Göring was a great man, *Unser Hermann*, and to visit Karinhall was an unimaginable honor. The two sisters appeared, but not the mother; she could not endure to meet an American, no matter how good a German he might be.

Promptly on time the big six-wheeled baby-blue Mercédès drew up at the door. An orderly leaped out and rang the bell, saluted Herr Budd, and took his surprisingly light bags. The guest rode alone to the *Residenz;* then came the Reichsmarschall with a couple of his staff and a couple of civilians. *Der Dicke*, enormous in a fur-lined overcoat, looked pale and bloated at that hour; his flesh was unwholesome, and there were pouches under his eyes; Lanny felt certain that he had gone back to his drugs again. His greeting lacked ardor; but when Lanny told him what the comedians had said about him last night, he cheered up. Apparently it didn't matter in the least what they said, so long as they were not forgetting him.

One of the civilians proved to be Doktor Bunjes—pronounced Boonyez—director of the "Franco-German Art Historical Institute" in Paris. That high-sounding title meant that he was Göring's chief plunderer in the conquered land. He had recently issued an elaborate manifesto in answer to Vichy protests against the looting of the national art treasures of *la patrie*. Lanny read this while in Karinhall, and learned that *objets d'art* had to be seized because they might be exchanged for tanks or planes, though how the French could have managed this was difficult to see. Also, the French efforts to protect art works might become espionage; and most of the works being "safeguarded" were of German origin anyhow, or at least "under the influence of the German spirit."

The other civilian was the fat man's "Curator," a small chap with reddish hair and little dark eyes, very shifty. His face seemed familiar, and Lanny discovered that he had known him in the old days, when he had been a salesman for an art dealer, his brother-in-law, who happened to be a Jew. So Walter Andreas Hofer had become the head of the firm and had managed to impress Göring with his authority as an expert. Naturally he would look upon this American as a rival, and Lanny, who surely didn't want to make a single enemy in Naziland, made haste to reassure both these gentlemen by agreeing with everything they said, praising their taste and judgment, and telling Göring that he was not merely Germany's greatest judge of art works, but Germany's greatest judge of art experts.

Curator Hofer, Lanny learned, had refused to take any salary, but worked only on commission, and never since the art of painting had been discovered in the caves of early Aurignacian France had there been such an opportunity to get rich out of that form of activity. All that Herr Hofer had to do was to tell Göring that a certain painting was no good, and he could have the painting for his own and sell it; all that he had to do was to threaten to discover that a certain collection *was* good, and the owner of that collection would be ready to pay him a fortune to say that it was bad.

Lanny had had a decade to learn about Göring's taste in paintings. *Der Dicke* adored the enormous beefy women of Rubens, the more naked the better; they were Nordic, Aryan, Teutonic, and glorious; *Der Dicke* could imagine himself rioting with them, and the more of them there were, the more German heroes would result. There was an Austrian painter of the last century who had imitated Rubens' fleshliness; Makart was his name, and Göring wanted everything of his that could be found. He wanted the sixteenth-century works of Cranach, because he, too, was German, and because he painted naked figures, even though they were symbolical and sexless, and even though a great proportion of them were not genuine. How could Göring tell, or how could he find an honest man to tell *him?* Honesty was a quality they had banished from their Third Reich. Had not their all-powerful Führer declared that the bigger the lie the more easy to get it believed? *Der Dicke* was surrounded by art experts who were trying out that maxim on him, and one of the best-established among them was the son of Budd-Erling.

VIII

The time Lanny had first come to Karinhall, it had been a hunting lodge in a royal forest, elaborate, but in harmony with the surroundings. Now Göring had been working on it—that is, setting other people to work on it—for ten years, and it was a colossal structure of stone and concrete, wandering here, there, and everywhere, all in the clumsy Hitler style of architecture. Whenever *Der Dicke* acquired a new lot of art works, he needed room for them, and even in wartime his new buildings received priority. Here were row upon row of great rooms, called anything fancy—banquet halls, drawing-rooms, ballrooms, libraries, studios, billiard-rooms, and so on and on. Here were the rows of nude ladies of all ages, climes, and colors. Here were the statues of ancient German heroes with cow's horns in their helmets, and Nazi athletes, male and female, with or without G-strings. Here were all the presents that had been made to the *Nummer Zwei* since the first day that he had become Reichsminister without Portfolio: jewels, massive silver plate, war trophies from all the Axis world. Göring had promised to present all this to the nation on his sixtieth birthday, and was planning a special railway to be built from Berlin, so that it might become the greatest showplace and Mecca for tourists in all the world. For the rest of time mankind would say: "Hermann Wilhelm Göring did this!"

When you entered this unusual building you went through a long corridor that grew narrower, like a funnel. An indirect lighting system revealed rows of art works on each side and the most beautiful rugs underfoot. There were little alcoves with chairs and tables where you might sit with a friend and sip the host's wine and chat about these treasures. At the end of the corridor was the most spacious drawing-room that Lanny had ever beheld; he didn't have a chance to pace it, but he guessed it as a hundred feet by a hundred and fifty, with lavish decorations, including paintings in unbroken rows. There were real masterpieces here, hundreds of them, and a lover of the arts might have spent a long time without boredom.

It was also undeniably pleasant to eat wholesome food without having to hunt for it; to have a warm room, and a bath with hot water, and your laundry done quickly, so that you could dress and feel like a civilized man. Lanny attended to these physical things, but he got only fleeting bursts of pleasure out of the old masters, because he had to be thinking how to impress this Nazi and that, and how to avoid making any of them jealous or suspicious. No easy task for an enemy alien; the fact that he carried a letter from *Die Nummer Eins* and enjoyed the favor of *Die Nummer Zwei* was not sufficient, for both these great ones were known to have their weak spots. They were susceptible to flattery, and everybody around them was using it, after the fashion of courtiers from the dawn of history.

Others of the Reichsmarschall's art staff were waiting for him at Karinhall. It was quite a convocation. Lanny had met one of them, Baron Kurt von Behr, who was head of the *Einsatzstab* office in Paris, the engineer who drove the powerful plunder machine. This nobleman was the criminal son of an old and honored family; he had had to give up a diplomatic post when his name became involved in swindles in Italy. Now, an old man, he had become head of the German Red Cross as cover for his collecting operations. He had been one of the swarm of locusts that had descended on Paris following the German armies, and Lanny had met him in Göring's suite in the Crillon. The Baron's first action had been to reserve a table at Maxim's every evening for two years, and there he entertained distinguished French and international personages, giving them the best food and wine in return for hints as to the location of art treasures.

Here was another creature dominated wholly by vanity and love of display. The Baron was not a military man, but he designed for himself elaborate uniforms. His manners were those of a potentate engaged in impressing his primitive followers. Everything he had was for sale, including his honor, and Lanny found him insufferable, but knew exactly how to deal with him. It was only necessary to hint that the son of Budd-Erling possessed influence that might enable him to take art works out and to deposit money in Argentine banks, and the Baron at once became his flattering friend. He wanted to know what kind of works would have a ready sale, and Lanny suggested those modern French schools which the Führer had declared decadent, and which therefore had no place in Karinhall. Renoirs, Cezannes, van Goghs, these were magical names on Fifty-seventh Street, Manhattan Island.

Only one trouble, the suave P.A. explained; he could not offer for sale works which might have any flaw in the title. "I would have to be in a position to assure my client that the painting had been voluntarily sold by the owner."

"*Aber, Herr Budd,*" said the equally suave Baron, "*I* would be the owner in every case."

"*Ja, Herr Baron,* but I mean the owner who preceded you. You know how it is in America, my client might have the idea that the former owner had had some pressure put upon him."

"I assure you, Herr Budd, that is *never* done."

"I don't question your word, my friend; but you know the anti-German propaganda that has been published in my country. In order for a sale to be possible, I would have to interview personally the former owner of the paintings, and perhaps pay him a sum for a quit-claim deed to the work. You will understand, I am sure, that I would not want to go to that trouble unless it was for some works of unquestionable value."

"Certainly, Herr Budd, I understand your point of view, and perhaps I shall be able to submit something when you return to Berlin."

IX

There were a number of guests at this overgrown hunting lodge. Several were Göring's Swedish relatives—he had been married to a Swedish baroness named Karin, and she had stood by him in the bitter days after World War I when he had been a drug addict and she a tubercular patient. He had named this estate in her honor, and had a sort of Nazi shrine to her memory. One of the things he wanted to talk to Lanny about was this adored lady, and where Lanny thought she would be now, and under what conditions. *Der Dicke* knew, of course, that Hess had been a devotee of spiritualism, astrology, and other occult arts, and that Lanny had experimented with him. What conclusion had Lanny come to? Did he believe that Göring would ever see his beloved Karin again? Could he take seriously any of the innumerable communications that alleged mediums were continually trying to bring to his attention?

Lanny could only say that he had never been able to make up his own mind on these subjects, and surely wouldn't dare try to make up his friend's. *Der Dicke* seemed disappointed, also very nervous when he talked about it, and Lanny could guess that he had had some experience that had shaken his skepticism. He had always been rather contemptuous of Rudi's gullibility on this subject, and now it might be hard to admit that he was changing his mind.

Something was happening to his mind, that was certain. He was erratic, irritable, and restless. He would get up and leave the room frequently, and Lanny would be left to wonder if it was to swallow a pill or get a shot of dope. He wanted to hear all that Lanny had told Hitler about the outside world and its attitude to Germany; but in the middle of the messenger's discourse he would start talking about a wonderful Vermeer that he had brought from Holland, and what did the American art expert think about it. "Christ and the Adulteress," it was called, and Göring had been so anxious to get it that he had traded with a Dutch syndicate and let them have a hundred and fifty paintings of which Göring did not think well, although their estimated market value was one million, six hundred thousand Dutch guilders. Now somebody had infuriated Göring by suggesting that the work was spurious; he wanted Lanny's opinion, and Lanny said that he could see no reason for holding such an idea.

The visitor would have said that in any case, for he would surely have been in hot water if he hadn't. As it turned out later, he was one of many experts who were "taken in." It was proved that the work was a forgery, done by a Dutchman named van Meegeren. He had painted half a dozen "Vermeers" that had fooled the entire art world; he had made such good imitations of the old master's style that the experts refused to accept his own confession, and he had to paint one in jail in order to convince them. And even then they wouldn't believe!

A strange mad world that Lanny was in! A palace fit for a Nero, and a prince who served his guests an immense eight-course banquet, knowing all the while that his subjects had every scrap of food doled out to them for tickets. And in the midst of the meal the host took out of his pockets great handfuls of jewels—rubies, sapphires, emeralds, amethysts, pearls, and diamonds—spread them out on the table, held them up to the light for his guests to admire, and poured them back and forth from one hand to the other, just for the joy of showing off such treasures. If any guest had admired one especially, he might have been told to keep it—but apparently no guest thought this a wise thing to do.

Soon after the meal word came that Allied planes were over Germany. Karinhall might be a mark, for enemy spies provided with radio-sending sets might report when the lord of the estate was at home. The guests were shepherded into an underground shelter, an immense and elegantly furnished drawing-room. At one side was a sort of dais, and on it a great chair, and there sat *Der Dicke;* his guests came by as at a reception, and he chatted for a few minutes with each. When that was over he clapped his hands and ordered his servants to bring his toy trains. This was a complicated set of contraptions—tracks and switches and trains to run over them and across toy bridges and into toy stations. Göring sat in a chair beside a switchboard and maneuvered all this by pressing buttons, and the trains raced and tooted whistles, and it would have been a delightful amusement for any half-grown boy.

The mental boy inside this two-hundred-and-eighty-pound man soon tired of the sport, and he disappeared from the room. To the amazement of everybody, he returned clad in black. He asked the guests to accompany him to the "chapel," and there, before a shrine containing a bust of Karin, everybody was asked to stand with bowed head and maintain silence for one minute in honor of the departed spirit. This while the present wife, Emmy Sonnemann, was in the company. Everyone wondered what she thought, but no one said a word, even after the group dispersed. Lanny was gracious to his hostess, but careful to have no word with her alone. He had decided that her husband was not entirely sane.

X

Among the Swedish guests at this strange week end was one who had been born in Brooklyn, so he told Lanny with a smile. His name was Eric Erickson, and he had an oil business in Stockholm, and evidently had some kind of deal on with the host. Lanny could guess that Göring's sister-in-law, Fru Lily Martin, was also in on it, because these three held more than one conference in the course of the next day and didn't trouble to retire to a private room. Mr. Erickson was a large man, somewhat older than Lanny, with a ruddy complexion. "My friends call me 'Red,'" he remarked, and perhaps he meant for Lanny to take it as a hint, but Lanny perferred to stand on formality.

The grandson of Budd Gunmakers and the son of Budd-Erling had had an interim period of several years during which he had been the scion of New England-Arabian Oil. That had been shortly after World War I, when Robbie had done what was called "dabbling" a bit; he had made what he called a "barrel" of money—representing many millions of barrels of oil. There had been a deal with Zaharoff, the "munitions king," and Robbie had been one of Sir Basil's "men" at the San Remo Conference, where the statesmen of Europe and Asia had presented themselves to the eyes of a young "Pink" as so many office boys running the errands of Zaharoff, Deterding, and the other big "oil men."

Such men were a special breed, and Lanny had come to know them well. They were big, hardy, and tough; they had fought their way up in a battle of wits and endurance that eliminated the weaklings. Mostly they had started from the bottom—it was no game for second or third generations. They traveled to all parts of the earth and learned to get along with all sorts of people, mostly bad. Many failed for every one who succeeded; and when that one had "struck it rich," his troubles were only beginning, for then he came into competition with the big fellows, the "majors," who set out to break him with the deadly weapon of price cutting. If that failed, they would buy him out, and he would move on.

All this was an old story to Lanny; he knew the lingo, and how to talk to "Red" Erickson. He understood that business is business, and that a man who plays that game has to meet his payroll every week, cover his overhead, and distribute a few dividends to the people who have entrusted their money to him. He understood also that Sweden had to have oil, and the principal source was the synthetic product of Germany. Sweden had to pay for it with the rich iron ore that Germany needed for her blast furnaces, also with all the machine tools and electrical goods she could make. No need to explain such things to a man who was here to purchase the "degenerate" art of France and smuggle it somehow to dealers in New York. These two were pals and spoke the same language, giving it the delightful twist of American humor. "Do unto others as they would do unto you, but do it first." Lanny could even employ the special dialect that a Swedish boy had heard in grammar school and high school in Brooklyn; in that "City of Churches" it would have been said that Red Erickson was buying "erl," and that Lanny was buying "pitchers."

XI

This pair took a "shine" to each other and exchanged reminiscences about international conferences and the persons who had been there. Erickson had known some of them, but more recently; his beginnings in the oil business had been of the humblest: he had been a "pipe-line walker," his job being to clear the right of way and look after leaks, all the way from Negley, Ohio, to Bayway, New Jersey—quite a stroll. He had saved his money and put himself through college, and then had become assistant manager of an American oil concern in Japan. So it had come about that he was in the British-American Club at Yokohama on the first day of September 1923, and the story of what had happened to him there interested not merely Lanny Budd, but a group of the Reichsmarschall's guests, sitting before a log fire in one of Karinhall's many drawing-rooms.

Upon what small details do the fates of man depend! Red Erickson wouldn't have been here, telling his tale to Germans and Swedes and one American, had it not happened that that day was a holiday, and that one of the men standing at the bar of the Yokohama club had suggested going out to the veranda to watch the *Empress of Australia* leave the port. The group went out and stood facing the Bund, about thirty-five feet from the waterfront; they watched the tugs pulling the great liner toward the opening in the breakwater, and suddenly they saw one of the tugs sink down five or six feet in what seemed to be the calm waters of the bay. At the same time Erickson noticed a strange rumbling, and said to the man next to him: "Brother, this is no place for me!" He leaped over the railing to the street, and had hardly touched the sidewalk when the entire building of four stories collapsed behind him into a heap of rubble. More than ninety white men were killed and only three escaped.

The oil man went on to describe the dreadful scene of that Tokyo earthquake. Since cooking in Japan was done with small charcoal stoves, tens of thousands of collapsed wooden houses burst at once into flame. Erickson ran to the American consulate and tried to persuade the vice-consul and his wife to come to the harbor with him; but they thought that a park would be safe, and subsequently he found their roasted and bloated bodies in this park. He himself stood five hours, holding onto a pier with water up to his neck, obliged to dunk his head every few minutes against the intense heat. At last he had swum out to the *Empress of Australia* and been taken on board.

"Something extra in the life of an oil man," remarked the narrator. "I stayed among those ruins for another year and helped to distribute the relief supplies that America sent." Lanny would have liked to point out that the Japanese hadn't shown proper gratitude for this assistance; but of course one didn't make such a remark in Naziland, where the small sons of Nippon had acquired the status of "honorary Aryans."

XII

In his secret work a P.A. met few persons whom he could like; it was a danger he had to guard against, for if he liked them he might let slip some suspicious remark. Now he had to be especially careful with this Swedish-American, for he was tempted to like him very much. Erickson didn't seem at all like a Nazi in any of the ways that Lanny had learned to know well. He wasn't fanatical, he wasn't mean, he wasn't especially greedy, at least no more so than a businessman is compelled to be if he wants to stay in the game. Erickson had lived most of his life in America, and everything he said indicated that he liked that country and shared its free and easy ways. He never said anything about politics unless he had to—that is to say, unless there was a Nazi present.

All that was understandable enough. The man was here to make a business deal of some sort, and perhaps he needed the money and had offered a "rake-off" to Göring's sister-in-law, and so had been invited to Karinhall. What puzzled Lanny was the lack of a certain atmosphere that went with that kind of activity. The P.A. described it to himself by the world "smell." Red Erickson didn't smell Nazi, or Fascist, or pro-either. He didn't have the cynicism by which men justify such attitudes; he didn't seem to despise his fellow men, rich or poor; he didn't have the toady spirit, the power-worshiping spirit. In short, he appeared to be a decent person, and what the devil was he doing in this *galère?*

All this meant that Lanny was becoming suspicious of Erickson; and the disturbing thought occurred to him that Erickson might as easily become suspicious of him. Perhaps Lanny also was being too decent; perhaps he didn't have the "Nazi smell." Lanny thought it over and decided that he had better explain himself a bit more clearly. "You know, Mr. Erickson, I don't want you to think that I have taken this trip into Germany just to buy paintings. Ever since this war broke out my father and I have been trying to figure out a way it can end short of the complete ruin of Europe. I find myself in an unusual position, because I have so many friends who happen to be persons of influence in the different countries. I have constituted myself a sort of messenger—not official, but just human. Some may call me a meddler; but I find that Göring likes to hear what important people are saying in Washington and London, and when I go back they are interested to know Göring's reaction to their thoughts."

"It is too bad that more people aren't in a position to do that," opined the oil man. "May I ask, why don't you visit Sweden? We have many of your way of thinking, and some are influential."

"I have thought of coming, Mr. Erickson. Perhaps some day I shall."

XIII

The result of that *démarche* was that Red Erickson invited the peace messenger for a sleigh ride, a pleasure that guests at this hunting lodge might enjoy for the asking. Presently there stood before the door a shining sleigh for two and a pair of eager horses breathing steam into the frosty air. Erickson drove; he loved horses, he said, and rode and hunted much at his home. Lanny sat beside him, sharing a bearskin robe over his knees. They enjoyed the sights of this magnificent forest, which had once belonged to the Prussian State and now belonged to Hermann; he ruled it in two capacities, as Prime Minister of Prussia and as Chief Forester of the Reich. They stopped for a while to watch the stags and their families at the feeding racks; these splendid creatures had long since forgotten how to take care of themselves in the snowbound forests, and behaved exactly like humans who discover that they do not have to work. Lanny remarked about this, and the other smiled; he had seen it often, he said.

This conversation would have been amusing to an auditor who knew the situation. Both men were "fishing," both "sparring for points," trying to get the other fellow's secrets without imparting his own. Erickson asked what Lanny thought about the war and is prospects; Lanny could say only what he had said to Hitler and to Göring, that Germany would always be the bulwark between Russia and Western Europe. Surely it wasn't the part of wisdom to tear down that bulwark; the Swedes, of all people in the world, ought to understand it.

The oil man said yes, but the Scandinavian lands had strong ties with Britain, too; their political systems were alike, and they were lovers of personal liberty. This was a bid for Lanny to say that he was a lover of liberty; but how could he say that while he was being pulled by Göring's horses, and with a letter from Hitler in his pocket? He had to say, somewhat lamely, that the problem was to appease all the nations, to work out a compromise and make an agreement that would last.

Then the P.A. took a turn at baiting a hook. He talked about the oil business, and about Zaharoff, whom Erickson had never met; he told about the old spider's efforts during World War I to keep the Americans from building airplanes to bomb his steel and munitions plants that were in the hands of the Germans. He told about some of the intrigues of this present war; then he remarked, quite casually: "I am wondering how you get along without being blacklisted by the Allies, Mr. Erickson."

The other answered promptly. "They have had me blacklisted from the beginning. But it doesn't worry me because my business is exclusively with Axis customers. How I'll make out afterward is something it would take a soothsayer to tell." Then, having answered frankly, he came back: "I have been wondering the same thing about you, Mr. Budd. How can you ship paintings to New York?"

Lanny had to pretend to be no less frank. "Before America got into the mess, I was all right. Now I'm not sure just what I'll do. Perhaps I'll store them in Sweden till the war is over. I've been wondering if I had the right to ask you for advice."

"I'll tell you anything I can, Mr. Budd. Why don't you come with me to Stockholm? I am one of those fortunate persons who will be furnished with a car to Stettin, and I'll be glad to take you along."

"How kind to a comparative stranger! Unfortunately I have to go back to Berlin for at least a day or two."

"I have to go there for several days. Let us meet there. I am deeply interested in your ideas about the war and the peace. I should like to introduce you to some of my friends in Sweden. Prince Carl, junior, of

Belgium, is a good friend of mine; he is the Swedish King's nephew."

"I have heard of him," Lanny said. "I have played tennis with your King on the Riviera. I'll think the matter over and let you know. Unfortunately my passport doesn't cover Sweden, but that, I suppose, could be fixed up."

XIV

Lanny looked over the list of his achievements on this trip to Germany, and it seemed to him that it was pretty poor pickings. The things he had hoped to get had already been sent in by Monck; and while this was good to know, it didn't help Lanny's score. His talks with Hitler and Göring—the terms of peace, the guaranteeing of the British Empire and the presenting of Latin America to the United States—all that was just so much wind. The only real things he had learned were that Hitler was more nervous and hysterical than ever, and that Göring was an advancing case of paranoia. He might have stayed at home and guessed as much with less trouble.

He just hadn't had any luck. To be sure, Göring had taken his guests into the map room, a wonderful place with detail maps covering whole wall surfaces. The guests had stood and looked at a map of the eastern front, with little red pins showing the Russian troop units and green pins for the German. Lanny might have tried to memorize some of that; but would it have been worth the trouble? The front was shifting continually, and the Russians had their observation planes taking photographs and their swarms of spies all over that snow-covered land. What chance would there be for a guest of Karinhall to bring anything that was still valid?

If he had been superstitious he would have knocked on wood or carried a rabbit's foot. If he had been religious, he would have prayed. As it was, all he did was to think continuously and to wish mightily; perhaps that had something to do with it—we should have to know a lot more about the subconscious mind and its infinitudes before we could be sure. Be that as it may, there arrived at *Der Dicke's* hunting lodge another art plunderer, Bruno Lohse by name, Baron von Behr's assistant and deputy on the *Einsatzstab*. He was introduced to Herr Budd by Göring's competent and devoted secretary, Fräulein Gisela Limberger, and at first he was rather standoffish, wondering what the devil an American was doing in this Nazi shrine. But, as it turned out, he knew Kurt Meissner well; and then he recollected that Kurt had told him about having an American friend who had known and appreciated the Führer from a long way back. Lanny showed his magic letter, and all was well.

The P.A. liked Bruno Lohse as much as it was possible to like any Nazi. To put it another way, Bruno Lohse was as good as it was possible for any Nazi to be. He was a sincere believer in his creed; he made Lanny think of Heinrich Jung, in the days of Heinrich's youth, when he had been inspired, and before he had become a cog in a Party machine. Lohse, unlike so many Nazis, was a physical examplar of his faith; he was tall, blond, and handsome, and if he was a cruel looter, it was because he was convinced that he was preparing a master cultural instrument for the master race of the world. He was a genuine lover of art, and a genuine student in the systematic, hard-working Prussian manner.

So he was interested in Lanny Budd's stories about art adventures, such as his finding of "The Comendador," a well-known Goya, in a decrepit mansion in a lonely part of the Spanish province of Aragon. Lanny did not forget to mention how he had found a couple of representative Defreggers for the Führer, and how the Führer had ordered half a dozen Detazes and put them in the Bechstein house at Berchtesgaden. Lohse had never been to Berchtesgaden, and knew the Führer only as most Nazis did, as a figure on a platform and a voice over the radio. He decided that this American was a very important person indeed, and a true authority on his specialty.

The *Einsatzstab* man had just come back from a trip to Norway. Some wealthy collector had spirited his art treasures out of Oslo and hidden them in a hut on a mountainside. The secret had been betrayed, and Lohse had gone to see if the works were any good, and if so, to bring them to Karinhall. The best of them, including a Rembrandt, were on their way now, and the deputy told about them, and hoped they might arrive in time for Herr Budd to inspect them. It was near a town called Rjukan, he mentioned, and Lanny said he had never heard of it. Lohse described it as being in the southern part of the country, not far from the coast; a really lovely spot, on a little river, between two mountain lakes. Then he added one sentence: "They have lots of hydroelectric power, and it's where we are making heavy water."

Lanny almost ruined himself by betraying his excitement. Only many years of practice enabled him to keep from catching his breath. "Heavy water?" he said. "What is that?"

"I don't know," replied the young Nazi. "It's something they do to water that makes it weigh more."

"Funny thing," commented the American. "Modern physics and chemistry have gone so far these days that we laymen don't even know the language. The Führer sent me to meet Professor Doktor Salzmann, at the Kaiser Wilhelm Institute, and honestly, it was as if I were listening to a man from another planet."

The P.A. went away from that casual chat, saying to himself: "Rjukan! Rjukan!" It became a little tune to which he wanted to dance!

25

Farewell the Tranquil Mind

I

HERMANN GÖRING was a dominating and blustering host. His unresting ego did not permit him to permit his guests to do what they pleased; he told them how to entertain themselves, and he told them what to think. When he was with them, he took charge of the conversation; when he chose to be funny, they all laughed, and he laughed loudest. In the map room he delivered a lecture on the state of the war. When he received a telegram informing him that the Russians had taken Krasnograd and Pavlograd, he read the news to the guests and made it all right by explaining that these were strategic withdrawals, that the Germans were allowing the Reds to exhaust themselves, and meantime were accumulating and training a million and a half new troops for the final spring offensive.

Lanny understood this application of the *"Führerprinzip"* and accommodated himself to it. Alone with his host, he would joke and be saucy, but never when there was any other person present. Jokes *à deux* were intimacy, but jokes *à trois* would have looked like rivalry and caused hatred and mistrust to be generated in the depths of a tormented soul. *Der Dicke* had too good a mind and too sound a military education not to know that his country had fought and lost its "Gettysburg." Alone in the night, he must have shuddered at the prospect of defeat, of the Red hordes sweeping onward into Poland and through

Poland into Germany. The ideas and images must have been madness to him, and the secret agent in his household kept saying to himself: "*Achtung! Achtung!*" Look out!

The master of men summoned the guest into his private office. The guest went, and spent a couple of hours, one in listening to Göring, and the other answering his closely pressed questions. Here the Reichsmarschall made little effort to conceal his anxiety; but Lanny didn't make the mistake of agreeing with him. Lanny wasn't supposed to be a military expert, and it was possible for him to pretend to believe that the scrapings of the German manpower barrel, the lame, the halt, and the wounded, the too young and the too old, the tubercular and the syphilitic, the criminals released from jail and the foreigners impressed into service—that all this miscellany could be trained in three months and sent out to halt and overcome double their numbers of fresh and sound Russian peasants armed with British and American weapons. Lanny pretended, and the other was so mentally weakened that he was glad of the pretense.

What Göring wanted at this stage of the war was the same thing that Rudolf Hess had been wanting since way back. "Our diplomacy has blundered criminally," he confessed. "It is that malevolent jackass, that *Grobian* Ribbentrop who is to blame. He went to England and made a fool of himself before the King, and because the King behaved as English gentlemen do in the presence of a fool, our champagne-salesman diplomat decided to punish the whole Anglo-Saxon race. I tell you truly, Lanny, there is nothing on this earth I would not give, including my life, to see Britain and America helping in this war against Bolshevism."

"You are absolutely right, Hermann," said the P.A. "I have done everything in my power, including the risking of my life. I am ready to go on, with my last breath."

"I am powerless to understand it, Lanny, and I ask myself: Are the Anglo-Saxon statesmen mad, or is it just that they are ignorant? Can't they read one of Lenin's books, or one of Stalin's, and see the program of world domination that these Reds have so carefully explained to their followers?"

"Statesmen seldom read books, *lieber Freund;* they read newspapers, and the reports of their agents, and sometimes the public-opinion polls. After that, their minds are tired, and they want a murder mystery to put them to sleep."

"There has never been murder on such a scale as the Reds are committing now, wherever their power extends. And as for mysteries, I am going to take you into a secret, Lanny. Tell it to some of the Allied statesmen. Take it as my word to Churchill."

"It would be rather difficult for me to get to Churchill—coming out of Germany. In fact it may be impossible for me to get into England."

"Do what you can. Tell it in America and ask them to send it back. In November of 1940, half a year before we blundered into our attack on Russia, Molotov was in Berlin, discussing with Ribbentrop the subject of a postwar settlement and what Russia expected in it. Here is a transcript of the discussion"—Göring had his hand on a thick and heavy typescript bound in black leather—"and I am going to leave it with you overnight. I cannot let you take it out, but you have my permission to make notes of it, and to take those notes out with you."

"That is certainly an extraordinary favor, Hermann."

"It is a favor that you will be doing me, if you can convince the Allied statesmen what kind of men they are dealing with. What Molotov demanded of us when he was certain that we had Britain licked is what he will demand of Britain and America, if and when he considers that Germany has been licked. Any Allied statesman who can read it without shivering in his boots must indeed be a mental defective."

"*Na nu, Hermann.* I can only regret that you did not entrust me with this secret earlier in the game."

"You were here, Lanny, and you know that the matter was not in my hands. It was Ribbentrop and Goebbels against Hess and myself, competing for the Führer's mind. The wrong side won out."

"*Welches Verhängnis!*" said the sympathetic guest. He had heard only recently that the champagne salesman had referred to the over-decorated Reichsmarschall as "that Christmas tree," so he understood the enmity between them.

"Understand," said Göring, "I wasn't present at these conferences, but both Ribbentrop and the Führer discussed them with me in detail, and these are my notes on what they told me, and also official documents connected with the negotiations."

II

Lanny took that document, more precious than all the handfuls of jewels that *Der Dicke* carried in his coat pockets and fondled at his dinner table. He took it to his room and locked himself in, and stayed until the small hours of the morning, reading it in bed. He made no notes, for he knew that he could not take any such papers out of Germany without having one of Göring's men accompany him to the border and see him across; even then, it might become an issue among the various gangs that were competing for the Führer's favor—and Lanny had heard from the Führer's own lips that it was not Göring who was "tops" at the moment. Who it was, Lanny didn't know; probably Himmler, and the P.A. surely didn't want any encounter with the fanatical head of the Gestapo, the ex-schoolteacher who was, by all accounts, so mild and amiable personally, and had men and women killed by tens of thousands without disturbing his smile or his breakfast.

There was no need of notes. Lanny knew the world situation, and every word he read now was stamped upon his mind. What Molotov had put forward was the age-old Russian demand for access to warm water—both from the Baltic Sea and the Black Sea. The Skagerrak and the Kattegat must be "open," and the Dardanelles must be under Soviet control. All during the morning of November 12 the champagne salesman had listened patiently to these demands, and had insisted politely but firmly that the proper way for Russia to reach warm water was by the Persian Gulf. That meant the taking of Iraq and Iran, with all their vast treasures of oil—a very generous offer indeed, except that the oil now belonged to Britain and America, who would hardly give it up without war. During the afternoon of the same day Hitler had joined the conference and had listened, but not so politely. He was quite willing for the Russians to conquer Finland and to keep the Baltic states which they already had; but they must go southeastward, not southwestward into the Balkans, which he had marked for his own. Berlin to Bagdad!—the slogan of the *Kaiserzeit*.

All the three-day arguments, pro and con, had been carefully recorded. Not merely what Ribbentrop and Molotov had said, but what their deputies had said, and what the German military, diplomatic, geographic, economic, and scientific specialists had reported and advised on the subject! There were also secret reports on what the Russians had done and said among themselves; for this conference, held in Berlin, had been fully covered by dictaphones, telephone-tappings, and other devices for spying.

When Lanny put the black-bound tome into the Reichsmarschall's hands, he said: "Why don't you try making a deal with the Russians now?"

"Between you and me, we have," was the reply; "but there has been too much blood shed on both sides."

Afterward Lanny wondered: Would Göring regret having said that, and would he blame his guest for having heard it? Lanny decided once more that it was time for him to be getting out of Hitlerland!

III

The traveler thought the matter over and decided that he might just as well go out by way of Sweden, a country he had not visited since the pre-Hitler days when he had been cruising on the yacht *Bessie Budd*. But he thought it would be the part of discretion to go out alone and not advertise to the Nazis his acquaintance with the plausible oil gentleman. He told that gentleman that his stay in Berlin was uncertain, but that sooner or later he would get to Stockholm and look him up. Erickson said: "If you change your mind in the next few days, I'll be at the Adlon." To which Lanny replied: "I hope the Adlon will be there." There had been another air raid the night before.

The art expert was driven to the city in one of his host's staff cars. By his side rode a Nazi-trained scientist, Dr. Stoffel by name; young and aggressive, tremendously proud of himself and his knowledge and his regime. He was distantly related to Göring, and proud of that, too. He had heard that Lanny carried a letter from Hitler, and said that he had never seen such a treasure, and would esteem it an honor to look at it. Lanny granted the request, and was touched as well as saddened to see the reverence with which the document was handled. From then on the P.A. was a great man to this young chemist, and he talked freely about the wonders that the Fatherland was achieving in his specialty, which happened to be wood.

Yes, wood! The Herr Doktor Stoffel was preparing to remake the world out of wood and wood synthetics. Germany's enemies had shut her off from so many natural resources, but in her noble and carefully tended forests her scientists had found the means of making up for many of her deficiencies. Three pounds of wood sufficed to make one pound of fiber equal to a good grade of cotton. Four pounds of wood were equal to one pound of gasoline, and five pounds would produce a pound of sugar that could not be told from cane. "You have been eating it, Herr Budd," said the enthusiast, and Lanny said that he hadn't noticed the difference.

Germany had a wood cartel, said the Nazi. Wherever her armies had gone, economic commissions had followed without delay, and they had bought up the forests and put them under German control. Wherever there were Fascists there were representatives of the wood trust, getting information and planning fresh campaigns. The young scientist was especially boastful of all this because he held it to be the work of his cousin, the Reichsmarschall; already five years before the

Party had taken power—so said Doktor Stoffel, speaking a Germanized English—Göring had this *Holzprogram* foreseen, and had outlined it at one of their *Bierkeller* assemblies in Munich. So now, in spite of *die Einkreisung,* Germany had alcohol, plastics, and rosins, fertilizer for her fields, fodder for her cattle, and foods for her people. Now in the papers you would see advertisements of *Holzschnitzel,* wood cutlets and *Holzwurst,* wood sausage. *Heil Hitler!*

Lanny listened with his two ears and remembered what he could. He learned that the converting of sawdust into sugar by the sulphuric acid process was known everywhere; but the Germans had a new process by which twice as much sugar could be obtained with simpler and cheaper equipment. That sugar could be converted into, not the poisonous wood alcohol, but ethyl alcohol, from which synthetic rubber, explosives, medicines, dyes, and textiles would be made. This discovery had been made by a chemist named Heinrich Scholler, who had been Dr. Stoffel's teacher, and of whom he boasted. Lanny, taking a shot in the dark, observed: "I have heard that a Jew had something to do with it."

This, as he expected, brought an instant reaction from his companion. "*Niemals, niemals, Herr Budd!* There were Jews working at our Hamburg plant, but that was five years ago. When we knew that Germany was going to be attacked, we cleaned them all out. You can be sure there are no Jews in any German war industry today."

"*Juda verrecke!*" remarked the friend of the Führer, and without the trace of a smile.

IV

Lanny's first move in Berlin was to mail a note to Monck, under his name as butler. It was the most inconspicuous note imaginable, written on plain stationery in uncertain German script, as if by an uneducated person, and addressed to Konrad Kraft at the house of Professor Plötzen. The letter said: "I look forward to meeting you Tuesday evening at ten. Baldur." Any name would do, for Monck would have no doubt whose script this was, and he would understand that it was to be the same corner as previously. If anyone else opened the letter, he would get no information, except that he might follow the butler on Tuesday evening, and that wouldn't be easy in the blackout.

At the Donnerstein palace Lanny found a letter for him. Hilde had thoughtfully put it away and handed it to him personally. It was a fashionable-looking note in a woman's handwriting, and he hastened to relieve the curiosity that he knew his hostess must be feeling. "It's from my sister Marceline," he said and put it into his pocket unopened.

Hilde remarked: "I have seen her dance, and she is charming." It was a possibly awkward situation, because he didn't want to introduce those two ladies, both of whom were indiscreet talkers and knew far too much about him.

He went up to his cold room and read the note. Marceline was in Berlin; she had learned about his presence through a musician-friend of Kurt Meissner's, and of course she wanted to see him. Lanny couldn't very well get out of seeing her, and he had to take time to plan what to say. He decided to tell her that he had come to see Göring on a confidential mission of Robbie's. That would satisfy her, because she thought of Robbie as an important and powerful person, able to work any miracle.

Lanny telephoned her apartment, which was in the fashionable suburbs to the west, which had few military objectives, and where, therefore, few bombs had fallen. He offered to have lunch with her, and to bring food—something that etiquette required. He was rich in coupons because he had been fed at Karinhall, free of both coupons and money. He stood in a queue in front of a *Kolonialwarenladen,* as the Germans somewhat ponderously call a grocery. With an armful of packages a man could be sure of a warm welcome at any woman's apartment, and the news that he brought from the families on three continents made this a red-letter day for a dancer out of a job.

That was what the all-out war effort meant to Marceline Detaze. No dancing until— "When, Lanny?" He told her that only *le bon Dieu* could answer. He had just come from Karinhall, and *Die Nummer Zwei* didn't know. Lanny was going to Sweden, and from there to London, Washington, and Newcastle, to report what he had heard. The world was ruled by madmen, and who could control them? That satisfied Beauty Budd's daughter, who had never been interested in political conversation and was willing to believe that nobody really knew any more about it than she did.

V

He looked at her and saw that worry had not marred her charms. She was only twenty-five, and he thought she had never appeared lovelier, though, of course, he couldn't be sure about her color, because the ladies learn to put it on so skillfully. She kept herself in trim, practicing to the music of a phonograph, so there was no superfluous flesh upon her. She had her father's brown eyes and hair, and wore the latter long, and sometimes danced with it loose. She gave hours every day to keeping herself perfect, and reveled in the admiration of everyone who saw her, including, surely, this half-brother, who had taught her dancing steps when she was barely able to toddle, and had defended her right to have her career and to live her life as she chose.

What she wanted now was to tell this old confidant about her problems. "Lanny," she exclaimed, "what a terrible thing it is to love a man whom you don't *like!*" A curious bit of psychology, but it was really true, she insisted. Oskar von Herzenberg, blond and handsome, was a Prussian aristocrat and a God-awful snob, by cultivation as well as by birth. He had despised the French half of his mistress, and now he had come to despise the American half still more. In addition, he was a Nazi, which meant that all women were dirt under his feet. Yet he loved Marceline, and she loved him, and so they had been having a cat-and-dog time of it.

"He is fighting the Russians," explained this spoiled child of fortune, "and under the most dreadful conditions you can imagine—ice and snow and freezing winds and men dying all around him. He has been wounded twice, and when he comes home he needs me, and how can I refuse to help him? How can I desert him, even when he says the most horrid things to me, even when he threatens to have me sent to a concentration camp?"

"Does it go as far as that?"

"It has gone so far that he has slapped me, and I have wanted to kill him. Love is a terrible thing, Lanny. I vowed I would never submit to it a second time, and yet here I am, a slave. I even admire his arrogance."

What could a half-brother say? Almost nothing. He couldn't offer to take her out of Germany; he might have been able to do so, but he had no right to use his influence for any such purpose, and besides, she wouldn't want to go! She was an adult and had chosen her own bed to lie in. Years ago he had warned her what an Italian Fascist husband would be like, and she had spurned his advice. When he had seen her "falling" for a Nazi, the P.A. had been in a position where he couldn't warn her again, and she wouldn't have heeded him any more the second time than the first.

"I never know," she told him, "at what hour I may get word that he's dead. I think I'll be glad; but then a few minutes later I am sorry I had the thought, and then I am grieving because I miss him. I am a fool, Lanny, and you must know it."

"Bless your heart, old dear," he answered. "You are a woman, and you were taught to expect too much of life, and to have it all free of cost. What I think now is, you ought to get out of Berlin and live in the country, preferably in the south, where it's easier to keep warm."

"And then if he comes back with another wound, what will I do? What if he gets a leave, as he writes me he may when the eastern front has been stabilized, as he calls it? I'll come running back, right under the bombs."

"Have you enough money?" he asked, the one useful question he could think of.

"I have a lot in the bank. But what will happen to it if the bank is hit by a bomb?"

He could hardly keep from smiling at this somewhat primitive idea about money. "The *Regierung* won't let the banks break," he assured her, "but they may limit the amount you may draw out. You have plenty in New York, you know, and I might be able to smuggle some in to you in case of need."

"Lanny, you are good to me!" she exclaimed. "I have been a selfish creature, and I still am."

"I know it," he answered frankly. "It may be that a little suffering will be good for your art."

VI

Lanny had given thought to the extremely precious secrets he had obtained. It would have been a great pleasure to walk into F.D.R.'s bedroom and remark: "Well, Governor, I have brought home the bacon!" But Lanny was a long way from the Governor's bedroom; and suppose it was written in the book of fate that a bomb was to drop upon the P.A.'s head in Berlin, or that he was to have another plane wreck on the way to Stockholm or to London or to Washington? No, manifestly it was his duty to get that information to headquarters as fast as possible, and the way was through Monck, alias Branting, alias Capitán Herzog, alias Braun, alias Kraft, alias Vetterl.

Going to his evening rendezvous, Lanny groped his way through the blackout as rapidly as he dared. He knew that he was in danger, and not merely from Allied bombs and the street traffic. The wartime increase in crime in Berlin was great, and in the working-class districts there was intense bitterness against the rich, encouraged by the demagogy of Jüppchen Goebbels. In their early days the leaders of the National Socialist German Workingmen's Party had laid the emphasis upon the second and fourth words of that name; after their success, they had gone over to the first and third words; but now, with the shadow of defeat hanging over them, they were all for names two and four again, and were telling the embittered poor that their troubles were due to the rich shirkers and parasites.

Here was a well-dressed foreigner, his pockets stuffed with bank-notes both French and German; but fortunately he was inconspicuous in the darkness, and he reached the agreed corner safely. He was wondering: Would Monck have received his note, and would he have been able to get off in time? Lanny passed the corner twice before he realized that there was someone close to him; he said: "*Guten Abend*," and the reply came in the new butler's familiar voice. Lanny took his arm and led him away. "Is everything all right?" he whispered in English, and the other replied: "O.K."

"I won't need but a minute," Lanny said. "You still have ways to send out news?"

"So far as I know there has been no change."

"Listen carefully. You remember the special and peculiar kind of water?"

"I remember."

"Learn the name Rjukan, Norway. R–J–U–K–A–N. That is where it is being made. Take time and fix it in your memory." Lanny listened to hear if there were footsteps, and he swept his arm around to be sure there was no one near. Then: "Next, see if you can locate any Jewish technicians who were employed in the synthetic sugar plant at Hamburg."

"Do you know their names?"

"I do not. I only know that they were cleaned out. They may be in a concentration camp, or they may be dead. If you can find one, he may know an important process. Wood into synthetic sugar."

"I get you."

"Is it all right for me to write you as I did?"

"O.K., but not too often."

"That's all. The synthetic sugar plant in Hamburg. Good luck." The two conspirators turned in opposite directions and disappeared into the blackout.

VII

Lanny kept his promise and phoned to the elderly financial fox with the odd combination of names. He was invited to lunch at the very exclusive Herrenklub, which numbered among its members eight genuine *Fürsten*, thirty-eight genuine *Grafen*, and forty-seven genuine *Barone*. Lanny went prepared for two things: a choice repast and the fanciest possible exhibition of diplomatic tongue work. In neither case was he disappointed.

Dr. Horace Greeley Hjalmar Schacht had on another of his immaculate and stiffly starched collars, and had brought Lanny a present of a couple of pounds of fresh butter from his farm. *Timeo Danaos et dona ferentes!* He had already ordered the meal, which included plovers' eggs and venison. The eggs were served hard-boiled, and, as usual, one had a young plover in it; Lanny found the others tasteless, but he knew they were extremely fashionable, so he sang their praises.

He watched this tall, large, and odd-looking Prussian gentleman, reflecting that from his brain had come the ideas which had made possible World War II. It had been his glib tongue that had persuaded Wall Street bankers that there was big money to be made out of German reconstruction bonds, and these bankers had passed on the glad tidings to their investing public. The Herr Doktor and his friends had made some four billions of dollars in this way, and had built great railroad stations and hospitals, and also warships, munitions plants, and fighter planes.

Then had come Hitler, providing the inspiration, and enabling Doktor Schacht to work quietly, as financiers really prefer. Out of his brain had come the "blocked marks," whereby the neighboring lands were persuaded to part with their lumber, grain, cattle, and ores in exchange for money, which could only be spent in Germany, and when Germany had goods to spare. By a succession of such devices the Nazis had extracted from the neighboring lands a total of eighteen billions marks' worth of goods, all of which had gone into the stomachs of the German *Volk*, or else into preparations for the conquest and subjection of the other lands. Now those peoples were working as the slaves of Germany, and Adolf Hitler was carrying out the promise he had publicly made, to see that all the other peoples of Europe starved before the Germans starved.

What did the ex-finance minister of this criminal Reich want of an art expert from an enemy land? First of all, to find out why and how he had come here; and Lanny amused himself by being smilingly evasive. Second, to pour out his tale of woe, the old tale of the ingratitude of princes. Once more Lanny recollected Cardinal Wolsey: "Had I but served my God with half the zeal I served my King, He would not in mine age have left me naked to mine enemies." The last time Lanny had heard that lament, he had half believed it, but now he didn't believe it the tiniest fraction. He was sure the old courtier would not have dared to talk that way if he had meant it. It was a role that he had been told to play; he was being groomed by the Nazis for a possible defeat. The ex-resident of Brooklyn was going to visit Wall Street once again and tell the bankers that he had always opposed the Nazis in his heart!

Lanny was sure of this when the ex-minister came to the real meat of his discourse. He wanted this terrible war ended, just as he knew the son of Budd-Erling did; and he had his own clever formula for settling the problem. He didn't suggest, as Hitler and Göring had done, that Britain and America should come in against the Soviet Union; no, something much slicker, just that Britain and America should go easy on the western front, so as to give Germany time to put the Bolsheviks out of the fighting. Just a little more of what they were doing now, at the end of February 1943! And if Lanny had said they were doing it, or that he and his father would advocate doing it, the Herr Doktor would have something he could report to the Russians, to increase their suspicions of British and American intentions in the matter of a second front!

The knobby-headed and red-faced Prussian signed a memo for this lunch, and Lanny wondered: Would he put it on his expense account, and would the bill be paid by Ribbentrop's Foreign Office, or by Goebbels' Department of Popular Enlightenment and Propaganda?

VIII

Lanny had promised to call up Baron von Behr, and it would have been very bad tactics indeed to forget that. He remembered it, and the head of the *Einsatzstab* said he had some real treasures to show his new friend. He sent his car to the Donnerstein palace—such a distinguished address to give!—and Lanny was carried to what had until recently been the fashionable art shop of the dealer Diamant—such a distinguished name! Unfortunately a bomb had hit not far down the street and blown in all its windowglass; the windows were boarded up and the firm was out of business. Before that afternoon was over, Lanny had come to the conclusion that the firm had been out for some time, and was being used as a camouflage, either by the *Einsatzstab* itself, or by the Baron and his associates, operating a black market. Inside this luxurious establishment, perfectly equipped for showing fine paintings, were half a dozen of the most charming examples of French Impressionist art that this expert had ever seen. Each had its own reflector, and a chair in front of it, so that the would-be purchaser might sit in comfort and admire. Only one light was turned on at a time, so there was nothing to distract the visitor's eyes or mind. No too eager salesman stood by, singing the praises of the work; a tactful clerk said: "I am told, Herr Budd, that you are competent to form your own opinion of paintings, and therefore I leave you to examine them at your leisure. In the corner of each frame you will find a card with the necessary information and the price of the work."

Nothing could have been more to Lanny's taste. All he had to do was to read the card and make a memo, and then sit and study the work. When he asked for a magnifying lens, it was brought to him. When he was through with the inspection of one painting, he turned on the next light and turned off the other. If only all dealers would be equally tactful—and if they could have the same confidence in their customers!

Here was a Monet, a lily pond and a little stone bridge in bright sunlight. Here was a van Gogh from the Arles period, when he had been drunk with the sunshine and warmth of the Midi, and had made all his work a hymn to the Sun God. Here was a Gauguin, when he had fled from the blasé and cynical art world of Paris to the bosom of Mother Nature in Tahiti, where the natives were peaceful and happy, or so it had been possible for a distraught painter to believe. All these works were "degenerate," according to the official classification established by a former painter of picture postcards from the home for the *Obdachlosen*, the shelterless of the Vienna slums. Their prices were low, but not too low, because it was well understood that the degenerate non-Nazi world put a high valuation upon them. Lanny might have these old masters—for so they had become in the year 1943—for approximately eighty thousand marks, which was about thirty thousand dollars at the official rate, but less at the real rate. He had no doubt that some of his clients would be glad to pay double the price.

Buying paintings was Lanny Budd's camouflage, and making money was the only way he could keep the rank-and-file Nazis from being suspicious of him. He had kept money in Berlin banks to cover such deals, and he would take the paintings out to Sweden and put them in a bank vault there. He would tell his Boss what he had done, and if the Boss approved, the all-knowing Baker would get the necessary permit, and the paintings could be brought to America and sold to Mr. Winstead or other collectors, and the profits given to the Red Cross.

IX

Lanny said that he would buy those paintings, provided that he could receive the necessary assurances as to their former ownership. The clerk said that had all been arranged for, and submitted for the customer's inspection two documents, one a bill of sale signed by Baron von Behr, and the other a quit-claim deed signed by one Rosika Diamant, stating that she had been the former owner of the specified works, that the sale to Behr had been voluntary, and that for the sum of ten marks she hereby ceded to Lanning Prescott Budd any and all claims that she might have to the said works.

There was brought into the room an elegant-appearing young woman, concerning whose race he would have had to ask no questions, even had it not been for the yellow Star of David which she wore upon her bosom, according to Nazi police requirements. She was evidently a person of refinement, and it was not her fault that she was also ripe and luscious. She reminded Lanny of Olivie Hellstein, when that daughter of a great Paris banker had been presented to him as a possible wife, and had started an impressionable playboy to quoting from the Old Testament. "What thing shall I liken to thee, O daughter of Jerusalem? What shall I equal to thee, that I may comfort thee, O virgin daughter of Zion?" Like Olivie, this one had large dark eyes, such as poets are wont to compare to a gazelle's. "Turn away thine eyes from me, for they have overcome me! How fair and how pleasant art thou, O love, for delights!"

The clerk, or salesman, or whatever he was who was handling this deal, said: "This is Fräulein Diamant, who was the owner of the paintings, and will tell you about them."

"I am pleased to meet you, Fräulein," responded Lanny politely. "I should be grateful for the information."

The young woman—she could not have been much more than twenty—began her story in a soft voice, which became her style of beauty. Her father had acquired the paintings in the course of his art business; the father was no longer living, and she was his sole heir. Inasmuch as the war had made matters difficult for her, she had been glad to dispose of them, at a price that she hoped would make the deal worth while to Herr Budd. This she said with gazelle's eyes looking straight into Lanny's, and without a trace of hesitation.

Lanny was fairly sure that this was a frame-up on the part of Baron von Behr, but what could he do or say? He might pin the young woman down, but she would surely have learned her story and would do nothing but repeat it. He would surely not be doing her any service if he were to break her down in the presence of any Nazi; and the same would be true of himself in his relationship to Göring and staff. A business deal is like a love affair—it is better not to start it if you mean to break off in the middle.

The P.A. said: "I accept your assurance, Fräulein. The price is satisfactory, and I am glad to hear that I can be of service to you."

X

He had been to his Berlin bank and got a checkbook. His account had been sequestrated when Germany declared war upon America, but that would hardly apply to a payment to the *Einsatzstab*. Lanny could guess that this must be a favorite way of making deals, to sequestrate a man's funds and let him know that there was just one person to whom he could draw a check. Lanny wrote the check and handed it to the clerk, and received the bill of sale and the other document. The precious paintings were taken out of their heavy frames, and each wrapped in a soft cloth; Lanny stayed to see that it was done properly and that he got what he was paying for. They were not large paintings, and were packed in two parcels, which could be handled without difficulty. They were put into the Baron's car and taken, along with their new owner, to the Donnerstein palace. All this was an old story to an art expert; he had been doing it for more than twenty years and always carefully watched all kinds of tricky persons.

He saw the treasures safely stowed in his icebox room, and told Hilde about them, so that she might not be worried as to his doings. He went about other affairs, and when he came back to the palace in the evening the elderly manservant told him that there had been a telephone call for him, a lady who declined to give her name but said that she would call again. Lanny at once guessed that it had been Fräulein Diamant, because he knew of no other lady who might have anything confidential to say to him. He was not surprised when he was called to the phone soon afterward and heard the soft voice of the daughter of Jerusalem; nor was he surprised that she did not give her name, but said: "This is the person with whom you made a business deal today."

He did not make the mistake of naming her. He knew that she was taking her life in her hands, because it was forbidden for Jews to use either telephone or telegraph. "I understand," he replied, and she told him that there was something she urgently desired to say to him. Would he be willing to meet her at the Brandenburg Gate at nine on the following morning? He recognized a device of the Berliners who wanted to discuss some confidential matter in safety; they went for a stroll in the Tiergarten. Lanny had done it himself, with Laurel and with others.

His mind was busy with the problem: What was it this young woman wanted? To back out of the deal? Manifestly he couldn't do that without jeopardizing his standing with the Nazis. The Fräulein was in a trap, but so was Lanny. He would have to take the paintings out; but, if she had been robbed, he might promise her the profits. Or could it be that she wished to tell him that the paintings had been extorted from other persons and that his title was worthless? In that case he would have to hold them in Sweden and see what developed after the war. He debated these matters until his bed got warm and he fell asleep.

XI

In the morning, when he saw the young Jewish woman strolling through the great monument to Prussian arrogance, he did not make the mistake of greeting her. He passed her by and walked slowly into the snow-covered park, leaving it for her to catch up with him when she chose. She was clad in a coat that might have been worn by her serving maid, and he could guess that she had parted with her furs and jewels. When she joined him he did not stop, but kept walking, and passers-by would be free to assume that it was one of those assignations which do not cease with war—quite the contrary. "*Pflücket die Rose, eh' sie verblüht!*"

"Herr Budd," she began, speaking low, almost in a whisper, "I apologize for troubling you—"

"Not at all, Fräulein. Do not be uneasy. I am here to listen to whatever you have to tell me."

"I am a stranger to you," she went on, increasing the tempo of her speech, "but it is sometimes possible to tell a great deal about a person from a brief glimpse. I beg you to believe that I am an honest woman."

"I can assure you on that point, Fräulein. I think I know a lady when I see one."

"I mean more than that, Herr Budd. I mean that I am a woman with a heart and a conscience."

"I am prepared to believe that, too," he declared promptly.

"I no longer have any standing in this world where I live; but I have my sense of honor, and I am capable of gratitude that would never die."

"Proceed, Fräulein, upon the belief that I accept your statements."

"I am about to make what must seem to you a mad proposal. It is born of my utter desperation. I am a Jewess. I had a father and a mother, two brothers and a sister, and a good family position—you know, perhaps, of my father's business, which was prosperous. Now, as you have seen, it is in the hands of others. All my family have disappeared; I have not heard a word from any of them for months, and I have no hope of hearing. I have given up asking, because it brings only angry words, and I have had to make up my mind whether I wish to live or not."

"A dreadful position, Fräulein."

"I am employed in the business because I used to help my father and so I have knowledge that they need. I am at the mercy of these men, and it is more horrible than any words can tell. I give them pleasure, but do not earn any gratitude or affection—these things are not to be had by any person of my race, no matter by what services."

"That I can understand—"

"Today I met an American, the first I have seen in more than a year. I saw a kind man, and I read in your face that you did not think I deserved the badge of shame that Jews must wear in Germany. It is no shame to us, of course, but to those who force us to wear it."

"You are right in your guess, Fräulein Diamant."

"Do not use my name. Words may be overheard, and I am doing something that might cost me my life. It is my thought that you might help me to get out of this land where I am not wanted."

"How could I help you, Fräulein?"

"There could be only one way—to marry me and take me to America as your wife."

"Oh!" he exclaimed involuntarily.

"It would be in name only," she rushed on, her voice trembling and almost breaking. "You could divorce me, or have the marriage annulled. If I had a fortune, I would offer it to you. As it is, I can offer only my services. I would be your secretary, your servant, I would work my fingers to the bone to repay you; and it would be for all the rest of my life. I would never ask to be released from the bargain. I ask only to live, and to have a chance to do something useful. This is the cry of a frantic woman—"

"You must spare yourself further effort, Fräulein," he interposed. "I might do what you ask, but as it happens, I have a wife and baby in New York."

"*Ach, Gott!*" she exclaimed, and her voice died away.

"I am truly sorry, but I am helpless in the matter."

The kindness in his tone caused the spark to revive for a moment. "Do the people here know that you are married?"

"No, but they could easily find out."

"It might not occur to them. Surely your wife would understand; and a Nazi marriage would mean nothing in America. I could go away and never see you again, just send you my earnings—"

"*Leider, Fräulein*, there is no possibility of it, and you must put it out of your mind. My circumstances make it impossible."

XII

He could not say any more; he had to pronounce what both of them knew was a death sentence, and without any explanation. They walked in silence for a space. Then the woman said: "Forgive me, Herr Budd. I had no right to trouble you."

"It was a natural thing for you to think of," he assured her.

"Tell people what is happening here!" she broke in. "They are exterminating our race. Not merely do they deprive us of our property and of the chance to earn our bread; but they are determined that there shall not be one of us left alive here, or in the lands that they have taken. They are shipping us away in cattle cars, to camps they have built for the purpose of wholesale murder."

"Can that really be true, Fräulein?"

"There can be no question that it is true. Thousands of our people are perishing every day. They are making Jewish bodies into fertilizer and soap. There has been no such horror since the beginning of history."

"I have heard such statements made, Fräulein, but it is difficult to believe."

"Every Jew in Germany knows it. We no longer accept the tales that are told us, that we are to be taken to Poland to be settled on the land. We are taken to be killed wholesale in poison-gas chambers and then burned in furnaces or boiled in rendering vats. Jewish bodies become a choice kind of German soap. And the harder the war goes with Germany, the more determined these fiends become that there shall be none of our race left to share the benefits of victory."

He took one glance at that lovely face, drawn with anguish; then he turned his eyes away. He couldn't say: "I will report these statements in my country, Fräulein." He couldn't even say: "I believe you."

He could not forget the possibility that this so plausible approach might represent a plot by some of Göring's henchmen who suspected him and would be glad to get something against him. He had to harden his heart and say: "I regret that I cannot do what you ask, Fräulein. All that I can do is to assure you that what you have said to me will be locked in my heart, and that whatever may happen to you in future will not be because of this appeal to me. Good-by."

They had come to a parting of the path on which they walked. He waited to see which one she would take, and he took the other. Such was his duty, and he did it; but the doing made him sick to the soul.

XIII

It wasn't much of a walk to Göring's *Residenz,* and there the dependable Furtwaengler made regretful note of the fact that Herr Lanny Budd was ready to depart from the Fatherland. He could have a seat on a plane to Stockholm in a couple of days, and the General-Major would see to it that the rules concerning baggage were set aside so that he could take his paintings. His exit permit would be ready for him, and Göring's own cashier accommodated him by taking several of his ten-thousand-franc banknotes and giving him good National Socialist marks—at a rate in favor of the latter. That was the modern way of bleeding a country that you had conquered: you just declared your money worth several times as much as the other country's money, and then your soldiers could walk into the shops and strip them bare. So the silk stockings and wines and watches of France had come to Germany, and the French had nothing to complain of.

A consequence of the closing of the cafés was that the white-collar workers and officials of the *Hauptstadt* had to bring their lunches, decorously hidden in a little satchel or something equally respectable. In cold weather they made up parties in one another's offices; and Lanny phoned Heinrich Jung and was invited to one. He would bring his own, of course; so he went out and strolled, looking for a queue that was not too long. Many were a block long, and the trouble was that when you waited your turn, you might find the shop sold out. But in the better-class districts were shops that had more goods—the luxury articles, for which no prices had been fixed. Lanny bought anchovies packed in olive oil, and ripe olives and dried figs from Portugal and Spain; also a loaf of rye bread, and some cheese that he knew Heinrich liked. The American millionaire—all Germans thought him that—

didn't mind spending coupons, for he was going out, and before he went he would make a present to Hilde that would balance the account against his Puritan moral code.

The admiring Jugend official begged to be allowed to bring in a couple of his superiors, and the three Nazis listened with stuffed mouths to an account of the visit to Karinhall, which was the same as Walhalla or Mount Olympus or Hollywood to them. Lanny described *Unser Hermann's* oblong dining-hall, which seated twenty-four persons, each in a big armchair, at a long table; and the magnificent leather-bound copy of *Mein Kampf*, which the Führer had presented, and which stood on a lectern with a candle on each side of it, always burning; and the cages with the grown-up lion cubs, each of which had been named Kaiser, and now were known as Kaiser Eins, Zwei, Drei, and Vier; and the wonderful toy trains, which dashed and tootled and obeyed signals just like so many *Jugendbeamten*. Lanny repeated what Göring had said about the new armies being formed, which would end the war in the east before the West had a chance to get started. All this added immensely to the enjoyment of *Delicatessen*.

It was really too good to last, and it didn't. There came a screaming of sirens, and these middle-aged and slightly paunchy bureaucrats had to gather up the remains of the food and hustle down into the air-raid shelter in the basement and sit crowded on uncomfortable benches. Daylight planes were always American, and this was embarrassing to a visitor who had to apologize and murmur that he had done his best to prevent it and now was trying to stop it. Fortunately the American bombers aimed at objectives such as factories where war goods were being made, and these were mostly in the poorer and more dingy neighborhoods; so Party officials didn't have to worry so much.

XIV

The traveler went out on the street again and looked at Berlin after an air raid. He didn't see any signs of damage, and the afternoon paper told him that a large flight of planes had been driven off by the city's accurate defense fire. He guessed that it had been an observation raid, for the purpose of taking photographs. The newspaper informed him also of a concert, and that item would probably be accurate. Music was now the only thing in Germany that was both excellent and cheap, and he decided to remind himself of the good Fatherland, the one he had known and loved as a boy. There must have been some of that left in people's hearts, or why would they come out of their homes in cold weather and spend their small savings for Mozart and Beethoven?

So Lanny spent a couple of hours in the presence of supernal loveliness, moved almost to tears at the thought of the spiritual treasures that were disappearing so rapidly from the earth. "Stay, thou art fair!" had been the cry of Faust; but this music did not stay, it spoke to you and then vanished, leaving nothing but a memory, and a soul ill satisfied with a world of cruelty and hatred. Lanny thought, as he had always done in the presence of any form of beauty: Why can it not be appreciated, and why cannot the world be built to guard it and keep it, instead of blowing it to pieces with explosives dropped from the air? He would have liked to voice that thought to the people about him, but he had to hold his tongue. In all Germany there was but one person to whom he would dare to speak his mind, and that person, Monck, was forced to live as an outcast and criminal, under an assumed name and carrying papers that were forged.

Coming out from this heaven of the spirit, Lanny walked again, and bethought himself of his bodily needs. He was planning to have supper with the Donnerstein sisters, and he stopped at a food shop where the queue seemed not too long. Living in a palace and visiting in others, Lanny hadn't met many of the German *Volk*, and this was the one way that was open to him. Mostly it was old people in the line, for they were the ones who had the time to spare; nine out of ten of them were women. It was late afternoon, and cold, and the would-be customers, mostly with shawls over their heads, stood hunched and silent, their hands under the shawls for warmth, their bundles clutched to their sides. The stranger hunched himself like the others and kept his fur-lined gloves in his pockets, trying to appear as unfashionable as he could.

There were some who talked, and Lanny discovered that most of the conversation had to do with food and where you could get it and what prices you had to pay. This was a poor neighborhood, and the women's faces were pale, all but some noses that were red with cold; they were standing and enduring in an effort to get something for the hungry children who would be coming home from school, and for the men who would be looking for a nourishing meal after a hard day's work. When the women did not find what they wanted, they grumbled, and the things they said about the *Regierung* would have made Jüppchen Goebbels' ears burn. Lanny was astonished by the violence of the complaints, and by the loud tones in which they were voiced.

XV

He made his purchases and headed for the Underground, knowing that it would be jammed and uncomfortable at this hour. His duties were done, and how glad he would be to step into a plane and fly out of this giant Nazi jail! His walk took him by the great Schlesischer Bahnhof, and there he saw a crowd and wondered if the place had been bombed. There was some shouting, and he ventured to ask a question and was told that a trainload of wounded men had just come in from the eastern front. Lanny had seen that sight in the past, and could imagine it; the cripples barely able to hobble, the men with bandaged heads, with arms in slings, and some having to be carried in litters; always they were ghastly pale, and some greenish; they were unshaven and dirty, pitiful wrecks of the sturdy soldiers who had gone away.

And here were women waiting for them, tense with anxiety, some of them beside themselves with grief; they had broken through the barriers that were supposed to hold them, and that was a strange thing in this land of order. Some began wailing and screaming, cursing the regime that kept them at war, clamoring for the war's end; the tumult increased every minute, and there were so many of the demonstrators that the police were helpless—at least until more had been summoned. Lanny didn't wait to see that happen, for in such a place a round-up of war shirkers was apt to occur, and he didn't want to have to produce his papers and explain how an enemy alien came to be there.

A little later the P.A. was crowded into the Underground. He found it indecent; it offended every sensibility of a fastidious gentleman, who had always had his own car and traveled where he pleased. He hugged his food bundles, and swayed this way and that with the standing mass, and tried hard to tell himself that he had no right to complain, that he was completing his education in the meaning of capitalist war. This modern style of conflict was bringing the great ones down to the level of the small; it was bombing the statesmen and the diplomats in their offices; it was even getting a general or an admiral now and then. It was bringing the civilians into the front line—rich man, poor man, beggar-man, thief; doctor, lawyer, merchant, chief! It was teaching all of them a painful lesson, and maybe when it was learned they would take an interest in preventing World War III!

When he emerged from the subway it was dark, and when it gets dark in a blackout there is no mistaking it. Lanny knew the way and followed in the footsteps of other tired people seeking their food and sleep. On busy streets two lines formed, each keeping to the right; people wore tiny shaded lights fastened to their buttonholes, aimed downwards, and wired to pocket batteries. With these you could get along all right until you came to a crossing, and then you had to watch out for your life. Snow had begun to fall, and that made it worse; but Lanny was in no great hurry, he had a warm overcoat and gloves, and well-nourished, healthy blood.

He came to what he recognized as the steps of the palace. They were of marble, with marble balustrades on each side, and an area slightly below into which you might stumble if you were not careful. He had started to ascend when he heard a voice, speaking low: "*Wer kommt da?*" He thought the tones were familiar, and he asked: "*Wer fragt?*" The voice said: "Lanny?" And he answered, with great presence of mind: "Vetterl!"

It was Monck, and Lanny went down a step or two, and gave his friend a hand, to help him out of the area where he had been hiding. His hand was ice-cold—he had evidently been waiting for some time. "Can you take me in?" he whispered. Lanny asked: "Are you in trouble?" When the other said yes, Lanny took him by the hand and led him silently up the steps. The P.A. had a key, and he opened the door, and they went inside and upstairs to the second-story room, unseen by anyone.

26

The Bombs Bursting in Air

I

UP IN that elegantly furnished bedchamber, which had not been warm for several months, Lanny saw by the dim light that his friend's teeth were chattering and his lips blue with cold. "I have been waiting a long time," he said. "Ever since it was dark enough to hide in the area."

"And you have no overcoat!"

"I had no time to get it. I had to run like the devil."

"My God, man! Take off your shoes and get into bed." Monck did this, moving over to the far side, and Lanny followed, taking the near half of the bed. It was an established way to live in a time when coal was needed for factories and railroads, and when every able-bodied man who could be spared was at the front. People learned how to live in cold houses; they had heat only for cooking, and they ate in the kitchen by that same warmth. When they were not moving about they lay in bed, saving both fuel and food. Conversations could be carried on there perfectly, and if you arranged a light you could read and be warm, all but the one arm that was holding the book or paper. Civilized people have a lot of fancy notions that they can unlearn when they have to—such as having sleeping clothes different from those you wear in the day, and that clothing has to be pressed smooth, and must not have any patches or other signs of wear.

Monck said: "Are we safe here?" The reply was: "I have locked the door. There might be a servant at the keyhole, so keep your voice low and speak English. What has happened to you?"

"The Gestapo came to Plötzen's house. It was a piece of blind luck that I happened to go out by the basement door to set out a trash can and saw their cars draw up at the curb. I don't think they saw me; I was on my way in. They ran up the steps and rang the front-door bell. I hid and waited until they rang again and the housekeeper came and answered. I heard them ask: 'You have a servant named Konrad Kraft?' and then I beat it for the rear door that gives onto a yard. I had studied the land in advance, looking from both the yard and the rear windows of the house, so I knew what to do. I climbed the fence into the next yard, and so on for five houses. Of course the SS could follow my tracks in the snow, but it would take them a few moments. I came to a garden that gave onto a side street. I fully expected to be halted there, but they hadn't posted a guard. I saw a car coming and dashed out into the street and hailed it: 'The master is sick! Take me to a doctor quickly!' You see, I had on the right clothes, and it worked."

"That is what I call presence of mind," said the P.A.

"Believe me, I have been thinking about these things for many years, and trying to foresee all troubles. We came to a doctor's sign, and I thanked the driver and jumped out. I went to the door and pretended to ring the bell; the car drove on, and then I walked as fast as I could without attracting attention, turning corners and getting away from Plötzen's neighborhood. I knew that I was in a desperate way, because the police would be notified to look for a man in a butler's black suit and without any hat or overcoat. Fortunately I came to a cinema, and

I went in there and waited for darkness. Then I came here, on the chance that you might be able to hide me for the night. I know I have no right to do it—"

"Don't worry, old man. You must be saved. You are safe here for the night, and you will be warm; also, I have some food. The problem is tomorrow. There are two servants here, and they may be worshipers of the status quo; there is also a bereaved old lady, who hates and fears Americans, and nobody can guess what ideas she may have in her head. I don't want to ask questions that I shouldn't, but tell me if you have any plan of escape in mind."

"I have two contacts in this city; I'm only supposed to have one, but I got another through accident. The trouble is, I am under orders not to seek refuge with any other agent in case of trouble. I'm on my own. You can understand why that is."

"I understand well enough. I'm supposed to take the same attitude."

"I'm ready to walk out tonight if you say so, Lanny. I have a little capsule of cyanide, so they won't get me alive."

"Let's think up something better than that, old man. Tell me, do you have any suspicion as to how you were betrayed?"

"Not the slightest. Somebody may have weakened under torture; or somebody may have been an enemy agent posing as our friend."

"Do you think it can have anything to do with the information I gave you recently?"

"How can I tell? That information was supposed to go out the same night that you gave it. It was carried by a railroad man whose job takes him to Holland and back."

"Did he have anything in writing?"

"He wasn't supposed to. They were simple things to remember."

"Could he by any chance have heard my name?"

"Jesus, no! Wild horses couldn't have dragged it out of me."

"Well, then, we have tonight to make our plans. Have you any suggestions?"

"I have been thinking, as well as a half-frozen man could. The first thing, I must have different clothing."

"I may be able to arrange that. And a passport, I suppose?"

"A passport and an exit permit, though there might be other ways of getting out. I am an old-time sailor, you know."

"Yes, but it wouldn't be easy for me to get you a sailor's outfit; and I'm afraid I can't get you any papers."

"Papers were furnished me in Switzerland, and they had come from Berlin. The same group that attended to that could do it again."

"Have you a contact with them?"

"The individual who has been sending out my information would know about the passport. It is a question, of course, whether the police have caught that person, too. I have to go and try to find out; if I don't come back, you will know that I have been caught—and that I have taken the capsule. I shall have it already in my mouth."

II

The two men lay whispering for hours, canvassing every aspect of Monck's situation, and of Lanny's. Any moving about that the German did would have to be at night, and he had the idea of taking Lanny's suit and overcoat and going at once to make his contact. He would have to be there personally, to put his fingerprints on the documents. Lanny vetoed this suggestion for several reasons. His suit, which had been purchased in New York, and his overcoat, which had been purchased in Tunisia and was of French make, were "dead give-aways" for the Gestapo; and they would be extremely active that night, stopping all wayfarers and searching them carefully. By the next night they might have decided that the criminal had found a hiding place or had escaped from the city.

"Listen, Vetterl," whispered Lanny—for when you are taking up an alias you have to get used to it as quickly as possible. "This is what I will tell my hostess in the morning. You are a former employee of my father's, and I got to know you well in Berlin back in the twenties. The Fürstin met my father then, and this will sound plausible to her."

"Am I German, or American?"

"You are German. I went to see you and found you just after an air raid. Your home was destroyed and you escaped in your underwear. I put my overcoat on you and brought you here. Will there be anything in the papers about the escape of the butler?"

"The Gestapo doesn't work that way. The papers warn the public about enemy spies and agents, but they don't tell about individual cases, especially German nationals. They are not admitting that there are traitors and enemies of the *Regierung*—it would be too bad for morale."

"All right then; I can get away with that story. You are not wounded, just suffering from shock and grief—you had a wife and two children and you saw them killed by a falling beam, and they were trapped in the fire. You tried to free them, but it was impossible."

You want to stay in this room and sleep, and not be disturbed. That will do for the first day at any rate."

"Won't they be wanting to bring me food?"

"I had food that I had bought, intending to contribute it to tonight's supper. Now you will eat it. There is a bathroom adjoining, so you do not have to be disturbed. You can lock your door, and sleep or think out your plans."

"Have you any idea of what to do about clothing?"

"I am quite sure that Hilde—that is the Fürstin—will have clothing that belonged to her husband and her son. She will feel sentimental about it, but will realize that this is an emergency. I will pay her a good price, and that will help, even though she may be too proud to admit it."

"Tell me about this family," said Monck alias Vetterl, and Lanny told the details. The old woman brooding in her room and hating all Americans was not so good. Old family servants would doubtless do what the family told them, but could hardly be expected not to gossip. Whatever the conspirators were going to do ought to be done the next night. A bomb-shocked man lying in a room by himself and not calling a doctor might be all right for one day, but surely not indefinitely.

"Will I have to meet this Fürstin?" asked Monck.

"I'll have to see how she takes the story. I wouldn't want her to take up the idea that I was hiding a woman in the room." He didn't tell his friend of the special and peculiar reason that he feared such a possibility. He believed the Fürstin to be, fundamentally, a decent soul, so that she wouldn't cherish anger against him for what had happened in this room. But was there any woman living who wouldn't blaze with wrath against a man who turned her down in that fashion and then smuggled another woman secretly into her home? Was there a woman who wouldn't think of that possibility, and want to make sure?

III

A complicated set of problems for two middle-aged secret agents, lying side by side in a cold dark chamber and conversing in whispers! All the vast machinery of a highly organized civilization was against them, and they were staking their lives against their ability to foresee and to meet all difficulties that might arise. Fortunately Lanny had money, and that can do a lot; but it can do nothing against fanaticism, against the solidarity of an idea. Millions of men and women and even children were convinced that they were superior to the rest of the world, and that it was their destiny to remake the world, and that anyone who opposed them was a scoundrel, a criminal, a fiend out of hell. Such people were hard to persuade or to bribe.

Lanny had that letter signed "Adolf Hitler," and he could use it. But did he have the right to? His orders were to take care of himself and return to Franklin Roosevelt for more orders. He wasn't permitted to be self-sacrificing or noble-minded; he was an apparatus for collecting military information, a very special apparatus that had cost a lot of money and taken a lot of time to construct; there was only one of him, and he did not have the right to destroy or even to risk himself. Most embarrassing of all, he didn't have the right to explain this, but had to leave it for Monck to guess.

At any rate, that was the theory. But unfortunately Lanny Budd wasn't just a machine; he was a human being and had feelings of love and friendship. He had a wife and baby, and couldn't keep from worrying about what he knew his wife must be suffering at the present time, having undoubtedly been informed that her husband had perished over or on the Sahara Desert. In the same way his mind was tormented now by the idea of this old-time labor man and Social Democratic comrade falling into the hands of the Gestapo and having to break and swallow a tiny glass capsule filled with cyanide of potassium. He just couldn't let it happen, and he couldn't help taking risks to keep it from happening.

He told his friend about that congenial oil man whom he had come to know at Karinhall and was expecting to meet in Stockholm. "I know it's a dirty thing, trading with the Nazis; but it is a fact that Sweden has to have oil. No modern nation can get along without it for even a week or two—all transportation would come to a halt and the people in the cities would starve to death."

"Sure, and besides that, he gets a lot of money out of it," replied the Socialist, following his pattern.

"I cannot lose sight of the fact that my own father was trading with Göring as long as the government would let him do so. You perhaps didn't get a very good impression of my father, but I know him better, and have had his point of view hammered into my head since childhood. I know that a man can be a hard trader, and be making millions of dollars, and at the same time be personally very kind, even generous, to those he knows."

"I don't doubt that, Lanny; it's the system that poisons their minds. But what is your idea? To ask this oil fellow to help get me out of Germany?"

"It's my idea to go and sound him out. I'll tell him that you're a man I have known for ten years or more and that you rendered valuable services to my father. I'll tell him the same sad story as I'll tell Hilde, about your loss of family and home; that you don't like wars and want to get away and start life over. I'll put it up to Erickson that you are a valuable man who might work for him, and that if he doesn't find you satisfactory I'm sure my father will take you on as soon as he can get you into the United States."

"That doesn't sound so bad. What would I be, an oil man?"

"You could hardly get away with that. You could be a handy man who had traveled for Robbie and interviewed people. What my father valued was your trustworthiness rather than your technical knowledge."

"All right, Lanny—if I have the right to let you take such a risk."

"I had decided to go out by plane; but I'll take a chance and tell Erickson that I'll go with him as he so kindly offered. I'll have my Hitler letter if trouble arises; but I don't believe it will arise, because if you're in the right company the police won't have the suspicions they would have if you were alone. If the worst came, I would have to say that you had lied to me, and that I had had no idea of your illegal activities."

"Sure thing," replied the German. "No use throwing good money after bad!"

IV

Some time after midnight the two agents got reluctantly out of their warm bed into the still, deadly cold of a marble palace. Lanny, who was in his underwear, put on his clothes, including his overcoat. Monck took off his butler suit and went through the pockets, taking out all his belongings—a watch, a purse, a handkerchief, a fountain pen; these he put under his pillow to keep them out of sight, for obviously a man who escapes from a bombed building in his underwear might pick up his shoes and run with them, but he could hardly gather up these smaller objects for which he had no receptacle. He gave Lanny a small box of matches—very precious in Germany—and his identification papers in the fatal name of Konrad Kraft. Then he got back into bed and set to munching a chunk of bread for his supper.

The P.A. took the discarded garments and went to the door of the room and carefully turned the key. He opened the door without a sound, and stood in the darkness, listening. It was as it had been on the night before Christmas—"not a creature was stirring, not even a mouse." Lanny knew that the ladies used the rear rooms of this second story, and that the servants slept higher up; so, barring a possible burglar, he would have the lower part to himself. He crept down the carpeted stairs, feeling his way. He knew the ground floor because he had visited here in happier days; he knew approximately where the door to the basement was, because he had been taken there during an air raid.

He groped his way through the dining-room, step by careful step, for to upset a lampstand or other piece of furniture would be a calamity. When he had come to what he thought was the right part of the building, he struck a match and then marked in his mind where the door was. When he blew out the match he ground it against the sole of his shoe and then put it into his pocket. He groped his way and opened the door, not forgetting to have his gloves on. There was a flight of stairs leading to the basement. He went down them, and with the help of another match found the furnace-room. As he expected, the furnace was cold and the grate empty; it had been that way for a year, or perhaps two.

Still wearing his gloves, Lanny laid the clothing in a rounded pile inside the furnace, and used the Swiss passport and the residence permit of Konrad Kraft to set the clothing afire in several places. It was dry and burned not too slowly. Lanny laid the ends of the papers on top, and stayed there and poked the little fire about with a stick, until there was nothing but ashes and black bone buttons. These fell down through the grate; and Lanny, who wanted to make sure of a perfect crime, raked the buttons out one by one and transferred them to a half empty ashcan and raked old ashes over them. All this he managed in silence, even to the opening and closing of furnace doors. Then he tiptoed back as he had come, and when he was safely locked in the room he whispered to his friend that the telltale suit was no more.

Lanny took off his overcoat and suit and spread them over the bed as before. He got himself a chunk of bread—for he, too, had had no supper—and crawled into his bunk and munched while he whispered with the ex-*capitán*. They would have a good part of the next day to work out plans, so they decided that it was time now to sleep. Lanny had known this man of many roles for more than ten years, but had never before chanced to sleep in the same room with him. It happened that he snored loudly; but this wouldn't be fatal, for if members of the household heard him they would blame it on Lanny. So Lanny went to sleep, too.

V

Steel-gray clouds and a cold wind—that was Berlin on the next morning, the first of March, a day fateful for the whole city as well as for two anti-Nazi conspirators. The P.A. had adopted the odd program of putting on his clothes, including his overcoat, and then wrapping a towel about his neck before shaving. He used ice-cold water out of a pail, for the running water in the palace had had to be shut off and the pipes drained in winter, so that they would not freeze and burst. Lanny went down to the kitchen, which was warm, and there he was welcomed by the elderly servants. What kind and lovely people the old Germans were, he reflected. They fed him hot gruel and an ersatz drink, and he left a food coupon, according to etiquette.

He had sent word to the two sisters that he wanted to see them about a matter of importance, and they made themselves and their room presentable. Lanny told the tragic story, of which he had studied every detail with Monck. He and his father had an old friend in Berlin, a Prussian of education and high character who had been employed by Robbie in his oil days at a salary of six hundred marks a month, doing research work, checking accounts, carrying on negotiations. Lanny had gone to call on Anton Vetterl to see how he was getting along, and had found that the house in which he lived had that morning been hit by a bomb. Evidently the story in the newspapers that no bombs had been dropped was due to a misunderstanding— Lanny put it thus tactfully, and could be sure the ladies would accept his statement, for no intelligent Germans any longer believed Doktor Goebbels. The house was a smoldering ruin, and the man was at a neighbor's, weeping uncontrollably; his wife and two children had been in the next room and the roof had collapsed upon them and pinioned them in the fire. Vetterl had tried to claw his way to them, but in vain, and the firemen had had to drag him out of the house. He had had only his underwear on, and neighbors had wrapped him in a blanket. Lanny had put his overcoat on the man and got a conveyance and brought him to the palace—he hadn't known where else to go and hoped the two ladies would forgive him.

It was a shame to distress one's friends with such a tale, but Lanny thought it would be a still greater shame to let a valuable agent of the democracies fall into the hands of the Gestapo. So he piled on the agony; the man was both grief-stricken and shell-shocked, and the only thing to do was to leave him alone and let him get over it. No, he didn't need food, because Lanny had made purchases, intending to bring them to Hilde, and had given this food to Vetterl. The poor fellow was embarrassed by his lack of self-control and couldn't bear to meet anybody. Lanny had advised him to lock his room door, so that he could be sure of not being disturbed; he had had almost no sleep, but might get some during the day. Hilde asked with anxiety whether Lanny could be sure the man wouldn't commit suicide. He answered that his friend was a gentleman, and would not think of subjecting his hostesses to such distress.

There was only one problem: this bombing victim had to have some clothes. He had money, and so did Lanny, but new clothing was unobtainable; Lanny was wondering if these ladies would part with some of the men's clothing that might be in the house. He saw the two women look at each other, and saw the pain in their features. But they knew that the request was a proper one; Hilde said she had decided that the clothing of her lost ones ought to be put to use in such a time of scarcity. Anyhow, they had to vacate this palace in a week, and could transport only a small part of their possessions. What was the size of this Herr Anton Vetterl? Lanny said that he was not quite so tall as Lanny himself, but a solidly built man, and it was a safe guess that the late Fürst's clothing would fit him.

They went to the dead diplomat's room, where everything had been left as he had had it. From the clothes closet Lanny selected a winter overcoat of the best wool and a black suit of the kind that elder statesmen wore at all the international conferences that Lanny had attended from 1919 to 1939. Monck would look impressive in it, and Lanny would have fun teasing him about it after they got out of Germany. But then the P.A. reflected that he had just burned a black suit, and that possibly some ignorant passport official or border guard might not know the difference between a diplomat's costume and a butler's. Lanny decided upon an English tweed of a mixed pattern, such as businessmen wore. He found a shirt, and a tie to match, for of course without that nothing would have been right.

Hilde said that she wouldn't think of taking money for any of her late husband's belongings, but Lanny told her that he was going to make her a present to cover all the many favors she had done, and she would have no choice but to take it, because he would drop it into her lap and get out of her reach. To cheer her up he reminded her of the joke they had heard in the night club—that Ribbentrop's dream of bliss was to have a suit of real English wool and to be able to rub a real grease spot off it!

VI

So far so good. Lanny took the clothes up to his friend, so that if anything were to make it necessary for him to get out of the Donnerstein palace he wouldn't have to go in his underwear. Monck dressed himself, to make sure that everything was right; then he undressed and got into bed again, so that the clothing might not be rumpled.

Lanny telephoned to the Adlon and made an appointment to meet Eric Erickson. "I am going to change my mind and go out with you if there's still room in your car," he said. And the other replied: "Plenty of room." It had been some time since Lanny had heard any more welcome words. "Give me your room number," said the P.A., for he was known in that "Club" and wanted to slip in without attracting attention.

He managed this feat without trouble. The oil man greeted him, and the one-time son of New England-Arabian Oil set out to exercise his conversational skill to its utmost. He repeated the tragic story of an old friend who had lost his home and his family under bombs, and who was fed up with living under such conditions. He had been in the employ of Robbie Budd for many years, and wanted to join Robbie in America; of course that was out of the question in wartime, but at least he could get to a neutral country. Lanny could recommend him as a valuable employee, both honest and intelligent. If Erickson could use him, all right; if he couldn't get a job in Sweden, he would go to South America; he had money, and Lanny was willing to give him more.

The oil man listened with interest, then said: "That is all right, Budd, and I'll be glad to accommodate you. But what about your man's passport and exit permit?"

"He tells me he can arrange that."

"But I have to leave tomorrow morning. I have engagements that are pressing."

"He is sure he can get it today."

"By God, if he can he's a wizard. Even I couldn't do it, with the friends I have here."

"I think I could do it for him if I had to. You know, I have a letter from the Führer."

"Red" Erickson fixed his blue Swedish eyes upon his new friend and said with a touch of sternness: "Look here, Budd! Is this some political fellow?"

"I haven't asked any questions about that," responded the well-prepared P.A. (It was true, in a way.) "One doesn't want to bother a man who had just met with a calamity."

"Understand," persisted the other, "I take a lot of trouble to keep out of politics. We oil men have no country."

"That used to be Zaharoff's saying," remarked Lanny with one of his genial smiles. "Only he always added: 'Except where there's oil.'"

"Sweden has no oil, and we're in one hell of a fix, caught between two fires—the hottest fires in history. We have the problem of surviving, and believe me, it will take our best brains."

"I understand you, my friend. As an art expert I am trying to save a small part of the world's culture; incidentally, when I see a chance to put in a word to end this mass slaughter, I venture to do it." The emergency required that Lanny should say this with a straight face, and that he should gaze steadily into the eyes of the other man. At the same time he was thinking: Will he swallow that? Or will he think me the world's worst fraud?

Erickson continued in his quiet and even voice: "Many Swedes take sides in this war, and they become bitter about it. Some rage at me because I buy oil from the Germans. They do not stop to think what would happen if no one in Sweden would carry on this business. Quite certainly the Allies are not in a position to meet our needs, and in a short time all Swedish industry would come to a stop, and all the population except the farmers would starve to death. I take the position that I am a businessman, and it would be embarrassing to me to discover that I had been bringing either a German or an Allied propagandist into Sweden."

"I am quite sure that Anton Vetterl is nothing resembling that. When I last saw him in Geneva a few months ago, he was diligently digging in the public library, compiling a history of Swiss diplomacy during the Napoleonic wars. He was working here in the Staatsbibliothek on the same theme. You will find him a man of culture as well as of business acumen."

"All right, Budd, I'll take your word for him. If he has his papers by ten o'clock tomorrow morning I'll take him along. We have to leave at that hour to catch the steamer. Shall I come to the Donnerstein palace for you?"

"It will be a great favor if you will do so. And of course I'll pay our share of the cost of the car."

"There is no cost. It's a government car and chauffeur. Will you have a drink?"

VII

Lanny joined a queue in front of a delicatessen and bought some cooked food. In the old days no one would have dreamed of approaching a home of the aristocracy carrying a bundle wrapped in newspaper; but now it was the fashion, and if anybody saw you he envied you. Lanny went up to the room, tapped lightly, and waited while his friend got out of bed and opened the door. "Cheerio!" Lanny said, and told what arrangements he had made.

The ex-*capitán* had had the morning to lie and think. Now he said: "The time is short, and I am afraid to risk waiting until night for my papers. You understand, our friends have a place where they prepare such documents; but suppose they don't happen to have a Swedish visa stamp? Suppose they could get it in the daytime, but not after the office closes?"

"Anton, it would be suicide for you to go out on the streets in daylight!"

"I have a telephone number that you can call for me. I have sworn not to reveal it to anyone, but in this emergency I feel justified in giving it to you."

"I don't question that; but remember, your friends may be in the hands of the enemy now."

"My idea is for you to telephone from some place where you will be inconspicuous, and then get away quickly."

"Listen, Anton. If the police have raided your place, they will take the call and will trace it; it mightn't be ten minutes before they'd be asking questions at the place from which I telephoned."

"That is true. You must not phone from here, nor from a hotel or other place where they have a switchboard operator. It must not be from a shop or place where you have to ask permission. I suggest a small hotel, where they have booths into which you can walk without speaking to anyone. If you have reason to think that somebody has observed you, you don't have to put in the call. Act as if you got a busy signal, and go elsewhere."

"Even that is a risk, but not too great, I suppose. Am I to tell your friends what you want?"

"I will give you the exact words, and you are to repeat them. You say: '*Die Linsen sind geschliffen, Paket Nummer siebzehn, gehen nach Schweden und sie müssen nicht später als 5 Uhr morgens bereit sein.*'"

Lanny repeated these words. He could guess from the word "lenses" that the secret hideout of the conspirators must be in an optical shop; but of course he didn't remark this. He asked: "Do I give this message to anybody who answers the phone?"

"If the person doesn't understand it, he'll give it to one who will. If the person says: '*Richtig*,' or *Ja, mein Herr*,' or something like that, you may be sure it's O.K. If he asks you to repeat it, do so. But if he starts asking what it means, and which lenses, and what package number seventeen, and who is to get it in Sweden, and so on, you may suspect that it's the Gestapo, trying to hold you while they get busy on another line and trace the call. In that case, get out of that place fast. Don't walk on any boulevard or straight street; turn at every corner and zigzag out of the way."

"Trust me for that," said Lanny, smiling, for he had done that sort of thing more times than he was going to let Anton know. "I'll take a chance and help you, because I'd surely hate to leave you behind tomorrow morning."

"One thing more," persisted the other. "The most conspicuous feature of a man in winter is his overcoat. I suggest that you wear the Fürst's overcoat for this trip. You don't want the police to have a description of yours."

Lanny grinned. "Suppose I meet some of the Donnerstein family in the hall?"

"Fold the overcoat with the lining outside and carry it on your arm till you get away from the house. Nobody will recognize it that way."

VIII

The P.A. carried out this carefully thought-out program. He walked into several medium-class hotels, but the layout did not suit him. At last he entered one by a side door and saw the clerk busy in conversation. He slipped into a telephone booth, dropped his coin, and gave the number his friend had imparted. A woman's voice answered, and he gave the instruction that the finished lenses, package number seventeen, were to go to Sweden and were to be ready not later than five o'clock in the morning. The woman asked no questions, but repeated the German words carefully, and then added: "*Danke schön, mein Herr.*" Lanny hung up and walked out, still unnoticed.

He was quite sure he had got away with that one. However, he took the precaution to zigzag; and while he walked he thought about the code. He had been familiar with codes since the age of fourteen, when he and Robbie had been caught in Paris by the outbreak of World

War I, and a bright little boy had acted as his father's secretary, answering telephone calls from all the nations that wanted to purchase Budd guns, and coding and decoding messages on the subject. Obviously, "Seventeen" was Monck's code number, and "finished lenses" probably had no meaning, but was camouflage to fit the business of an optical shop. If Monck was going to Sweden they would know what papers he would require, and they would understand the time limit.

All right, these people would have half a day and a whole night to work in, and if they could produce a German passport and exit permit and a Swedish visa stamp that looked authentic, Bernardt Monck alias all the other names would stand a chance of getting out of the Nazi gangsterland. Incidentally, Eric Erickson could go on buying German synthetic oil and selling it to the Swedes at a profit. An American "Pink" admitted that a man who came into Berlin under the bombs and ate the ersatz foods of the Germans was surely entitled to some reward for his trouble.

Lanny had only one more errand, and that was to stop at *Der Dicke's* official *Residenz* and tell the General-Major about his change of plans. He wouldn't mention Erickson, but would say that he had a friend in Stettin he desired to call on. Furtwaengler would accept this and cancel the plane reservation; they would say good-by all over again, and Lanny would stop in a toy shop and order some small gifts to be sent to his friend's large family. Toys were still obtainable, oddly enough; perhaps because they were handmade, by old people who couldn't do anything else.

"By the way," said Lanny to the faithful staff officer, "I have a permit to take out six paintings that Baron von Behr's office packed for me. I am going to catch a steamer for Stockholm, and it won't wait if I am delayed. I know from past experience how stupid border officials can be; they have to telephone to headquarters, and perhaps the line is busy, or the chief is out to lunch, or whatever. I am wondering if it might not be wise to have a letter from *Seine Exzellenz's* office, stating that the transaction has been approved by him."

"Certainly, Herr Budd, if that will facilitate matters."

"I imagine *Seine Exzellenz* and the *Einsatzstab* are one and the same. At any rate, in this case I refused to have anything to do with the deal unless it had his approval."

"I know that, Herr Budd. *Seine Exzellenz* has left town, but I am sure he would wish me to write you such a letter. There would be no sense in selling you paintings that you couldn't take out."

"Write it on official stationery," suggested the art expert, "and put his seal on it, so that I may be able to overwhelm any officious subordinate." He said this with his best grin, and it was a tribute to the *Allmacht* of the *Allmächtige* Number Two, and therefore of the General-Major who served him.

The P.A. went out from that office carrying a document with a gold seal as big as one of Göring's medals; he was sure it would make his paintings safe against the touch of any subordinate in Naziland. Too bad that he didn't have something really secret to put into those packages; for example, if he had been able to steal that priceless dossier of the negotiations in which Molotov had been invited to join the war against Britain at the price of the Baltic states and the Near East with its oil!

But, alas, he didn't have a thing but the six "degenerate" paintings—and one Monck! He smiled to himself as this not so brilliant jest occurred to him. It warmed his heart, because it made him think of F.D.R., and how inevitably, if the Boss had had dealings with the ex-*capitán*, there would have been a Bernie the Monck to join Harry the Hop and Tommy the Cork and Henry the Morgue and the rest of them. What a blessing to a nation to have in this crisis a leader who possessed gaiety of spirit as well as courage and vision!

IX

The P.A. went shopping for the last time. The Berliners spent a good part of their day at that duty, standing in lines or wandering from place to place looking for something that did not exist. Usually it was the women who bore this burden; but Lanny had plenty of time, all the time until ten the next morning. When he had his arms full he went back to the palace; he gave one bundle to Hilde's woman servant and took the other upstairs for his friend. The two men ate a meal, and then Monck covered himself up again—you couldn't stay out of bed in that room unless you were moving continually.

Lanny went to pay his respects to the two ladies and told them his plans for departure, and also, of course, about Vetterl. The unfortunate man was getting himself together. He might go out later to look for a place to stay; Lanny would go with him for safety. "It might be better if he spent another night with me," said the friend, and Hilde replied that this would be quite agreeable. Lanny added: "Before he leaves, he wishes to meet you and thank you for your kindness." To this Hilde said that they would always be ready to meet any friend of Lanny's.

He put a thousand marks into her lap, as he had threatened. That was somewhat more than the proceeds of two of his ten-thousand-franc notes, and she protested that it was too much; but he assured her that he could spare it and that she would need it for her moving. "Put your pride aside, old dear," he said. "Tell me your situation and I may be able to give you some advice."

So he heard one of the sad stories of the old aristocracy, which was fading out all over Europe before the power of the big-business class. In Germany the process had been enormously accelerated by the Nazis; they had called themselves a workingmen's party, but all they had given the workingmen was the Blood Purge of ten years ago, and from that time on they had been the party of steel, coal, chemicals, and munitions producers. The great cartels were making fabulous profits out of the war, and did not worry because they had to put it all back into plant. They were looking forward to victory, after which all the profits in Europe would be theirs.

Hilde didn't say any of that; what she said was: "Alas, my husband owned very few stocks. He was a conservative man and put his savings into bonds. These pay no more, as you know; and what has happened to the money? The prices of the common things are fixed, but the result is that the goods become scarcer every day; the quality deteriorates, and if you want anything good you have to pay black-market prices."

"You will find it easier in the country," he assured her. "You will be farther from the bombs and nearer to the sources of food."

"Yes, but how are we to get our things moved? Motor transport is unobtainable; and are we to tie our goods up in bundles like the refugees and carry them on our heads?"

Lanny didn't know the answer to that. He could only say, lamely: "Call in some of the secondhand dealers and sell what you cannot carry." Lacking the faculty of prevision, he had no idea how simply that problem was going to be solved for the Fürstin Donnerstein and her household—and before that first day of March had passed!

X

He went back to Monck, and they lay in bed and discussed in whispers all the troubles they could imagine. So much safer to think them out in advance than to be confronted with sudden emergencies! Monck had to go to that unnamed place for his papers, and he might be caught in a police round-up on the way, or he might find the place in the hands of the enemy. His own fingerprints had to be put on the passport, because he might be required to make fingerprints for comparison before he was allowed to board the steamer. He and Lanny discussed at length the possibility that the police might have sent the prints as well as the photograph of the much-wanted man to every exit station in Germany and to roadblocks on the way. They might even have enlarged them and sent them by telegraph. No one knew better than this man of many aliases the deadly efficiency of the *Geheime Staatspolizei*, or the marvelous devices with which modern technology had provided them. He told Lanny that they now had a device for printing code messages in microfilm, so tiny that it could be fitted into a dot or period as printed in a newspaper or by a typewriter key. That must surely be giving the Allied Intelligence services a lot of research to do!

The German said: "I will blur the fingerprints as much as I dare, because the blame for that will be attributed to the official who made them. If any question is raised or delay is suggested, it will be up to you, Lanny, to make use of your magic letters. But you mustn't go too far with them."

The reply was: "Forget it, Anton! If I have to choose between sacrificing you and sacrificing my ability to come back into Germany, you know which it will be. For your comfort let me tell you that my Boss forbade me to come here, and I only did it because I couldn't help it."

They argued the problem back and forth and came to two conclusions: first, they would move heaven and earth to get Monck on the steamer; and second, if this could not be done, Lanny would not stay behind. If Anton Vetterl were held, it would mean that the Gestapo were going to make an investigation, and they would certainly be able to identify him as Konrad Kraft, and it might even be that they would identify him as Bernhardt Monck. Lanny's effort to save him might lead to Lanny himself being caught in their net.

"We can die only once," said the ex-*capitán*, "and when I go out of this place I shall have the capsule in my mouth."

"I know," replied Lanny. "They gave me one a year and a half ago, when I set out for Germany to try to meet Professor Schilling." Then, changing to a less gruesome subject, he inquired: "What do you expect to do when you get out?"

"How can I tell? I'll report to the O.S.S. and do what they tell me. I suppose they'll send me back here."

"Then what is the use of going out?"

"I have to get new orders, and I suppose a new layout. Perhaps I'll be an old peasant woman." They both chuckled, and it made their parting a bit easier.

XI

Monck estimated that he could get to his destination, attend to his affairs, and return by ten o'clock in the evening. So Lanny agreed to be in front of the palace at that hour. If Monck wasn't there, Lanny would come again at eleven, and again at twelve. If the man had not come by midnight, it would mean that he was in trouble, or that for some reason he had not been able to get his papers until morning. The next appointment would be for seven in the morning, when it would still be dark.

Lanny cautioned: "Remember, the hour when the car leaves is ten. I'll hold it in front of the house until that moment, and you can take a chance on coming by daylight." The other replied: "I'll be on hand if it's humanly possible."

Lanny put out the light and moved the heavy window curtains and looked out. He wouldn't let his friend go until it was completely dark. They went together, silently, and not meeting anybody in the house. They walked together only as far as the corner and then parted. Monck said: "So long, and good luck to you." His friend replied: "And to the cause." He knew that Monck lived for that.

Lanny had to pass some time, and he decided to see what Doktor Jüppchen Goebbels was feeding his public. He went into a cinema "palace," and watched the unfoldment of a story about the love life of a beautiful golden-haired farm girl, a perfect examplar of the Aryan ideal, who raised healthy animals for the Fatherland and made speeches about the Führer that closely paralleled what the old Sunday School books had said about Jesus. According to this movie, each aspect of farm life was more like a colored valentine than the one preceding it; the sun shone all the time, there was never any mud or manure, and the sturdy young lover who came home from the war hadn't a spot on his uniform.

After that came a newsreel, full of heiling and goosestepping, and with no depressing scenes. Then came Jüppchen himself—it was part of the speech he had tried to make in the great Sportpalast of Berlin on the thirtieth of January, the tenth anniversary of the assumption of power by the Nazis. Göring had been scheduled to speak in the morning and Goebbels in the afternoon, but the malicious Allies had sent their bombing planes on purpose to spoil both occasions. Evidently the

Minister of Popular Enlightenment and Propaganda had made this recording in a studio, for no air-raid sirens and no ack-ack interrupted his eloquence.

He had been driven from his usual line that victory was certain. How could he hold it, with the Allies in North Africa and the calamity of Stalingrad being whispered all over the land? No, he told them that they were fighting for their national existence, and he pictured the horrors that lay before them if they did not win. It surely didn't make cheerful entertainment, and entirely spoiled the idyllic picture of German farm life.

Lanny was more interested in the audience than in what he saw on the screen. He was pleased to observe that the public didn't like this odious little man of hate. There was no applause when he appeared and made his smiling bow; and as he went on, there began a murmur that became almost a snarl—the equivalent of what American schoolboys call a "raspberry." Lanny had been told of these demonstrations, and that it had become the practice of the Gestapo to flash on the lights and arrest persons caught taking part in them. Evidently the audience knew about it, for they were cautious. Nobody stood up, nobody shouted; they just groaned as if they were sick and couldn't help it, or as if they were distressed by the bad news about the plight of the Fatherland. Lanny was glad, for he surely didn't want to be caught in a raid and have to explain himself to any SS men.

XII

He stood it until after nine-thirty, and then he went out and groped his way to the Donnerstein palace, arriving exactly at ten. He spoke the name of Vetterl, not too loud, but there was no response. He strolled away, and returned two or three minutes later, but still there was no sign of his friend. He started up the steps to enter the building, and at that moment came the shriek of the sirens. This was not what was called a "pre-alarm," this was the real thing and meant that enemy bombers were nearing the city. Lanny went up the steps and let himself into the house; he ran up to his room and threw his few belongings into his two bags. You could time yourself in these raids because you would hear the anti-aircraft fire in the distant suburbs before the bombers were overhead.

The packages containing the paintings were light, and the bags still lighter, so Lanny could carry them all. He went out into the dark hallway and heard the ladies emerging from their room. "Are you all there?" he inquired.

Hilde's voice replied: "Mother is not coming. She is tired of air raids."

"Don't you think we ought to bring her?" he asked. The answer was: "There is nothing to be done." He could guess that there had been family arguments, and that an old woman who had outlived her time had gone on strike against sitting in a cold basement.

The servants had come from the floor above, and five people groped their way down the stairs. The cellar room to which they went was next to the furnace-room where Lanny had committed his "perfect crime." It was a storeroom and contained trunks and boxes. Lanny lighted a feeble gas jet, and they sat, not talking much, because cold and boredom and fear are not conducive to sociability. The crack of the anti-aircraft guns began, and presently it was near, and you could feel the earth shaking. Berlin boasted itself the best-defended city in the world, and the firing mounted in intensity until it became like the rattle of machine guns. This meant that the air was filled with flying fragments, all of which had to come down, and many civilians would be wounded by them. Some shells failed to explode, and when these fell they might penetrate the roof of a house.

There came the bombs, a heavier and more massive sound. Lanny had been under bombing in cities all the way from London to Hongkong, and was something of an expert on the subject. He could tell small ones that were near from big ones that were distant, and he said that these must be the one- and two-ton bombs. Every time one exploded you felt as if someone had taken you by the wrist and shaken you. The crumping sounds became louder and the shakes more violent, and it was evident that the bombers were overhead or near. When that happened, it meant, as a rule, that soon they would be gone; but this time they appeared to stay on, and the clamor and shocks mounted to a bedlam. "Why don't they go?" Hilde cried. And Lanny answered: "More keep coming."

That was undoubtedly the explanation. This was no ordinary air raid, this was one of the big ones that the Allies had been promising and at which Doktor Goebbels had scoffed. They had been experienced by Cologne, Essen, Hamburg, Bremen, all the great ports and centers of industry; and now it was the turn of the *Hauptstadt*. Alfy had told Lanny about the preparations for these thousand-plane raids: the lines of Lancasters and Blenheims taking off from a score of different fields and falling into formations, a sky train one hundred, two hundred, three hundred miles long. A train of three hundred miles would take an hour and a half to pass a given spot; and now an unkind fate had brought it about that Lanny was sitting on that spot!

It was the most nerve-racking experience of his life. It reduced the human creature to an animal, cowering in a hole, utterly powerless against the calamity that surrounded and possessed him. He was shaken until his teeth rattled, and the sounds, even in an underground basement, deafened his ears. The women were moaning and weeping; the woman servant began to scream and had to be ordered to silence by her mistress. Lanny sat with his nails dug into the palms of his hands, waiting, waiting, and thinking that it must surely end now, but each time it started up again, seeming nearer and more deadly. He learned later that nine hundred tons of explosives had been dropped that night.

Hitherto the bombing of Berlin had been aimed at the war plants, which were all on the outskirts of the city; but this time, evidently, the enemy had made up his mind to go after the government, the bureaucrats, those leaders who were making the world sick with their vaunting and their lying and their crimes. It was plain that these bombs were falling in the heart of this cold proud capital, among the public buildings, the centers of administration. They were being aimed at the brain of Nazism.

XIII

The missiles screamed as they came; but there were so many that the sounds made one continuous uproar. So it was that the particular one that had the name "Donnerstein" on it gave no warning. The door of the storeroom, which had been closed, was suddenly burst in and hurled across the room. Blast has the speed of light, and also the hardness of steel. The five people were knocked off their seats and half stunned by a deafening concussion, an all-enveloping roar. Every door in the building had been burst outward, and many doors in near-by houses burst inward; there was not an unshattered pane of glass within two or three blocks.

The five victims, stunned and bruised, some of them bleeding, lay on the floor until their senses began to return and they realized that they were still alive. The first thing they became aware of was a pungent odor of chemical smoke, and the next was that they couldn't see at all, the dust was so thick in this basement room. Was it dust of half a century that had accumulated here, or was it plaster and masonry blown to dust? Lanny staggered to his feet; then he thought about the others and began calling, but without much result, because the uproar continued; there were other bombs exploding and shaking the ground.

He groped here and there and found the two sisters and helped them to their feet; he shouted into their ears: "We must get out! There will be fire!" He found the old man lying in a corner, able to get up when he was told to. The woman servant was unconscious and they had to carry her.

They groped their way out of the storeroom. The place was littered with debris, but they climbed over it and reached the stairway. The door at the top had been blown down to the bottom; they stumbled over it, and up the stairs, choking, the ladies crying. The ceiling of the room above had come down, and the rooms were littered with wreckage; they climbed through it, and got to the front door, which had been hurled out into the street. They were just about overcome by the sulphurous fumes, but were revived by the fresh air.

A man came running up the steps, an air-raid warden with a helmet on his head and an electric torch in his hand. Hilde started crying: "My mother! Save my mother!" The man ran into the house and Lanny followed, and stood looking up at what had been a marble staircase. The steps were still there, presumably, but they were covered with debris, and the opening at the top was plugged solid with beams and other parts of the upper stories; it appeared as if the explosion had tried to force all the wreckage down through one opening. "It will take a lot of time to get up there," said the man, "and nobody could be alive." Lanny had to agree.

They went back to the door and reported the situation. The two ladies were weeping hysterically and wanted to make an effort at rescue, but the warden took one and Lanny the other, and led them through the rain of shell fragments to the house across the street. Getting in was a simple matter, for the front door had been blown inward. With the help of the warden's torch they found the way to the basement stairs and went down and joined a group of people sitting in a shelter. Nobody said: "By your leave," or made any apology; the situation was obvious, and it proved the old saying that "Misery loves company."

The fresh air had revived Lanny, and he bethought himself of Monck. It was about midnight, and his friend might be waiting. Lanny went up with the air-raid warden, and by the glow of the searchlights in the sky looked at the Donnerstein palace. The entire front of the upper stories had been blown into the street and the area and side-walk were littered with debris. Taking chances on the steel falling from the sky, he ran over to the house and shouted: "Vetterl! Vetterl!" There came no answer, and the warden asked: "Is there somebody else in the house?" Lanny said: "There may be."

He bethought himself of those paintings, which might easily be saved. He said: "Let us make another search in the basement." He tied his handkerchief over his mouth and nose to keep out the dust, and they went into the wrecked building and down the stairs—it didn't take long when you had a light. Lanny made a pretense at searching for a man, and then in the storeroom he picked up his belongings—the two bags, which he handed to the warden, and the paintings, which he carried himself. They staggered outside again, and Lanny thanked the man and gave him a ten-mark note, which made up handsomely for the risk he had run.

XIV

The bombing ceased, the All Clear sounded, and the burghers of Berlin came up from their cellars and bomb-proof shelters. The dead remained, and twenty thousand were homeless. Fires were blazing and new ones starting; there was hardly a block in the central part of the city that did not have one or more conflagrations, and it would be three days before a crippled fire department could extinguish them all. Lanny Budd, with a splitting headache, lay on a couch in the drawing-room belonging to one of the city's wealthy families, and when he was told that the Donnerstein palace was blazing, he did not get up to look at the sight. He had done all he could for Hilde's mother; that unhappy old lady who hadn't wanted to live was having a magnificent funeral pyre. Peace to her ashes!

Lanny thought about Monck, and about Erickson, and the car in which they were to travel. What might have happened to these? And what would a P.A. do if one or more of them were gone? To his new hosts he explained that he was due to leave Berlin at ten in the morning, and that he had an engagement to meet a friend here at seven; they gave him a bed and promised to waken him at six-thirty. So he slept for a while, twitching and starting now and then as he dreamed of dangers. It would be a long time before his subconscious mind was free of that night's memories.

In the morning he ate a little food, and then he tried to call the Adlon, only to learn that the telephone was out of commission. He went out at a few minutes before seven and found the palace still burning; the flames turned early dawn into daylight. Lanny strolled and watched, and when he saw the familiar figure in the clothing of the Fürst Donnerstein, he hurried toward him and led him to a darker neighborhood. "You are all right?" he asked. Monck replied: "I was in a part of the city that was not bombed. I have been able to get the passport and the exit permit, but not the Swedish visa. What shall we do?"

Lanny had thought of this contingency and told him that they would go anyhow and take a chance on fixing it up with the Swedish authorities. The problem was Erickson and the car. The P.A. said: "I will go to the Adlon and find out. Where will you stay meantime?"

An awkward situation: it would not do for this much-wanted man to be walking about the streets in daylight. Lanny decided to take him back to the house at which Lanny had just been a guest. It was easy of access, because there was no front door. A woman servant sat on guard, and Lanny explained that this was a friend who had been staying in the palace and had no place to go until the car came for him. Monck caused a sensation by offering to put the door back on its hinges if the woman would get him the tools. Men's labor being all but unobtainable in Berlin, this was indeed welcome, and Lanny left him at the job.

The traveler walked through streets littered with rubble and illuminated by fires. He saw the insides of many Berlin offices and homes, exposed to view by the blowing out of the front walls. He had to detour several times to avoid blocks roped off by the firemen. Everybody had his own troubles at that hour, and no one paid attention to a solitary pedestrian. He came to the Adlon and thought it was intact—until he got inside and discovered that one corner had been struck. He went up to his Swedish friend's room and found him already dressed and breakfasted. "So glad to see you!" exclaimed Erickson. "We must start early. God only knows how long it will take us to get out of the city."

"The sooner the better," was the reply. "Is the car all right?"

"Everything is ready," declared Erickson, and added that he had spent the hours of the bombing in the hotel's comfortably appointed shelter. Lanny knew it well, having sat out an air raid there two years previously. "My ears are still ringing from the blasts," said the oil man. Lanny told him what had happened to the palace.

Erickson put his belongings into his bags and they went down to the lobby. So simple a thing as phoning for the automobile could not be done; the secretary had to walk to the garage to order it. Lanny, knowing the blocked streets, was able to tell them how to get to the Bismarckstrasse. There they found that Monck had just finished putting the house door on; they stowed the bags and the paintings in the trunk of the car; the secretary rode in front with the chauffeur, and Lanny contrived to have Monck ride between Erickson and himself, the least conspicuous position. They started westward, to get out of the central part of the city where the bomb damage was; they turned northward and then eastward to the *Autobahn* which took them to the great port of Stettin.

Berlin, viewed from several miles away, was covered by an immense pall of smoke, illuminated by flames on its under side. The oil man said: "By God, if ever I was glad to get out of a place, this is it!" Lanny echoed agreement. The mysterious Anton Vetterl didn't trust himself to open his lips.

BOOK NINE

The End of This Day's Business

27

'Twas Heaven All Unawares

I

"*A*BER *es ist strengstens verboten*"—most strictly forbidden. The speaker was an SS *Feldwebel*, standing by a roadblock at the northern boundary of Berlin. A black-and-white painted barrier had been let down, and half a dozen armed men guarded it; one had a machine gun, another a motorcycle in case a pursuit might be necessary.

"*Aber, Herr Feldwebel*," said the son of Budd-Erling, "this gentleman's exit permit was issued to him only yesterday."

"*Ja, aber*"—the everlasting BUT—"my orders were issued only this morning. No able-bodied man is permitted to leave the city unless he has a special permit, later than this date. Women and children, *ja, aber kein männlicher Bewohner*." In the old days he would have added "*Mein Herr*" to every sentence. But the Nazis were not polite.

"*Aber, Herr Feldwebel*, this is most inconvenient. We have to catch a steamer for Stockholm."

"There is nothing to prevent your going. The orders do not apply to *Ausländer*."

"*Aber* this gentleman is my special assistant, and I cannot accomplish my mission without him."

"That is not in my province. *Befehl ist Befehl*." If he had been an American noncom, it would have been the same: "Orders are orders."

"*Herr Feldwebel*, I warn you that you are delaying a matter of the utmost state importance."

"I shall be sorry to learn it, *aber*—"

Lanny guessed that it would not be good tactics for an *Ausländer* to lose his temper. He put on his most winning smile and said: "*Lieber Herr Feldwebel*, did you ever meet the Führer?"

The other, looking startled, replied: "I have never had that honor."

"Have you ever seen his handwriting in facsimile?"

"*Ja, gewiss.*"

"Would you be interested in seeing his actual handwriting?"

"*Freilich, mein Herr.*" The *Feldwebel* had suddenly become polite.

Lanny took the precious letter from an inside coat pocket, handed it to the man, and watched while he opened it and stared at its impressive superscription: "*Kriegsleitung Oberkommando Hauptquartier.*" He saw the man's eyes go down to the signature, and then to the top of the letter again. Lanny gave him time to read, mark, and inwardly digest, and did not let any suggestion of superiority or triumph appear in a foreigner's glance. It was a different *Feldwebel* who folded up the letter and returned it to the owner. "*Natürlich, meine Herren, das ist freilich ein ganz besonderer Fall*"—an unusual case.

"The Führer says 'All courtesy,'" quoted Lanny. "You must surely admit that it would not be courtesy to cause me to miss my steamer, and therefore to fail in the mission with which the Führer personally has charged me. *Heil Hitler!*"

"*Bitte um Verzeihung, mein Herr,*" replied the other. "*Bitte zu passieren. Heil Hitler!*" He saluted, and all his men did the same; they could not have done more if Lanny had been Reichsminister for the Extermination of Heretics and Unbelievers. The barrier rose, and the car sped onward to the north. The three men in the back seat permitted themselves to glance at one another and exchange smiles, but they did not speak a word, for this was an official car and the chauffeur was an SS man.

II

For ten years the Führer had been building these *Autobahnen*, four-lane motorways that underpassed or overpassed all other roads, and on which one could drive at eighty miles an hour if the car would stand it. It was the great engineer Doktor Todt, now a general, who had planned them, putting them at exactly the places where the armies would need them when the time came. Robbie Budd had told his son that it was a mistake, for Hitler wouldn't have enough gas or rubber and would have to fall back upon his railroads. He had plenty of coal, but, alas for him, he neglected the building of locomotives and freight cars. That was the reason he had been beaten at Stalingrad—he could not bring up enough supplies. He had lost there a hundred and twenty thousand trucks, something more serious to him than the loss of three hundred thousand men.

The trouble did not show on this highway, for Stettin is the port for the *Hauptstadt*, and the great steamers came from Sweden, loaded with ore, wood, and products such as synthetic rubber, machine tools, and ball bearings, to pay for the oil and coal that Sweden had to have. Military vehicles shot past—diesel trucks, and some powered with the fumes of charcoal, a confession of the difficulty the Germans were having. They reminded Lanny of what the chemist, Doktor Stoffel, had told him, and because it was to the credit of the Fatherland, this was a proper subject for conversation. A Gestapo agent might find it suspicious if they sat in silence, so the three of them sang the praises of German science and the marvels it was achieving with wood.

Past the flat snow-covered fields of Brandenburg and Pomerania they sped, and in a couple of hours came within sight of the Oder River and the installations built along it. Stettin was one of Germany's great shipbuilding centers, and the Allies had bombed it, but the damage did not fall under the travelers' eyes. It is an old city, but they saw little of it, for the route took them along the river, straight to the Bollwerk, where the passenger steamers dock. Here, they knew, would come their great test, and Lanny braced himself for it. He had told Erickson that Vetterl had no Swedish visa, and Erickson had advised against bringing him, but Lanny had wanted to try, and it could not do the oil man any harm.

The entrance to the quay was guarded by a high fence, topped by barbed wire, and there was the customary group of uniformed officials, mostly old men since the recent military draft. By prearrangement Erickson and his secretary presented themselves first. Their papers were in order, and they signed a declaration that they were not taking out more than the lawful amount of money; their baggage underwent a search, their steamer tickets were inspected and stamped, and in they went. In the meantime Lanny was buying tickets for himself and friend, and when it was discovered that the friend had no visa he was told that the steamer regulations required him to deposit money for double passage, to cover the event of his having to be returned to Germany.

Lanny, shaking in his boots, approached the officials, each of whom had a little table or stand on which to do his writing. Lanny's own papers were correct, and his letter from the Reichsmarschall's office saved the need of opening the packages of paintings. It caused him to become a personage of distinction, and produced much bowing and apologizing and *"mein Herr-"*ing when the discovery was made that his friend's passport lacked the Swedish visa. Lanny explained that it had been intended to get the visa this morning, but the terrible bombing had made it impossible to get about the streets of Berlin. There was a Swedish consul here in Stettin, but the office was up in town, and there was no time for such a visit. (The real reason, of course, was the certainty that Vetterl would be investigated.)

Surely, argued Lanny, the lack of a Swedish visa was the problem of Sweden, and might be dealt with by the authorities in Stockholm. But no, the officials insisted, it was the German regulations that had to be complied with. No one could leave for any country unless he had the right to enter that country.

After exhausting all other arguments, Lanny produced his all-powerful letter. That literally terrified these humble bureaucrats; their hands trembled and the perspiration came out on their foreheads. Never in all their lives had they seen such a document, or had such a dilemma presented to them. There were four, of as many different services, and they called in others and put their heads together. Apparently all wanted to give way save one, but he unfortunately was the most important. An old-style Pomeranian of the *kaiserliche Regierung*, with big white mustachios, he insisted that rules were rules, and they were not made to be broken at the discretion of any minor *Beamte*. How could they know that the letter was genuine? Courtesy, *ja*, and they were surely showing it; but the letter did not say that the American Herr's friend or assistant or whatever he was should have any special privilege, and if the Führer had intended that he would surely have said it. Why wasn't this *Kunstsachverständigenstellvertreter*—the Germans do actually have such words and speak them without a trace of a smile—why was he not mentioned in the letter from the Reichsmarschall's office? *Befehl ist Befehl, Pflicht ist Pflicht*—so it had been ever since the days when obedient and dutiful Pomeranians had driven the Swedes out of this land.

III

All this time Monck stood there, not speaking a word. The officials were staring at him; and might not one of them recognize him as a sailor who had come to this port, a labor leader who had spoken here twenty years ago? He let his employer do the talking, the American millionaire, the friend of *Nummer Eins* and *Nummer Zwei*, the glib one who had talked himself and others out of so many different plights. The steamer whistle began to blow, and the would-be passenger had a right to fly into a passion and speak like a Pomeranian. *Dummheit, Borniertheit!* Here he was, bound on a personal errand for the Führer, confidential to the point where anyone who discussed it, or even knew about it, might be taken out and shot without a trial, and they proposed to cause him to miss the steamer and balk the Führer's plans! They were proposing to delay Herr Vetterl while they showed the passport to higher officials up in the town. *Aber* what would these persons know about it? And what was the good of a letter signed by the Führer's own hand, for one who had been guest a score of times in Berchtesgaden and elsewhere, if a tenth-rate official at a shipping port could set it aside and thwart it?

"Telephone the Führer himself," cried the outraged traveler, "and ask him if he gave such a letter, and if he permits me to have an assistant in his work!"

"*Aber, mein Herr,*" pleaded the agonized *Beamte*, "how can such as we reach the Führer?"

"His secretary in Berlin will tell you how to reach him. Call the Führer's private telephone number."

"*Aber* who has that number?"

"I have it! Call Berlin one-one-six, one-nine-one, and you will hear the secretary's voice. He has already consulted the Führer's headquarters at the Russian front and verified the genuineness of the letter and informed the Berlin *Polizeiamt* of that fact. He will tell you."

There were telephones on some of the stands, and the friend of the great pointed to one with a gesture of command. The call was placed, and the answer was, as Lanny had expected, that the Berlin exchange in which the New Chancellery was included was temporarily out of commission. The steamer whistle was rumbling again—Lanny learned afterward that Erickson had been pleading with the captain to hold it for a minute or two while his secretary came running out to see what the situation was. Lanny became frantic, as the Führer himself would have done and a Führer-friend had a right to. He shouted to these paralyzed *Beamten:* "If you compel me to miss this steamer, I shall make it my business to see that every one of you loses his job and his pension! And as for you"—shaking his finger under the nose of the elderly Pomeranian with the white mustachios—"as sure as I stand before you I will see to it that you are shot!"

So wahr ich hier vor Ihnen stehe, werde ich dafür sorgen, dass Sie erschossen werden! Pomeranian flesh and blood, nourished on *Ersatz-Wurst* and *Kartoffeln,* could not stand such a threat. The old fellow's knees gave way, and his heart. "*Gut, gut, mein Herr!*" he said. "*Auf Ihre Verantwortung, passieren Sie beide.*"

It was the greatest surrender since Stalingrad! Monck seized the two packages, and Lanny his two bags, and they raced to the gangplank and up to the vessel's deck. The plank was raised behind them, and the heavy mooring ropes were cast off. The two conspirators stayed only long enough to exchange handshakes with Erickson, and then both went to their cabin and locked themselves in. They knew that it would be several hours before they were out of German jurisdiction, and they surely didn't want to be inspected by anybody on board, now or later.

IV

The steamer went down the Oder River, kept open all winter by icebreakers; it entered a sort of estuary or bay, part of which is the Kleines Haff and the other the Grosses Haff. From there the river finds its way into the Baltic by three channels, the westernmost of which is the river Peene. At the Peene's mouth is an island covered by sand dunes and pine forests, and on it had been erected a number of camouflaged constructions. That island is Peenemünde—the name that Lanny had been seeking for so long; he was going to pass within a few miles of it. He would have given all the earnings of his lifetime to be able to spend a day there and look around, but not even the life earnings of his father would have sufficed to buy that privilege. He was not even permitted to view the various installations along the way to the sea; being non-German, he was required to stay in his cabin, and a cover was put over his porthole and made fast by a seal.

To avoid the silting of the channels, a deep canal had been dug through to the sea, and by this all steamers passed. At the canal entrance, and again at the exit, nothing would have been easier than for SS men to step on board and take two suspects off. Even after they were in the Baltic they would not be entirely safe, for there were armed vessels guarding the entrance to the port, and a wireless message could cause one of them to halt the steamer. So, lie down and rest, and don't talk much about what has happened; although this is a Swedish vessel, it is at the mercy of the Nazis, and who can guess what spying or listening devices they may have installed? Better not talk frankly anywhere until you are in Stockholm, and can go for a walk in the Berzelius Park and be certain that no one is overhearing!

The two men were content to rest after the strain they had been under. The cabin was warm, and they fell sound asleep. When the steamer entered the Baltic they woke up, for a March gale was blowing and the vessel pitched violently; it was just as well that the pair had had so little to eat that day. However, it wasn't many hours before they were under the lee shore of Sweden, and after that the passage was quieter. They did not go to the dining-room, but had a meal brought to them, and they slept the night through, disturbed by no bombs, only by memories manifesting themselves in dreams.

Monck couldn't feel yet that he was safe. The Swedish authorities might order him back to Germany, and then his identity would be rigidly investigated and he could not hope to get by with a false passport. Erickson had offered to try to fix matters up, and he was a man of influence; but the trouble was that the Swedes would feel it their duty to ask a lot of questions about Anton Vetterl, and he might not be able to think up a satisfactory life history.

Lanny said: "What good would it do you to be turned loose in Stockholm with no connections? Our Intelligence people who operate there surely don't go about with labels on them, and how would you find them?"

There could be no answer to that; and Lanny explained how he was planning to proceed in his own case. He could cable his father from Stockholm, but it might be days or even weeks before a message got by the Swedish and the American censorships, not to mention the British, who got in on most cable lines somewhere. It was Lanny's idea to take the American Minister into his confidence; and if he was going to entrust one secret, why not two? Surely the American Minister would have influence in such a case as Monck's. Lanny said: "I'm guessing that the Swedes are favoring the Allies wherever they can without the Nazis finding it out. And this ought to be one of the cases."

Monck agreed, and Lanny added that the Minister would be pretty sure to know the identity of some O.S.S. representative in Sweden; this person could get a message through to Washington and verify the secret agent's story. So they decided to ask Erickson to lay off, at least until they could see how matters shaped up. This vessel would surely not be sailing back until several days after it had arrived.

"Yes," assented the ex-*capitán;* "but don't forget, there will be other vessels." Years of bitter experience had taught him to take the worst possible view of a situation.

V

The steamer came into the magnificent harbor of Stockholm, facing a sunset after storm. The porthole had been unsealed, and the two men took turns looking through it at the city, built on two peninsulas and a number of islands, all joined by bridges and covered by a palace and many public buildings. It was the first peaceful land that Lanny

Budd had been in for a long time, and his relief and joy were beyond telling to anybody but Monck. Lanny remembered a poem that he had read about a man who was killed in a battle at sea: "And sudden the horror faded—'twas heaven all unawares." This hero had had to die to have the experience; but Lanny had it just by getting out of Naziland into free and peaceful Sweden.

The steamer docked at a brightly lighted pier. The three men who had visas were passed readily and quickly. The case of the man without a visa was explained, and the officials looked grave. Many people tried to get into the country without permission, and the Swedes were sorry for them, but they had their regulations, which must be respected. Lanny said that this was a special case that he hoped to bring to the attention of the higher authorities in the morning. The officials answered that of course they would allow time for such action; meanwhile Mr. Vetterl would have to stay in durance. Lanny could guess that it wouldn't be too vile.

The P.A. was driven to the Grand Hotel. Imagine that there were taxicabs, and no blackout! And that you could register in your own name and have a jug of hot water whenever you called for it! He sat down and wrote a note to Mr. Herschel V. Johnson:

> My dear Sir: I am the son of Robert Budd of Budd-Erling Aircraft, and I met you once when you were First Secretary in London, eight or ten years ago—though probably you don't remember that meeting. I have just come out of Germany on a secret errand for the President, and I have a message of the utmost urgency. This is strictly between us, for reasons which I will explain. I would like to see you this evening if it is humanly possible. Please telephone me to the Grand Hotel.

This Lanny double-sealed and marked it "Personal and Private," and handed it personally to the servant who answered the doorbell at the Legation. Then he went back to the hotel, had a bath, and had barely got shaved before the telephone rang, and there was the Minister, ready and eager to see this mysterious arrival from a land that was supposed to be double-sealed against all citizens of the so-called democratic but really Jewish, Bolshevik, and plutocratic Vereinigten Staaten von Amerika.

VI

The American Minister to Sweden, a career diplomat a few years older than Lanny, came from North Carolina. He was large and rather heavy, with a grave face, watchful dark eyes, a determined mouth, and a soft Southern voice. He welcomed his guest politely, not saying whether he remembered him from the past. He led the way into his private study and did not waste any time on preliminaries. "Now, Mr. Budd," he said.

The visitor began promptly. "For the past six years I have been serving President Roosevelt as confidential agent, coming to Europe for him and returning to report. I have kept the pose of a Fascist sympathizer, and only the President and a few friends who have aided me over here know the truth. I have been sending reports through the ambassadors in London, Vichy, and Bern, who have been instructed by the President to forward them by diplomatic pouch, unopened. As I did not expect to come to Sweden, no instructions were given to you."

"I have not received any such."

"I last saw the President at the Casablanca Conference. He arranged for me to be flown to Cairo and from there to Moscow, with the idea of persuading Stalin, whom I met a year ago, to arrange for a conference with the President and Churchill. The plane was shot down over the desert, and so I had to come to Berlin instead of Moscow. This may seem a strange sort of credential, but at least it will amuse you." Lanny presented the Hitler letter.

The Minister examined this document with unconcealed surprise. "How on earth could an American get such a thing, Mr. Budd?"

Lanny explained how he had met the Führer and come to know him; and how, for years before he had entered Roosevelt's service, he had been picking up information among the Nazis and imparting it to anti-Nazi friends in England and France. "My connection with the President is ultra-secret," he said. "Not even my father or mother, not even my wife, knows about it. I have to ask you to keep this visit from your secretary, and even from your family."

"I am a bachelor, Mr. Budd." And then: "You must understand that in my official capacity I ought to have some credential."

"What credential could I have brought through Naziland, Mr. Johnson? The President gave me one of his engraved visiting cards, on which he had written: 'My friend Lanny Budd is worthy of all trust.' He signed it with his initials. But I had to eat that."

"*Eat* it?"

"When I saw that the Bedouin caravan that brought me out of the desert was entering German-held Tunisia, I tore the card into tiny pieces and put it into my mouth. It would have cost me my life if I had not managed to swallow it before I encountered the first German military detachment. Now I have spent a month in Hitler's realm and have a mass of information that I ought to present to the President as quickly as possible. I have come to you as the one whose duty it is to help me."

"What, precisely, do you ask me to do?"

"First of all, to let the President know that I am here. I have written out the message I should like you to send." Lanny handed over the message: "Traveler arrived Stockholm desires transportation London. Remain three days then proceed Washington. Requests notify father safe and well." Lanny added the explanation: "Traveler is my code name, and the President will know who is meant. A message signed by you would surely reach him, whereas one signed by me would probably not, because his secretaries know nothing about me."

"But you must understand that I do not communicate directly with the President. My messages go to the State Department."

"Yes. But if you send a message marked 'urgent and confidential for the President,' would the Department delay to deliver it?"

"I trust not."

"If they do I shall have to ask you to break a rule on my behalf. Let me assure you, the President has told me that what I have brought him has been of use to him, and that he has never yet failed to act immediately on my request. I should like you to know that I am one of those dollar-a-year men—although I have never had the dollar. The President put a hundred thousand dollars to my account in a New York bank, and I have distributed some of it where it could be used to advantage, but I have never taken any of it for myself."

That was the way to impress a career man of "State"!

VII

That was all Lanny had to ask for himself. He didn't put the direct question: "Will you send the message?" He thought it better tactics to go on, and let conviction sink into the Minister's mind little by little. The son of Budd-Erling understood well that members of the ruling and privileged classes are under continual siege from strangers, from pushers and climbers, intruders and self-seekers, and they have to learn to hold themselves in reserve and take time to form their judgments.

The P.A. went on: "There is another matter, even more urgent. I have brought a man out from Germany with me, under rather difficult circumstances. He is a German who has been for some time in the employ of our O.S.S., and the Gestapo was on his trail. He was able to get a false passport and exit permit in Berlin, but he could not get a Swedish visa, so he is being held by the authorities here. It is important that he should be freed, and without any publicity that might destroy his usefulness."

"You know positively that the man is in the employ of the O.S.S.?"

"I personally told Colonel Donovan about him in Washington and arranged for him to be taken into the service. I have known the man for some thirteen years, and he was vouched for by the German woman who later became my wife and who was murdered by the Nazis in Dachau. This man Monck helped me in the effort to save her, and showed himself both brave and competent. When I ran into him in Berlin I was on the trail of an important story having to do with German discoveries in nuclear physics. I won't burden you with the details—suffice it to say that I was trying to make contact with a certain German physicist, and I found Monck working for this man as his butler, photographing his notes and sending them out. That was why the Gestapo was after him, I assume."

"Mr. Budd," said the Minister, "this is like having a motion picture brought into my study and run off for me."

"Quite so, Mr. Johnson," said the P.A. with his number-one smile. "Colonel Donovan could run off hundreds of such reels for you. Such things are going on all over Europe."

"This world continues to take me by surprise. Tell me what you want me to do about this man."

"First, to get permission from the Swedish government for him to enter and stay for at least a few days. This ought to be done without their questioning him, if that is possible."

"There are some persons in the government who will do small favors for me if they are sure that scandal can be avoided."

"No man works more quietly than Monck. He is a self-educated man, and carries on historical researches in libraries—so well that he has been able to keep the very strict Swiss government satisfied about him."

"And what else, Mr. Budd?"

"As soon as possible he should be put into contact with the O.S.S., so that he can make a report and receive further orders."

"You must know, surely, that our Minister is not supposed to know anything about espionage activities being carried on inside a friendly country."

Was there possibly a tiny twinkle in this Minister's eyes? There was one in Lanny's as he replied: "I thought it conceivable that you might have heard some whisper and be able to recall some person who might be in touch with Colonel Donovan's organization."

"And if I don't?"

"Then I would ask you to include in your code message a request to inform Colonel Donovan that Bernhardt Monck is at the Grand Hotel. I should be sorry to have it done that way, because there is always the possibility of even the most carefully guarded code being read."

"All right, Mr. Budd. I will make inquiry and see if I can find somebody here who will call upon your friend."

"Thank you," said Lanny gravely. "I have here the names for your convenience," and he handed over another slip of paper on which he had written: "Real name: Bernhardt Monck. Working name: Konrad Kraft. Present name: Anton Vetterl." He added: "Would it be possible for you to get that message off to Washington tonight? Let me explain that my father is in Newcastle, Connecticut, my wife in New York, and my mother in Marrakech. All three must have been informed that I have been lost in the Sahara, and I am anxious to relieve their minds. It is about midday now in New York and there is time for the President to get my message and act upon it."

"I will do what you ask, Mr. Budd. At this time of night there may be delay in getting hold of our code man, but I will do my best."

VIII

The P.A. had got what he had come for; so, naturally, he felt pleased with Mr. Herschel Johnson. He decided that he liked all Southerners. Laurel was one, and would have known how to get along with this one. "Thank you ever so much," he said. "I am in your debt both personally and professionally."

"Not at all, Mr. Budd. May I hope to have the pleasure of seeing you again before you leave?"

"Certainly, sir, if you wish. But it had better not be in the Legation. Don't forget that I am supposed to be a Nazi sympathizer, and not a fit person for you to associate with. I expect to be seen about town in the company of Mr. Eric Erickson, whom I met at Karinhall, and with whom I traveled out of Germany."

"Eric Erickson!" echoed the other. "Tell me, how on earth did you find out that he is one of ours?"

"One of *ours?*" Not all the training of a lifetime could keep Lanny from showing his amazement.

The Minister's face revealed embarrassment. "Dear me, I am afraid that I have made a slip. You didn't know his position?"

"I took him to be a businessman making money out of the Nazis. I was playing the role of an art expert; buying some of Baron von Behr's unwanted French paintings. But I must admit that I was puzzled about Erickson because he didn't have what I thought of as the Nazi smell."

"He has been bringing us a mass of information. For God's sake, don't mention it to any living soul."

"Rest assured on that, Mr. Johnson. If I have not told my devoted wife what I am doing, you may be sure I have learned to keep the secrets of the underground. Neither Monck nor I have ever told each other anything that wasn't needed for our duties."

"I think it might be better if you do not let Erickson know that you have learned about his position."

"Of course not. I couldn't tell him without at the same time revealing that I myself am not what he thinks me."

"Be careful, Mr. Budd. It doesn't seem to me that you yourself have much of what you call the Nazi smell."

Lanny grinned. "You should hear me talk when I am among them. I have been studying them for almost twenty years, and I really do know their lingo. I assure you, the day I never have to speak another word of it will be a red-letter day in my life."

Lanny went out from the Legation building, chuckling to himself, now and then snapping his fingers and exclaiming: "By heck! He fooled me!" Somehow that seemed to him an especially good joke. He hadn't really taken it for granted that he was the only American agent in Naziland, but he had acted as if he believed it, and now to discover that there was somebody as smart as himself entertained him vastly. He almost wanted to say "smarter," but then he reflected that he had fooled Erickson. Or had he? Could it be that Erickson had got on to him and had been too tactful to hint it? Or was Erickson in the same position that Lanny had been, speculating as to how a man could be a Nazi and still be decent?

IX

Anyhow, the P.A. was relieved, because he wanted to like this oil man and now was free to do so. He would tease him a bit by showing his liking and letting the oil man wonder if he ought to have friendly feelings for a traitor! Early next morning Lanny sought out "Red" in his hotel room, and they were free to talk about their adventure without fear of dictaphones. Lanny didn't say that he had been to see the Minister, but let this remain a mystery. What he said was how grateful he was to his Swedish friend, and that he would never forget it. Did Erickson ever come to America? Or to England? They might get together again somewhere, perhaps after the war was over. Lanny gave his various addresses, Newcastle and Bienvenu and Wickthorpe, and they promised to meet and fight their battles over again.

In midmorning Anton Vetterl came out of his durance. Nobody told him how or why; the officials just said that it had been decided to let him in. He went to one of the smaller hotels and booked a room, and then phoned Lanny's hotel and left a message. As soon as Lanny got it he went to an outside booth and phoned the Minister, saying: "This is your visitor of last evening; the man we talked about is ready for business." Lanny gave the address, and Mr. Johnson said: "A Mr. Halperson will call upon him this afternoon." The P.A. observed with satisfaction how bureaucrats and officials appeared to have been transformed by the war; they now acted promptly, where hitherto they had postponed; they remembered, where hitherto they had been apt to "forget."

Lanny phoned his friend, and they had their promised meeting in Berzelius Park, named after a Swedish scientist—a good example to other nations. Stockholm of course would be as full of Nazi agents as Geneva had been, and Allied agents would need to take precautions to avoid being shadowed. They looked behind them before they joined each other, and they did not delay for sociability. Lanny gave the name of Halperson, Monck's new contact; also Lanny stated that his best mail address would be in care of his father. If something special should come up, Monck would write one of his letters about art works. They exchanged a handclasp and parted—it might be for years and it might be forever.

Lanny had politely declined the oil man's offer to meet some of the latter's aristocratic friends. He said he was suffering from blast shock, which was true; but the real reason was that he couldn't be sure what sort of people they would be, and he was tired of intrigue and uncertainty as to every word that passed his lips. He thought it a good axiom that no two spies should ever be seen in public together; that would be telling the enemy something he had no business to know.

What Lanny wanted was to stroll about and look at the unusual city of Stockholm. It had been called the Venice of the North, but that didn't fit, for the canals of the Italian city were not so clean, whereas the water that crept around the islands and under the bridges of this Swedish capital came from cold mountain streams. At present everything was frozen, and people skated. Lanny, raised on the Riviera, had learned to propel himself through water, but not on top of it, and he was content to watch the skill of others. There were skating ponds in the parks, and he envied the young men their lovely blond partners; he stamped his feet, and was glad that Hilde had insisted upon his keeping that pair of fur-lined gloves. Lanny Budd wasn't as young as he had been.

Some fifteen years ago the yacht *Bessie Budd* had sailed into the Baltic, bearing the Robin family and Beauty Budd and her son, on a delightful summer's holiday. Hansi Robin had just been married to Bess, and Freddi had brought his fiancée, Rahel; they had all been so happy, having no idea of tragic fates that lay before them and the world. They stopped for several days at this shining city; they swam in these waters and watched the sailboats, canoes, and other craft from the bridges. They improved their education in the National Museum, which contains examples of most of the schools of painting in Europe.

This last was the place for the son of Budd-Erling, and he spent his time renewing impressions of many individuals and schools. He had an unfailing memory for everything about art works, and this included what his dearest friends had said about them. So, when he looked at Rembrandts and Raphaels he saw not merely these painters, but the spirit of Freddi Robin, at once gentle and heroic, dreaming of a free and just world, and never resting in his determination to bring it about. This boy and young man was an undying part of Lanny Budd's being, and the foul murder that the Nazis had committed upon him was one of the reasons why a P.A. would never rest in his war upon the infamous system.

When Lanny last heard from Hansi and Bess this pair of musicians had been in Leningrad, making their contribution to the defense of their beloved Soviet Union. They were a couple of hours' airplane flight distant, but, alas, the Luftwaffe was in the way! If it had not been for that circumstance, Lanny might have gone on to Moscow and completed the commission that F.D.R. had assigned to him. He consoled himself with the thought that what he had got in Germany was important enough to be delivered, and if the Boss still wanted the Moscow trip taken he could arrange it. In these days, when you could fly two thousand miles in a day, you spoke of "hopping" to places that had taken your forefathers several weeks to reach.

28

Land of Hope and Glory

I

A MESSAGE came for Mr. Budd, and he called at the office of the airline and was informed that a place had been reserved for him on the plane flying to Britain the next day. Those planes had to pass over German territory, and their number was limited and their routes strictly defined. Germany could not entirely deny this right to a neutral nation, most of whose trade she was seeking to absorb. Lanny packed his few belongings, bought some English newspapers and weeklies to read, and had an uneventful trip across Norway and the North Sea. The moment when he set foot on the soil of the blessed isle was one of the happiest he had known for months.

A man who had come through Hitlerland might expect questions to be asked, and Lanny had spent some time figuring out how to meet that situation. But to his satisfaction there was his friend Fordyce waiting for him; he could guess that Baker had taken the trouble to notify B4. When Fordyce said: "The P.M. wants to see you as soon as convenient," Lanny could imagine Roosevelt remarking in one of his transatlantic telephone chats: "By the way, Lanny Budd is arriving, and I suspect he may have a story."

Lanny replied that he would be delighted to meet Mr. Churchill, and Fordyce asked: "Will this week end be too soon?" Lanny answered: "I'll be at Wickthorpe Castle, awaiting your call." The British agent told him that things were rather crowded now, so he had taken the liberty of engaging a room for him at the Dorchester. Lanny could understand that Fordyce might be curious to hear how a man had got from the Sahara Desert to the Venice of the North. Lanny was willing to "spill it" to the head of their government, but not to any common or garden variety of agent. On the drive to the hotel he entertained his host with news as to the situation in Sweden, and then about what he had seen in North Africa; but not a word about places and people in between.

613

Lanny's first action in the hotel was to send a cablegram to his father, addressing it as usual: "Robert Budd, President Budd-Erling Aircraft Corporation"—this for the benefit of the censor. Now he wrote: "Arrived safe and well love to all returning soon." This sounded like a proper family message and no code. He did not mention Laurel; Robbie could get her on the telephone in less than a minute, and he would be sure to do so. Also Robbie would cable to Beauty, something he could do because of his position. Lanny tried it from London, but with no assurance of success. He began: "Dear Mother"— but would that have any effect upon a censor who might well have Lanning Prescott Budd on his list as a Nazi sympathizer?

The traveler telephoned the Castle to ask if his presence would be welcome. Irma said: "We have been terribly upset about you. Come as soon as you can. Frances is wild with joy that you are alive." He told her: "I can hardly believe it myself. I'll take an early morning train." They made an appointment for him to be met at the station.

II

Lanny wanted to see Rick, and the flying sons if it were possible. When he phoned to the paper for which his friend was writing, he heard a voice, deeply moved. "For God's sake, Lanny, what happened to you?" It appeared that in newspaper dispatches from Algiers he had been reported as missing on the Sahara Desert and presumed dead. Nobody knew why he had gone out in a fighter plane and nobody knew what had happened to either him or the pilot. Lanny said: "Maybe I'm dreaming, but I have the impression that I'm still alive."

He had decided after much thought that he wasn't going to tell anybody in England with the exception of Churchill that he had been through Germany. The story was sensational, and it would be difficult to keep rumors from getting into the press—something which Lanny dreaded above all things. It was enough that the man who was dead had come back. The son of Budd-Erling would go about surprising many people, and would tell them casually that he had got out of the desert all right and there wasn't much of a story to it. If any newspaperman got after him he wouldn't be mysterious, but just offhand, English fashion. "Nothing to it, old boy; it happens out there all the time; chaps get lost and they find their way in."

What could he tell Rick that would be of any use to a journalist? Certainly nothing about Peenemünde, nor yet about Rjukan, nor any of the German scientists or what they had said. The various messages

that had been entrusted to him by Hitler and Göring were all just rubbish, "springes to catch woodcock"; Rick had heard them many times
before and knew them by heart. The condition of the people in Berlin, their grumbling, their behavior at the movies and at the railroad
station when the wounded were brought in—Rick could have made an
A-1 article out of that, but hardly without pointing to Lanny as his
source. The alert Gestapo would surely not fail to know when the
Führer's friend had left Stockholm and when he had arrived in London, and they would pounce eagerly on any signs that he was doing
harm to the Nazi cause. If they found out that he went to see the
P.M., that wouldn't be so bad—for the Führer had requested him
to get a message to Churchill!

Lanny said: "I'm sorry, but this time I'm not free to talk. However,
I can tell you about North Africa, where there's a story that won't
be out of date for a long time."

Yes, for General de Gaulle had come back from Casablanca not the
least bit reconciled with Giraud or with the American occupation. He
was determined to have power for himself and was using the radio that
the British provided to persuade the people of France that he was their
heaven-sent deliverer, the one man who could lead them to freedom
and security. A man of boundless ambition, a driving ego, he was in
Lanny's view the traditional French "man on horseback." He stood
for the army caste, for aristocracy, and clerical privilege—forces which
had ruled *la patrie* since the days of the St. Bartholomew massacre.
President Roosevelt distrusted him, and more than ever since the exhibition he had given at the Casablanca Conference. "Thumbs down!"
F.D.R. had said.

What was the attitude of the British? Rick said: "Winnie hoped to
use him, and gave him every facility to set himself up. Winnie hated
Darlan and all the Vichy crowd that had betrayed him when he went
to France just before the end. But by now, I guess, he's pretty tired
of Big Charlie's intransigence. Our Labor people don't know what to
make of the situation. They see the Americans putting the old Vichy
gang in power, and they ask if that's what we're fighting the war for."

"I know, Rick, and I've done my share of worrying over it. We've
invited De Gaulle to come and take a part of the responsibility, but
with him it's everything or nothing, and how can we undertake to
clean out a government and set up a new crowd about whom we don't
know anything—except that they don't know anything about the job
in North Africa? Our Army people have to decide whether we're
going to fight the Germans or the French civil war. We are saying to

the French: 'Wait, and if you have to have your civil war, have it after the Germans are out of the way.' "

III

Rick, the eager publicist, plied his friend with questions, and there was no reason why Lanny shouldn't tell all he knew about the invasion and what he had seen at that time. Rick, in turn, told the news about Britain. Politics had come to an end for the duration, and everybody, high and low, was doing what he could against the villainous foe. A man of the Left found it hard to say anything good about a Tory, but Rick had to say that Winnie's speeches were magnificent, and the fact that he tried them out on everybody he knew made no difference to the public that heard them for the first time. The radio had brought back the art of public speaking, which had seemed to be put on the shelf by the more powerful art of printing.

Rick reported that the American forces were still pouring onto these small islands in spite of so many going to North Africa. They were training incessantly, and with the vigor they had learned on their football fields. Ways had been found to make them feel at home, and Rick said that the islands would never be the same after the long sojourn of these easygoing and free-spending visitors. In spite of the food shortages the British people were living better than ever in their lives before, the reason being that what there was got distributed more fairly. The man of the Left proclaimed: "Winnie and his Tories will never be able to hold them this time!" His friend replied: "I hope not," but he remembered the high expectations with which the pair of them had seen World War I come to its end, and the bitter disillusionment when the old crowd had come back stronger than ever.

The baronet's son reported that his family was well. "The Pater," now in his seventies, was standing punishment marvelously; he was bossing all the war work in their district. Alfy, a flying instructor, had been advanced in rank and responsibility; and the younger was piloting a bomber—he had taken part in that recent tremendous raid over Berlin. "Well, I'll be switched!" said Lanny, but he didn't say what for. He saw himself cowering in the cellar of the Donnerstein palace, and wondered if his friend's plane had dropped the bomb that had fallen on that particular building.

IV

Lanny took the morning train, and there was Frances with her little pony cart and a groom riding behind for safety. She rushed into Lanny's arms and burst into tears right there on the platform of the little station. "Oh, Father, Father! They wouldn't tell me what had happened to you!" He soothed her down as soon as he could, for he knew that her mother disapproved of emotionalism. "I was where I couldn't get word to you, dear; but I'm all right again and you have nothing to worry about."

It was all right to thrill her by describing how it felt to come down out of the sky in a parachute, and how hot it had been in the desert, and how pleasant to hear the bells of a camel caravan, and how those great brutes had grumbled and complained. He didn't say that the caravan had taken him into the German lines, but just that he had had a long way to travel with them and so had been delayed. That satisfied her, and it would be enough for everybody, both in Britain and America. He made up his mind that he wouldn't tell even Laurel that he had been into Naziland; it would only terrify her and make it harder for her to be happy the next time he went away. Some day after it was all over—then she could write a novel about Germany in the midst of war!

At the Castle nothing was changed very much. Irma said: "I'll have to put you up at Mother's again," and Lanny replied: "All right, if Mother can put up with me." Mother was a little more subdued, and Uncle Horace a little more feeble. Ceddy was the perfect country squire, talking about the tremendous crops he had had last autumn and about his spring plowing. A few refugee children were still on the place because, although the bombing had practically ended in the cities, the scarcity of homes remained an insoluble problem. Lanny played bowls with his little daughter—he would have to learn to call her his big daughter now, and that delighted her. He met her governess and her music teacher and her playmates; she was at the age where girls have wonderful "crushes," and Frances was in a state of rapture over the little daughter of Ceddy's London lawyer, who was staying at the Castle. Patricia, called "Patty," must be in on everything, and Lanny had to agree that her red hair and freckles were lovely. He was pleased to do so, and told stories about the Dark Continent and its strange sights; altogether he was a delightful and romantic father home from the wars. England had known such fathers ever since men had lived upon its shores.

After she had gone to bed Lanny sat with the mother and the step-father and a couple of friends who had the right point of view. They thought that Lanny had come directly from North Africa, and he answered their questions with discretion. He was interested to discover that the famous "Wickthorpe set" was beginning to shift its position. The realization was dawning on them that maybe Britain was going to win after all, and that afterward, with American help, it might be able to restrain the predatory impulses of the Red hordes. Some of the things that the fourteenth Earl of Wickthorpe had said to Lanny scores of times, he now managed to forget that he had ever said—and Lanny would surely not have the bad taste to remind him.

V

Next morning the guest had a talk with his former wife. They had agreed that the welfare of their child required them to be friends in spite of any impropriety the world might find in that course. Now Lanny had an idea that his father had suggested and that he had been considering ever since. Employing that tact which he had spent a life-time in acquiring, he began: "There is something serious that I ought to tell you, Irma. I know you have information that the Germans are preparing new weapons against Britain—jet-propelled missiles, rockets— that may develop a speed greater than any airplane and may carry a warload ten times as heavy as the present bombs. There will be no defense against such weapons, so far as I have been able to learn. I don't know when they will begin coming, it may be a long time or it may be this year. One thing is certain, they will come suddenly, prob-ably some night, and surely without warning. So I do not like to think of Frances being in England."

Irma's face went white. "You think they will be aimed at places as unlikely as Wickthorpe?"

"My guess is they will be aimed at the biggest target in this war, which is London. But they may be flying hundreds of miles, and they may not always be accurate. I think Newcastle would be a much safer place for our daughter than Wickthorpe. I am not proposing to take her now. I am asking you to think it over, as something to be done when I come again."

Irma drew a deep breath, and her voice betrayed her emotion.

"Lanny, she has never been separated from her mother. I cannot bear the thought!"

He tried to divert her with playfulness. "There is another aspect of the matter. If the bombs begin falling on London, you will have what you had before—hundreds of refugee children having to be put up and cared for here. You found that so inconvenient, you remember; Frances was associating with children of whom you disapproved."

Irma saw no humor in the idea. "All this is dreadfully hard for me to face," she exclaimed.

"Hard for you, Irma, but best for Frances. She would have Robbie's and Esther's other grandchildren for playmates. And it would please Robbie and Esther to have them all together for a while. She would have everything a child wants, just as she has here. It would be good for her in many ways, as you will realize once you have thought it over."

"But what about the danger of such a trip in wartime! It seems a terrible idea to me."

"The Germans are not troubling the planes to Lisbon—they need to use the same port themselves. From there to the Azores and Bermuda; hundreds of planes are making that trip every day; it is like one of the ferries across the Thames."

"You say that after having two crashes in a year and a half!"

"In one of them I was shot down over enemy territory; and the other was in a storm near the Arctic. There is nothing like that to be expected by the southern route."

Irma had known that this was bound to come sooner or later; and always it brought to her mind a fear even older than the war. Frances was an heiress, and America was the land of gangsters and kidnapers! She brought up this argument now, but Lanny only chuckled. "The kidnapers are all in the Army, getting ready to work upon the Germans!" Then he added: "I'll tell Robbie and Esther you are thinking it over. You can write to them, or to me."

VI

A telephone call came from Fordyce asking if it would be agreeable for him to take Mr. Budd at nine that evening. Lanny said: "Fine," knowing all about the nocturnal habits of Churchill. He understood that he was going to the very agreeable estate called Chequers Court, which he had visited once as a boy, when it had belonged to Lord and

Lady Lee, and they had given a grand garden party for some charity. Now it had been donated as a national home for the head of the government, a British "White House" without an office. The brick building dated from the days of Queen Elizabeth, and the grounds comprised some two or three square miles. The place, like Wickthorpe, was in "Bucks," and not more than a half-hour's drive distant.

The B4 man entertained Lanny with talk about the submarine situation, upon which the whole war depended. The armies in North Africa were being supplied with very small shipping loss, only about two per cent; but this was at the expense of the rest of the Atlantic, where losses were running dangerously high. Fordyce said there were new detection devices; he didn't claim to know about them, but those who ought to know declared that they were in production and soon would be in use, and they would give the U-boat crews a very unhappy summer. The wonders of radar were multiplying fast, and our technology was fast outstripping the enemy's.

They drove through the elaborate iron gates into the grounds of Chequers. Whatever week-end guests may have been there saw nothing of Lanny, for he was taken upstairs by what was presumably a servants' stairway and escorted into a large sitting-room. They sat before a grate fire, waiting until the hunched figure of the Prime Minister appeared. He was wearing what he called his siren-suit, a costume he had devised for war emergencies; it was made like a child's teddybear costume, all one piece and closed in front by zippers—the idea being that you could slip into it quickly and hop to an air-raid shelter without exposure to cold. Winnie was proud of it and wore it on all possible occasions; he had even made the mistake of wearing it on his recent trip to Moscow, but the Russians hadn't liked it; they considered it undignified and something of an affront.

Fordyce excused himself, and the other two settled themselves for a long chat. Churchill confirmed Lanny's guess, that Roosevelt had mentioned him in one of those telephone chats that had become almost a nightly habit. "How the devil does a man get from the Sahara to Stockholm?" demanded the P.M., and when Lanny told him, he exclaimed that he would give up his present honors to be young enough to go and have an adventure like that. The son of Budd-Erling replied: "I'm really not young enough, and I only had it because I couldn't help it. Now I try to apply Cicero's principle, and look back upon my past pains with pleasure."

To quote Cicero was an elegant and English thing to do, and put the visitor upon a plane of equality with his host. Lanny was subjected to

an elaborate inquisition as to whom he had met in Germany and what
he had seen there. When he told about the Führer's rage over the fall
of Kharkov, the Führer's antagonist chortled with glee and exclaimed:
"We've got the bastard worried!" When Lanny repeated the message
he had been asked to deliver "if possible," about how Britain was to
come over to Adi Schicklgruber's side and accept his permission to
live, the Duke of Marlborough's descendant snorted. "All that tripe all
over again!"

Lanny said: "Excuse me for mentioning it. It's what he said, and of
course I had to pretend to take it seriously and promise to do my very
best to get it to you."

"Righto, you have done it," said Winnie.

Lanny went on to tell about Göring and then about Schacht. "That
old rogue!" the Prime Minister called the former president of the
Reichsbank, and seemed to know him well. "He wants us to go easy
on the western front, does he? Well, we'll oblige him—for a while! I
have stood out for the principle that we shall not cross the Channel
until we have such forces that we can drive and keep driving and not
let up until we get to Berlin. That's the schedule, Budd!" Like all
Englishmen, he pronounced it "shedule," but he didn't say that he had
learned the pronunciation in a "shool."

VII

The Right Honourable Winston Spencer Churchill lighted one of
those big Havana cigars without which he could not be happy for very
long. He took a couple of puffs and slid his pudgy body a little deeper
into the armchair. Then he started plying his visitor with questions
again. What were the conditions in Berlin? What were the people eating and wearing? What were they saying? He enjoyed the jokes from
the night club; and then he wanted to know about the damage from
the recent bombing, and the reaction of the populace to it. Everybody
knew how the British had taken it, and now everybody wanted to
know if the Germans would do as well. "Better they couldn't do,"
boasted the P.M.

Then the business of rocket bombs. Lanny told about his adventures
with the professors and what he had learned about Peenemünde. "Yes,
we have that from several sources," declared the other. "We haven't
done anything about it, because it appears that they are still in the
construction stage. If you bomb a place then, you get nothing but a
bunch of common workers; but if you wait until they have finished

their installations and have started production, you get the skilled workers and the experts, and possibly even some of the scientific devils."

"I guessed that might be it," Lanny answered. "And one thing more, their heavy-water project. I suppose you know that that has to do with the efforts at atomic fission. I was assigned to get the facts from Germany a year and a half ago, but I got smashed up in a plane. I don't know how much you may have learned in the meantime, but I happened to get the name of the place where they are making the heavy water. It's called Rjukan, in southern Norway. I sent the name in by the O.S.S. I don't know if it will have come to you."

"When did you send it in?" demanded the other, peering at his guest through sharp eyes well surrounded by flesh.

"I'd have to figure up the exact day," was the reply. "I would guess about the twenty-sixth of last month."

"Well, it will interest you to know that we blew the insides out of the place on the night of the twenty-seventh."

"That was certainly quick work!" exclaimed the P.A.

"Don't fool yourself!" chuckled the other. "We have had the spot marked for the past year and a half, and have been working on the wrecking project for I don't know how long. It was an inside job—sabotage—and don't mention it to anybody, but we're not through yet. I am sorry if you wasted time on it."

"As it happens, I didn't," said Lanny. "A young SS officer dropped the name by accident, and I caught it. That's the way it goes if you stay around among the right people."

"You have shown discrimination in your choices!" remarked the head of the British Empire. He meant it for a compliment, and Lanny did not miss it.

VIII

It was the visitor's duty to offer to leave, and he did so. But the P.M. liked to talk, and apparently he had found a satisfactory listener. He had heard some of Lanny's adventures, and now he wanted it to be known that he, too, had not lived without them. He told how, when he was young, he had been sent as a war correspondent to South Africa, and how the Boers had captured him and what they had done to him. He told the story at length; what Louis Botha had said to him and what he had said to Louis Botha, how he had escaped from Pretoria by climbing over a garden wall and hiding in some coalsacks on board a "goods" train. He had no doubt told that story many times, and he knew every point that counted, every gesture, every intonation. He had told it once before to the son of Budd-Erling, by the swimming-pool of Maxine Elliott's villa on the Riviera, six years ago—but he had forgotten that.

This genial British bulldog hadn't, it appeared, the slightest remorse over having helped to conquer the Boers. He believed in "the Empah," and held it as worth what it had cost. In those days an "Empah" had had to have gold and diamonds, and nowadays it had to have oil. Winnie was deeply concerned about the oil in the Near East, and said it was a race with the Russians, and no use blinking the fact. He was troubled because Roosevelt kept trying to blink it, and wrapping it up in fine phrases about democracy and internationalism. It appeared as if he wanted this P.A. to help persuade his Boss to revise the country's military plans and make some landings in the neighborhood of that oil, so as to be on hand when the time came for the dividing up. "You know how it is at the end of a war," he said.

Lanny replied: "Oh, yes, I was at the Paris Peace Conference. I remember how you came over to try to persuade them to go in and lick the Bolsheviks before it was too late." A broad grin spread over the old gentleman's face. There was a lot that he might have said if he had known this American better; but possibly he, too, might be tainted with Red ideas.

He went on to talk about that dinner in the White House where he had renewed his acquaintance with Lanny. He remembered "that fellow Adamic"—pronouncing his name with the accent on the second syllable, perhaps because that gave a hint of what he would like to do to him. He wanted to know if there was any chance of the President's taking up that "fool idea" of sending "democratic Americans" over to run the Middle European lands from which they had originally come. "They would turn out to be a bunch of Socialists," declared the staunch old Tory, "and the Communists would be running *them*." Lanny quoted what the author had said to him, that some day he was going to publish an account of that dinner. The P.M. growled: "I ate the dinner, but I don't have to read the book!"

29

Home Is the Sailor

I

LANNY received notice that a seat was available for him on the plane to Lisbon. He flew the familiar route, and was warm again, after being very cold in the half-heated Castle. He looked down on the bright blue waters around the Azores, and again on the island-dotted harbor of Hamilton, the town in which automobiles were being admitted for the first time. Bermuda was being Americanized.

Lanny was going back to his wife and baby, and his thoughts were on them. The baby would be more than four months old; Lanny thought how Laurel had wanted him because he would be Lanny's son. This aspect of parenthood had never come into his mind before—the love for a child being due to love for the other parent. He loved his little daughter, not because she was Irma's child, but because she was his own. But Laurel had said that she wanted Lanny's child, and she had her wish. This thought of her made her seem closer to him. It made his young son something they shared, the symbol of their love for each other.

He hoped the young Lanny would be like Laurel, who was kind, unselfish, and clear-minded. Yet he admitted that he had a somewhat egotistical desire that this son might closely resemble his father. He wanted to see himself as a child again in this child. Now he told himself that he must not hold this idea; he must hold the other—that his boy's mother would live again for him in his son. He would have more of Laurel that way! He found himself smiling with amusement at this line of thought; a strange idea, that wanting his son to be a reincarnation of the woman he loved should be a sort of renunciation! Never mind, he said to himself, you will live in your work; you have helped the Chief in this hour of world travail.

Lanny's thoughts moved on. How fortunate he was to have found a woman who would leave him free to do his real work! She must have suffered cruelly during that time when he was "missing"—just as he

624

had suffered when Trudi had disappeared. Did a man have the right to cause a woman so much grief? Laurel had said that he did. She loved his cause and his zeal for humanity. Because she had the same zeal, she would always understand him and never be resentful. So they could be happy; and now his mind became occupied with the problem of how to make her happy, to give her some sort of holiday, as repayment for her sufferings. He had a clear sense of having earned a holiday himself, and he meant that they should have it together.

II

Set down at the Washington airport, the P.A. called Baker, but the President's man wasn't in; Lanny left word that "Traveler" would call in one hour. Then he was free to try New York, and after some war-time delay he heard Laurel's voice. Her excitement was painful; she couldn't keep from crying, and that brought tears to his eyes. "Lanny, I wouldn't give you up! I never did give up hope!" He told her: "It was terrible, but I was in a position where I couldn't possibly get word to you. I will tell you about it."

"Are you all right?" she wanted to know, and he assured her that he was entirely well. He asked about the most wonderful baby in the world, and learned that it, too, was thriving. He couldn't say yet when he would be able to leave Washington; he had to make a report to two different persons. "I'll let you know as soon as I can," he said. "How is the book coming on?"

"The book? I finished it, but then I forgot that it existed. How could I think about a book when they told me my husband was dead?"

"Darling," he went on, "we're not supposed to talk more than three minutes. Phone Robbie for me and tell him I'm here, and we'll come to see him soon. I'll probably take a plane to New York tomorrow after-noon. I'll let you know."

Lanny tried to reach Baker again, and this time got him. The President's man said that he would get word to the Boss—no names over the telephone—and Traveler was to call again in two hours. Traveler said he would have to spend the night, and Baker told him what hotel to go to and promised to have a room reserved. That was the way with the V.I.P.'s and their families—sometimes even their dogs!

Lanny had time for a bath, and for dinner, and to read the evening papers and discover that the Russians were being slowly brought to a halt in the Ukraine, and that the British and Americans were holding on desperately in Tunisia, bombed incessantly in their muddy foxholes.

The Germans had moved an army across from Sicily, and Rommel was holding fast to what was known as the Mareth line, near the seafront at the border of Tripoli. More than four months had passed since Lanny had seen the Americans come ashore, full of hope and determination; they had been learning the bitter lesson that war is not all victories, but tedious waiting, and seemingly endless toil, repairing roads and bridges, laying new airfields, and bringing up supplies, mostly in the night, to dodge the bombs. All the dirty work that men had done at home, but much more of it, and under conditions of exposure and discomfort such as they had never dreamed.

The son of Budd-Erling, clean and elegant, sat reading this news in an overstuffed armchair in a well-heated hotel room. He thought, as usual, that he was far too comfortable; but was he to wish himself back in the Sahara oven or the Donnerstein icebox? No, he would take things as they came, the thunder and the sunshine. Promptly on the minute he called the President's man, and was told to be on the corner near his hotel in fifteen minutes. He could guess that F.D.R. had put off some other engagement, or perhaps the viewing of a film, in order to hear how his P.A. 103 had managed to get from the Sahara Desert to Stockholm.

III

In the familiar large bedroom there was an open fire burning, and the "Governor" had on his large blue cape for protection against the "sniffles"—but he had a few, even so. His face so lighted up with pleasure that it was only after a while that Lanny noticed how tired he really looked; he reached over and gave his friend one of those hearty handclasps and then exclaimed: "So you had your way and went into Germany!"

"How did you know that?" Lanny asked, and the answer was: "Winston told me last night."

"Believe me, Governor," the P.A. hastened to explain, "I had no idea of disobeying orders; it was my only way. I had to parachute in the desert, and the caravan that picked me up took me into German-held Tunisia. I had to chew up your visiting card and swallow it."

The hard-worked executive opened his mouth and enjoyed a roar of laughter. "How did it taste?"

"Sort of rough and sticky. I had to get it down fast because there was a German roadblock ahead of us, and I had to be ready to slide off my camel and say '*Heil Hitler!*'"

"Tell me the story," exclaimed the other. "Don't leave out a single detail!"

That was quite an assignment. It started in Algiers and led by a rocky and sun-scorched route to Tozeur, and from there to Tunis, Rome, Nürnberg, and an unnamed place in the western Ukraine; then Stubendorf, Berlin, Karinhall, Stettin and Stockholm—quite a journey. "I've thought it all over, Governor," remarked the traveler, "and I'm embarrassed to realize that I didn't accomplish a single thing of importance, unless you count the fact that I came out alive."

"I count that, Lanny."

"I thought I had achieved a real coup in the name of Rjukan, where the Nazis are making their heavy water in Norway. I sent the name out by my friend Monck, whom I had put in touch with the O.S.S.; but I learned from Churchill that he had it for a long time."

"The competition is getting keen, Lanny; we have the field well covered, and you won't find it so easy to bring in scoops from now on."

"Well, I'm not working to build up a score, and if others can do the jobs, that's O.K. But I thought, while I was there I might as well pick up what I could."

"You don't count having talked with Hitler and Göring?"

"I learned that Hitler is wild with nerves and that he's dosing himself with nostrums; but I might have guessed that and saved my carfare. I heard him tell me his peace terms, but it's the same old story as a year and a half ago. He wants you and Churchill to quit and let him polish off the Soviets. He's very generous with you; he offers you Japan and all that the Japs have taken, and the whole western hemisphere; you can help yourself to Mexico and Central and South America. I promised to tell his good friends in America about it, and I assured him that they would be deeply grateful."

"Tell me everything you can remember that he said, Lanny. It may possibly mean more to me than it does to you."

That was another considerable assignment; and after Lanny had finished with Hitler he had to tell about Göring and the drugs he was taking and the art collections he was looting—such an odd combination of esthete and pirate! Then there was Schacht and others of the lesser lights; and there was the German *Volk*, the food they were eating, the newspapers they were reading, the jokes they were hearing. There was the bombing of Berlin and what Lanny had seen of it, and the story of Professor Plötzen's butler, and of the Swedish-American oil man who had helped him out of Naziland.

It was the longest session Lanny had ever had with his Chief; and on top of that the Chief wanted to do some talking, too—to tell about what had happened since he and his secret agent had parted in the Villa La Saadia in Marrakech. F.D.R. was in a happy mood, not merely because of the continued landing of an army in North Africa without losses, and getting them so promptly to the front, but also because of what the American Navy and Air Force men were doing on the other side of the globe.

"We have made sure of the outcome of that war," he said. "First we sank or burned the greater part of a Japanese Fleet in the harbor of Kavieng, and a month later we destroyed a whole convoy trying to get to the same harbor. Those were air-versus-sea battles, and the significance lies, not so much in the number of vessels destroyed, as in the power we have established to do such damage at almost no cost. We did it first in the Coral Sea, and then at Midway, and now twice again. When we have built up our air forces, we can do it as often as necessary. The Japanese Air Force and Navy will be powerless against us."

Said the P.A.: "That surely sounds good to a man who was under their bombs at Hongkong."

IV

At the first lull in the conversation Lanny put in the question: "Am I to make another try at Stalin?"

The answer was: "I sent somebody else, and I'm satisfied that he doesn't intend to meet us until we have come through with the second front that he demands. You know how it is, we are pretty much at his mercy, because if he should choose to slacken up in his efforts, he might set the whole German Army free to come at us, and we couldn't match it. I doubt if we could ever win the war alone."

"I can tell you this, Governor, from my talk with him; he's going to be mighty sore if we don't cross the Channel this spring or summer."

"I should like to do it, and Beetle Smith is sure that we could; but our British friends are set against it, and I dare not force the issue. What it comes down to is air power; you can't move anywhere in this war until you can put an air cover over your troops and keep it there. We tried it in Tunisia, and you saw what happened."

"Are we going to get the air power there, Governor?"

"That is a compartively small job, and we are doing it already. We are. bombing the enemy bases, their harbors and airports, and their ships coming across. You know, the Germans in Tunisia are just as if they were on an island, and if we destroy their communications they can't put up much of a fight. We've got them to the point where they are trying to send in supplies by air; and you can imagine, those heavy transports are fat ducks and geese for our flyers."

"That is certainly a change since I was there!"

"It was just a question of making the airports bigger and getting in the planes and supplies. The British Eighth Army is beginning to move on Rommel now, and our boys will be threatening his communications behind the Mareth line. They tell me that Rommel is ill and has had to go to Germany for treatment."

"I read that in the Berlin papers. They all put up a bold front to me, but Göring gave me to understand that he considered it was a blunder to send any army over there—it's a trap. That is the Führer's great weakness: he cannot bear to give up any territory that his troops have taken; he'd rather lose the troops."

"Well, we are already building the prisoner pens for them. If you go back to North Africa you'll be surprised to see how we are getting things straightened out."

"There was surely a lot to be done. By the way, you'll be interested in something the Herr Doktor Schacht had to say about our financial doings there."

"What does *he* know about them?"

"Lord! That old vulture misses nothing that happens in the money world; he gets his beak into every carcass. When we came into North Africa you could buy a hundred and fifty francs with a dollar, which was fine for our troops. But our occupation authorities pegged the franc at seventy-five; and then Jacques Lemaigre-Dubreuil persuaded Murphy to raise it to fifty to the dollar."

"You must know the reason for that, Lanny. We wanted to make it possible for the people there to buy our goods. Those poor natives never had but one shirt to their backs, and now that one is in tatters."

"Yes, Governor; it's like the talk about the widows and orphans that the insurance tycoons put out. The people who got the benefit of the deal were the big bankers and the Comité des Forges gang. Lemaigre has been the good friend of those fellows from away back, and they got the tip-off and shifted their money from Paris to Algiers. Schacht thought it was the joke of the century; he estimated the amount at twenty billion francs, and we raised the value of it to sixty billion, which meant forty billion net profit—that is about four hundred million dollars at one stroke of the pen."

"That's terrible, Lanny. But you see how those economic royalists have us sewed up. We can't do anything for the people, at home or abroad, that the speculators don't get there first. I can't solve that problem for the American people, let alone for the French."

"Yes, Governor, but here is something more. Schacht didn't tell me, but I happen to know that the Germans own fifty-one per cent of all those companies, so we have made the enemy a free gift of a couple of hundred million dollars, which he will transfer to Spain and Switzerland and Sweden and use against us."

"I must admit I didn't realize that, Lanny. That was State's boner."

"Yes, and you may be sure that State isn't going to let you do anything about it if they can help it. If you don't mind my butting in, you might let Treasury have a go at the problem. Henry Morgenthau is one who really hates the Nazis—even when they are very rich." Lanny had been a little dubious about making that suggestion, but the way the President chuckled over it let him know that he hadn't gone too far.

V

"What do you want to do next?" demanded the Boss. And the P.A. said: "My wife had a terrible fright, and I'd like to give her a little time to get used to the idea that I'm still alive. Unless there is something urgent, I'd like to take a little furlough and watch you pull the drawstrings on Rommel and Arnim. Then, if you say so, I'll go back and see how Hitler takes it and what he plans to do next."

"You can get in again?"

"He practically gave me orders to return. I'm to interview the leading appeasers in this country and find out when and how they plan to kidnap you and take control of the government."

"Golly!" said F.D.R. "You might find out about that for me, too!"

"That's not so easy," replied the P.A., smiling. "The big fellows talk about it freely, but they don't get down to places and dates. I think it more likely that there will be an attempt to kill Hitler, and I might get on the trail of that. I should have to play a double role, doing what the O.S.S. people call 'turning.' "

"All right, but don't worry about it now. Enjoy yourself listening to the radio—the news will be good this spring."

"One thing more, Governor, before I go. At Karinhall I found myself in the midst of the fat boy's art looters, and I thought I ought to make myself secure with them. You know, buying paintings is my camouflage, and the only way I have to keep them from becoming suspicious of me."

"Certainly, that is all right."

"I had some money sequestered in a Berlin bank. I couldn't pay it to anybody else but I could pay it to Göring's gang; so I bought half a dozen French paintings from them and brought them to Sweden and left them in a bank vault there. Technically that was trading with the enemy, and I ought to report it somewhere and clear myself."

"Are you planning to see Bill Donovan?"

"Yes, I promised Monck I would report on his situation."

"Tell the Colonel about it, and tell him I say to have his people get the paintings and bring them home. You can fix it up so that your name won't be involved."

"It was my idea to wait till after the war and then perhaps restore them to the family from whom Göring stole them. They are Jews, so they may not be alive. I intend to turn any profit I make over to the Red Cross."

"You can do that if you wish," responded the President, "but you are surely not under any obligation to do it. You refuse to let me pay you for the work you are doing, and tell me that you earn your living out of picture deals. Surely you're entitled to it!"

"Yes, Governor, but I can't deal in goods that I know were obtained by fraud and force." Lanny said this and then began to chuckle. "I have stayed too late, but you ought to hear the story of how I was tempted to commit bigamy. Perhaps you will give me permission for that! Or is it in Colonel Donovan's department?"

He told the story of Rosika Diamant, which wasn't really funny but horribly tragic when you stopped to think. Roosevelt laughed first and then he frowned. He didn't often use profanity, but he took time off from his sleep to curse those Nazi demons, and to say: "Some day we're going to hang them, Lanny, every last one of them, as an example to the world for all time!"

VI

Lanny went out from the presence uplifted, as always. He returned to the hotel and slept soundly, and in the morning phoned Laurel, telling her that he would take an afternoon plane. Baker had undertaken to arrange it; also to make an appointment with "Wild Bill," so that Lanny might be passed into that amiable gentleman's office without having to explain himself to secretaries.

Lanny had three stories to tell: first Raoul, then Denis, and finally Monck. The proper heads of departments were called in to listen and make notes. All three of those foreigners were valuable men and ought to be given responsibility. Lanny laid particular stress upon the ex-*capitán;* with "State" it was a black eye to say that a man had fought for Republican Spain, but he hoped this wouldn't be the case with the Intelligence service. And apparently it wasn't; they were using Socialists, Communists, anybody who could get information and carry on sabotage against the enemy.

The visitor suggested: "You might arrange to fly Monck to this country and let him give you advice. You will find nobody who knows Germany, high and low, better than he does. You might want to put him at the head of a department, or at the least let him teach a class of those who are going into Germany."

The stout and rosy Colonel said "Fine!" Some of his assistants looked worried, but Lanny labored to clear up their doubts. He gathered that there was a certain amount of friction in the office, because its head trusted too many people and put all sorts at work somehow. They were as busy as a hive of bees, learning in a few months a job at which the nations of Europe had been working for generations and even centuries.

Lanny told about his paintings, and the informal Colonel made note of the fact that Presidential Agent 103 had permission to trade with the enemy in works of art. Lanny advised that the paintings be left where they were for the present; also, he thought it worth while to mention that he had learned the secret of Eric Erickson, although Erickson did not know about Lanny's secret. If he went back into Germany it would probably be through Sweden, and he might make use of Erickson's friendship in a pinch. He underwent a thorough questioning as to what he had seen and learned in Berlin. Too bad that he hadn't been able to get any idea where the Führer's headquarters was situated! Also, that he hadn't got the names of those generals whom the Führer had been cursing; they might by now be ready to be approached by some Allied agent!

VII

Taking a taxi from La Guardia Field Lanny arrived at his apartment. The sailor was home from the sea, the airman from the air, the desert man from his camels. "Rejoice, for I have found my sheep which was lost!" Laurel was so happy that she couldn't bear to think about how unhappy she had been; she choked up with tears when she tried to tell about it—she was at that stage where laughter and tears are mixed together and it is no longer possible to be sure which is which. "Oh, Lanny, I'm so glad! Thank God, oh, thank Him!" She held on to her husband, her face against his shoulder, to hide her tears. "I don't want to be emotional, but I can't help it. I thought I was never going to see you again."

He drew away and took her face in his hands and looked into her eyes, laughingly. "What a big baby you are, after all!" he chided. He kissed her on both cheeks, smoothed her hair, and kept on smiling.

"Lanny," she sobbed, trying vainly to regain her usual air of practicality, "it is really terrible to love someone as much as I love you. Truly, it isn't rational! There were hours during those nights when I couldn't see myself going on with life without you. I nearly suffocated when I thought of it." She buried her face against his shoulder again. He held her tightly, his cheek against her hair. "Women have to cry, don't they, my dear," he mused aloud. "Even you who are so brave and matter of fact." He knew this would draw a retort.

"Troglodyte!" she cried mockingly and drew away. "Come, look at Baby Lanny. See how tall he has grown. He is going to look like you, I'm afraid."

"Afraid?" he countered.

"Well, I thought you wanted him to look like *me*."

"What an absent-minded lover I am! But it's all right, because he *is* the image of you. Look at that scornful little curl of his upper lip. Just the way you looked at me the first time you met me."

They stood together, arm in arm, looking at the sleeping infant. Laurel said gravely: "I wonder if anyone has the right to bring a child into the world today. What a gamble the future is! What might happen to our helpless baby if the Nazis were to win this war!"

"Life must go on," said Laurel's husband. "You and I can only do our best to make things better. This justifies us in what happiness we take for ourselves."

"I wonder," persisted the wife. "I sometimes feel that no one has the right to pause for anything personal until the world has been made safe from war."

"I have been told that I have earned a furlough," he told her, "and I'm going to have it. First, I have a lot of adventures to tell you; then I want to read the last chapters of that literary masterpiece; then we're going to take a run up to see the family. I have another scheme in my head, but I won't tell it all at once!"

He told what he was free to tell about North Africa: the failure of the plane—he didn't say it was shot down—and his finding a caravan, and his long ride in the desert. "But Robbie said you had cabled from Stockholm!" she exclaimed. He answered: "It was a long journey. There are secret routes, and I am under pledge not to mention them." That was literally a fact and saved his conscience. He was resolved to be careful and not speak the word Germany to anybody. The chance to go back there was too important to be risked on any careless word, including his own. To tell his wife that he had visited Hitler wouldn't add anything to her happiness, but on the contrary would engrave marks of fear into her soul. She, too, had visited Hitler, and knew what a den of hyenas he made for himself.

VIII

The returned traveler called for the last chapters of the manuscript, those written after his departure. Laurel had sent the whole thing to a publisher who had shown interest in her short stories, but after receiving the news of Lanny's disappearance she had given it no thought. Now he read a carbon copy, while the anxious author looked at a newspaper with one-half her mind and with the other half awaited his occasional comments.

It was all right, he was happy to tell her. She had told adequately the tragic story she had outlined to him two years ago. After many interruptions—including their long journey through China—the work was done, and he had no doubt that some publisher would appreciate it. He could help her with bits of local color here and there, and correct a few slips in her German. All languages are tricky, and this one not less than the average. She had spoken of von Papen and von Ribbentrop, the almost universal American custom, but he told her that it was not correct; you would say Franz von Papen and Joachim von Ribbentrop, but if you left off the first names it was plain Papen and plain Ribbentrop.

There is a saying that misfortunes seldom come singly, and if this is true it should apply to good fortunes also. The next morning brought a letter from the publishers. They had been greatly pleased with the manuscript; it was exactly what the public needed at present, and the firm would be happy to make a proposition for it. Lanny let out a whoop of delight and frightened the baby, which was contrary to regulations.

He agreed to put off his trip to Newcastle and went with her to the publishers. He waited in a near-by hotel; they were not to know him, of course, and were to know Laurel only as Miss Mary Morrow, and her address in care of Agnes. She brought the contract which they offered her, and husband and wife studied its complicated provisions. The subject was a new one to them, and they might have consulted a lawyer; but like most new authors, Laurel wanted to see her first book on any terms, and this elaborate printed document was presumably what other authors signed. She signed it and sent it by messenger, and they hurried back home so Laurel could nurse the baby, for nothing was allowed to break that regimen.

IX

The happy novelist didn't want to go to Newcastle; she wanted to work over the manuscript and put in the corrections Lanny had suggested. He took the train, and had a long talk with his father, and saw the amazing things that had happened to the town of his grandfathers. The Budd plant had been multiplied half a dozen times, and the same was true of Budd Gunmakers, with which the family no longer had much to do. There were other Budd plants out in the Middle West and the Far West, in places that were named only in whispers. Whole new villages had sprung up around Newcastle, built of any sort of material that could be found in a frantically crowded market; the planes were pouring off the assembly lines—that was the way air cover was being provided for the boys in Tunisia, and those in the Solomons and farther out. Budd-Erling planes were being flown across Africa to Cairo, and from the head of the Persian Gulf to the Russians; pretty soon they would be flying from Winnipeg to Alaska, and from there across Siberia. Lanny had to hear all about the new "job" that was the world's wonder, and he had to go and see it.

Lanny told his father what he had learned about the performance of the plane in North Africa and in England, and about the progress of the war. He had dinner with the family and then drove one of his father's cars back to New York. In his pocket was one of those little folders full of coupons that you had to have in order to get gasoline. If you had the support of the president of Budd-Erling you could get what you wanted from the local ration board.

Lanny spent the next two days going over that precious manuscript with his wife and getting it into shape for the printer. When that was done and the package had been delivered, he looked out of the window and saw the month of March acting up to its bad reputation. A belated snow was falling and turning to slush on the sidewalks; a disagreeable wind was driving into people's faces and turning umbrellas inside out. Lanny said: "I was told by my Boss that I had earned a holiday, and to take it. Why shouldn't we?" When Laurel asked: "Where to?" he said: "If it were peacetime I would fly you to Marrakech and let Beauty see her new grandson. The sun will be rising there in a few hours, shining on pink walls and red roofs, and the mosque towers will be casting long black shadows on the gardens full of roses."

"But it's wartime, Lanny; so what?"

"So we have to stay on the ground. Let's put a few things into the car and drive south as far as the gas will take us."

"And how will we get back?"

"We will wait a month or two, and some more coupons will come due. Then it will be springtime in New York and the trees in the park will be green and we can sit outdoors."

It sounded crazy at first, but lost that aspect gradually as he talked. They would put the baby into a wicker basket and set it on the back seat, with several suitcases stacked on the floor in front of it to keep it from sliding off. Agnes would sit in the other back seat and Laurel would ride at Lanny's side and give the customary advice about safe driving. Lanny loved nothing better than driving a car, unless it was driving Laurel. They had coupons for eighty gallons of gas, and that would take them to the tip of Florida and leave them enough to drive about and find a bungalow on the ocean front. The "season" was about over, and there would be plenty of room and of quiet. They would sit on the sand and watch the pelicans and maybe Lanny would catch a fish and they would cook it. Since the baby was breast-fed, they wouldn't have to worry about his diet, only about his mother's!

Laurel had come to realize that she was married to a rich man's son, who was accustomed to have what he wanted. He would think of something, and then: "Let's go!" She was ready to believe that he had earned a holiday; if he wanted to have it with her it was surely not her job to object. "We can be in the Florida sunshine by the day after tomorrow," he insisted; and when she answered: "It must be a thousand miles," he said: "I have never thought anything of driving six or seven hundred in a day, but of course we can't do that in wartime. You can lean back and sleep, and we'll only stop for meals. What are we waiting for?"

X

They put their summer things into bags, and some odds and ends of belongings into carton boxes that the janitor of the building brought them; they did not forget a box of books they had been hoping for time to read. Last among the bearers came Lanny with the precious infant lying on a pillow in a clothes basket, well covered against the cold. They packed the basket so that it would not slide or topple; they stowed themselves, with rugs over their knees, and away they went, down Park Avenue, across to the West Side, under the Hudson by the Holland tube, and by the Pulaski Skyway to Newark and the south. It was the familiar Highway No. 1, four lines of speeding vehicles, two in each direction. Lanny kept a space between himself and the truck in front, so that the one that crowded behind him might have room to shove him along in case of a jam.

It was that way to Trenton, and to Philadelphia, Baltimore, and Washington. Thirty-five miles was the established wartime speed, and it was rarely that you could pass a car ahead of you. It was dark when they reached the capital, and slow driving through the dimmed-out streets; but in the open country of Virginia they could turn on the lights and make time. They had brought a basket of food, and Laurel would put a sandwich into the driver's hand and he would take a nibble when circumstances permitted. The road led through the "Wilderness" country, scene of many battles; there were tablets by the roadside, but they did not stop to read the inscriptions. Few travelers did, for America was not interested in history at present—she was too busy making it.

They drove until late and spent the night in a hotel in North Carolina. They were up early next morning and on their way; when the sun rose they no longer wanted rugs over their knees, or overcoats, and they took the covers off the baby. When you moved south you were placing yourself under the sun and enjoying springtime prematurely. The road was still a perfect pavement, but there was far less traffic; the country was pineland, or hilly fields with the topsoil long since washed off; poverty ruled the land, and the cabins were small and unpainted. "Hound-dogs" chased rabbits, and one ran under the wheels of the car to his great misfortune.

Out of the hills the highway brought them to Savannah, city of magnolia trees and live oaks drooping with Spanish moss. From there on they followed the coast into Florida, and came to St. Augustine, oldest of American cities, deliberately keeping itself picturesque with old-style horse carriages. They spent the night there, and next morning they sped on, and by late afternoon were in the middle of Florida.

Lanny said: "How about cutting over to the West Coast; fewer tourists go there, and you see more of the country." Laurel answered that she had no preference, so they took the road through Lakeland, flat country with endless yellow-pine woods, dotted with lakes of all sizes. The movement of the car made a pleasant breeze and was too fast for flies or mosquitoes. They stopped for supper, and then drove on through the night, with the lights of the car outlining the straight ribbon of road. Three times a deer showed up in these lights, and once Lanny had to jam on his brakes to keep from running into a cow.

They spent that night in an old hotel in the city of Tampa, and in the morning went on, driving slowly and watching the shore. They came to a tiny village on a cove, and found a modern and comfortable cottage just vacated by its northern owners. An agent rented it to them for a small price, and there they were; they unloaded their belongings, and put on their bathing suits, and were all right so long as they did not stay in the sun too long, or sit on the ground and expose their skins to the tiny red bugs called chiggers. "If the chigger were bigger, as big as a cow, and his digger had the vigor of a subsoil plow, can you figger, picknicker, where you would be now?"

They could catch all the fish they wanted without trouble; but it was a trouble to clean and prepare them, and they were pleased to discover a tiny café where an elderly Italian with a handle-bar mustache was prepared to feed them on a sea-food "gumbo," thick with fish, shrimp, oysters, and crabs, and hot with red pepper. One such meal just after sundown, and they could get along the rest of the day on the fresh fruits and green vegetables, which were abundant. Lanny, who had sailed a boat all over the Golfe Juan, hired a catboat and took his wife out to watch the sponge fishermen—Portuguese and Greeks mostly, all middle-aged or old men, for the younger ones had gone to war. Lanny caught a small shark, and once was enough of that. For the most part they were content to stay indoors during the heat of the day, well screened against flying and biting insects.

XI

America had covered itself with a network of radio stations, and Lanny with his portable set could get Tampa and Pensacola and Key West. All stations gave the war news at frequent intervals, and the favorite commentators in afternoon and evening. So, while the baby practiced his arms and legs on a rug, the three adults would sit and follow the dénouement of that melodrama, the earlier acts of which Lanny had helped to write in North Africa. He saw the British Eighth Army cut around behind the Mareth line, through the same country of baking-hot rocks and sand and salty *shotts* where he had traveled with the camels. They forced Rommel's bedraggled Afrika Korps out of its last strong position, and northward up the coast, into the trap the Mediterranean had prepared at the northeastern corner of Tunisia.

The Americans released their air cover and blasted the Luftwaffe out of those skies; and then began desperate fighting in the rain and mud, for the capture of one hill after another. British, French, and Americans were attacking along a line some two hundred miles long; the Germans were resisting furiously, and the Italians with considerably less ardor. All that country, and the men, the tanks, the planes, were so familiar to Lanny Budd that he could supply the local color to the two women; he could hear the guns and smell the smoke of battle while the radio eyewitnesses talked.

A curious experience for a P.A. on vacation: Early in April an enemy force was cut off at a place in southern Tunisia called El Guettar, close to where the camels had brought Lanny in. A great number of Italians had surrendered, and Lanny listened to an American correspondent who had interviewed some of the prisoners. Standing near the microphone was Il Maggiore Vittorio di San Girolamo; his voice wasn't heard, but the correspondent quoted him as saying that the Germans had seized all the trucks and other vehicles and made their escape, leaving their allies in a trap.

When the broadcast was over, Lanny said to his wife: "Did I ever mention that Italian name to you? He was my half-sister Marceline's husband, and when he needed money he stole some of Marcel's paintings and sold them to a dealer in Nice. When Marceline had it proved to her, she divorced him and he went back to Italy. Then he was a *capitano*, and now they have made him a *maggiore*, but he is still grumbling about his fate and blaming other people. Handsome fellow with coal-black eyes and hair—he puts oil in the hair—and he can't keep his eyes off the ladies."

"What will we do with him?" asked Laurel.

"I suppose we'll ship him over here and put him in some comfortable summer hotel. We can't make the officers work, you know, and we have to treat them well lest the enemy do worse to ours. If Vittorio is ever turned loose, he will come to me and try to borrow money."

XII

In mid-April began the general attack, all along the narrowing line. The battle lasted for a month, and Lanny could hardly keep away from the radio; he had maps and marked the positions with a red pencil. The line had been shortened to a hundred miles, and every day it was still further reduced. The enemy was in a pocket, with no place to go but the sea, and the British and Americans controlled that with fighting ships and planes. Step by step the drive continued; resistance collapsed, and the enemy forces were driven back upon Tunis and the great naval base of Bizerte. There was another Stalingrad preparing— some three hundred thousand enemy troops being driven toward a peninsula called Cap Bon, where they would have to choose between surrender and destruction.

A woman novelist wasn't very good company for listening to events such as these. While Lanny kept talking about military strategy, she was thinking about human beings. She was like Little Peterkin, not content with a glorious victory, but wanting to know what good was going to come of it. She was ill satisfied with what Lanny had to tell her about the government that had been set up in North Africa, and was hardly to be persuaded to entrust decisions to the State Department gentry and the brass hats in command. "Big business will be there and will take over," she insisted. "What sort of democracy are we going to teach the people of Europe if we leave it to the military and the profiteers?"

It was a good time for Lanny to clarify his ideas, and he found his wife's mind an excellent grindstone upon which to sharpen his wits. "This war is either a world revolution or it is a world calamity," she insisted; "and what part is America going to play? Our businessmen haven't the remotest idea about a social democracy—they don't know what the words mean. They will have only one idea, which is to set up the old system in Europe and turn the control over to the big exploiters, including themselves. You know and I know what that will mean in the end, a Communist revolution and a new kind of dictatorship all over Europe."

"I am putting my faith in Roosevelt," he told her. "I know from his own lips that he understands all that."

"Yes, Lanny, but if he can't find men to carry out his orders? If he has to please the Catholic Church, and the Southern senators, and the big-business crowd who are the only ones who know how to restore industry, and mean to have it exactly as it was before? Are we going to overthrow Nazi-Fascism and set up a polite American brand of the same thing?"

Lanny had had these same thoughts, but oddly enough he didn't like hearing them from his wife's lips; he had the impression that she was going to an extreme. The Vichy gang was being curbed in North Africa, the Jews were getting a better deal, a good part of the political prisoners had been released, and so on. But Laurel said all that was just window-dressing; what counted was the fact that the bankers, the landlords, the trading magnates, were inviting the American "brass" to their dinner parties, introducing them to their wives and daughters, and perhaps letting them in on a "good thing" now and then. "When the war is over they will form a solid phalanx, and the ragged proletariat will be outside, starving."

It took no special gift of seership to foresee what was coming to the postwar world. There would be three great powers, the Communist, headed by the Soviet Union, the capitalist, headed by America, and the democratic Socialist, hoped for in Britain, France, and the Scandinavian lands. Laurel said: "We Socialists will be out in No Man's Land, under the fire of both extremists; it will be our task to teach the Russians that democracy in industry is nothing without democracy in politics, and to teach the Americans that democracy in politics is nothing without democracy in industry."

"Will you write a book about that?" he asked.

"I was about to ask what *you* were going to do," she answered. "We must both work at it, with all we have. Let us both save our money, and prepare for a long battle. It will be that, and Roosevelt cannot do it all. We must help to carry his cross!"

BOOKS BY UPTON SINCLAIR

A WORLD TO WIN
DRAGON HARVEST
PRESIDENTIAL AGENT
WIDE IS THE GATE
DRAGON'S TEETH
BETWEEN TWO WORLDS
WORLD'S END
EXPECT NO PEACE
YOUR MILLION DOLLARS
LITTLE STEEL
OUR LADY
THE FLIVVER KING
NO PASARAN!
THE GNOMOBILE
CO-OP: A NOVEL OF LIVING TOGETHER
WHAT GOD MEANS TO ME: AN ATTEMPT
    AT A WORKING RELIGION
I, CANDIDATE FOR GOVERNOR AND HOW I
    GOT LICKED
THE EPIC PLAN FOR CALIFORNIA
I, GOVERNOR OF CALIFORNIA
THE WAY OUT: WHAT LIES AHEAD FOR
    AMERICA
UPTON SINCLAIR PRESENTS WILLIAM FOX
AMERICAN OUTPOST: AUTOBIOGRAPHY
THE WET PARADE
ROMAN HOLIDAY
MENTAL RADIO
MOUNTAIN CITY
BOSTON
MONEY WRITES!

OIL!
THE SPOKESMAN'S SECRETARY
LETTERS TO JUDD
MAMMONART
THE GOSLINGS—A STUDY OF THE AMERICAN
    SCHOOLS
THE GOOSE-STEP—A STUDY OF AMERICAN
    EDUCATION
THE BOOK OF LIFE
THEY CALL ME CARPENTER
100%—THE STORY OF A PATRIOT
THE BRASS CHECK
JIMMIE HIGGINS
KING COAL, A NOVEL OF THE COLORADO
    COAL STRIKE
THE PROFITS OF RELIGION
THE CRY FOR JUSTICE
DAMAGED GOODS
SYLVIA'S MARRIAGE
SYLVIA
LOVE'S PILGRIMAGE
THE FASTING CURE
SAMUEL, THE SEEKER
THE MONEYCHANGERS
THE METROPOLIS
THE MILLENNIUM
THE OVERMAN
THE JUNGLE
MANASSAS, A NOVEL OF THE CIVIL WAR
THE JOURNAL OF ARTHUR STIRLING

Plays

PRINCE HAGEN
THE NATUREWOMAN
THE SECOND STORY MAN
THE MACHINE
THE POT-BOILER
HELL

SINGING JAILBIRDS
BILL PORTER
OIL! (DRAMATIZATION)
DEPRESSION ISLAND
MARIE ANTOINETTE

CONCERNING THE CIRCULATION OF THE *WORLD'S END* SERIES

In the following record the volumes of the series are indicated by their numbers in order of publication:

Vol. I	*World's End*	1940
Vol. II	*Between Two Worlds*	1941
Vol. III	*Dragon's Teeth*	1942
Vol. IV	*Wide Is the Gate*	1943
Vol. V	*Presidential Agent*	1944
Vol. VI	*Dragon Harvest*	1945
Vol. VII	*A World to Win*	1946
Vol. VIII	*Presidential Mission*	1947

In the United States the totals, including book club editions, are as follows:

Vol. I, 177,394   Vol. V, 65,779
Vol. II, 44,695   Vol. VI, 135,063
Vol. III, 52,190   Vol. VII, 736,191
Vol. IV, 50,072   Vol. VIII, first printing, 50,000

In England, the publishers, Werner Laurie, Ltd., report the following:

Vol. I, 31,550   Vol. V, 32,250
Vol. II, 30,000   Vol. VI, 58,530
Vol. III, 42,326   Vol. VII, 67,300
Vol. IV, 33,750

All paper obtainable was used in printing these books, and editions were sold out in a month or so. Foyle's Book Club offered to take 140,000 copies of Vol. II, but paper was not obtainable.

Other countries are listed in alphabetical order:

ARGENTINA   Editorial Claridad, Buenos Aires, Vol. I, *El Fin Del Mundo;* Vols. II and III issued.

BELGIUM
(French language)   Editions de la Paix, entire series contracted for.

BRAZIL   Cruzeiro, Rio de Janeiro, Vols. I to IV published, V and VI in preparation.

BULGARIA	"Haemus," Sofia, entire series to be published this year (1947).
CZECHOSLOVAKIA	Lincolns-Prager, London, Vol. I, *Konec Svëta*, published; entire series contracted for.
DENMARK	Thaning and Appel, Copenhagen, Vol. I published; entire series contracted for.
HOLLAND	N. V. Servire, The Hague, Vol. I, *Einde van een Wereld;* Vol. II, *Tussen Twee Werelden;* entire series contracted for.
HUNGARY	Lincolns-Prager, London, First three vols. published; entire series contracted for.
INDIA *(Tamil)*	S. Shanmugan, Terunelveli, Vol. III in preparation.
ITALY	Mondadori, Milan, entire series except Vol. V contracted for. Casa Ed. Sansoni, Rome, Vol. V in preparation.
NORWAY	Aschehoug, Oslo, Vols. III to VII contracted for.
PALESTINE	Ideal Publishing Co., Tel-Aviv, entire series contracted for.
POLAND	Roj Publishers, Warsaw, entire series contracted for.
RUMANIA	Cultura Nationala, Bucharest, Vol. VI, *Balaurul*, published; Vol. VII in preparation.
SWEDEN	Axel Holmström, Stockholm, Vol. I, *De Sadde Vind;* Vol. II, *Mellan Två Världar;* Vol. III, *Drakens Tänder;* Vol. IV, *Förtappelsens Väg;* Vol. V, *Presidentens Agent;* Vol. VI, *Drakskörd*, published; Vol. VII in preparation.
SWITZERLAND *(German language)*	Alfred Scherz, Bern, Vol. I, *Welt-Ende*, 12,-600; Vol. II, *Zwischen Zwei Welten*, 9000; Vol. III, *Drachenzähne*, 6000; Vol. IV, *Weit ist das Tor;* later volumes in preparation.
U.S.S.R.	Goslitisdat, Moscow, condensations of first five volumes published.